Oregon Country

THE STORY OF THE 1843 OREGON TRAIL MIGRATION

Oregon Country

THE STORY OF THE 1843 OREGON TRAIL MIGRATION

T. J. Hanson, Ph.D.

PORTLAND • OREGON
INKWATERPRESS.COM

Oregon Country
Copyright © 2006 by T. J. Hanson, Ph.D.
Photos © 2006 by T. J. Hanson, Ph.D.

Cover: This is a scene along the pass at Scott's Bluff in present day western Nebraska. Although the 1843 Oregon Trail passed to the south of this point, later routes crossed the bluff. Scott's Bluff became a recognizable landmark along the Oregon Trail.

Originally published in 2001 under the title Western Passage, ISBN 0-9705847-0-9. Original copyright © 2001

Cover and interior design by Masha Shubin

All rights reserved. No part of this book may be reproduced or transmitted in any form or by any means whatsoever, including photocopying, recording or by any information storage and retrieval system, without written permission from the publisher and/or author. Contact Inkwater Press at 6750 SW Franklin Street, Suite A, Portland, OR 97223-2542. 503.968.6777

www.inkwaterpress.com

ISBN-10 1-59299-235-8
ISBN-13 978-1-59299-235-5

Publisher: Inkwater Press

Printed in the U.S.A.

Dedicated to the many Indian nations who have called the American West home for ten thousand years.

Unending hardships shall come to pass,
As we enter a land of trees and grass.
We will build our homes with love assured,
Yet never forget the troubles endured.

We are the first, but there will be more,
People with dreams of that distant shore.
They will look with awe at the road we dared,
And say we had courage, more than our share.

Table of Contents

Preface xi

Preface to the Second Printing xiii

Chapter 1: Homesteading 1

Chapter 2: Independence, Missouri 34

Chapter 3: The Trail to Oregon 106

Chapter 4: Oregon City 585

Appendices 597
    Appendix A: The Oregon Migration of 1843 599
    Appendix B: Slave receipt 638
    Appendix C: Calendar for 1843 639

Index 643

Preface

The Oregon Trail had its beginnings in 1843 beneath the wagon wheels of the Oregon Emigrating Company, a group of disparate Americans with a common goal: to seek a new land and make it their own. The trail met its end in 1869 with the completion of the transcontinental railway. Oregon Country is a detailed account of the Oregon Migration of 1843 in a "historical fiction" setting. In this context, the reader can enjoy the adventure as a participant, rather than as a student or scholar.

During its twenty-five year history, the Oregon Trail essentially changed every year. From its rough beginnings grew an organized route. By 1846 ferries serviced most of the major river crossings, and fully-stocked supply depots awaited hungry travelers. Due to all the livestock driven west, the trail became a mile-wide swath of trampled ground, providing an easy road with no need for a guide. During the summers of 1849 and 1850, over 100,000 miners also followed the Oregon Trail, en route to the California gold fields. By the 1850s, Mormons were using the trail as a source of income, supplying emigrants with food and equipment. As the railroad extended further west, many people took the train as far as they could before switching to the trail.

Only the 1843 migration held the true adventure of entering an unknown land. Guides were needed to show the way; dangerous river crossings taxed the courage of everyone; the existing fur trading posts were unable to supply necessary food and other equipment; and the first emigrants had to build their own road because the Oregon Trail did not yet exist. Wagons had never been taken all the way to Oregon, and it was entirely possible that this great experiment might end in tragedy. It is this migration, 1843, to which we often attribute the adventure and romanticism of the Oregon Trail.

While researching this book, I found information to be both scarce and scattered, requiring many months to form an outline of the complexity of this event. The popular myth of western migration, championed by film and television, depicts a wagon train of smiling emigrants, traveling down a well-worn road and fighting Indians at every turn. The truth is considerably different.

Research sources included the Oregon Historical Society, several Oregon historical libraries, the Oregon State Archives, numerous probate records, military discharge papers, newspaper clippings, trail diaries, and cemetery headstones. I suspect that other sources of information are hidden away in the attics of various descendents, information that is essentially not available to the public. Appendix A provides a listing of the known emigrants that were part of the 1843 Oregon Emigrating Company, along with some brief biographical data. This appendix is nonfiction, providing new knowledge to the scholarly community and, it is hoped, inspiring other researchers to help fill in the gaps.

The Oregon Migration of 1843 was a watershed moment in American history. It marked the end of the trapping era and the beginnings of civilization on the Western frontier. You are about to become part of that experience. Enjoy the journey!

T. J. Hanson
July, 2001

Preface to the Second Printing

For the second printing I have included a number of photographs that were taken along the trail in western Nebraska and across Wyoming. The landscape depicted in these photos looks the same today as it did in 1843. I have also included a number of photographs for Appendix A. These pictures were taken in various pioneer cemeteries throughout the Willamette Valley in western Oregon.

Many people have expressed their appreciation for telling the story of the "1843 Oregon Trail Migration" in a historical fiction setting. This format allows the reader to become part of this great adventure—experiencing the wonder of discovery while also enduring the hardships of trail life. The trail is still visible in many places—looking much the same as it did 163 years ago. After reading this book, you may find yourself planning to see part of the trail on your next vacation.

T. J. Hanson
September, 2006

Oregon Country

THE STORY OF THE 1843 OREGON TRAIL MIGRATION

CHAPTER 1

Homesteading

"Do you, Abigail Hanley, take Caleb Meacham to be your lawful wedded husband, to have and to hold until death do you part?" asked Reverend O'Donald.

"I do."

It was done. On a cold clear Saturday in January 1841, Caleb Meacham and Abigail Hanley began their new lives together. They kissed and received congratulations from friends and family in attendance at the Hanley's farmhouse. That evening there would be a dance to enjoy and a celebration that would bring friends and family together from miles around.

Caleb, the youngest of five boys, still lived on his parents' farm. He was a hard-working young man who loved children and had a smile that could melt the heart of any young woman. Now, at the age of twenty, the time had come to take a wife. Most of his friends had families of their own by now, and those that did not had left Greene County, Ohio, for some faraway adventure. Although Caleb wanted a family, too, the right woman had not come along, at least not until Abby. Caleb knew his parents needed help running their frontier farm, so rather than going off on an adventure of his own, he stayed on to help his father. After today, all that would change.

Over the last few months Caleb and his brothers had built a small cabin on an eighty-acre parcel owned by their father. This would be the home he and Abby would call their own. With twenty acres already clear of trees and brush, the farm would begin to take shape during next spring's planting. Caleb, the most educated in his family, completed the eighth grade by the age of fifteen. That education and a gentlemanly charm had helped him catch Abby, the local schoolteacher.

Abigail Hanley had been twenty-four years of age when they met, considerably old to still be single. Most other women married before they turned eighteen, but Abby had a different mind. Getting married as a form of social acceptance held no interest. Rather, she wanted exactly the right man—strong, handsome, loving, and caring. With so many men in Greene County to choose from, it was a difficult decision. A number of men had asked for her hand in marriage, but none could entice her to give up the freedom of being single. For miles around, bachelors considered Abby to be the ultimate prize, and those who had not met her had certainly heard of her. She had jet-black hair, thick and straight, parted haphazardly on top and reaching halfway between her chin and shoulders, where it curled slightly inward. This simple hairstyle suited the harsh life of a frontier woman. Her brilliant smile lit up her big brown eyes, accenting her high cheeks and smooth complexion. She had a slight frame, only one hundred pounds, but stood five foot six and could handle a team of horses with the best of men.

Like Caleb, Abby too came from a farm family. Her two brothers and three sisters often wondered when she would settle down with a family of her own. At Saturday-night socials her dance card always filled before the music began. Since turning sixteen, she had been the envy of most women and the irritation of quite a few more. Some women said she had broken the heart of every young man in Greene County. The envious ones put it that way. Now, all that would change, for today was her special day. She now belonged to the man she had been waiting for, and a new life filled with love and family awaited.

Relations and friends of the Hanleys and Meachams made up a guest list of over fifty people, with each woman bringing one or two dishes of food. There were several types of bread, cookies, cakes, casseroles, preserves, and dried fruit. Rebecca Hayward even brought an ice cream machine with all the necessary ingredients, including rock salt. This week's Saturday-night social would be one to remember. No one would go hungry.

The location of dances moved from one barn to another across the county. With the wedding of Caleb and Abby, the Hanleys were hosting tonight's social. They had decorated their barn with various colored ribbons, signs of congratulations, and colored banners. January in Ohio yielded few flowers, yet the small wood-frame barn still made a festive sight. Makeshift tables on sawhorses held the banquet. As each guest passed through the reception line, they received a plate upon which the ladies piled mounds of food. It took almost an hour for the newlyweds to greet all the guests and receive their good wishes. Last through the food line were Caleb and Abby.

Some men were heading back for seconds when the couple finally sat down. A few minutes later, Zeb Josse stood and offered a toast:

"I would like to propose a toast. I am sure I echo the sentiments of everyone here today when I welcome Caleb and Abby as the newest family in our community. I sincerely hope their future will be bright with happiness, good health, and bountiful harvests."

A cheer went up, and glasses clinked throughout the barn. Before people had a chance to finish that toast, Henry Meacham, the groom's father, got to his feet and added, "And plenty of little mouths to feed!"

The statement prompted more applause, with embarrassed smiles and laughter.

Caleb, normally quiet and reserved at social events, surprised even himself when he rose with his glass to propose his own toast.

"Here's to the most beautiful woman in Greene County, my wife!"

The guests hurrahed and raised their glasses. Abby was smiling too as she grabbed Caleb's shirt to pull him down into his chair. That simple act won another shout of laughter from the crowd.

The room remained a bustle of noisy conversation, eating, laughter, the playful sounds of children, and men returning to the banquet table for seconds. Women made sure their own plates were full the first time. It simply wasn't ladylike to go back for seconds. Conversations reflected the rich heritage of the immigrants who had settled Greene County. At one point, Caleb could hear Norwegian, German, Polish, and English, with each language vying for space in the festive gathering of friends and family.

With so many interruptions, Caleb and Abby were the last to finish eating. As soon as they took the last bite of food, Elsa Johnston and Mary Erdman entered the barn with a beautifully decorated three-layer cake. The frosting and candy decorations were a remarkable sight, almost too good to spoil by cutting. Sarah Kinkade quickly cleared an area for the cake on the table in front of the couple. Abby stood as Mrs. Kinkade handed her a knife. Caleb got up too after Abby gave him a quick hand signal. Together they cut the first piece amidst another cheer from the guests. It was a large cake, yet with fifty people to feed Abby made sure the pieces were small. After she cut the first few servings, Mrs. Kinkade and Mrs. Johnston took over. Mrs. Kinkade continued cutting while Mrs. Johnston handled the plates and forks. Within a short time everyone was served.

After a few more toasts by close friends, and when the last piece of cake was eaten, the guests got up to stretch their legs before the dance. Most of the gifts brought for Caleb and Abby sat on a side table for everyone to see. There was a crocheted tablecloth from Emma Hankins and several tatted doilies from Anna Helmerson. Four ladies, Cornelia Robb, Mary Jane Freeman, Sarah Reed, and Martha Kerron, gave a large quilt that they had been working on since the fall harvest. George and Letitia Hanley, Abby's parents, used part of their harvest income to buy four place settings of the finest dinnerware from Freeman's general store. Henry and Margaret Meacham, Caleb's parents, gave the most valuable gift of all. They were leasing Caleb and Abby the eighty acres of land needed for their farm. Additional gifts consisted of candles, candle holders, candle molds, a kerosene lamp, an odd assortment of utensils, a Bible, and to the amusement of everyone, a money belt for Caleb.

"It'll come in handy for carrying corn when I go out to feed the chickens!" he joked.

He and Abby thanked each guest individually for their generosity and kindness. As people admired with envy the assortment of gifts, Joe Freeman began the dance by playing a lively tune on his fiddle.

Adam Erdman also brought out his fiddle and played along as best he could to tunes that ranged from waltzes to polkas. Caleb received the first dance from Abby. After that, it was every man for himself.

Abby did not need a dance card tonight, for she was the center of attention. Every man in the room, married and single, received at least one dance. A fair amount of food still remained, but that would disappear before the guests left for home. It was a wedding and a Saturday-night social to remember.

The first guests to leave were the Farnhams. They had seven miles to ride in an open wagon on a chilly night, and a light snow had just begun to fall. During the next hour most of the other guests said their farewells, carrying empty baking dishes and any other household items they had brought to the social. By ten o'clock only Caleb, Abby, and their immediate families remained. Caleb's brothers, Adam, Michael, and John, brought the wagon around to the front of the barn while Caleb and Abby bundled up for the ride home. They boarded the wagon and, with a snap of the reins, were off.

During the dance Caleb's brothers had tied several old cowbells to the back of the wagon, each on a short rope that allowed the bell to bounce on the ground. With a final cheer from their families, and a very noisy wagon, Caleb and Abby set off for their new farm and for what they both imagined would be a life of love and caring for each other.

Caleb's sparsely furnished cabin reflected the tough frontier life facing all young couples of meager means. The cabin stood at the edge of a clearing, facing west. Caleb and his brothers had constructed it from logs taken from a nearby woodlot, so it was crude, but weatherproof. Its two rooms measured approximately fifteen feet by twenty feet. The small side room was a bedroom, with a piece of canvas acting as the door. The main room served as a kitchen and everything else. The fireplace consisted of rocks taken from a nearby stream during the previous spring, dried out over the summer, and mortared together with a mixture of clay, sand, and water. It had a spacious opening, six feet by four feet, with a large mantle made from a single plank of white oak. Caleb's brothers had installed grates and pot hangers, since Abby would have to use the fireplace for cooking until the couple could afford a woodstove.

There was one window at the back, a single window on the side opposite the fireplace, and one window in the front. The side window provided light for the bedroom while the door, back window, and front window lighted the main room. Glass was hard to come by and too expensive for a young couple just starting out, so each window closed with outside shutters. With the shutters open during winter days, the cabin remained comfortable as long as there was a good fire and a hot bed of coals.

The plank floor, made from rough-hewn white oak, came from the same tree as the mantle board. This was a special feature, as most new cabins had no floor at all, only dirt.

Window glass, a bedroom door, and a woodstove were on the top of Caleb's wish list. The sale of logs from his woodlot would provide some winter income and allow the purchase of a few items before the arrival of planting season. Farm implements and seed would constitute other primary expenditures.

In the main room was a simple table about five feet by three feet with wooden benches on each side. During the previous week, Caleb had managed to construct a few shelves and a counter along the back wall—and none too soon, since those wedding gifts needed a home. One special gift, a rocking chair, was hand made by Caleb's brother Adam. Abby placed the rocker in the middle of the room facing the hearth and sat down while Caleb went back outside to unhitch the team and move them to a makeshift corral. These two horses comprised all the livestock he owned. There would soon be more, for neighbors were always generous toward young couples.

There had been no time to build a barn. That would happen next summer at a barn-raising social. His brothers promised a barn raising as soon as the spring crops were in. This would be an event as important as a wedding, for it was a time of social gathering, friendship, and food. For the present, Caleb kept his farm implements under a small lean-to.

As Caleb stepped back into the cabin, Abby met him with the kind of hug reserved for lovers who have not seen each other in a long time. It was their first moment alone after a long and tiring day.

With unending kisses, Caleb picked up his bride and walked toward the bedroom, bumping into the bench and table along the way.

"Should I stoke the fire?"

"We won't need it," came Abby's reply, muffled with more kisses. "Besides, we have that new quilt."

The next morning five inches of new snow lay on the ground, providing a beautiful pastoral winter scene. The horses were patiently waiting for feed when Caleb came out of the cabin. He wore only homespun pants and a shirt, so it was not long before Abby came running after him with a jacket and hat.

"You're going to have to take care of yourself if you're going to take care of me." She barely got the words out before her arms were around him and she was kissing him as if he had just returned from a weeklong absence.

"I think I'm going to enjoy married life. Will every morning be like this?"

"Yes!" replied Abby. "Every morning and more, for the rest of our lives. We're going to have lots of children and bountiful crops and livestock and everything good in life."

Through more kisses and a constant hug, Caleb finally managed to say, "Let me get some hay and water for these horses, then we can go back in and talk about the future. First off, we're going to need some furniture and other household items. We have a few months before planting season, and … and Abby, we're going to have the finest farmhouse in Greene County! I have some money left from last season, so first thing Monday morning we'll hitch up this wagon and go into town. Mr. Freeman down at the general store should have most everything we need, at least for now."

"That sounds wonderful." Abby was still hugging him while smiling at his dreams and intermittently kissing him on the neck whenever the opportunity arose.

"We'll need a baby basket, on rockers, don't forget that."

"I haven't forgotten." He smiled back and added, "I think we'll probably wear a couple of 'em out."

"I'll bring in some firewood and start breakfast. Don't be long."

Abby finally broke her grip from around his neck and ran over to the woodpile. It did not matter that they were as poor as church mice, for they were happy and the future was theirs.

The winter months passed quickly, and soon it was time for planting. Before the last remaining frost seeped out of the ground, Caleb found himself down at the general store looking at the available plows, seed drills, hay rakes, and garden tools. Abby needed several hand tools for her vegetable garden, and Caleb needed a plow and seed drill. Borrowing such equipment was not an option, since other farmers needed these implements at the same time. Joe Freeman, the store owner, accustomed to selling equipment on credit, simply opened a new account. Caleb paid what he could, with the rest due next fall after harvest. It was an equitable deal.

Joe Freeman's general store, like all general stores, smelled of new textiles, fresh varnished wood, and raw iron. A large front window provided adequate light, while a woodstove kept the front room warm and comfortable. Sitting around the stove today were two men Caleb did not recognize. They wore buckskins, looked as though they had recently journeyed a long distance, and were, possibly, only passing through Greene County. Caleb introduced himself and learned that they were trappers, previously employed by the Rocky Mountain Fur Company. They had given up their adventurous profession to return East and try civilization for a year or two. He pulled up a small barrel and sat down to listen to the stories they were relating to the other men around the stove.

"Well, I don't know how long I'll last," said one trapper, a big burly man with a year-old beard, greasy buckskins, and an odor that proclaimed cleanliness was not a priority task. "All these buildings and people are closing in on me. If the price of plews hadn't fallen, I'd still be setting my line up on the Beaverhead."

"That's the bare truth," replied the other trapper. He was a wiry man who, Caleb thought, was probably a lot stronger than he appeared. He too had a five- to six-inch beard, blonde hair that fell down around his shoulders, and a filthiness equal to his partner's.

"This child never smelled anything so foul as the air in Cincinnati," remarked the burly trapper. "When I first got scent of all that coal smoke in St. Louis, I almost turned around right there. I thought Cincinnati would be better—not so. I don't know how anybody could live there, certainly not this child."

Caleb wondered how they could smell anything above their own odor—but odor or not, it was impolite not to join the conversation. When the trappers paused to light their pipes, Caleb interjected his own image of the West.

"I once heard that west of St. Louis is a vast desert. Trapping must be the only work people can do out there. Certainly never sounded like a place for farms and families."

"Well now, I'll agree with you there, son," replied the wiry trapper.

Caleb thought the trapper could not be more than ten years older than himself, so being called "son" seemed odd. The manners, dress, and speech of these strangers were all a little odd.

"You have to go past that desert till you get to the Rocky Mountains. Now there ain't nothing prettier than those mountains. They reach right up into the clouds—and with eternal snow up on top. The forests and water out there are the finest in the world, and there's no such thing as sickness in those mountains. In all the years this child spent out there, I never once saw anyone get sick."

"None? I mean nobody?" This news brought another farmer into the conversation.

"Not a one. Sure, I saw Blackfeet kill plenty of trappers, but nobody ever got sick! That's the bare truth. Yes sir, out there is a continent intersected by great rivers, snowcapped mountains, and fierce Indians. A man can't go wrong making his home out in those mountains."

"I'm a farmer, not a trapper," said Caleb. "Those mountains don't sound like anything that would suit me or my family, except that it would be something to see. You say they got snow in the summer?"

"Sure do," replied the wiry trapper. "If you're looking for good farmland, you got to go beyond those mountains. There's good farmland in California and Oregon. I suspect someday those areas might even get settled. The land's too good to pass by."

"How much does some of that land cost, and who owns it now?" It was Joe Freeman, the storekeeper. He had been standing by listening to the conversation with the interest of any entrepreneur.

"Nobody owns it, and you can have as much as you want. Just go out there and stake your claim," replied the wiry trapper.

"Nobody!" Caleb sat up straight on the barrel. "How can nobody own it? You mean it's there for the taking?"

"That's right, son. You go out there and take what you want. Now, that Oregon Country is where I'd go. The Spanish missions down in California have cattle and horses, but they don't take kindly to strangers. They threw old Jed Smith and some of our boys in jail simply for passing through. Now then, the British Hudson Bay Company controls all of Oregon Country. I don't much care for the British either. My Daddy had a run-in with 'em back in 1812, and since then they've done whatever they could to stop us trappers. Pushing them out of Oregon Country would suit me just fine."

"Who's going to tell them to leave?" asked one of the farmers. "That's over two thousand miles away, so you won't be getting any help from the United States. Those British probably think they own all that country."

"Well now, that depends on who you talk to," responded the burly trapper. "Old Lewis and Clark were the first to get out there, and that means that country should be ours. If we don't do something soon, those HBC boys will surely move in for good. I heard that a number of them have already moved into the Wallamet Valley and started farming. The trapping fields have dried up for those boys too. Farming!—I can't see it, but there they are. If we don't get some American farmers out there, you can say farewell to the whole Oregon Country."

"Oh, that might sound good to you, but where could we buy dry goods and other supplies, and where would we sell our crops? There's more to farming than planting seed." Caleb was trying to be practical.

"The Hudson Bay Company will buy any and all of your crops. They got gristmills and a considerable number of mouths to feed. They also got trade routes going to the Russian settlements on the northwest coast and the Sandwich Islands out in the Pacific. You won't have any trouble selling crops in a land as new as Oregon."

Both trappers seemed pleased with that description as they reloaded and relit their pipes.

"They're going to need supplies," announced Joe Freeman again. "Sounds like a good opportunity for us merchants. If they got a seaport we could get our supplies by sea, around the Horn."

"Tell us about that land," asked Caleb. "How good is it for farming?"

"To start with, it's already cleared," replied the burly trapper. "Not a single tree to remove. You put your plow into the ground and you've got a farm. That's the Wallamet Valley. You don't need to worry about timber, 'cause the surrounding mountains got that—and that timber's not the least of it. The best thing about that Oregon Country is the climate. The summers are warm with no insects to pester you—and the winters, well, the winters never happen. I don't know of anyone that's ever seen snow in the winter. Your livestock can graze all year. Now you try that here in Ohio! Yup, that Oregon Country is a place to see."

"You mean people can farm all year?" Joe Freeman was thinking about potential markets for his dry goods.

"All year," replied the wiry trapper. "You get all the land you want, several crops a year, and markets to sell them to. Now you can't beat that. Yes sir, that Oregon Country is something we Americans should have. Right now, all we got out there are a few missionaries and trappers like me. It's going to take a lot more people, farmers and such, to get that land for the United States."

Caleb sat mesmerized as the trappers continued their description of the country. Everything they said sounded too good to be true. Was it really a land without winters, without insects, and without sickness?

Free land that doesn't need to be cleared, Caleb thought. *How could I go wrong?*

The discussion continued for several hours until it was time to go. Joe helped Caleb load his new plow and seed drill into the back of the wagon.

"Wait till Abby hears about Oregon," Caleb said laughingly. "She probably won't believe a word."

"Let me know if you have any trouble with that drill," Joe called out as Caleb stepped up onto the wagon, "and give my best to Abby. We miss seeing her in town, and they surely miss her down at the schoolhouse."

"I will do that. Till next Sunday, Joe." Caleb snapped the reins and was off. As he turned a corner and headed out of town, his mind was swimming with news of Oregon.

Could it really be that good? Could any land be that good? His mind spun with future plans all the way back to the farm, but he soon would put them aside as the reality of starting a new farm in Greene County took precedence.

The cabin adopted a warm and cozy look with the addition of a few more pieces of furniture and an afghan knitted by Abby. The remainder of their savings went to seed, farm equipment, and a woodstove during this first spring. Caleb bought most of the equipment on credit, while some items he borrowed from his brothers, such as a honing wheel.

Felling trees provided some income from the local sawmill. To get the land ready for a plow, stumps needed to be burned out, and that was slow, hard work. By the end of each day, Caleb returned to the cabin almost too tired to enjoy one of Abby's meals. The days were getting longer, the weather warmer, and to the young couple's great joy, Abby was expecting their first child.

Life on a new farm was hard. Chores such as sewing and washing were strictly "women's work," and chores such as plowing and weeding were strictly "men's work." The vegetable garden was Abby's domain. Such a clear division of labor made life, and sustenance, considerably easier. Marriage was more of a necessity on the frontier than a convenience. No man would ever consider starting a farm without the labor of a woman—and as children came along, there would be chores for them, too.

Sunday provided a needed respite from a week of hard farm labor. The white wood-frame church with its modest steeple served as a gathering place where people could socialize and catch up on weekly news. Because farms were so isolated, Sunday at church stretched into an all-day affair. Ladies brought food dishes for the noon meal along with crafts and quilts to work on, while men usually gathered around the two woodstoves to discuss current affairs, the difficulties of farming on the edge of the frontier, the varying availability of equipment, quality of seed and market prices—and of course, the weather. For most of this year their conversations had revolved around the current economic depression. Crop prices were at an all-time low with no end in sight. Several men wondered whether they would be able to continue farming if they did not receive top dollar for their produce during the coming harvest.

"Have any of you men considered going out to Oregon Country?" Caleb had not stopped thinking about those trappers. Several months had passed, but their descriptions were still vivid.

"I need to hear a lot more than what we currently know," said Isaiah Johnston. "The wild descriptions of a few trappers aren't enough for me. Has anyone else heard about this Oregon Country?" He surveyed the group sitting around the woodstove.

"The Cincinnati *Gazette* might have something to say about it," replied Bill Robb. "I'm going down there next month, so I'll ask my brother. If there's been anything written, I'll bring it back."

For the remainder of the day, and for several Sundays afterwards, the men casually talked about the opportunities offered by this new land of Oregon. Sunday presented one of the few times for these discussions, for the women did not want anything to do with this type of foolishness. Some women would not even allow the talk in their homes. Such was the summer of 1841—but things would soon change.

After the spring crops were in and the warm summer sun slowed the pace on many farms, Caleb's brothers organized a barn raising. Almost everyone who had attended the wedding, and then some, helped with the new barn. Neighboring farms and the local sawmill donated all the necessary building materials. Women again brought enough food for a large banquet, so nobody went hungry.

In less than a day Caleb had his new barn. It had a loft for storing hay and enough room for six horse stalls. There was also room to store tack, a hay rake, a plow, and other farm implements, along with the wagon. With this barn up, and his first crop greening in the fields, Caleb's dream now looked like a real farm.

The summer passed quickly, and before long the hay was ready to cut, dry, and bundle. In another month the corn would be ready. Most of it was sweet corn, and Caleb hoped to get a good price at the Greene County fall market. The remainder was field corn to feed chickens and supplement the diet of their two horses. Abby's garden contained necessities that would carry them through the winter and into next summer: pumpkins, tomatoes, squash, potatoes, cucumbers, raspberries, onions, carrots, beets, and an odd assortment of other vegetables. The work of preserving would keep Abby busy for several weeks. In seven or eight years, the fruit trees Caleb had planted last spring would add to their harvest and fall preserves.

The Depression of 1839 turned disastrous for many. By 1841 creditors had taken possession of farms from families unable to pay their debts. For those remaining, the owner's income related to the size of each crop, which in turn depended almost entirely on the weather. Warm weather, not too hot and with adequate rain, was the hope of everyone—but hope can give way to despair on many occasions. This year was average—better than many, but not the best. August had been a dry month, and September about average. It was October now, and Caleb was busy from morning 'til dusk with the harvesting chores of cutting, shucking, and baling. His creditors would not be paid in full this year, but he was not selling the farm.

Abby's first child was due sometime in November—late enough so that all of the fall harvesting chores would be complete. It pleased her that she would have the winter to devote to the baby without all the work of the growing season. As she put up preserves and tended to a multitude of other chores, her thoughts fell more and more to the new baby. She hoped it would be a boy, for Caleb wanted a boy—a strong lad to help him with the farm—but as long as the baby was healthy, they would both be happy.

On one of those beautiful autumn days, between the heat of

summer and the cold, snowy days of winter, Abby's child began to stir. The brilliant fall color now lay on the ground while only the oaks clung to their leaves, reddish brown and dry. Everywhere hung the distinctive autumn odor of dry grass and foliage, for the season was rapidly changing to winter. While Abby collected the remaining squash from her garden, the baby decided to make an appearance. She instinctively knew it was time, but had a few more squash left to pick, so she kept working. Caleb, out in the fields gathering the remaining harvest, would not be back until evening. Abby headed back to the cabin by herself to await the arrival of their baby.

Abby had never decided where to have the child. Their bed now had a new straw mattress that she did not want to damage—and the wedding quilt had become a treasured item, along with the afghan. The time for decision had passed, so she lay down on the cabin floor to await the return of Caleb.

"Caleb better hurry," she thought, "and I could use the help of Sarah Reed. She said she would stop by regularly to check on me. Well, now is the time Mrs. Reed! Where are you?"

Abby could tell that this baby was not going to have the courtesy to wait for guests. The time had come, so she gasped for air and grit her teeth.

"Ahh ... Ahh ..." She often made this sound when some momentous event occurred, a soft gasp of despair and helplessness, as if she could do nothing but await the outcome. It escaped involuntarily and happened when fear, despair, and courage all collided in a maze of confusion—like when Mrs. Kerron fell off the footbridge near the church last summer. That episode had been quickly followed by laughter as soon as everyone saw she was not hurt, just wet and embarrassed when she landed on her feet in the small creek. This time it was Abby's turn. She closed her eyes, and within a few minutes it was over.

Abby picked the baby up to clear its mouth, then held it to her chest with both hands as she lay back on the floor to rest. It was a girl, with ten toes, ten fingers, and a head full of hair—jet-black like Abby's. After a few minutes the movement of the baby prompted her back to the situation at hand. She was still alone and this baby needed washing. She bit off the umbilical cord and got up slowly to walk over to the wash basin. She wrapped the baby in a flour sack that was in use as a dishtowel. In the next hour she cleaned herself and put on another dress, washed the baby, nursed and diapered her, then wrapped her in a small blanket prepared for just this moment.

"Won't Caleb be surprised when he gets back! Now Jessica Anne, I want you to smile when your father comes in."

Jessica Anne was a name they had chosen a few months earlier. They had still been discussing a name for a boy, now a moot point. Jessica Anne would be the main attraction at church next Sunday.

"When your father comes in I will hand you to him and watch his face. He won't believe his eyes."

Jessica Anne did not gain weight as quickly as other babies and her color was of a slight bluish hue. The doctor passing through Greene County told Caleb and Abby not to worry and that her color would come around after a few months. They still worried though, for the baby did not seem to have as much energy as other babies in the community. This did not dampen their feelings, for they loved her dearly and devoted their time to keeping her healthy and happy.

As winter progressed, more and more people began talking about Oregon, a Western land described by returning missionaries and trappers as a "land of milk and honey." Caleb and some of his friends had been quietly talking among themselves about Oregon since last spring. Now, other men took up the call. Early in February a missionary, named Mahoney, who was passing through Greene County stopped at their church to give a sermon. His main purpose was to solicit the parishioners for financial help to aid Jason Lee, a minister who ran a Methodist mission out in Oregon.

Reverend Mahoney focused his sermon on the work Lee was doing with the Calapooia and Molalla Indians in a place called the Wallamet Valley. After a considerable harangue, he asked if anyone had any questions. Nobody spoke. In church, speaking aloud was the preacher's job, not the congregation's—but all eyes stayed on the visitor, so he changed his tactics.

Tell them what they want to hear, the missionary thought. *Tell them about Oregon Country!*

"Now let me tell you a little about that country we call Oregon."

"Finally," Caleb thought, "I don't need to hear anymore about those poor Indians!"

"In Oregon it never snows," Mahoney began, "and sickness is unknown. The cattle can graze all year, and the land is already clear of trees. It's as fertile as can be and, most importantly, it's free."

Caleb and the other men listened intently. Could anything this good be believed? After services the congregation spent the next few hours socializing until the noon meal. This was typical, yet today all talk was about Oregon. The men conversed in loud excited voices at the prospects of being the first people in a new land. They talked about how they could shape Oregon to their liking, and maybe even gain statehood. By being the first settlers they would have the largest say in organizing a territory. The idea quickly took hold. Caleb and several other men took the missionary aside to ask some pointed questions concerning details of starting a farm in the Wallamet Valley.

The ladies did not want anything to do with the men's grand ideas. They kept their social circles separate and talked about more commonsense things associated with raising a family and keeping a farm. Each Sunday someone brought a new recipe or craft to share. Mrs. Reed, Mrs. Johnston, Mrs. Helmerson, and Abby continued to work on a quilt they had begun two months earlier. Jessica Anne and several other babies lay in their baskets, while the older children played outside. It was that time of week when the isolation of farm life gave way to socializing with friends and family.

The ladies thought that leaving their homes, friends, and family spelled anything but an exciting prospect. Oregon was over two thousand miles away.

"One would have to cross deserts and mountains, probably filled with hostile Indians," said Sarah Reed. "That's a fool's journey."

"Have any women ever gone to Oregon?" asked Elsa Johnston.

"Have the missionaries got wives?" asked Abby. "If so, then they must have crossed all those mountains."

"Well, it's not natural, leaving one's home to go off chasing in the wilderness for a few more acres of land. It's just not natural." Elsa sounded firm, as if she was going to give her husband a good talking-to as soon as she got home.

The men soon learned that Reverend Lee recently had begun another mission at a place called Wascopam on the Columbia River. Apparently this new mission was situated near extensive fishing grounds visited by many different Indian tribes. Mahoney asked the men for help and financing for Lee's latest work in Oregon Country.

"There are thousands of lost souls in this country, and we can use all the help we can get," he argued.

"Yes, but what about this Columbia River area for land? Is there good bottomland within the floodplain? How big is this river?" George Robinson was looking for new land, not missions.

"Not along the Columbia," replied Mahoney. "There's land at Wascopam, but nowhere else. Mountains hem in most of the river. You need to go to the Wallamet Valley to find good farmland. I can tell you straightaway that the Wallamet Valley has the best farmland in all the world, already cleared and ready to plow."

"We've heard there's timber in nearby mountains," said Joe Freeman. "The trees are so big you could make an entire house from a single tree! We even heard that with some trees you could make two or three homes! Is there any truth to that? The men last spring talked of clear streams to water livestock and run any kind of mill. Is that true?"

Mahoney nodded his assent. It was all true!

"What kind of yields does this Lee fellow get from his fields?" Bill Robb's tone was gravely serious. Leaving one's home for another country was serious business.

"A bountiful crop every year," came the reply, "and the Hudson Bay Company will buy anything you grow. It's a guaranteed market. There's no depression out in Oregon Country, no sir, not like here."

"If several hundred new farms get established, the Hudson Bay Company would never buy all of those crops." Caleb was goading the missionary to keep talking.

"You're on the Pacific Coast son," replied Reverend Mahoney. "Merchant ships sail up the Columbia and dock right there at Fort

Vancouver. I know that the Hudson Bay Company sells their surplus cheese to the Russian settlements up at Sitka and down in the Sandwich Islands. Whoever starts a farm in Oregon has the world as a market. You can't go wrong."

Caleb had heard this from those trappers last spring. The missionary's confirmation was welcome news.

"What about a government?" asked Adam Erdman. "You need laws and some type of court system to uphold those laws."

"That's where you come in," said Mahoney. "If enough of you people go out there to settle, then you can start your own Provisional Government. Imagine that. You can actually start your own country! Make the laws you want!"

"Schools, what about schools?" asked Caleb. "I want my daughter to have good schooling. Are there any schools?"

"You bring your own," smiled the missionary. "I'm saying you can start your own country, or state if that land becomes part of the Union. Right now all the missions run their own schools, so we could use some schoolteachers out there, beside you farmers."

"My Abby's a schoolteacher, but I'll need her on the farm to raise my family. We'll have to take a schoolteacher out there alright. I mean, if any of us go." Caleb looked around as if he had spoken out of turn.

A number of men were thinking of going—but thinking and doing were two different things. For the present, Sunday discussions would have to do.

Mahoney rose to go over and talk to the ladies, leaving the men to discuss Oregon.

"Free land is fine," Caleb's brother Michael said, "but where can you sell your crops?"

"Hudson Bay Company," replied Zeb Josse, "didn't you hear that man? What they don't buy you can sell to the different missions."

"Don't forget the settlements in California," added Isaiah Johnston.

"By being on the Pacific coast we'd have all those markets available across the ocean, ain't that right?" Hank Farnham looked for approval and received it in the form of several nods.

"Don't forget that man said there's timber for building homes, barns, and furniture. Not all the land is clear and ready for farms, yet it sounds to be about as perfect a place as any man could want. Yup, about as perfect as any man could want." Adam Erdman drew a puff on his pipe with that last remark, eliciting another round of nods.

Caleb listened intently to each man, adding his own remarks about the great possibilities that awaited them in Oregon.

"If enough of us want to go, maybe we should form some sort of emigrating company. I'd hate to miss out on an opportunity like this. It may never come again." More nods, this time with raised eyebrows as some men realized the potential benefits of embarking on such an adventure.

The day passed quickly, and before dark Caleb, Abby, and Jessica were on their way back to the farm. Caleb began telling Abby about the wonders of Oregon and how it was said to be everything a farmer could want. Talking was not harmful, but when he began getting serious about emigrating, Abby put a stop to it. She would not hear of such childish thoughts.

"Abby, this missionary talked about the importance for Americans to settle the region to prevent the British from taking over. Now isn't that reason enough to go?" After two wars within a single generation, few Americans had any time for the British.

"The U.S. Congress is talking about enacting a land law that would allocate 320 acres to every male and another 320 acres if he has a wife. That's you, Abby. What do you think about that? That's 640 acres, eight times more than I have now, and it's already cleared."

He continued with an excitement in his voice that Abby had never heard. "With a farm that size we would be set for life! The climate is healthier, maybe that's what my Jessica needs." Mahoney had painted a picture that was hard to resist.

Abby remained silent, holding Jessica in her lap. She thought about their new farm and how much work they had done over the past year. It was home. Even if the country was experiencing a depression, that would soon turn around.

"Caleb, we have a home, a good one. Our home is here in Greene County, and that's where we're going to stay. Oregon is over two thousand miles away, and I have no intention of going through the work of starting another farm. Besides, all our friends and family are here, so I don't want to hear any more foolish talk about going to Oregon. You can dream about it all you want, but we're staying right here in Greene County."

"But, Abby!"

"Caleb, now you forget this foolishness, 'cause we already have a farm. Our friends and family are here. We have a good life, so you just forget this Oregon Country." The determination in her voice brought Caleb back to reality. He knew that when she made up her mind it was hard to change.

"It doesn't hurt to talk about it. I hear George Robinson is planning on going by himself. He doesn't have anything here, and Oregon sounds like a great opportunity. Since we have to lease our farm, it might be years before we'll have enough money to buy it. Land in Oregon is free—and good farmland. Going to Oregon would be a great adventure and a great place to raise a family."

"Caleb!" Abby said his name with a look that could stop a runaway horse. That was all she needed to say. He knew he had better change the subject.

Unlike other women, Abby was not subservient. If she had an opinion, she let Caleb know, and Caleb knew better than to challenge her. For the present, the subject of Oregon would have to wait.

During that winter there was constant talk of Oregon every time Caleb went to town or to Sunday services. The missionary, who had only visited Greene County that one weekend, stirred something in Caleb that Abby had not counted on. It was a desire for adventure, a desire to be the first in a new land. She did her best to discourage him, but it seemed to be of no use. Although she would do anything to improve Jessica's health, there was no guarantee that moving to Oregon could help.

The winter passed quickly, and soon it was time for planting, April of 1842. The winter had seen a good snowpack, which folks often referred to as farmer's fertilizer. By the end of April the fields were dry enough for plowing and planting. While Caleb tended to getting the crops in, Abby worked in her garden and watched Jessica in her basket alongside the neatly furrowed rows.

Jessica was almost six months old and still very weak. Abby tied a small red ribbon in the infant's black hair, which was now thick enough to cover her ears. She wore a simple dress made from homespun cloth and an old folded flour sack for a diaper. She was a quiet baby who always had a smile for strangers. Caleb and Abby enjoyed showing her off at church every Sunday and whenever they had occasion to go into town. It seemed as if everyone wanted to hold her.

Caleb still spoke idly about Oregon Country, and Abby had begun talking about having a second child. She still wanted Caleb to have a son. With their farm rapidly taking shape, and with more and more acreage plowable, Caleb would need help. On this and any other farm, such help could only come from a large family. Both Caleb and Abby had grown up on farms with large families, and for Abby, a farm would not be a farm without one. Jessica was just the start, for there would be more. She loved taking care of Jessica, working in her vegetable garden, and building this small frontier farm into a beautiful home.

The interior of their cabin now had several more chairs and a woodstove for cooking. The rocker was Abby's favorite, especially when nursing Jessica. During those quiet moments she often thought of the life she once had as a schoolteacher. She had always enjoyed working with children, and being single had certainly had its benefits—but marriage brought a whole new dimension to life. There was commitment and responsibility. It was a life she and Caleb had adapted to easily. Caleb's talk of free land in Oregon and the restlessness caused by the current depression did not alter her feelings. Abby loved the farm and her family, a love that would last forever.

It happened on one of those warm May afternoons when the sun felt more like July than May. Caleb was plowing a five-acre parcel that he had managed to clear the summer before. There were many needs, especially with a sick baby, that income from this additional acreage could address.

Abby was sitting in the rocker nursing Jessica when Pearl, Caleb's plow horse, walked up to the cabin and halted in front of the window. Abby looked out at the horse with surprise, wondering why Caleb was back so early. Usually he stayed out in the fields until early evening.

"Maybe he broke a harness," she thought. It was probably nothing to get alarmed about, for Caleb usually left Pearl outside the cabin before giving her feed after a long day.

Today, however, was different. The horse stood looking in at Abby for several minutes before she noticed that Caleb was not tending the animal.

"Maybe he stopped off at the barn, or maybe he's getting a drink of water from the well." Surely, there was a simple explanation.

She stood up and walked over to the front door. Caleb was not around, and the plow, still harnessed to Pearl, lay on its side. It looked as though she had dragged it in from the field. Abby stood looking at the plow, not knowing what to think other than that something was very wrong. Seeing what looked like blood on the face of the plow, she slowly walked over to it, fearful, but trying to convince herself that it was only the color of wet soil.

It was blood. That distinctive gasp issued forth from her lungs, somewhere between a cry of despair, the need to understand, and a want of courage all rolled up into a single utterance. She ran to the side of the barn where she could see the newly plowed field. There was a form, Caleb, lying in one of the furrows on the far side. Without hesitation and still carrying Jessica, Abby ran as fast as she could to the spot where Caleb lay. Stopping about ten feet from him, she could see immediately the seriousness of his injury. A wide gash had torn through his shirt under his rib cage, and the ground was bathed in blood.

"Caleb!" He did not move. "Caleb!" She ran up to him, but still saw no movement. She reached out with her left hand, grabbing his right shoulder and rolling him over on his back. Another muffled cry of despair, for she could see immediately that he was dead.

Her breathing came rapid and shallow as she knelt alongside him for a few moments, not knowing what to do. It was that unimaginable moment of encountering news so bad that it could not possibly be true.

"There must be some mistake, this must be someone else." Yet reality would not allow for such disbelief.

"Caleb!" His name issued forth as she fell back into one of the furrows, holding Jessica and crying uncontrollably.

She did not know how long she lay there. It might have been ten minutes, or thirty. At some point she stood up and walked back to the cabin, hugging Jessica tightly while continuing to cry. Her tears fell on Jessica's back, wetting her small dress.

"What should I do?" she thought. Abby had always been a clear thinker. She could easily resolve the most complicated problem, and without hesitation—but this situation was unknown, and she could not think of what to do. Her mind was blank.

Confusion replaced time. Not until Jessica began to make a fuss did she look at the baby in her arms. Her mind was still a blank, absent of purpose and direction. Then she saw Pearl, still standing patiently in front of the cabin.

"That's what I need to do," she thought. "The Farnhams will know what to do and they're only a half mile down the road."

Within a few minutes she had removed the plow harness and looped a makeshift bridle over Pearl's head. She led her over to a stump Caleb used for woodcutting, stepped up on the stump and sat down on Pearl's back. Still holding Jessica, she rode down the dusty lane never going faster than a walk. She could not, for she was still crying and hugging Jessica tight to her chest.

Emma Farnham came out on the porch as Abby rode up. She could see instantly that something was very wrong, so she yelled out to the barn for Hank, her husband. He came running up as she took Jessica from Abby's arms and helped her down. Abby could not stop crying long enough to say what happened, so Hank mounted Pearl, then quickly glanced at his wife as he spoke in a voice of urgency.

"Take Abby inside and look after her. I'm going down to the Meacham's to check on Caleb." With that he dug his heels into Pearl's sides and was quickly out of sight.

Abby looked after him, not knowing if she should go with him or with Mrs. Farnham. With Jessica in one arm and her other arm around Abby, Emma spoke quietly and assuringly. "Come, child, let's go inside. There's nothing we can do out here."

Caleb's funeral came two days later. The small, white, wood-frame church filled with friends and family of Caleb and Abby. Abby held Jessica in her lap during the short service given by Reverend O'Donald. His words floated in the air around her, but were not heard. Her thoughts lay with Caleb, Jessica, and the future. She was no longer crying, but rather in a state of shock and numbness.

The accident had been one of those freak occurrences that happen when working with animals and equipment. According to Hank Farnham and a few others, Caleb had stopped to adjust Pearl's harness, placing himself between the horse and plow. Pearl must have spooked, maybe from a bee sting, and Caleb was not able to get out of the way in time. He fell, and the horse dragged the plow over him.

How it happened did not matter to Abby. The fact was that it did happen. Caleb was buried in the churchyard along with the other pioneers of Greene County. His parents bought a simple headstone with his name, date of death, and age in years, months, and days. At the top of the stone were the simple words, "At Rest." The graveside service was short, after which several ladies took Abby by her arms and led her back into the church. Many of the ladies had brought food for the post-service meal. A good meal always helped provide constancy and signaled the beginning of a time for healing.

Abby ate what she could, then went home with the Farnhams. She was staying there, unable to bring herself to go home since the accident. Hank Farnham and two of Caleb's brothers finished the plowing and got the crops in before June. Finally, two weeks after the funeral, Abby went back to her cabin. Mrs. Farnham stayed the first few nights until she was able to take care of herself. She was beginning to adjust to life without Caleb.

It was a long hot summer, but the work of running a farm kept Abby busy both in body and mind. Henry Meacham, her father-in-law, gave her the eighty acres after Caleb's death. He could not see leasing the land to anyone else and did not want to burden Abby with such rent. It was a fine gesture, and she tried to show her appreciation with a good home-cooked meal. Her energy was not yet back to normal, but that would come in time. Ladies from surrounding farms stopped in on a regular basis, checking on both Abby and Jessica. The two were never in want of food.

Abby knew she could not run a farm by herself, and Jessica seemed to be getting weaker every month. She would need help getting the crops in—but then what? In July she took in some sewing to make a little money, yet Jessica was taking more and more of her time.

The area doctor stopped in to see Jessica on several occasions. Sadly, he could do little. He tried to comfort Abby, stating that many babies have poor complexions during the first few months after birth. They were kind words, but Abby knew Jessica's color was not improving, and the baby had less and less energy. Other women could also see this on Sundays when families gathered at church. Recently, Jessica's breathing was sporadic and often shallow. People could see she was not growing as other babies did, and her fingers were always sore and swollen.

It was September now and the corn stood ready for harvesting. Caleb's brothers brought in the hay during the latter part of August and the first week of September, and would bring in the corn next. Abby's vegetable garden required attention too, but she was too busy taking care of Jessica to work outside or put up preserves. Hank Farnham, being the good neighbor he was, harvested the garden and brought the bounty back to his farm so that his wife and Abby could put up preserves together.

Abby again went to stay with the Farnhams at Emma's invitation. Everyone could see that Jessica's health was continuing to deteriorate and that it was now only a matter of time. When Jessica's time came, Mrs. Farnham did not want Abby to be alone.

Jessica's funeral was held in early November. Abby buried her in the churchyard next to Caleb with a simple marker that read, "BABY JESSICA AGED 11 MONTHS 2 DAYS." Although Abby was distraught, she had had time to prepare for this death and was ready when it came. In the six months since Caleb's death, she had become accustomed to living without him. Now she would have to become accustomed to living without Jessica.

After a few weeks of adjustment, Abby began tending to work around the farm. It was winter, and there was time to get the farm in order before next spring.

She continued to earn a little money taking in sewing, but not enough to live on, and the farm was too much work for her to manage alone. Such concerns haunted her during the long winter nights. Then one Sunday in late January, while attending church services, a new family of immigrants approached her and asked if her farm was for sale.

"Well, I don't know," Abby replied. "I've never given it much thought."

Her response was simply one of courtesy. She had given it thought, weeks of thought. The memories of Caleb and Jessica had prevented her from acting.

"Ma'am, we're looking for a good spread and would be pleased to come out and look at yours. My name is Riley Ennes, and this here's my wife, Sarah Jane."

"Pleased to meet you, and you, Mrs. Ennes. If you would like to come out tomorrow, I can show you what I have. It's a good farm and I'm sure you'll like it." Abby smiled, although she knew not why. This was her home. She wondered if she had the courage to sell—but if not, she thought, it would not hurt to show these kind people what she had.

She quickly located her father-in-law before people began sitting down for the noon meal.

"Henry, I know you gave me those eighty acres, but they're too much for me to farm alone. I don't know what to do, especially now that someone might make an offer to buy the farm. Do you want the land back? What should I do?" She stood with her hands folded, looking directly at Henry.

"Abby, that is your land and your farm. If you want to sell it, then that's your business. It's more acreage than I can handle with the farm I already have. If you want to sell, then go ahead." His voice was quiet and reassuring. He had always wanted Abby to have the best in life, and the events of the last year were more than any woman should bear.

"Thank you, Henry," she replied. "I wanted to make sure it would be acceptable to you."

"Anything you want, Abby, is alright with me."

"Maybe you could help me determine a price. Besides the eighty acres, there's a good farmhouse. Well, it's only a cabin, but it's warm and comfortable. Then there's a barn, a few implements, some chickens, and two horses."

"Tell you what Abby, I'll stop by late this afternoon and we can walk around and see exactly what you have. Then we'll set a price and see who wants to bite."

"That sounds wonderful, Henry. I'll be expecting you." Abby was smiling again. This was the first positive step toward the future she had taken in months.

On Monday morning Riley Ennes made an offer of $2,300 that, according to Henry Meacham, was a fair price. That included everything—land, buildings, equipment, and livestock. Mr. Ennes was polite and understanding in his offer, and said he would return in a week to hear her decision. That gave Abby time to consider selling and what her future would be without the farm.

The week passed quickly as she considered the offer. If she sold, what would she do?

"I can go back to teaching school," she said to herself. "There's always a need for that. Maybe I can find a schoolhouse that has an extra room where I can live." Her thoughts were random now as she contemplated the future. She was certain about going back to teaching—but where?

Then one evening it came to her like a flash of bright light. All those months of listening to Caleb talk about Oregon and his dreams of a better life—dreams previously suppressed because of the foolishness of utopia. Suddenly it all came into focus. The thought of beginning a new life and leaving the pain of Greene County behind was too much to ignore.

"I will go to Oregon! It's what Caleb wanted, a new beginning, and now that's what I need. I'll go back to being a schoolteacher. They must certainly need schoolteachers out in Oregon!"

Abby said these words aloud. Everything began to fit together as she surveyed her situation.

"If the Ennes family buys the farm, then there's nothing holding me here. My family will certainly try to discourage me, but I need a new beginning—and most importantly, it's what Caleb wanted."

Oregon was young and fresh. New land awaited farmers, merchants, and other settlers. She repeated her logic.

"With so many families planning on undertaking the adventure, surely there would be work for a schoolteacher! If not, men will pay good money for a home-cooked meal, washing, and sewing. No, I want to go back to teaching. It's something I know and something I'm good at. I'll be working with children again." This was sound logic, logic she could not ignore.

"I will sell the farm and then find out all I can about Oregon. There must be people going there after the spring thaw. Someone in town will surely know."

On Monday Abby accepted Mr. Ennes's $2,300 offer. They would move their belongings from Pennsylvania, arriving in Greene County sometime in March. That gave her several months to prepare for the journey to Oregon.

By traveling alone her needs would be few and baggage light. She already owned one small trunk, and acquired three more from her family and in-laws, who all the while tried to talk her out of going—all except Caleb's brother Michael. He showed the same interest in Oregon as Caleb had, except that his wife quickly put a stop to it. Abby would have to travel alone.

It was difficult to determine what to pack for such a long journey. Friends advised Abby not to take any furniture, for she could buy those items in Oregon. Rather, sell all the furniture and take money instead. She decided that she would buy all items necessary for the trail when she got to Independence, Missouri. This town, according to the missionary, was the last settlement on the Western frontier. She learned that emigrants going to Oregon and other Western destinations were assembling at this community in early May. Apparently, this town served the Santa Fe traders and could equip emigrants going to Oregon. Independence was a town built around supplying traders, trappers, emigrants, adventurers, speculators, mountain men, military excursions, and any other faction heading West.

"They will have everything I need for such a journey, including a wagon and stock. They'll also know what to take and what to leave behind, better than anyone here in Greene County." Her skill at logic never failed as she considered all the details.

By early April she was ready to leave. She had four trunks packed with clothes, household items, a few keepsakes, and her diary. One of the trunks had a false bottom, in which she kept Caleb's money belt and the $2,300. Establishing a home in Oregon would take whatever money was not used in Independence for securing an outfit. The Enneses were staying in town, and the Farnhams would make sure they got settled. On the previous Sunday, family and friends at church had wished Abby a safe journey. Now, only that final moment of farewell remained.

Caleb's brother Michael picked Abby up in an old farm wagon on the morning of April 6. As they rode down the dusty single lane, Abby looked back, knowing it would be the last time she would ever see the farm she loved so much. It now held bad memories, memories better left behind. Michael drove her back to his farm, where everyone was waiting.

The farewells took almost an hour, for everyone knew they would never see Abby again. She knew she would never see them again either. After taking on several loaves of bread and some dried fruit in a cloth sack, and shedding several hundred tears, she got back in the wagon and Michael drove her down the lane toward town. From there she planned to take the local stage line down to Cincinnati, where she could secure passage on a steamboat heading to St. Louis.

As they passed the church, Abby asked Michael to stop and wait for a few minutes. She went out into the churchyard, back to the graves of Caleb and Jessica. About ten minutes later she returned to the wagon.

"Thank you for waiting, Michael. We can go now."

Cincinnati was a booming town on the Ohio River. Barges and steamboats moved goods from producers to markets, upriver and downriver. The docks were a maze of confusion as livestock, businessmen, roustabouts, emigrants, and merchandise all vied for room. Michael, who had traveled with Abby on the stage, helped her to secure passage on a steamboat named the *Importer*, a stately steamboat engaged in moving farm implements down the Ohio River to Louisville, then continuing on to the Mississippi River and St. Louis. Abby loaded her trunks and gave Michael one last hug, then took off on the adventure of her life. It was April 13, 1843.

The *Importer* stopped at Louisville for a day while roustabouts unloaded Cincinnati cargo, replacing it with new cargo for the Western settlements. The passage down the Ohio River from Louisville to its confluence with the Mississippi passed quickly and uneventfully. But the trip up the Mississippi to St. Louis became a harrowing journey as the helmsman continually swung around sawyers, trying to avoid the strongest current. The steamboat landed at St. Louis on April 22, nine days after leaving Cincinnati.

St. Louis was already the jumping-off point for adventurers traveling to the West. Fur traders, Army personnel, land speculators, Indian traders, and a myriad of merchants gave the city an excitement and bustle Abby had never seen. This was her first exposure to the world outside of Greene County, and it was like magic. Steamboats lined the wharf with their bells clanging and whistles blowing. Crates and merchandise jammed decks and holds, along with draft animals, parts of disassembled wagons, plows and other farm equipment. There were tons of supplies ordered by merchants from the settlements of Westport and Independence. Other steamboats held mountain men, emigrants, Negroes, some Indians, Santa Fe traders, gamblers, speculators, and adventurers, all going west. Everyone seemed to have a purpose and destination. It was an exciting time.

Abby quickly secured passage on another steamboat heading up the Missouri River to Independence. Roustabouts moved her trunks from the *Importer* to her new quarters on the *Osage*, a smaller steamboat more suited to the waters of the Missouri. The boat was not leaving until the following morning, so that gave Abby the rest of the day to explore the waterfront businesses. After washing up from her previous journey and putting on a clean dress, she was ready to venture out into St. Louis and see for herself what all the excitement was about.

St. Louis overlooked the Mississippi River a few miles below the confluence of the Missouri. Since the time of Lewis and Clark, St. Louis had acted as a gathering place for people going West. By 1843 the city referred to itself as "The Gateway to the West," and it truly was. The waterfront warehouses were filled with furs from Indian Country and emporiums that boasted every type of article needed by Santa Fe traders, mountain men, Indian trading posts, and Oregon- and California-bound emigrants. Inns, billiard parlors, and saloons lined every street. Residents lived up on the bluffs, away from the noise and confusion of the waterfront.

Abby walked up the steep board sidewalk from the wharves to the business district. As she turned a corner and stepped out onto the main street, a whole new world opened in front of her—wagons, people, horses, merchants, and what seemed to be an uncontrollable, exuberant bustle in every direction. The city presented an excitement that a farm girl from Greene County could have never imagined.

Abby spent a few minutes gawking at the scene before her, then cautiously started down the sidewalk looking in each store window. The buzz was infectious, so she picked up her pace to walk in step with the other emigrants, speculators and frontiersmen. A dry-goods store caught her attention, and soon she was wearing a new dress made from good homespun cloth, tough enough for the trail.

"From now on," she thought, "everything I buy will have some function for getting me to Oregon."

Abby spent most of the afternoon shopping for small items she thought might be of use on her journey, enjoying the delicacies of St. Louis cuisine, and turning the head of every man on Main Street. Her beauty had never failed to make her the center of attention. Doors opened and hats tipped wherever she went. It was an afternoon to remember.

The passage from St. Louis to Independence aboard the *Osage* took six days, with the boat occasionally getting caught on a snag for two or three hours at a time. After three days Abby could see signs of the great Oregon migration. Party upon party of emigrants with their wagons and livestock moved west along the south shore of the Missouri, all on their way toward Independence. Seeing Oregon emigrants for the first time brought a sharp sense of realism to the journey. Greene County now seemed so far away, while uncertainty and danger lay ahead. Yet, whatever lay ahead was her destiny. Abby watched the emigrants slowly wend their way west on the road to Independence.

"Oregon," she whispered, "I'm going to Oregon."

CHAPTER 2

Independence, Missouri

The steamer *Osage* docked at Independence during the afternoon of Saturday, April 29. Other steamboats lined the shore, unloading their cargoes of manufactured goods, foodstuffs, and Indian trade goods. Some emigrants rolled their wagons down gangplanks, while others reassembled theirs on the dock. A few wagons already had canvas white-tops, but most did not. These additional trail accouterments could be acquired in town. Emigrants and emigrant baggage were everywhere. Stevedores continued to move massive quantities of cargo while drovers unloaded braying livestock and moved them to a holding pen near the dock. The scene appeared to be mass confusion and pandemonium, yet order prevailed within the madness. People knew where they were going.

All around Abby, teamsters loaded a variety of wagons belonging to local merchants with cargoes destined for traders, trappers, adventurers, speculators, emigrants, and of course, the local population. Roustabouts located Abby's trunks and placed them on the dock. Before paying these laborers, she questioned them about transportation up to the city of Independence and the availability of overnight accommodations. One roustabout quickly secured the services of a hack and its teamster, directing him to take Abby and her belongings to Hannah Greer's Boarding House. Mrs. Greer was a good woman who could provide lodging and meals for Abby during her stay in Independence.

The steep road up to Independence flattened out into rolling hills of row crops and pastureland. The town itself lay six miles from the wharf and twelve miles from the western state line, which signaled the start of Indian Territory. While riding up from the wharf, Abby received some comfort in viewing the small farms and homes of town merchants. They reminded her of the rural communities back in Greene County. In addition to the farms she could see hundreds of cattle, several dozen wagons, and a number of families camped out on the prairie west of Independence. Abby drank in the exhilarating scene as she contemplated her upcoming adventure.

"These people must be part of the Oregon migration. They will become my good friends!"

The emigrant wagons appeared to be typical farm wagons, with the addition of a canvas white-top fitted over five to seven hoops. Some wagons displayed only hoops without a canvas white-top cover, at least for now. The wide expanse of prairie framed a pastoral, tranquil scene of people sitting around campfires and cattle, oxen, horses, mules, and donkeys grazing on the surrounding prairie. The only activity came from children playing around the wagons.

Upon arrival at Hannah Greer's the teamster unloaded Abby's trunks and carried them up to the porch. Hannah Greer was a stout woman of forty years, muscular, and with a strong voice but a soft kind face. Her brown hair, haphazardly tied up with various strands, fell down around her ears and face. Her husband had died several years earlier, and she now made a living by taking in boarders. She wore a print dress with a well-stained, blue bib apron. As Abby climbed down from the hack, Hannah smiled and offered a boisterous greeting.

"Welcome to the finest home in Independence!" Abby smiled back while Hannah wiped her hands on her apron, surveying her new tenant.

"I have straw mattress beds and hot meals twice a day. If you want a bath, Mrs. Skow down at the general store will let you bathe in her new tub for half price as long as you're staying here with me. There's a washtub out back if you need to do your laundry. I charge two dollars a day, including meals."

After sixteen days on two different steamboats, the warmth of a home and the kindness of this woman were a welcome change. Abby quickly pulled four dollars from her cloth drawstring purse and gave it to Hannah.

"I will stay two nights and maybe more. I have many questions about outfitting for a trip to Oregon and hope you can advise me on such a venture."

Hannah quickly responded, "Where's your husband? I charge an extra dollar as long as you both use the same bed."

Abby smiled with a look of independence and determination. "I'm traveling alone, Mrs. Greer. I'm going to Oregon to become a schoolteacher."

Hannah's smile disappeared when Abby said "alone." Her face grew pale and perplexed, and she wondered if this young woman had lost her mind.

"Oregon! You can't go to Oregon by yourself. You'll need a wagon, and stock, and a man to handle them. Why, girly, you wouldn't get past the Kansas River. You get those trunks inside, and tonight at dinner I'll talk some sense into you."

Her comments did not affect Abby. She simply smiled back, knowing that the opinion of this one woman could not alter her determination.

"She has surely heard stories of the road to Oregon," Abby thought. "She will know the quantity and type of supplies needed for such a journey. She will also know the best places in Independence to buy such supplies." Abby considered herself lucky to be staying with Hannah, even if the woman did not have a high opinion of her future plans.

Abby wasted no time getting settled in her room. She opened each trunk to air out the contents after the long journey from Greene County. Next came the laundry. She located the washtub, soap, and a line to hang her clothes out to dry. It was her first chance to do the laundry, and there was a considerable amount. These times of physical labor provided Abby an opportunity to contemplate her situation—problems she had encountered in traveling to Independence—and how to modify her needs to reduce or eliminate various problems in the future. Right now the biggest problem at hand was the laundry. She decided to wear each piece of clothing for as long as possible before committing it to the wash.

"When I get on the trail to Oregon, there's no telling how often

I will get to do my laundry. I better get accustomed to wearing dirty clothes."

That evening at dinner Hannah served a stew that appeared to contain leftovers from the last four days. Two other guests at the table welcomed Abby to the house. One was a young boy who was staying with Hannah while attending school. His parents had a farm on the other side of the Missouri River from Independence. They were determined that their boy should receive a good education—something he could only get in Independence. Abby introduced herself and asked his grade in school.

"Seventh," he replied smartly. "Next year I'll be in eighth and then done." To Abby, he sounded as if he would be glad when his schooling was over.

"I'll be the most educated person in my family, both sides. I'll probably be the most educated farmer in Clay County. When I finish my schooling, I'll get myself a right smart bride too. I'm fourteen now, and I plan to get married and have my own farm in a few years."

Abby couldn't help smiling at this young boy's resolve.

"I'm sure you'll be a very successful farmer." The boy smiled back, but was too busy serving himself more stew to reply.

The other guest was a young woman from New Orleans. She had long brown hair, hanging loosely over her shoulders and combed straight, a fairly plain face, and was a little plump. She wore a beige cotton dress of homespun cloth. The dress was clean, but had clearly seen a year of wear. She was answering an ad placed by a young adventurer looking for a wife. The man was going to Santa Fe and had agreed to meet her here in Independence during the first week of May.

"My name is Sarah," she smiled. "Welcome to Independence and Hannah Greer's."

"Thank you, it's quite exciting." Abby sat straight in her chair with her hands folded in her lap. "Where is your husband from?"

"Illinois, and he won't be my husband until we get hitched here in Independence. I expect to meet him any day. Then my name will be Mrs. Clayman."

Abby shared in the young woman's joy, wishing her well. Life on the frontier was difficult for any couple and almost impossible alone. People often married more for convenience than love. Couples needed to share the work, and with any luck, love would come later.

After sitting down, Hannah wasted no time in telling Abby of the problems associated with a journey to Oregon. "First of all, you'll need a wagon to haul those trunks and all the supplies you'll need along the trail—such as food. Storekeepers are selling two hundred pounds of flour and one hundred pounds of bacon for each person. Then there's salt, coffee, pepper, dried fruit, and any other food you might think you'll need. Once you get a wagon outfitted, what kind of animals you gonna get to pull it? Lots of people are buying oxen, but I don't know nothing 'bout that. Have you considered what to do if the wagon gets stuck in the mud? Who's gonna unstuck it?" These were all good points, and Abby listened intently.

"Maybe some of the other men in the company could help me with my wagon over the rough terrain."

"They got wagons of their own!" Hannah blurted out. "They ain't got time to help you, girly girl!"

"I could pay for some help," Abby said in defense.

"They still got wagons of their own. Taking care of their own families out there in the mountains will be trouble enough. You better find yourself a husband, girly, or just forget about going to Oregon." It was sage advice and Abby knew it. She straightened up in her chair, not allowing Hannah to discourage her resolve.

"Well, I don't plan on getting married simply to go to Oregon. There must be some single men on their way West that I could hire. A hired hand is as good as a husband." She made this last statement with an expression of absolute resolve while looking directly at Hannah.

That tickled Hannah. With a hearty laugh she boomed, "Why, girly, a hired hand is better. When they get ornery, you just fire 'em." Everyone had a good laugh from this last remark.

With that, Hannah offered Abby more stew. The innkeeper knew that Abby would be going to Oregon no matter what, so the least she could do was to offer her best advice.

"You go see Mrs. Skow tomorrow. She'll help you make a list of all the necessary items. Her husband can help you find a good wagon. There are several kinds, so learn all you can before buying one."

"Thank you, Mrs. Greer."

"Call me Hannah," she boomed. "You'll need all the friends you can muster. I'll have breakfast ready at six tomorrow morning. You'll need most of the day to learn about all the supplies you'll need—and don't hire the first man you see. Ask around. Find someone you can depend on and who won't run off when the road gets rough."

Abby helped Hannah clean up after dinner, then went back to her room to start making a list of needed items. Without knowing exactly what to take, the list was not very long. It would get longer tomorrow. She opened her diary and recorded the events of her arrival in Independence. She was still moving forward, still going to Oregon.

The next morning Abby put on one of her clean dresses and walked down to the general store run by the Skows. Independence was a frontier town with small buildings and considerable room to grow. While walking down Main Street toward Courthouse Square, Abby drank in the wild, uncivilized, and almost unbelievable scene before her—a scene consisting of wagons and coaches, mules and oxen, businessmen and mountain men, farmers and adventurers, saddlers and gunsmiths, general stores and land offices, innkeepers and saloons, livery stables and carpenter shops, and even some Indians. She had seen local "civilized" Indians back in Greene County, but these were Western Indians. Their garb was a combination of animal skins and cotton cloth. Some wore military pants, while others had buckskin leggings and a cotton shirt. She even saw one Indian with a silk top hat. They were a motley bunch, but seemed harmless enough.

Scattered throughout the town were the usual complement of commercial vehicles preparing for the journey to Santa Fe. These vehicles were Conestoga wagons, large and sturdy outfits pulled by mules. The Santa Fe traders, all men, engaged in a lucrative business with the Mexican population hundreds of miles to the southwest. Unlike the Oregon emigrants, these men were not taking their families and household possessions. Instead, they carried supplies to Santa Fe for profit. On the return trip their wagons would carry furs, woven blankets, gold, and silver. It was the Santa Fe trade that had created Independence twenty years earlier. With this beginning, the town could easily adapt to equipping Oregon- and California-bound emigrants. Independence was quickly becoming the jumping-off point for a new Western migration.

Abby continued down the street, smiling as she went and acknowledging the men who tipped their hats. Civilized men did that. Mountain men were more apt to howl or make rude remarks. As in St. Louis, Abby's looks did not escape the attention of every man on Main Street.

As she passed Courthouse Square, she could see groups of men going through their supplies and discussing the particulars of a trip to Oregon or California. One man, standing in the back of an open wagon, held up a box of various kitchen utensils while a trapper standing nearby motioned with negative gestures to leave those items behind. Courthouse Square appeared to be a general meeting place for people to discuss and learn about the trail ahead, and the supplies they would need on the journey.

A constant buzz of noise came from a half-dozen blacksmith shops as they helped teamsters prepare. Some liveries displayed wagons in all stages of repair, while others contained a line of oxen, horses, and mules, all waiting to be shod. One of the liveries had several new wagons parked out back. In front, a blacksmith worked on attaching a hot rim to a new wheel—and from the looks of things, he had sufficient work to last many days. Emigrants were keeping all the merchants of Independence busy.

Main Street consisted of widely spaced brick buildings and homes surrounded by large cottonwood trees. A menagerie of traffic jammed the street with farm wagons, livestock, and Conestogas. The people provided even more variety, with Indians in blankets, Mexicans in sombreros, mountain men in buckskins, and businessmen and speculators in tall beaver hats and long frock coats. Most emigrants wore homespun cotton of a tough weave. The street echoed with the sounds of animals braying, anvils clanging, wagon wheels squeaking, and people shouting orders to mules and spouses.

"Could all these people be going to Oregon?" Abby's attention kept jumping from one wild scene to the next, trying to digest the maze of confusion. "Surely, these people will know about outfitting for a journey to Oregon."

Storekeepers were selling merchandise as soon as it arrived. The item that one emigrant chose not to buy became a valuable purchase for the next. Each emigrant had different ideas on what supplies they would need in crossing the Great American Desert and the Rocky Mountains. While men discussed the needs of the journey, women, some carrying parasols, busied themselves looking at all the store goods and picking out items they felt were essential. As Abby continued down the street, she came upon a building with a large sign, "General Merchandise." Hannah had said she could find Mrs. Skow here.

Hannah had said to look for a slight woman, just over five feet tall and about one hundred pounds. Abby walked in and introduced herself to a woman matching that description and wearing a bib apron made from old flour sacks. She presented a note written by Hannah stating that she was one of her guests.

Upon reading the note, Mrs. Skow replied, "You wanna bath? Lord knows you need one."

"Yes, Mrs. Skow, a bath would be nice. Then I need to start making a list of supplies to take to Oregon."

Supplying emigrants for Oregon constituted the Skows' main business. Mrs. Skow turned around and walked toward the back of the store. Without looking at Abby she said, "Bathtub's this way. I'll talk to your husband 'bout what supplies you'll need."

"Thank you, Mrs. Skow, but I don't have a husband."

She stopped in her tracks and turned to face Abby. "Well then, I'll talk to your hired man."

"I haven't hired anyone yet. Maybe you can help me find someone I can trust. For now, there's just me."

Mrs. Skow stood staring with a look of disbelief and confusion while Abby smiled back for what seemed to be an eternity. Finally,

Mrs. Skow turned around and continued toward the rear of the store.

"I'll start heating some water. Bath costs fifty cents."

———•:◆:•———

By the time Abby finished her bath, Mrs. Skow had written a preliminary list of needed supplies. Along with food, there were tools, clothes, and camp equipment such as cooking pots and a small portable woodstove. Mrs. Skow read the list as Abby dressed.

It felt good to be clean and to put on a clean dress. Abby retrieved a comb from her purse and walked over to a small mirror on the wall. "Can Mr. Skow advise me on the type of wagon I should buy?" She started to comb out her wet, jet-black hair.

"He can tell you 'bout what you'll need, but we don't sell wagons here. You'll have to go down to the livery and see what they got. All I know is that you need cured wood. I've heard the wheels will fall apart if it's not. Lord knows why." She moved toward the door that was a piece of canvas hanging over the doorway. "Come out to the front of the store when you're decent, and I'll get my husband."

Mr. Skow was of Spanish ancestry with black hair, dark eyes, and a dark complexion. He wore a bib apron with several pockets sewn in as an afterthought. He stopped sweeping and listened as Mrs. Skow explained Abby's desire to travel to Oregon and her need for various supplies. His eyebrows raised when he heard she was traveling alone. Without saying a word, he scanned her frame from head to toe. Abby couldn't tell if his look was that of disbelief, humor, or an amorous leer. Was he silently laughing at her plans to travel to Oregon?

Whatever his thoughts, she stood straight and tall, responding, "Pleased to meet you, Mr. Skow. I've heard you can advise me on what type of wagon to buy."

"Sure can—but who gets the wagon after the Indians get you?" He let out a loud laugh and added, "That hair's gonna look right smart on some brave's lodge."

"Mr. Skow, I am going to Oregon no matter what you or anyone else says. I will be appreciative if you could provide some useful information." Abby wore a look of determination and was not a little upset with Mr. Skow's comments.

Glancing at the scowl from his wife, Mr. Skow knew this was no longer a joke.

"I can tell ya 'bout wagons, but you'll need a hired hand to drive it, and I can't help ya there. Maybe the folks down at the livery know someone." He leaned the broom against a cabinet, wiped his hands on his apron, and went on to explain the type of wagon needed for such a journey.

"Assuming you can find one, it has to be made from strong hardwood—not too heavy mind you. Heavy wagons require more animals to pull and will get stuck easier. The bed needs to be sturdy with tight seams, tight enough that with some caulking they'll be waterproof. It should be twelve feet long, four feet wide, and at least two and a half feet deep. That's so you'll have some freeboard crossing the deeper rivers. The most important part is the running gear. This needs to be the best available. A two thousand-mile journey over deserts and mountains will test its endurance. You'll need to take tools and spare parts to effect repairs along the trail. You'll also need hickory wedges to tighten loose rims. We can supply you with the tools." He motioned to the side of the store at several shelves of assorted tools.

"Besides being a two-horse wagon with good workmanship, it needs to have a falling tongue. You're going to be crossing hollows that have steep, short banks. Without a falling tongue you'll just get stuck, or worse yet, break the tongue. Even so, you should carry an extra tongue strapped to the underside of the bed. There're not many blowdowns along the way that could break a tongue, but that also means you won't have timber to make one. You'll have to carry an extra."

"Will the livery have extra tongues?" asked Abby.

"They should. Another thing to look at is the top board of the bed. It needs beveling, else water will leak in during a rainstorm. During heavy storms that canvas white-top will eventually leak, so you'll need beveling."

Last came the canvas white-top. Mr. Skow sold both the hoops and sheet.

"Once you buy a wagon I'll attach the top myself, assuming you buy the hoops and canvas white-top here. Wagon sheets, tents too, are best made from heavy brown cotton drilling. We have plenty here at the store." He shifted his weight as if to present some new and important information. "The sheets should be double and not painted. Painting makes them crack, then they'll start leaking. You should have at least five hoops, and seven is better, all well made. I have everything you'll need."

"Thank you, Mr. Skow, that's a fine offer, and I might take you up on it." Abby was holding the list of supplies given to her by Mrs. Skow. "Now, before I can buy any of these supplies I will need that wagon to carry them. Can you recommend an honest livery that can help me with all the details you described?"

"Sure can. You go talk to Jim Smithy, he'll fix you up with what you need. He's two blocks back … well, I'll go with you. Jim needs to know what you'll need. Let's go."

He untied his apron and moved off before Mrs. Skow could say anything. Abby hurried to keep up with his long strides.

"Thank you, Mr. Skow," she called out as she partly ran to catch up. "Thank you, Mrs. Skow!" she said, turning around and holding up the list. "I'll be back later today to start gathering these supplies."

Jim Smithy was a tall, lanky man ready to help any emigrant. When he heard of Abby's desire to travel to Oregon, and alone, he led her and Mr. Skow out behind his livery and showed them five wagons suitable for such a journey. Without hesitation he walked up to one of the wagons and grabbed a sideboard.

"This is the one you want, Missy."

He then began explaining the construction of the bed, the quality of the running gear, the strength of the tongue, and the quality of the wheels. With a quick glance around, Abby could see this was the best of the five wagons. Its construction was of cured sugar maple, a strong hardwood but not as heavy as oak.

"How good is the wood in the wheels?" she asked. "It should be cured properly. I don't want them falling apart."

Jim raised his head at that last remark. This woman must know something about wheels!

"The wheels are made of hickory, which was cut last year and cured up until a few months ago before being made into wheels. You won't have any trouble with them, Missy. Those spokes are tight and they'll stay tight."

"It looks like a fine wagon. What do you think, Mr. Skow?"

Mr. Skow placed his thumbs inside the bib of his apron and rolled back onto his heels as he surveyed the wagon.

"If Jim says this wagon can make it to Oregon, then it can make it to Oregon. It looks like a fine outfit to me."

Abby was nervous about the next question—but it needed to be asked. "What is your asking price, Mr. Smithy?"

"My price is four hundred dollars. You can find cheaper wagons, but you won't find any better."

That was a considerable sum of money for only a wagon, and Abby was expecting something a little cheaper. You could get a decent farm wagon back in Greene County for about two hundred dollars. But not as good as this one, she thought.

"What about stock? What type of stock do you recommend?" she asked.

"Oxen, Missy—oxen are the way to go, and I'll tell you why. Oxen are slow but have more stamina and can subsist on poor vegetation. They're easier to handle, seldom stray, easier to round up in the morning, cheaper to buy, and Indian theft is minimal." Jim shifted his weight and continued. "They cost twenty-five dollars a head here in Independence, but you can sell them for four times that amount in Oregon. At least that's what I've heard. You should also know that in case of an emergency you can use them for food."

Abby did not care to think about that.

"Now, mules will cost seventy-five dollars a head and will give you nothing but trouble. They're as stubborn as can be and will run off if you don't keep 'em tied every minute. Horses are just as bad 'cause they don't have the endurance. Yes, Missy, oxen is the way to go."

Abby knew he was right. She had heard this same reasoning while traveling on the *Osage* up from St. Louis.

"With a loaded wagon, how many oxen should I have to pull it?"

"On flat ground you can get by with two yokes—but on the grades you'll probably need three," replied Jim. "One ox will pull as much as two mules, and four in mud. They should be three to five years old, well proportioned and compactly built."

Abby knew that this was also the best type to have on a farm. Caleb always commented on how good she was at judging animal flesh.

"They shouldn't be too big or heavy 'cause their feet will not hold up, and they don't need to be shod. A lot of people are getting their oxen shod, but it's a waste of money. Did I tell you they'll graze on most anything? They're not picky, and they'll make an effort to get to good grass, even if it's on the other side of a stream. They'll eat willows along stream banks when grass is in short supply."

"Thank you, Mr. Smithy, your description is very complete," Abby smiled, grateful that these men were being so helpful.

"Swimmers, they're good swimmers, and that's important," added Mr. Skow.

"You better plan on a few of them dropping dead," interrupted Jim. "That's just the way it is. If you want my opinion, if I were going to Oregon, which I'm not, but if I was, I would take four yokes—three to pull and one to rest. Then I'd rotate them around so that no two animals ever get too tired. Keep the same two animals together in a yoke. If you mix them up they might get confused and not pull as hard."

"Well, Mr. Smithy," replied Abby, "if I was to buy both the wagon and oxen here, can you offer me a decent price?"

Jim Smithy looked to the corral behind the livery, tipping his hat back and wiping his brow.

"Tell you what I'll do, Missy. I'll sell you this wagon and eight oxen for six hundred dollars. To show you my heart's in the right place, I'll throw in four yokes free of charge. Now you can't beat that."

It was a good deal, and Abby knew it. If she was to save money now by buying a cheaper wagon, she might never make it to Oregon. Getting stranded somewhere out on the trail was not in her future plans.

"Your offer is acceptable, Mr. Smithy—although I want to pick out the oxen. I want strong, well-fed, healthy animals. They have to last all the way to Oregon. Dead oxen aren't worth anything in Oregon, so let's go pick out some good ones." Abby started walking over toward the corral, with Jim and Mr. Skow quickly following. It wasn't long before she isolated eight of the best. Caleb was right, she always had an eye for picking good stock.

"If you can hitch them up with the yokes you promised, I'll be back to pay you this afternoon. Right now, I have other business to attend to. Thank you, Mr. Smithy, thank you, Mr. Skow. I'll be back to your store later today to start gathering those supplies."

Buying a wagon, oxen, and supplies was the least of Abby's concerns. Getting everything to Oregon would be the hard part—and by now she knew she couldn't do it alone. During the trip from Greene County, she had considered hiring a young adventurer—but it was only a passing thought. The comments people had made since her arrival in Independence, and what she had seen of other outfits, now persuaded her to hire someone—but whom? Most men and older boys had families of their own. And though a few single men were going West for the adventure, these people were not knowledgeable about the difficulties ahead, not any more than other emigrant farmers and merchants. Also, a young man might take a shine and spend more time courting than working. These thoughts raced through Abby's mind as she walked back down Main Street.

Numerous men milled around the storefronts preparing for the journey ahead or upcoming farming season. They came in all ages and sizes, from civilized dress to buckskins, and from various nationalities and occupations—but outward appearance said nothing of the man inside. Abby then noticed a small building across the street with a sign that read, "US Indian Agency."

"I will start there," she thought. "The proprietor must know of some hard working, knowledgeable, and honest men—and if he doesn't, maybe he can direct me to someone who does."

Abby crossed the dusty street, stepped up on the board sidewalk, and entered the agency. A rough-looking man of medium build in a buckskin shirt stood behind the counter smoking a pipe. As she walked up to him she noticed that chewing tobacco stained his beard and that he wore some type of Indian necklace. She stopped short of the counter as if preparing to run for the door if necessary.

The shelves of the agency contained blankets, knives, beads, cooking pots, shirts, gunpowder, lead for ball, tobacco plugs, and even sewing awls, all Indian trade items. Do the Indians come here, she wondered, or are these goods sent out to trading posts?

"Howdy, ma'am!" boomed the man behind the counter. Abby had let her gaze wander, and his greeting startled her. "How can I be of help?"

"Well," Abby replied, "I've just arrived from Greene County in Ohio, and I'm going to Oregon." The agent stood silently listening as she continued. "I've bought a wagon and stock, and now I need to find a knowledgeable and trustworthy man that I can hire to drive it to Oregon. Do you know of anyone with such character that I may talk to?"

The agent stood scratching his beard, as if trying to remember someone specific.

"No, ma'am, I don't know of anyone right off. Men come and go all the time. None come to mind right now—least not anyone going to Oregon." The man paused for a moment, took a puff on his pipe, then added, "With the beaver trade drying up, thar's plenty of experienced mountain men around—yep, plenty. None going to Oregon, though."

Abby started, "Well, do you know where …"

"Mountain men ain't farmers. They don't much care for wagons," he interrupted. "How you gonna get a wagon over the Rocky Mountains?"

Abby started again, "Well, sir, I …"

"Yes, ma'am," he again interrupted, this time with a smile. "Wagons over the mountains?" He let out a loud laugh and added, "You'll need a farmer to drive it and a mountain man to show you where to go."

Abby thanked him and added, "If someone should come by that

you feel would make a good hand, I'm staying at Hannah Greer's, and I'd be pleased to hear from you."

"Yes, ma'am, Hannah Greer's."

Abby turned and left, not knowing if she should feel disappointment or relief. She started to walk back toward Hannah's to get the money needed for Mr. Smithy and at least three hundred dollars more for supplies. Once she bought an outfit, there would be no turning back. It did not matter, though, for the fever pitch of Independence was infectious and turning back was not an option.

"I'm going to Oregon," she said aloud as she surveyed the busy scene of Main Street. "Yup, I'm going to Oregon."

Abby returned to Jim Smithy's livery around noon. The wagon sat out front with six oxen yoked and chained to the tongue. Tied to the back of the wagon was the fourth yoke. She recognized the animals by their distinctive markings as the ones she had picked out earlier.

"Here they are, Missy, ready for the road to Oregon. You ever driven oxen?"

"No sir, I have not," she replied. "I've driven horses and mules, but not oxen."

"Well, there's nothing to it. You walk alongside the lead yoke and keep 'em moving with this here quirt." Jim handed her a willow rod about four feet long with a one-foot length of rawhide tied to the end. "They need to be prodded to keep moving, and even then they only move at about two miles per hour. It's slow, but at least you'll get to Oregon."

"Thank you, Mr. Smithy," Abby replied. "I believe our agreement was for six hundred dollars." She opened her cloth drawstring purse and pulled out a handful of twenty-dollar gold pieces. Jim held his hands open as she counted out thirty coins. She knew this would be one of the most difficult parts of the journey—paying out hard-earned money that still held memories of Caleb and Jessica.

"Eight, nine, ten." The words started to come hard, and she could feel her throat tightening up. *Caleb worked hard to make that farm productive,* she thought. *He was so proud of his first crop.*

"Fifteen, sixteen, seventeen." She wiped her cheek with the back of her hand. *If I could only get a drink of water, she thought. Jessica, I miss you so.*

She continued as best she could, her eyes filling with tears as she finished counting. "Twenty-eight, twenty-nine, and thirty." She looked up at Jim with tears running down both cheeks. With a weak smile she added, "Thank you for your kindness, Mr. Smithy, I will take good care of these oxen."

Jim stood staring at the tears, not knowing how to respond. He shifted his weight uneasily and said, "Once they get to know each other, they'll almost yoke themselves. You set the yoke on one animal, and its partner will move into place. Nothing to it."

Abby started to hand the quirt back, but he quickly added, "You keep it, you'll need it to get these beasts back to Hannah's."

"Why, thank you, Mr. Smithy, that's very kind of you." The words came hard.

"You take care of this outfit, and it'll take care of you." Jim paused for a moment. "I wish you good health and a safe journey, Missy."

Abby half-smiled without saying thank you again. She couldn't. The tears were rolling down her cheeks now, and she knew her voice would crack. She walked up to the lead yoke, snapped the quirt on the flanks of the oxen, and headed down the street to Mr. Skow's general store.

Mrs. Skow stood outside the front door as Abby pulled up with her team and wagon.

"Have you found someone to hire?" Mrs. Skow called out.

"Not yet. If you hear of someone with good character, please get word to Hannah or me." She glanced back at her wagon and the eight oxen. "Well, as you can see, I'm ready to start gathering those supplies."

Abby followed Mrs. Skow into the store and over to the dry goods counter.

"Let's take care of clothing first," Mrs. Skow remarked, "then we can look at tools and camp equipment. Food can come last."

Abby had brought several dresses from Greene County, but some were a little threadbare.

"I will need a pair of good shoes and at least two bonnets," she said as she surveyed the various shelves filled with clothing. The smell of new textiles filled the air. "Hankies, do you think I'll need hankies?"

"You'll need everything you need if you was running a farm," replied Mrs. Skow. "Don't forget warm jackets. It gets cold in the mountains, even in the middle of summer."

It was good advice, so Abby picked out several jackets and tried them on.

"I can always take clothes off if it gets too hot," she thought, "but I can't put them on if I don't have them."

Over the next hour Abby bought enough clothes for a six-month journey. This included four cotton dresses, two pairs of strong shoes, two jackets—one lightweight cotton and the other of heavy wool—two bonnets, and smaller items like socks, belts, and hankies.

Mrs. Skow then explained the importance of having men's shirts to trade with the Indians.

"You never know when you'll be needing them, and the ones you don't use are worth plenty in Oregon."

That made sense. Whatever she did not use she could sell for a profit in Oregon. "That sounds like good advice, Mrs. Skow. Will ten shirts be enough? Well, I guess there's no way to know. I'll take ten of those calico shirts, the ones for seventy-five cents each."

Mrs. Skow pulled down a stack of shirts and counted out ten.

"For camp equipment, you'll be needing a couple lanterns with oil for six months. An extra globe would be useful, but I don't know how you'll carry it." She stacked the shirts on the counter.

"I can pack it with the shirts," Abby replied. "I'll need some cooking vessels. That small woodstove sounded like a good idea. At least I can bake bread. Then there's rope; I'll need that, but I don't know how much—also a bucket for carrying water and chain for repairing the wagon tongue hitch. I have sewing materials, but I'll need some heavy thread." Her mind swam with ideas as she surveyed the general store. Once she left Independence, there would not be another store until she got to Oregon, and maybe not even then. It was critical that her outfit contain everything she would need on the trail and upon arrival in Oregon.

"Make sure she gets plenty of rope," Mr. Skow called out from the back of the store. "You'll need it to cross rivers and to manage your stock at night. Then there's no telling how many times you'll need rope while crossing those mountains."

"That's on the list," Mrs. Skow shouted back.

"Thank you, Mr. Skow," Abby called out.

"Now let's look at tools." Mrs. Skow started walking to the other side of the store, motioning for Abby to follow.

"You'll need extra iron bolts for your wagon along with some linchpins, skeins, paint bands for the axletree, and a few pounds of different-sized wrought nails—and don't forget a cold chisel." She surveyed the array of tools and hardware while adding items to the list. "You should take several papers of cut tacks and some hoop iron. Then you'll need a punch for making holes in the hoop iron, a hand saw, a drawing knife, and some axes. Well, at least one axe. Then there's small tools like an auger that don't weigh too much."

"Seems like a lot, but if I need it, then that's that," Abby said, folding her arms and looking up at the shelves of hardware.

"An emigrant yesterday bought a hand scythe—claimed he could use it to load his wagon with cut grass before venturing out on some of those dry stretches where there's no feed. Seemed like a good idea to me."

"It is a good idea. Add a small hand scythe to that list."

"Another thing you'll need is a good shovel. I've heard that in some places you'll need to dig a pit for a campfire else the wind will cause too much trouble."

"A shovel," Abby repeated, nodding her head.

"Besides a few cooking vessels, you'll need a pot hook and a pair of heavy leather gloves. You got any of that stuff with you?"

"No, Mrs. Skow. All I have are a few trunks. A pot hook and gloves, yes, add those to the list."

Mrs. Skow stopped to add those items while glancing at the stock on her shelves.

"If I'm going to carry grass during some parts of the journey, then I'll probably have to carry water too. Stock need water more than grass."

"We got water barrels," replied Mrs. Skow, "different sizes, but I recommend the twenty-gallon, and get two of 'em. My husband can secure 'em to the outside of your wagon bed."

"Yes, ma'am."

"Then you'll need a bucket to carry water to your stock. One or two buckets, it doesn't matter. Just be sure to have at least one."

"Yes, ma'am. Add one bucket to our list."

"Don't worry about a grindstone," Mr. Skow said as he walked up to pull two twenty-gallon barrels down from a shelf. "These are farmers, and someone will have a grindstone."

"I suppose that axe will need sharpening many times before I get to Oregon."

"Shovels and knives will need sharpening, too. Don't forget that," added Mrs. Skow.

"I won't."

"Now, instead of that small stove, maybe you'd prefer to use a Dutch oven. Once you become skilled at using one, they're as good as a stove. You can even bake bread in them, and they're a lot lighter than a stove."

"I've used Dutch ovens before—and I like the idea of avoiding the weight of that stove, no matter how small it is. Put two Dutch ovens on my list so I can cook two things at once."

"You know about preheating those things?" asked Mr. Skow. "You have to get them hot like a regular oven before using them."

"Have to preheat the lid too." Abby smiled as she responded. Mr. Skow could see this woman knew how to use a Dutch oven.

"Before I forget, I think I should take some parfleche for repairs. Maybe two yards, and a good awl and thread."

Mrs. Skow nodded and added the items to her list. "Two yards should be enough."

"Blankets! How could I forget blankets? I better get two. Maybe I should have one or two extra in case it really does get cold in those mountains. Do you think four blankets are enough?"

"For yourself four is enough. If you hire someone, I mean when you hire someone, make sure he brings his own blankets, else you'll have to supply them, and four won't be enough."

"Oh, he'll be prepared, whoever he might be." Abby again smiled. The excitement of preparing for Oregon had started to show through. She was not all that different from the male emigrants preparing for a trip across the continent.

"You'll need a washtub—and it'll come in handy for more than the wash. You can use it to carry your pots and pans during the day, and in the evening it'll serve as a stool."

"Yes, that sounds useful. One small washtub."

While Abby and Mrs. Skow went through an array of supplies inside the store, Mr. Skow attached seven hoops to her new wagon. He took extra care to tightly secure each hoop, knowing she was going to have enough trouble without the added inconvenience of her wagon cover not holding up.

After attaching the last hoop he went back into the store to retrieve the two twenty-gallon water barrels and the hardware needed to attach them to the wagon. In another thirty minutes, they, too, were ready for the trip to Oregon.

"Now let's get your stores together," said Mrs. Skow. "We can start with the flour." She walked over to several large barrels containing different varieties of flour.

"We've got both shorts and middlings, most of it kiln dried. You can get it in twenty-gallon barrels or sacks, doesn't matter. We charge extra for the barrel. You should have at least two hundred pounds for yourself and another two hundred when you hire a man."

"We use shorts back in Greene County to feed the hogs. I've never heard of people eating that. I'll stay with middlings. Superfine whole wheat would be nice, but I can do without the added expense. How pure are your graham middlings?"

"Take a look." Mrs. Skow pulled the top off one of the large wooden barrels.

Abby drew her hand through the flour, looking at the color and texture. She picked up some and squeezed it. It adhered slightly to her hand, but more importantly, it retained its squeezed shape when she let go.

"These middlings will do. It's coarse enough, and I don't see too many impurities. I'll need a flour sieve before I leave."

Mrs. Skow added one flour sieve to her list. "We've got cheaper middlings, but it's not kiln dried like this."

"No, thank you, I'm only interested in kiln dried. This has to last all summer, and I don't care to throw out spoiled flour."

"That's smart thinking—we've enough kiln dried."

"Have you any rye cornmeal? That always improves the flavor of middlings. One fifty-pound sack should do."

Mrs. Skow jotted down, *Rye CM, 50 pds.* "You sure you're not interested in our prime flour? It's been cleaned and well winnowed. Probably won't turn sour or stale, and it'll make fine bread."

"I'm sure it will, Mrs. Skow, but at $2.75 for one hundred pounds, I'll stay with the middlings."

Mrs. Skow placed the lid back on the barrel of prime flour.

"I can use food to help pay for help on the trail. Crossing rivers will take many hands, and fresh bread is good payment. I'll take five hundred pounds, and put it in double-thick sacks." She pointed to a pile of white flour sacks on a shelf above the barrels. "I don't need the added weight of wooden barrels."

"That's good thinking." Mrs. Skow leaned over to Abby and in a low voice added, "You can get almost anything from a man as long as you feed him." She smiled as she leaned back to pull a stack of flour sacks down from the shelf.

Abby also smiled, but did not respond. She crossed her arms as Mrs. Skow opened one of the sacks.

"Hold this, and I'll fill it." She handed Abby the sack and picked up a large flour scoop while Mr. Skow retrieved some strong cord and a large needle to close the bags.

Five hundred pounds required ten sacks. As each one filled, Mr. Skow sewed it shut, then placed it into another sack for double thickness, sewing the second bag too. He then carried each one out to the wagon.

"Now, cornmeal, I'll need cornmeal," asserted Abby, looking around at the other wooden barrels. "Both regular and parched. A fifty-pound sack of each should be sufficient."

"Over here." Mrs. Skow walked to the end of the same aisle of barrels, pulled down another flour sack, and handed it to her. Abby again held the sack as Mrs. Skow dipped her large scoop into the barrel of regular cornmeal.

"I should probably get more, since this is easy to cook and doesn't spoil or turn sour." Abby contemplated the quantity as Mrs. Skow finished filling the sack. "Yes, I'll take another fifty pounds."

Mrs. Skow handed Abby another sack to hold open.

"I'll need eggs, so I'm hoping I can buy some from farmers with chickens. If I can't, then the cornbread will be a little heavy—but cornbread without eggs is better than no cornbread at all."

"It'll be edible with or without. Without eggs you can always make mush. At least it's something to eat. Parched cornmeal is over here."

Mr. Skow double-sacked the fifty-pound bags, sewed them shut, and carried them out to the wagon.

"I should take along some bacon. Not too much, though, since it spoils so quickly. Wrap one hundred pounds; that should last me until we reach buffalo country—and I'm going to need a good butcher knife for slicing."

Mrs. Skow grabbed her list and wrote, *1 B knife*.

"I'll start on this bacon right away. If I run out before buffalo country, well, that's not a problem, since I have other food. I hate to think of throwing out spoiled food."

Mrs. Skow wrapped two fifty-pound sides of cured bacon, and Mr. Skow carried them out to the wagon.

"You'll need beans," said Mrs. Skow, "plenty of 'em. We have both dried white and Jacob's cattle."

"Dried white please, and 150 pounds. I've always loved that type."

"No Jacob's cattle?"

"No ma'am, just the white. Three fifty-pound sacks please."

"They might have cranberry beans over at Lynell's store."

"These whites should be enough. I'll need a big pot for cooking them, with a lid. Better make it four fifty-pound sacks."

Mrs. Skow added a lidded pot to her list. "I have a pot that will cook several days' worth at a time."

"Thank you, that should be fine. Now, sugar. What kind of sugars do you have?"

"Havana's the only kind we can get. It comes up from New Orleans, and all we got are ten-pound cones. Same with every other merchant this year."

"I'll take three cones then, wrapped. You can add a sugar nippers, mortar, and pestle to that list."

After jotting these items on her list, Mrs. Skow took three pre-wrapped cones of sugar down from a shelf and handed them to Mr. Skow to carry outside.

"You'll need rice. Besides having it alone you can add it to the corn mush to give it some flavor."

"I never had much rice back in Greene County." Abby hesitated, contemplating all the food. Purchasing enough food to last four or five months was an ominous task. Mistakes made in estimated needed quantities could not be remedied on the trail. It was better to have too much food than not enough.

"Rice won't spoil, so I better take a sack. Fifty pounds should be enough."

"You won't regret it," Mrs. Skow said as she picked up another flour sack and handed it to Abby to hold open. "Easy to cook, all you do is boil it."

In a few minutes it was ready for Mr. Skow to carry out to the wagon.

"What else can you think of? How about coffee?"

"I never cared for coffee, but it's a good drink to socialize with. A hired man might want some. Ten pounds should be enough, but I want to pick out the beans."

"We have a big selection with Havana, Java, and Rio. Most of it arrived over the last month." Mrs. Skow pulled the lids off three medium-sized barrels for Abby to inspect.

"The Rio and Java look too green—probably picked last. Havana looks better." She picked up a handful of beans to examine them. "They're light, that's good. I'll take ten pounds of the Havana. No, wait, make it fifteen."

"Fifteen pounds it is." Mrs. Skow started filling a small cotton sack.

"Do you know how well the Havana roasts? I mean does it burn easily?"

"I've never had any trouble—like any bean you gotta keep 'em moving in the pan."

"I want to get some tea too. I prefer that over coffee."

"We sell Gunpowder, Imperial, and Young Hyson. There might be other brands in town, I don't rightly know."

"Gunpowder is fine, that's my favorite. Five pounds should be enough since it's just for me. Well, make it eight pounds. Oregon's a long ways off."

"Eight pounds it is." Mrs. Skow pulled eight packages off the shelf behind her and set them on the counter next to the other articles that Abby had picked out.

"Saleratus and cream of tartar?"

"Over here." Mrs. Skow walked past the flour barrels to where she kept the saleratus in tins.

"These tins are waterproof. I'd say you're going to need at least ten pounds. That's two tins."

"Have you tried any of this soda?" Abby asked. "I mean, how effective is it?"

"Always works for me. Don't add too much tartar—just a pinch."

"A pinch, thank you." Abby was holding one of the tins and reading the label.

"I'm going to miss milk. Seems like most every recipe calls for milk."

"Why not get yourself a milch cow?" questioned Mrs. Skow. "You have eight oxen already; another animal won't slow ya down any. She'll give ya fresh milk, cream, and butter. You'll need all of that."

Abby did not reply, contemplating the advantage of taking a milch cow.

"A glass of milk would be a welcome change from water," she thought, "and I'll surely need cream and butter."

"I might do that," she said to Mrs. Skow. "Yup, I just might do that. A cow would be worth plenty in Oregon. With a cow, I'll need a milk pail."

"We got pails. You'll have to ask at the livery about cows. Maybe a local farmer will be willing to sell you one."

"Maybe. If I do get one, I'll be back for that pail and a butter churn."

"Before I forget," added Mrs. Skow, "about that soda. If you run out, I've heard you can find natural soda near the Sweetwater River. I don't know 'bout the quality, but it might be worth trying."

"I'll remember that, thank you. I should also get pilot bread. I saw some over there." Abby pointed to some shelves against the back wall. "Do you know how old it is?"

"Made within the last four weeks. It's good and hard, so it should last all summer. How much do you want?"

"Forty pounds should be enough. You can pack it in a flour sack."

Mrs. Skow started stuffing chunks of pilot bread into the sack Abby held.

"When it's rainy you won't have any fire, so hardtack will feel good on an empty stomach."

"Yes, it will. Better make that sixty pounds, not forty."

"You can make your own hardtack if you got a slow oven."

"Sixty pounds should be enough."

Mrs. Skow set the full sack down next to Abby's other supplies.

"Do you have Kanawha salt?"

"Yes, in five-pound lots."

"I'll take ten pounds, please."

Mrs. Skow set two packages on the counter and faced Abby, waiting for her next instruction.

"You can forget the pepper, I never use that—but I'll need something to prevent scurvy, like pickles. Do you have a gallon?"

"We do. It's in the back, wait here."

In a minute she was back, carrying a gallon of pickles. She set it on the counter.

"I'll need dried fruit like apples, pumpkins, onions, raisins, and ... what other dried fruits do you have?"

"We have those plus peaches, tomatoes, and cherries."

"How about ten pounds of each? That would be ..." she counted the different types of dried fruit and vegetables, "... six, seven, seventy pounds—that should be enough."

Mrs. Skow bagged each item separately and set them on the counter.

"We have meat biscuits this year," Mrs. Skow said as she set the last bag down, "and portable soup—you ever had any of that?"

"No, I've never heard of it. Portable soup?"

"Just add hot water. Good for emergencies, and it don't taste too bad either."

"I don't know."

"Why don't you get a few envelopes now? If you like it, you can get more before leaving."

"Good idea. I'll take two envelopes and a package of those meat biscuits."

"If you decide to get more, you'll need a tin to store them so they don't get wet."

"Tins will come in handy for storing a number of items." Abby paused, looking around the store as if to jog her memory for some forgotten item. "A man on the boat from St. Louis told me I'll need brandy for medicinal purposes."

"We have brandy, also bourbon and scotch. From what other people are buying, I'd say you're gonna need five gallons."

"Five gallons!" Abby took a breath. "I couldn't possibly get that sick. One gallon of brandy will be more than sufficient, thank you."

"One gallon it is, at twenty cents a gallon."

"I should get some laudanum too. One quart jar should be enough."

"The pickles, brandy, and laudanum need to be packed in something that won't break. Glass won't do on the trail. They can all go in canteens, but keep one canteen free for water—and make sure you got 'em labeled."

Another hour passed while Abby packed her food purchases in a provisions box in the back of her wagon. Other items included a few salted hams that she planned to eat before leaving, beef jerky, dried peppers, tartaric acid, store cheese, peppermint essence for flavor, and a five-pound block of dark chocolate. The latter was for medicinal purposes, in the form of hot chocolate drinks.

By late afternoon she had purchased over $250 worth of supplies. Besides the food she bought kitchen utensils, such as a camp kettle, frying pan, several tin-plated cups, two tin dishes, two spoons, two bread pans, a rolling pin, two stir spoons, a spatula, two mixing bowls, one pie tin, a butcher knife, twelve dozen tallow candles, a spider pan, a half-gallon milk can, and a coffee mill. She had decided against buying an oil lantern because of the weight of several gallons of oil and the almost certainty of breaking the globe along the trail.

While she and Mrs. Skow were consolidating her supplies, a short, stocky trapper surveyed Abby's plunder from across the store. "Don't depend on any game for the first two hundred or three hundred miles, ma'am," he blurted out. "Buffalo all been run off."

Abby turned to look at the man. He wore fringed buckskins that looked as if they had been rolled in a combination of grease and dirt. On his head sat a fur hat with a tail and head such that she recognized the animal. It was a muskrat. The man wore high-cut moccasins and carried a rifle with a powder horn and bullet pouch draped over his right shoulder. In his belt was a butcher knife. He had shoulder-length hair, a beard, and smelled like a horse stall.

"Thank you sir, I will remember that."

"You'll find game somewhere on the other side of Grand Island out on the Platte," he added. "Make sure your man has a good buffalo rifle. Those squirrel guns of farmers couldn't stop a Comanche much less drop a charging bull." Looking at Mrs. Skow, he raised his head a little and said, "I'll take five pounds of salted jerky."

Mrs. Skow walked behind the counter and quickly produced his order, wrapping it in an old St. Louis newspaper.

As he turned to leave, he looked back at Abby and with a half-smile added, "Good luck to ya, ma'am. I know this child would never take a wagon over those mountains, but good luck to ya, ma'am."

Mr. Skow helped Abby load her remaining supplies into the back of the wagon. It was obvious to Mrs. Skow that the numerous small items of food and cooking utensils needed a storage box.

"Wait here," she announced and walked back into the store. In a minute she returned carrying a small wooden crate.

"You'll need this to keep from losing things and to have some semblance of order."

"Thank you, that's very kind." Abby loaded the crate with the loose items lying on the floor of the wagon bed. "There, that should work out well."

"No charge for it. You've bought enough already."

"Thank you again. It looks to be the right size to hold all my small kitchen gear." With tools, food, and clothes, Abby could see she would either need a couple more chests or more crates. "I'm going to do some serious reorganizing when I get back to Hannah's. I might need more trunks or storage crates. There's probably other supplies I haven't thought of, but this will do for now."

"You talk to the other emigrants and see what they're taking," said Mr. Skow. "That should give you some idea of what other items you might need."

"I will do that."

"I'll send word to Hannah's if I hear of any man wanting to hire on," said Mrs. Skow as she brushed the dust and dirt from her apron.

"A man of good character," smiled Abby.

"You come back if you need anything else," offered Mr. Skow. His attitude was of genuine concern, very different from when he had first met Abby earlier in the day—but Abby's smile did not fool him or Mrs. Skow. They could both see that buying all these supplies was traumatic. Once again tears streaked down her face as she paid with coins from her drawstring purse.

"Must be difficult leaving friends and family." Mrs. Skow's voice was quiet and concerned.

Abby did not answer, only smiled. Words were starting to come with greater difficulty. The Skows could see her determination and did not interfere with words of discouragement.

"Thank you, Mr. Skow," Abby said as she closed her drawstring purse and picked up her quirt. "The canvas top looks wonderful, and I'm sure it will keep me dry during the heaviest rainstorm." She turned to Mrs. Skow, thanking her for her kindness and help, then added, "I will take inventory of all my belongings to see if I need anything else. I'm sure I will see you again before I leave for Oregon, especially if I find someone to hire."

"I wouldn't trust my life to any of these scoundrels. You'll need help, though. If I hear of someone acceptable I'll come and get ya."

"Thank you, Mrs. Skow. Thank you, Mr. Skow. Well, I'm off." Abby walked up to the lead yoke and snapped her quirt on the oxen's flank, causing the wagon to lurch forward. The crowded streets of Independence prevented turning the team around, so she headed around behind the Skows' store, then out onto Main Street in the direction of Hannah's.

After dinner that evening, Abby looked through each of her four trunks and isolated those items that would be useful on the trail and those that she would not need until reaching Oregon. Of the $2,300 she had had when leaving Greene County, only $1,392 remained. She had spent over $900 in traveling to Independence and in purchasing an outfit and supplies.

"I should have at least $1,000 left when I get to Oregon," she thought. "That leaves about $400 for additional supplies and money I may need along the trail." She placed the remaining coins back into Caleb's money belt and then into the false-bottom chest.

Abby spent three more nights at Hannah's boarding house. Then, after breakfast on the fourth day, she bid farewell to Hannah Greer and her other guests. It was time to move down to camp with the other emigrants.

"I need to meet the people I'll be traveling with," Abby said with resolve as she loaded her last chest into the back of the wagon. "I want to look at their outfits to see what I might be missing. By camping with these people now, I'll learn what to expect on the trail."

This made sense to Hannah.

"Well, good luck to ya, girly," Hannah boomed in her usual loud voice. "Lord knows you'll need it. If they give you any trouble, well, you get back here 'cause I got plenty of room."

"Thank you, Mrs. Greer. I'm sure I will see you again before I leave for Oregon." Abby picked up her quirt, walked up to the lead yoke, and snapped the oxen into motion, heading toward one of the many encampments on the western outskirts of town.

Numerous groups of emigrants surrounded Independence as they prepared for the journey to Oregon or California. There was constant activity and communication between the many camps as men organized their outfits and talked about various community needs, such as a guide to lead them and a provisional trail government to settle disputes. As Abby approached the camps, she could smell smoke from the many campfires. It was a peaceful scene with livestock grazing nearby, women finishing their breakfast chores, and children playing.

Abby pulled up about fifty feet short of one of the camps and called out. "Morning to camp!" She thought that should be sufficient warning. It would be rude to walk into someone's camp unannounced.

A number of people looked up upon hearing her greeting, but only two women came out to meet her. They were both young, in their twenties, and wore drab, threadbare cotton dresses that had seen their share of hard work. They both wore aprons that once were white but now displayed the harshness of pioneer life and the absence of a scheduled wash day.

"Welcome. My name is Mrs. Sarah Rubey, and this is Mrs. Levina Blevins. Have you had breakfast?"

"Yes, Sarah, I had breakfast at Hannah Greer's Boarding House. My name is Abby Meacham, and I'm going to Oregon. Have you got room that I may set up my camp nearby?" She forced a smile while holding the yoke of her lead team with her left hand and her quirt with her right.

"There's room in front of our outfit," replied Levina, pointing to her wagon. "You're more than welcome to set up there. There's fresh water in that creek and we've organized a privy over there." She pointed to some shrubs a ways from camp.

"Is your husband in town, Mrs. Meacham?" asked Sarah. "He'll be happy to see that you got one of the better campsites."

Abby straightened, throwing her shoulders back to muster courage before responding. "My husband was killed last year. I'm going to Oregon by myself, and you can call me Abby, I'm not married anymore." She tried forcing another smile; it helped give her courage. Talking about Caleb was more difficult than going to Oregon, and she hoped these ladies would understand. "I hope to make many friends during the journey."

"You're going to Oregon by yourself?" interrupted Sarah. "I don't believe it. You can't go by yourself, who's going to drive your wagon?"

"I hope to hire a man," replied Abby. "He needs to be someone with good character and a hard worker."

"Land sakes." Levina stood staring and shaking her head. "I would give anything not to go to Oregon, and you're going by yourself? Don't you have family? Where you comin' from?"

"I'm from Greene County in Ohio. I have family back there, but Oregon was a dream of my husband's. I'm going out there to start a new life in a new land, as a schoolteacher. They must need schoolteachers out there with all these emigrants."

Levina and Sarah briefly looked at each other, then back at Abby.

"Well, I'm sure they will," Sarah answered after a moment of silence. "We have little ones, and they'll need schooling. After you get your outfit set up," she motioned at the empty campsite, "you come over to our camp. We wanna hear more about your plans for Oregon."

Abby smiled without responding. With a quick snap of her quirt on the lead oxen's rump, the wagon lurched forward toward her first campsite. What would these people think of her and her plans? Would they try to discourage her? Would they criticize her decision?

"Well, whatever happens," she said firmly, "they won't discourage me 'cause I'm going to Oregon no matter what."

Abby unhitched her oxen, removed the yokes, then drove them over to the stream to water them. After twenty minutes she moved them to an area with good grass. Using some of her new rope, she cut eight twenty-five-foot pieces, securing one end to an ox and the other to a stake. This gave each animal a twenty foot radius in which to graze. The stakes and hammer had been Mr. Skow's suggestion. The prairie offered few options for tying off stock.

Before joining Sarah and Levina, Abby arranged a bed inside her wagon with several blankets. She straightened the contents of a trunk, closed the tailgate, and walked over to talk to the other emigrants.

The men of this small band were now aware of Abby's plans. Dan Waldo, a sickly-looking man, greeted her as she came up.

"Ma'am, you really traveling alone? You sure 'bout that?"

"Yes, sir," responded Abby with a resolute demeanor. "Going to Oregon to start a new life is really quite thrilling. I've organized my outfit over the last few days, but I still have work to do. I'd be pleased to learn about the different types of supplies you people are carrying."

"I'll say you got work to do." A second man walked into the conversation. "I'm Pete Burnett, and I'd like to know how you gonna get that wagon over the Rocky Mountains without a man? I hear there isn't even a road past Fort Laramie. I'm not sure any of us is gonna make it, much less a woman travelin' alone."

"I plan to hire a man of good character to help me," Abby said with a serious tone. "I haven't found one yet, but I've only been in town a few days and I'm sure someone will become available."

"Well, I hope you do find him," replied Dan, "'cause we can't have you goin' with us by yourself."

"That's right," agreed Pete. "We got problems enough without having to take care of a stranded woman."

"Thank you for your concern. I'm sure I will find someone to help me 'cause I'm going to Oregon, that's a fact."

Sarah hid a smile with that last comment. She enjoyed Abby's spunk, but couldn't understand why she would embark on such a perilous and unknown journey. The women of this small group of emigrants were going to Oregon to keep their families together. Men made the decision to go, and it was not something for their wives to dispute. Talking among themselves provided some comfort, although nothing could replace the friends and family they were leaving behind. The trauma of leaving a comfortable life to chance the dangers of Indian Country, the Great American Desert, the Rocky Mountains, and the wild Columbia River, to finally arrive in Oregon to an unknown future was more than any woman should have to bear. Now this woman, traveling alone, was doing what they all dreaded. It was a conflict of reasoning.

The small group Abby hooked up with consisted of four families and six wagons. The families were the Rubeys, the Blevinses, the Burnetts, and the Waldos. Phil and Sarah Rubey had two children, aged twelve and fourteen, and a single wagon pulled by six oxen. They also had several milch cows and a horse. Alex and Levina Blevins had four children, of whom two were teenage boys capable of helping to drive cattle and move their two wagons. They had six head of cattle along with their six oxen. The Burnetts also owned two wagons. Pete Burnett was a storekeeper who was going to Oregon to escape the current economic depression and to improve the health of his wife, Harriet. She had been ill for some time and Pete had heard that Oregon was a healthier climate where illness was virtually unknown. With six children, and a young Negro girl to help with the chores, there was always activity near the Burnett wagons. Dan Waldo was also ill with what people referred to as ague. This disease was unheard of in Oregon. So at the age of forty-three, he packed up his family of a wife and three children and headed for Independence, the embarkation point for Oregon and California migrations.

It was Wednesday, May 3, 1843, and the spring flush of growth was in its full glory. An early spring chill hung in the air, and Abby wore her new cotton jacket. As she sat down with the other emigrants around one of their campfires, Pete Burnett pulled a pipe from his shirt pocket and addressed the group.

"Looks like we'll be leaving in less than three weeks. Some people are talking about meeting at a place called Elm Grove on May twenty-second—that's a Monday. Can't leave before that 'cause there won't be grass enough out on the prairie, and if we leave any later we might get caught in the mountain snows next fall. Hard to tell what the best day is. Looks like it'll be in a few weeks. Everyone should be ready by then."

May twenty-second, Abby thought. It was the first time she had heard a specific date. It felt good.

"Families still gettin' their outfits together got time," Pete continued. "We gotta have good grass with all these livestock—there must be over a thousand head."

Abby nodded in agreement. Since arriving in Independence, she had seen several emigrant groups with over one hundred head of cattle each.

"It'll be quite a sight with all these wagons and cattle leaving at once. How many people do you think there are?" Abby posed the question to anyone around the campfire.

"I've counted over seventy-five wagons," Dan Waldo responded. "Probably gonna be over one hundred by the time everyone is ready, so I guess there's gonna be eight hundred or nine hundred people—although some are going to California. I don't know how many are going to Oregon. I suspect the majority will."

Dan paused to take a puff from his pipe, then added, "The missionaries were able to take their wives out there, so the trail must not be that bad. I don't expect we'll have too much trouble." He stood up and walked over to a nearby wagon to retrieve more pipe tobacco from a small sack hanging from the side.

"Maybe so," responded Pete. "It's good to be moving to a mild climate and fertile farmland. All the missionaries I've talked to say disease doesn't exist."

Abby had heard all these arguments back in Greene County.

"The biggest draw for me is free land," added Phil Rubey.

Dan stepped back into the warmth of the campfire adding, "I wanted to leave last year, but I couldn't get my outfit together in time. I heard about a hundred people took pack animals and some carts out there, no wagons though. When we get there, we'll more than double the population of Americans."

"Leaving the United States forever is a big step." Pete lit his pipe with the end of a burning stick that he retrieved from the fire. "Nobody I've talked to ever plans on returning. It'll be a new life, that's for certain."

"It'll be a better life," added Phil. "Some of these people are Missouri farmers escaping the slave system of farming. They don't agree with that lifestyle—then I've noticed a number of other people are taking their slaves with them, including you, Pete."

"Hattie's a good worker," responded Pete in defense. "I wouldn't be without her."

"I'm sure she is," Phil replied. "It's just that this migration will be full of a lot of people with different backgrounds and different ideas. Sure hope we can all get along."

Alex Blevins, who had been quietly listening to the conversation, added his concern. "We'll need some sort of guide to get us across those mountains, both the Rockies and those mountains out in Oregon Country. That means we'll have to hire one of those mountain men. I don't know how we can find one trustworthy—they're a rough-looking bunch at best. Helping farmers is probably of no interest."

There was a moment of silence. None of the wives had spoken since the conversation began. Such were the social mores of 1843, social mores that Abby was learning to resist. The silence presented an opportunity for her to speak.

"I don't know how so many determined people could ever fail. This is all quite exhilarating—I mean all the people and their wagons. Everyone going West to start a new life."

"I liked my old life just fine," Sarah added abruptly. As soon as the words were out, she knew she had spoken out of line. Her husband did not look up at her. There was more silence, then she stood up stating, "I need to straighten up some things." She walked back toward her wagon, wiping away a few tears.

Abby knew this woman shared the sentiments of many of the emigrant women. Leaving a home, family, and friends to travel to an unknown country was not natural. There had to be some driving force. For emigrant families, it was usually the man looking to improve their economic condition or health. The woman simply went along to keep her family together and to continue her wifely duties. A few newly wed couples were going for the free land, and a number of single men looked for adventure. Abby stood alone as a single woman starting a new life.

"Where you gonna find a man to hire?" asked Pete, staring directly at Abby. "There're mountain men around, but none that I would trust. We're gonna have to hire someone to guide us, and I'm not even sure who we can trust for that. Those people are half Indian and just as wild."

"We'll have to have an organizational meeting to pick a leader and a guide," added Dan Waldo. "Right now we've enough time, so we'll probably find someone suitable."

"And I will too," she added to Dan's concern about finding a trustworthy guide. "There are several people in town that will notify me if someone shows. Tomorrow I'll go back into town to tell Hannah and Mrs. Skow where my camp is so they can find me."

Abby knew that any organizational meeting would be for men only. Women had no say in the affairs of government, even a provisional trail government. The normal subservient role of women no longer suited her, especially since she was the sole proprietor of her outfit. Since leaving Greene County she had felt an uneasiness about the accepted behavior of women in the face of her new independence. It gave her a feeling of freedom, struggling to be released from the restraints of social mores and the societal duties of women that no longer fit the life she had chosen for herself. Those years of being single and enjoying the associated freedom from family responsibilities had set her apart from other women. Only Caleb was successful in bringing her back to a strict role where society rigidly defined female behavior.

Now, those unwritten rules seemed frivolous. The journey down from Greene County had been, in itself, an education. Abby had learned that a woman did not need the defined structure of a role with specific wifely, motherly, and family duties. Her innate independence and intelligence were in conflict with the social mores of the time, and this conflict was bound to dog her relentlessly in the United States. She needed a new land, a land where rules did not exist, a land like Oregon. The lure of Oregon was stronger now than when she had left Greene County, for the preparations and whirl of activity around Independence were contagious. She had caught the fever!

That afternoon Abby became familiar with some of the supplies carried by the four families. The Blevinses, with their two wagons, were carrying a considerable quantity of supplies that they planned to sell at inflated prices in Oregon. The Burnetts had a beautiful chest of drawers made from Honduras mahogany, too valuable to leave behind. It was clearly one of their prize possessions and would make them the envy of their neighbors in Oregon.

Abby spent part of the afternoon familiarizing herself with her outfit, organizing the storage in her wagon, and making notes of small articles she still needed to buy. The Blevinses had nailed cleats to the bottom of their wagon bed to prevent trunks from sliding around. That was a good idea.

"Cleats." Abby spoke the word as she wrote it on her list. "The Skows will surely have cleats, and if not, someone in town will."

The Burnetts had several containers made of rubber, a new material from India. It was a strange, smooth substance impervious to water. After looking carefully at the containers and considering the need to keep certain items dry, Abby decided against buying one.

"It's too new," she thought. "It might start leaking half way to Oregon—then what? I'll stay with tin until I learn more about this rubber."

Before long, the interior of Abby's wagon took on a more homey appearance. She had an area for sleeping set up along one side, with a blanket to sleep on and another to cover up with. The area was small, but so was she. She stowed the kitchen gear and other equipment needed each night in the rear where it would be easily accessible—cooking pans, food, rope, the axe, shovel, and a few other tools like the hammer to drive in stakes. She stowed clothes and other personal items up front. Over the front axle she stacked the sacks of flour and cornmeal, with smaller loose items filling up each little nook and cranny. The need to properly distribute weight in a wagon was common knowledge for a farm girl.

Several of the other wagons had a spare tongue suspended underneath the bed, in case the tongue in use broke while turning a corner or encountering a steep drop along the trail. Abby had considered carrying an extra tongue ever since her discussions with Mr. Skow and Mr. Smithy, but considering the difficulties of hauling one, she decided against it. It was good insurance, but weighed over a hundred pounds, weight she could use for food and other necessities. If her wagon tongue broke, she could borrow one from another emigrant until they reached a timbered region where she could make a new tongue. Besides, she was carrying enough weight with just her supplies.

Two other large groups were camped on the outskirts of Independence preparing for a journey West—but not as emigrants. The first group was a government survey team under the leadership of a Colonel John Charles Fremont. This group of men had surveyed the first part of the route to Oregon and California during the previous year. They planned to continue their surveying mission where they had left off, somewhere near the Continental Divide.

The other group was a private entourage belonging to Sir William Drummond Stewart, a member of royalty from Scotland. This adventurous man was going on a hunting expedition, or rather a pleasure trip. He had taken other such excursions in the American West and was returning for additional "sport." His party consisted of about sixty men, all using pack animals and carrying all the comforts a royal hunter could want.

Not far from Independence lay the small town of Westport. This remote community also acted as an embarkation point for people traveling to Oregon and California. Emigrants gathering there, although less in number, were just as enthusiastic as the groups camped near Independence.

Late that afternoon word passed through all the scattered camps that on May 22, everyone would rendezvous at a nearby place called

Elm Grove. From there, everyone would start west together. Although some families were on their way to California, the vast majority were traveling to Oregon. Because of this, people referred to themselves as part of the Oregon Migration of 1843.

Pete Burnett now estimated there would be around one hundred twenty wagons, over nine hundred people, and several thousand head of livestock. Prior groups in 1841 and 1842, associated with California emigrants and the Rocky Mountain Fur Company, had taken carts as far as Fort Hall on the Snake River; however, these were only a few token vehicles driven by hardened trappers. The Oregon Migration of 1843 would be much bigger. For the first time entire families, including children and elderly, were going to cross the North American continent with all their worldly possessions and dreams of starting a new life. It would be a watershed moment in American history.

Abby retrieved her diary to continue the entries she had been making since her arrival in Independence: *"All these people are leaving everything behind and going west. If only Caleb could be here, we would make such a fine looking couple. He would be proud of the outfit I've organized. Right now, I'm as prepared as any of these emigrants. Oh Caleb and Jessica, you both are always with me in heart and mind. Tomorrow we will go back into town to pick up a few more items, and maybe I'll find someone to hire. Maybe tomorrow."*

The evening arrived with a cloudless, windless, scene of tranquillity on the American Prairie. To the east, in the distance, stood Independence. Six miles north of Independence ran the Missouri River, still somewhat swollen from the spring run-off—and due west was a beautiful sunset.

The panorama was intoxicating. It was wild, it was adventurous, and it was uncertain. Abby sat staring at the solitude and beauty before her. She could smell campfire smoke as it drifted from over a hundred encampments, while cattle and other livestock grazed lazily throughout the valley. In the distance she could hear the sweet music of a fiddle. It was a setting that belied the difficulties ahead.

"If these cattle knew about the journey to come," she thought, "they might not be so calm."

Darkness was coming on, and it was time to try out that new bed. Abby checked her oxen one last time, made sure everything was secure in case a wind blew up during the night, then retired to her wagon bed.

The next morning Abby walked the two miles back to Independence and the Skow's general store. Besides cleats, she needed to buy another bucket for watering her oxen. One bucket for eight oxen was simply not enough. As soon as she entered the store, Mrs. Skow asked if she had heard from Hannah.

"She came around here yesterday lookin' for ya—said she found someone you might want to hire. He's a mountain man, though, so I'd be mighty careful. He got into town yesterday and is heading back out West."

"Does he want to go to Oregon?" Abby asked, "and do you know if he wants to travel with emigrants?"

"Don't know 'bout that," said Mrs. Skow. "Hannah Greer recommended him, so you better talk to her. Now, buckets are over here." In a few minutes Abby was walking out with a new wooden bucket and the hope of finding a good man to hire.

"Thank you, Mrs. Skow. I'll talk to Hannah directly."

Hannah greeted her as if it had been weeks since her departure, rather than simply one day. Referring to the mountain man, she said, "He arrived on a steamboat from St. Louis and wants to go to Oregon. I heard he worked as a free trapper for the Rocky Mountain Fur Company. When the price of beaver fell, he wandered back to St. Louis and has been there since last fall. Apparently six months in a city was more than he could tolerate." Hannah paused, holding the straps of her apron and looking toward the business district of Independence. "Someone said he was inquiring to hire on with one of the emigrant families. I don't know why, but that's what I've heard."

"That sounds wonderful, Hannah," Abby said with a smile, "but is he of good character?"

"Well, as good as a mountain man can be, I suppose," replied Hannah in her usual boisterous voice, her hands on her hips, shoulders thrown back, and a few strands of undone hair hanging in her face.

"Hiring any mountain man is risky, girly. If ya want to get to Oregon, though, then that's the kind of man you need." She then suggested checking the liveries in town. "He needed to get his horse shod, so he shouldn't be too hard to find. Ask for a Jacob Chalmers."

After leaving Hannah's, Abby went straight to Jim Smithy's livery. As she walked up to the front entrance, Jim called out a greeting.

"Morning to you, Missy. I figured you'd be by sometime today."

"Morning, Mr. Smithy. Hannah told me …"

"I talked to Jacob Chalmers this morning," Jim interrupted. "That's who you want to see, isn't it? He seems like a right smart fellow. This here's his horse." Jim motioned to a large gray mare tied up near one of the front stalls. "He was going across the street to the gunsmith. I suspect you can find him there."

"Thank you, Mr. Smithy, I appreciate your help." Abby crossed the dusty street to a shop with a sign that read, "Hawken—Gunsmith." Inside, two men stood behind the counter, talking to a tall third man wearing a full buckskin regalia. To Abby's surprise, the one who must be Chalmers had white hair and a well-weathered face.

This man is old enough to be my father, Abby thought. He stood over six feet tall and wore several necklaces ornamented with Indian-type artifacts. He also wore a leather belt with a large butcher knife stuck in it, just like the trapper over at the Skows had; however, this man's buckskins were not as filthy. Along with high-cut moccasins, this man wore an additional knife strapped to the lower part of his right leg. Abby looked at this knife with caution, not understanding its purpose. He looked strong and agile and was cleanshaven; only recently, though, for his face bore the fresh cuts of a man not accustomed to a razor. Abby's thoughts raced in random confusion as she surveyed this wild man. *What kind of a man carries a knife strapped to his leg? Is that really Indian jewelry? How can such an old man be of any use on the trail? Well, it won't hurt to talk to him.*

"Sir," Abby said to the man, "are you Mr. Chalmers?"

"Yes, ma'am," he said turning around. "That I am, and whom might you be?"

"My name is Abby Meacham, and I'm on my way to Oregon. My outfit is a few miles west of town, and I need to acquire the services of a hired hand to assist me in getting my wagon to Oregon. I hear you're looking for a stake."

"That I am, ma'am," replied the man in a rough voice. "I've had all of civilization I care for, so I'm headin' back to the mountains and beyond—the sooner the better. If you do the cooking and some washing, I might hire on. You send your husband around so we can discuss the particulars."

"I'm not married, sir. I'm traveling to Oregon alone, and I need a man to help me with my outfit."

The shop grew silent, with the only remaining sounds filtering in through the open front door. Chalmers stood staring at Abby, as did both men behind the counter. No man spoke, nor did any expression give away their thoughts.

Abby waited for a reply as long as she dared, finally saying, "Well, sir, are you interested in assisting me?"

The room continued in silence for what seemed like another minute, but was really only a few seconds.

"Alone!" The reply came from Chalmers. "Alone!" He repeated himself while looking at the other two men, who were both equally bewildered. He turned back toward Abby. "Where's your husband? Did he run off?"

"No, sir, he did not run off. He was killed last year in an accident. It was his dream to go to Oregon, and now I am going out there to become a schoolteacher." She stood tall and straight, giving no sign of weakness that these strangers could exploit.

"Well, ma'am, you've got pluck, I give that to ya."

That sounded like a compliment—she could not be sure. Without allowing him time to berate her, she continued. "If you have good character, I will pay you a fair wage, and I will cook your meals and do your wash if you will help me in transporting my outfit across this continent to Oregon."

Chalmers slowly nodded several times as he leaned up against the counter. To Abby's determination, it was a nod of approval, but not an agreement to go with her. She could see in his eyes that he had his doubts.

"Well, we might be able to strike up some sort of agreement." His reply was slow and deliberate as he lit his pipe. "I need to see your outfit first, and the stock you have to pull it. If I do agree to go, you'll do what I tell ya, even if you are hiring me. I know those mountains, and you'll be lucky to keep all that hair."

He had as many doubts about Abby as Abby had about him. It was a good beginning.

"I'm out at the Burnett's encampment. You are welcome to come out anytime and look at my outfit."

"Fair enough," came the reply, firm and steady. "I'll be there first thing tomorrow morning."

"I will be expecting you," Abby replied. "Good day, gentlemen." She smiled at the men behind the counter and stepped out into the morning sunshine.

The daily bustle of Independence was just beginning as she started walking back down Main Street toward Hannah's.

"Am I making a mistake with this man?" Abby wondered, "or is he the best available? I have to hire someone," she thought. "I will consider him today and make sure my outfit is in good order for tomorrow. If he is of good character, I will know by tomorrow."

A second night in camp revealed a few more needs for her stock of supplies. A second small canteen would be useful during the day when she was driving her oxen and unable to go back to the wagon. Also, some type of poker for the campfire was essential. The fire needed to be good and hot to cook on, and that meant a poker to stir the coals.

It was ten o'clock before Chalmers showed up. He rode his gray mare and held a Hawken rifle over the horse's neck. He also had a pistol shoved into his belt, an item Abby had failed to notice the day before. When he was within twenty feet of her wagon, he lifted his right leg over the horse's neck and slid down on the horse's left shoulder. Both feet met the ground simultaneously, and his hands never left the rifle.

Fairly agile for an old man, Abby thought.

"Morning, Mr. Chalmers," she said with her usual warm smile. "Welcome to my outfit."

Chalmers merely nodded, without facial expression. He walked over to the wagon and started to examine it. He leaned his rifle against the bed, then began checking the tightness of each seam by running his hands along the side. At one point he pulled out his belt knife and tried to force the blade through one of the seams. He continued checking everything including the sturdiness of the hoops, the canvas top, and the quality of the tongue. Then he slid underneath the wagon on his back, examining every detail. He knew the running gear was the most important, so it had to be of the highest quality and in good condition. He pushed on both axletrees at several points, checking for any movement or hairline cracks. Next came the wheels. He straightened up and grabbed one of the wheel spokes with both hands and tried to twist it free. This one was tight. He repeated the procedure with several other spokes on each wheel. They all appeared to be tight.

"I see you're not carrying a spare tongue."

"No, sir," replied Abby. "If I need one, I figure I can borrow one until we reach timber where we can make a new one."

"You got a hewing axe?"

As soon as his words filled the air, she realized the deficiency. *How could I forget something so obvious?* she thought with embarrassment. "No, sir. I still have some additional supplies to buy."

"Well, you'll need that and some tools for repairs and for taking this rig apart. You never know when you'll have to remove the running gear, like when crossing a large river."

"Yes, sir, I already have some tools. They're in the back." Abby walked over to the tailgate, opened it and pulled a small wooden crate out containing the tools and hardware recommended by the Skow's.

"I'm open to your advice on additional supplies," she said as she stood back for him to go through her toolbox. It was obvious that this man understood wagons. It would be only prudent to listen to his advice. She quickly produced a small notebook, pen, and ink to write down his suggestions.

"Is there anything else you feel I should carry?"

"Before I agree to hire on, I want to look at your oxen and the supplies you already have to make sure you're not carrying anything you don't need. Then we can talk about additional items. You got a gun?"

Abby had thought of buying a gun, but had not because of a lack of knowledge of what to get.

"No, sir, I do not own a gun. I did not know how to go about that."

"You can drop the *sir,* ma'am. If we're going to be riding together you better start calling me Jacob."

Did he agree to hire on? She could not be sure.

"You can drop the *ma'am;* my name is Abby."

With a look of paternal kindness, Jacob smiled as he slowly nodded his approval.

"Abby it is."

He continued to examine every detail of her outfit. Nothing escaped his keen eye, and by the time he finished Abby had two new lists: one consisting of a few additional items she needed to buy, and the other of items she should discard before leaving. Of the first list, the most expensive item was a rifle. Jacob agreed to help her buy that and the additional supplies on the following day.

The second list, items to discard, was more difficult to deal with. Some of them were wedding gifts, and all contained memories of Caleb, Jessica, and their farm in Ohio: the set of dinnerware given by her parents as a wedding gift, four place settings of plates, bowls, and cups; a serving platter, also a wedding gift; a small vase; and her writing box. This box contained paper, pen, ink, and her diary. How could she leave them behind? It would be difficult, if not impossible to discard all these things—but Abby knew Mr. Chalmers was right. Not only did she need to lighten her load, but some items would never survive the rough journey through two thousand miles of wilderness, over most of which there was no road at all.

Does this mean he will be hiring on with me? Abby was still not sure if this was the best man to hire—but how could she tell? Hiring any man was risky.

They completed going through the last items in her outfit and walked back out to his gray mare. Jacob Chalmers seemed to be a man of good character—she could see this in his meticulous manner as he considered her situation.

"I figure we'll reach the Wallamet Valley in Oregon in late October," Abby said to him. "That's approximately one hundred seventy-five days from now. I will pay you two hundred dollars upon my safe arrival in Oregon City. That's a fair wage, and most likely better than you'll get anywhere else."

Again, he nodded his approval—a slow careful nod that extended down to his shoulders.

"Meet me tomorrow morning at that gunsmith, and we'll fix you up with a suitable rifle. In the meantime, get rid of those items we talked about."

"I will be there." Abby walked a few steps back to her wagon, crossed her arms, and turned around just in time to see him mount his horse. He was holding his rifle in his right hand and the horse's mane in his left. A second later he sat astride and was ready to go. She had never seen anyone mount a horse by simply throwing their right leg up and over the horse's back, especially a tall horse such as this gray mare—and a horse that was as wild as its owner. The horse only wore a hackamore and probably had never seen a saddle. Jacob tipped his leather hat and rode off.

This insignificant gesture did not escape Abby's attention. Only a gentleman would tip his hat to a lady. *This man does have good character!*

During the remainder of the day, Abby talked with Sarah Rubey and Harriet Burnett about equipage and supplies. All the flour bought by the Burnetts were shorts. By doing so, they were able to buy an extra fifty pounds for the same price as middlings. They also carried both regular and parched cornmeal.

"I'll be interested to learn how they compare after we've been out for two or three months," Harriet said.

"Won't we all," replied Sarah. "I have such a hard time trying to determine what to take, and how much."

"Amen to that," answered Harriet, "and we have an extra mouth to feed with Hattie."

Abby had seen a Negro man while passing through Cincinnati on her way from Greene County—he was the first black person she had ever seen. Now, she couldn't help being curious, especially since Hattie was a slave!

A human being, Abby thought, *bought for a price.* She decided that when the opportunity should present itself, she would talk to Hattie to find out what her life was like. The opportunity came later that same day when both she and Hattie found themselves at the nearby creek fetching water.

"I don't believe we've properly met. My name is Abby Meacham."

"Pleased to meet you, Miss Abby," replied Hattie.

"Have you been with the Burnetts long?"

"Two months or so. They bought me before leaving Kentucky, figuring they could use the extra help on the trail." Hattie spoke clearly and distinctly, the result of being a house servant for a well-to-do plantation owner.

"It will be work, you can be sure. I'm looking to hire a man to help me with my outfit. That man you saw me with this morning might be the one; I simply don't know yet."

"I hope you find a good strong man, Miss Abby, one that ain't scared of nothing. The more men the better. The thought of crossing two thousand miles of Indian land scares me to death. Aren't you scared, Miss Abby? It's as if we're all marching to the cemetery!"

"It's not all that bad, Hattie. Other people have gone before us. I'll admit, nobody with wagons, but we're going to change all that. We're going to be the first, and more people will come next year. It's a whole new, exciting world out there. With so many people going, we should be safe enough. We can take care of each other."

Those were comforting words, but not reassuring for Hattie.

"That might be fine for you 'cause you have a choice. I have to go where my master says, and I'll never see my boy again, or any of my family."

Abby paused for a few seconds, not knowing how to respond. "How old is your boy?"

"Turned four last month. Wish I could have been there."

"You mean the Burnetts separated you from your son? Why didn't they take your son along?"

"Cost too much. They paid $450 for me. My boy would be worth at least that much. Men are always worth more 'cause they can do heavier work. My old master wouldn't sell anyway—he's got a big plantation and needs all the help he can get."

"But he sold you!"

"Must have needed the money, don't know. I never did anything to hurt him. He's the father of my boy."

"Maybe your boy will eventually make it out to Oregon with another family." The statement sounded hollow, but it was all Abby could think of saying.

"Don't matter 'cause I'm going to die on this trip. I know that, sure as I'm standing here. Don't know when or where, but I'll surely die, as God is my witness. Now, if you don't mind, Miss Abby, I need to get back before Miss Harriet misses me."

Hattie turned and began walking back to the Burnett's wagon at a brisk pace. The weight of her three-gallon water canteen did not seem to slow her effort.

"Thank you for talking, it was good meeting you!" Abby called out.

Abby filled her canteen and slowly walked back to her wagon, occasionally glancing at the Burnett's outfit. There would be much to learn on this journey. Much more than the adventure of a new land.

The following morning, Abby hitched two yokes of oxen to her wagon and drove them into town. Her first stop was Hannah Greer's. Relieving her outfit of wedding gifts was almost unthinkable, yet she had no choice. The gifts would be good payment for the innkeeper's kindness and help. Hannah understood, agreeing to take the items and promptly return them should there be a change in plans. That promise was merely a formality, for she knew that nothing could deter Abby from her desire to go to Oregon.

As Abby made ready to leave, Hannah invited her for dinner, a request she could not refuse. She left her oxen and wagon tied up at Hannah's and walked to the business district.

Jacob Chalmers was already at the gunsmith when Abby arrived.

"Morning, Abby. Here's the gun you'll need." Without hesitation, Jacob handed her a formidable-looking weapon. "This here's a Hawken, made by Hawken himself out of St. Louis. After twenty years in the mountains I've seen about every type of gun there is, and this one's the best. A genuine Hawken."

It was heavy, requiring both hands just to hold it.

"Really," Abby said as she turned the gun over to look at both sides. Then she lifted the rifle to her shoulder and took aim at a storefront across the street. The weight of the gun caused the barrel to waver back and forth—a situation that more than alerted the men in the store. Everyone froze, not knowing what she was going to do, though the rifle was not loaded, or even cocked. A few moments passed as the men wondered if she had the strength to hold the gun, much less steady the barrel.

As she took aim through the window, a young man passing on the sidewalk happened to look in. Instant fear crossed his face. He dove below the windowsill and crawled the next few yards down the board sidewalk.

Abby held the rifle to her shoulder while all the time the barrel wavered in a six-inch circle. She was holding it correctly, with the stock seated against her shoulder. The barrel, however, was too heavy for her to hold steady.

"I have heard of this type of gun." She lowered the rifle, looked at the gunsmith and asked, "How much are you selling it for?"

"Fifty-five dollars, ma'am," the gunsmith replied, "and I'll throw in a pound of powder, five pounds of lead, a ball mold, and a box of flints."

Fifty-five dollars was a considerable sum of money, but Abby knew a good rifle was expensive. And she did need a gun that could withstand the rigors of travel without failure. There would not be another gunsmith for over two thousand miles, and once in Oregon she could probably sell it for considerably more than fifty-five dollars. It was a good deal. Like many of her supplies, she only needed it for the journey. It was merely an investment of her and Caleb's hard-earned money—an investment she would get back after reaching Oregon.

"What do you think, Jacob? Is that a fair price?"

"As fair as any I've heard, especially for a genuine Hawken."

The talk Abby had heard on the steamboat from St. Louis simply verified Jacob's opinion that a Hawken was the best gun available.

"Then I'll take it, along with the powder, lead, and flints."

"You'll need more powder and lead than that to get you all the way to Oregon." Jacob walked over to one of the shelves and grabbed a small lead barrel.

"Here, we'll take this powder, and you can deduct the cost of that one pound." The barrel was waterproof and contained ten pounds of powder. "Then we'll take twenty pounds of lead along with those five pounds—and flints." Jacob pointed to some small boxes on a shelf behind the counter. "We want two of those boxes over there."

"That will be an extra $5, no, $8."

"Here's $4 for my share. Pay him the rest, Abby." Jacob handed the gunsmith half and stepped back.

Abby wanted to protest the speed of the transaction and not being a part of it, other than providing the money—but Jacob had knowledge about travel in the West, knowledge that Abby and all the other emigrants lacked. She quickly produced $59 from her cloth drawstring purse, knowing that she was receiving good advice and that she could recover the money upon arrival in Oregon.

"I'm going to need a powder horn and bullet pouch. Do you sell those items?" She looked at the gunsmith.

"I do," he replied. "I'll charge you a dollar for the horn and throw the pouch in for free."

"Fair enough." Abby produced another dollar and handed it to the gunsmith while glancing at Jacob to check for approval. His stoic manner betrayed no emotion.

Abby placed the flints in her purse, slung the powder horn and bullet pouch over her shoulder, and picked up the gun. "I will be back later today with my wagon for the powder and lead."

"I'll set them aside, ma'am," the gunsmith replied.

Soon she and Jacob were walking down Main Street in the direction of Hannah's. As Jacob began to talk about other supplies, Abby thought the two of them must look like a pair of fairly rough characters. They were both carrying rifles.

People are going to think I'm a mountain woman, she thought.

Abby looked around to see if anyone was staring. Several men from across the street had stopped loading a wagon to watch. She quickly turned her head forward to avoid eye contact, while at the same time hoping she looked presentable. It was a reflex and emotion that all attractive women knew well.

"Let's stop in here," Jacob said as they passed a general store. Independence had a number of stores selling general merchandise to emigrants, and other than size, each store had a similar appearance and wares. He was inside before Abby could respond. Jacob walked over to the counter and promptly asked the clerk for twenty-five plugs of tobacco. In a moment the wrapped tobacco was on the counter.

"Pay the man, Abby."

That was more than she was willing to tolerate.

"Mr. Chalmers, I have not yet agreed to hire you, and you are spending my money like there is no tomorrow. I do not chew tobacco, and if you would like some I suggest you pay for it yourself." Her voice was stern and determined, as she often got when making a point. She was not going to back down, and Mr. Chalmers needed to realize that.

"You want to get to Oregon?" Jacob asked in a quiet, reassuring voice.

"Of course I do." She wondered how he could ask such a question. Had that not been obvious?

"Then you'll need me, and that means you'll need tobacco." He towered over her as he looked down for a response.

Abby hesitated, considering the situation. He was right, she did need him to get to Oregon. He had experience in wilderness survival, he was strong, he knew the mountains and probably the route to

Oregon, and he was of good character. Chances were she could not find another man as good.

"Well, Mr. Chalmers, I will hire you for the agreed wage, but I expect you to be up front with me. This is not a pleasure excursion for your amusement. It will be hard work, and I expect you to do your share."

That was exactly what he wanted to hear. The determination of a woman who would not turn back at the first sign of danger or the first hardship—and there would be plenty, he knew that. He also knew that traveling with this woman would be better than traveling with any of the other emigrant farmers. They were too independent. They liked to do as they pleased, no matter what the danger or available advice. Abby was different. Although she was independent, she was intelligent and she would listen to reason. She could recognize the knowledge of more experienced people and heed it. Likewise, she could recognize poor advice, the type often given by inexperienced emigrants. She was a woman he could trust and a woman he could count on during a crisis. He no longer entertained any doubts—he would go to Oregon with her.

"That will be $3, ma'am," announced the clerk. He was smiling at the friction between the two, no doubt entertaining for someone not risking the dangers of the trail.

Abby quickly produced $3, picked up the tobacco, and shoved it into Jacob's ribs. "Here's your tobacco, let's go."

Jacob smiled while nodding at the clerk, then left the store behind her as she quickened her pace.

"You got any trade items like bells, mirrors, and beads?" Jacob asked. "You'll need plenty when we meet tribes wanting payment to cross their lands."

"I have ten calico shirts for Indian trade. That should be enough, shouldn't it?"

"Good, you'll need shirts, but that's not enough. You'll need baubles, awls, and other items for the squaws—and another five shirts. Squaws can be useful when you need a new pair of moccasins."

"Well, let's get them now while I'm in a disagreeable mood. That way I won't have to be disagreeable tomorrow." Abby turned around and headed back to the general store. Jacob followed close behind, and they soon had all the Indian trade goods they could carry.

That evening, Jacob enjoyed Hannah Greer's home cooking and the company of Abby and the other houseguests. After dinner they all gathered around the hearth while Jacob told a few stories of his adventures in the mountains. He went into great detail about the Battle of Pierre's Hole back in '32. It was the first true Indian battle Abby had heard from an eyewitness account. She listened intently, then quietly hoped they would not meet any members of the Gros Ventre tribe.

The evening passed quickly, and soon it was time to leave.

"I'll be around Independence talking with other emigrants," Jacob said as Abby untied her lead oxen from the hitching post. "I'll stop by every day or so until the time of departure. If I think of anything important that should be a part of your outfit, I'll let you know."

"Thank you, Mr. Chalmers, I appreciate that—and thank you for your help today. I will see you soon."

Jacob mounted his horse and started back toward Main Street. Abby turned her wagon toward the prairie and quirted the oxen back to her encampment.

Several more emigrant families joined Abby's encampment during the following week. Like others, they were looking for land, opportunity, and a new life. The economic depression of the previous four years had seen many casualties, and the Oregon emigrants represented a wide cross-section of these people. Farmers, merchants, land speculators, adventurers, and newlyweds made up the 1843 Oregon and California migrations. They were independent thinkers, accustomed to making their own decisions in the manner of a truly free people.

They were, for the most part, middle class. Poor people could not afford the cost of an outfit, while wealthy people had no reason to go. The exceptions were young adventurers hiring on with emigrant families as general laborers. These were young single men looking to make their fortune in a new land. They signed on as teamsters, cooks, and even as babysitters.

During the following week, Abby returned to Independence several times to pick up additional supplies. She added ten pounds of portable soup to her stock, but no meat biscuits. She also added a small butter churn, knowing she could get cream from the emigrants with milch cows. She had decided to buy a milch cow should one become available. Otherwise, buying cream and milk from other emigrants would suffice.

On another visit to the Skows she bought flint, steel, a large bag of cotton wads, and low-grade gunpowder for starting campfires. She wouldn't need enough to start a fire each evening, since she would always be camping with other people and they would have fires. Still, it was important to contribute her share and start the fire on occasions.

Jacob stopped by about every other day to check on Abby's equipage and any news of departure. On one of those visits he took her over to a small draw where she could learn how to use her new Hawken rifle. She quickly mastered the mechanics of a muzzle-loading gun, even to the point of wetting the ball with saliva before ramming it down. She could not reload with the same speed as Jacob, since she did not have his strength and experience.

After a few trial shots at some branches across the ravine, they both agreed that she should always balance the muzzle on something before taking aim. If nothing was available, then sitting down on the ground and balancing the gun on her knees would do. During several more target sessions, she began to feel comfortable with the big gun and knew she could handle it during an emergency.

On another visit, Jacob brought a tar bucket for the wagon. They had discussed this earlier, and Abby was expecting it. She reimbursed Jacob and hung the bucket on the back of her wagon below the bed. It was an item each wagon needed in order to keep the running gear well lubricated.

Each evening Abby cooked and ate her dinner with Sarah Rubey and her family. The prairie air would fill with the sweet smell of over a hundred campfires and the odors from a myriad of ethnic foods.

In the distance one could often hear the melodic and relaxing sound of several fiddles. From some encampments came the noise of men gambling, while in others there was dancing and singing. Religious hymns were popular and often filled the night air. Above all else were the sounds of children, hundreds of children, always at play.

After dinner one evening, as Abby sat on her overturned washtub enjoying the scene about her and the company of Sarah and their friend Harriet, she looked over at her wagon and suddenly realized it would be her home on wheels for the next six months.

"Sarah, are you going to give a name to your wagon—like the Applegates named theirs?"

"A name!—for our wagon? I wouldn't know what to call it other than home. I've heard the names several other families have given to their wagons, like 'Oregon' or 'Trail Home.' They don't seem very original. What do the Applegates call theirs?"

"The 'Little Red Wagon.' I think one of their children named it."

"Are you going to name yours?" asked Harriet, who was sitting nearby sipping a cup of hot tea.

"I've given it considerable thought over the last week. A few names have come to mind, but the best is 'The Western Passage.' That has an adventurous sound and is certainly appropriate, since our journey needs to discover a 'western passage' for wagons. What do you think?"

"The Western Passage?" Sarah repeated the name, smiled, and nodded. "I like it. It sounds warm and friendly."

"Much like an address," added Harriet, "something none of us will have for the next six months."

"I hadn't thought of that," said Abby. "I needed to call it something other than 'the wagon.' It is an address, I like that."

"We should all name our wagons," Sarah said with enthusiasm. "We all need homes and an address, even if it is on wheels. That's certainly better than nothing. Abby, what should I name ours?"

"Oh, my, whatever you like. How about something related to the home you're leaving? Like the name of the county or town you're from."

"We're from Weston in Platte County," said Harriet. "We could call ours 'The Weston.'"

"We could call ours 'Philly,' for Philadelphia," said Sarah. "We're not from the city, but I always liked the name Philly, and we are from Pennsylvania!"

"Then that will be our little group." Abby smiled at the enjoyment Sarah and Harriet were feeling. "I'm sure the Weston, Philly, and Western Passage will be very happy together."

They all laughed at her suggestion and the thought that they all now had addresses. Over the past week these three ladies had become good friends—a friendship that would last to Oregon and beyond.

As the days passed, Abby conversed with other emigrant women while waiting for the start date. Many people talked about "seeing the elephant"—a term descriptive of a great adventure. People were preparing to see a land they had only heard about from returning trappers and missionaries. The stories tended toward embellishment a little more each time until nobody really knew what was true. Now it would be their turn. They were all going to see the elephant.

Abby continued to take notes of the many articles emigrants were taking. Some people, like John Boardman, did not have a wagon. Instead, he was using mules as pack animals to carry all his baggage. Without shelter from the weather, the trip would certainly be more uncomfortable—but possibly more certain. By not having a wagon he eliminated a major concern, thereby increasing his chances of getting to Oregon.

Conestoga wagons, popular on the Santa Fe trail, were too big and cumbersome for a trip to Oregon. The Santa Fe trade had existed for over twenty years and was a staple for the economies of Independence and St. Louis. The well-worn Santa Fe trail could handle the larger Conestogas, but the trail to Oregon did not exist for wagons. For such a long and dangerous trip, small farm wagons were a better choice.

Many people packed their wagons full with farm equipment, from plows to butter churns, while others carried heirloom furniture they could not bear to part with. A few entrepreneurs loaded their wagons with goods they could sell in Oregon at inflated prices. Along with articles for use in Oregon, everyone also needed to pack the normal complement of consumables for use along the trail. It was obvious to Jacob and Abby that many of these farm wagons would not hold up under the weight of their loads and the roughness of the road. Pulling these wagons across the American Prairie might be possible, but there would be rivers and mountains to cross. The migration was to be a great experiment into the unknown, and nobody knew for sure if they would be successful. It was not unreasonable to imagine a situation where they would have to abandon their wagons. Should that occur, survival would certainly be in doubt.

Two Santa Fe traders visited Abby's camp on several occasions after hearing about her in Independence. They were of Mexican ancestry and had made the trip to Santa Fe every year for the past ten years, claiming St. Louis as their adopted home. It might have been Abby's jet-black hair, or her smooth, almost tan complexion that attracted these men. Whatever it was, they clearly showed an interest in persuading Abby to stay in Independence until they returned from Santa Fe at the end of the summer or early fall. The caravan to Santa Fe never included women, and the traders clearly felt that an unknown trail to Oregon was no place for a young señorita. On two separate occasions Abby invited them into her camp for dinner. They always behaved in a gentlemanly manner, unusual for Santa Fe traders. Abby maintained the friendship only for the sake of convenience. She questioned both men at length about the dangers and privations of the trail. She and the other emigrants at her encampment appreciated their honesty and suggestions for consumable supplies. Abby was leaving nothing to chance.

The advice Abby had heard from other emigrants, trappers, and Santa Fe traders was to load her wagon light and to put one-third more oxen on than necessary for the load. Jim Smithy recommended not taking any more weight than two yokes of oxen could pull, then using three yokes and keeping a fourth yoke in reserve. This was the guideline Abby had used, so she felt confident in her outfit. Even so, there might still be weight she could do without. On several more occasions she went through her entire wagon looking for any item that she could forego on the trail and could replace after arriving in Oregon. After much reorganization, her load consisted almost entirely of provisions and equipment needed for the trail. She felt good not having the added weight of furniture. Instead, she was carrying money she could convert into furniture upon arrival in Oregon. Only a few keepsakes of Caleb and Jessica remained. These could fit into a cigar box, consuming hardly any space or weight.

On a visit to Hannah Greer's, Abby had learned of a local farmer willing to sell several of his milch cows to the emigrants. Abby's social visit turned into a $30 expense and a walk back to camp with a milch cow in tow. The cow was a good addition to her outfit, providing a welcome supplement of milk to any meal and most recipes, including bread. Furthermore, if the cow made it to Oregon, it would be worth at least $50 and maybe $100.

It was now mid-May and Abby had been in camp for almost two weeks. During one evening she roasted a pound of coffee beans, setting them aside for Jacob. She would grind them as needed to ensure freshness. Mrs. Skow had been right—the Havana brand did roast easily, with very few burned beans. Abby had obtained a fair amount of skill in cooking on an open campfire with a Dutch oven and in keeping her wagon and camp efficiently organized, much like a home—for her wagon was her home and would remain so for the next five or six months. She rearranged the wagon contents several times to balance the weight and to store everything needed to efficiently set up a new camp every night while on the trail.

Now it was ready to go, with clothes and equipment packed in convenient locations. She kept the cooking equipment in the back for easy unloading at night, while daytime needs such as a warm jacket and food were in the front. At nighttime her diary and other items, such as a candle and an extra blanket, were within easy reach of her bed.

Her outfit was now complete, and she was eager to leave.

Emigrant families came from many different backgrounds. They included college graduates and people who never once attended a school; the country-bred and the city-bred; the sociable and the unsociable; law abiding folks and possibly some criminals; people accustomed to the discipline of work, and individualists unaccustomed to any cooperation. Most of the emigrants were going West to improve their fortunes and to gain free land. Others proclaimed a nobler calling in expressing a desire to secure Oregon for the United States, while still others were making their way West to escape the institution of slavery.

"This group is such a menagerie of people," Abby said to herself one evening. "So different from the life I knew back in Greene County." Her enthusiasm for going had not diminished in the few weeks since arriving. The influx of more emigrants had only helped solidify her resolve.

Constant discussions were held between the men concerning the organization of such a large caravan: *Who will lead? Who will maintain law and order on the trail? Will there be enough water when we cross the Great American Desert?* Most considered this desert an obstacle equal to the Rocky Mountains. The lack of water and infertility of the soil precluded any hope of settlement. The land was strictly for the plains-dwelling Indian.

Discussions also focused on the future of Oregon. Great Britain and the United States were in contention for Oregon Country, and the question of ownership was still open. The War of 1812 had only postponed a decision of ownership, and Oregon could still go to Great Britain. There was cause for concern over Oregon's future. After fighting two wars with Great Britain, many people opposed British claims on any land in the Oregon Country. Other people felt that such a large number of Americans going to Oregon would surely tip the scales in favor of the United States.

Senator Lewis Linn of Missouri had recently pushed a bill through the Senate that would encourage people to emigrate to Oregon by donating land to settlers. Although the bill still had to go through the House of Representatives, and then be signed by President Tyler, many people felt it was a foregone conclusion. A bill of this type would cause many more Americans to travel to Oregon, which in turn would guarantee admission to the Union. The bill had no reason to fail.

One evening, a gentleman named Aaron Layson visited Abby's encampment and informed everyone that there would be a meeting on the following Thursday, May 18, to elect leaders for the migration. Abby had already recognized Pete Burnett as a good orator, so he would probably play a prominent role. The meeting would take place at nearby Fitzhugh's Mill and was open to all males over the age of sixteen. Women could attend, but could not vote. Although Abby had as much at stake as any emigrant family, she knew this male-dominated society was not going to change to accommodate her. She would attend the meeting, voice her opinion if necessary, and nothing more. She would have to accept whatever their final decision might be. With this in mind, she informed Jacob of the meeting and asked that he represent her interests.

On that following Thursday, Abby was one of the few women in attendance. People gathered around the front entrance to the mill in lively discussion concerning the loading of wagons and the number of livestock some families were taking. Men posed questions of herding, night guards, and rounding up strays. To Abby, these men appeared quarrelsome, undisciplined, and resentful of anything that threatened their freedom. When they had assembled, Aaron Layson stepped up on the mill's loading dock and called the meeting to order. He stated that he would serve as chair until they could choose a permanent leader.

"Now I know we've all got opinions on how we should organize for this journey across the continent," Aaron addressed the group of approximately one hundred fifty. "I want everyone to have a chance to be heard before we make any decisions. I'm sure there are many good ideas, and we want to hear them all. Now, I'm asking Pete Burnett here to act as secretary for this meeting and record anything of note. Is that acceptable to you, Pete?"

"It is; continue." Pete sat on a small barrel, ready with a piece of paper, pen, and ink.

"We're going to need a permanent captain to take charge of the whole group, much like a president. Under him will be other officials to handle smaller matters, so let's hear some opinions. What kind of a trail government do you folks want?"

Several men raised their hands, and Aaron pointed to one, giving him the floor.

"We need to look at ..."

"State your name, please," Aaron requested of the lanky man as he stepped forward wearing a home-spun shirt and tattered pants.

"Bill Parker. I think we need to look at the loading of wagons. Some people are carrying too much to make it over the mountains, and others probably haven't got enough provisions. We need to make sure everyone is ready 'cause anyone who can't make it will become a burden on the rest of us."

There was a general rumbling of agreement and nodding of heads.

Aaron pointed to another man with his hand raised. The man looked nervous.

"Isaac Hutchins. Along with overloading, we need to look at the quality of wagons and the stock to pull 'em. I've seen some wagons that couldn't make it to the Kansas River, let alone Oregon!"

"Ben Wood," said a younger man who stood on a wagon bed for a better view. "I agree, but what are we going to do about people who are unprepared? We can't force them to get more provisions, and we can't abandon them on the trail."

Several more men offered their opinions, and a lively debate ensued. It remained civil, and Aaron Layson kept a tight rein on meeting protocol. Upon suggestions from Aaron and several other men, they decided that a committee of seven men would inspect each outfit and advise the owner of necessary improvements, both in provisions and equipment. Aaron asked for volunteers, and the committee quickly filled.

"I'd like to say a few words concerning this venture and my desire to offer my services as a leader." Pete Burnett, who was cleanshaven and wearing a frock coat and tie, stepped up next to Aaron. "I know you people have concerns about heading out across the continent with your families and all your worldly possessions. Well, let me say a few words about Oregon. We're here today because the Western states of Missouri, Illinois, Kentucky, Tennessee, and others are getting overcrowded with too many farmers, merchants, speculators, and everyone else. We need to go somewhere that has sufficient elbowroom for the expansion of our own concerns, our own enterprises, and our own genius. It's the duty we owe ourselves and posterity—to strike out in search of a more extensive farmland and a milder climate.

"We need a place where the soil will yield the richest return for the smallest amount of cultivation. We need a place where the trees are heavy with perennial fruit. We need a place where the streams crowd with salmon and other fish. Yes sir, we need a place where the principal labor is keeping our gardens free from the inroads of buffalo, elk, deer, wild turkeys, and other game. I appeal to your patriotism by picturing the glorious empire we are going to establish on the shores of the Pacific—an empire that will soon become part of the United States. We need to drive out those British usurpers and establish our dominance. That's what I think!"

There were cheers and applause all around.

Pete continued, "Now we need to draft out some rules and regulations for folks to follow. Much like laws. These rules will set down who is to be in charge and what authority they have. Trying to draft something like that during this meeting won't be possible, so I'd like to propose that a committee of five men sit down and draft out a set of rules. Then we can get back together in a few days and vote on it."

Aaron pointed to a bearded man wearing a black coat and waving his hand for recognition.

"Hank Sewell. That sounds reasonable to me. In the meantime, I'd like to propose that Pete Burnett here take over as a temporary captain until we get down the trail a piece. Right now I don't know many of you men, and wouldn't know whom to vote for when it comes to leading this migration."

"Jim Athey." A tall, lean man stood to be recognized by the chair. "I think we need to provide for the recall of leaders in our list of rules. We can still make a mistake no matter how well we get to know someone. I think if maybe one-third approves of a recall, then so be it. Then we can have another election."

"Abram Olinger here." A stocky man in a home-spun shirt stood and looked around to be sure he was not interrupting anyone. "Besides a leader, we ought to have some type of legislative group like the U.S. Congress. This group should be able to pass laws that our leader could accept or veto. If he vetoes something, then the legislature—I'll call it a council—could vote again and maybe overturn the veto. Checks and balances, that's what I say. We gotta have checks and balances."

"I'm Dave Lenox." Another tall man, only with the solemn voice of a preacher, stood to speak. "A council's a good idea 'cause we'll need a jury. You know, people to decide what to do about discipline problems."

"You want twelve people on this council?" Aaron questioned the assemblage.

"Ten or twelve," responded Pete Burnett. "It doesn't matter, but we do need a council for checks and balances."

"John Baker here." A husky man stood and gained everyone's attention with his rough, loud voice. "I'll go along with a recall, like Jim Athey said. As far as your council of ten, I think it would be better to have nine. There shouldn't be any ties if they have to vote."

"Ed Constable here." A small-framed, fastidious man stood to be recognized. "This group, I mean this council, should act as a judge and jury for any criminal proceedings, like Mr. Lenox says. We have to consider that. There won't be any law where we're going, so we gotta make our own."

"I'm Clay Paine—how about the Kansas River?" A middle-aged man stood and turned to face the crowd, giving a furrowed brow expression and holding the straps of his bib overalls. "As soon as we cross the Kansas we can have an election for leaders and a council. That should give us enough time to get to know each other."

Another discussion ensued resulting in general agreement to the proposal. Pete asked for volunteers to serve on a temporary council until the election. They would act as a legislative body, reviewing rules and resolving disputes. Nine men quickly volunteered for the council, along with five other men to serve on a committee to draft organizational rules.

As the afternoon wore on, several other committees formed. Bill Martin and Dan Matheny agreed to engage Captain John Gantt as a pilot. The previous year's government survey team, commanded by Colonel John Fremont, did not get past the Continental Divide, so the land beyond that point was unknown. The emigrants would need to hire a guide, and Captain Gantt was familiar with the route. Unfortunately, he would be traveling with several wagons of California-bound emigrants who planned to turn south after Fort Hall and journey down the Humboldt to California. So those bound for Oregon would need the services of an additional guide beyond Fort Hall. Several people had heard that another man, Reverend Marcus Whitman, could handle that task.

Reverend Whitman ran a mission out in Oregon Country at a place called Waiilatpu. The American Board of Commissioners for Foreign Missions had sent Marcus and his wife, Narcissa, to Christianize the Cayuse Indians and other Columbia River tribes. During the previous year he had returned East to visit his various constituencies and reaffirm their dwindling financial support. With that business accomplished, he was now in Independence preparing to return to Waiilatpu. Several young men who had met Whitman the week before volunteered to ask him to guide the migration from Fort Hall to the Columbia River. The Columbia River flows toward the Wallamet Valley, so a guide would not be needed after encountering that river.

Another small committee formed to obtain information from Reverend Whitman concerning the practicality of the journey and any special equipment they should take along.

On a motion from Aaron Layson, and a second from Pete Burnett, the group agreed to reconvene in two days to hear the various committee reports. Aaron closed the meeting by reaffirming Monday, May 22 as the date they would start west.

Bill Martin and Dan Matheny, assigned to hire John Gantt, a 53-year-old frontiersman and army officer, completed their task the following day. Gantt agreed to conduct the migration to Fort Hall, charging a price of one dollar per person. His title of captain was a remnant of his military career that he carried proudly.

The men who volunteered to engage Reverend Whitman as a

guide from Fort Hall to the Columbia River also made their arrangements the next day. Because of some additional business in Westport, Reverend Whitman agreed to catch up to the migration along the trail.

The committee of seven men inspecting each of the emigrant wagons for soundness and overloading had the largest task of all, for there were over one hundred wagons. The committee could make recommendations, but had no power to stop people from going or to prohibit heavy items such as furniture. The men started their inspections on Friday morning, but soon realized the enormity of the task. They would never be able to inspect each wagon before the Monday start date, so they decided to split up.

By Friday evening they had given each outfit a cursory once-over. They made recommendations concerning the loading, both weight and balance; the carrying of repair tools and parts; the quality of stock; and especially the quality of the running gear. Several wagons were in such poor shape that the owners agreed to effect repairs or replacement before starting west. These people would have to catch up to the main body.

John McClane, a man from the inspecting committee, rode up to Abby's wagon shortly after the noon meal. Both she and Jacob were waiting. John started his inspection by crawling under the wagon bed to look at the running gear and soundness of the box. Jacob knelt down next to him to watch while Abby stood by with her arms folded, hopeful her outfit and preparations would make a good impression. Her meticulous attention to detail and resolve to be ready for any contingency would prove invaluable on the trail. The inspection reaffirmed her confidence. John complimented her and Jacob as having one of the finest outfits in the migration.

Dan Waldo, however, was not as fortunate. John found several problems with the forward running gear—problems that needed repair before starting out. The rear axletree was in even worse condition, with a hairline crack. This meant the entire axletree needed replacement, with an estimated delay of up to a week. Other emigrants had similar problems, both with their wagons and with loading. Not everyone would be ready to go on May 22.

On Saturday morning, May 20, the men reconvened at Fitzhugh's Mill. Meanwhile, the majority of emigrants rendezvoused at Big Spring near Fitzhugh's Grove. It was the first time all the emigrants from the various scattered encampments around Westport and Independence had congregated in a single group. Wagons, people, and livestock made a dizzying scene of confusion as everyone came together.

Abby brought her wagon up while Jacob attended the meeting. Without voting privileges, there was not much else she could do. The short trip helped her become accustomed to the difficulties of moving a fully loaded wagon, eight oxen, and one milch cow. The day went without incident, but was exhausting.

At the mill, committees reported their findings concerning the hiring of a guide, the preparedness of emigrants and wagons, and the rules for the provisional trail government. The committee on rules picked emigrant Jim White as their chairman. Jim was a well-educated family man with long blonde hair and a demeanor that commanded respect. Jim stood up and addressed the group.

"Mr. Chairman, my name is Jim White and I have the rules my committee drew up last night." He held up several pieces of paper. "If it's acceptable to everyone, I'd like to read them."

"Proceed," replied Aaron Layson.

"We can modify them as we see fit, then vote on 'em. When we get a final version we need to read it to everyone, women included. I'll leave that up to you, so here they are." Jim began reading from the first sheet of paper.[1]

"First off, we put together an opening paragraph that goes like this: *'Whereas we deem it necessary for the government of all societies, either civil or military, to adopt certain rules and regulations for their government, for keeping good order and promoting civil discipline. In order to insure union and safety, we deem it necessary to adopt the following rules and regulations*

---

[1] Letters of Peter H. Burnett, Oregon Historical Quarterly, Volume 3, 1903, pp. 406-407. Peter Burnett included the trail government rules in a letter he wrote to James G. Bennett dated January 18, 1844. The *New York Herald* printed this letter on January 5, 1845.

for the government of our migration.'" Jim looked out at the crowd for any disapproval. He continued.

"Our first rule is this: *'Every male person of the age of sixteen or older shall be considered a legal voter in all affairs relating to the company.'"*

Again, Jim surveyed the crowd. "Rule number two: *'There shall be nine men elected by a majority of the company whose duty it shall be to settle all disputes arising between individuals, and to try and pass sentence on all persons for any act for which they may be guilty, which is subversive of good order and military discipline. They shall take special notice of all sentinels and members of the guard, who may be guilty of neglect of duty, or sleeping on post. Such persons shall be tried, and sentence passed upon them at the discretion of the Council. A majority of two thirds of the Council shall decide all questions and subject to the approval or disapproval of the captain. If the captain disapproves of a decision, he shall state to them his reasons, when they shall again pass upon the question, and if the same decision is again made by the same majority, it shall be final.'"*

Jim looked at the gathered crowd. "We discussed that one at length. It works for the U.S. Government, so it oughta work for us. We can talk about it some more if you want. I'll continue. Rule three: *'There shall be a captain who shall have supreme military command of the company. It shall be the duty of the captain to maintain good order and strict discipline, and as far as possible, to enforce all rules and regulations adopted by the company. Any man who shall be guilty of disobedience of orders shall be tried and sentenced at the discretion of the Council, which may extend to expulsion from the company. The captain shall appoint the necessary number of duty sergeants, one of whom shall take charge of every guard, and who shall hold their offices at the pleasure of the captain.'"*

Jim paused, then moved to the second page. "Alright then, here's rule four: *'There shall be an orderly sergeant elected by the company, whose duty it shall be to keep a regular roll, arranged in alphabetical order, of every person subject to guard duty in the company. He will then make out his guard details by commencing at the top of the roll and proceeding to the bottom, so every man gets an equal tour of guard duty. He shall also give the member of every guard notice when he is detailed for duty. He shall also parade every guard, call the roll, and inspect the same at the time of mounting. He shall also visit the guard at least once every night, and see that the guards are doing strict military duty. He may at any time give them the necessary instructions respecting their duty, and shall regularly make report to the captain every morning, and be considered second in command.'"*

Jim cleared his throat, shifted his weight, and moved on to the third sheet of paper. "Now rule five: *'The captain, orderly sergeant, and members of the Council shall hold their offices at the pleasure of the company, and it shall be the duty of the Council, upon the application of one third or more of the company, to order a new election for either captain, orderly sergeant, or new member or members of the Council, or for all or any of them, as the case may be.'"*

Jim glanced up. "We talked about that one at the last meeting. I'll continue, rule six: *'The election of officers shall not take place until the company crosses the Kansas River.'* We talked about that one too. Now the final one, rule seven: *'No family shall be allowed to take more than three loose cattle to every male member of the family of the age of sixteen and upward.'"*

As soon as Jim read the last rule, a vocal protest arose among many of the men who owned large herds of cattle. They could never agree to such a rule. A heated discussion followed with most men, cattle owners or not, opposing the final rule. After a rousing speech by Pete Burnett, the men accepted the rule on a trial basis.

After the reading, several men expressed concern about rules enforcement. Aaron reaffirmed that if someone broke the rules, the council would have the final say on discipline. Several wording changes were agreed upon, amounting to more of a cosmetic improvement than meaningful change. After thirty minutes of discussion, a voice vote adopted the rules.

"Mr. Chairman." It was John McHaley, a heavyset gentleman of about fifty years of age. Aaron recognized him, and he stood up.

"I'm John McHaley, and I think we're going to have some serious problems crossing all those rivers. None of these rivers have ever been crossed with wagons before, so we don't even know if it's possible. Now, we have all our worldly possessions in these wagons, and I for one don't want to see any wagon roll over in a river. So I've got this to say—I think this new provisional trail government ought to get two large boats and two wagons to haul them in. We'd take turns driving these wagons. It would mean extra work, but it would be well worth the effort whenever we got to the big rivers."

There was stunned silence from the crowd as most men were in disbelief of what they had just heard. A few voiced their opinions of having enough work to do with their own wagons and certainly not wanting to get taxed to pay for so-called "government" equipment. Clay Paine made a motion to abandon the proposal. Pete Burnett quickly seconded, and nothing more was said.

"Mr. Chairman." A middle-aged gentleman stood up. "I'm Dan Delany."

"Mr. Delany," Aaron recognized him.

"This council, captain, and government are fine, but what about laws? I'm from Tennessee, and we got laws for our courts. So I'd like to propose that our trail government adopt the laws of either Tennessee or Missouri. It don't matter which, long as we got laws."

Dan continued making a good speech about adopting proven laws rather than writing their own. Several other speeches responded in favor of using a set of established laws. During the discussion it became obvious that there were major differences of opinion depending whether the emigrant was from a slave state or a free state. The antislavery people did not want to adopt Missouri laws, while people from slave states did. This was especially true for slave owners such as Dan Delany, Pete Burnett, and a Miles Cary. The abolitionists eventually won a compromise by adopting Missouri laws, minus all slave-related statutes.

Alex McClelland, an elderly gentleman traveling with the Applegate families, proposed the company take along a penitentiary. He rose, introduced himself, and then stated his case.

"If we're going to try and sentence people, we're going to need a jail."

He continued to make a good speech, but people treated his proposal similar to John McHaley's proposal for boats. Nobody cared for the extra work of driving "government" wagons, and even fewer wanted to pay for them. A voice vote eliminated the proposal.

Joe Chiles, a veteran from a previous California venture, introduced himself and explained his intention to guide a group of eight wagons and thirty people to California. They would not be ready to leave until after May 22, but still wanted to travel with the main migration. After some discussion, Chiles agreed catch up to the main Oregon migration and help Captain Gantt guide the group to Fort Hall. At that point the California-bound emigrants, including Captain Gantt, would turn south to follow the Humboldt River.

Aaron Layson suggested that they call their provisional government the Oregon Emigrating Company. This small formality provided a framework by which diary and other recordkeepers could identify. The new name quickly passed by voice vote.

The meeting also produced an estimate of the size of the migration: approximately nine hundred people and over one hundred wagons. Work animals, consisting of mules, horses, and oxen, numbered about one thousand, plus an additional thousand head of loose stock, consisting of goats, beef cattle, and milch cows. Many emigrants were also carrying chickens in wire cages attached to their wagons—and of course, many dogs.

The meeting ended with the appointment of Captain Gantt as guide and a reaffirmation of Monday, May 22 as the start date. On this first day, everyone who was ready would move west to Elm Grove, about ten miles from Fitzhugh's Mill, just across the Missouri state line. The slow start was beneficial to many emigrants not fully prepared. Riders could return to Independence to buy a forgotten tool, a few more pounds of coffee, or some other innocuous item.

Several men stated that their families would not be ready in time for the Monday-morning start. They agreed to leave within a week, perhaps with Reverend Whitman, and catch up to the main body. Dan Waldo offered to lead this group of stragglers.

"I'll be in Independence for at least another week," Dan said as he addressed the small crowd. "I'll talk to Whitman and the others so we can head out as a group. Nobody should start out alone, since we have rivers to cross and other unknown dangers. The trail you people make should be sufficient for us to follow, so we'll catch up as soon as we can."

Two other groups, Colonel Fremont's government survey team and Sir William Drummond Stewart's hunting brigade would also leave within the next ten days. Along with these groups, there were many long lines of Conestoga wagons preparing for their long journey to Santa Fe. Everyone would follow the same wide, well-worn road for the first few days. The Conestogas, loaded with manufactured goods, would return with gold, silver, and finely crafted rugs, baskets, pottery, and other items. This road had been theirs for the last twenty years. Now they would share the first few miles with the white-sheeted farm wagons of Oregon- and California-bound emigrants.

Beyond the western Missouri state line lay Shawnee Indian Territory. These Indians had adopted white-man customs, and most owned good farms and comfortable homes. Some were excellent mechanics, and most spoke English. It would be later in the week before the migration finally left civilization completely.

After the meeting, Jacob walked back to Abby's wagon at the Big Spring rendezvous and informed her of what had transpired. They decided he would join her the following evening, Sunday, and move on to Elm Grove in the morning. That short distance might show problems that they could correct while still near Independence. No matter what, on Monday morning they would be ready to go.

Sunday morning dawned clear with blue skies and a slight breeze. Lew Cooper, a meticulous gentleman from Illinois, could not wait another day and so started out for Elm Grove. He and his hired hand, a teamster named John Jackson, were both traveling to Oregon Country to make their fortunes. Apparently, they aimed to get there a day sooner than everyone else.

In the evening, Jacob rode into the Big Spring camp on his gray buffalo horse, leading two pack animals. Abby offered him some coffee, and he accepted. It was the first of many evenings that Abby and Jacob would enjoy each other's company around a warm campfire in the midst of a great migration.

CHAPTER 3

The Trail to Oregon

On Monday Abby was up before sunrise, stoking the fire and starting breakfast. She glanced over at the large black lump on the ground. It was Jacob underneath his buffalo robe, peering out at the activity.

"Morning, Mr. Chalmers. When we leave, you can tie those pack-horses to the back of my wagon."

"Abby." Jacob sat up while surveying the movement of emigrants in nearby camps. "Call me Jacob, everyone else does."

Breakfast consisted of a few pieces of bacon and bread, along with fresh milk. The excitement of getting underway was too much to dawdle with a large breakfast, so before Jacob could finish, Abby was cleaning the pans and putting them away for the day. Jacob quickly finished and went out to bring in the oxen.

By the time Abby finished with her kitchen chores, he had the oxen yoked and ready to go. He chained three teams to the tongue and tied the fourth to the back of the wagon. He then loaded his two pack animals and tied them off next to the fourth yoke of oxen and the milch cow. Then he asked Abby if she was ready to go.

"Have you made a final check of your camp?"

"Final check?"

"It's a good habit to get into. You never know when some small article will get misplaced or left on the ground. Anything that gets left behind is gone forever."

It was sage advice. Abby surveyed the campsite and could not find any missing items. Everything was in order, packed and ready to go.

The Rubeys and Blevinses were planning to leave shortly after Abby. Pete Burnett and his family had left for Elm Grove the day before in order to have time to converse with the other appointed leaders. Each leader had previously agreed to meet up at Elm Grove, if possible. If not, there would be time on the trail to nurture their friendship and discuss the particulars of organizing the migration.

It was a cool morning, and Abby wore her new cotton jacket over a well-worn dress. The dress was of homespun cloth that could take the punishment of trail life and could be easily repaired should it get torn on brush. She pulled her quirt from two rawhide loops on the side of the wagon and held it up for Jacob to see.

"I've fixed up a place for my quirt so it won't get lost at night. What do you think?"

"I think you're probably as prepared as any of these emigrants, even more so." He shoved his skin hat to the back of his head, "You're going to do just fine, Miss—now let's get this outfit shook down. The next few days should tell a story."

Abby walked up to her lead team and with a snap of her quirt was on her way to Oregon. The wagon lurched forward, only this time leaving camp was different. She was not going back to Independence to get more supplies. Instead, her outfit was moving south, away from Independence and all she had ever known. By noon, the trail would veer southwest to Elm Grove. She considered her situation as she walked alongside the lead yoke.

"I'm leaving the United States for good," she thought, "and my friends and family—but I'm going to a new land that will probably become part of the United States. I'll be a schoolteacher again! But I will miss Greene County."

Abby's family had tried their best to discourage her from going, along with a number of other people from Cincinnati to Independence—but this was a journey of destiny. It meant a new beginning in a new country and an escape from the tragedies of Greene County. Emotions bounced back and forth, but there was never any doubt. Abby and her outfit were not turning around. She was going to Oregon.

May twenty-second was a sunny, blue-sky day that boosted the already exuberant spirits of the many emigrants. The white-sheeted wagons, all moving in unison toward a common goal, were an inspiring sight. Abby could hear singing from several wagons and the laughter and play of children everywhere.

The ten miles to Elm Grove demonstrated some of the problems of handling six oxen and a loaded wagon over rough prairie terrain. Every mile offered several steep ravines that proved to be a challenge for all teamsters. Abby and Jacob spent most of the day learning how to handle her wagon on a steep hill without losing control. With Jacob's advice and encouragement, Abby rapidly caught on to handling the oxen over these difficult situations. Her firm yet gentle approach proved more effective than the harsh manner of many other teamsters.

Jacob handled the wagon's brake during several descents into ravines. In some places, they found it necessary to tie a rope on one side of the wagon while traversing a side hill. Jacob held the rope on the high side, thereby preventing the wagon from rolling over. On steep hills, or when the hill extended for some distance, he tied the rope to the saddle of a pack animal for extra strength.

As the Oregon Emigrating Company turned southwest, they passed a sign that read "Shawnee Indian Territory." This was the western Missouri state line.

When the wagon in front of Abby's passed this sign, the teamster stepped back from his oxen, turned around, waved his hat and called out, "Farewell to America!" It was John East, a good-natured man Abby had met the day before. His antics made her smile, but drove home the seriousness of the venture.

"He's right. I'll probably never see the United States again, unless Oregon becomes a state—and it will. It has to! How can so many Americans ever fail?" She was still giving herself encouragement, except now it was easy. The slow-moving white-sheeted wagons signaled a defining moment in American history and she knew it.

The first wagons arrived at Elm Grove around two o'clock, with Abby and Jacob arriving shortly after three. Elm Grove consisted of two elms. One was a single old stump, almost gone from the Santa Fe traders using it for fuel. The other was a small sapling.

"So two trees constitute a grove on the American Prairie. I wonder what they call a forest?" Abby's education in the ways of the American West had just begun.

Jacob requested that she steer her wagon over to a creek approximately one-half mile from the trail, where there were willows for fuel and water for the animals. Upon doing this, she wisely stopped in a spot where they would have shade for the remainder of the day. While unhitching the oxen they discussed problems encountered during the day, what they had learned, and how they could do better tomorrow. It had been an exhausting day, but they were now considerably more knowledgeable about the difficulties of handling a loaded wagon over rough prairie terrain.

Jacob watered and hobbled the stock, then walked over to hear what Burnett, Layson, Jim Nesmith, and the other leaders were saying about the day's march. Above all else, the day had demonstrated the independence of each emigrant. This was something they would have to correct if they were to help each other during the difficult sections of the trail. Crossing rivers, securing food, and self-defense all required cooperation. Jacob had learned that when he first went up the Missouri with General Ashley's men back in '23. The Oregon Migration of 1843 would have the same need for survival and the same reasons for cooperation.

By six o'clock Jacob was enjoying one of Abby's meals and the quiet repose of an evening camp. The meal was simple, beans, bacon, and rice—more than adequate for the trail.

"Well, Abby," Jacob said between mouthfuls. "I think we did alright."

"I think we did wonderfully. We were always moving and didn't get stuck or have any breakdowns."

"That wagon won't be too hard to handle out here on the prairie—crossing major rivers and the Rockies, that's something else." He wore a look of concern—a look that did not affect Abby's spirit.

"We'll learn how to do that when the time comes," she said as she handed him the large camp spoon for him to refill his plate. "So far we haven't discovered any additional item we need. That's a good sign we're prepared."

"That it is—and the quality of your wagon is already visible. As long as we keep those axles greased they shouldn't give us any trouble. Tomorrow we can start caulking the seams on that bed with a mixture of ash, tallow, and tree sap."

"I'm interested in learning how to do that. In fact Jacob, I would like to learn many things about living in the West. I'm sure you can teach me a great deal."

Jacob half-smiled and gave a few slight nods of approval. "Burnett and Nesmith would like to travel in groups of ten wagons until we cross the Kansas," he said. "That should show these farmers what it's like to cooperate, or at least acquaint them with the idea of cooperating. After the Kansas, whomever we elect as a leader will probably modify that organization."

"That's fine with me—I prefer some semblance of order. I don't understand why some of these people have to be so ornery. Don't they know that we need each other?"

"They'll learn soon enough."

After dinner Abby washed the pans, dishes, and utensils, then put everything away, keeping items needed for breakfast easily accessible. She would learn this routine well. In an hour, she and Jacob were again sitting beside their campfire—Jacob with a cup of coffee and Abby with a cup of tea. The sweet sound of a fiddle drifted up the creek from another camp, and also that of a wooden flute. The air was filled with the smells of a hundred campfires, and the sounds of children playing and dogs barking.

"How long did it take you to become accustomed to sleeping on the ground?" Abby asked. "I mean, the wagon bed is plenty hard, but isn't the ground worse?"

"That buffalo robe is waterproof and plenty comfortable. Old Mud Flat, that's that sand packhorse, old Mud Flat's been packing that robe and other possibles for most of five years. He's a good animal, seen most of the Rockies and then some—Dog Town, too. That's my gray mare."

"I'll probably become accustomed to the hardness of that wagon bed before too long," Abby replied. "If it starts raining you are welcome to sleep underneath the wagon."

"That's acceptable to me, Abby. I'll get along."

The evening wore on with very little conversation. Both were lost in thoughts of the future, and being one small part of a great migration, and the many unknown privations yet to come. Listening to the fiddle and enjoying the warm evening and western sunset belied future dangers. Before the last flicker of sunlight disappeared under the western sky, Abby looked over at Jacob and broke the silence.

"Where are we going, Jacob? What wondrous things are we going to see?"

He gave no reply. He only sipped from his cup and nodded his understanding of her questions and concern.

The next morning Abby arose before dawn, fixed a quick breakfast, and made ready to go an hour after sun-up. Yoking the oxen proved to be a fairly simple task. With one animal yoked, its partner moved into place without any coaxing, just as Jim Smithy had said they would. By the time Abby was ready to go, Jacob had the teams hitched and his packhorses loaded and tied to the back of the wagon, along with the fourth yoke of oxen and the milch cow.

Tuesday went better and faster. When they encountered a ravine to cross, or a steep side hill, they each moved into position without speaking a word. By using a rope tied to the high side of the wagon, Jacob and one of the pack animals managed to keep the wagon stable while Abby kept the oxen moving with her quirt. She also managed the brake when necessary. They operated smoothly together, almost as if they were professional teamsters and not just starting out.

Six miles from Elm Grove the trail split. Twelve Conestogas, each being pulled by a team of eight mules, veered southwest onto the Santa Fe trail. The Oregon-bound emigrants continued in a more westerly direction. Unlike the Oregon and California emigrants that used oxen, the Santa Fe teamsters used mule teams and rode in their wagons, while the other traders bound for Santa Fe were on horseback.

About a mile before the intersection, Abby's two admirers from the Santa Fe caravan rode up to say "Adios" and to wish the pretty señorita a safe and speedy journey. It was a quick and happy farewell, as Abby could not stop her team without disrupting the entire line of wagons. In a moment, the men were galloping off, waving their sombreros and shouting in Spanish their wishes for good health and a safe trip.

Abby watched them disappear into the trail dust, wondering what Santa Fe was like, how the people there lived, and what kind of world they all were traveling toward. She faced forward again, snapping her quirt to urge the oxen on—westward, toward the endless prairie. It stretched as far as she could see, and only seemed to get larger as the day wore on.

Jacob picked the next campsite and it was a good one—close to water, good grass for the stock, and a level place for the wagon. The surrounding prairie filled with emigrant wagons as they converged on this singular spot—but not everyone found a good campsite. Fistfights broke out over minor territorial squabbles. Abby watched in disbelief, wondering how these people would ever get along during the next five months. Jacob, a veteran of many Rendezvous, simply took it in stride.

"It won't be long before they'll be too exhausted to fight at night," Jacob said. "The bruises they get along the trail will suffice for injury. Before long these squabbles will be nothing more than name calling. I'll never forget that trip up the Missouri with Andrew Henry, most of twenty years ago. I was full of vinegar and itching for adventure and a fight. After the Arikaras satisfied that need, I decided caution was the better part of adventure. This child was lucky to get past those dogs with my hair."

"Well, I think these farmers could act a little more civilized. With all this prairie, as far as the eye can see, you'd think they could find a campsite to their liking."

"They are an independent bunch, that they are. When they come on hard times and need each other, they'll be friendly enough. I suspect they're lucky they don't know what's ahead. If they did, most of 'em would turn around."

Jacob unhitched the oxen and moved the stock over to an area of good grass, where he staked and hobbled each animal. In the meantime, Abby unloaded her cooking gear and organized the camp. The wagon's tailgate had already proved its worth as a countertop for preparing meals.

It was still early afternoon, so after a brief rest from the day's march, Jacob engaged several other men in conversation about the problems of driving wagons and caring for the stock. Abby climbed a nearby hill to get a view of the area. From there she could see the surrounding prairie, green with new grass and dotted with a multitude of encampments, several thousand head of livestock, and over one hundred wagons with their white-sheeted tops. Such a spectacle had never before been seen on the American Prairie.

Before long, she came down from the hill to converse with the other women. She was not going to leave anything to chance. Independence was still close enough to ride back and pick up a forgotten item that might prove useful on the trail.

During that evening the Oregon Emigrating Company rules were read. The rules committee had implemented suggested modifications, and now all the emigrants heard the organizational rules of their provisional trail government. Jim White and Pete Burnett read the articles at several locations so that everyone of age sixteen and over had an opportunity to listen, including the women.

Again the air filled with the smoke from a hundred campfires and the occasional sound of a fiddle. With almost two thousand animals grazing around the many encampments, it was a pastoral scene of peace and tranquillity, providing no reason to turn back.

After dinner Abby checked the stock to make sure they had adequate water. For the past three weeks she had considered names for each of her oxen, but resisted until she got to know their habits. Now, after two days travel, it was time.

She addressed her oxen. "First of all, there's you with the mottled coat. I will call you Patchy—and I will call you Lashes for those long white eyelashes. Now, you are going to be Loafer 'cause you seem to always lag behind—and you're the opposite, so I'll call you Jumpy. Then there's Dinnertime, you must know why I'm calling you that.

I don't think you've missed a blade of grass between here and Independence—and speaking of Independence, that will be your name since you always seem to have a mind of your own." She placed her hands on her hips and looked around. "Who else? Oh yes, there's Perky, since you're always perkin' those ears up at the slightest sound. And finally—you're the one I couldn't decide. I think I'll call you Flowers 'cause you always want to eat the prairie flowers before the grass." She wiped her hands on her apron. "There, that should do it. There's Patchy, Lashes, Loafer, Jumpy, Dinnertime, Independence, Perky, and Flowers."

"Don't get too attached. One of those fellas might be our dinner in a few months."

"Mr. Chalmers, I didn't hear you come up. Well, I have to call them something—and what do you mean, dinner? We're going to take good care of these animals."

"Oh, we will—but they still might be dinner. The buffalo run out past Fort Hall, and we'll still have a long way to go. Those Snake River Plains are unforgiving, and these animals will certainly be spent by the time we get there."

"Well, I'd rather not think about that right now. There will be time for sadness later."

They both walked back to the wagon in silence. As they sat down next to the campfire, Abby asked, "Do you, I mean, have you ever regretted leaving the United States?"

"Never considered it. Oregon will be part of the United States soon enough, and I suspect someday all the country from here to the Divide. I was never one for civilized living. Once you've breathed that clean mountain air and seen snow in August, you'll never want to return. It'll hold you like a spell. A man can live good in those mountains, with plenty of game and no sickness. No, this child doesn't care much for living in the United States."

"Yes, but this is a lifetime journey. I'm leaving the United States for good, and Oregon could go to the British. I'll surely never see any of my family again. It's a lot to take in."

Jacob looked at her with raised eyebrows. "Do I detect some misgivings?"

"No, you don't, not at all. I'm going to Oregon and that's a fact. I'm considering my situation, and there's nothing wrong with doing that—but I've found that not all these women share my desire. Only the young newlyweds that I've met. Most of the other women don't want anything to do with Oregon—they're simply going to keep their families together. Doesn't seem right. They should have more to say about their future."

"I can't speak for the women. If I had a family, I surely wouldn't be hauling them across the Rockies. I know what's up ahead, and it's no Sunday picnic. No, if I had a family I'd stay put. No sense in gettin' everyone killed."

"You have a way with words, Mr. Chalmers, a way that does not exactly convey comfort. I don't mind your directness, but other people haven't been supportive and that does bother me. Earlier when you were out I talked to two women over in that camp—" Abby motioned to several wagons about fifty yards away— "and they were very much against me going to Oregon. They were critical of my plans, and they don't even know me. Why can't strangers accept me for who I am?"

"Because you're different. I knew that right off. People fear those who are different, and frightened people can say terrible things. Don't you let them bother you none—you do what's in your heart."

Abby thought those last words did not sound as if they came from an old mountain man, yet they had.

"You are an interesting man, Jacob. I will enjoy traveling with you."

He gave a slight smile and the usual nod.

"They also said you'd run off whenever you decided to. What do you think of that?"

"I think those ladies might be trouble before we get to Oregon."

With a slight laugh she added, "When I told them you were a mountain man, they got real quiet. Maybe they were changing their minds about you."

"Maybe."

"That group of wagons next to them had the cutest baby girl. Sarah Owens is the mother, and the girl was born in February. She let me hold her for awhile. I couldn't help but think of my baby. I'm glad I didn't start crying again."

Jacob looked up—it was the first mention Abby had made of a baby.

"Where's your baby now?"

"With my husband. She only lived a year."

Jacob hesitated for a few moments, considering this new information. Abby's last statement had caught him by surprise. He had known since they first met that some personal, singular event had driven her to Independence—but an unwritten code of mountain men says a person's past is their business. A number of men left for the mountains to escape an unhappy marriage or an infraction with the law. In the mountains, everyone was equal and a man's past was of no importance. They all respected that.

"I am sorry, Abby, I truly am. I will not burden you with talk of it."

"I thought I was over it until that baby this afternoon—and then if that wasn't enough, I met another lady named Sarah Jane Hill with that same group, and she lost a baby last month. I told her about my Jessica, and we talked for an hour. It felt good."

Jacob had no response—it was a subject best left alone. The sun was now going down, and only the sweet sound of music broke the silence of this makeshift prairie town. They could hear fiddles, squeezeboxes, flutes, singing, and dancing. Everyone was in high spirits and excited to be on the trail.

Jacob lay back on the ground with his hands clasped behind his head, listening to the distant music and mesmerized by the flickering light of the campfire. Abby retrieved her diary box from the wagon. She wanted to record the events of the day while enjoying the solitude of their camp, the warmth of the fire, and the joyful sounds of the many nearby encampments.

As she sat back down, Jim Nesmith, one of the interim leaders, rode into camp. Jim was twenty-two years old and going to Oregon to make his fortune. He did not have a family or property, so there was nothing to hold him back. Like Jacob had been some years before, he was full of vinegar and looking for adventure. He dismounted and walked into the light of the campfire.

"I'm told you're Abigail Meacham from Greene County in Ohio."

"Yes, that's me."

"I'm Jim Nesmith from Maine, going to Oregon to see the elephant. I heard talk of you from some other people. They said you were traveling alone, but I see you've got your father. I don't know where they got the idea you were alone."

"This is Jacob Chalmers," Abby replied. "He's traveling with me, but he's not my father. This is my outfit, and I'm going to Oregon to become a schoolteacher."

Jacob eyed the young man but did not move from his position. He was still lying on the ground with his hands clasped behind his head. A slight nod acknowledged Jim's presence.

"Yes, sir, pleased to meet ya. Ma'am, should you two need any help I'd be glad to give you a hand."

"That's very kind of you Mr. Nesmith."

"Just Jim, ma'am, just Jim."

"Yes, Jim, and I'm Abby."

"Well, Abby, there's another reason I've come over here, I mean to your camp. I don't really know how to say this, but there's this young man, well, he's really a farmer's son. I mean he's traveling with a family, not his own, mind you. He's hired on as a teamster." Jim stopped and looked at Abby, seemingly for some approval.

"Yes." Abby assumed this other man was looking to hire on with her for part of the journey. Maybe the family he hired with was going to California and he wanted to go to Oregon.

"Yes, ma'am, I mean, Abby. He's a teamster alright. Well, that's not really why I'm here, I mean, not to tell you 'bout that."

"Jim, if you don't say what's on your mind, you might end up standing there for most of the night."

"Yes, ma'am, Abby. Well, Sam, that's this man's name, Sam, and he says he'd like to meet ya. Yup, that's what he wants to do alright, and he asked me to see if that would be acceptable to you."

Abby quickly glanced over at Jacob in time to see him remove a smile. Young men taking a shine to her was nothing new. It was flattering—a feeling she'd not experienced since before marrying Caleb.

"You tell Sam that if he wants to meet me, he's going to have to come over here and introduce himself."

"Yes, ma'am, I will tell him that. Yes, ma'am. Good night to you, ma'am, and you, sir."

Jim mounted his horse and quickly disappeared into the evening twilight. Abby glanced over at Jacob again, but this time he was sitting up and his smile did not disappear. He stirred a stick into the campfire.

"Like I said earlier," he said, "this should be an interesting trip."

On the following morning, Charley Applegate rode up to Abby and Jacob's camp. Charley was one of the three Applegate brothers who were traveling to Oregon with their families, possessions, and large beef herds. He was riding between encampments explaining that until they elected a leader on the other side of the Kansas River, everyone should travel in groups of about ten wagons.

"This should help ease some of the congestion, both on the road and in camp." He addressed Jacob as if it were his outfit.

"We need to have some type of fortification during the night for protection. If ten wagons could organize into a circle, then we'd have a corral for the working stock, with no chance of any animal getting stolen."

"That's fine with us," replied Jacob, "but what about all those loose cattle? They're going to need watching to keep them out of our camps."

"Maybe a third of those belong to my brother Jesse. He's got drovers to keep them moving during the day and herded up at night. Just wanted to let you know about traveling in groups so we don't get all tangled up. As soon as these wagons around you leave, I'd just fall in behind one."

"Thank you, Mr. Applegate," said Abby, "we'll be ready."

Charley looked over at Abby and tipped his hat. "Ma'am."

As he rode away, Abby walked over to where Jacob was standing. They both watched him ride off.

"Do you think he knows this is my outfit?"

"I suspect he does, just too proud to do business with a woman."

"Well, we'll see about that. Oregon's a long way off."

"I didn't have the heart to tell him that no Indian with any self-respect would ever steal cattle."

Abby smiled and walked back to finish her morning chores and prepare the Western Passage for the day's march.

During the previous day she had devised a system to keep track of each ox and its position. Each of the four yokes would rotate every morning. The lead team would move to the back of the wagon while the team that walked behind the wagon during the previous day would move to the third yoke, directly in front of the wagon. Then each yoke would move up one. She felt this system was equitable; however, Jacob was quick to point out the drawbacks.

"What if one ox gets a sore foot and can't pull? Or what if one drops dead?"

"Jacob, I appreciate your frankness, but let's deal with those problems when the time comes. For now, I think my system will work just fine."

"It's a good system, alright. My apologies, Abby. You have the best outfit I've seen, and I have no cause to discredit it. You let me know if I speak out of turn again."

"Thank you, Jacob."

Soon each yoke of oxen was in place and Jacob was attaching the tongue chains to the yoke rings. It was nine o'clock, a little late for starting, but this was a big morning. Many people were slow to organize their outfits after the celebrations of the night before. People were not yet trail-tired and were still celebrating the start of the journey. That energy would soon subside as the realities of traveling with wagons set in.

As Abby waited, she could see a number of wagons already in motion, moving out across the prairie. In a few minutes the wagons around hers pulled out, and she and Jacob were on their way.

Abby established her position, walking alongside the lead team on the right side and carrying her four foot-long quirt. On this third day she wore her usual brown homespun cotton dress, a new pair of shoes, and a bonnet. In the morning the bonnet provided warmth, while during the afternoon it served to shield her eyes against the sun. Always prepared, she stowed her cotton jacket in the front of the wagon, so she could get to it in a hurry should a rainstorm appear.

Jacob rode his horse slightly behind the wagon and off to the left, far enough to get out of the way of the dust kicked up by the caravan. Tied behind the wagon were his pack animals, the fourth yoke of oxen, and the milch cow. He carried his Hawken rifle across his horse's neck as all mountain men did. Although such preparation at this point in the journey was not necessary, it was an old habit and hard to break. His fringed buckskins and otter-skin hat gave him the appearance of a man more wild than civilized. Abby surveyed his form as he rode, knowing that as long as he was with her, she would get to Oregon.

Shortly after midday the entire migration stopped for a nooner, with each wagon keeping its position on the road. Not only was this easier, but it would save time when getting the caravan back in motion. Abby, now covered in dust, vowed to become accustomed to such conditions, which she considered to be only a minor inconvenience. In a few minutes she had bread and dried fruit ready for herself and Jacob. During this brief respite, she hung a canteen along the right side of the wagon, so she could get a drink without stopping. She'd gone all morning without a drink of water—a lesson well learned. She also retrieved a handkerchief from one of her trunks. This she tied around her face to keep from breathing too much dust. After twenty minutes, she and Jacob were fed and ready to go. However, she proved to be a little too efficient, for families with children required a nooner anywhere between forty-five minutes to an hour.

The afternoon passed more comfortably with an accessible canteen and a mask against the dust—but not everyone was ready to accept these road conditions. A number of teamsters pulled out of the long line and started hurrying their oxen to get to the front, away from the dust. For some, it became an outright race as they whipped their oxen into a frenzy. Abby watched the spectacle as wagon after wagon passed hers.

Jacob, too, watched the foolishness of the many farmers exhausting their oxen. He had more important things on his mind. Abby watched as he rode off to a nearby draw, returning shortly with an armload of firewood. He rode up to the rear of the wagon and tossed it in. As soon as other people saw this, they followed his lead and began to gather firewood from along the trail whenever available. After disposing of the firewood, Jacob rode up alongside Abby to hear what she thought about the racing.

"What are these people doing? They're going to wear their oxen out before we get to the Kansas, and some of those wagons are overloaded. There's no need to race, is there?"

"You never pay them no mind. We're doing fine and we'll keep doing fine. They're going to end up with a lot of dead oxen before they're halfway to Oregon."

"It's not right to exhaust those poor animals for no reason at all."

"Those pilgrims are a little over-spirited right now. After the first few weeks, and after they've crossed some rivers, got stuck in mud, and broke a few wheels, well, they'll slow down."

"How far do you think we'll go today?" Abby's interest was in the business of getting to Oregon safely rather than quickly. She did not intend to join the foolishness of racing.

"We have good conditions today. The road is flat and dry, so if we'd started out at sun-up we could have made fifteen to twenty miles. As it is, I'd say more like twelve, and less if these fools don't stop racing. Anything over fifteen is a good day. There will be days when we don't get out of camp because of weather, and other days when we only make a few miles because of mud. Whenever conditions are like today, we should go as far as we can before making camp, as long as we got good grass and water."

At five o'clock the lead wagons came upon the Rockariski River. The river was only twenty yards wide with clear water and a gravel bed. Crossing it presented the first major obstacle.

The steep banks created a formidable problem in getting down to the river and an even bigger problem getting up on the opposite bank. Before Abby's turn came, Jacob surveyed the procedure in use by the other teamsters and readied Abby's outfit accordingly. He tied two ropes to the back of the wagon so he could use the pack animals to ease the wagon down the bank to the river. He also chained up the fourth yoke of oxen so that upon reaching the other side, the wagon was fully double-teamed and easier to pull up the steep bank. Crossing this small stream was hard work for everyone, but continued smoothly without loss of property or injury to animals.

Once across, Abby pulled her wagon off to the side while Jacob helped other people. By seven o'clock he rejoined her, wet and tired.

"Not everyone will get across today, so we might as well set up our camp over there." He pointed to some high ground with good grass. Abby snapped her quirt over the rumps of the lead team, and they moved quickly away from the Rockariski toward higher ground.

On this third night out they were able to execute their camp set-up routine with precision and efficiency. While Jacob unhitched, watered, and hobbled the stock, Abby set up her kitchen and fixed dinner. Organizing into groups of ten would have to wait another day, for crossing the Rockariski scattered wagons on both sides of the stream for the remainder of the night.

This evening was quieter than the previous. Men collapsed from exhaustion after a long day of travel, especially those who had chosen to race. Some boys tried their hand at fishing, but the Rockariski at this point yielded few fish. The weather continued clear, and a quiet, relaxing evening fell over camp. Captain Gantt came riding in, catching up to the migration. Tomorrow would be his first day as guide.

Abby cleaned up after dinner while Jacob sat near the fire and lit his pipe. She soon joined him, sitting down on her overturned washtub. Just before dark, she made out three Indians approaching from the southwest. They were riding tall horses complete with martingales, bridles, and saddles. Pete Burnett and Jim Nesmith rode out to meet them and learn their business.

They turned out to be from the Potawotomie tribe, on their way to visit a trading post that served the Shawnee farmers of the region. After a brief and friendly exchange, they were on their way, not caring to risk their safety among such a well-armed caravan. For the

Indians, the encounter made a lasting impression. Never before had the American Prairie witnessed a scene like the Oregon migration. White-sheeted wagons and several thousand head of livestock made an imposing display.

As Abby sipped her tea and Jacob his coffee, a young man came riding in from one of the many encampments farther back from the river.

"Ho to camp!" The man dismounted and began walking in, leading his horse and carrying his hat in hand. He wore a plaid shirt, with suspenders holding up homespun cotton trousers, cut off about six inches above the ground. The most distinctive thing Abby noticed was that he was barefoot.

"Is this the Abigail Meacham camp?"

"It is, I'm Abigail Meacham."

"Yes, ma'am, well, I'm Sam. Sam Oakley, ma'am."

"So this is Sam," Abby thought. "He's right handsome."

"I'm a-going to Oregon and I thought I'd introduce myself. That is, my friend Jim Nesmith said it would be alright if I, well …"

"Pleased to meet you, Mr. Oakley." Abby stood and held out her hand in friendship, an act that caught Sam by surprise. Most women were not so bold.

"Pleased to meet you, ma'am," he said as he shook her hand hard enough to shake her whole body. His nervousness was obvious. "I've signed on to help John Copenhaver and his family get to Oregon. I've got no family of my own, though—I'm going to Oregon to make my fortune. They say there're opportunities out there for everyone, and I aim to get my share."

"I'm sure you will, Mr. Oakley. Why don't you tie your horse up and join us at the fire?"

"That's right neighborly, ma'am. I shall do that."

"Can I get you a cup of coffee or tea?"

"Well now, ma'am, I don't want to be a burden, but coffee sounds right kind of ya."

Sam sat down wanting to speak to Abby, yet knowing he had better make his good intentions known to Jacob first. After an uncomfortable introduction, for which Jacob never stood to shake Sam's hand,

Sam asked the trapper about his experiences in the mountains. That was all it took.

For the next hour they shared stories of the past and hopes for the future. Jacob's stories of adventures in the mountains paled the former experiences of Sam, while Sam's dreams of fortune in Oregon paled any future expectations of Jacob. Abby spent most of this time listening, since she did not care to discuss her past, and her future was simple: She wanted to be a schoolteacher.

During that hour, Abby sensed that Sam might prove to be more than just an acquaintance. It was going to be a long journey, and there would be time to get to know each other. *He is handsome,* she thought, *and he's going to Oregon, and he is interested in me. It won't hurt to be friendly, but I'm still going to Oregon!* As darkness came on, Sam said his good-nights and slowly rode back to his encampment.

Tonight Abby's wagon bed was warm, inviting, and home. In a few moments, thoughts of Sam, possible Indians, and the adventure of a lifetime elapsed into sleep—a sleep that passed far too quickly.

With the crack of a gun and a guard calling, "The sun's a-coming, everyone up!" Abby crawled out from under her blankets and started preparing breakfast. Everyone was up before daylight, preparing for another day of travel. People were settling into standard routines, giving a smooth appearance to the Oregon Emigrating Company's morning preparations. While Abby cleared the morning dishes and completed her kitchen chores, Jacob rounded up the oxen, yoked them, but did not chain them to the tongue. It was still early, and few people were ready; however, he loaded his two packhorses and tied them to the back of the wagon.

They spent the morning waiting for the remaining wagons to cross the Rockariski. Some emigrants began to show considerable uneasiness, Abby included, about the time required to cross such a small stream. People generally felt that such delays could not continue if they were to cross the final mountain range in Oregon before the first winter snows.

During the morning, Abby shared her concern over the delay with Sarah Rubey and several other women, only to learn that most of the ladies enjoyed the respite. These women, accustomed to the difficult life of running a frontier farm, were still adjusting to the requirements of trail life. There were no buildings to provide a feeling of civilization, and the white-sheeted wagons made a poor substitute for their warm, comfortable homes. As Abby had learned back in Independence, their lot was not one of open dissent. They were going to Oregon to keep their families together, since their husbands made all monetary and subsistence decisions.

Jacob did not chain up the oxen until almost noon, when the caravan was ready to advance. As wagons finally began to pull out for the day, a few stragglers were still crossing the Rockariski. These people would have to catch up on their own.

When the order to march came down the long line of wagons, Jacob chose to walk with Abby for the first hour, leading his horse. The slow start provided an opportunity to discuss the logistics of their outfit and to plan for future needs. One of the primary concerns was the health of their oxen. In the first few days, grass and water were plentiful, and would probably remain so until Fort Laramie. Most everyone knew that this would not always be the case.

"After we pass Fort Laramie in a few weeks, the water gets bad, poison to horses," said Jacob.

"Poison!" Abby looked up at him while keeping a firm quirt on the lead oxen's rump. "How can water be poison out here in the desert? It might be muddy, but any water is better than nothing."

"Not so. This water is full of alkali and will kill any animal that drinks, especially animals that are in a weakened condition."

"Alkali—you mean salt. It's saltwater?"

"That's about it. We might need to depend on Indians to show us where to find good water."

"What about Indian attacks? Will they attack us, or show us where to find water?"

"Don't you worry none about Indian attacks. They won't bother us as long as we treat them fairly."

"If the oxen are thirsty, how are we going to keep them from drinking that water? Won't they start running toward it if they smell it?"

"They might," replied Jacob. "We'll have to be careful. Let's make sure they're as healthy as possible when we get to that region. That'll improve their chances considerably. These emigrants that are racing will never make it past the Sweetwater, leastwise not in one piece. When their oxen start dying, they'll have to lighten their load. If they come to you wanting to buy your spares, you tell 'em no. We need all the oxen you got."

The next few miles were uneventful until Jacob pointed out several depressions in the prairie.

"Those are buffalo wallows. Buffalo get down in them and roll around, giving themselves a dust bath. Helps to keep the insects off and probably just feels good."

"Are you sure, Jacob? People say we won't get to buffalo country for several hundred miles."

"Not mistaken, those are wallows alright. Buffalo moved out of this area and gone farther west. This is too close to civilization to suit them—those wallows probably been fallow for ten years. Make sure you keep the wagon away from them. They're probably soft sand, and you'd sink in to the hubs."

Abby immediately looked forward to see where her oxen were heading. More sage advice. From now on, she would be more watchful of trail conditions.

"Looks like we got a good afternoon coming up, ten miles easy." Without another word he mounted and rode over to the south side of the column, about thirty yards out at his normal position. Far enough to avoid the constant cloud of dust put up from the wagons and ox teams.

That evening they made camp about a mile north of the Kansas River. After today's march, people could easily see the advantages of traveling and camping in smaller groups. Charley Applegate was right. There were too many wagons, working stock, and loose cattle for the entire migration to stay together.

Tonight was the first attempt at an organized camp, and it went well. Teamsters drove their wagons into a circular corral with the tongues pointing out. Then people set up their tents and kitchens outside this makeshift corral, using the tongue of their wagon as a place to sit. The working livestock, oxen, mules, and horses grazed on the open prairie during the evening before being brought into the "wagon corral" for the night. Two wagons on either side of the so-called gate simply turned their tongues toward each other to close the gate. Loose cattle remained out on the prairie under guard. This arrangement, with the tongues pointing outward, allowed for easy team hitching in the morning. The teamster simply backed each pair of yoked oxen into position and chained them to the tongue.

The new arrangement also meant that people had to move their kitchen equipment to the front of the wagon, and the gear previously in the front to the rear. With Jacob's help, Abby easily accomplished this chore. Overloaded emigrants faced a considerable dilemma of reorganization. Tonight's campsite provided no water, so after "corralling" the wagons and helping Abby rearrange her kitchen gear, Jacob drove the oxen and horses south to the river.

Each group of wagons set up a makeshift latrine with a piece of canvas. Privacy wasn't perfect—but one had to make do. During the day women would hide each other behind their skirts for privacy.

While watering his oxen up on the Kansas, Phil Rubey chanced upon a honey tree. A large honeybee hive sat in a hollow part of a cottonwood, and it was loaded with honey. In Missouri, raiding honey trees was illegal. The Missouri legislature set those trees aside for the Osage Indians, both as a food source and as a trade item. However, this wasn't Missouri, and the honey was theirs for the taking. After retrieving several large pots from his wagon, Phil succeeded in obtaining a substantial amount. After dinner that evening, Sarah stopped by with a quart. Abby thanked her profusely, since sweets were a welcome addition to the usually bland dinner fare.

While Phil was gathering honey, Jacob filled a container with tree sap from a few boxelders growing near the river. When he returned to camp, Abby could see that there would be something new to learn.

"We're going to fill the seams on that wagon," he said. "We'll be crossing the Kansas River soon, and you're not going to want water leaking in on your trunks and supplies."

"Well, let's have some dinner, and then you can show me what to do." By now, she knew that she had hired the right man. To herself, she said, "Most men would probably not bother with such work. There's a great deal this old trapper can show me, and I'm going to learn everything I can."

While she cleaned up after dinner, Jacob secured some ash from their campfire and a half dozen tallow candles she had bought at the Skow's general store. Waterproofing her wagon was a good use for the candles. In a cooking pot, Jacob created a mixture of ash, tallow, and tree sap that had the consistency of molasses and stickiness of animal glue. As soon as it was ready, he picked up the pot and walked over to the Western Passage.

"Now, here's what to do. Take some of this mixture on the end of a knife and work it into each seam, inside and out. Try to push as much as you can directly into the seam before moving on. We won't get completely done tonight, but by working together we should finish by tomorrow night."

"I'll get another knife. When do you think we'll get to a part of the Kansas where we can cross?—and will this caulking be dry in time?"

"Probably tomorrow or the next—and don't worry about it drying, it'll still keep the water out. We should do the entire outside first before moving on to the interior. That way we'll be ready no matter when we get to the river."

Later, as the sun began to set, Lindsay Applegate, one of the Applegate brothers, stopped by to inform their group about organizing for an eventual Indian attack. People from each of the wagons in Abby's corral gathered around to hear what Lindsay had to say. He remained on top of his tall mount so people could see him.

"I've talked to several groups already and there's a general feeling that we ought to run some drills, or at least let everyone know what to do. Don't you think so, there, Mister?" He looked at Jacob. Those fringed buckskins and fur hat made him stand out from the other emigrants. Lindsay could see he was a mountain man, and figured that he would confirm his concerns about an Indian attack.

Jacob slowly lit his pipe while the eyes of all emigrants trained on him.

"Well, there's nothing wrong with being prepared. My advice is to not lose any sleep over worrying about Indian attacks. I never met an Indian that would be foolish enough to attack such a large, well-armed caravan."

"Just the same, we need to be ready." Lindsay felt strongly on this matter, and a lack of concern by this mountain man could not deter him.

"Now, here's what I've discussed with the other groups. Whenever you hear the alarm, we want women and children to get in the wagons while all able-bodied men above the age of sixteen should grab their gun and come a-running. That means your gun should be ready at all times."

"What are you proposing we use for an alarm?" asked a boy named Ed Lenox. Ed was just fifteen, traveling West with his parents and three siblings—but he considered himself a man and capable of joining in the defense of the caravan.

"A rifle shot, followed by the cry, 'Indians!'" replied Lindsay. "You folks have guards watching your loose cattle all night, so it'll be up to them to give the alarm."

"During the day we'll all be watching," Ed added.

That was enough for Jacob. He stepped forward.

"So you're asking these people to carry loaded rifles in their wagons or on their person at all times? Is that what you're saying?"

"That's right, Mister," replied Lindsay. "We're gonna be ready."

"You're gonna be dead!" replied Jacob in a bold manner that startled some of the men and most of the women. "Half these farmers never handled a rifle, and the other half never fired anything more than a squirrel gun. You'll kill more people from accidents than from Indian attacks!"

"I don't see any cause for being against preparedness. What would you do if Indians attack and we're all sitting around with empty guns? What then, Mister Trapperman, what would you do then?"

"I'd invite 'em into camp for some dinner. They're probably just hungry." Several people smiled at this last comment. It broke the tension and encouraged a few other men to offer their comments.

A tall, lanky man named Matt Gilmore, agreed that everyone should be ready and know what to do in case of an emergency. He addressed the crowd with a serious, concerned tone. "I think every family here should have a place set up in your wagon where the women and children can hide. Everyone should keep their head below the edge of the wagon, out of the way of arrows."

"Don't worry 'bout that," answered Jacob. "Most Indians use trade guns, plenty strong enough to pass a ball through the side of a wagon."

"Now that's enough there, Mister Trapperman," interrupted Lindsay. "You can laugh at us if you want, but we're going to be ready to defend ourselves. If you want to lose your hair, then that's your business. There's no call to make a joke of our situation. I consider this to be serious business, and we're going to be ready."

There was a muffled grumbling of agreement.

"I'm Joe Hess." A rough-looking man with a heavy German accent stepped forward. "I have my whole family out here. I am not about to let anything happen to them." He looked over at Jacob. "You are traveling alone, and it does not matter what happens to you. I think your attitude is frightening our women and children. This is not called for."

Another rumble of agreement.

"Maybe so. I still say there'll be more injuries with loaded guns than with Indian attacks. You mark my words."

"We'll mark 'em alright. We'll mark 'em on your headstone!" It was John Hobson. The tall, solidly built man with a week-old beard stepped forward from the back of the group. He spoke firmly, sure of his purpose. "I have my whole family out here, too, and I aim to be prepared. We know how to handle guns, probably better than most Indians, and we can certainly fight better; I'm sure of that."

"Now, that's another thing," answered Jacob. "Have any of you fought Indians before?" There was silence. "That's what I thought. You go up against a group of Sioux warriors and you'll be going up against some of the finest fighting forces on this continent—certainly better than any army. You take my word when I say you'd be well advised to avoid any conflict and make friends with the Indians we meet."

"Making peace first sounds fine with me." Sam Oakley had just arrived to hear the last of the conversation. "There's no cause to go spoiling for a fight. We have enough problems driving these wagons—don't need any more problems than that."

"We're not going to start anything," replied Lindsay, "but if the Indians do, we'll sure finish it."

Jacob wanted to make an additional comment. Something like the number of people they'd be burying if they should inadvertently kill an Indian. He thought better of it and kept silent.

Lindsay continued, "Now let me reiterate. If we should get attacked, the night guards will sound the alarm, and all women and children will get into their wagons as fast as they can. All men above the age of sixteen will get their gun and come a-running. Is that understood?" There was a nod of agreement from all the male emigrants and most of the women. Other women, either too confused or too frightened, stood mute, wishing they were back home and not out here on the American Prairie.

"It's settled then, we'll all be ready. Now I got to move on and tell the next camp."

While Lindsay rode off, everyone dispersed toward their wagons to discuss preparations. As Abby walked back with Jacob and Sam, she couldn't help remark on Jacob's lack of concern.

"You know Western Indians better than anyone here, Jacob. Do you think they will let us pass through their country unmolested?"

"There's no reason for them to get upset, unless we wantonly kill buffalo or, worse yet, start a fight. With all these frightened farmers someone might be dumb enough to shoot."

"I must admit, it doesn't hurt to be prepared. I don't want that gun going off when the wagon hits a rock, so what should I do?—leave the gun empty?" Abby's voice showed genuine concern.

"I keep mine loaded all the time, but I've carried it for over twenty years. I shouldn't expect you to respond with the same experience. Tell you what, Abby, we'll compromise. You keep the gun loaded, but tie a small cord around the hammer. That way you won't be able to pull the hammer back until removing the cord. If the gun gets jostled around, or something brushes up against the hammer, it won't get pulled back and there won't be any spark to ignite the powder. How does that sound?"

"Sounds good—and I'll tie the cord so that I can remove it easily but it won't come off by itself. I can also wrap the gun in one of my blankets so it doesn't get jostled too much during the day. I'll keep it beside me at night."

Sam listened quietly as he walked on with the pair. He had nothing to add, but the conversation convinced him how he should carry his gun, with a safety cord.

"You better practice more at loading," Jacob said. "Back when I was trapping for the Rocky Mountain Fur Company, we figured a man could get two shots off every minute. You'll probably never get that fast—and you won't need to as long as these pilgrims don't start anything. You do the best you can."

"Tomorrow, if we make camp early enough, can we go out and shoot some more? I mean, I want to get accustomed to handling that big gun." Abby spoke with a seriousness that Jacob could see in her eyes.

"That we will, Abby, that we will—but tomorrow we need to finish caulking your wagon. Now, if you don't mind, I'll see you in the morning."

"Good night, Mr. Chalmers," Abby called out as he walked away. There was no reply. At times like this she felt that calling him Mr. Chalmers recognized his experience, knowledge, and advice.

He moved off toward his gear, leaving Abby and Sam to talk.

The sun had set, and the flicker of campfires dotted the prairie landscape.

"It's not too late, Miss Meacham. Would you like to walk for a few more minutes?"

"That's kind of you, Sam, and you can call me Abby." The evening was cool, so she folded her arms to keep warm. They started walking around the corral of wagons, out far enough so as not to disturb the kitchens of other emigrants.

"I hope all that talk about Indian attacks didn't frighten you. I think Lindsay just wants everyone to be prepared. His brother Jesse has over two hundred head of loose cattle, so I suspect they're worried about losing some. Although I can't see Indians driving off cattle, especially when they have buffalo. I mean, why should they risk a fight? 'Course, they know this country better than we do and could probably hide cattle in some canyon where we'd never find them." He trailed off, then continued almost to himself. "I don't see why they should mind us crossing their land. We don't plan on staying, and they don't really own land. I hear they think of land like we think of the air and water—it belongs to everyone. So if we pass through on our way to Oregon, they shouldn't mind at all."

He looked Abby in the eye. "I'll keep my gun loaded like Lindsay says. You know, just in case—and that safety cord Jacob mentioned, that's a right smart idea. Just tied in a bow, so I can get it off fast." He addressed her with forced confidence. "Yes, ma'am, that's what I'm gonna do. I'll keep it in the front of Copenhaver's wagon where I can get to it. I drive their ox team, you know. I could keep it up front where I could run back and get it. You know, if something happens. Not that anything will, 'cause ..."

"Sam," interrupted Abby, "are you afraid of an Indian attack?"

"Who, me? Why, no, ma'am, not me—not afraid at all. Like I said, I have my gun and I'll keep it real handy, like all these other men. You know, I think that old Jacob is right. Any Indian would be plumb crazy to attack a caravan this well-armed. Why, they wouldn't stand a chance, and what do we have that they want? These emigrants are carrying farm tools and furniture. What would any Indian want with that? Don't most of them live in teepees? There's not much room for furniture in a teepee—and I can't see Indians farming. They'd need some sort of barn for their hay, 'cause you can't store hay in a teepee. No, ma'am, I'm not afraid of Indians. Not with this group of emigrants, especially since we've all got guns. I'll keep mine in the front of the wagon where ..."

"Sam," Abby interrupted again, "do you always talk so much?"

Sam paused for a moment. "No, I ... I don't. Was I talking too much?"

"So, you're not afraid of Indians?"

Sam paused again, considering how to respond. "Now, there you go again. I think you must be afraid, Miss Abby. Afraid is not such a good word for men. Cautious, yes, that's what I am, cautious. It doesn't hurt to be a little cautious. I just want to …"

"I'm glad you're not frightened, Sam," Abby smiled, then tactfully changed the subject. "Why don't you tell me what made you decide to go to Oregon."

"It's like I said the other night. I'm from Springfield, Illinois, and I'm a-going West to make my fortune."

"Yes, well, what did you do in Springfield?"

"I worked on my parent's farm. Well now, don't that beat all. You want to know about me. I never would have guessed. You're the first person in this whole caravan that ever bothered to ask. Even the people I'm working for never bothered to ask. I guess they don't care. As long as I drive their wagon and look after their oxen, they don't much care about where I came from. Least they never …"

"So you grew up on a farm. What kind of crops did you grow?"

Again, Sam hesitated. "Corn, beans, and squash—sold them in town. Well, Abby Meacham—here you're asking what kind of crops I grew. Nobody ever asked me that—not even once. Even back in Springfield, whenever I went into town, the people they just …"

"We grew corn too, back in Greene County. How about family—have you got any brothers or sisters?" Abby was having fun now—she sensed Sam's nervousness.

He might be doing all the talking, she thought, *but I'm in control.* She had been smiling for the last few minutes, for she hadn't had this much fun with a man since before getting married.

"Three brothers and two sisters, all younger. They're all still back on the farm. They were sorry to see me leave, but a man's gotta move on, can't stay on the nest forever. Here we are, Abby, back at your wagon. That sure went fast. I guess I did talk some. Hope I didn't bore you, I just …"

"I enjoyed it, Sam. Thank you for walking with me."

"My pleasure, Abby. Maybe I could see you again, I mean for another walk."

"That would be fun, Sam."

"Well, I better be getting back now. You take care, and if you need any help, you come a-hollering."

"I will do that, Sam. Good night."

"Good night, ma'am." Sam hooked both thumbs in his back pockets and took a few steps backward. "I will call on you in a day or so."

Abby smiled and repeated her good-night as Sam turned to walk away. She watched him disappear into the darkness while continuing to smile at his behavior.

"Well, Sam," she said to herself, "you're tall, you're handsome, you're strong, and you're certainly afraid of Indians."

Campfires were still burning when Abby walked over to the Applegates' to visit Malinda and Cynthia, two women whom she had befriended while still back at Independence. Cynthia, the 29-year-old wife of Jesse Applegate, had several children to care for, in addition to adjusting to living from a wagon and cooking on an open fire. Her sister-in-law Malinda, Charley Applegate's wife, faced the same dilemma, but was less accepting of her new situation. Charley had not bothered to consult her when the three Applegate brothers decided to go to Oregon. Both ladies, accustomed to the benefits of slave labor, considered the menial trail chores of washing and cooking an unwelcome burden.

"Abby." Malinda looked up from kneading a large ball of dough as Abby approached. "Please come in." She motioned for her to sit on a small barrel.

"Thank you, I hope it's not too late for a visit."

"Not at all," replied Cynthia, poking her head out of the wagon. "Let me get these children tucked in. Betsy," she called over to her other sister-in-law, "bring some pap over—we've got hot water. Abby's here!"

"Looks like you're getting settled with your trail homes," Abby said as she sat down. "There certainly is a lot of work with these wagons."

"Worse than I ever imagined," said Malinda. "I'd give anything to go back to our farm. At least there the kitchen didn't keep moving around!"

"We're just new to this life," added Abby. "After a few weeks we'll all be settled into daily routines."

"Maybe for you, Abby," said Cynthia. "Me and Jesse have two wagons to drive and a lot of little ones to feed—I just don't know how we'll do it. The 'meat wagon' is overloaded, but at least we've got a teamster to drive it."

"Meat wagon!" exclaimed Abby. "That's a good name for it. I see you're carrying farm implements too."

"Everything we can." Betsy said as she entered the kitchen carrying a small tin of pap and some cups for Abby and her sisters-in-law. She handed Abby a cup, then sat down on the tongue of the wagon that Cynthia's children had christened the "Little Red Wagon."

"I saw you walking next to your oxen today, Abby," said Malinda while she poured hot water into each lady's cup. "Aren't you exhausted by the end of the day?"

"Our teamster is going to start walking too," Cynthia added before Abby could answer. "That trunk he's sitting on isn't all that comfortable and the roughness of this prairie is taking its toll."

"Are you able to keep those herds together out here?" asked Abby. "You Applegates must own the majority of the loose stock."

"It's a chore," answered Cynthia. "Jesse's already told me that he should have kept a few of our slaves as drovers."

"They're just extra mouths to feed," added Betsy.

"Yes, but we can certainly use more camp help," mused Malinda. She took a sip of pap while closing her eyes. The exhaustion of trail life, without slave labor or any say over her family's destiny, weighed heavy on her expression and drooping shoulders.

"This is only the first week," said Abby in a voice of encouragement. "We all need a little more time to adjust to these new routines. Everything will work out."

"Maybe so," said Cynthia. "But our husbands really have no reason to go to Oregon. We've all got large, productive farms—and the depression hasn't hurt us at all. It's just that a land full of opportunity like Oregon is too tempting for those Applegate boys to pass up. Maybe if we'd been less successful, Jesse would have been too busy to go chasing off on some faraway dream."

"Does your teamster help with the camp chores?" asked Abby as she looked over at Cynthia.

"Not at all," blurted out Cynthia in a tone of disgust. "George Beale is one of the most ill-tempered and useless men I've ever met. He doesn't have any family or friends, so I rather suspect he's going to Oregon to escape some infraction with the law."

"Cynthia," scolded Malinda. "We don't need to talk about that."

"Abby, you've caused quite a stir among the men of this migration." Betsy abruptly changed the subject. "Our husbands don't quite know what to make of a woman traveling alone."

"I've got a good man to help me, Jacob Chalmers," Abby said in her defense. "He's a hard worker and knows about the West."

"We can use more men like that," sighed Malinda. "This journey is just more than our families should have to bear."

The ladies continued their conversation until the pap was gone and it was time for bed. When Jesse, Lindsay, and Charley returned from securing their herds, Abby thanked the Applegate women for their kindness and returned to her wagon. Having friends in the same corral made the encampment feel like a friendly village, something that everyone could take solace in. There would be many other evenings for social visits.

It had been a long day of travel and a tiring evening, what with the added work of preparing for the upcoming river crossing. But after less than a week on the trail, Abby was beginning to feel confident in her new life. While she had much more to learn, crossing a major river was a challenge that she felt up to. The diary received almost a page of quick notes concerning events of the day. These included the assignment of traveling and camping groups, the formation of circular corrals; the rearrangement of kitchen gear to be accessible at night; the quart of honey from Sarah Rubey; the recipe for caulking the wagon bed; the concern for a potential Indian attack; and the walk with Sam. Each note would be expanded when time allowed.

After organizing her Hawken so that it was within easy reach, she lay down on her wagon bed and was soon asleep.

After breakfast the next morning, Friday, May 26, Abby became more familiar with her Hawken by practicing loading. Powder was irreplaceable, so the practice only involved going through the motions of loading and handling the heavy gun.

Jacob tore a fringe off the shoulder of his buckskins to use as a safety cord. He stopped short, looking at the fringe.

"I'm going to back off what I said about keeping this gun loaded. Your loading skill is good enough that you can load it when you need it, so keep it empty during the day. That way we won't have any problems carrying it over rough roads. You can load it during the night if you want, but I'd recommend against it."

"Didn't you tell me once that discharging a gun in camp was against camp rules, at least for you mountain men?"

"That's right, so when we go out to practice we'll get far away from these wagons and stock. The worst case I seen of discharging a gun in camp happened up on the Yellowstone about ten years back. We had a number of Crow in camp trading buffalo robes and other hides. Things were tense and everyone was ready for trouble. The Crows were our friends most of the time—but they could be treacherous. If they thought they had a stronger force or the advantage in any way, well, you better watch your hair. Old Joe Meek started the ruckus when a young buck began to strut back and forth in front of his wife. She was beading moccasins outside his lodge while Joe was lying down inside. She didn't pay this buck any attention, so he rode up and thumped her on the shoulder with his bow. Well, old Joe wasn't much for conversation, so he stepped out and shot that Indian dead. The whole camp erupted, and by the time things calmed down, one trapper was dead and several men wounded. Gabe was plenty upset with old Joe. Joe said he was sorry about the trapper, but no Indian was going to whip his wife."

"Jacob, your life is so different from the people I've known, I never stop being amazed at the stories you relate. Do you really expect me to believe this fellow Joe would kill an Indian for trying to get the attention of his wife?—and why would he take his wife way out into a wilderness? Your story is a little made up, now, isn't it?"

"If I said it, then it's true. His wife was the prettiest thing you ever did see. From the Snake tribe, Mountain Lamb, yep, that was her name, Mountain Lamb. Too bad she stopped that Bannock arrow the following summer. She was a fine-looking squaw. We must have killed a dozen Bannocks that day in retaliation for their attack on us—but no women and children. We never had the stomach for that."

"So, you're saying that Indians do attack."

"Now you're getting things confused, Abby. One of those Bannocks tried to steal old Gabe's horse, so Gabe's Negro friend shot him dead—seemed to be the natural thing to do. Then the other Bannocks got a bit unfriendly, so we killed ten or so more. We chased them back to their camp and rode straight through. All the braves, squaws, and children came running from their lodges, jumped into a nearby river, and swam out to an island. We held them there for two days, killing any brave that poked his head above the brush. I guess we got tired of the sport and finally left."

"Jacob, your stories get more and more wild. How can you kill people for sport? I don't believe a word of it."

"You can ask old Joe yourself. Last I heard, he and Doc Newell were taking some carts west out of Fort Hall, the first ones. I don't expect they got very far, leastwise not past Fort Boise. Probably abandoned them at some river crossing. Those boys should be in the Wallamet Valley by now, so you can ask old Joe yourself—and we'll probably see old Gabe when we get past South Pass. I heard last winter that Gabe was building a trading post for emigrants down on the Green. You can ask him if you don't believe me."

"Does Doc Newell practice medicine in Oregon? We can always use another doctor."

"Doc's not a real doctor. I don't know where he got that name. After the fur trade dried up he told me he was going out to Oregon to become a farmer—him, Caleb Wilkins, and Joe Meek. Can't much see Doc as a farmer, same with old Joe—but that's what they said. You'll probably meet Doc out in Oregon too."

"You can be sure I will talk to him and Joe and this Gabe fellow. I assume that name is short for Gabriel. He must be from a religious family."

"Don't rightly know how Gabe got to be called that. He's also known as the Blanket Chief. Not sure how he got that name either. His Christian name is Jim Bridger. I've known Gabe since he and I went up the Missouri with Ashley and Henry. He'll tell you stories you won't believe either, but you ask him anyway."

"It seems like your trapper friends all have nicknames. How about you—what's your nickname?"

"Never got one. Now let's get this outfit ready to travel."

Within the hour the order to march came down the line and, as usual, Abby and Jacob were ready and waiting. The long line of white-sheeted wagons slowly moved forward to their next big challenge, the Kansas River.

After a ten-mile trek, the caravan reached the Kansas River shortly after midday. Because of spring rains and snowmelt, the river was running high and presented an extremely dangerous obstacle to cross. It was approximately a quarter mile wide with sandy banks and a sandy bed. The water was muddy, similar to the Missouri. Timber grew thick and varied along the river's floodplain. Sycamore, elm, bur oak, black walnut, boxelder, linden, coffee bean, honeylocust, white ash, red ash, cottonwood, sumac, and plum offered more than enough wood for campfires—and more importantly, wood to build a raft.

By midafternoon a discussion ensued with the migration leaders and other emigrants concerning the best way to cross. The river at this juncture flowed from west to east, and the migration needed to cross to the north shore. Nearby, a Frenchman named Pappin had built a flatboat to ferry wagons across. This man, a farmer from outside Independence, was taking advantage of a new moneymaking opportunity. The Kansas River was relatively close to Independence, and he knew the migration would have to cross it. With a business venture in mind, Pappin had arrived in early April with two of his boys to make a raft for ferrying people and wagons across the river. He employed several Indians of the Osage tribe to pull the flatboat across using ropes and horses. Today, four other Osage warriors, wrapped in blankets, watched the proceedings from the opposite shore.

The council appointed a committee of three to make arrangements for crossing on Pappin's flatboat. Unfortunately, his price was too high. The council considered five dollars for each crossing an outrageous price, so in retaliation they decided to build their own flatboat. Cottonwood logs in the floodplain were the right size, so by late that afternoon, men were felling trees and hewing them into squares to build a raft. For Abby and Jacob, this seemed to be a lot of unnecessary work. The price Pappin was asking was high, but the service greatly needed. Abby had planned for such trail expenses.

By three o'clock she and Jacob had their wagon down next to the river, second in line to get across the Kansas on Pappin's flatboat, followed by a handful of others. Several men expressed anger at the independence of Abby, Jacob, and the others preparing to pay Pappin's high price. This discontent grew when they all got their animals and wagons across in time to make camp before the dinner hour. Most of the men's anger was directed at Abby. The fact that a woman, traveling alone, could cross a major river so easily irked them. They quickly attributed her success to the prowess of Jacob—but he posed another problem. This trapper, in his buckskin regalia, did not fit into the emigrant social circles—and people who did not fit in could not be trusted. Now, he and Abby had just crossed a difficult river with ease. That was reason enough to dislike her and not trust him.

Jacob directed Abby to move the Western Passage out of the Kansas River floodplain and up onto the prairie near Black Warrior Creek. It appeared to be a comfortable place to wait for the rest of the caravan. The camp afforded fresh water for the livestock and shade from the afternoon sun.

The rest of the migration camped on Soldier Creek, two miles south of its confluence with the Kansas. River crossings disrupted the orderliness of wagon corrals by scattering wagons on either side. The next few days would see the corrals slowly disappear from the south side and reform on the north as wagons crossed the river, one at a time.

Abby was not the only teamster interested in hiring Pappin. Even with his high price, he stayed busy with more work than he could handle.

On the following morning, Saturday, May 27, a man named Steve Fairly demanded that his entire outfit cross on a single trip. At five dollars a crossing, splitting his outfit into two raft trips would be simply too expensive. Against the wishes of Pappin, he loaded his wagon (an overloaded wagon), eight oxen, and his entire family onto the flatboat.

As the flatboat approached the far shore, several anxious oxen shifted their positions, which changed the center of gravity too fast for the boat to recover. In a moment the oxen were falling off the tilted platform, followed by the wagon and Fairly's entire family. His two daughters could not swim and began to flounder as the current carried them swiftly downstream. Without hesitation, two of the Osage warriors on the opposite shore threw off their blankets and jumped into the river, pulling both girls to safety. The Fairlys' wagon, now floating, lodged in a shallow backwater several hundred yards downriver—stuck in the mud on the north side. All their belongings were wet, and their trunks were floating inside the wagon. Only the canvas white-top prevented the trunks from disappearing with the current.

Steve and his wife, along with the eight oxen, swam to the north shore. By the time they pulled themselves up on the bank and regained some of their composure, the two Osage Indians were walking back, each carrying a daughter. They were wet, but alive and healthy. The frightened girls jumped from the arms of their saviors and ran for their mother. Steve immediately approached the two Indians and, without thanking them for saving his daughters' lives, asked for their help in getting his wagon and provisions out of the shallows. They agreed to help, but wanted two dollars each. Although they were Plains Indians, they knew the value of money at the local Indian Agency. Saving his girls was simply a common courtesy they would perform for anyone. Recovering gear from the river was something else. That was worth payment.

Steve, already upset about losing his outfit, lost his temper when the Indians asked to be paid for recovering his gear. He berated them for their selfishness, claiming that they were taking advantage of his situation. In a few minutes his wife came over to express her concern about recovering their provisions quickly, before the river claimed everything. Steve agreed to pay the two Indians four dollars as long as they got his wagon out as quickly as possible. Within the hour, they used two yokes of his oxen to pull the wagon up on shore. Water poured out of the bed and all of their trunks, but they did not lose anything.

The Rubeys crossed on Sunday morning along with the Burnetts and Blevinses. They joined Abby and again formed their little encampment, not unlike the one outside Independence. With the delay in crossing, there was time to make needed repairs and to socialize—but the wait proved to be an exercise in frustration. People who were already across were consuming valuable provisions as they waited for the rest of the caravan. They did not dare go on because of a lack of knowledge of the trail and a general fear of Indians. Before long, they began referring to their encampment as Camp Delay—an appropriate title that women could refer to in their diaries.

Without wagon corrals, the white-sheeted wagons randomly dotted the green landscape of the American Prairie. A formal government with a guard detail could not be selected until the entire migration was across, so people with loose cattle continued their chores of guarding and herding the animals.

The prairie was a perfect picture of magnificent beauty, unmarred by the hand of civilization. It shone as a sea of grass under an intensely blue sky. All was natural, beautiful, and undisturbed. To Abby, crossing the Kansas felt like stepping suddenly from the known world of western Missouri and Shawnee farmland into the uncivilized, unspoiled American West. Seeing such a vast area at once, unbroken by trees and buildings, was awe inspiring. Her preparations, both emotionally and in her outfit, would now prove their worth as she left the United States and all that she knew behind. She would never again see its luxuries, comforts, and most importantly, society, friends, family, and home. Ahead lay untold hardships, privations, and dangers. What wondrous things were there to see beyond this sea of grass? The wild rivers, the immense forests of Oregon Country, the eternal snows of the mountains, and a thousand other curiosities awaited her and the other emigrant adventurers.

Sam and the Copenhavers crossed just before noon on Sunday. After getting settled, Sam did not waste any time locating Abby and catching up on the news. The organization of trunks and equipment in Abby's wagon had taken on the look of a well-manicured home, with a storage place for everything and everything in its place. Accustomed to the ragtag affair of the Copenhavers' wagon, Sam was quick to compliment Abby on her outfit. With two children it was difficult, if not impossible, for the Copenhavers to stay organized. They were always misplacing one item or another and subsequently wasting time looking for it. Sam avoided this hassle by carrying his gear on two pack animals, thereby shielding himself from dealing with the interior of their wagon.

During that same afternoon a 21-year-old adventurer named Billy Vaughan suffered cramps while swimming his horse and pack animals across the river. The man's distress was obvious to everyone on shore, but he was too far out for anyone to help. Jim Nesmith, who happened to be crossing on Pappin's flatboat at the time, jumped in to help him. However, Billy panicked and started to pull Jim down. Jim had all he could do to release Billy's death grip and keep himself from drowning. Another man, Pete Stewart, was watching from the north shore and jumped in to help. He got to the pair in time to help pull them to shore before Jim became completely exhausted. Billy was unconscious and given up for dead by several men who helped carry him up to level ground. Young Ed Lenox got a small barrel from his parents' wagon so they could lay Billy over it, belly down, and pump his arms to discharge river water and try to get him breathing again. They were about to give up when he came to and started to cough and gag as he gasped for air.

It took Jim Nesmith the remainder of the day to regain his strength from the ordeal. He was traveling with the Otey brothers, who had a single wagon for the three of them. As soon as they got across, they tried to make Jim as comfortable as possible. Pete Stewart made up a bed in his wagon to keep Billy Vaughan warm, dry, and well fed for the next few days. The delay in crossing proved beneficial, for it took Billy three days to recover.

Late Sunday afternoon a heavy rainstorm disrupted the crossing for about an hour. Mules refused to move during the storm, while most people sought shelter in their wagons. To make things worse, Pappin's flatboat broke apart and several men, women, and children almost drowned. Luckily, the incident occurred near the north shore, so all escaped with their lives and almost all of their property.

Earlier that afternoon, Jacob went out on the prairie for purposes of hunting and just plain solitude. His fondness for being alone came from many years in the mountains. Also, he needed time away from the quarreling farmers. Shortly before dinner he brought in a deer that he generously shared with the other people in Abby's small encampment.

On Monday, May 29, the large entourage associated with Sir William Drummond Stewart arrived at the Kansas River crossing. The expedition consisted of about seventy-five individuals, all men, each riding his own horse and leading two pack animals. To avoid any confusion or conflict, they crossed the Kansas about a half-mile west of where the Oregon contingent was crossing. They then set up camp just south of the trail where there was good grass and water. This was only their third day out from Independence, and they needed time to reorganize their packs based on the experience and knowledge gained from the trail.

By noon, the emigrant raft begun on Saturday was ready. It consisted of ten logs laid between two dugout canoes and was large enough to hold only one wagon at a time. To get it across the river, men employed three towropes and six horses. The time needed to load a wagon and tow it across the river was a point of contention for anxious teamsters, and a test of everyone's patience. With over sixty wagons remaining, and about twenty crossings each day, it would take another three days to get the entire migration to the other side.

Later that day a group of Kaw Indians rode into Camp Delay. This area, north of the Kansas, was Kaw land. The mounted group consisted of eleven warriors who were on a hunting excursion. When they first appeared, there was some momentary confusion, as a few men thought the encampment was under attack. Fortunately, reasonable minds prevailed.

These Indians were poor, not having ready access to the buffalo herds that had been pushed farther west several decades earlier. Their dress, what little they had, consisted of a menagerie of skin and cloth garments, while their hair, cleanliness, and odor indicated a lack of concern for civilized life. They were a nomadic race of hunter-gatherers, rendered poor by advancing civilization. Several of the Indians possessed trade guns, but the remainder carried bows and quivers of arrows.

Shortly after declaring their friendly intentions, they began to go from wagon to wagon begging for food. Most of the emigrants were callous to their needs and refused their requests. A few did not. Abby and Jacob calmly watched the proceedings until the Indians got to within a hundred feet of the Western Passage. At that point, Jacob turned to Abby to ask for some bread.

"Like this?" Abby was already holding the remains of a loaf. She had been holding it for the last five minutes, waiting for them to get closer.

"I don't see why these other people are so stingy, it's only a little food. We'll be moving on soon, so it's not as if we're inviting them to Oregon."

"They're probably frightened, or proud, or confused," Jacob responded. "Most of these emigrants have never seen Plains Indians—but it is interesting. I'll bet if these Indians were clean and well dressed, those farmers would be happy to share their food." Jacob was a keen observer of people, and the basis for social prejudices exhibited by these emigrants did not escape his attention.

"If you don't feed them, they might be back to steal something. I suggest you not leave anything out tonight. If they return, they won't remember you were the one that gave them food."

This was more sound advice that Abby vowed to follow.

Later on, Abby again spent the evening with Sam. They had been apart for two days during the crossing, and Sam did not want that to happen again.

On Tuesday morning eight people, including Overton Johnson and Bill Winter, decided not to wait for the remaining wagons to finish crossing. They hitched up their wagons and started out, following the trace of Sir William Drummond Stewart, assuming that the Oregon migration would eventually catch up. It was another example of emigrant independence, an example that more than concerned Abby and the others. These impatient farmers would miss the upcoming elections for a trail leader.

After the mishap with Pappin's flatboat, all livestock—working animals and loose stock—were swum across. Drovers hired Kaw Indians to engage in the dangerous work of swimming the stock. A curiosity never before seen was the manner in which these Indians swam—dog-style. With the mishaps and slowness of the crossing, the main concern was getting the livestock across with minimal loss. The Kaw performed this job flawlessly. Drovers compensated the Indians with small trade items of little value, such as beads and other ornamentation.

Meanwhile, two Catholic missionaries, Father Pierre-Jean De Smet and Father De Vos, arrived and crossed the river by swimming their horses and pack animals. Like the Stewart entourage, they used pack animals to avoid the problems associated with wagons. They were traveling to a mission located near several villages of the Flathead Indians north of Fort Boise. After crossing, they chose to continue on without bothering to spend the day with so many "godless" farmers.

Later that morning a small band of Kaw squaws appeared in camp for purposes of trading. One of the Kaw warriors had gone back to his village to inform everyone of the large number of whites passing through their country. The squaws carried moccasins and dressed skins to trade for shirts, metal tools of any kind, food, and general gewgaw for ornamentation.

Shortly after the squaws appeared, Jacob traded a small handful of blue beads for two pair of moccasins and a small deerskin. Twenty years in the mountains had taught him the comfort of moccasins and the importance of carrying an extra pair on a long journey. After spending the previous winter in St. Louis where he endured the often tight and always uncomfortable "white man's" shoes, replacing his old worn-out moccasins was a welcome relief.

"I suggest you do the same, Abby. Your feet might not be hurting now, but we've just begun, and this prairie is the smoothest road we'll have. When we get into those mountains, or any rough terrain, you'll be cursing those store-bought shoes."

Abby was quickly learning to adhere to Jacob's counsel.

"How many beads will I need for a pair?"

"Ten or twelve should do, or you could trade one of those sewing awls. You should get two pair for something like that. Save the shirts. though. You'll need those when we get to buffalo country and beyond."

"Wait here, I'm going to need you." Abby went back to her wagon and in a moment returned with a sewing awl, one she had bought specifically for Indian trade. "Come on, you can translate."

Without saying a word, Jacob followed her over to where the squaws were displaying their wares.

"Tell her I would like to trade this awl for two pair of moccasins."

Jacob was enjoying Abby's spunk as she engaged in her first Indian barter. She stood tall and straight in her usual defiant stance as she surveyed the display of new moccasins. These were everyday moccasins, without ornamentation. They had double skin-thick soles, were ankle high, and tied with a single piece of rawhide. The squaw sat on the ground looking first at Abby, then at Jacob. Before Jacob could say a word, the squaw lifted Abby's dress far enough to see her shoes. In a moment she was speaking a tongue Abby had never heard. It was loud, fast, and unintelligible to both her and Jacob.

Jacob sat down and started speaking to the squaw in English, but using sign language for every sentence. Such was the way of mountain men. Their use of sign language when speaking was so common that many men spoke to each other in the same manner. It was simply habit. Being fluent in sign language was essential for any mountain man. During a single year they could come in contact with fifteen different tribes, all speaking a different language. Sign language was the common denominator. This method of communicating had been used by tribes of the Great Plains and Rocky Mountains for untold centuries, long before the incursion by white trappers. The value of such a common language was obvious. Since the time of the Lewis and Clark expedition, all white trappers had learned and used sign language in the pursuit of their nomadic, adventurous, and dangerous profession.

The squaw watched Jacob intently as he signed out their intention to trade for two pair of moccasins. Abby stood watching the squaw, who, after Jacob mentioned and signed the awl, quickly looked at Abby. She handed the awl to the squaw for her to examine.

Her keen interest in the item prompted Jacob to continue.

"That awl is worth two pair of moccasins and a good piece of hide. It will last you many seasons and is strong enough to pierce buffalo."

The squaw nodded her approval and gave Abby a pair of moccasins to try on. She quickly sat down on the ground, unlaced her shoes, and pulled the moccasins on. They felt loose and comfortable as she stood to walk around.

"I can feel everything, every stone, every clump of grass. They're comfortable, but my feet will have to become accustomed to them."

"You might have sore feet for the first few weeks until the bottoms toughen up. Right now you've got white man's feet. In a few weeks you'll never go back to shoes."

"Can we trade for two pair?" Abby walked back toward the squaw and Jacob. "You mentioned a hide, what do I need that for?"

Jacob continued signing as he emphasized the awl was worth at least two pair of moccasins and some hide. "With this awl you can make many more moccasins, faster than ever before." He motioned to another pair of moccasins about the same size as the first pair. Then he pointed to a dressed deer hide amongst a pile of folded hides behind the squaw.

The squaw agreed to a second pair of moccasins and handed them to Abby. The dressed hide was pushing the bargain. She turned and started looking through the pile of hides until she pulled out a small deerskin. She had several otter skins, but those were far too valuable. A small deerskin would complete the transaction.

While holding her second pair of moccasins and the deerskin, Abby picked up her shoes and asked Jacob to thank the woman for the trade. As they returned to the wagon, Jacob knew what her next request would be.

"Jacob, I want you to teach me sign language. You communicated with that woman as if you both spoke the same language, yet neither of you could understand a word. I want you to teach me to converse like that. I will pay you extra, since that was not part of our original agreement. Will you do that for me?"

Turning toward her, Jacob signed while speaking, "Yes, I can teach you to speak with signs."

"Thank you. Now what am I going to do with this hide? It looks like something extra to carry."

"Put it in your possibles sack. You never know when you'll need to patch something."

A possibles sack was a key element to any trapper's outfit. In it, he carried various miscellaneous items that could be useful in repairing a gun, a saddle, or a buckskin shirt. A scrap of cloth or piece of metal that may appear to have no value could prove indispensable when the nearest store was over one thousand miles away.

"Mr. Chalmers, you are going to turn me into a mountain woman before we reach Oregon. I will put it in with my other sewing materials, so I can use it to patch these moccasins."

"You'll find many uses. I suggest you start wearing those moccasins while we're still out here on flat ground. At first you'll have to watch your step to avoid sharp stones and prickly pear. After awhile you'll develop a general sense of where and how to walk. Your feet will toughen up soon enough. On a trip out to California a few years back, we ran into some Paiutes who go barefoot most of the time. The rocks in the summer get so hot you could cook on them, yet those Paiute kids played their games without any notice of the heat."

"California! Why haven't you ever told me you've been to California?"

Jacob paused in silence for a few moments, trying to think of a good answer.

"Never seemed important, and we're not going to California. No sense in cluttering up your Oregon plans with news of California."

"Well, maybe tonight at dinner, rather than feeding your face in silence, you could enlighten me on some of your exploits in California. Maybe Captain Gantt and his group will want to hear your stories."

"Gantt's been to California, so I'm sure his group knows enough. I will humor you if you wish. California is a paradise, that it is. They have dry sunny weather all year, no winters—and those Spaniards run thousands of horses and cattle in valleys bigger than most states. I was with Joe Walker's brigade when we first entered the California mountains. Well now, the beauty of those mountains, that's a story. I'll tell you about it tonight at dinner. Right now I feel like dropping a line into the Kansas."

In a few moments he had retrieved some fishing line from his packs on the ground underneath the wagon and was walking down to the river. It was still morning, and the emigrants' flatboat would need another two days to transport the remaining wagons across the Kansas. For Abby, it was a warm spring day without much to do but watch the stock and rest. At noon she carried a small plate of rice and bread down to the river for Jacob. In exchange, he gave her four trout to clean and prepare for dinner. These would be a welcome change from their usual fare.

That afternoon a French trapper, traveling east, rode into Camp Delay. He was leading two pack animals—one loaded with furs and the other with his outfit. When Jacob returned from the river, Abby immediately informed him of the visitor and the opportunity to send a letter home.

"He plans to go all the way to St. Louis, so if you want to send a letter to any of your family, you're welcome to use some of my writing paper."

Jacob scanned the other wagons, looking for the Frenchman.

"Did he give his name?"

"No, and I never thought to ask. With the excitement of sending a letter back to my folks, I never thought to ask—how rude of me. A number of other people are writing letters, and he's agreed to carry them all. I think he might be talking with Captain Gantt."

"You finish your letter, Abby. This might be someone I know."

"Jacob, don't you have any family? I mean it's none of my business, but ..."

There was no answer as he handed her two additional trout and walked off toward the Gantt encampment. The appearance of someone fresh from the mountains could provide valuable information as to the condition of the road ahead and the condition of Fort Laramie's supplies. Could they handle the needs of nearly a thousand emigrants? Had Gabe finished his trading post on the Green River?—and what were the condition of his supplies? Were there any scrapes with the Blackfeet or Gros Ventres that the migration should know about? How about Crow parties west of Fort Laramie engaged in their favorite sport of horse stealing? Captain Gantt was probably already quizzing the trapper for this information. Jacob wanted it firsthand.

The trapper turned out to be Louis Mathiot. Louis had originally gone West with Nat Wyeth and had been with Jacob during the Battle of Pierre's Hole back in '32. As Jacob approached, Louis, Captain Gantt, and several other California-bound emigrants were sitting on the ground discussing the news from Fort Laramie. In an instant Louis jumped up and grabbed Jacob by both arms.

"Jacob! Mon ami, mon qui a bon coeur ami!"

"English, Louis, English. You know I don't speak French."

"Oui, monsieur, oui. It is good to see you. You are going back to the mountains, no—but with these farmers? These people will die in the mountains!"

"Oregon, Louis, going to Oregon. There's nothing back East for this old child. Almost died last winter choking on coal smoke, wearing all them store-bought clothes and being civilized. There's no sight prettier than the Rockies, and I aim to go far enough west where civilization won't ever catch up."

Jacob sat down with the other men to begin a long discourse that lasted until dinner. Three years had passed since Jacob and Louis had enjoyed the 1840 Rendezvous. That year marked the last Rendezvous and the end of an American era. The gathering took place on the Green River near Horse Creek, in the shadow of the Wind River Mountains. This oasis had both water and a luxuriant carpet of grass, necessities for the horses and pack animals brought in by scores of trappers and their Indian allies.

The Green River site had served as a gathering place for the summer rendezvous six times between 1833 and 1840. The 1840 Rendezvous was smaller and more subdued than any previous, for each trapper knew that his lifestyle was coming to an end. Silk hats were replacing beaver hats, and the price of plews had fallen to an all-time low. The life of pure freedom they loved so much was falling victim to technology and advancing civilization. After that rendezvous, not all trappers went back to their secret haunts for another season of trapping. Some went to California, some to Oregon, some to Taos and the Mexican settlements, and a few returned East with the annual pack caravan of furs.

Jacob and Louis had chosen to stay in the mountains and sell their furs at Fort Laramie and Bent's Fort. After two years, Jacob returned to St. Louis to cash in his furs along with most of his outfit and to become civilized. That had been in November of last year. After only a few months, he realized that his life had moved beyond the constraints imposed by laws and society. Jacob spent most of the winter waiting for the spring flush when he could return to the West. Louis had stayed on for another winter and was just now returning from the mountains.

"Oui monsieur, there's nothing back East that can hold me either. As soon as I get a good price for these furs, I aim to load up with farmer supplies and head back to Bridger's trading post."

"So old Gabe got that place built did he? Where's it at?"

"On Black's Fork of the Green. He's got good grass and is far enough from Fort Laramie that these pilgrims should need just about everything."

"That's a fact," Jacob nodded. "In the past week, this child's seen things I ain't never seen, not before Ashley, not ever. When their oxen start dropping dead and they run out of food, they might start being less foolish, but maybe not even then."

The conversation wandered through the many seasons, adventures, and dangers these men had witnessed in the mountains. Jacob and Captain Gantt learned about the condition of the trail ahead, the depth of last winter's snowpack (which would determine the difficulty of river crossings), and the availability of supplies at Fort Laramie. The afternoon turned into a pleasant respite for Jacob. The last week had tried his patience, and it was good to converse with an old friend.

The dinner hour arrived with Jacob inviting Louis to join him and Abby.

"The woman I'm working for is a tolerable good cook, and we have fish tonight. I want you to meet Abby, she's got pluck, as good as any squaw."

By the time they got back to the wagon, Abby had dinner ready, all except for frying the fish. Jacob's conversation did not disappoint her this evening. He and Louis talked about old times, leaving Abby hardly a chance to get a word in. Their stories of adventure and danger more than satisfied her curiosity about Jacob's past life in the mountains.

During the afternoon Abby finished two letters, one to her folks and another to her brother. They were short so as to not waste paper, and contained the simple information of good health and a bright future. She made no mention of hardships or of the quarreling of other emigrants. Her family did not need to know of these problems. News of her outfit and hired man were enough. She knew her family would find comfort in knowing an experienced mountain man was watching for her safety in crossing the continent. She gave the letters to Louis and thanked him for his kindness.

After dinner Sam stopped by as usual. He and Abby were enjoying each other's company every evening, and on more than a friendship basis. Their walk tonight drifted away from the light of campfires, down toward the river. Tonight Abby wore her new moccasins, something that Sam did not know whether to like or dislike. All he knew was that she was unpredictable. If she wanted to try something new, then that's what she did.

"You sure those moccasins will hold up on the trail? I mean they don't look all that sturdy," he said.

"They're sturdy enough for Indians, so they should be strong enough for me," Abby replied. "I suppose they'll hurt for a few weeks until my feet toughen up. Jacob says I've got white man's feet. I guess that means soft."

"Jacob seems like a good man—probably real good in an Indian fight. You be careful, though. Those mountain men have a way about them."

"Oh, Sam, you shouldn't be so concerned about me. That is sweet of you, though. I'll be careful."

They found an old cottonwood log and sat down to watch the river current flicker by in the partial moonlight. The spring evening was chilly, so Sam was quick to take advantage of the opportunity to put his arm around Abby.

"Thank you, that feels good." She put her head on Sam's shoulder while holding his other hand between hers. His cheek pressed against her hair, and after a few moments he gave her a soft kiss on her temple. She did not move. The warmth of Sam and the comfort of being with a man felt good. "Our folks will be glad to hear we're getting along to Oregon without too many problems. How much did you write in your letter?"

"Just one page. I didn't want to waste paper, and I didn't have that much to say. I told them that I'm well and getting along fine. I also told them that I met you and how much I've started to care for you. I mean, you know, that we're seeing each other."

"Sam, you didn't. What did you say about me?"

"That was easy. I said you're the prettiest thing I ever did see, and you can cook, and sew, and drive a team, and you're on your way to Oregon to become a schoolteacher."

"Your folks will probably think I'm crazy. Almost everyone else does."

"It doesn't matter what they think. I have some deep feelings for you, Abby. I don't rightly know why, they just started when we got here to the Kansas. My folks will just have to accept you. I know as soon as they meet you, they'll be as happy as I am."

"Sam, if we're going to Oregon, and your folks are staying back East, I wouldn't get my hopes up about seeing them in the near future."

"You know what I mean, Abby. I mean, if they could meet you."

"Sam, it's only been a week since we met. Don't you think you're moving a little too fast?"

"Not at all. I seen the way other men look at you, and I want you to know how I feel."

"Well, I like our evenings together, and we have a long way to go before Oregon, so let's not go too fast." She looked up at Sam.

Sam's enthusiasm suffered a momentary setback, but Abby was right.

"Whatever you say, Abby, whatever you say."

Several minutes of silence passed while they watched the river flow by. A cool breeze kept the mosquitoes down and made their embrace even more reassuring. Abby moved her head closer to Sam's neck, closing her eyes and hoping he would kiss her again. Another minute passed, but it seemed like five. Finally, Sam kissed her forehead. This time she was ready, turning her head to meet his. His kisses were soft and sensuous, so she returned the sensuality with a style all her own. Each kiss was soft and sweet. They could feel the warmth of each other's breath and the feel of each other's tongues. Sam's hand slid around her waist as they stayed locked in an embrace, falling in love and not wanting to let go.

This love came as a surprise to Abby, for she was on her way to a new life in Oregon. Her plans were definite, not open to change—and Sam was not part of those plans. Yet his kindness and charm addressed her loneliness as nobody else could. The feelings he aroused in her had been absent for too long.

The two continued to embrace and intermittently kiss for some time, not speaking, for there was no need—just the quiet warmth of love and affection between two adventurers in search of El Dorado; a search for that mystical, legendary land of wealth and beauty. It was late before they returned to camp.

They walked close together on the way back from the river, with Abby holding Sam's arm with both hands. As they came into the light of campfires, Sarah Rubey was the first to notice, smiling her approval. Being seen arm in arm was a sure sign of a new romance. Abby knew that if Sarah knew, the whole camp would know by morning. She mentioned that to Sam, but it was of no matter. They both wanted everyone to know, for it was the kind of news that one could not keep secret.

Upon arriving at the Western Passage, Sam tipped his hat, said his good-nights, and walked back to his outfit. Public displays of affection were not acceptable.

Tomorrow was an organization day, not a travel day. The last wagons should be across, so there would be preparations for getting underway. It did not take Abby long to crawl into her wagon and ready her bed. After lying down and lighting a candle, she wrote about her first meeting with Plains Indians and the excitement of trading. The matter easily filled a page. She stopped long enough to reach down and feel the soft leather of the moccasins and smell their rich leather scent—then she wrote another page about Sam. This was the evening of their first kiss. It was a special and tender moment that needed recording.

On Wednesday morning Jesse Applegate swam his large herd across the river. For the past few days he had allowed the two hundred head to graze in an area of good grass for as long as possible. He knew the remaining wagons would be across by day's end, so it was time to drive his herd down to an area where they could scramble up on the opposite bank without disturbing the many encampments. During the crossing he lost six head, which wasn't bad considering how they interfered with each other as they swam for the far shore. After crossing, he drove the herd past Abby's encampment and over to another area of fairly good grass.

By early afternoon, the last wagon floated across the Kansas to join the rest. During the previous six days, three horses and twenty cattle had drowned—a small price to pay for such a large, inexperienced caravan. Except for the incidents with Steve Fairly's wagon and Pappin's flatboat breaking apart, the migration lost almost no provisions and very little equipment.

The completion of the crossing meant it was time to elect a leader. The previous week had seen several knock-down-drag-out fights, teamsters racing, quarrels over campsites, preparations for an Indian attack, and a great learning experience of how to move 100 wagons and 2,000 head of livestock across the prairie while maintaining some semblance of order. People had made friends and angered others, learned who were the hard workers and who were not, and most importantly, who could lead and who could not.

Numerous discussions took place on Wednesday evening as people submitted names of men whom they thought could best keep their group organized. They already had a guide, Captain Gantt, to lead them to Fort Hall. After that, Marcus Whitman would take over until they reached the Columbia. These guides were only that, guides. The Oregon Emigrating Company still needed someone to manage the caravan while on the trail. This leader would assign guards to watch over loose cattle, organize hunting parties when they reached buffalo country, pick campsites that afforded good grass and water, provide leadership at river crossings, and keep the wagons organized into smaller groups for camping and traveling.

The next morning, Thursday, June 1, all men over sixteen years of age gathered several hundred yards from the river on a level spot of ground. There were four candidates who accepted nominations and agreed to lead if elected. Rather than marking a ballot, the four candidates walked out on the prairie with their backs to the company, and men then began to line up behind the person they chose. At a given signal the office seekers began moving out across the prairie with their supporters in tow. Each line gained and lost supporters as men switched lines in hopes of being behind the leader. Soon the lines began wheeling about the prairie looking more like a whip than a legitimate election, for curling the lines helped to confuse the judges. Abby watched the proceedings, wishing that she could vote, but glad not to be a part of such foolishness. Soon the judges declared the longest line the winner. It was truly a free and honest election with each candidate literally "running for office."

The winner was Pete Burnett. Three cheers went up for Captain Burnett and Oregon. The runner up, Jim Nesmith, received the appointment of orderly sergeant. These two leaders immediately eliminated the rule of three loose cattle per man over the age of sixteen. This created some discord among emigrants who did not own large herds, yet the change did not surprise anyone. They next appointed an advisory council of ten men, including Captain Gantt. After a brief discussion with the new council, they decided to divide the migration up into four platoons, each with a leader. Appointed to these subcaptain positions were Dan Matheny, Dave Lenox, Jim Waters, and Hank Lee. With over twenty-five wagons in each platoon, the corrals would be large enough to easily hold all of the working stock. Over the next hour the council laid down camp routines for each night. These included organizing four wagon corrals (now called platoons); latrine locations; campfire numbers, size, and location; grazing locations and the time for bringing the working stock in for the night; night guard duties; and wagon positions during the day, so no one family would have to eat dust all the way to Oregon. The council also agreed to Captain Gantt's original request of one dollar per emigrant for his services to Fort Hall.

With these arrangements made, many emigrants now felt they were finally on their way and could take comfort in the safety of a well-organized and secure assemblage.

According to the original rules set down by the provisional trail government, Jim Nesmith now needed to take a written census of the migration. He would eventually count 294 men aged sixteen and over, approximately 130 women aged sixteen and over, 290 boys, and 312 girls for a total of 1,026 people. There would be 111 wagons, 106 going to Oregon and 5 going to California. Livestock would total 698 oxen, 296 mules and horses, and 973 loose cattle for a total of 1,967 head.[2]

---

[2] Appendix A provides a listing of adult members of the 1843 Oregon and California migration.

Several groups had not been able to leave Independence on May 22, so Jim would add their counts when they caught up. These included Chiles's California Column and the Oregon-bound stragglers being led by Dan Waldo. Marcus Whitman could attach to either of these groups or come in by himself.

While taking the census, Jim collected one dollar per emigrant, so the council could pay Captain Gantt upon arrival at Fort Hall. The stragglers would have to pay their dollar when they caught up. He also used the four-platoon arrangement to organize guard detail. Men quickly learned they would have three nights in bed and one night on guard.

With the work of elections, organizing platoons, taking a census, and individual families getting their outfits ready to travel again, people spent all day Thursday in camp. Many, including Abby, used this opportunity to do domestic chores such as the laundry.

Later in the day, two Kaw Indians entered Camp Delay and asked for a toll for crossing their lands. They requested twenty-five cents for each wagon, an amount they thought was reasonable. Their begging for food a few days earlier had not been successful, and the squaw's efforts at trading had met with similar failure. Also, the Indians had earned very little for their efforts in swimming the migration's stock across the Kansas. Charging a toll to pass through their country seemed like a legitimate way to acquire money—money they could exchange at the local Indian Agency. With a lengthy harangue, Burnett belittled the Indians for their begging and claimed that the land was free. It did not belong to anyone except the United States Government, and the Indians were lucky the government allowed them to live on it. The exchange was heated and short, leaving the Indians bewildered at Burnett's anger for what they considered to be a reasonable request. The warriors rode back to their village, about a half-mile upstream from Camp Delay.

Burnett and the others thought that this would be their last encounter with the Kaw, a tribe they considered to be nothing more than despicable beggars—but they were wrong. The next morning, Friday, June 2, various items left out overnight were missing. Items such as pots and pans, laundry hung out to dry, and several blankets were not to be found. Since nobody saw anything taken, people could not be certain who the thieves were. But the general feeling was that the Kaw had returned to extract their toll by way of trade goods rather than money.

Burnett discussed the matter with Nesmith and several others. Under the advice from Captain Gantt, Burnett determined that not taking any action was the best course to follow. Only a few items had been stolen, and with little value. By attempting to get them back, someone might get killed, and that simply wasn't worth the risk. The Indians could have the items in exchange for crossing their lands.

While Burnett, Nesmith, and others were considering what action to take, Abby, Jacob, and the rest of the migration readied their wagons and stock for a day of travel. They had spent six days in Camp Delay—valuable time that, had they been moving, would have placed them over one hundred miles closer to Oregon. The delay inspired a general urgency among many emigrants. A week's delay now might mean the difference between getting through to the Wallamet Valley in Oregon or getting caught by early snow in the Blue Mountains beyond Fort Boise.

Sam stopped by after breakfast to help Abby with any last-minute chores. He had already hitched the Copenhavers' ox teams and packed his own gear shortly after sunrise. Visiting Abby was not part of his agreement with the Copenhavers, so he completed all preparations at an early hour. That would allow him a few more minutes with her. When he arrived, she was cleaning up after breakfast while Jacob was off collecting the oxen.

"Morning, Abby. I thought you might need some help loading your wagon." They both knew Jacob was more than capable of helping, but it was a courteous gesture, and Abby welcomed the company.

"I missed you last night," she said, "so I figured you might be with the other men discussing all the new camp rules and reorganization."

"I wanted my voice heard," Sam replied. "Oregon is a long way off, and I feel I should be part of our provisional trail government. You never know what they might decide if you're not there."

"I agree, you should be there—and just as important, I should be allowed to participate. I have my whole life tied up in this outfit, and it's not right that I'm not allowed to vote or participate."

"You're a woman, Abby. Politics is no place for a woman. I mean, it's not ladylike. It's not natural. We men know what's best for the group." Sam said this with the confidence of a man who knows his place in American society. What he failed to consider was that Abby no longer subscribed to such behavior. There had been a time when she did—but that was long ago and far away. Things were different now.

At first, Sam had no idea that his statements had touched a nerve with Abby. She walked over to him, stood tall and straight with her face about a foot from his, then gave him the look of determination that had served her well since leaving Greene County. She spoke no words. Her cold stare told Sam he had better find a new subject.

"You know what I mean, don't you?"

Abby did not move.

"I mean, we men are natural leaders."

Her stare intensified.

"Well, Abby ... Well, I just ... You know what I mean, don't you?"

She still did not move.

"You're real pretty when you're angry."

Still nothing.

"You know, I think I'll help you load this kitchen gear." Wisely, Sam walked over to the kitchen box and readied it for loading. Jacob was coming in with the oxen, which gave Sam another moment of relief in changing the subject.

"Morning, Jacob. Looks like a clear day for travel."

"Sam." Jacob acknowledged Sam's presence with an expressionless face and the solemn voice of a parson meeting a sinner.

"How many miles do you think we'll make today?" Sam was hopeful this would start a conversation, for anything was better than silence. He could still feel Abby's stare.

"Twenty maybe, if we're lucky, maybe less. There'll be some adjustments to make with this new organization. We're traveling with the Burnett platoon, how 'bout you?"

"We, I mean the Copenhavers, are assigned to platoon number four. Don't know who's all in it—guess I'll find out this morning."

Abby was now moving about the camp, picking up loose items and stowing them in their regular place in the wagon. She had not spoken, but to Sam's great relief, she was at least moving.

"Ready for this kitchen box?" Sam squatted, preparing to pick it up.

"Just a minute." Abby pushed a chest toward the center of the wagon to make room for it. "It goes here." She started to walk over to help him lift it, but he already had it in both arms. He set it down on the wagon bed and slid it into place. In a moment he had the foregate closed and locked.

"There you are, Abby, ready for the day."

"Thank you, Sam. That was very kind."

"Now, Miss Abby, I hope nothing I said offended you. I mean that's the last thing I want to do. I care about you, and I get too protective. I know you can take care of yourself, so if you'll forgive me, I'll try to keep my mouth shut next time."

"Well, why don't you stop by after dinner tonight? I missed our walk last night."

"Oh, yes, ma'am, I mean, Abby. I will do that." Sam was all smiles now, crushing his hat with both hands and backing away.

"You have a fine day, and I will call on you this evening." He turned to go, placing the crushed hat on his head and looking over at Jacob hitching the team.

"So long, Jacob."

Jacob nodded in his usual fashion. Sam made him feel more like a father figure than the mountain man he was. Abby was happy, though, and that was enough. Her mood had changed since meeting Sam, ever so slightly, but noticeably. She was smiling more, talking more, and showing more confidence in her ability to get to Oregon. Most of that confidence was because of himself, although Sam played a part. Abby's positive attitude was a pleasant relief from the disposition of many other emigrants.

The prairie came alive with activity as men hitched teams to over a hundred wagons, brought in the loose stock, and pointed everything west. Loaded pack animals, drovers, teamsters, riders, and walkers all waited for the order to march. A few stragglers were unable to join their platoon in time to travel together. That would soon change. Their penalty was to eat dust from the rest of the column. It would not take too many days before each wagon would be ready to go on time.

After the lead wagons started out, almost fifteen minutes elapsed before the slow ripple of movement passed down the column to the Western Passage. With a snap of Abby's quirt, the oxen jolted forward. Jacob took his usual position left of the column, thirty feet out from Abby's wagon and far enough not to eat dust. Abby walked beside her lead team on the right. It felt great to be moving again, for the wait at Camp Delay had seemed interminable. The excitement of going to Oregon had not diminished, and the wait had probably served to increase the excitement. With a new provisional trail government, people felt a sense of obligation to their neighbors. This new dedication to success seemed unstoppable.

Spring flowers covered the prairie in every direction. The hues of black-eyed Susans, ox-eye daisies, pearly everlasting, yarrow, and a myriad of other colors provided a welcome sight for the travelers. Abby's gaze wandered between the prairie, the column of white-sheeted wagons, and her oxen, which needed a gentle prod now and then. She was adjusting to her moccasins with an occasional glance at the road to avoid sharp stones. They felt warm and snug on her feet. It looked to be a clear day for travel, and indeed the day passed without incident.

Sam dropped by after dinner and found both Abby and Jacob several wagons away, with a small group of people listening to the stories being told by a fellow named Jim Wair. As Sam approached, Abby motioned for him to sit next to her. She shushed him before he could speak, then grabbed his left arm with both hands and faced forward to listen to Jim.

Jim Wair was a pleasant, witty fellow with a dry sense of humor. Tonight he was talking about his travels in the United States and some of the events surrounding these travels. His graphic descriptions, including gestures, dialects, accents, and exaggerations of social proprieties, provided great entertainment for the small crowd. The biggest laugh came when he impersonated a solemn Irish preacher addressing the town drunkard.

Wair was an old bachelor, old being in his forties, and his entertaining manner would help boost the morale of the company during many evenings over the next few months. He continued his sojourn of humor for almost two hours before stopping for the evening. As everyone returned to their wagons, Abby declined Sam's request for another walk. It had been a long and tiring day.

"I'll see you tomorrow, Sam. Sleep well."

"And you, Abby. Thank you for spending your evening with me."

"Good night, Sam." She turned and crawled into the Western Passage without waiting for Sam's reply. He obviously wanted to spend more time with her, but that could wait. Even the diary would have to wait until tomorrow. Right now, her blanket bed was irresistible.

Saturday, June 3, was also uneventful, and the caravan made almost twenty miles on a hard, flat prairie. In the early evening it began to rain and continued well into the night. Nobody was able to light a campfire, which resulted in everyone enjoying their first "pilot bread" dinner.

The four platoons and livestock presented a peculiar sight amid a sea of prairie grass. The one exception to this orderly encampment was the Miles Eyre outfit. Miles was a farmer, about sixty years old with a wife and three children. Every evening when the four platoons formed their wagon corals, Miles would take his wagon and family about a quarter mile away and camp alone. Nobody really knew if he was afraid of getting sick with smallpox or cholera, or if he was just too independent to be a part of the company. Whatever his reason, few people got to know him or his family.

After dinner several Kaw chiefs rode in from the west, apparently returning to their village. Burnett and Gantt smoked with them in an attempt to learn the condition of the road ahead. Unfortunately, they could not provide any new information and were soon on their way.

Sunday, June 4, was a travel day. A number of people debated working on the Sabbath versus the fear of getting caught in Oregon snows. With the insistence of Captain Gantt, the logic of travel prevailed. There would be time to honor the Sabbath at the noon stop and during the evening.

The morning was less than comfortable due to a light rain the previous night. Everyone packed up a wet camp and made ready for travel over a muddy prairie. As the caravan moved out, people quickly adjusted to staggering their wagons to avoid the ruts of previous wagons. The day went fairly well with only one water crossing, the Big Sandy Creek. By late afternoon the prairie was dry and easier to negotiate.

People had spent the last two days adjusting to their new platoon structure and the knowledge that there was a controlling authority in charge of the migration; however, not all was well. Many men who did not own loose cattle complained that the large herds were slowing them down. Also, having to stand guard over somebody else's cattle was simply not acceptable. There were some rumblings among the ranks, yet for now, the organizational structure stood firm.

By the time the platoons started forming their wagon corrals for Sunday evening, they had made thirty-four miles in two days, a productive advance by any standard. Jacob always made sure that the oxen received good grass and water every evening. It was as if he knew something the other teamsters did not, or did not care to know. With this extra attention, Abby's oxen remained strong, healthy, and ready for the hardships to come. This stood in stark contrast to some of the other teams in the migration. Some were not healthy at the outset, while others took a beating during the first week when people engaged in racing. Abby's concern for picking healthy, strong oxen had been wise, evident only a few weeks out from Independence.

Sam showed up after dinner—a little later than normal. He had attended a meeting with Burnett, Nesmith, and others concerning management of the large herds. "There's gonna be trouble," he announced to both Jacob and Abby as he came into the camp kitchen. "I can feel it. Most people have all the work they can handle with their own wagons and stock. Asking these farmers to take care of loose cattle belonging to other people is a bit much."

"They haven't asked me to stand guard," replied Jacob, "probably 'cause they know I'd refuse. I don't look like the farmer type."

"Well, since they won't let me vote, I wouldn't stand guard if they paid me," protested Abby.

"Oh, they'd never ask a woman." Sam started to smile, but caught himself. He didn't want to paint himself into a corner again.

"Even though you'd make a fine guard, Abby. You know how to handle a gun, and that's more than most women around here. Yes, ma'am, you'd make a fine guard, although they'd never ask you."

"I'm sure you're right, Sam. Which reminds me, Jacob, I'd like to do some more target shooting whenever you've a mind to. A little more practice with loading that gun can't hurt."

"We need a place where we won't disturb all these loose cattle. Maybe sometime this next week, we'll camp where we can set up some targets. Sam, you want to join us? I'm sure Abby would like to see your skill at shooting. Wouldn't you, Abby?"

Jacob was smiling, something he seldom did. Abby wondered if he had an ulterior motive, like a contest of some sort. Actually, he had no idea whether Sam knew anything about guns, much less shooting, but this would be a chance to find out. Besides providing an opportunity to test Sam's skills, Jacob knew that Sam wanted to spend more time with Abby. Even a veteran mountain man doesn't forget the power of young love. If Sam was the man Abby wanted, then they should be together.

"Thank you, Jacob," said Sam, "I'd be pleased to join you. Although I'm sure not equal to your skill, I can still shoot fairly straight. You let me know when."

"Come on, Sam, let's walk a bit."

Abby took Sam's arm, turned him around, and began walking out from the wagons onto the prairie. It was only dusk, so they had to be discreet. Even though their arms fit together like two spoons in a drawer, a certain protocol had to be followed. The absence of civilization did not dismiss the need for established social mores. Since there were no closed doors out on the prairie, their only privacy was the darkness of night.

Soon the two disappeared into the evening dusk. Their arms

slipped around each other in a walking embrace. Abby put her head on Sam's shoulder as they directed their walk out toward the loose cattle. Guards would be on duty, so they felt safe enough. Their conversation varied from the lives they had left back in the United States to the lives they expected to gain in Oregon. They had not yet begun to talk about life together, although it was on their minds. Courting etiquette prevented Abby from approaching the subject. However, once Sam brought it up, it was fair game.

Sam still responded with that nervous, head-over-heels feeling whenever he was with Abby. The feeling was normal enough, although with Abby it did not go away; at least not yet. Abby was the prettiest and most eligible woman in the entire migration, and it was an honor just to spend time with her. Conversations about marriage could wait until those evening hugs and kisses became an important daily need rather than a passionate, nerve-wracking desire.

Their romance was no secret among the Oregon Emigrating Company—and what is more important, everyone approved. Almost everyone in the caravan had come to know of Abby, if not to meet her directly. A woman traveling alone was news, and it pleased the many parents to know there would be a schoolteacher in Oregon. A school was a sign of civilization, providing comfort to those unsure of their final destiny. Sarah Rubey and the other women were happy with Abby's budding romance, for a woman needed a man to take care of her. At least that was the view of people who did not know Abby well. Earlier feelings of uncertainty about a woman traveling alone would have to be put on hold. Apparently, with Sam as a romantic companion and Jacob as her hired hand, she was no longer alone.

These evenings with Sam and Abby off on their walks provided Jacob with some time for himself. Each evening he lit his pipe and stared into the campfire in quiet reflection. Such peacefulness was an enjoyable respite from the frustration of being around so many greenhorn farmers. The new organizational structure seemed to calm them down a little; however, there would still be trouble. These emigrants were too independent and too free to abide by a set of rules for very long. He knew eventually a split would come. For now though, there was peace, a quiet evening, a warm campfire, a good smoke, and thoughts of past and future adventures.

Abby returned to the wagon an hour after dark. She walked in with her arms folded, looking down at the ground with an expression of love donned with a slight smile. Her mussed hair told Jacob things must be getting serious. He lay inside his buffalo robe on the ground near the campfire, saying nothing as she approached and walked over to the Western Passage.

She crawled into the wagon, not paying him any attention. Mornings on the trail came early, before sunrise, so most folks had already bedded down. Even so, she lit a candle to write a few paragraphs in her diary. Although thoughts of Sam were taking up more and more pages, she still kept a log of the day's events. Maybe it was for the memories, maybe for advice to help future emigrants, or maybe she thought about writing a guide. Whatever her reason, that diary received some attention almost every evening before bed.

The next day, Monday, June 5, they crossed the East Fork of the Blue River. This was a large creek and a tributary of the Kansas River. Its shallow water and gravel bed made fording an easy job. The company delayed only momentarily as Captain Gantt determined the best place to cross.

A slight shower passed through during the early afternoon, but not enough to muddy the trail. After crossing the East Fork of the Blue, they continued for a good day's travel, stopping shortly after six o'clock.

The caravan set up their encampments near the Black Vermillion River. As usual, Miles Eyre and his family camped separately from the platoons. Everyone understood that and left him alone. However, tonight the Richardson and Rossin families, who were part of Hank Lee's platoon, also chose to camp by themselves, next to the Black Vermillion. They did so in order to be the first to cross in the morning. These two families had waited six days to cross the Kansas, and they had no intention of being last again.

Sam showed up as Abby and Jacob were checking a sore hoof on one of her oxen. Sam knew she had given each animal a name and that their yoking was alphabetical. At first this seemed like something rather humorous, something only a very orderly person would do. On reflection, it made sense. She explained to Sam that by pairing the oxen alphabetically, the team members would remain constant and she could rotate them so each animal received one day of rest out of every four. This new knowledge about her organizational ability pleased Sam, and only enhanced the way he felt about her. He was already in love, and anything she did was acceptable to him.

Abby and the rest of her platoon set up their corral near some bluffs, which suited Jacob for a place to help her work on her skills at handling a gun. Sam was looking forward to shooting and was more than willing to forgo their evening walk. On their way out of camp, the three stopped by the Copenhavers' wagon for Sam to pick up his gun. In a moment he was ready to go, carrying an old squirrel gun, bullet pouch, and powder horn. Mrs. Copenhaver took a few minutes to introduce herself and meet Sam's new belle. She, like all the women in the migration, had heard of Abby and wanted to meet the schoolteacher.

"Miss Meacham, you don't know how pleased I am that you and Sam are seeing each other. My, you must certainly be happy."

Abby smiled without really knowing how to respond. A private romance was certainly not something for public discussion.

"I'm pleased to meet you, too, Mrs. Copenhaver. One can always use another friend on a long journey like this."

"Call me Henrietta, please. Do you know where in Oregon you and Sam will settle? I want my children to have their schooling—that's important."

Me and Sam! Abby thought. *She's got me married, and Sam hasn't even asked!* Sam just shuffled his feet in silence.

"I don't rightly know where I'll settle," she said. "There are several Methodist missions out there that must offer schooling. I'll have to see where most of these farmers locate. Maybe I'll stay in Oregon City, I don't rightly know."

"Well, I'm sure you and Sam will find a wonderful place to raise your family. I'm so happy that he found you."

Abby was ready to take off running. *Does everyone think of Sam and me like this?*

She quickly changed the subject. "It was a pleasure meeting you, Henrietta, but we need to practice target shooting before dark." She turned to walk away, adding an abrupt, "Come on, Jacob. Let's go, Sam."

"Good night, Miss Meacham," Henrietta called out. Abby smiled back at her, but kept walking. This conversation was out of control, and she needed to place some distance between herself and Henrietta Copenhaver.

As they walked around the bluff to avoid the loose cattle, Jacob handed Abby a small piece of white rabbit fur and pointed to some willow brush.

"Here, Mrs. Oakley, hang this fur on that brush over there, then count back thirty paces."

Abby snatched the fur from Jacob's hand, smiling broadly at his little tease. In a few minutes all three were loading and priming their rifles.

"Sam, why don't you take the first shot," Jacob said as he thumped the butt of his rifle on the ground to drive home the ball. "See if you can knock that fur down."

Now it was Sam's turn to be uncomfortable. Sam planted his feet perpendicular to the target, took careful aim, and fired. It was a clean miss with no notice of movement in the target or nearby foliage. Sam took a step back, hoping that either Abby or Jacob would also miss.

Abby knew she didn't have the arm and shoulder strength to balance her rifle while standing, so she sat down to brace her elbows on her knees and steady the barrel. She carefully lined up the sights as Jacob had taught her, then gently squeezed the trigger until the hammer fell, igniting the powder in the pan. The momentary delay between powder ignition and rifle discharge was always the most difficult for keeping the barrel steady—but steady she was, and the target jumped as the ball passed through.

Now Jacob took aim and made the target jump again.

They started reloading.

"I can see I'm up against some fairly good competition," Sam said. "Maybe I better steady the barrel."

During the next round Sam joined Abby on the ground and was able to make the target jump. Abby's next shot hit the target too, while Jacob's shot knocked it to the ground.

Their target practice went on for close to an hour before Abby had had enough. Her shoulder was sore from the recoil, and her ears rang from the noise. It had been a good practice session and an enjoyable social hour. This was the first time Jacob, Sam, and Abby had spent any time together, and it felt good. These three adventurers were looking more and more like an impromptu family.

On the way back to the wagon, Jacob took Abby's rifle from her grip stating, "Here, I'll carry that. You and Sam probably want to go for a walk. I'll take that bullet pouch and powder horn too. Sam, you want me to carry your gun back?"

Sam didn't give Abby a chance to voice an opinion. In a few seconds Jacob was carrying all three rifles and heading back toward the platoon.

"That was right neighborly of Jacob," Sam remarked as Abby took his arm. "I think he looks at you like a daughter."

"Oh, Sam, he's just a sentimental old mountain man—too free to settle down and too wild to tame. He's glad I met you though, that's the truth."

"Seems as though he's worried about you. I mean, you being alone and all. Well, he doesn't have to worry any more 'cause I'm not going anywhere." Sam pulled Abby closer, and she put her head on his shoulder, then pulled away.

"Sam, not yet. We're too close to camp, and it's not dark enough. You just wait a minute." They walked on without speaking.

After a while, she said, "I wonder if Jacob's worried that if I don't meet someone, he might get saddled with me when we reach Oregon. Do you get that impression?"

Sam thought about his response, for getting saddled with Abby was exactly what he wanted.

"I've never considered Jacob as anything more than your hired man. It's only been recent that I've noticed he treats you like a daughter. I don't think a mountain man could get saddled to anyone. It doesn't matter, though, 'cause I don't plan on letting go." Again, he pulled her in close. This time they were far enough away from the wagons to grab a quick kiss. It was not yet dusk, much less night, so a warm embrace would have to wait.

Their walk tonight took them past the camp of Miles Eyre. As they approached, Abby called out.

"Good evening, Mrs. Eyre, it's a beautiful evening out here on the prairie."

Abby's appearance startled the woman, but she quickly recovered. "Yes, a beautiful evening. You must be Miss Meacham. It's a real pleasure to meet you. Please, come into our camp. I want you to meet my children." She turned toward her children, who were playing nearby.

"Children, come meet the schoolteacher."

Miles was off moving his stock over to better grass. After seeing his wife invite Abby and Sam into camp, he made no attempt to join them. Instead, he remained with the oxen until they left. Which, as it turned out, would be over two hours later.

Abby, still holding Sam's arm, was all smiles as the children came running over.

"This is Emily, and this is Tom and Pete. This here is Miss Meacham. She's a schoolteacher going to Oregon, and maybe she'll become your teacher."

"Howdy, Miss Meacham." Tom, a youth of fourteen, stepped forward offering a handshake in a very adult manner.

"Howdy, Tom, pleased to meet you."

With this encouragement from their brother, Emily and Pete also stepped forward to shake hands with Abby.

"I really want to go back to school, Miss Meacham," said Emily. "Last year I was in the first grade, but had to leave early 'cause we were going to Oregon. Are you going to be my new teacher?"

"I would love to be your new teacher, Emily. If your new farm is nearby, then I will definitely be your teacher." Still smiling, she looked at the other two children. "What grades are you two in?"

"I'm in fourth," stated Tom, "and he's in second." He pointed at Pete, who stood mute, just staring at Abby.

"Wouldn't it be wonderful if we all ended up together out in Oregon!"

"It would," said Mrs. Eyre. "I'm so glad to know they'll be able to continue their schooling. Won't you and Sam stay and visit for awhile? There's so much to do with living out of this wagon that I don't get to visit with the other ladies. I have a pot of hot coffee brewing. Won't you please join me?"

"We'd be delighted, Mrs. Eyre," said Abby. She could see the woman was lonely. Her husband's unsociable behavior was an added hardship to an unwanted journey. Like other women, Eliza Eyre was reluctantly following her husband to Oregon. Leaving friends and family behind had been particularly painful for her, since they were her only contact for any type of social life. The opposite of her husband in character, Eliza loved social gatherings. Camping away from the rest of the migration was a lonely, difficult burden.

The coffee sounded good to Abby, and the campfire looked warm and friendly. A short visit could not hurt. She and Sam drew closer.

"That's wonderful. Please," she motioned to two small barrels near the campfire, "please have a seat, and you can call me Eliza."

Time passed quickly, as there was much to talk about—past, present, and future endeavors. Finally, Abby and Sam excused themselves, for the hour was getting late and tomorrow would be another long day of travel.

"Do come back and visit. It was such a pleasure meeting you!"

"You too, Eliza. You and your family are welcome in my camp anytime. Thank you for the coffee, and say goodnight to your children for me." The children had been in bed for an hour.

"I will, and it was a pleasure meeting you, too, Sam."

"And you, ma'am. Good night now."

By the time Sam dropped Abby off at her wagon it was close to midnight. The campfire had died to a few coals, and Jacob lay in his buffalo robe nearby. Abby tried to be as quiet as possible as she got out some soap and a towel. She had not seen a bath since the Kansas and was not going to let this opportunity pass. The entire camp was asleep, and the Black Vermillion was only a few hundred yards off.

On Tuesday morning Pete Burnett decided that the Richardson and Rossin families should not be the first to cross the Black Vermillion. They had intentionally disobeyed his direct orders about staying with their platoon, and that could not be tolerated. He called for a meeting with Jim Nesmith and the council to discuss what type of penalty to impose for their actions. As they discussed their options, a guard rode in informing them that the two wagons were preparing to cross ahead of the rest of the column. Burnett immediately sent two men, Burrell Davis and John Pennington, on horseback with the orders, "Shoot to kill," if they did not stop.

As Davis and Pennington approached, Joe Rossin drew his rifle first. With a quick exchange of heated words, it was clear to the men that Joe would shoot if they tried to interfere. That was the end of Burnett's threat. They allowed the wagons to cross without attempting to stop them.

The entire caravan was across and continuing west by ten o'clock. After less than ten miles, Burnett chose to halt early due to the appearance of a severe thunderstorm. Platoon leaders formed their wagon corrals with slightly more urgency, as oxen and other cattle were beginning to spook at the continuous flashes of lightning and rolling, rumbling thunder. As soon as Abby got her wagon into position, Jacob unhooked the yoke chains and led each of the three teams around to the back of the wagon. He had already hobbled his horse, two pack animals, the milch cow, and the fourth yoke of oxen. When the corral closed, he untied the stock and let them wander among the other animals.

This storm was exceptionally violent. The wind tugged at canvas tops as if to tear them to pieces or at the very least, tip the wagons over. Many people followed Jacob's lead in tying a rope to the windward side of their wagon and staking it to the ground to prevent getting blown over. These independent emigrants did not agree with

Jacob's lifestyle, but they were quickly learning to heed his advice and follow his lead.

Normally, Jacob sought shelter from storms by staying underneath the wagon. This time Abby invited him in. The rain started coming down in sheets and the ground under the wagon flooded instantly. They both crouched down behind the foregate watching the storm pass, mesmerized by the sudden violence and beauty of a prairie storm.

The storm passed as quickly as it arrived. By six in the evening the sun shone through cloud breaks, and people ventured out to survey the damage. There were several torn white-tops, a dead horse among the loose stock, and some of the cattle needed rounding up. The horse had been on a high point of ground and was struck by lightning. The wagons suffered no major damage other than wet equipment. Everywhere, the fresh smell of new growth, wet soil, and rainwater mixed with the smell of wet livestock. It was quite distinctive. The drenching rain seemed to give the entire migration that bath they so dearly needed—a refreshing change after a week of eating trail dust.

The storm prevented anyone from lighting a campfire that evening, so there was cold food all around. For Jacob, pilot bread was better than nothing.

"Meat's meat," he proclaimed as Abby handed him a piece of bread.

"Meat? We don't have any meat."

"That's just a saying. It means, any food is better than nothing. I was out with Joe Meek once on the Snake River Plains, and we hadn't eaten in four days when we came across a large anthill. Old Joe and I kicked it open, then stuck our hands in until they were black with ants. Then we licked them off like a couple of kids with ice cream. Meat's meat, and we were glad to have it."

"Jacob, that's hardly talk for the dinner hour," Abby scolded. She let a few seconds of silence go by, then added, "Did you really eat ants?"

"We did. You get hungry enough, you will too—and it's not all that bad. Some critters are better than others. Moth larvae can get right tasty, especially if you roast them first. Most of the Indian tribes I'm familiar with eat insects."

"If you don't mind, I'll stay with beans, bread, and bacon—at least until we reach buffalo country. How much farther do you think we need to go?"

"Not far, maybe another week, maybe two. We'll probably start seeing sign any day."

Sam made his appearance after dinner. This time he brought news of the impending split between cattle and non-cattle owners. Also, Pete Burnett had taken about all of the complaining he could stand, and was threatening to resign.

"I left before anything could be decided, but something is sure to come of that meeting." Sam said. "I probably should have stuck around. Jacob, maybe you'd like to have your say. They might listen to you, since you know the country. Nobody wants to listen to Burnett or Nesmith anymore, that's for certain."

"I could go over and hear them out, but these farmers are heading for a split no matter what."

As Abby began to clean up from dinner, Jacob took the scrub brush from her hand and said, "Here, I'll do that, you go with Sam."

Abby stepped back, her mouth agape, staring at Jacob. She had never seen such attention to domestic duties by any man, much less an old mountain man.

Now I've seen it all, she thought. *This old fool's a hopeless romantic!* She quickly recovered with a smile, pulled off her apron and threw it into the front of the wagon, grabbed Sam's arm, and was off.

A few people had put their tents up before the storm struck. Now they were tightening guy lines or putting them back up after getting blown down. Some people had all their belongings drenched, while others fared well. Tonight Abby and Sam chose to walk around the four platoons to survey the damage. The prairie was too wet to go far. They were back at the wagon before dark.

That night, shortly after midnight, the cry went out: "Indians!" The corral sentry fired his gun and yelled again, "Indians! Indians! Everyone up! Indian attack!"

In an instant there was pandemonium. Abby jumped from her

bed still half asleep. As the call went out again, she grabbed for her rifle—gasping for breath with that sound of despair and fear heard only in times of tragedy or mortal danger.

"My gun, where's my gun?" The wagon was pitch black as she frantically scrambled on her hands and knees feeling for the barrel.

She kept it wrapped in a blanket near her bed for instant use, yet tonight it became entangled in the blanket. She threw back the corners in wild, frantic motions to free the weapon. Again came that frantic, uncontrollable sound of despair. Finally, the rifle was free. The bullet pouch and powder horn were right where they belonged. Grabbing them, she fell down behind the foregate, knowing that she would have to load the gun in a prone position. Men filled the camp shouting orders at no one in particular, while women ran screaming and children began crying. The corralled stock panicked at all the excitement and would have taken off running had the opportunity presented itself.

The noise and confusion created enough curiosity in Abby for her to poke her head above the foregate to see the commotion and panic. In a nearby corral, a man named John Roe jumped out of his wagon, gun in hand and wife in tow, screaming at the top of her lungs. He tried to free her grip, but it was no use.

In Abby's corral several women were running through the stock, screaming at the top of their lungs. The oxen responded with frightful calls of their own in an effort to escape the confines of the corral. Children looked out from underneath the wagon white-tops with tears and cries for their mothers.

A Mrs. Beagle jumped from her wagon, ran about ten feet, and fainted. Another man fell out of his wagon and started running out across the prairie away from the platoon. This was enough to get Abby to smile, since the unarmed man was dressed only in his underwear.

Another man was running around the corral yelling, "God help us, we're all going to die!"

"At least he remembered his gun," Abby thought. "Too bad he didn't remember his pants!"

The scene of people running around in their underwear had Abby holding in the laughter. It was obvious that this was only a drill: There were no Indians, just a lot of foolish farmers.

Abby peered out over the foregate far enough to see Jacob leaning up against the inside of one wheel. He was holding his rifle and watching the spectacle in disbelief.

"How you doing down there?" she called out above the noise.

He looked up at her with an expression of slight anger and mostly frustration. "They're going to scatter these cattle from here back to the Kansas." He looked back at the ridiculous commotion.

Abby wondered if a shot in the air might bring people to their senses—but the sound of a gun might make things worse. They would have to calm down on their own.

"When these fools get hoarse from screaming and tired of running, they'll realize there aren't any Indians and calm down," Abby called down to Jacob.

Jacob just shook his head in disbelief. The spectacle did not merit any comment, only a reaffirmed disgust for greenhorns.

The next morning people were talking about how they would do better if there were a real Indian attack. Apparently, Burnett and several other men had wanted to demonstrate that the caravan could not get along without cooperation. To prove their point they decided to hold a practice drill. It was an education for everyone.

The original orders requested women to stay in their wagons with their children. Now the women who had run after their husbands, or fainted, swallowed their embarrassment and promised that next time they would stay in the wagons. The men who had panicked had nothing to say. They knew their behavior was nothing short of cowardice, and such a subject was not a point of discussion. They, too, silently vowed to do better next time. There was a general air of gratefulness that it was not a real attack, and a feeling that the drill had exposed weaknesses and provided some cheap lessons.

Everyone had recovered their composure when, about an hour after sun-up, Isaac Mills came walking back into camp. He was the man Abby had watched run out onto the prairie without a gun or trousers. After running for an hour he had found a small ravine to hide in until morning. He now had to face the laughter and ridicule of the rest of the platoon. His wife, carrying his trousers, met him before he could reach their wagon. As she handed them to him, the camp erupted in gales of laughter. Another roar of laughter burst forth as he fell to the ground trying to put them on. It was a moment Isaac would never forget.

Today was another good day of travel. The Oregon Emigrating Company crossed the West Fork of the Blue River, a small but dangerous tributary about fifty yards wide. This river presented a greater problem than the East Fork because of its depth and swift current. Men cut a number of logs from trees growing in the floodplain and used them to prop up wagon beds by tying a log to each side. As soon as a wagon crossed, boys floated the logs back for attachment to the next wagon. With almost twenty logs in use, the entire company crossed in less than three hours.

The caravan was now moving across level ground toward the Blue River. This crossing would again test the ingenuity and mettle of everyone, and provide the first major challenge to the new leaders. Burnett and Nesmith were already discussing their options and devising several plans, but nothing could be decided until they reached the river and surveyed the physical situation.

Jim Nesmith, Captain John Gantt, and Bill Martin, along with a few other men, went ahead of the company in what they called the "advance guard." In midafternoon they encountered about ninety warriors of the Osage and Kaw tribes, traveling east. The brilliantly painted Osage warriors had shaved heads and rode fleet ponies, also painted with various animal and sun images. Their chiefs possessed a scalp with the ears still attached, and were quick to display their trophy to Burnett and Gantt. The scalp had long black hair, which they had divided into five pieces with ears, or other pieces of flesh, dangling precariously alongside.

Captain Gantt and one of the chiefs had a brief exchange of friendly words by way of sign language. The Indians openly bragged about killing a number of Pawnees several days previous and displayed severed human fingers to prove their claim. The battle had not been without cost, for two of their party displayed severe wounds, now bandaged in deerskins.

The grotesque display did not surprise Gantt, but nearly sickened Burnett and Nesmith. Burnett pressed Gantt for information about the road ahead and how soon they would reach the Blue River. "Three or four days' march" was all they could learn, for these Indians had little concern about supplying useful or correct information.

Burnett hastened a quick end to the conversation, then gave a signal for the wagons to start moving again. There was still enough daylight to make four or five more miles.

Most people considered these Indians as the most miserable, cowardly (because of the scalp), and dirty Indians they had ever seen. Although they did not steal, while in camp they annoyed almost everyone with their begging. At Burnett's direction, several families gave them bread and a calf after they claimed they had not eaten in three days.

After a long day the company camped on a beautiful, dry, level plain next to the Blue River. The river was high from recent rains, so Burnett and the council gathered to determine the best way to cross.

The beauty of the river and surrounding prairie did not mask the trouble brewing, for tonight saw the first mutiny. Men without loose cattle refused to stand their watch guarding the large herds. There were also numerous complaints lodged about the herds slowing the progress of the entire migration. Current arrangements were no longer acceptable.

Two men, John McHaley and Jesse Applegate, had more than two hundred head of cattle each. These two herds, along with the other loose cattle and over one hundred wagons, required a nightly guard detail of fifty men—twenty-five for the early watch and twenty-five for the late watch. These men also had families to care for, along with the work of tending to their own working livestock. Each evening several wagons were in need of some type of repair that prevented their owners from assuming guard duty. The provisional trail government would have to make new arrangements for guarding the caravan.

To calm the vociferous farmers, Burnett persuaded the people with large herds to supply meat at a fixed price when necessary. This helped, but discontent still lingered. Men managing their own outfits did not have the time or inclination to guard another man's stock.

The four platoons, each with a subcaptain assigned by Burnett, consisted of both cattle and non-cattle owners. This arrangement saw these two groups coming together in some rather vocal exchanges around evening campfires. Part of their discontent came from the stress of living out of wagons and being exposed to the elements twenty-four hours every day. The cattle question only compounded the problem and gave people an excuse to protest. For the present, those with large herds would have to stand guard themselves or pay somebody else. Jacob was right, a split was sure to come.

In the area where Burnett halted there was good grass in the floodplain along with water for the stock. Here they encountered Overton Johnson, Bill Winter, and the several other men who had ventured ahead following the trace of Sir William Drummond Stewart's entourage. After leaving the main body at Camp Delay, these emigrants found that they needed help in getting across the Blue. Nesmith informed them of the election results and company rules, counted them in his census, and collected one dollar per emigrant for Gantt's services.

In an area that appeared to be the only good place to cross, several Kaw Indians had cleared the brush, thereby providing a place for wagons to approach the river. These warriors had learned about the migration back at the Kansas River and realized an opportunity to gain American coins, exchangeable at the nearest trading post. Consequently, they rode ahead of the migration to gain control of this crossing. The Kaw wanted fifty cents for each wagon and would assist the teamster in getting to the other side. However, Burnett, Nesmith, and most of the other wagon owners had no intention of giving these Indians money. They decided to cross on their own without the Kaw help. Bill Winter, who had scouted the area while waiting for the caravan to catch up, reported that the next nearest place to cross was at least one mile upriver. It was already the dinner hour, so crossing would have to wait until tomorrow.

Another violent thunderstorm blew in that night with hard winds and torrents of rain. Half the tents blew down, and nearly the whole camp flooded as the Blue overflowed its banks. People sleeping in tents spent the night in their wagons with what little they could salvage before being flooded out. The incident was a major inconvenience, but caused no serious damage. Everything would dry out.

In the morning eight inches of water covered the entire encampment. With this disagreeable situation, the first order of business was to move one half mile to what appeared to be higher ground. Jacob had removed to higher ground during the middle of the night when the river began rising. Now he returned to hitch up Abby's oxen and help her extricate the Western Passage from the flooded encampment.

Abby waded through the water in her bare feet, holding up her dress as she retrieved two floating yokes. She had taken Jacob's advice several weeks ago about not leaving anything out overnight, so the flood caused little havoc with her outfit. Men pushed a number of wagons out of the mud, and by eight o'clock the wagons and stock were on high ground and ready to roll.

The offer made by the Kaw Indians to help each wagon across was still open, but the frugal farmers showed no interest. They thought that paying the Indians fifty cents to cross was a waste of good money, especially since there was another place to cross one mile upriver.

Abby could not understand why the men were being so obstinate. Driving the wagons one mile upriver, then one mile back down on the other side seemed like an enormous waste of time and energy—certainly not worth the savings of only fifty cents.

"Jacob, we have these Indians to help us, so what do you think? The oxen will have two less miles to pull the wagon, and I don't mind paying fifty cents. Do you think it's safe to cross here?"

"Safe as any. Having several Indians lead the oxen should reduce the chance of a panic. I say we do it."

That was Abby's choice too. Her wagon was about fortieth in line when Burnett gave the order to march. As each wagon came up to the Indian crossing, the teamster turned south toward the other crossing. The patient Indians merely waited, hoping someone would take their offer.

As Abby approached, she looked over at Jacob, who now rode up to the back of the wagon and tied off his horse next to the two pack animals, the fourth yoke of oxen, and the milch cow. When they got to the crossing, instead of turning her lead oxen south, she halted the wagon and walked over to the Indian who appeared to be in charge. Reaching into her dress pocket, she pulled out fifty cents and handed it to him. He immediately signaled to several other braves, who ran over and took control of her teams. She and Jacob then climbed into the front of the wagon while four Indians, two on each side of the ox teams, drove the wagon down the embankment and into the river.

As soon as the other nearby teamsters saw what was happening, dissension arose in a vocal protest. Several men engaged in name calling as the wagon entered the river, berating both Abby and Jacob for their independence. They vocalized their mistrust of the Indians and Abby's nonconformity to the rest of the migration with yells of, "Indian lover!" "Traitor!" and "They're going to steal everything!" Abby and Jacob simply looked at each other in silence, for it was too late to turn around.

"Don't you pay them any mind," said Jacob. "We'll be across and can spend the remainder of the day resting the stock."

The river was not deep, rising only chest high on the Indians. As they crossed, the lead brave on the right side of the team kept looking back at Abby. She had first noticed his attention when she paid her fifty cents. Accustomed to the leer of interested men, she instinctively ignored him. Now Jacob took notice of this brave's attention.

"Looks like you've got a new admirer."

"Don't look at him," Abby snapped. "Don't make eye contact and he'll leave us alone."

Such reserved behavior was not Jacob's style. Besides, he was enjoying this young brave's attention to Abby.

"Are you sure you don't want to meet him? I could interpret for you." Jacob smiled as he looked at her.

She knew he was only teasing, but this was serious. "I have Sam, and I don't want to make this Indian angry. We've already got everyone angry with us for crossing here. Don't look at him, and he'll go away as soon as we get to the other side."

Jacob watched for the next time the brave turned around to look at her. When he did, Jacob smiled broadly and doffed his hat.

"Mr. Chalmers!" Abby exclaimed with pure astonishment. "I can't believe you did that." She continued to face forward, not looking at the Indian or Jacob.

"Now what will I do if that Indian wants to speak to me? I can't believe you did that!"

Jacob continued to enjoy his little taunt, much to the dissatisfaction of Abby. They were silent for the remaining few minutes until they reached the opposite shore.

As the wagon pulled up onto land, water poured down from the running gear and all the stock. Jacob's waterproofing had kept the bed and its contents dry. They both stepped down, with Jacob walking back to untie his horse and Abby walking briskly forward to the lead oxen to take control. The brave stood waiting for her, but only received a quick thank-you, in English, and no smile. She snapped her quirt on the flank of the lead oxen without bothering to see if Jacob had untied his horse. He had not. When the wagon lurched forward, he had to scramble to free the rein.

Abby did not look back at any of the Indians, or Jacob. Instead, she drove her team up the embankment to level ground and away from her new admirer.

The appearance of Abby's outfit on high ground on the opposite side of the river served to anger several more men on the east shore—but the ladies held a different opinion. Here was a woman traveling alone and doing a better job at driving her wagon than most men. She was safely across, and it was still morning. Unknown to Abby, she had made a number of new friends that morning.

Jacob rode up alongside, telling her to head toward a grove of cottonwood about a quarter mile distant and directly on the trail. The rest of the caravan would probably not catch up until sometime tomorrow. Upon reaching the spot, Jacob unhitched all the stock, moved them to good grass, and hobbled them. Abby set up her usual kitchen around the tongue of the wagon. It was still early, and they had the rest of the day to make repairs and just rest. For Abby, this provided an opportunity to mend two dresses that had torn on trail brush during the past two weeks and to catch up on her diary entries.

A light rain continued all day, preventing the main company from crossing. Around noon Chiles's California Column caught up to them. Soaked from the rain of the last two days, they welcomed the respite of high ground and a day of rest before crossing the Blue. After learning of the dissension between cattle and non-cattle owners, and the improved efficiency of traveling in smaller groups, Chiles decided to remain separate rather than join the Oregon migration, and to simply shadow them all the way to Fort Hall. Jim Nesmith again updated his census and collected the required fee.

Because of the steepness of the west bank, the emigrants' crossing was not as good as the one controlled by the Indians. Wagons needed to be double-teamed to make it up the west bank, and that took time. With the rain and over one hundred wagons, Nesmith estimated the crossing would take two, maybe three days.

That evening after dinner, while Abby was doing kitchen chores, her new Indian admirer approached their camp and signed for permission to enter. The Indian led three fine buffalo ponies. On one was a travois loaded with furs, blankets, and other paraphernalia—mostly Indian trade goods. Jacob walked out to meet him, then brought him into camp. After tying the lead rein on one of the wagon wheels, and not looking at Abby, he joined Jacob at the campfire.

They both sat on the ground signing their greetings and peaceful intentions. The Indian had a pipe slung over his shoulder that he now produced and lit. His manner was slow and methodical, meaning his intentions were serious. For Plains Indians, the formalities of a smoke and general conversation about the country always preceded serious talks.

"Abby, bring another plate of food over here. Our guest is hungry."

Reluctantly, Abby dished up the leftovers and brought them over for the Indian. He watched her approach, eyeing every move and making her most self-conscious. She handed him the plate, then retreated to her chores.

Abby normally enjoyed company visiting her camp. She was quick to offer coffee and a seat at the campfire—but not with this guest. The sooner Jacob could get rid of him, the happier she would be. She decided to finish cleaning up the dinner dishes so the Indian wouldn't think that she took the slightest notice of him. Then she would join them for the pure necessity of protecting her interests. She trusted Jacob implicitly; however, there was no need to be careless. This Indian wanted something, maybe trade goods for crossing his land. Joining them at the campfire was simply business and nothing more.

Jacob and the Indian continued signing, paying little attention to Abby after she joined them. Jacob was not speaking as he signed, so Abby remained confused over what they were discussing. After a few minutes they both stood up and walked over to the three ponies. Jacob looked them over carefully, as a man about to make a purchase. He checked each hoof, their teeth, and any twinge from muscle soreness.

"Jacob, we don't need any horses," Abby called over to him. "Our animals are in good shape and horses would just be another burden to take care of."

Jacob and the Indian walked back to the campfire and sat down.

"You could at least tell me what's going on. You've been signing for a half-hour. I can't imagine what could possibly be so intriguing."

"You."

"Me!"

"You are intriguing," Jacob replied looking up at her. "He wants to buy you with these three ponies and those other items—and he thinks I'm your father."

Abby, too astonished to speak, sat for the next few seconds with her mouth agape, staring erratically between Jacob and the Indian.

"Me! Sell me?" She stood up. "Jacob, I have never heard of ..."

"Sit down," Jacob blurted out angrily. "Women don't speak during such negotiations."

His blustery voice caused her to sit back down in a reflex motion.

"Jacob, I don't ..."

"Quiet, you don't speak here." His tone was serious.

After several weeks of adhering to Jacob's accurate advice, Abby's natural inclination was to do as he said—but her heart, and now her mind, were not in agreement. She tried to get the words out, but with nothing more than her lips moving.

He's going to sell me, she thought. *I can't believe this, he's going to sell me!*

Jacob continued signing, only this time speaking so that Abby could understand.

"Those are fine horses, good for running buffalo, and the blankets will keep me warm against the cold winter wind."

The Indian signed back, but by now Abby was ready to get her gun.

She stood up and walked back toward the wagon. "Jacob's going to sell me!" she repeated to herself. "He doesn't think I'm worth more than three horses—but then he'll get my entire outfit! That's what he wants! That's why he's going to sell me!" Without hesitating she climbed into the back of the wagon to retrieve her Hawken, bullet pouch, and powder horn. Jacob could see her from the corner of his eye as she emerged and began to load the gun.

Jacob's conversation remained peaceable, but now the Indian noticed Abby loading her gun. He began to shift his weight with slight agitation as he asked Jacob what her intentions were. Jacob calmly responded that she was a difficult woman to understand and that he never knew what she might do, especially when she was angry.

Abby walked back to the campfire carrying her Hawken, ready to chase the Indian out of her camp. As she approached, both men stood.

"I have no intention of being sold—not tonight, not ever—so you can leave my camp, else I'll ..."

Jacob grabbed the barrel, pushing it skyward with a slight jerk. Abby already had the weapon cocked and her finger on the trigger, so his action was enough to cause the gun to discharge—fortunately, into the night sky. The Indian jumped backwards with a look of surprise and fear. Jacob took the gun.

"I've already declined his offer," Jacob announced. "You don't have to shoot him."

Abby hesitated, looking at Jacob, then at the Indian.

"Declined, really. Well, I wasn't going to shoot him, just scare him off. You didn't have to grab my gun."

"I'm not so sure about that. Is this any way to treat a guest, by shooting him? And especially one with such good intentions."

Abby had no response.

"We're going to sit down now and finish our smoke. You may join us if you wish." As soon as they were seated, he added, "It would be proper if you offered him a gift for his proposal to you, and the fact that you almost shot him."

"Gift ... I can do that, if he promises to leave." Abby started back toward the wagon.

"Now would be a good time to use one of those plugs of tobacco."

Abby whirled around, looking back at Jacob, suddenly realizing the meaning of a previously unknown quantity. "Of course," she thought, "that's why he hasn't used any of that tobacco. That's why he had me buy it back in Independence!"

As she headed back to the wagon to retrieve the tobacco, Jacob called out again, "Only one plug, Abby, only one plug."

She quickly returned with a single plug of tobacco, sat down, then handed it to the Indian.

The Indian nodded his approval, then started searching his possibles for a gift of equal value to give in return. He started to untie a knife sheath, hesitated, then continued. He handed her the sheath and knife.

Abby smiled slightly as she accepted the gift, not knowing if it was something she needed or even wanted. She glanced at Jacob to make sure accepting the gift was the right thing to do. He nodded his approval. She could see in the light of the campfire that the sheath had beaded outlines and a buckskin fringe, and enclosed a knife with what appeared to be a handle made of bone.

"Thank you," she said. Jacob signed her response.

With that exchange, and the completion of a smoke, the Indian gathered his horses and left camp.

Abby took the Indian's dinner plate back to her kitchen and started to prepare for bed. Jacob checked the stock, then rolled out his buffalo robe next to the campfire.

A few minutes after they both retired, Abby lifted up the edge of the white wagon sheet and looked over in the direction of Jacob.

"Thank you for making me buy that tobacco."

"Good night, Abby."

Unknown to Jacob and Abby was Pete Burnett's resignation that evening over in the main encampment across the river. The complaints of farmers had taken their toll, so Burnett submitted his resignation to the Oregon Emigrating Company Council after being their leader for only a week. In it, he made reference to ill health. This was only a formality, though, because everyone knew he simply no longer wanted to deal with ornery farmers. His choice of the camp that had flooded the night before had finally solidified the mutiny of many men, prompting his decision to resign.

On Friday morning, June 9, the main body flooded again. People were eager to get across the Blue and did not care to delay another night, so men hitched their teams and began crossing. The steep bank on the far side required double-teaming each wagon. It was difficult work for a rainy, muddy day. As soon as each wagon made it to the other side, the teamster continued on for five miles to a grove of elm trees on high ground. Although the rain and muddy, miserable conditions lasted all morning, by early afternoon everyone was on the west side of the river and on high ground.

Abby did not get up that morning until Jacob went out to water the stock, shortly after sunrise. Next to the wash tub lay the Indian's knife. The beautifully decorated sheath displayed red and blue trade beads along the perimeter with an image of the top half of the sun or moon in the center. Underneath was a symbol depicting a buffalo. The knife had a metal blade with a handle made from a black horn that fit well in her small hands. She had never seen an antelope, but from the description given by Jacob the horn could only be from this animal.

As she examined the knife, she knew exactly where she would keep it. With a glance toward the stock to make sure Jacob was not watching, she lifted her dress and tied the knife to the lower part of her right leg. There were a thousand uses for a good knife, especially on a journey to Oregon. Unknowingly, Abby was adopting the ways of a Western adventurer.

When Jacob returned, she had his breakfast waiting. Today, for the first time, she ate in silence while assimilating the events of yesterday and especially last night. There would be time later in the day for recording the details in her diary.

"Jacob," she said as he finished breakfast and leaned back against a wagon wheel in his usual cross-legged position. "Did you ever seriously consider selling me?"

"Not for a minute, Abby, you're too good a cook." He set his empty plate on the ground, then rested his elbows on his legs.

"Mr. Chalmers, you are the most incorrigible man I've ever met. I hope you know I never would have shot that Indian. I just needed to get his attention."

"Well that you did—he showed disappointment up until then. By the time he left I think he was glad to be getting out of here with his hair. You certainly know how to make an impression."

Abby smiled back with no response, then began to clean up from breakfast.

By ten o'clock, wagons were rolling past their encampment. Women greeted Abby warmly with "Morning, schoolteacher" and "Please join us for dinner sometime." The men had nothing to say, and a few gave her what she considered to be rather unfriendly looks. Her success in crossing the Blue was still fresh in their minds. Whatever their personal feelings toward her action, they all knew she was right.

As soon as the Copenhavers crossed and found a place to camp, Sam wasted no time in locating Abby. The rest of the caravan would spend the remainder of the day regrouping and trying to dry out gear.

"Abby," Sam called out as he rode up, "you wouldn't believe the stir you caused by crossing with those Indians! Several men wanted to expel you from the migration, but their wives put a stop to that. You're certainly the most well-known person in this company."

"Really."

"Most men blamed you, Jacob, rather than Abby. It was really quite a joke. Those humiliated men were too proud to admit they'd been beaten by a woman."

"Sam, it wasn't that important," responded Abby.

"It was to them; I guess it was principle. I made sure they all knew I was seeing you on a regular basis, so they didn't say much after that, leastwise not when I was around. I tried to get the Copenhavers to hire those Indians, but they wouldn't have anything to do with it."

"What's happening with Burnett?" asked Jacob.

"He quit!"

"Quit! Now what do we do?" asked Abby.

"Nobody knows, least not yet. Burnett was so frustrated with people that won't take orders that he just up and quit. We'll probably have to elect someone else—but there's no sense in doing that until the cattle people split from us non-cattle people."

Jacob gave his usual nod of approval.

"A split is probably for the better," added Abby. "We have a long way to go with trouble enough moving these wagons. If a split calms people down then I'm all for it."

"How many more wagons to cross?" Jacob's interests were in getting underway rather than in appeasing ornery farmers.

"They should all be across by now. I took my turn at helping them double-team each wagon—worked about three hours before being relieved. You know, there are quite a few men who won't help in situations like that. They've always got some excuse to avoid work, doing the minimum and no more. Then there are others who are always willing to help. It's them that are making this trip to Oregon possible. Shouldn't be that way, but it is."

"Where's everyone camping tonight?" asked Abby. "Are they re-forming the platoons, or is everyone on their own for another night?"

"We're all moving to that high ground over there." He motioned to a grove of elm trees. "Everyone's on their own, and we might not have any more platoons. When the cattle owners split off they'll take half the wagons with them. We need those corrals, so I don't know what will happen."

"Fewer wagons the better," said Jacob, "I'm tired of listening to all this complaining. Maybe we can make a few additional miles each day without all this controversy."

"Maybe." Abby stood with her arms folded as she listened to Sam's news. "I want to get going. We've wasted another two days here."

"With good weather we can make up a few of those miles," Jacob responded. "We'll be underway first thing tomorrow."

"Well, here I've been doing all the talking," Sam said with a smile. "Has anything happened to you two? I missed you last night, Abby."

Abby glanced over at Jacob, who was obviously not going to answer.

"Nothing to speak of," she said. "We just had a good rest."

"Well, I thought I heard a gunshot from over in this direction. I thought you might be target practicing, but it was only one shot and it was already dark."

"That was me," Jacob interrupted. "Took a shot at a prowling coyote and missed."

Abby stared at him in mild surprise. She was becoming accustomed to this old mountain man—this wild, uncivilized, domestic, romantic, lying old fool. *He's certainly unpredictable,* she thought.

Sam looked relieved. "I knew there was nothing for me to worry about, especially with Jacob here to look out for you."

"Sam, how about some coffee." Abby felt the conversation was getting out of control, so an offer of coffee was in order.

At noon the rain stopped, the weather began to clear, and by two o'clock the sun started showing through. People came out of their wagons and started hanging wet clothes on nearby trees and shrubs to dry in the afternoon sun.

Those with loose cattle formed their own encampment separate from the other wagons. Jesse Applegate, one of the instigators, called for a meeting that evening of the people with more than five head of loose stock. They needed to form their own leadership and rules for traveling. Without much fanfare, they elected Jesse their commander and christened their new group the "Cow Column."

The split was a bittersweet parting as many women said farewell to friends and established campfire social circles. Even so, everyone knew this was for the best. By splitting now, they might all reunite as friends upon reaching Oregon.

The council of the provisional trail government ordered new elections for the remaining emigrants. There was little enthusiasm for holding an election, so Steve Fairly suggested the council appoint someone. This was acceptable to everyone in attendance. After a short discussion they appointed one of the council members, Bill Martin, as leader of the company without cattle. His appointment seemed to be a logical choice, since he was one of the most avid proponents of a split. Emigrants knew they needed a leader, and the exhaustion of trail life could excuse dispensing with the formalities of democracy. At this point, general consensus was as good as an election.

Upon accepting command, Bill Martin announced he would use the title of colonel to distinguish his authority. He also labeled the new group the "Light Column." His first order of business was to organize four new platoons and appoint a captain and orderly sergeant for each. The captains he appointed were Dave Lenox, Jim Waters, Hank Lee, and Dan Matheny. A quick census revealed that the Light Column had almost 60 wagons and about 160 men. The new platoons consisted of 15 wagons each. To Abby's joy, her platoon contained the Burnetts, Rubeys, and Blevinses. Their campfire social circle remained intact.

Colonel Martin chose the number four simply because there had been four platoons since their first organization by Burnett. These new platoons were smaller and could operate more efficiently. The same general marching orders remained in effect, with wagons alternating positions to give each family a turn at the lead and an opportunity not to eat dust.

The Cow Column consisted of over 30 wagons and about 110

men. Jesse chose to divide the group into 8 platoons of 4 wagons each for purposes of sharing a common kitchen and keeping some semblance of order. During the evening they formed one large corral for the working stock, and like the Light Column, the platoons and wagons alternated positions during the day.

The next day was surprisingly uneventful. Even with new leadership, all columns were ready to march by eight o'clock. This included the already separate column of Chiles's California-bound emigrants. On this first day, the Cow Column fell in behind the Light Column. The weather was clear with blue sky and sun. Unfortunately, the rain of the last few days had created a road that was wet and soft. The miles came hard, but at least the columns were moving.

Today Abby experimented with an idea she'd had before crossing the Blue. Making butter with her churn required a fair amount of effort during the evening—energy she could use elsewhere. Last night she had loaded the butter churn so that today she could allow the rough road to turn the cream into butter. When the wagons set out that morning, her butter churn was tied to the tailgate. At the noon stop she could see that her experiment was working. By evening she would have butter.

About midafternoon the advance guard encountered a company of four wagons traveling east from Fort Laramie. The wagons contained furs from last winter's harvest and were en route to Independence. The Fort Laramie men were also driving several buffalo calves. These buffalo, the first most emigrants had ever seen, evoked great curiosity.

Gantt, Martin, Jesse Applegate, and the other leaders obtained a description of the road ahead. To their disappointment, they learned that Fort Laramie could not supply such a large group of emigrants. But at least the establishment did have a blacksmith shop that would prove invaluable.

Before parting company, many women quickly dashed off letters to family and friends back in the United States. With the remoteness of their journey, they dared not miss an opportunity to send a communiqué.

Both columns traveled about ten miles that day, camping within sight of each other near a grove of cottonwood on the north side of the trail. Nobody had seen any game since before crossing the Kansas, except for a few isolated deer. Buffalo country still lay ahead. Seeing those calves meant it would not be long before they would be enjoying buffalo hump and tongue.

Early that evening several men guarding cattle in the Cow Column came across the body of a mutilated Indian. They immediately informed the Light Column, so Martin, Gantt, and Nesmith came out to investigate. Gantt suggested that the band of warriors whom they'd met a few days earlier had killed the Indian—but they had said they'd killed several Pawnees, displaying fingers they claimed to be from each kill. Now, the leaders could see that they had killed only one Pawnee, a Pawnee with all his fingers severed.

Over the course of the evening almost all emigrants in each column, children included, hiked the full mile out onto the prairie to see the dead Indian, a curiosity they could not resist. Several people found arrows that they kept for souvenirs.

This event, in combination with the Indian drill fiasco, was enough to upset a number of families. Several talked about turning around, while others tried to persuade Burnett to take charge again. That evening saw a general feeling of uneasiness in each column. Would this be the night of an Indian raid? Everyone took extra precautions, making sure to load all guns and secure all stock.

Shortly after dark a young guard named Nate Eaton took a shot at what he thought was an Indian. The camp immediately woke, and Colonel Martin doubled the guard. Few people slept that night, sure that an attack would come at any minute.

———◆•◆•◆———

In the morning several men ventured out to find the Indian Nate had shot. Instead, they found a dead mule belonging to the O'Brien brothers, Hugh and Humphrey. The mule was worth about three hundred dollars back in Independence. The news came as a great relief for the entire migration, but was a terrible disgrace for poor Nate. From that point forward, the other young men teased him unmercifully.

It was Sunday, June 11. The weather remained clear and it looked to be a good day for travel. All columns were moving by eight o'clock. Those individuals who previously had wanted to spend the Sabbath in camp were now more than willing to travel. There had been too many delays, with some people feeling that they should already be at Fort Laramie. The road today was considerably drier, so people expected to make more miles than the day before.

The advance guard, called the "pioneers" by some, always consisted of Gantt and Nesmith. Other single men usually joined them, along with Bill Martin and Pete Burnett. Today the guard traveled up the north side of the Blue River, staying two to four miles from the river on high, mostly dry ground above the floodplain. Meanwhile, a number of older boys rode over to the Blue to gather firewood from the cottonwoods growing along the riverbanks.

Shortly after the noon stop, the Light Column passed Chiles's California Column. Jesse's Cow Column chose to stop early, so by chance, all three columns came together late in the afternoon.

That evening the Light Column and Chiles's Column camped together on the west side of Horse Creek. Jesse's Column was just a short distance away, also on the west side of the creek. The migration had traveled fourteen miles—a good day, considering that the prairie was not completely dry from last week's rain. The creek had steep banks and a fast current that did not deter the teamsters. Everyone wanted to cross before making camp, though not all would make it. Water obstacles had taxed the patience of everyone, so most people were not willing to wait until morning. Darkness arrived before everyone could cross, but the majority were now on the west side of Horse Creek.

Jesse's Cow Column was camped within sight of the main group, thereby affording an opportunity to exchange news and visit friends. Although people were now traveling in separate columns, they did not forget their friends.

For dinner, Abby fried up some bannock bread for both Sam and Jacob, a pleasant change from their usual fare. Sam took Abby for their walk away from the wagon corrals and out toward the night guards and cattle. As long as the Cow Column was nearby, there was comfort in knowing that guards were on duty.

Unfortunately, a light sprinkle cut their walk short. They returned to the Western Passage as the sprinkle increased to a steady rain. Sam made a quick farewell, then ran back to the Copenhavers' wagon for shelter.

During the night a heavy thunderstorm blew down all the tents and tipped one wagon. With this disagreeable weather, the next morning saw more frustration from people angry at being constantly wet and the prospect of another muddy road.

Because of the havoc wreaked by the thunderstorm, wagons were not ready to start rolling until ten o'clock. To make things worse, some of the company had still not crossed Horse Creek and were now having trouble with the muddy, slippery banks and high water.

During the thunderstorm a number of loose cattle wandered away from the Cow Column herds. Several short-tempered wranglers immediately blamed local Indians for stealing them. After finding the animals grazing in a hidden ravine, they realized that Indians would have little use for slow-moving cattle. Wranglers would have to be more watchful for any tracks leading away from the herds—an indication of the overnight wanderings of one or more animals.

Shortly before noon the advance guard spotted a buffalo bull on a ridge about two miles north of the trail. Jim Nesmith, John Gantt, Mr. Kerritook, Bill Newby, and two other men quickly rode off in pursuit. Mr. Kerritook was the half-breed son of a trapper and had spent his entire life on the edge of the frontier. The 1843 migration provided him the opportunity he needed to set out on his own, breaking the ties of family and civilization. Bill Newby was a farmer who could not miss the prospects offered by Oregon. With a hired teamster to help drive his wagon, he chose to join the adventure of a buffalo chase.

The buffalo saw his pursuers at two hundred yards, surveyed the situation, and then fled at full speed. He ran for a half mile before Gantt finally caught up and discharged two pistols into the bull's shoulder. Nesmith shot the bull in the neck below the backbone and Mr. Kerritook fired a pistol and a carbine. After seven shots the bull finally stopped, reeled, and fell. The men butchered him and returned to the company, now a distant five miles away.

Meanwhile, each column traveled ten miles on a muddy prairie that day. They all finally made camp near a small grove of timber on the south side of the trail about a mile north of the Blue River.

That evening expectations ran high among the people of the Light Column about getting their first taste of buffalo. Cooks doled out small portions so everyone would have a few bites. Sadly, it was a great disappointment. This was an old bull that could not keep up with the rest of the herd, and the meat it gave was lean and tough.

Jacob warned Abby that the old bull might be less than tender. Consequently, she was ready with fresh dumplings for herself, Sam, and Jacob.

The following morning, Tuesday, June 13, was clear, yet damp. A heavy dew the night before meant that any equipment left out was wet. Jim Nesmith, Jim Williams, and Ed Otey, all mounted on mules, went out early to hunt for more buffalo. Williams was traveling to California with three brothers, so he had plenty of help to manage his packhorses while he was out hunting. Ed's brother, Morris, continued to drive the Otey wagon so Ed could join Nesmith on the hunt.

They crossed the Blue by rafting their gear (saddles, blankets, guns, and clothes) and then swimming their mules. To reconnoiter the country and see if there were any buffalo in the area, they rode a distance of ten miles to the dividing ridge between the Republican Fork of the Kansas and the Blue River. Once on the ridge, they traveled several more miles but could not see any buffalo. Rather than buffalo, they came upon five elk. Williams was close enough to take a shot, but missed. Soon all five elk were out of sight.

The hunters had started moving down the ridge toward the Republican Fork when they spotted an Indian leading two horses and riding another. As soon as he spotted the hunting party, he disappeared down into the Republican Fork floodplain. Nobody had reported any missing horses, so they apparently did not belong to anyone in the migration. They recrossed the ridge and spent the evening camped on the south shore of the Blue River.

Nesmith's hunting party had unknowingly caused quite a commotion among the rest of their column after crossing the Blue earlier that morning. They had discharged two loads of ammunition to clear their guns. When Hank Hyde heard the two gunshots, he assumed Nesmith's party had killed two buffalo and immediately informed Colonel Martin in order to retrieve the meat before the Light Column took up the day's march. Martin sent Pete Burnett and two other men with packhorses to load up on meat. The men crossed the Blue and searched for an hour, but could not find any trace of buffalo or Nesmith's hunting party. They returned empty-handed to start the day's march.

Back at camp during breakfast, Jacob enlightened Abby on the change in local Indian tribes. Now that they were well past the Kansas River and approaching the Platte, they were in Pawnee Territory. To Abby, Jacob seemed a little more talkative than usual. Maybe because he was getting farther from civilization, or maybe due to a good breakfast. At first light she had bought two eggs from Jane Linebarger to make cornbread, enough for both Jacob this morning and Sam later in the day.

The columns traveled ten miles and camped on Ash Creek. The evening provided another beautiful sunset for Abby, Sam, and other young couples enjoying their own private romantic rendezvous. Even the migration's new lovers had established a daily routine.

On the following morning Abby prepared another pot of white beans. She began by soaking the beans all day in a pot with the lid tied down to prevent spillage. At night she placed them in her second Dutch oven and allowed them to cook all night. In the morning they were ready. One pot would last her and Jacob about three days.

Nesmith's hunting party caught up to the Light Column at noon. Colonel Martin and Pete Burnett were a bit agitated at the trouble caused by the false-alarm gunshots, and even more frustrated at their unsuccessful hunt. Everyone hoping to enjoy a buffalo dinner this evening would have to settle for some other fare.

The Light Column traveled sixteen miles over a dry level plain and again camped on the Blue River. Surprisingly, the Cow Column had not fallen behind as expected, and camped within visiting range. Today the caravans passed over an area of rich prairie soil that evoked discussions of future settlement. A number of farmers thought the land might be good for farming, although their opinion was not in the majority. The lack of trees, except in the river bottoms, gave most people the impression that the land was only good for buffalo and Indians.

The grueling work of moving a wagon across a prairie where no wagon road existed, and all the difficulties of journeying to Oregon with hundreds of other people, did not dismiss the divisions of labor so well established in American society. During the day the men toiled at driving their ox teams and loose cattle. When a wagon got stuck, they helped each other by either pushing the wagon free or double-teaming it with additional oxen. It was backbreaking, difficult work.

In the evening after corralling the wagons and letting the cattle out to graze, the men relaxed while the women took over. During the day women walked alongside their wagons, or at least out far enough to avoid trail dust. Some women carried infants, while others held the hands of small children who were old enough to walk the entire day. Some children were too big to carry, yet too small to walk the entire day. They rode part of each day in their parents' wagon. Several elderly people also chose to ride. Few teamsters rode in their wagons unless pulled by mules. These they controlled through a standard harness. For wagons pulled by oxen, it was easier to control these slow trudging animals by walking alongside and urging them on with a long quirt. The majority of emigrants were young, middle-class farmers in their twenties and thirties, fairly physically fit for the hardships of the trail. Few people were over fifty, and those who were traveled West with their children and grandchildren.

Women did not consider walking a hardship, since it allowed them to visit. They walked together while watching each other's children and making friends for life—for a friendship made during hard times is a friendship forever. Since Abby had to drive her team, women were constantly coming over to walk with her. Although not everyone approved of a single woman doing a man's job, they all admired her courage and fortitude. She made many friends during these long days on the trail, and she welcomed the company. There was enough curiosity among the women in the migration that most wanted to meet the schoolteacher.

After the wagon corrals formed, women set up their kitchen areas near the tongue of each wagon, outside the corral. Men helped unload small seats, stoves, and cooking paraphernalia as each woman went to work making dinner for her family. Women also did the washing and any clothes mending. Laundry fell under the domain of women's work, so no man with any shred of decency would engage in doing the wash. The social mores of sewing were not as strict, as men engaged in repairing canvas tops, harnesses, and other equipage; however, mending clothes always fell to women.

This division of labor served people well as long as everyone knew their duties and performed as such. Unfortunately, the emotional strain of trail life often erupted with men criticizing their wives' cooking—such as when the fire was not hot enough to cook the beans properly. They apparently expected home-cooked meals out on the trail. Their criticism frustrated Abby, for there was no call to deride their loved ones—trail life was hard on everyone. She noted the discontent in her diary: *"If I had a husband like that, it would be his last meal for a week!"*

Emotional changes started to show in more ways than rude remarks at dinner. Absent was the original joy first experienced after leaving Elm Grove. In its place came a daily routine of ten to twenty miles, with constant work and constant dirt. People soon abandoned any attempt at trying to stay clean. It was simply easier to accept and acclimate to trail dust. Men used profanity liberally when something went awry, such as a wheel getting caught on a stone. The stress of trail life seemed to encourage a godless society. Back in the United States people reserved Sunday for rest. Now, the emigrants' main concern was the need to travel. The closer they got to Oregon, the less chance of getting caught by snow in the Blue Mountains. Sunday rest and religion could wait until they reached the Wallamet Valley.

Abby knew her choice in hiring a mountain man provided the best possible situation. Jacob did not complain like the farmer emigrants. He was strong, willing to work, took good care of the stock, and ate whatever food she put down in front of him. For Jacob, having a woman do the cooking was a real pleasure, something he had not enjoyed for almost twenty years. He also proved himself quite handy in repairing the wagon, harnesses, packsaddles, and even his own clothes. Mountain men did not adhere to the same social mores as farmers, and mending clothes was just part of living.

That afternoon saw another steady, heavy rain. It began shortly after the noon meal, and by three o'clock the road was too muddy to continue. Men helped each other free wagons from ruts and move them to higher ground off the trail. As usual, there were workers and shirkers. Once a shirker's wagon was on high ground, the owner often had some excuse to avoid helping other men, such as a need to clean the running gear or tend to their stock. This pattern would persist all the way to Oregon.

The land they were now moving through was a wild region with rolling prairie intersected by timbered bottomlands. Flowers grew everywhere. Black-eyed Susans and ox-eye daisies sprinkled the hillsides, along with yarrow and mullein. The timber along the streams consisted of eastern cottonwood with some boxelder and rock elm. These shady areas in the bottomlands abounded in bunchberry, trillium, and bracken fern. The beauty of the land seemed to subside during the rain, only to spring back in a profusion of color and charm with the warming sun.

Trail-life difficulties made strange bedfellows with the land's beauty. Though moving forward was a continual struggle, exhaustion was rewarded by scenery and beauty no emigrant had ever seen or even imagined. Each day brought new sights that were foreign to the mostly uneducated men and women. Curiosity about such a mysterious and new land helped to maintain the spirits of many during these long days on the trail. Abby was no exception. She had heard descriptions of the country, although no description could replace the experience of seeing it firsthand. This was an adventure of a lifetime; she knew it, and relished it.

Thursday, June 15, was a sunny, bright day and a welcome relief to yesterday's rain. The camp arose at the usual predawn hour, fixing breakfast and readying the stock for another day on the trail. Today's start would be a little later than usual, as many people were still drying out from the day before. Women laid various items of their families' personal belongings out on the prairie grass to dry in the morning sun.

"You notice those wagons over in Lee's platoon?" Jacob said as Abby cleaned up after breakfast. "A number of people are throwing out food that got wet yesterday. Most of it looks like cornmeal, which would surely dry out in a few days."

"Won't it spoil?" she said. "They'd have to throw it out eventually."

"They could eat it as soon as it dries out. It might not taste good, but meat's meat. It's just wasteful throwing out good food. They'll wish they'd been more conserving when they run out of provisions."

"When the buffalo become more numerous, we'll all be eating better."

"True, but we pass straight through their territory. Once we get out on the Snake River Plains, the only available food will be insects, snakes, rodents, and whatever fish we can pull out of the Snake—and I wouldn't count that. The Indians have all the good fishing areas staked out, so we'll probably end up trading for fish. Those farmers might get through without any problems, although I wouldn't count on it, not with all these mouths to feed."

"Well, there's nothing we can do Jacob, other than to make sure none of our stores get wet."

After crossing the Blue, the trail headed northwesterly, paralleling the river for a number of miles. Numerous side streams flowing into the Blue intersected the road and made watering the stock easy. These creek bottoms also contained firewood for each evening's camp—yet crossing them was an exercise in patience. The first ten wagons halted the entire column as men cleared underbrush and moved rocks from the streambed to make a path for the wagons. By the time twenty-five wagons had passed, the trail displayed sufficient wear from hooves and wheels to make passage fairly easy for the remaining wagons.

The three columns, Chiles's California, Martin's Light, and Applegate's Cow, traveled sixteen miles and again camped on the Blue with good grass and water. During the afternoon Mr. Kerritook killed an antelope and brought it back to camp. Abby, Sam, and many other emigrants walked over to see the curiosity.

John Gantt came over just as Mr. Kerritook untied the carcass from his packhorse and let it fall to earth. Folks gathered around to examine the animal's coloring and size. "It's a member of the deer family," Gantt explained to the onlookers. "Except that it runs gracefully and smoothly, not in irregular bounds like a deer. It's wary, difficult to approach. I've seen Indians wear out a number of horses trying to bring down a single antelope." Mr. Kerritook nodded in corroboration. "They work in relays chasing the animal into one group of Indians with fresh mounts who then chase it toward another group with fresh mounts. It takes a while, but when the antelope finally tires, someone on a fresh horse can usually catch and dispatch it. Another way to hunt them is for the hunter to hide behind a hillock and wave his hat on top of his gun barrel. Antelope are curious enough that they'll want to investigate and soon come within range of the hunter's gun." Captain Gantt looked back down at the carcass. "Meat's right tasty."

Abby noted the animal's markings for a description in her diary. Its antlers consisted of two black pronghorns with a slight inward curve at the end. The animal was a beautiful tan color, with two white markings under its neck extending from side-to-side, and a white belly. Its two-toed hoofs, like its antlers, were black. It also had a white rump that acted as a flag to other antelope when danger approached. In all, it was a most unusual spectacle—an animal never before seen by most everyone in the migration.

The government council met that evening to settle a dispute between two families, something that did not interest either Abby or Sam. Without saying a word, they slipped away from the people around Kerritook's antelope and went for their evening rendezvous.

The council needed to settle a dispute between John Howell and

Elbridge Edson. Apparently, one of Elbridge's oxen had strayed over to the grassy area where John had hobbled his oxen. This had happened on one other occasion, and John warned Elbridge that the next time he would shoot. Unfortunately, he had held true to his threat. Now the council would decide what to do about John Howell's short temper for shooting an ox. The crime itself was inexcusable. Shooting an ox over grazing rights in a sea of luxuriant grass made the crime absurd. Pete Burnett agreed to preside as judge after Colonel Martin refused to get involved, expressing a desire to stay impartial.

After deliberating fifteen minutes, Burnett handed down the sentence: John Howell would have to pay Elbridge Edson twenty dollars plus an ox. That was a stiff penalty out where there were no new oxen to buy, and with Oregon still over fifteen hundred miles away. Howell meekly apologized, hoping to get the sentence reduced, but to no avail. Others took note of the penalty, vowing to be more tolerant of their neighbors.

On Friday morning, June 16, Abby and Jacob passed several trunks, chairs, and a dresser left alongside the trail. People were beginning to understand the importance of taking only provisions. Many families debated the need for reducing weight as oxen weakened and the difficulty of trail life provided a new incentive. The most peculiar abandonment was a complete, full-size stove. It was a beautiful cast iron Franklin stove that must have given the owners a great deal of pride. Sadly, the rain and muddy roads brought a taste of reality to this family and many others.

The first few days of racing had given way to common sense. People knew that if they had to reduce weight out here on the prairie, then they would surely have to abandon more keepsakes before crossing the Rocky Mountains. Stubbornness pervaded and many people chose to hang onto those items until the last possible moment.

Most women now knew of Abby's butter experiment. Ladies in each column were making butter during the day by tying their churns to the back of their wagons. They loaded the churns the night before, so the cream would have a chance to clabber. On cool nights the cream did not turn until later the next day. Since the wagon jostled the churn all day, the exact time of turning was not important. By the time the migration stopped for the night, the butter was ready.

Early in the afternoon the Cow Column (who were a few miles behind the Light Column) encountered eighty to ninety Pawnee warriors. Upon seeing this group of Indians, a man named Jacob Myers rode up to the front of the column and urged Jesse to strike a treaty to protect the herds. He felt the Indians would surely steal as many cattle as they could get—but Myers stood alone. Several other men labeled him a coward for even mentioning the idea of a treaty. Most men felt they could protect their property well enough. If the Indians should attempt to steal from or attack the column, there would soon be a considerable number of dead Indians. At least that was the general feeling among the greenhorn farmers.

After a friendly exchange where both groups expressed peaceful intentions, they lit a beautifully decorated pipe and passed it among the leaders. Jesse gave the chief and three lesser chiefs some shirts and tobacco as payment for crossing their lands. John McHaley told them of the war party of Osage and Kaw Indians, and the one dead Pawnee passed a few days earlier. The chiefs met this news with excitement and a vow to take revenge.

These Indians were part of a Pawnee hunting party returning from a buffalo hunt in the south. They did not shave their heads like the Osage Indians; rather, they wore their hair similar to white men. Because of this feature, most of the emigrants thought they were a fine-looking tribe. They led numerous pack animals loaded with buffalo meat, dried in the sun and then cut into thin strips and pressed between two pieces of wood to produce a smooth appearance. The encounter with the migration was fortuitous, for the Indians were eager to trade some of their meat for various items such as shirts and metal arrowheads. Jesse ordered the Cow Column to halt for an hour during this friendly exchange.

While trading, several Indians expressed amusement at the wrangler's efforts to drive cattle, something they had never seen. A few warriors tried to imitate the drovers, having their efforts met with great laughter from everyone. After an hour of trading, the Indians continued east and the Cow Column resumed their march up the Blue River Valley.

At about three o'clock, an antelope flushed from some brush and ran parallel to the Cow Column wagons, about two hundred yards out. As the antelope came down the line, dogs ran out to chase it until they realized the futility of catching such a fleet animal. As quickly as the antelope left one dog behind, another dog would continue the chase. It provided good entertainment for everyone, and soon the antelope disappeared over a hill, unharmed.

The day was productive in that all columns, the Light, Cow, and Chiles, made eighteen miles and again camped on the Blue River in sight of each other. The Cow Column formed one large corral with all their wagons. The corral was then subdivided into groups of four wagons each, for purposes of setting up common kitchens. Similar to the Light Column, they brought their working stock in from grazing to be corralled for the night.

While the Cow Column was trading with the Pawnees, a number of men in the Light Column rode out in small groups for purposes of hunting buffalo. The weather was cool and sunny, and the road was dry. This freed some men from the task of keeping wagons rolling, so they could go hunting. By evening they brought in one deer and another antelope. Andy Baker, a young man in Abby's platoon, shot the antelope. He divided the meat as best he could, so everyone enjoyed a few small pieces with their evening meal. It provided a good side dish to Abby's boiled rice mush. She saved a small piece of antelope for Sam, who showed up promptly after dinner.

A beautiful red sunset dressed the Friday evening sky, along with a slight breeze to keep the mosquitoes down. The pleasant evening came as a welcome relief after a long, hot day on the trail. Sam and Abby walked along one of the small streams, away from the wagons and toward the Cow Column. So far, the Cow Column was keeping up with the Light Column, a surprise to most.

"This land's not much good for farming," said Sam. "The bottomland could produce a crop, but not up here on the prairie."

"I know what you're thinking, Sam. Just because there aren't any trees doesn't mean the land up here's not fertile. Some crops might do quite well, like wheat."

"People can't live on wheat alone. The best use for this country is to keep it as Indian Territory. They don't need good land, and we farmers do."

"Indians are people, too, Sam. It's not right that we should always push them onto the worst land."

"That's just the way it is, Abby. I wonder what kind of Indian trouble we'll have out in Oregon where there's good farmland? Besides, we need timber for cabins, barns, tools, furniture, fence lines, and fuel. You can't have much of a farm without a nearby source of timber."

"Why does there always have to be trouble? Why can't we live together in peace? Even if our cultures are different, we should be more charitable toward each other."

"Maybe, Abby. Can we talk about something else?"

"Like what?"

They were now out of sight of the wagons, and Sam had no interest in conversation. He put his arm around Abby's waist, pulling her toward him for a warm embrace. As soon as he had both arms around her and she placed her arms around his neck, he gently walked her backwards into the brush. This was just a little more private than being out in the open where cattle guards could be watching. She laughed at his discreetness, and after a few minutes of passion they found a small cottonwood log to sit down on. From here, they could see in the distance the white-sheeted wagons and campfires of the Light Column—a peaceful, serene, and romantic close to another day on the trail.

On the following evening, Saturday, June 17, several families in the Light Column decided to have a dance. They had traveled sixteen miles during the day, and this would be their last night in the Blue River Valley. Tomorrow they would strike north to the Platte River. Their camp also appeared to be the last timber until they reached the Platte. A few sprinkles had fallen in the morning, but the afternoon had cleared and now they had a beautiful summer evening. In addition to this good weather, late in the afternoon Waldo's Straggler

Column caught up with the migration. With them was Reverend Marcus Whitman, the company's future guide, who had chosen to travel with the Straggler Column for both food and protection. All these considerations, and their new-found freedom from the Cow Column, provided excuse enough for a dance.

As people were finishing their dinners and preparing for the dance, Jesse's Cow Column passed by to the north, making a few more miles before the close of the day. It was a sobering reminder that having loose cattle did not slow one's progress.

Before the dance began, Jacob cut several bushels of grass and placed them in the back of the wagon. He also gathered firewood from the nearby elm, bur oak, and ash trees and made sure the water barrels were full. Preparation for the estimated two-day journey to the Platte was more important to him than the upcoming dance.

Among the emigrants there were two fiddles, one wooden flute, and one squeezebox. Two other men could play the fiddle and offered their services to spell the owners of the instruments. Word of the dance spread like a prairie fire through the four wagon corrals. Shortly after dinner, people began to gather on the outskirts of Dan Matheny's platoon, where brush and tall grass had been trampled or pushed aside to create a level dance area.

Saturday-night socials were a common occurrence among farm communities throughout the United States. To the emigrants who had left the states and were now traveling through a strange and exotic country, the Saturday-night social was a touch of home that nobody could resist.

Abby and Sam showed up as the music began and dance lines were forming. Square dances and polkas were the favorites. A new dance, the waltz, was also gaining popularity among rural folks—especially with the young men who viewed it as an opportunity to meet or be close to a particular lady.

As Sam was tall and good-looking, he became an immediate hit with most of the young ladies, a situation that was quite alright with him. He enjoyed dancing, and was now meeting women he had never had the nerve to speak to. The first few dances seemed to be going quite well until he noticed Abby dancing with a young, good-looking man. He quickly decided that this man was enjoying himself far too much. Unfortunately, in his excitement to meet the other young ladies, he had completely overlooked the fact that every man in the company had been eyeing Abby since they left Elm Grove. The schoolteacher's dance card filled before the end of the first reel, with additional men hoping for an opening. Crossing the Blue a few days earlier no longer seemed important, especially when there was a chance to dance with the schoolteacher.

It became obvious to all the women that Abby was the most sought-after, and this was quite acceptable. Everyone knew she and Sam were serious, so why not have some fun? Besides, this was a Saturday-night social.

As the evening wore on, new fiddlers took over while people clapped, sang, or stomped their feet in time with the music. Even Hattie and Rachael, two of the several young slave girls, stood on the outskirts clapping their hands in time to the music. Men took their turns dancing, but poor Abby, there was no rest for her. To Sam's dismay, one man after the next kept her out on the dance ground. Without his name on her dance card, Sam had to stand and watch or dance with the other ladies. The fun and laughter increased on several occasions when a jealous wife came out to retrieve her husband from Abby's arms. It was all in good humor, with a round of applause given to each unlucky husband.

The dance lasted late into the evening, when people started to wander back to their wagons. Tomorrow would be Sunday, and they would be traveling. As usual, people would observe the Sabbath while on the move.

Sam walked Abby back to her wagon. It was the first time all evening that he was able to put his arm around her, so he wasted no time in getting chummy. Abby had finally caught her breath, but was wringing wet with sweat. She gave Sam a quick hug and a kiss, then sent him on his way. A small stream ran nearby, and this was an opportunity for another bath.

On Sunday the company left the vicinity of the Blue River and started to cross a waterless plain of about thirty miles. People were quick to notice the lack of firewood and poor quality of grass on the Great American Desert. The barrenness of the land reaffirmed everyone's support of a national policy to keep this area for the non-agrarian Indians. A few people also noticed the peculiar absence of bees and small game. These creatures, too, farmers concluded, needed a land filled with trees.

Captain Gantt informed everyone that they would encounter the Platte River at the other side of this dry stretch, a crossing he expected to take two full days. This meant that Sunday evening would be the first night the entire migration would be without water. Families would be on their own, and livestock would go without.

By noon they were crossing the dividing ridge between the Blue and the Platte. Because of the lack of water, Colonel Martin requested that everyone keep moving until dark before making camp. At nine o'clock in the evening, just as the sun was going down, they came within sight of the Platte River Valley. It was a beautiful and serene scene with the sun setting over the meandering river and endless prairie. The Platte at this point wound around an island that Captain Gantt referred to as Grand Island. The island contained thick stands of timber that stood in stark contrast to the grassy barrenness of the north and south shores of the river.

The migration continued down toward the Platte and camped about two miles from the river. They were now within the river's floodplain, where there was good grass for the stock, although wood for fuel was still absent. After setting up the wagon corrals, teamsters drove their stock down to the river for a drink.

Jacob removed the grass from the wagon and tossed it aside. Because of his foresight, Abby had one of the few campfires. After dinner she and Sam chose to sit next to the fire rather than walk. It had been a difficult and tiring day, so it wasn't long before they kissed and parted for the night.

On the following morning Colonel Martin and Captain Gantt got everyone up and moving before breakfast. Without campfires, breakfast could wait.

The caravan met the Platte at the head of Grand Island, then turned westward along the south shore. Trappers gave this river the colloquial description of "a mile wide and a foot deep" or "too thin to plow and too thick to drink." Still, the Platte was a beautiful, wild river. The Light Column, now behind the Cow Column, traveled five miles down the south shore before stopping for breakfast where they found some small willows for fuel.

The morning breakfast stop lasted three hours while people kindled fires and unhitched their stock to allow them to drink. Abby walked down to the river where Jacob was tending her oxen.

"Jacob, when we get to an area where there are buffalo, I would appreciate it if you could show me some of the finer points of hunting those animals."

He nodded. "I can do that. Somehow your request doesn't surprise me. In fact, I was expecting it. You never miss an opportunity to learn something new, or gain a new experience."

"Knowledge of hunting could be useful, especially out here."

"Is that all?" he was smiling.

"Alright, so I enjoy learning. I might never get another chance to do this, and I don't want to miss an opportunity."

"Well, Miss Meacham, I'd enjoy showing you the finer techniques of buffalo hunting. I think we can dispense with running buffalo—that's only done efficiently with bow and arrow. I'll show you how to approach and secure meat with that Hawken."

"Thank you, Jacob."

"Have you been working on your signing?"

"I have. The next time we encounter squaws I plan to trade for more moccasins. This time, I'll do the talking."

While they were down by the river, Jacob pointed to the distant forms of three animals running across a hill on the north side of the river. The Platte at this point was about two miles wide, and the animals were mere specks.

"Wolves. You ever seen wolves?"

Abby peered at the far hill, shading her eyes from the sun.

"No, I haven't, and I can hardly see those."

"They're wolves, alright, good sign—we're getting close to buffalo country."

"How can that island have so much timber, yet there's not a single tree on this shore, only a few small willows?"

"Don't rightly know, maybe 'cause of buffalo. They can trample most anything. You see these paths leading down to the river?" Jacob pointed to a number of trails extending down from the hills directly south of the river. "Those are buffalo trails, and they're going to present a problem for the next few days. Some can get to be a foot deep. We'll need to take care not to break an axletree."

Abby stood with her arms folded, staring at the paths and the general beauty of the country around her.

"Here, grab some of this driftwood."

His request brought her wandering stare back to reality.

"At least we have good grass and water," she said as she started walking over to the driftwood.

The column continued for another five miles before making camp. Jacob was right about the buffalo paths. They varied from six inches to a foot deep, contained soft sand, and led directly to the river. During the afternoon two heavily laden wagons did suffer broken axletrees. Fortunately, the wagon owners were carrying extra axletrees and were able to effect repairs.

Bill Martin's Light Column passed the Cow Column while they were stopped for a nooner. It was good to be in the lead, yet everyone noted that Jesse was easily keeping pace with the non-cattle people.

Shortly after making camp, a small party of Pawnees heading east encountered the Light Column. Colonel Martin met the group with a warm, peaceful greeting, then sent a runner for John Gantt and Jacob to act as interpreters. The Indians were returning from a buffalo hunt and led packhorses laden with buffalo hides, tongues, meat, bladders, sinew, horns, and other useful items. With Jacob's help, Colonel Martin provided presents of a shirt and tobacco to their chief, and tobacco to each of the warriors.

The Indians continued east, passing the Cow Column and beyond before making camp. Maintaining this separation provided both groups with some cultural comfort. Although everyone's intentions were peaceful, there was no need to test the gap in social proprieties.

After their departure, Colonel Martin commented on how polite and well kept these Indians were. Other men involved in the meeting agreed.

"These men are proud and honorable," said Martin, "unlike those beggars we dealt with back on the Kansas."

To Jacob, this was simply a farmer's way of accepting people who had a like appearance. Similar to the Pawnees met a few days earlier, each Indian had his hair cut like a white man's, however, that was the only similarity. The nomadic nature of Plains Indians was as different from white farmers as anything could be. Jacob returned to Abby's platoon without making any attempt to enlighten Colonel Martin or his sergeants.

As dusk came on, hordes of mosquitoes erupted from the Platte's riverbanks, engulfing the camp. Wagons, and even campfire smoke, did not provide an escape from the bloodthirsty pests. Instead, most people rolled their bedrolls out near a campfire or under their wagon in the crisp, fresh night air. With cloth protection over one's face, a good night's sleep was still possible.

Chiles's California Column and Waldo's Straggler Column camped nearby, while the Cow Column camped about a half mile behind the Light Column. With the nightly wanderings of their large herd, there was no need to antagonize people by getting too close. Wisely, Jesse stopped his column and herd in an area where they had good grass and water without getting tangled with the others.

The Cow Column enjoyed some light entertainment that evening as an antelope, confused by the intrusion into its territory, ran through the center of their camp. Lindsay Applegate's black dog named Fleet did not waste any time in running after the antelope—no doubt in an attempt to take it down. The dog ran at full tilt, slowly gaining on the antelope as it crossed a slope in front of the camp. When the dog got within fifty feet, his excitement took over and he gave a loud yelp. With that sound, the antelope took off at full speed, leaving the dog to stop and stare in astonishment. The dog looked back at the camp, then at the speck of dust that was the antelope disappearing in the distance. There was a roar of laughter from the camp and a round of applause for the effort. The dog returned to camp both humbler and wiser.

On Tuesday, June 20, the four columns continued west along the south shore of the Platte. Captain Gantt estimated the length of Grand Island to be approximately seventy-five miles, which meant it would be in view until Friday or Saturday. Seeing a forested area was a pleasant change from the endless prairie, yet there was irony in its presence. The inaccessible island contained needed wood resources for fuel, wagon tongues, and other repairs. Unfortunately, the shallow, muddy Platte River made a formidable barrier.

Today Colonel Martin commissioned Jim Nesmith and twenty other single men to hunt buffalo and scout for a safe place to cross the river, after it forked and became the South Platte. Volunteers were plentiful since the Oregon Emigrating Company contained a substantial number of single men ready for adventure and looking to make their fortune in a new land. They did not have wagons or families to slow them down or hold them back, so a hunting excursion would provide great entertainment. They agreed to wait for the Light Column when they reached an acceptable crossing—a distance that might be as far as eighty miles.

The warm summer sun and lazy pace of the oxen posed an additional challenge to the teamsters—staying awake. Men driving mules often fell asleep at the reins, as the swaying motion of the wagon proved too much to stay alert. Other men riding horses would also doze off in the saddle. Even the oxen were not immune to this lazy atmosphere. Teamsters had to continually prod their animals to prevent them from stopping in the humid, sunny afternoon, nearly drifting off. This need for constant vigilance kept Abby busy with her quirt and vocal encouragements.

There seemed to be a new buffalo trail to cross every thirty or forty yards. These trails, cut down by the hooves of thousands of animals over centuries of use, were difficult to cross without sustaining damage to the running gear. After about twenty-five wagons crossed a trail, the wagon ruts and hooves of oxen wore down the trailsides enough to permit easy passage for the remaining wagons. In situations like this, it was better to be back in the pack eating trail dust rather than out in front as one of the lead wagons.

During the afternoon, men and boys not driving teams rode down to the Platte to pick up driftwood for the evening campfire. While Abby was watching one of the returning riders, the wagon directly in front of hers almost capsized when it dropped two wheels into a buffalo trail. The quick-thinking teamster turned his lead team into the tilt and whipped them forward, righting the wagon. Drivers were trying to meet these paths at an angle to minimize the chance of breaking an axletree. In this case, the softness of the ground nearly proved disastrous. After this incident, Abby was more than cautious when crossing the many buffalo trails.

Jacob spent these days walking alongside Abby, since each trail crossing required both their efforts. As she drove the team, Jacob and other men knocked down the sides of steeper trails using picks and shovels. There was no telling how long this condition would persist, but Captain Gantt had a vague memory that it continued for thirty or forty miles after the western end of Grand Island. The next week would be exhausting.

After dinner Sam waited for Abby to roast another pound of coffee beans before going for their evening walk. Lately, hordes of mosquitoes along the river were interfering with their time together and cutting their walks short of sunset. Going to bed early to cover up from the insects seemed to be the only relief.

On Wednesday, June 21, there was a cold hard rain all day. Abby did her best to stay warm, but her jacket, dress, and moccasins hung wet, heavy, and cold. The muddy road presented a challenge: not to slip under the hooves of the oxen while continuing to keep them moving. In all, it was a very disagreeable day.

Today Nesmith's hunting party secured a buffalo bull, one calf, and two antelope. Although the men had fresh meat for dinner, the rain made their camp as uncomfortable as any so far. With clothing soaked through and wet blankets to lie down on, their misery was enough that they named their campsite Camp Disagreeable.

On Thursday the Nesmith party encountered a herd of about fifty buffalo. Over the next hour they pursued the herd on horseback in an exhilarating chase over sweeping hills and ravines in a sea of grass. After a number of miles and rifle shots, they managed to secure three young bulls. The animals fell at various places along the chase, so the party was spread out over four miles when they finally started the task of butchering each animal for its hump and tongue. The remaining carcass was left for the wolves.

By late afternoon Nesmith's party had traveled fifteen miles and camped in an area with shelter from the wind and wood for a fire. In contrast to the previous night, they called this campsite Camp Satisfaction. During the afternoon on Friday they obtained four more buffalo, eating well every night.

Emigrants continued to gather firewood during the day when it was available. Driftwood on the Platte provided the only available source, since the timber out on Grand Island was simply too difficult to collect. People also thought it possible that the caravan would encounter easily accessible firewood at any time. With this in mind, most everyone felt that a dangerous ford out to the island was not necessary. Instead, firewood scarcity continued until everyone had to adopt a practice used by Indians for uncounted centuries, namely, the burning of buffalo chips. Captain Gantt and Jacob, who had used chips for many years, acquainted everyone with their value. Dried buffalo chips provided a hot, steady heat adequate for cooking.

The thought of using buffalo dung for cooking was repugnant to most of the emigrants, especially the women. However, it wasn't long before everyone adjusted their routines after recognizing the value of chips for fuel. Some folks even considered it to be superior to wood since it came in small pieces, easily collected and easily ignited.

After making camp, the children went out in search of dried chips, using pieces of canvas to carry them back to the kitchens. Most girls simply used their aprons. Soon it became a daily ritual for the children, and almost a contest, to see who could collect the most chips.

Prairie winds along the Platte forced people to dig a fire pit every evening, just as Mrs. Skow had predicted. The pit usually measured three feet long by one foot deep and eight inches wide. This narrow width allowed cooks to span the distance with large pans while leaving enough room for the coals to develop a hot fire. With a pit this size, and a cache of chips, cooks were able to keep a hot fire stoked all evening.

Over in the Cow Column on this Thursday evening, Jesse Applegate put his hat over a globeless lantern to prevent the wind from extinguishing the flame. Soon the Captain had a large hole burned in the top of his hat. This amused several men in his column, spurring comments about his ability to lead if he didn't know enough not to burn his own hat. News like this passed quickly between the four columns, since every evening people from each camp visited the others. People gladly shared news and events. Although the Light and Cow Columns had separated, they had done so in a civil manner, thereby retaining their many friendships.

On Thursday afternoon as Abby drove her wagon amid the long line of white-tops, she watched a small herd of buffalo running at a leisurely pace on the opposite shore of the Platte about two miles away. Although they were mere specks, their black forms contrasted against the green prairie, flush with new growth. It was a wild scene of Western beauty, never before witnessed by these Eastern emigrants. They were truly seeing the elephant.

The buffalo ran parallel to the river and did not see the large migration of white-sheeted wagons and loose cattle—but as soon as they came into its downwind air stream, the beasts turned at right angles and increased their speed, now away from the river. Later that evening, Abby noted in her diary that the buffalo's sense of smell is much better than its vision!

The sight of these buffalo provided enough incentive for Jacob to prepare for a hunt. On Friday morning he went out alone, returning in the evening with both of his packhorses laden with meat. After securing the meat, he had spent the remainder of the day catching up with the migration during their fifteen-mile advancement. Each wagon in Abby's platoon received a share of the meat, since Nesmith's main hunting party had not yet returned. The grateful emigrants consumed the entire store in a single evening, prompting Jacob to prepare to head out again in the morning.

On Saturday morning, June 24, cloudy conditions and a stormy sky presented an ominous outlook for a day on the trail. With twenty men gone from the company, Jacob thought it prudent to remain rather than journey out for more meat. If the trail turned into a muddy quagmire, freeing stuck wagons would require all able-bodied men.

Unknown to the Light Column, Nesmith's hunting party had split up. Four men stayed in camp to dry meat while the others went out in search of more game. The hunters soon came upon an immense herd, and the chase was on. Within the hour they had secured five additional animals.

Colonel Martin started the caravan at the hour of seven o'clock. The morning remained cloudy, yet dry, allowing a good advance on a dry prairie. While the column stopped for their nooner, distant rumblings began in the southwest where storm clouds were darkest. Without trees for protection, Colonel Martin ordered each platoon to form their wagon corrals, secure the stock, and wait out the impending storm. It was a wise safeguard, considering the havoc created by previous violent storms. Rather than the typical corral with wagon tongues pointing out, this time teamsters kept their teams hitched, pointing the tongues inward. This arrangement corralled the oxen, but still allowed the caravan to get underway as soon as the storm passed. In addition to the corral, Jacob secured all their livestock by hobbling them—an action that prompted other teamsters to follow his lead. A little extra precaution couldn't hurt. Men also corralled loose stock such as horses, pack mules, and milch cows. With the caravan as secure as possible, people climbed into their wagons to await the coming storm.

What Jacob knew, and the other emigrants did not, was that this was not a storm. It was something worse than a storm. The distant rumblings belonged to a large herd of buffalo on the run. If they passed close to the caravan, livestock would surely panic. That was reason enough for hobbling.

Even Abby thought the thunder was an approaching storm. She did not show any fear, just an urgency to make her outfit safe. After tying down the side flaps and making sure everything was protected from the impending rain, she invited Jacob into the rear of the wagon. It was an offer that he quickly accepted. He knew the ground was no place to be during a buffalo stampede. Even the wagon itself was not safe, although the platoon bunched together should offer adequate protection.

Jacob jumped up into the wagon carrying his rifle. Since it was usually part of his person, Abby did not give it any thought. He sat down on the bed, resting the barrel on the tailgate. Only then did he begin to enlighten Abby.

"You see any lightning flashes in that distant cloud?"

Abby scrutinized the black ominous mass to the southwest. "No, none—it's probably just a rainstorm."

"If it were rain, you could smell it—no rain in that cloud. You might want to get that Hawken loaded, just in case."

Her calm expression turned to anxiety as she considered the possibilities. "Is it Indians? It's Indians isn't it?" She quickly grabbed for her Hawken before he could respond.

"No, not Indians, buffalo—that dull rumbling is from a large herd on the run. If we're lucky they'll pass by. If they come straight into us, there will be a few tipped wagons, that's for sure."

Several men were still standing outside the wagon corral watching the black, massive cloud as it moved toward the river. They, too, began to notice the lack of lightning flashes and the constant steady rumbling, unlike the sound of thunder. Phil Rubey commented on how the cloud color was not like those associated with a severe thunderstorm.

Miles Eyre, the company's loner, joined the group of men after hobbling his animals. This so-called "storm" was enough for him to abandon his solitary ways and seek shelter with the rest of the platoon.

"How come there aren't any thunder booms?" Miles asked as he came up to the group.

"Don't rightly know," responded Bill Hobson, a stocky character with shoulder-length hair. He wore homespun pants and a stained shirt that had once seen use only on the Sabbath. "Seems rather peculiar," he pondered, "not like any rainstorm I've ever seen."

"Look how low that cloud is," said a stout young man named Levi Boyd. "Seems to be moving toward the river." Levi, thirty-one years old and still single, was looking for his place in America. He came from a well-to-do southern plantation family, but was abandoning that leisurely pace for the adventure of Oregon.

"It's moving with the land," added Phil. "I mean it's following the contours and even looks to be turning away from the Platte. My God, it's Indians, and they're charging us! To your rifles, men!"

"Not Indians." It was Jacob. He thought it only prudent and neighborly to come out and tell these men to take shelter.

"That cloud's from a herd of buffalo heading this way. I suggest you men take shelter in your wagons, and keep your women folk and children down. We should be safe enough, just get off this prairie."

He then turned around and headed back toward the wagon. The men looked at each other for a few seconds, then parted without speaking. They had never taken a liking to Jacob, but they knew his advice was sound. Taking shelter was simply the best thing to do.

As Jacob got back to the wagon and climbed in, the ground began to tremble—slowly at first, much like that of an approaching locomotive. A sudden burst of wind from the Platte lifted the cloud to reveal a black mass of moving bodies heading straight for the caravan. The buffalo were not veering to either side. It looked as though they would pass straight through, with streams of animals flowing between and around the four corralled platoons.

Soon the wagons began to shake violently. As the first animals entered the fortress, hanging pots clanged together and trunks and other baggage rattled and bounced around the wagon beds. The noise was deafening, and the dust blinding. Abby tried to speak, but Jacob could not hear her shouts above the roar of the stampede. She tapped him on the shoulder and pointed to a shovel about to fall over the side. He grabbed it and shoved it behind a trunk.

Abby continued holding onto several trunks as the wagon filled with choking dust, shaking like a rail car moving at top speed. Jacob sat at the rear watching the herd pass, more concerned about the safety of the wagon's running gear than its contents. Animals were now flowing around both sides of the platoon, so close that a person could reach out and touch one of them.

Through the front of the wagon Abby could see oxen and other stock in a noisy, braying panic, wanting to break free of their restraints. The makeshift corral and hobbling were their only protection, for if these animals got mixed up with the stampede, they would surely be killed. As she glanced forward she saw a wagon on the other side of the compound jump up in the air twice, then tip over, dumping its baggage and occupants. The people quickly scrambled for shelter underneath the overturned wagon. She again tapped Jacob on the shoulder to get his attention, pointing to the overturned wagon. He nodded his acknowledgment while looking to see if the occupants had survived. He soon turned back to the tailgate, rifle in hand, ready to drop any bull that might tangle with Abby's wagon. The deafening noise and blinding, choking dust continued for almost twenty-minutes before the herd finally passed.

When it was over, the emotionally shaken emigrants needed time to recover. Colonel Martin decided to spend the rest of the day at this spot, repairing nerves and some baggage. Fortunately, there were no injuries and all animals were safe.

Almost everyone expressed their gratitude in getting through the ordeal uninjured. But one emigrant, Alex Zachary, derided Colonel Martin and the council as being unable to protect the company from even buffalo. Zachary was always quick to fix blame and had never had a kind word for anyone. People had become accustomed to his abusive language, and simply ignored his calls for a new election.

After the herd passed, Sam was quick to locate Abby. He had originally wanted to join Jim Nesmith on the buffalo hunt, but the Copenhavers had insisted he stay and help with their wagon. Now, with the trauma of a buffalo stampede, he was glad he had. As soon as he came up to Abby's wagon, she jumped down and threw her arms around him. They could ignore social protocol during times of great emotion; public affection in the form of a hug was certainly acceptable after a buffalo stampede. Abby was in tears as she held on for a good cry. It had been an experience that nobody would ever forget.

Jacob and the other men unhobbled their working stock as soon as the animals calmed down. They then formed standard wagon corrals and took the oxen down to the Platte where they could get water and grass.

The tipped wagon belonged to the Wheeler family. They were a deeply religious couple, traveling to Oregon to start a merchandising business to service the expected rush of emigrants. Elizabeth Wheeler's wedding dishes were in a thousand pieces, and several trunks had cracked during the mishap. Their wagon bed suffered a few broken boards, but was still usable. Most importantly, there was no damage to the running gear. Neighbors helped to right the wagon and put things in order. The loss of the dishes weighed heavy on Elizabeth; however, she would have had to abandon them eventually. Their overloaded wagon could never make it through without a reduction in weight. Right now, Elizabeth needed time to recuperate from the ordeal. Two other families offered to make dinner, an offer that Newt Wheeler quickly accepted. His wife was in no condition to do any chores.

People spent Saturday evening in quiet repose, compared to the day. Women cleaned dust and dirt from their wagons while men made repairs to trunks, wagons, and other gear. Abby kept Sam for dinner, not letting him return to the Copenhavers until after dark. Her outfit and animals were unscathed, but her emotions had taken a beating. She and Sam sat arm in arm next to the campfire, mostly without conversation. The mesmerizing effect of the flames gave comfort of a known quantity, providing a healing for frayed nerves. Jacob sat on the ground leaning up against the wagon tongue, smoking his pipe. His experiences with running buffalo and various Indian scrapes had satisfied his curiosity for excitement many years ago. Today would only be a footnote.

"You think they'll return?" Sam broke the silence.

"Not likely." Jacob calmly started to reload his pipe. "Something must have spooked that herd for them to stampede like that. Maybe a lightning strike—hard to say, certainly wasn't Indians. Indians are smart enough not to do anything like that."

"It never did rain," added Abby. "I guess all those clouds in the southwest were just buffalo."

"Maybe, maybe a lightning strike, maybe something else."

Sam sat up straight, shifting his weight. "Well, whatever it was, we can do without any more trouble like that."

"Amen to that," Abby said as she leaned over, putting her head on Sam's shoulder. Their camp fell silent again as the campfire flame worked its comforting magic.

Fortunately for the Cow Column, their group was four miles behind that afternoon and they avoided the stampede. Had they been in its path, they would have lost their entire herd.

The next morning, Sunday, June 25, brought a new concern. Two teenage boys belonging to the Parker family had slept near their campfire, each with a quilt for warmth. Since it was still warm, they placed the quilts at their feet when they lay down. In the morning the quilts were gone. Jesse Parker, a hot-tempered farmer going to Oregon for the free land, was ready to accuse another man of the theft when Jacob pointed out the moccasin tracks of two Indians entering the camp and passing by the boys. An instant feeling of alarm shot throughout the column.

"How?" demanded Colonel Martin. "How could Indians get past the night guards undetected?"

"They could have killed my boys!" Mrs. Parker cried, visibly shaken from the thought of Indians in camp.

"They weren't here to kill anyone," Jacob intervened. "If they were, your boys and plenty more would be dead. They simply wanted to steal a few items, so I'd check around. There's probably a few more things missing, like cooking pots—those are always useful items."

"They should have never gotten past the guards." It was Colonel Martin, still demanding a reasonable explanation. "I want to know which guard fell asleep!"

"Nobody fell asleep, Bill," replied Jacob. "A number of tribes take a great deal of pride in their ability to steal—it's a matter of honor. The only way to prevent loss is to not leave anything out overnight. These could have been Omahas, or Ottos—doesn't look like the work of Pawnees. If they were Crow, our horses would be missing."

"Will they be back?" asked a woman from the back of the gathered crowd.

"Maybe," responded Jacob. "If not them, then some other tribe. You're in Indian Territory now, and a little extra vigilance won't hurt. Just don't leave anything out overnight. Now let's get rolling, looks like a good day ahead."

That last statement stole some of Colonel Martin's thunder, but everyone knew they needed to break camp. Daylight was burning.

In an hour they struck camp, and Colonel Martin gave the order to march. Jacob was standing next to Abby when the order came down, so he chose to walk a piece, leading his horse.

"Jacob, is that why you've taken to carrying your rifle all the time? Since we crossed the Blue I hardly see you without it. Is it because we're in Indian Territory?"

"Just an old habit—makes me feel at home out here away from all those settlements on the Missouri frontier. I've carried this rifle for over twenty years and it feels natural—many a time it saved my life."

"You think I should carry my Hawken? Even when I'm driving the team?"

"You drive the team and don't worry about Indians. We're doing fine and will get through to Oregon without much trouble, that's a fact."

"Jacob, what do you think of Sam? —I mean, really think of him? You think he's a good man?"

Jacob hesitated as Abby abruptly changed the subject. She had something more on her mind than simply a desire for his opinion.

"Has he asked you to marry him?"

"No!" Abby snapped back with surprise at his bluntness. "I just want your opinion of him. I don't know if I'll ever get married again. Well, I didn't mean that. I simply want your opinion."

"I think he's a good man and would make a fine husband. He's a hard worker, doesn't drink, and he's devoted to you. Yes, ma'am, he'd make a fine husband and a good father. That's what you want to know, even if you deny it. I'm not blind."

"I don't know why you or anyone else thinks I should get married.

I'm getting along quite well on my own." It was a poor defense, but sounded acceptable for now. They walked on in silence for another minute.

"Besides, who could marry us way out here?"

"That's what I thought." Jacob smiled at her frankness, turned and mounted his horse. "How about Reverend Whitman?" He rode off, leaving her to contemplate his final words.

This Sunday, like many Sundays, saw the gathering of various prayer groups during the noon stop. A number of religions were represented, each with their own customs, prayers, and ceremonies. To be considerate of each sect, Colonel Martin allowed a little extra time during the Sunday nooner before giving the afternoon order to march. Not all emigrants engaged in religious activities, and Abby and Jacob were among the few who didn't. They usually sat down on the ground near the wagon to enjoy the noon respite before another ten-mile march in the afternoon sun. Their customary meal of last night's leftovers now consisted of cold buffalo hump. This meat, and some bread, provided more than enough food while conserving Abby's store of beans, rice, and other foodstuffs. There would be close to eight hundred miles to traverse between the end of buffalo country and the Wallamet Valley in Oregon. Conservation of supplies was an ongoing necessity for survival.

"How do you like that bread?" Abby waited for Jacob to answer between mouthfuls.

"Just fine, even tastier than usual—you change something in the way you make it?"

Her face lit up as she leaned forward with laughter.

"Well I'm glad you like it 'cause I call it 'Buffalo Chip Bread.' Buffalo contributed more to your meal than just meat." She grinned broadly while taking another bite from her sandwich.

"I knew there was something special about this bread," Jacob said smiling, "and you can serve it anytime 'cause it's better than any civilized bread."

"I have the recipe written down in my diary. I want to give it to some other ladies, so I've written it out here." She handed him a piece of paper with the following inscription:

Buffalo Chip Bread

1½ cups warm water
4 cups flour
5 pinches saleratus
1 pinch cream of tartar

Mix water, saleratus, and tartar, then add flour and mix well. Let rise. Punch down, knead, then form a loaf. Let rise again. Bake for about thirty or forty minutes in a hot oven or until done.

"I think that steady heat from the chips makes a big improvement over regular trail bread. I want Sarah Rubey to have this recipe, and Levina Blevins too—her children will enjoy it."

"I'm sure they will." He handed the recipe back. "You have good handwriting Abby, easy to read."

"Thank you." Abby sat in silence, contemplating his compliment. It had never occurred to her that Jacob might not be able to read, although it should have. Most people on the frontier are deficient in proper schooling—but he could read, and well enough to judge handwriting.

"Jacob, I apologize for not considering the possibility that you might not be able to read. I guess a lot of mountain men can't read. You seem so smart that it just never occurred to me."

"Oh, I can read, although there's not much need for it out in the mountains. During those long winters we'd have what we called the Rocky Mountain College. We covered about everything you'd need to know to survive in those mountains. Men would learn various skills during their summer wanderings, mostly from friendly tribes. Then during the winter months we'd exchange such knowledge. It was quite an education, all without a single book. Some of the men had small Bibles to read, but most of our education was in practical knowledge. Yup, it was the Rocky Mountain College, best school I ever attended." He paused while looking over at Abby. "Now what are you smiling about?"

"You," she replied, "you're always so silent, I was enjoying listening to you. How much formal schooling did you receive?"

"Completed secondary school by the time I was seventeen."

Abby looked back in astonishment. Secondary school was a tremendous education and certainly not expected from a mountain man.

"Jacob, secondary! That's wonderful. You certainly are full of surprises. I'm sure Oregon could use an educated man like you. Secondary! My, I never would have guessed."

"For all the good it's done me—and I don't rightly know what I'll do in Oregon. Heading out there seems like the best thing to do right now—certainly better than dealing with all those people back in St. Louis. Oregon should be part of the United States, and the more people that go out there, well, the less claim Old Man McLoughlin and the Hudson Bay Company will have on that land. If there's going to be a fight then I'll be there. I've had my fill of British trapping brigades. They never could understand boundaries, always encroaching onto this side of the Divide. If we can secure that Oregon Country for the United States, then that would make up for hundreds of lost beaver and years of irritation."

"I hope you're right; I prefer living in the United States. Who's this McLoughlin person, another trapper?"

"He's chief factor at the Hudson Bay fort on the Columbia. He's in charge of all British operations, sending out trapping brigades and making sure the British get a strong foothold all through the region. He helped old Jed Smith years ago, so maybe he won't be so tough. We'll see. We'll see."

"With all these emigrants and educated men like you, I don't see how Oregon could be anything but part of the United States. We've already got a number of missions out there, and if the country is as good as I've heard, then, well, it'll be part of the United States. I just know it will."

"Maybe, we'll see. Looks like those prayer groups are starting to break up. I thank you kindly for this meal." Jacob stood and handed Abby his empty plate.

"You're welcome Jacob. Looks like another good afternoon for travel. We should make upwards of ten miles before camp."

"That's good enough for this child."

Jacob mounted his horse and started toward the front of the

column to explore the road ahead. Abby cleaned up the noon dishes by placing them behind the foregate. Washing always waited till evening. In a few minutes the order to march came down the long line of white-tops, and the column slowly creaked forward and westward.

It was a twelve-mile afternoon, with the caravan stopping just after six o'clock. As wagon corrals formed, eleven men from Nesmith's hunting party rode in, their pack animals heavily laden with buffalo humps and tongues—enough for several days' rations for everyone in the Light Column. The remaining nine men of the hunting party were continuing down the South Platte looking for a crossing. The returning men hobbled their horses and set about their bachelor duties of cooking a dinner of buffalo hump.

As they related their adventures of the past few days, it became evident to Jacob and several other emigrants that the hunting incompetence of these men had caused yesterday's buffalo stampede. Instead of moving downwind from a large herd to gain a favorable position, they had ridden directly into it and panicked every animal into a headlong flight. These buffalo then ran into, and panicked, another nearby herd, which formed the massive group of animals that had stampeded the Light Column.

Although Jacob remained silent on the matter, other men were not so kind. There were some hot exchanges that evening; however, the event was over and nothing could be done. Exhaustion and a tasty dinner of buffalo hump served to placate the camp.

After completing evening chores and with the arrival of dusk, Sam and Abby stole away for another private rendezvous—away from the light of campfires and prying eyes. It had been a good day of travel, food, company, and now some quiet moments of romance. Other couples were also out on the prairie or down by the river for their secret trysts. The 1843 migration, with all its quarrelling and malcontents, was not without young love.

On Monday, June 26, the Light Column arrived at the confluence of the South and North Platte Rivers, approximately 102 miles from where they first encountered the Platte. Here the South Platte deepened and veered to the southwest, away from the main trail to Fort Laramie as indicated by Captain Gantt.

Jim Nesmith and the remaining hunters returned in the morning, unsuccessful in their attempt to find a suitable crossing. The column was now at the normal crossing, but because of rain and snowmelt from the Rockies, the river was too high to negotiate. Their only alternative was to continue up the South Platte in hopes that the river level would drop or they would find a place wide enough to provide shallow water with a solid bottom. It was critical that such a crossing be found before the company strayed too far south. Colonel Martin and Captain Gantt decided to ride ahead to look for a crossing, leaving Jim Nesmith in charge of the column.

By chance, the Light and Cow Columns came together for a combined nooner. Chiles's California and Waldo's Straggler Columns caught up as well. It was a time for friends to visit and discuss the problems posed by their newest obstacle, the South Platte.

When the Cow Column stopped for their midday rest, the wagons in each of their kitchen platoons came up alongside each other, four abreast. This way people could visit while eating. It was a practice permitted by the wide-open prairies, but one they would have to abandon in the mountains.

After nooning, the Light Column continued up the South Platte for a day's total of sixteen miles before making camp on the riverbank. The Cow Column was four miles to the rear. For tonight's campfire, trees were absent, but chips were plentiful—as they had been every day for the last week. Soon there were over fifty chip fires dotting the beautiful prairie landscape.

After dinner Matt McCarver hitched up his oxen and drove his outfit back to the Cow Column. Matt was a middle-aged businessman who had visions of a political career on the Western frontier. By moving his family to Oregon, he felt he could easily break into politics if Oregon became a territory, and hopefully, a state. Matt was a free and independent thinker, not afraid to voice his opinion in the affairs of the trail government. Although disagreements about loose cattle were over, other disputes continued. Matt did not like the leadership of the Light Column and thought they should have chanced crossing the South Platte earlier in the day. He drove his wagon past Abby and Sam, who were out for their evening walk. As he passed, Sam waved and Abby called out a friendly greeting, but he gave no answer.

"If I knew there would be so much arguing, I might have changed my plans while still back in Independence," said Abby.

"I've heard some people talking about turning back," Sam replied, "but then they'd have to cross those rivers alone. I don't know how they could do that."

"Well, I'm not turning around. As long as I have you and Jacob, I'll get through to Oregon. I don't know what I'd do without you two."

"I'll never leave you, Abby." He pulled her in close as they continued their quiet stroll down to the shore of the South Platte. It was another warm summer evening with a beautiful sunset. Only the hordes of mosquitoes rising from the Platte could interrupt such a romantic interlude.

On Tuesday morning a warm wind blew up from the southwest and lasted for thirty minutes as each column readied for the day's march. It seemed to follow the course of the river, but then dissipated as quickly as it had appeared. Abby and Jacob exchanged no words while they both scanned the sky for some sign of the weather to come. It looked to be a clear day. The appearance and then disappearance of that warm wind was inexplicable.

During today's nooner seven buffalo crossed the South Platte from north to south, unaware that they were swimming toward the column. By the time they caught the scent of the caravan, it was too late to turn back. They scrambled up the bank in front of the lead wagons and started running. At the time, wagons in the Light Column stretched out along the south bank of the river for over a mile, so people in the rear never saw the buffalo. About ten men rode after the animals and succeeded in killing three and wounding the others.

The day passed without incident with all columns advancing twelve miles. On each evening for the past week, Jacob and Abby had enjoyed a substantial meal of buffalo tongue, hump, or ribs.

After a long, hot summer day, the evening presented a quiet serene picture of the four platoons, grazing livestock, and wisps of smoke rising from the many chip fires. This had become a familiar scene of home and security for everyone, and provided comfort to those women homesick for family and friends.

"Jacob, I've decided I like this buffalo better than any other meat I've had. In fact, I've been eating more out here on the trail than ever before. Antelope is good too, even better than deer meat."

"Everyone eats more buffalo—don't know why. It tastes better than beef and doesn't fill you up. I can't understand why some of those farmers over in the Cow Column still insist on eating beef. They are a stubborn lot."

"Have you been considering how we're going to get across the South Platte? I mean, we can swim the stock and float the wagon—but what about all my provisions and baggage? There's too much weight to keep everything in the wagon, even if we do have it caulked good."

"When we get to an area that we can cross, we'll see if it'll float with all that gear. A little test near shore should show us if our caulking job is holding up. The problem will be with these other pilgrims—few people have bothered to caulk their beds. They'll have to make bullboats, which will take more time, something we're running short of."

"Bullboats. I guess I'll be learning about that too."

Jacob did not reply, only packed down the tobacco in his pipe and leaned up against one of the wagon wheels.

"Sarah was telling me that she's still apprehensive about getting to Oregon safely. I tried to calm her, but didn't do a very good job. I'm still a little apprehensive myself. We haven't gotten to Fort Laramie, much less started climbing up into the Rocky Mountains. Taking wagons to Oregon is such a risky journey—but if we can get through, others will follow. I mean when we get through." She looked over at Jacob.

"We'll get through, although that won't be true for everyone. Some will drop out and some will break down. After Fort Laramie things should start to get interesting. The air dries out, water becomes scarce, wheels shrink, and the people with poor running gear may have to switch to pack animals."

More silence followed his last statement. Sam had not shown up, and Abby did not have enough energy to start cleaning up after dinner. Quiet reflection and the flickering warmth of a campfire provided needed comfort. The dangers of the trail would come soon enough.

"Tomorrow is my birthday," she quietly said as she stared into the flames.

Jacob looked over at her, then back toward the fire, saying nothing.

"I'll be twenty-seven. Seems like I should have accomplished more by now. I'm not married, I don't have a home or family, and now I'm way out here in Indian Territory. I haven't contributed much to society."

"You're a schoolteacher, that's a noble profession—certainly more than I've done. You've got more pluck than any white woman I've ever met." He relit his pipe, feeling that he had probably said enough.

"Sometimes I wish I was back in Greene County. Then I wish I was done with this trip and settled in Oregon. The truth is that I'm enjoying this adventure. With all the troubles and uncertainties, the beauty of this country is infectious. I think I can see why you mountain men love your solitary life in the West. Living in a wild land filled with wonder and beauty, not being held back by the restraints and demands of society …"

"Now, you wait till we get to those mountains. They're so tall and white you might decide to stay right there and not go on to Oregon."

"Oh, Jacob, I have to go on to Oregon. These people are going to need schoolteachers. Besides, Sam is going to Oregon—but I would never give up the adventure of getting there, no matter what difficulties we encounter. It makes me feel more alive."

After a few more quiet moments, Sam walked into camp and took his place on the ground next to Abby. They immediately held hands and started talking about their day. Jacob sat by like an old patriarch, watchful and concerned, but pleased that she was happy.

"You think we'll find a crossing soon?" Sam looked over at Jacob.

"Can't say. I've never been this far south. We shouldn't go on much farther, we're too far off the trail as it is. We'll have to cross at some point no matter what, then double back some."

"Even if it's too deep?" asked Abby.

"I'll give us one or two more days of travel, then we'll have to take our chances. We have a fair distance to cover between here and Fort Laramie, and to get into Oregon before the snow flies we should be at the fort right now. I knew these wagons would be slow—well, we should be farther down the road by now, that's all."

"You think we can get resupplied at Fort Laramie?" asked Sam. "The Copenhavers are running short of just about everything. They threw out the cornmeal that got wet—probably shouldn't have done that."

"Laramie's not equipped to handle a migration this large—those Laramie teamsters last week verified that. During the last two years they saw only a handful of emigrants, and most without wagons. They've got a blacksmith shop that we'll need, but certainly not enough food or other supplies. They need to take care of their own people."

"I have enough supplies for the two of us," Abby responded, "and for you too, Sam, if the Copenhavers run out. We're in good shape, so Fort Laramie will simply be a pleasant rest stop."

"You did a right fine job getting prepared back there in Independence." Jacob took a puff from his pipe. "When this caravan falls on hard times, you'll know what I mean."

The trio sat in silence, watching the campfire and listening to the sounds around them: children playing, pots clinking as women did their kitchen chores, mules braying, dogs barking, and a myriad of other sounds of civilization. These were sounds never before heard on this prairie landscape—from a caravan of dreamers moving west on a nomadic journey to El Dorado. These interludes of quiet reflection around the campfire provided peaceful repose from a day of toil.

Sam broke the silence. "One of the Applegate boys rode up with a pack of playing cards left at last night's camp. Ransom Clark claimed them. Even with all this quarreling, I guess we're still watching out for each other." He paused for another few moments, then addressed Abby. "You want to walk?"

"Not tonight, Sam. I've been walking all day. Let's just sit here and enjoy the fire." She leaned over with her head on his shoulder. He put his arm around her while continuing to hold her other hand. With this snuggling position, they leaned back on the wagon tongue while watching the mesmerizing flicker and warmth of the fire. Their love affair was now common enough to show some display of affection in public. Besides, this was her kitchen and her campfire. They were still adhering to social protocol.

On Wednesday, June 28, the Light Column continued up the south shore of the South Platte until three o'clock in the afternoon, making fifteen miles. At that time Colonel Martin and Captain Gantt came riding in from their excursion to find a suitable crossing. Martin halted the caravan and called for a meeting of the platoon leaders and council. The column was now fifty-seven miles up the South Platte, farther than anyone wanted to be. The remaining company made camp while the leaders discussed the logistics of what to do next. Their success and possible survival depended on making a correct decision now.

Another beautiful prairie evening had brought with it a slight breeze to keep the mosquitoes down. There had not been any rain since June 21, and it looked as though the good weather would hold for another few days.

After dinner while Jacob and Abby were again enjoying their campfire, Sam walked in carrying a small cake decorated with a single candle. Behind him came John Copenhaver and his entire family. Jacob had informed Sam of Abby's birthday, who in turn told Mrs. Copenhaver. After stopping for the day she had prepared a small dessert. At first Abby looked on in confusion, wondering how Sam had found out it was her birthday. In an instant she glanced over at Jacob. He was the only one who knew! With her piercing glare Jacob's eyebrows went up in a pious look of innocence that made her smile. This old, unconventional, romantic trapper never failed to surprise her.

The cake quickly disappeared, and everyone spent the remainder of the evening in friendship and conversation. Sam and Mrs. Copenhaver even did the dishes so Abby could enjoy her special day. It was an evening to remember.

The Light Column started Thursday's march at nine o'clock, continuing up the South Platte, with the advance guard looking for a place to cross. It was a late start, but people knew they could not go much farther before crossing. Part of this morning's delay was the result of loose stock wandering off overnight. Rounding them up took almost two hours. Few people hobbled their livestock, so each morning saw a slight delay as people rounded up strays. For Abby and Jacob, the delay presented the usual morning frustration as they stood by waiting for the order to march. Eventually, they got underway.

Over in the Cow Column a buffalo bull had wandered in amongst the herds overnight. Guards quickly dispatched and butchered it for the hump and tongue. Since the emigrants felt that buffalo would always be plentiful, they left most of the carcass for the wolves and vultures. The whole incident did not delay the column's morning preparations. They started on time, keeping pace with the Light Column.

After only two hours of travel, Colonel Martin halted for a nooner near a small pond of brackish saltwater. Captain Gantt referred to the water as sulfate of soda and warned all teamsters to guard their livestock from drinking. Here, the South Platte provided the only safe drinking water for both livestock and emigrants.

The column stopped for an hour, then continued on for a total of ten miles, halting at a grove of cottonwood trees along the river's south shore. These were the first trees they had seen up close, other than some small willows, since the migration encountered the Platte River, over 150 miles back. Colonel Martin and Captain Gantt determined to cross here, even though the river was still too deep to provide a safe passage. They were now sixty-seven miles from the confluence of the North and South Platte Rivers, a distance that might create additional problems in trying to regain the trail after crossing.

Wagon corrals formed at six o'clock, after which people scattered about doing their various chores. Some started gathering firewood, others washed clothes, while still others went out in small hunting parties. Martin, Gantt, the platoon leaders, and the council gathered to discuss the logistics of crossing such a deep and swift river.

Before dusk the hunters brought in the butchered humps and tongues of eight buffalo. They also brought in the hides in response to a request by Captain Gantt. Crossing the South Platte would require boats, namely bullboats. These were boats made from buffalo hides stretched over willow frames. The hunters left the hides with Captain Gantt, who began instructing several other men how to make boat frames from willow boughs.

Sam stopped by after dinner as Abby was writing in her diary. News of the buffalo bull found amongst the Cow Column's herds had prompted a paragraph on the gregarious nature of this animal. *"They are seldom found alone,"* she wrote, *"and need the company of other animals, even if they are domestic cattle."* She quickly finished, stowed the diary, and was off for an evening with Sam down by the river.

On the following morning, Friday, June 30, Captain Gantt continued supervising the construction of four bullboats along with the conversion of three wagon beds into boats. Men constructed the "wagon boats" by sewing two green buffalo hides together and then stretching them with the flesh side out over the outside of an overturned wagon bed. They then tacked the hides to the wagon bed and placed them in the hot summer sun. After they became thoroughly dry, Jacob brewed up a mixture of his tallow, tree sap, and ash recipe to help the men caulk the seams and render the boats impervious to water.

While Captain Gantt demonstrated the finer techniques of making a willow boat frame, Colonel Martin sent out several more hunting parties to secure additional hides. Gantt estimated they would need at least ten more to complete the bull and wagon boats.

Women named their new camp Sleepy Grove. They knew the crossing would take several days, so they made themselves as comfortable as possible by setting up their wagon corrals in the shade of a stand of tall cottonwoods and a nearby bluff. A camp name was also useful for those women recording the journey in a diary.

Early in the afternoon, Sam and Jacob tested Abby's wagon bed for water leaks. The rough road traversed since crossing the Kansas had taken its toll, and water seeped in at three separate joints. After they dried, Jacob recaulked these areas to make the bed entirely waterproof—except for the gates. He would caulk these the evening before crossing. The test also demonstrated that it would take six men to control each wagon boat during the crossing. The river at this point was about a half-mile wide, much too far for the use of towropes. In addition to the width, the many quicksand beaches complicated their efforts. Men needed to construct paddles to pilot the boats to the north shore.

By evening, the hunters had brought in several more buffalo hides. The willow frames were ready, so Gantt estimated they would complete the first bullboats by noon the next day. While men engaged in boat building and hunting, women engaged in cooking, washing, mending, cleaning wagons, and other domestic chores to keep their moving homes in order. Abby was no different. As soon as Sam and Jacob returned from the river with her wagon, she supervised reloading it with everything in its proper place.

On Saturday morning, people began drying the meat brought in by hunters the day before. They cut the large humps into thin strips, then draped them over their white canvas tops to dry in the hot summer sun. Boat builders completed their tasks by noon, with the first baggage being ferried across shortly after. Some men waded and swam alongside the wagon and bullboats, while other men swam ahead with a three hundred-foot towrope. After a few crossings and learning more about the logistics of such an operation, Colonel Martin estimated that it would take five or six days for the entire column to cross. He assigned everyone a number for crossing, placing Abby's turn on July 3, two days from now.

Transporting baggage to the other side was only half the problem. At the end of the day, the empty wagons needed to be ferried to the other side. Teamsters hitched oxen to each of the empty wagons, then chained the end of each wagon's tongue to the tailgate of the next wagon directly ahead. They then drove the entire train across as one large vehicle. The first train had only five wagons. Subsequent trains contained as many as fifteen, depending on how much baggage the wagon boats and bullboats had transported to the north shore during the day. On this first day, by the time the first wagon reached the north shore, the last wagon in the train had drifted downstream, creating an additional unforeseen problem. The oxen in the final wagons had to swim against the current as they scrambled to keep moving. Fortunately the power of the other oxen was enough to pull these final wagons out of the river.

Moving baggage, wagons, and livestock to the north shore was not the only activity that Saturday. Early in the afternoon, Becky Stewart gave birth to a daughter. Abby took a loaf of bread over to the Stewart family, only to meet twenty other women bringing food. The ladies spent the next few hours helping Becky, washing the baby, and visiting. The pleasant afternoon passed quickly, with the difficulties of trail life momentarily left behind.

The Cow Column, Waldo's Straggler Column, and Chiles's California Column were going through the same consternations of determining the best way to cross the South Platte. The Cow Column had camped eight miles below the Light Column as a courtesy to prevent their herds from disrupting Sleepy Grove. Waldo's and Chiles's columns were also nearby, just below the Light Column. This afternoon Jesse Applegate rode up to converse with Colonel Martin on the logistics of crossing. Marcus Whitman, who had been traveling with the Cow Column over the past few days, also came along to check on Mrs. Stewart. With him was his thirteen-year-old nephew, John Burch McClane.

After dinner as Abby started cleaning up, a sentinel's gun went off, accidentally wounding a mule. Jacob, Gantt, Martin, and the platoon leaders came running up just in time to see the mule's owner dispatch the crippled animal. Since it was an accident, there would be no retribution. Jacob wanted to voice his concern about farmers and loaded guns; however, he knew it would be of no use. He returned to Abby's kitchen without saying a word.

On Sunday a strong, cold wind kicked up from the southwest. Since this would be another day of waiting, Abby saw no need to venture out into the cold wind at an early hour. Seven o'clock would be soon enough for breakfast.

The crossing continued all day, with both wagon boats and bullboats ferrying equipage to the north shore. The men swimming with ropes often had to hold the ropes in their mouths, which resulted in swallowing a fair amount of bad water. This caused an emigrant named Pierson Reading and several other men to become violently ill before the day's end with chills followed by high fevers. Dr. Long, who was part of the Light Column, wisely confined the men to their beds until the fever dropped.

Early in the afternoon two men, John Umnicker and Rich Goodman, returned from a buffalo hunt. While approaching a herd, John's gun accidentally discharged, striking Rich in the arm. They had been crawling up a ridge to get a clear shot at a herd on the other side when the accident occurred. John had already cocked his rifle in anticipation when it snagged on some brush and went off. The small herd quickly disappeared while John tended to Rich's arm amongst a profusion of apologies. It was only a flesh wound, with no broken bones. When they returned to camp, Dr. Long stopped the bleeding and organized a sling. Rich would be of little use for the next month, a situation that frustrated him greatly. He was always one of the first to volunteer for work, so becoming an invalid would be difficult, even if it was only temporary.

After dinner that evening, Abby and Sam helped Jacob recaulk her wagon's tailgate and foregate. Her turn to cross would come sometime the following morning.

As they finished with the last seam, Jim Nesmith rode in with news that he had discovered a place where teamsters could easily cross the river with empty wagons. It appeared to be shallow, which would be an improvement over the current crossing. If wagons could keep their wheels on the bottom, the last wagons in the chain would not drift downriver. As a test, Colonel Martin agreed to allow a small group of wagons to cross there in the morning. If everything went well, the remaining wagons would also cross there.

On Monday morning, July 3, Abby drove her wagon down to the river staging area to have its contents loaded into bullboats for the crossing. In the meantime, Jim Nesmith guided eleven empty wagons upstream to the new crossing that he'd found the day before. Instead of chaining wagons together, the teamsters merely started driving their wagons across as if they were crossing a shallow creek. About halfway over, the hard sandy bottom gave way to mud and each wagon quickly sunk in, sticking fast. The oxen began to flounder, so drivers hurriedly unchained them, allowing them to swim for the far shore. The stranded train of wagons presented a lonely sight, with eleven empty vehicles stuck fast in the mud, out in the middle of the South Platte without an ox in sight. Eleven frustrated teamsters released some energy in the form of verbal abuse toward Nesmith. His hope of an easy crossing had turned into a potential disaster. Men on the south shore could see their distress, and soon twenty-five additional bodies were wading out into the river to help. Other men gathered the oxen on the north shore and triple-teamed them, with towropes leading out to the wagons. With two men on each wheel, and four towropes leading to two triple teams of oxen, they slowly extricated each wagon from the riverbed. By evening the eleven wagons were safely up on the north shore. It had taken all day and almost fifty men.

Around noon Joe Chiles's California Column and Dan Waldo's Straggler Column moved up from their encampments to cross with the Light Column. Leaders of the Cow Column had decided to cross in the same manner as the Light Column and requested use of the bullboats as soon as the Light Column was across. To avoid any further delay, both Joe Chiles and Dan Waldo thought it best to cross with the Light Column rather than to wait for the Cow Column and compete for the availability of bullboats.

As soon as Abby's wagon was empty, she drove it upstream to where George Brooks was supervising the chaining and crossing of empty wagons. George, one of the migrations newlyweds, always volunteered his services when the company needed help. Like other young couples, he and his bride wanted their share of the adventure and fortune offered by Oregon. Sam stayed with her baggage to make sure it got across safely while Jacob went with her to help with the wagon. This crossing area was shallower and considerably wider than where the boats were operating.

Abby took her place in line, then Jacob chained the lead yoke to the wagon directly ahead. While the train formed, men raised each wagon bed six to eight inches by placing wooden blocks between the running gear and the bed. As soon as ten wagons were ready, they ventured out into the river with thirty to forty men swimming ahead with a towrope attached to the lead wagon. Abby sat in the front of her wagon, urging her oxen on as best she could with a piece of rope attached to her quirt. Horse- and mule-drawn wagons led the train, with ox-drawn wagons in the rear. She counted her position as seventh in line—a dangerous position, but not as bad as the last two wagons. Water came up the side of each wagon bed, leaving very little freeboard. Forty-five minutes later the whole party landed on the north shore, over two miles downstream from where they had entered the river. During the crossing, Jacob and the other men rode alongside the column urging oxen, horses, and mules as they floundered for solid footing.

The wagons at the end of the long line drifted downstream first, with men and teamsters trying to compensate by angling the teams against the current. The last wagon in the chain, belonging to John McHaley, broke loose and rolled over in mid-stream, panicking the oxen and almost drowning John and his wife, Sarah. Since the wagon was empty, they did not lose anything. It took twelve men and another hour to get the wagon to the north shore. Once up on shore, McHaley regained his composure and drove his outfit up to high ground, where Abby and the other wagons were waiting. He did not waste any time in announcing that he was the one who had suggested the company bring along two boats for crossing major rivers, and that the whole company could have crossed the South Platte in a single day. People knew now that he was right, but did not respond. There were other pressing demands, such as opening tailgates to let the wagon beds drain and dry. The interior of the Western Passage had remained dry, so Abby headed her team over to the boat landing to claim her baggage. With Jacob's help and a good caulking job, she was again ahead of the other teamsters.

John McHaley normally traveled with the Cow Column, since the size of his herd was second only to Jesse Applegate's. When their column was unable to find a suitable crossing, the danger of this river prompted him to rejoin the Light Column with his wagon only, leaving his herd and drovers with the Cow Column. His gamble that crossing with the more experienced Light Column would be inherently safer proved wrong—but then, at his age, this entire journey to Oregon was a gamble. After claiming his baggage and securing his wagon and oxen, John sat back to await the rest of the Cow Column.

That evening two men from the Cow Column came up to claim the bullboats as soon as the Light Column was across. Colonel Martin estimated that Chiles's California and Waldo's Straggler Columns would take another three days to complete the crossing. In the meantime, Jesse and his lieutenants could move both their wagons and herd to the north shore. When the boats became available, they would only have baggage left to ferry across.

The men also informed Colonel Martin and Captain Gantt that one of their drovers, Bennett O'Neil, had gone out hunting three days previous and never returned. Jesse sent out a search party that returned the next day without success. After that, all hunting parties from the Cow Column were told to be on the lookout for Ben. Gantt and Martin said they would inform their hunting parties to also watch for the man, or any sign of his demise. There was really nothing more they could do. If O'Neil couldn't find his way back, he might very well be dead. Although it was fairly easy to get lost in a sea of grass, all he had to do was travel north and he would eventually encounter the South Platte. Sadly, Ben O'Neil was an Eastern farmer, not an adventurer—and when panic sets in, even the simplest logic can be difficult.

As the two men were about to return to the Cow Column, Mr. Kerritook rode in with a severely lacerated and burned face. While shooting at an antelope, his rifle had burst at the breech, causing the injury and almost blinding him in one eye. He was able to stop the bleeding and return to camp by using his shirt as a bandage. Now he needed additional medical attention. Nat Sitton, a young single man, helped him down from his horse and tended to his wound. Reverend Whitman was down with the Cow Column and Dr. Long was already on the north shore, so Nat bandaged the wound and tried to make Mr. Kerritook as comfortable as possible.

The weather today remained clear and cool. By late afternoon most of the Light Column's baggage was on the north shore; however, a number of wagons were still on the south shore. Men planned to chain and move these wagons across in the morning.

Tuesday was the Glorious Fourth, the most important holiday of the year. Abby started the day by baking wheat bread, cornbread, and a pumpkin pie. Other ladies were also busy cooking, for tonight they would certainly be celebrating. Their families and friends back home would be enjoying mint juleps, soda, ice cream, cognac, porter ale, sherry wine, parades, dances, and flag waving. Although people in the Oregon migration consigned themselves to drinking cold water and swimming wagons and stock across the South Platte, there would still be food, dancing, and celebrations at the Sleepy Grove encampment, now situated on the north side of the South Platte. It would be a time for people to reminisce about the celebrations going on back in the United States—and also to rejoice in their journey to Oregon.

Sam was not a man to make the same mistake twice. Tonight he made sure his name was on Abby's dance card—only once, though, but at least it was there. Other men had Abby's card filled before the fiddlers began. Jim Wair provided his own entertainment by using the tailgate of his wagon as a dance floor, tapping out a lively step in tune to the fiddlers and applause from everyone.

The north shore Sleepy Grove camp was anything but sleepy that evening. Men lined up to get their dance with Abby as both embarrassed and irritated wives watched their husbands make fools of themselves. The dancing, eating, and imbibing of medicinal spirits continued until exhaustion took over and folks slowly returned to their wagons.

The next morning people were sluggish to get up and begin the day's chores. The weather turned warm and sultry, so teamsters rolled the canvas up on both sides of their wagons. Some wagons were still crossing, but by now all of the Light Column's baggage was on the north shore and claimed by its respective owners.

During their stay at Sleepy Grove, a number of men placed wagon wheels with loose spokes in the river, weighing them down with stones. These wheels, made from poorly cured wood, presented a problem the owner would regret all the way to Oregon. Cured wheel spokes did not shrink, and remained tight in the wheel. Poorly cured spokes became loose as the wood shrunk, a problem that could be remedied by keeping the spokes moist. Beyond Fort Laramie the dry air would raise havoc with any wood not properly cured—and they were still at least a week away from the fort. By soaking the wheels in water, they could keep the spokes moist, thereby delaying their shrinking.

Today was Ben Wood's birthday. Ben was a 26-year-old laborer, going to Oregon to claim his share of the wealth. He had no desire to be a farmer; he was looking to start a business to supply the needs of the many new Wallamet Valley settlements and farms. He was in Abby's platoon and had become a good friend over the last several weeks. During the dinner hour she surprised him with fresh cornbread and best wishes for "many more." They sat and talked awhile, but soon Sam showed up with news of Joe Chiles telling stories over in Gantt's platoon. Such entertainment was rare and would provide a pleasant diversion, so Sam, Abby, Jacob, and Ben went over to hear the tales.

When they arrived, Joe sat near the campfire with no less than twenty-five people gathered around to hear about his 1841 trip to California. In that year he traveled with a handful of emigrants in a group that called themselves the "Western Emigration Company." The group also consisted of several missionaries in need of protection and a guide. All total, they had fourteen wagons and fewer than sixty people. When they got to Fort Hall, nobody knew the route to California, so they split up. Their guide, an old mountain man, had never been west of Fort Hall and was of little value beyond that point. They decided to abandon their wagons at the fort and continue the journey using pack animals. Some went west to Oregon with a fur trapping brigade associated with the Hudson Bay Company. The few that went to California, including Chiles, barely got through. They ran out of food and water crossing the desert, avoiding certain death with the help of Paiute Indians. It was a harrowing tale of starvation and courage, but they finally got through without any loss of life.

Abby and Sam sat mesmerized by Chiles's detailed description of his exploits and the country that lay ahead. Holding hands in the warmth and flicker of the campfire provided a restful way to end their long stay at Sleepy Grove. Jacob sat nearby quietly smoking his pipe, no doubt thinking of his own experiences traveling to California.

Not everyone embraced a peaceful evening. The last wagons had crossed today, and those men who missed last night's celebration of the Glorious Fourth had plans of their own. They organized an all-male dance down next to the river on a sandy beach. They had two fiddlers, but that was the only resemblance to any dance. The men wrestled, kicked sand, imbibed, and cheered the Glorious Fourth until the wee hours of the morning. They knew their celebration would be rough, so they had intentionally left the women out. It had been a long, hard crossing, and they needed time to savor the nation's birthday and the completion of the South Platte crossing in their own rowdy way. Tomorrow everyone would be back on the trail, so tonight they would celebrate.

While listening to Joe's stories, Abby and the others could hear Nesmith's group carousing down on the beach. At first she felt a little left out, but when she heard about their raucous celebration, she expressed relief to Sam that they had not invited her. The quiet evening with Sam and listening to Joe's wonderful stories had been enough for her. Abby excused herself to go and rest up for tomorrow, a travel day.

On Thursday morning, July 6, the Oregon Emigrating Company continued their journey to Oregon—but instead of traveling west, they were now traveling east, down the north shore of the South Platte. During their search for a safe crossing they had gone so far upriver that they now had to backtrack to pick up the trail.

Colonel Martin decided to make it a short day, traveling only seven miles before making camp. Chiles's California Column and Waldo's Straggler Column continued for an additional three miles. Unfortunately, the short day for the Light Column was due to discontent among a number of its members. During the day a total of eighteen wagons from the Light Column broke off to join either Chiles's California Column, Waldo's Straggler Column, or Jesse's Cow Column, which was now on the north side of the South Platte. The number of wagons in the Light Column—now less than fifty—would vary daily as people switched groups. People could see that the Cow Column was able to keep up, so there was no need to show loyalty to the Light Column. For Colonel Martin, forming wagon corrals became more of a freelance operation than a precise military drill. The migration still needed wagon corrals, so teamsters formed them with whomever they were near at the end of the day. On some evenings there would be four corrals, while on other evenings there would be only three. The situation presented a modified, but cooperative type of discipline for the independent emigrants.

Shortly after nooning, Jacob went out hunting, returning in three hours with his packhorse loaded with meat. As he rode up to the Light Column, Alex Zachary, nicknamed "Old Prairie Chicken," pulled out of line and headed over to Waldo's Straggler Column. Abby and a number of other emigrants quietly expressed relief and a feeling of good riddance. Old Prairie Chicken didn't like anyone or anything. His cackling voice, which earned him his nickname, grated on everyone's nerves, especially since he never failed to be cantankerous, no matter what the situation. People were glad to see him go.

About midafternoon Bill Wilson, who had been traveling with the Cow Column, chose to switch to the Light Column. Bill was taking his family to Oregon for the free land, but had always doubted the possibility of taking wagons across the Rocky Mountains. His wife, Polly, had convinced him to take a wagon, rather than pack animals. While traversing a side hill, his wagon tipped over when it hit a large rock. Bill's three-year-old son, who was riding in the wagon at the time, got pinned underneath a trunk and broke his right leg just above the knee. Friends easily righted the wagon, then sent a runner to fetch

Dr. Long. Within the hour Dr. Long had the boy's leg bandaged with a splint. For the next few weeks riding in a wagon that bounced hard on every stone would be a painful experience for the boy.

After dinner that evening, the Wilsons received a visit from Jacob. He carried two long poles cut from willows growing down near the South Platte. With a few pieces of rope, Jacob showed Bill how to organize a travois for transporting the injured boy. It was primitive, but considerably more comfortable than a wagon. In three or four weeks the boy would be back to normal. In the meantime, a travois was the only way to travel.

After dinner Dan Waldo came up from his Straggler's Column to discuss the trail ahead with Bill Martin and Captain Gantt. During his visit he expressed his frustration with the lack of preparedness on the part of Reverend Whitman. Apparently Whitman had left Independence with only a single ham. This could not possibly sustain him and his nephew until buffalo country, so Dan had been feeding the two from his own provisions. The reverend showed little regard for the supplies of others—the result of a lifestyle accustomed to "living off the collection plate."

A light rain that evening prompted Sam to return Abby to her wagon just before dusk. It was still too light for a kiss, so they quickly said their good-nights before Sam ran back to the Copenhavers' wagon for shelter. Everyone expected tomorrow to be a long hard day as they tried to make up for all the time lost while crossing the South Platte.

On Friday morning the columns headed north by northwest, crossing the divide between the South and North forks of the Platte River. This area, known as Ash Hollow, was broken, rocky, difficult terrain. Jacob spent the day helping Abby get the Western Passage down the steep trail to the North Fork of the Platte. He handled the brake while Abby managed the oxen. The wagon slid most of the way, and by the time they reached the North Platte the columns had traveled a total of twenty-five miles through some of the roughest country yet. It had been an exhausting day when wagon corrals finally formed along the south shore of the North Platte. Chiles's California Column and Waldo's Straggler Column camped about two miles upstream from the Light Column, while the Cow Column was slightly downstream.

As soon as the wagon corrals began to form, two wagons from Chiles's Column came back to join the Light Column, while one wagon from Waldo's Column split off to join Chiles's Column. Company organization was in a constant state of flux, with arguments continually erupting between the irritable, independent emigrants. And the stress of crossing Ash Hollow brought out the worst in people. Some complained of trail damage caused by teamsters using their brakes too liberally, while others bemoaned the constant flurry of dust from livestock and wagons negotiating the dry terrain. Conflict and bickering had become the rule, so most people took the column desertions in stride.

Once the wagon corrals formed, stock was put out to graze, and dinner was served, the columns finally settled down into a series of peaceful camps. Abby cooked another three pounds of buffalo, as she had done each night since encountering the herds. It was good food, and she enjoyed it better than beef—though a little more variety would have been welcome. After dinner she began to roast another pound of coffee beans before the cooking fire cooled off.

"Jacob, you ever see any prairie chickens when you're out hunting? I haven't had chicken since Hannah's, and I don't dare ask to buy a chicken from any of these farmers. I think chicken would be a pleasant change for our dinner fare." She continued shaking the frying pan full of coffee beans as she looked over at him. He was leaning up against a wagon wheel, smoking his pipe.

"No chickens, haven't seen any since crossing the Big Blue—too dry out here. We'll start running into prairie dogs soon if you want a change. You prepare much small game back in Ohio?"

"All the time. Caleb secured squirrels and rabbits from around the farm. From what I've heard those prairie dogs are probably like squirrel. I could make some sort of stew if you can bring in a few." She stopped shaking the pan, looked at the beans, and picked one out that appeared burned. She poured the rest into a bowl, then retrieved her grinder from the kitchen box.

"Stew it is. Two dogs should be enough." He paused to relight his pipe. "You notice how people are throwing out their bacon since crossing the South Platte?"

"I certainly have. If I hadn't had the presence of mind to consume that first, I'd be throwing out bacon too. Those people back in Independence gave me good advice."

"These other people heard that same advice, they simply chose not to listen." Jacob leaned back against the wagon wheel, holding his pipe in his lap and closing his eyes. It had been a long day.

Abby started grinding the beans just as Polly Wilson walked up carrying a fresh-baked apple pie. Her boy was doing much better after spending the day traveling in a travois, and Polly wanted to show her gratitude. She had made the pie from dried apples, and it was still warm from her Dutch oven. Sam showed up in time to claim a piece for himself and some friendly conversation before he and Abby went for their evening walk down by the river.

Tonight they ran into Bill Fowler and Becky Kelsey. Bill was a thirty-year-old bachelor traveling with his father, Henry Fowler. Becky was twenty-four years old and traveling West with her parents. Her father, Dave Kelsey, hoped to escape the current economic depression and start a new farm in the Wallamet Valley. Bill and Becky had met shortly after leaving Independence, an encounter not unlike Sam's and Abby's. This evening, as on many previous evenings, the paths of these four El Dorado lovers crossed. There was a brief exchange of smiles as the couples parted for a more private rendezvous.

The next morning Jacob brought the oxen in from watering, along with news that three men had failed to return from a hunting excursion the previous evening. Jim Nesmith and three others went out shortly after dawn to look for them.

"Maybe they'll find Mr. O'Neil. That poor man, he must be terribly frightened and hungry." Abby continued putting her kitchen away.

"Old Bennett's probably gone under. I don't know how he could get himself lost. All he had to do was travel north and he would have run into the South Platte. Probably got thrown from his horse—don't expect we'll ever see that child again."

"Gone under?"

"Dead."

"Jacob, you could at least be a little more hopeful. Jim and the others might find him. There's always hope."

"Maybe."

Jacob finished hitching the oxen and walked back to his horse while Abby retrieved her quirt and stood ready for the day's march to begin. Ten minutes later the order came down, and soon the long line of white-tops slowly lurched forward along the North Platte, this time heading west. It was the first movement in a westerly direction in over a week!

Today's march along the North Platte revealed a country that nobody except Jacob, Chiles, Gantt, Whitman, and a few others had ever seen. Prairie dog towns stretched for several acres, absent of all grass and covered with hundreds of barking dogs. Abby also watched jackrabbits stand up on their hind legs as the wagons slowly rolled by, not allowing anyone to get closer than fifty yards before taking flight. The grass was both thinner and shorter than a few weeks earlier, but still thick enough to keep the stock well fed. The air too was getting drier, creating havoc with wagon beds, wheels, running gear, tools, and trunks.

The road during the morning consisted of soft sand in which wheels occasionally sank up to the hubs. Jacob spent most of the morning walking alongside the Western Passage to help extricate the wheels before they sank in too far. By working together, he and Abby kept the wagon moving continuously until they were past the sandy stretch, just before midday.

Shortly after the column stopped for a nooner, Jim Nesmith and his search party rode in with the three lost hunters. The men had spent the night approximately seven miles south of the North Platte after a successful day of hunting. By the time they had finished butchering two buffalo, it was too dark to find their way back. They chose to camp on the open prairie rather than chance getting lost. Also, they had failed to find Ben O'Neil and concluded that he was probably dead.

The trail hardened out during the afternoon, so Jacob reestablished his position on his horse about thirty paces from the left side of the column. Abby kept busy nudging her lazy oxen forward as the afternoon sun warmed the trail in waves of heat bouncing up from the ground. About midafternoon the wagon directly in front of hers stopped. It belonged to George Brooks. He had chosen to ride rather than walk that day, and in the afternoon sun he had managed to fall asleep at the reins. George's wife was walking with some other ladies and did not notice their wagon, so Abby walked forward to see what was wrong. She returned with a smile after finding George fast asleep. With a snap of her quirt she turned the oxen and went around George's wagon. The wagons behind Abby followed her lead.

The afternoon presented several distant landmarks that looked like ancient castles in a foreign land. Abby's gaze wandered back and forth between these rock monuments and a small herd of buffalo lazily grazing on a hill, north of the river. Occasionally she interrupted her gaze with a quirt to the flank of her lead oxen, for they too wanted to spend the afternoon sleeping.

When wagon corrals formed that evening, they were eighteen miles closer to Oregon. Their immediate destination was Fort Laramie, where men could repair wagons and, hopefully, obtain a few supplies. Tonight Sam joined Abby before dinner. The scenery of the day had filled most of the emigrants with awe, and Sam wanted to walk out on the prairie for a closer look at the landscape.

"People are calling those two mountains Courthouse Rock and Jailhouse Rock. They look like castles to me, what do you think? You ever seen anything like that back in Ohio?" he asked Abby as she began to soak a fresh pot of beans for use over the next few days.

"Nothing like that. All our hills have trees, and we certainly don't have hills as big as these. Courthouse Rock and Jailhouse Rock? Who came up with those names?"

"Don't know, but they sure caught on—I guess we have to call them something. Let's walk out toward them tonight so we can get a better look."

"Will you stay for dinner, Sam? We're having prairie dog stew, and I need someone to help finish it in case it's no good." Abby smiled broadly, knowing that he would probably eat anything she put in front of him.

"If you make it, then I'm sure it'll be good." Sam shifted his weight, put his thumbs in his back pockets, and looked over at Jacob. Jacob was sitting on the ground cross-legged, leaning against a wagon wheel. He seldom spoke while Abby prepared dinner, and tonight was no different. Prairie dog stew was something new, even for a mountain man. He would reserve judgment until after dinner.

As usual, Abby's cooking was more than acceptable—prairie dog was not as tasty as buffalo, but a good change. After dinner she threw the dishes in a bucket of water and headed down to the river to wash some clothes. A walk with Sam would have to wait for the completion of a few more chores. In the meantime, Sam had some coffee and a smoke with Jacob.

Down at the river, Abby was not alone. The pleasant evening provided many women an opportunity to do their wash in the North Platte. Some families strung clotheslines between their wagons, while others simply draped their wash over their wagon's white-top. With the warm, dry, summer air, most clothes were dry by dusk. Abby completed her wash in an hour so she could walk with Sam. The dinner dishes could wait until morning, for she too wanted to see the strange rock structures.

Jacob walked out of camp with the couple, then headed downstream. Sam took Abby's hand and headed toward a rise on the prairie to get a better view of the rocks. Earlier in the evening Jacob had seen several wolves prowling around camp, and a wolf hide has many uses in the mountains—uses that other emigrants would learn about before reaching Oregon.

As soon as Sam got Abby out of earshot of other people, and in view of Courthouse Rock and Jailhouse Rock, he brought up the subject that was foremost on his mind.

"Abby, you ever think about getting married again?"

She smiled slightly and looked down at the ground. They were still walking and Sam couldn't see her face. Her expression was one of warm feelings—and relief that he had finally mustered the courage to bring up the subject.

"Sometimes—I mean, I'll get married again sometime, I just don't know when," she replied. "How about you, Sam. You ever think about getting married?" She looked at him without flinching, continuing to smile, but now looking directly into his eyes. The situation gave Sam a fair measure of uneasiness.

"Not until I met you, Abby." He pulled her close and started walking again. Now it was her turn. He had brought up the subject and put her on the spot to continue the conversation. It was a challenge she couldn't resist.

"That's sweet, Sam, although there's no need for you to ask me 'cause there's no church or preacher way out here. Or have you forgotten? We're hundreds of miles from civilization." She continued to smile.

"Oh, you think so—well, what about Reverend Whitman? He's a preacher, and I'll bet he's married all kinds of folks—and what about Captain Gantt? I hear captains at sea can do the marrying."

"Sam, you're really serious!"

"Yes, ma'am. I never thought I'd meet you, but there you were—with your own wagon and going to Oregon. Abby, I just think it's destiny. You and I are meant to be together. We could start our new lives together out there in Oregon—and it's only practical 'cause a woman needs a man and a man needs a woman, especially when pioneering a new country. Life is too hard alone, and I know we'd make a fine couple."

They continued walking toward the monuments, talking about future plans and the life they would have starting a Wallamet Valley farm. The image was inviting, but Abby was still cautious.

"I'll give you my answer tomorrow, I need time to think about it. I mean, it's a lot to consider." She hesitated for a few moments, contemplating her future and the life she would have in Oregon. She still wanted to become a schoolteacher, but she was also deeply in love. Oregon was a new land where anything was possible. *Why couldn't a woman be a schoolteacher and also have a family?*

"No, just wait—I've thought about it enough over the last few weeks. Yes, yes Sam, I'll marry you! But not until we get to Oregon where we can have a proper wedding."

In an instant, Sam was holding Abby in both arms, and then twirling her around in a circle.

"Sam, oh, you're crazy—someone might see us."

"Let 'em! It doesn't matter now 'cause you're mine. Mine forever! Just wait till everyone hears. There's gonna be a lot of jealous men, even the married ones. A proper wedding it'll be, as soon as we get to Oregon City—and then we'll build a home, and I'll have a farm, and I'll even let you teach school if that's what you want. Nothing's too good for you, Abby. Come on, I don't want to stop here. Let's keep walking and talk about the future."

It was an hour after dark when they finally returned to the wagon corral. A quick kiss, and Sam was off. As Abby walked over to her wagon she noticed a fresh animal hide draped over one of the wagon wheels. It was a wolf. She glanced over at Jacob who lay in his buffalo robe next to the fire.

"I'll hear about that in the morning," she thought, "and he'll hear about me." She crawled into the wagon and pulled out her diary. Tonight's news would fill several pages.

Sunday morning, July 9, woke with a beautiful blue sky and the promise of a good day's travel. Jacob was already watering the stock when Abby poked her head out of the wagon. When he returned he received an earful of her engagement. Before things were in order for the day's march, most everyone in the Light Column was aware of the new union. Abby received congratulations from every woman in her corral. Several mothers expressed concern that she might not become a schoolteacher, but she quickly relieved their fears by telling them that she still planned to teach.

While Abby cleaned up after breakfast and received the well-wishes of the women and older girls, Jacob doled out wolf flesh to those people with dogs. By the time the Light Column was ready to march, Abby had the wolf hide partially scraped, bundled, and stowed in the back of the wagon.

Jim Nesmith dropped by to offer his congratulations along with news that Isaac Williams had fallen asleep on guard duty during the night. "If you hadn't killed one of those prowling wolves last night we might have lost some stock," Jim said, addressing Jacob. "Just wanted to stop by and thank you."

"Isaac Williams? If I recall, he's heading for California."

"I took his rifle as punishment. We'll auction it later, so he can buy it back if he wants—have to set an example for the other guards."

"He might go over and join Chiles's column; then you'll be short another man."

"Not likely, all his kin are traveling with us. I have to get back now. We'll be starting soon." He looked over at Abby. "Congratulations again to you, Miss Abby—looks like we have another good day for travel." Jim tipped his hat, then turned his horse around and galloped upriver to where Colonel Martin and Captain Gantt were making final preparations for the day's march.

The road that day was hard and the terrain difficult, with numerous intersecting ravines slowing the caravan's advance. By midday they had only traveled seven miles. Colonel Martin halted for the nooner on a hill where everyone got their first view of Chimney Rock. At this point it was a considerable distance away and looked like a tiny upside-down funnel. Jacob enlightened Abby and a few other nearby emigrants with the story of how this rock monument got its name.

"It happened back in '34," Jacob began. "When Bill Sublette brought the annual supply train out to our summer Rendezvous, he left about a dozen men at the Laramie River to build a trading post. Prior to that, the nearest trading post was up on the upper Missouri. We needed a supply depot to service us trappers in the Rocky Mountains, so Sublette had his men build Fort Laramie. That rock you see up ahead made a good reference point for describing the location of the new fort, which is not too far beyond. By telling folks the fort was just west of 'Chimney Rock,' they couldn't miss it. Soon everyone knew where to go to trade their furs."

Jacob continued relating his knowledge of the surrounding area until Colonel Martin rode back down the long line of white-tops, rousing people from their noon rest.

The afternoon march was as slow as the morning's, yielding a daily total of only fifteen miles. Wagon corrals formed on the south bank of the North Platte where the stock had good grass and water. Firewood, as usual, was scarce, so chips remained the fuel of choice.

After dinner Sam showed up as Jacob was demonstrating the finer points of dressing a hide. Abby watched his techniques, then improved on them by scraping the hide in the same manner that she had observed Indian squaws using a month earlier. Before long she would have a beautiful wolf skin that, once dried, she could make into a warm jacket.

Sam sat on the ground next to her, watching her scrape the hide.

"Did you see those three wild horses today?"

"I did. First ones I've ever seen—but they couldn't compare to the sight of the hills around here. There must be every color in the world in those hills. Did you see that one north of the river when that cloud came over?"

"Looked like a sunset at midday."

"I have to come up with a good description for my diary—something that will make me remember my feelings at the time I saw it."

"I thought it was like a giant painting with light and colors bouncing off those hills in every direction. No man could ever paint a picture that good."

"Those cracks where the light glittered out made them look like white marble columns in a huge church."

"Church, that's a good description, with stained-glass windows."

"I'll use that for some of my diary entries—too bad it lasted for only a few minutes. Even the darkness of those clouds drifting by was part of the beauty. I almost had to wake up when the sun came out. It was a sight."

"Let me help you finish so we can walk a bit before dark. I want to keep talking—things are different now." Sam couldn't contain his feelings. Every second with Abby was special, especially holding hands while walking out across the wild and beautiful American Prairie.

Abby smiled back as she continued to scrape the hide. "Chiles and Waldo are ahead of us," she said. "We can walk in that direction. Now, let's see if Jacob thinks I have this hide clean enough to start drying." In a few minutes, Jacob was stowing the hide, and Abby and Sam were off for their evening walk.

On Monday, July 10, the Light Column moved sixteen miles closer to Chimney Rock and Oregon. When they finally made camp on the south bank of the North Platte, the rock monument was about nine miles away. There were other rock mounds nearby, but nothing like Chimney Rock.

Several hours of daylight still remained, so after dinner Abby, Sam, Jacob, Jim Nesmith, and a fellow named John Boardman rode over to look at the monument. Abby used one of Jacob's packhorses, riding astride as she had observed Kaw squaws doing back on the Kansas. This was the West now, and Eastern mores did not always apply.

When they arrived they were not alone. People from all four columns converged on the curiosity. Eight people, including Abby, decided to ascend the mound on which the chimney stood. Jacob estimated the mound to be about 200 feet high and the chimney to rise another 150 feet more, for a total of 350 feet above the surrounding plain. The shaft was about 20 feet in diameter at the base.

Sam tried to talk Abby out of climbing Chimney Rock, but it was no use.

"I've been looking at this rock for the last thirty miles," she told Sam, "and I didn't come all this way from Greene County to just look. I'm not going to miss anything on this journey—come on." She grabbed Sam's hand and started up the mound.

Once on top, they found a place to sit and view the surrounding countryside. Here they could see the winding North Platte River and the trail taken over the last few days. Several miles to the south, a small herd of buffalo grazed lazily in the evening sun. More rock hills lay north of the river—and the way west was vast, as if one could see for a hundred miles. Sadly, there was no sign of Fort Laramie. That would take a few more days of labor and another river crossing. Near the river on the south shore was a large bluff that extended up to the shoreline. Obviously, the caravan would have to turn south in the morning to avoid this obstacle.

They stayed as long as they could, returning to the wagon at dusk.

Tomorrow looked to be a long day of travel, so Sam gave Abby a quick kiss before returning to his own outfit over at the Copenhaver wagon.

The early morning weather on Tuesday was warm, suggesting that the afternoon would be blistering. Before starting out, Jacob helped Abby roll up the sides of her wagon sheets, a practice most teamsters used to keep their provisions and possessions from getting too hot. As they finished their morning preparations, Captain Gantt rode up to their corral and addressed the emigrants.

"We'll be turning south for three or four miles this morning. You might be happy to know that those bluffs are about the halfway point for crossing this prairie—and they're called Scott's Bluff for those of you keeping diaries."

There was no answer or even a show of enthusiasm from the gathered crowd. The difficulties of trail life had taken their toll, and the notion of being only halfway across the Great American Desert was hardly cause for celebration.

"The road should be good, so we'll make over fifteen miles."

Still no response.

"Chimney Rock will be in view for several more days, so those of you who want to go over there will have another chance tonight."

"I'd like to say something." It was Jacob. "After we get past this here Chimney Rock, you'll see that the prairie dries out and the grass turns to sagebrush. The wind gets dry, and wheels shrink even more. I suggest everyone check your spokes and tires every day—wedge them if you have to. When we get back to the North Platte you might want to soak some of your wheels in the river. We're still four or five days out from Fort Laramie, so keep track of your wheels. That's all I've got to say."

"Good advice," replied Gantt. "We'll roll in about fifteen minutes." He turned his horse and galloped back to the front of the column.

The caravan traveled south for three hours that morning, then turned west and continued on for another hour before their noon

Chimney Rock. Encountered on July 10, 1843.

stop. During the nooner Reverend Whitman came up from the Cow Column urging everyone to keep traveling for as long and as far as possible.

"Nothing but travel will get you through," he said. "Nothing that slows your advance is good. There'll be plenty more obstacles to cross or go around, so we can't delay a minute in areas where we have a good road. Only travel, travel, travel will get us through to Oregon. I know it's tough, especially in this hot summer sun—but that's better than the cold snows of Oregon. Let's make a short nooner of it and move on."

The Reverend rode between each of the four columns giving the same advice. As he moved along, he stopped to confer with each of the column leaders, now strung out over a ten-mile stretch. His efforts had an effect, for the company was back on the road after a shortened nooner.

As they continued their march, Jacob chose to walk with Abby for a distance, giving his horse a rest. The surrounding landscape had a Western appearance that boosted his spirits, an attitude he wanted to share.

"This here Scott's Bluff has been a landmark for ten or fifteen years. I don't know which one of these bluffs is Scott's Bluff, so they simply call the whole range that name."

"They're all so majestic," replied Abby. "They have a quiet, sublime beauty all their own. I've never seen anything like it."

"They're named after old Hiram Scott. He was with Bill Sublette's pack train back in '28 when they were coming back from the Rendezvous at Bear Lake. Somewhere around the Black Hills old Hiram got so sick they couldn't move him. Bill had two men stay back to either bury him or take him on to St. Louis when he got well enough to travel. After a few days he was able to ride, so they continued."

Jacob shook his head. "That didn't last long, though. Hiram took ill again and couldn't stay on a horse. They were on the North Platte by then, so they made a couple bullboats and started downriver. They were making good time until they hit some rough water west of here—ended up losing all their supplies, including their guns. For the next week they carried Hiram on their backs and subsisted on anything they could find. Made it all the way to these here bluffs. Now, Sublette said he would wait for a week or so at the bluffs, but he'd gone on by then. The two men decided they couldn't keep carrying Scott and survive themselves. Without guns they needed to catch up to Sublette—and they couldn't do that with old Hiram in tow, so they just left him."

"Left him!" Abby exclaimed.

Jacob shrugged. "They probably gave him a robe and what little food they had. Then they just left him—right here near these bluffs. The two caught up to Sublette and told him Scott was dead and that they had buried him. Well that was just fine until the following year when Bill and his men headed out for the next Rendezvous. They found Scott's bones scattered over a wide area—probably finished off by wolves. Ever since then we've called this here place Scott's Bluff."

"Were you with that pack train?"

"I was out at the Rendezvous in Pierre's Hole that summer of '29. That's where I heard the story."

They continued walking on in silence. Abby drank in the beauty around her and considered the poor man who gave his namesake to the bluffs.

Jacob, too, surveyed the vastness of the surrounding country, when he spied two horsemen riding near the bluffs. "That look like Nesmith to you?" he asked.

"Could be, looks like his horse."

Jacob mounted and, without a word, rode out to see what they were looking at.

He found Jim Nesmith and Pierson Reading, riding between the wagons and the bluffs to inspect the formations more closely.

As Jacob rode up, Jim pointed to one of the odd-shaped hills. "We're calling that one Betzar's Bluff, Jacob. Looks just like a building back in Cincinnati with that name. I suppose we'll be seeing a lot of country like this from now on."

"You will," replied Jacob. "But not until we get past Fort Laramie. The air dries out and so does the land."

"You think we'll be able to find enough grass for our animals?" asked Pierson.

"Maybe, if we can keep near water." Jacob surveyed the sky as he spoke. "Looks like the next few days will be good for travel: hard road, and no clouds in sight. Keep your eyes open for game." He turned and rode back to the caravan, leaving Jim and Pierson to continue their explorations.

At about four o'clock they rejoined the Light Column, carrying the carcass of a badger. They, too, were adopting some of the ways of mountain men, in that "meat's meat." Jim, who was traveling with the Otey brothers, Ed and Morris, tossed the badger into the back of their wagon. There would be time to skin and butcher it before dinner.

By late afternoon the company could see the Black Hills. These hills were due west, about a hundred miles distant. The good news was that Fort Laramie was on this side of the hills. This news trickled down the long line of wagons, boosting the spirits of everyone—especially those in need of a blacksmith and those who simply wanted to see a sign of civilization.

Captain Gantt stopped the column near a small creek issuing from a cold clear spring at the foot of Scott's Bluff, about four miles from the Platte River. It had been a twenty-mile day, and Chimney Rock had been in view all day. This, along with numerous other rocky features, provided infinite variety to a beautiful Western landscape.

These geological features gave the country a wild appearance, as did the change in vegetation from short-grass prairie to sagebrush. Jacob put it best. "We're in the West now Abby—notice how everything is different? Even the air is drier. It's good to be back."

The immensity of the land had not escaped her attention. However, there were chores to attend to.

"We'll have more buffalo tonight," she said, "and we need to fill one of those water barrels."

"I'll take care of that while you're fixing dinner." As Jacob pulled the barrel down from its perch on the outside of the wagon, Sam walked in. "Sam, I could use a hand with this barrel."

"Yes, sir," Sam replied. Looking over at Abby, he added, "John Baker found some turtle shells over near that bluff." He pointed to a nearby hill, where a ravine between two bluffs extended all the way back to the North Platte. "I'd like to see that, so after dinner maybe we ..."

"I'd like to see that too, Sam, and you can stay for dinner."

As soon as the dinner dishes were soaking in a bucket, the trio headed over to look at the shells. At a point where the hills approached the river, and about fifty feet above the high-water mark, were a number of semipetrified turtle shells. The shells were from one to two feet in diameter and partially embedded in the sand. Many remained unbroken. Abby and Sam dug one out to examine it. Even Jacob was intrigued with this rare find. Nowhere on the Platte, or anywhere on their journey, had they seen a turtle like this. Abby wanted to take one of the shells as a curio for her Oregon classroom. Unfortunately, the weight and fragile nature of the shell prevented such extravagance. The novelty would remain a notation in her diary. Another wonderful, magical, and mysterious encounter on her journey to El Dorado.

Wednesday, July 12, started with the usual predawn gunshot. People awoke and began their morning chores: women cooking breakfast, and men rounding up cattle and yoking the oxen. All appeared to be random and in a state of confusion, yet there was an underlying order. Everyone had specific chores to do within their families or traveling companions. These including dropping and packing tents, cleaning and storing all kitchen gear, preparing saddles and harnesses, and securing everything for another rough day of blazing a new road to Oregon. Hitching normally took thirty minutes unless the weather was bad. On rainy mornings the entire caravan ran about an hour late.

At eight o'clock the order to march came down the long procession of white-tops, already lined up and pointing west. They continued their journey along the south side of Scott's Bluff and into the foothills of the Laramie Mountains. They were now in Sioux and Cheyenne Country, so Captain Gantt informed everyone of the need to be more vigilant. Colonel Martin, against the wishes of Jacob and Captain Gantt, requested everyone keep their guns ready for use at all times.

Since striking the North Platte, the four columns were seldom out of sight of each other and buffalo. The abundance of game prompted wastefulness as hunters took only the hump and tongue, leaving the remaining carcass for wolves and other scavengers. Abby gave numerous accounts of buffalo in her diary, covering a description of the animal, how trappers butcher the carcass, how to skin and dress the hide, how to prepare various dishes with buffalo meat, and so forth. Late the evening before, she had made the following entry: *"A description of the vast herds of buffalo would be too romantic to sound true. It is a sight one must experience, and an experience one must feel. In a land that has such breathtaking beauty merely from its enormity, life itself is sustained by this magnificent animal."*

The company struck the North Platte west of Scott's Bluff after traveling sixteen miles from their previous night's camp. They set up their wagon corrals near the river where livestock could get good grass and water. This excellent camp was a welcome relief after a long, hot day in the July sun.

After people completed their evening meals, Colonel Martin auctioned the gun belonging to Isaac Williams. It brought twenty-five dollars, which went into the Oregon Emigrating Company's treasury. Isaac would have to finish his journey to California unarmed. What was even worse, the availability of good-quality guns in California was almost nonexistent. The incident taught the other night guards a lesson they would never forget.

Auction participants, more tired than usual this evening, chose to retire early. It had been a long, hard day, so Abby turned down Sam's company in exchange for some needed sleep. There would be many other nights they could spend together.

On Thursday the columns continued up the North Platte through sandy, undulating terrain. Wagons continually bogged down in the soft sand, making a trying day for teamsters and oxen. Jacob spent the entire day walking alongside the Western Passage, helping to free wheels before they sank in too deep. Abby worked hard also, guiding her oxen around rocks and over ground that appeared to be more stable.

Around midafternoon the Light Column passed the original site of Fort Laramie. The original fort, called Fort William, had burned to the ground several years earlier, leaving only charred timbers to mark the spot. The new, renamed fort was still ahead. As the last wagons passed the remains of Fort William, the advance guard came riding in with news of an Indian village about two miles ahead. The guard assumed they were Sioux, so everyone took immediate precautions for an attack. After a brief conference between the column's leaders, the company chose to turn north toward the river and camp on the riverbank, rather than approach any closer to the vicinity of the Indians.

As soon as wagon corrals formed and teamsters had their oxen watered and put out to graze, men readied their rifles and made other preparations for an attack. Jacob and Captain Gantt tried to allay the emigrants' fears by explaining that the Sioux were simply there for purposes of trading at the fort and presented no danger to the migration. With complete disregard for this advice, the frightened emigrants continued to prepare for an attack.

The Light Column had traveled about twelve miles during the day and was sure to reach Fort Laramie sometime tomorrow. Except for men readying their guns, it was a quiet evening in camp. Growing along the banks of the North Platte were several redcedars that contained enough dead wood to feed a number of campfires. The aroma of burning redcedar hung heavy in the air, and was a refreshing change from the smoke of chips.

Sam carried his rifle as he and Abby went out for their evening walk. Abby chose to take Jacob's advice and leave her Hawken wrapped in its blanket inside the Western Passage. Besides, how could she hold Sam's arm if she were carrying a rifle? They walked along the river until they found a good place to sit and watch the current slowly drift by. Bill Fowler and Becky Kelsey were doing the same just a few hundred feet downriver. The dry air contained few mosquitoes, creating a beautiful evening for lovers in a distant, romantic land to watch the red and orange clouds of a Western sunset.

"You think Bill and Becky will get married like us? I mean when we get to Oregon?" Abby pulled Sam's arm in closer as she whispered.

"Probably so, no reason not to. Everyone's got to have a wife, especially in a new country. Got to have a family too—a farm is just too much work for one man."

"One of the missionaries out there could marry us, and Bill and Becky too!"

"You mean together? I mean at the same time?" Sam sounded a little confused.

"Different weddings, Sam, of course—but we could all get together afterwards. I mean everyone from both ceremonies. We've already met hundreds of people in this company, and quite a few will want to celebrate both our weddings. We could have a dinner and dance afterwards where we can invite everyone."

Abby smiled as she started laying out her plans for the type of dinner and whom she wanted to invite. Obviously these thoughts had been occupying her mind during those long days on the trail. Now as the words flowed out, her ideas started to come together with logical precision. Sam patiently listened as she mapped his future wedding. He, too, was smiling, enjoying her enthusiasm.

"Whatever you want, Abby, is fine with me. You just tell me when and where, and I'll be there."

Abby tightened her grip on his arm after his little tease. "We can do what you want, too, Sam. You tell me what you want, and I'll make sure it's part of our wedding."

"If I think of something, I'll let you know. For now we better keep our plans a secret. Bill and Becky haven't announced their engagement yet, so we'd be a little premature."

"I never thought of that!" Abby paused, realizing her mistake. "I never, well, I just assumed that—they're so much in love that—Sam, you know what I mean. How could I be so foolish? What if I had said something before Bill proposed?"

"But you didn't, so no harm done. We have a long way to go before reaching Oregon, so there's all kinds of time."

"If there's time, how come you proposed to me after only a

month?" Abby smiled, waiting for Sam's uncomfortable and embarrassed answer.

"'Cause there were just too many men looking at you, Abby. You know how many single men there are on this migration? Nat Sitton, Tom Brown, and John Cox have all been eyeing you ever since we left Independence—and you see the way the men line up at a dance—even the married ones. I decided that I better not wait too long, else I'd lose you—and that's why I did it. Yup, that's it. I'd have proposed eventually anyway, the sooner the better—and you saying yes has given me new strength to overcome any of the hardships we meet along the trail. All I have to do is think about the great life I'll have in Oregon, and I feel that I can do just about anything."

That was enough talk. She slipped her arm around Sam, and he pulled her in close—a warm embrace, a kiss, and another embrace with Abby putting her head against his shoulder and neck. They watched the river flow by in the moonlight, lost in each other's thoughts and love.

The next morning, Friday, July 14, the Light Column arrived at the Laramie River crossing at around ten o'clock. Chiles's California Column, Waldo's Straggler Column, and Applegate's Cow Column had crossed the day before and were already making use of the fort's facilities.

The Laramie River, a tributary of the North Platte, presented a formidable obstacle for the Light Column. Yesterday its flow had been normal for this time of year. Overnight the water from distant rains had caused the small river to overflow its banks, converting a simple crossing into a daunting task. Men obtained two small boats, one from Fort Laramie and the other from Fort Platte. Free trappers owned this second fort, situated about one mile below Fort Laramie. Both forts were constructed from adobe, but Fort Platte was smaller in both size and importance.

As soon as the two boats arrived at the point of crossing, men lashed them together and covered them with a platform made of three overturned wagon beds. Loaded wagons were then wheeled up onto the platform, secured, and ferried across with ropes. Although it was slow and dangerous, everyone understood such crossing logistics and worked together to expedite the effort.

The ferrying operation continued for the remainder of the day and most of Saturday morning. Abby crossed on Friday afternoon. Drovers swam the oxen and other stock across and let them out to graze while the wagons slowly caught up, crossing one at a time. As Abby got her wagon across and unloaded from the ferry, Jacob stood waiting with three sets of yoked oxen. In a few minutes they had the wagon moving up the road toward the fort. About halfway there, a hailstorm passed by, scattering the column's loose stock for several miles. A mad scramble ensued as teamsters and drovers ran to catch a horse, mount, and ride after the frightened oxen, mules, horses, cattle, and milch cows. It took the rest of the afternoon, but by six o'clock all animals were back in camp and hobbled for the night.

Fort Laramie, belonging to the American Fur Company, was originally built by Bill Sublette as a wooden palisade from cottonwood logs. Its first location next to the North Platte had experienced spring flooding on several occasions, so after Fort William burned they located the new structure on higher ground, constructing it from adobe. Not only was adobe fireproof, but wood had become scare since the original fort's construction. Adobe was the only choice for a building material.

The fort had always been a private fur trading center, serving Indian tribes for hundreds of miles in every direction. It sat on a hill above the Laramie River with a commanding view of the surrounding country. The occupants, employees of the American Fur Company, were mostly French with Sioux wives. The outside walls were 6 feet thick and 15 feet in height, enclosing a square of 150 feet on a side. Smaller buildings of various shapes ringed the interior, with the white adobe perimeter making up their back walls. These buildings, constructed of the same adobe material, consisted of a trading house, work shops, warehouses, and dwellings for the residents. There was also a small corral for the livestock. The fort had two entrances opposite each other, in the center of two sides. One was a main entrance, and the other was a small private door. Above the main entrance rose a square tower with loopholes. Two bastions in opposite corners of the adobe perimeter provided for additional defense.

Crossing the Laramie River prevented the formation of wagon corrals Friday night. Consequently, Jacob chose an area of level ground where the wagons in their platoon could join up as soon as they crossed. They would probably be at the fort for several days, so he made sure to locate an area where the grass would last until their departure.

Joe Walker, bourgeois of past trapping brigades, happened to be at the fort. He and Jacob got reacquainted around Captain Gantt's campfire that evening. Jacob asked Walker about last winter's snowpack, the condition of the road ahead for wagons, and possible routes to the new Fort Bridger and beyond to California. Chiles joined the conversation at this point, and Walker informed him that the best route was to move west from Fort Hall for a day or so, then turn south to the Humboldt River. Joe had no particular plans for the future, so before the end of the evening, he agreed to join Chiles's California Column and act as a guide for the new route after Fort Hall. It was an amicable agreement between free trappers.

Abby and Sam spent their Friday evening with a little more activity than Jacob. The free trappers down at Fort Platte held a dance that evening, inviting all the women from all four columns. They knew the men would show up too, so there would be a rousing dance for all. The trappers were hospitable enough, sharing what little food they had for a small banquet table. By midnight the tired participants drifted back to their wagons. Most camps were on the west side of the Laramie River by now, while about ten wagons still had to cross in the morning.

Martin's Light Column finished crossing the Laramie shortly before noon on Saturday, July 15. While the last wagon was being unloaded, a small band of Cheyenne came riding in to trade. They had been at the fort and were preparing to return to their villages when the Light Column appeared. The opportunity of trading with these new emigrants was too tempting to pass up.

When the Indians rode over to the column's encampment, Captain Gantt and Colonel Martin were up at the fort, the platoon leaders were organizing their wagon corrals, and Jacob and the other men were off tending to the stock. Consequently, the company was temporarily without leadership. The Cheyenne chief's initial encounter was with one of the Smith boys. Jim Smith was a brash teenager with a penchant for trouble and little patience for Indians. Without waiting for his father or any of the leaders, he began to belittle the Cheyenne chief by calling him a coward and a filthy beggar.

The chief, without a command of English, failed to understand Jim's words, but did understand the boy's tone and gestures. After the boy spoke his piece, the chief, without replying, walked slowly away in a show of indignant repose to the boy's harassment. About this time Pete Burnett came up, saw what was happening, and took immediate action to prevent any trouble. He ran after the chief, calling for Jacob to come and act as an interpreter. Pete explained, through Jacob's signing, that this young man was a fool and without good upbringing. He stated that the migration leaders would severely punish the boy. The chief nodded his approval of the apology. He understood human nature and knew this was only the action of an immature boy.

Upon returning from the fort, Colonel Martin had the platoon leaders assemble the men of the Light Column. "Now men," he addressed the gathered crowd. "I know you have repairs to make and would like to have a few days to recruit your stock and let your womenfolk catch up on their chores ... I'm afraid that's not going to be possible. I've talked to the trappers here at the fort, and they have only enough supplies for their own people. They'll sell or trade the little extra they have, but that won't be much. You'll see a sign of what they've got outside the trading house."

He let that sink in, then continued. "Now the way I see it, every day we spend here at the fort is one more day closer to winter—and while we're here, we're consuming our own supplies. Most of you are already running low. I don't know of anyone who has any bacon left, so it doesn't make any sense for us to stay. Get your gear together, make whatever blacksmithing repairs you need, then be ready to go by tomorrow morning. I want to be on the trail by nine o'clock." There were a few rumblings from some of the men who needed to make repairs. "We'll go slow for those of you that will need to catch up 'cause I suspect you won't finish all the blacksmithing by morning. We'll stop for Sunday worship as usual, which should help. For the rest of you, be prepared to go first thing in the morning."

Colonel Martin paused briefly while a few more men joined the gathered crowd. He stepped up on a small barrel so people could see him better. "You can tell your womenfolk to buy whatever they can. Now, I know how some of you would like to stay here at the fort and rest for several days, maybe even a week. You could do needed sewing and washing, complete all your repairs, recruit your stock and tend to sore hooves—but that's simply not possible. We have to get across the Blue Mountains before the first snows. We've already delayed far too long in crossing the Kansas and South Platte. We should be another ten days closer to Oregon, and that's probably 150 miles. Instead, we're here at Fort Laramie consuming supplies that are irreplaceable."

He cleared his throat, and went on in a more hopeful tone. "Reverend Whitman says we'll encounter five more outposts before reaching the Wallamet Valley in Oregon, and a man named Walker here at the fort says his friend Jim Bridger has built a fort just beyond South Pass for resupplying emigrants. This being its first year, Walker doesn't know how organized Bridger's new fort will be. He should at least have a forge and some blacksmithing tools. That'll be our next stop. After that we have Fort Hall, Fort Boise, Fort Walla Walla, and the Waiilatpu and Wascopam Missions. The Hudson Bay Company runs all the forts, and the missions are Methodist. Now, I know most of you don't care much for the British—but they might sell us supplies, so we'll just keep our opinions about Oregon Country to ourselves. It won't hurt any of you to be a little gracious."

Colonel Martin paused again to gather his thoughts. "That being said, we have to move out tomorrow morning. So get your washing and baking done, and we'll keep the blacksmith shop going all night. First thing in the morning, we'll hitch up and be on our way. That way if we're consuming supplies, well, at least we'll be moving."

The colonel's comments did not dampen the spirits of the gathered crowd. They already knew the fort could not resupply all their needs, and his logic for moving out the next day reaffirmed conversations men had been having for the last week. Still, the fort represented civilization—the first vestige in over seven hundred miles. As wagon corrals formed that afternoon, people displayed a noticeable excitement after almost two months on the trail. Just going into the fort was an occasion. Women put on their best dresses even though they knew there would be nothing to buy. Men readied wheels, wagon tongues, and other equipment that required the attention of a forge and skilled labor. The fort's blacksmith could not possibly handle all the work supplied by the teamsters, but was accommodating enough to allow the migration to use his tools and forge. The blacksmiths traveling with the caravan, Lew Cooper, Sam Cozine, and Jacob Reed, soon made good use of the facilities. With only one forge and one anvil, the activity at the shop continued nonstop until Sunday morning. Jim Athey took advantage of the fort's carpenter shop to help men repair cracked wagon tongues and tighten the boards on wagon beds shaken loose from the trail. The fort was a scene of hurried activity that Saturday afternoon, as over four hundred adults and six hundred children vied for their place in this island of civilization.

Not all emigrants had left Independence as prepared as Abby. Most were in need of supplies, such as additional clothing and the replacement of food discarded along the trail. Everyone had heard the earlier warnings that the fort could not supply such a large migration. Now those warnings became reality. Outside the door of the main trading house hung a sign that pronounced the scarcity of supplies:

Coffee	$1.50 /pt
Brown sugar	$1.50 /pt
White beans	$1.00 /pound
Salt	$0.50 /pound
Flour, unbolted	$0.25 /pound
Powder	$1.50 /pound
Lead	75 cents /pound
Percussion caps	$1.50 /box
Calico	$1.00 /yard

Some women stood gawking at the high prices, while others asked why there weren't any beans or flour. The reply was simple. People from the other columns, who had arrived before the Light Column, had bought all the fort could afford to sell. Fort Laramie existed for exploiting the fur trade business and nothing more. Nobody ever imagined a caravan of over a thousand emigrants arriving from the east, much less being able to supply such a migration. The items listed constituted only those goods the fort had an excess of, or was equipped to sell during their normal trade negotiations, such as lead and powder. Women could mend clothes and make some other items with the calico. Unfortunately, the quality of the material was inferior. It was a disappointing shopping trip for the ladies of the Light Column. Most knew they might not get what they needed, so they stood brave against their disappointment. For others, the joy of this island of civilization could not offset the tears of disappointment. Soon they would be back on the trail with what meager supplies they had left.

As men continued to repair equipment, women returning from the fort busied themselves with domestic chores such as washing clothes and cleaning trail dirt from their wagons and worldly possessions. Time was precious, so visiting with friends would have to coincide with chores as the emigrant women crowded the shoreline with piles of dirty clothes.

Abby's outfit was in better shape than most. The few minor problems could be corrected easily. Jacob checked each wheel spoke, tightening two loose ones with shims. He also repaired several loose joints in the wagon bed with the tools and nails brought out from Independence. Several other people in the platoon requested to use the tools—requests that Abby cautiously obliged. New tools were nonexistent on the trail, and she did not want people damaging hers, such as breaking a hammer handle. Still, most teamsters with wagons to fix recognized the rudeness of asking for her help. They knew they should have prepared better while back in Independence. Everyone did their best, reinforcing wagon beds by pounding existing nails into new holes for tightness and returning all tools promptly.

Abby had a myriad of chores to do while the migration was at the fort. Repairs to her wagon took priority—a job accomplished by Jacob. Also on the list were baking, washing, and reorganizing her gear for the continuation of the journey. After Colonel Martin's speech, Abby knew she would never realize her plan to bake as much bread as possible, for time was precious. She grabbed some soap and a pile of dirty clothes, and headed down to the river.

Late Saturday afternoon a group of Sioux warriors, not associated with the visiting village, arrived at the fort for purposes of trading. They had recently been in a fight with the Pawnees on the forks of the Platte, and had a number of wounded warriors in their party. They claimed to have killed thirty-six Pawnees, with only six or seven escaping—a number which several free trappers believed. The Sioux were a fearsome tribe whom trappers everywhere respected. They traded several buffalo robes for calico, which they used for bandages, then rode downriver to encamp with their blood relatives. The sight of so many white emigrants alarmed them considerably, so their time at the fort was brief.

On Saturday evening, news that three families had decided not to endure the hardships of the trail anymore passed through the various encampments of the four columns. It was still unknown if wagons could get all the way through to Oregon, and the difficulty of moving wagons across an open prairie had taxed these emigrants to their limits. Ahead loomed the Rocky Mountains, and no wagon wheel had ever rolled beyond Fort Hall. It was entirely possible that this great experiment could end in disaster. After Fort Hall lay an unforgiving desert of broken, rocky terrain that would strain every wagon's running gear to the point of breaking. After that came the Blue Mountains, assuming they could get safely across the Snake River Plains. There was no road over the mountains, or even a trail, and the timber might be so thick that getting wagons through could prove impossible. There was a good chance that they could get stuck in the mountains at the onset of winter. Should that occur, starvation and death would be certain.

These three families no longer had the mettle or enthusiasm to make it through to Oregon. Unfortunately, it was too late to turn back to Independence. Having to recross the South Platte and Kansas Rivers alone, along with the supposed danger from Plains Indians, precluded any dreams of returning to the United States. Staying at the fort was the first option; however, the chief factor of the American Fur Company put an end to such plans. The fort only had enough provisions to get its own people through the next winter. Taking on a number of greenhorn farmers and their families was simply not possible. Another option needed to show itself.

That option came in the form of a small group of free trappers on their way to Taos. Taos was only four hundred miles away, considerably closer than the fifteen hundred miles left to Oregon. Moreover, according to the trappers, the road was passable with wagons. The trip would entail some hardships as they traveled south past the front range of the Rocky Mountains, but with a concerted effort, they could be in Taos in only five or six weeks. For some, this option was too good to ignore. As this news filtered through the columns, two more families decided to drop out of the Oregon Emigrating Company. The roll call of those turning south to Taos consisted of the families of Nicholas Biddle, Alex Francis, Frank Legear, John Loughborough, and Jackson Moore. For the present, they would stay at the fort, recruiting their stock. When the trappers left they would follow them south to Taos and the Spanish settlements. It would be a bittersweet parting from their friends of the last two months, but that would pass. If Taos proved unsuitable, they could hook up with traders and follow the Santa Fe trail back to Independence.

Jackson Moore summed it up as best he could. "At least we'll still be alive!"

Other people couldn't give him an argument; he might be right. Taking wagons to Oregon was an unknown venture that could end in disaster. The Taos-bound families had more discretion and less valor than the people who wanted to go on. It was a gamble either way, although less so for those choosing Taos.

Colonel Martin understood their concern about the road ahead and the safety of their families. He did not try to change their minds with more descriptions of Oregon Country. They had heard it all. As a parting gesture, he returned half of their fee for Captain Gantt's services.

Abby listened carefully to their arguments and could not fault their logic. Even so, at no time did it alter her plans. She was going through to Oregon no matter what. Caleb always knew that when she made up her mind to do something, it got done—and Oregon was no different. When the company left Fort Laramie heading west, she would be with them.

When Sam stopped by, Abby was talking with Cynthia Applegate and Malinda Waldo. They had become good friends back in Independence. Traveling in different columns stifled the normal exchange of news, so there was much to talk about. Fort Laramie provided a brief moment to catch up.

"We're already short of flour and have no bacon at all, since we had to feed Reverend Whitman and his nephew until we reached buffalo country. I don't see how we can make it all the way to Oregon."

"Some people might have more than they need," answered Cynthia to Malinda's despair. "Like you, Abby, you don't have any children, so you must have supplies."

"I'm pretty well fixed, Jacob saw to that when we were back at Independence—but if I start selling things, then I'll be short. I think if we all stay together and help each other, and not be so independent, we'll all get to Oregon before winter and in good health."

As the women continued to talk, with Sam quietly listening, Susan Moore, Jackson Moore's wife, came up to say good-bye.

"Since you'll be pulling out in the morning, we might not see each other again, so I wanted to say my farewells now. It was a wonderful adventure, and I'll always remember you ladies as some of my very best friends."

"I don't think I'd use the words 'wonderful adventure,'" said Malinda. "You might be right in going to Taos. It's taken all our energy to get this far—now we're running short of supplies, and our wagon wheels are falling apart."

"You people are going to get through. It's just that my husband and I don't feel we have the strength to go all the way to Oregon. I'm sure you understand—we never thought it would be this difficult."

"Don't you fret about it," Cynthia said sternly. "You're the smart one. By the time we get to Fort Bridger, you'll be in Taos—and Taos has stores, like Independence. Fort Bridger might not have anything, so don't you fret none. I think you're doing the right thing."

"I do too," added Malinda. "We ladies never wanted to go to Oregon to begin with. Well, not you, Abby, you're different. Us women with families don't belong out here. I'll just thank God if and when we get to Oregon safely."

Sam and Abby listened, with Sam adding his sympathies. "You know, Mrs. Moore, there's never been a wagon taken west from Fort Hall, and that's still over five hundred miles from the Wallamet Valley. At least that's what I've heard, so there's nothing wrong with going to Taos. You do what's in your heart. Our good wishes go with you."

"Thank you, Sam. I'm going to miss your wedding." She smiled at Abby. "I just know you two will be happy together in a new land."

She held Abby's hands while looking around at everyone, adding her good wishes for the future and a safe journey. Within a few minutes, they concluded their farewells and parted. Tomorrow might be the Sabbath, but it would be another long day on the trail, and there were still chores to finish today.

At nine o'clock sharp on Sunday morning, July 16, Colonel Martin gave the order, and the Light Column began to move slowly toward the northwest, away from Fort Laramie. The other three columns were also leaving that morning, so they would be together at least until the noon stop for food and worship. Most emigrants, including Abby, occasionally glanced back as the white adobe walls of Fort Laramie slowly disappeared in the distance. Civilization was again fading from view, with only the privations and dangers of the trail ahead. Scattered around the fort were teepees of several visiting tribes of the Sioux Nation, along with the five white-tops of the Taos-bound emigrants. It was wild, unique, and beautiful—a sight Abby would never forget.

Everyone making wheel repairs at the blacksmith shop finished before sunrise. With a full complement of wagons, Colonel Martin kept the normal pace of around two miles per hour. They traveled eight miles before stopping for worship and the usual nooner.

The afternoon was shorter, only four miles, as they passed through a hard sandstone area that had never seen the mark of a four-wheeled wagon. At three o'clock they came upon a gushing spring producing a constant volume of water from a limestone outcrop. The availability of fresh water, and the day being the Sabbath, was enough to persuade Colonel Martin to set up camp at an area just below the spring. Captain Gantt referred to the small stream issuing from the spring as Sand Creek. The wagons from Chiles's California Column were also camping at the spring.

Trappers called this area Red Buttes. Traders at the fort had made a crude description of the country to Colonel Martin and the platoon leaders; however, their description was only for practical travel concerns and failed to capture the beauty of the land. Soon after the wagon corrals formed, Abby pulled her diary out to describe the surrounding country.

"Since leaving Fort Laramie, we have entered a country that is not like anything we have seen before. There are red-rock buttes in every direction, and a hard, difficult road that wants to shake my poor wagon to pieces. The area is a beautifully unique country, but nothing that could support towns or farms. The air is drier here, and the grass is poorer, making feeding the stock more difficult. Jacob says that this type of land will become more prominent, so water and grass will be a problem from here on. We've stopped at an area called Sand Creek. There is ample forage and water here, but that will probably not be the case for future campsites."

Jesse's Cow Column was also taking advantage of this area, camping several miles ahead. With each column encamped within a mile of each other, plus the herds of grazing stock, the smell of a hundred campfires, and the magnificent scenery of the red buttes and setting sun, Sam and Abby would enjoy another spectacular backdrop for their evening rendezvous.

"It's good to be moving again," Abby sighed. "I could have used a few more days at the fort for baking and other chores—chores that I'll have to do on the trail now. The sooner we get to Oregon, though, the sooner we can start our lives together."

Sam, too, was looking forward to arriving in Oregon, now more than ever. The work he was doing for the Copenhavers was getting old, yet they provided meals for a day's work along with a small wage. The money would be valuable in a new country.

"How big of a claim do you think we should make? I hear most people are going to take 640 acres straightaway. That way they'll have land for their children. You think we should take that much? I sure can't farm that much, but it would be good to own."

"It's more than enough, more than my family owns back in Ohio, and they had enough to give Caleb and me a stake. I think 640 acres is just right."

"Probably not all the acreage will be tillable. We'll need land that's watered with a good stream running straight through the middle. That way our children can have productive farms right next to ours."

"Really, and how many children are we going to have?" Abby was smiling.

"I don't know, Abby, enough to help us out on the farm. You can't really set a number, they just happen." Abby was enjoying his embarrassment as he reached for the words. She wanted to continue with dreams of her own.

"If this is new land that's never been surveyed, how are we going to claim 640 acres? I mean, how do we measure that much—and if we can figure that out, how do we stake a claim? There's no government out there in Oregon, only missionaries and farmland."

"Haven't you heard the other men talking? They're going to set up a provisional government. That's what Pete Burnett, Fred Prigg, and John Long are talking about—Jim Nesmith too. I'll bet those men will play a big part in organizing a new territory for the United States."

"We don't know that yet, Sam. Oregon could become a British possession. With the fort they have, they probably think they own everything already. How do you feel about being a British citizen?"

"I've thought about that and I don't much care for it. Oregon will become part of the United States—you just wait and see. With the people in this migration, we'll probably double the size of the Oregon population, and everyone I've talked to wants Oregon to become part of our country. We might be heading away from the

United States for now, but we'll be back in the U.S. in a few years. You wait and see."

"I hope you're right, Sam." Abby paused for a moment and then added, "I want you to know that no matter what happens, no matter how big our farm is or what country we're living in, I still want to teach school."

Sam pulled her in a little closer. "I wouldn't have it any other way. If that's what you want, then it's yours. Why, most of these emigrants are depending on you to teach their children. I'll bet if it wasn't for you, a few more families might have gone to Taos. You've seen the way the women treat you. You represent a piece of civilization."

"Some of the men haven't been too happy about a woman traveling alone, except when we have a dance." Abby laughed aloud at her last comment while Sam again pulled her in for another hug. They sat down together as the sun lit up the prairie sky with hues of red and orange, intermixed with wisps of clouds. Another spectacular Western sunset played out as they lay back in the grass, secure in each other's arms.

On Monday, July 17, the emigrants encountered rougher country, with high hills on either side of the trail. Chiles's California Column chose to travel behind the Light Column today, while Jesse's Cow Column and Waldo's Straggler Column were one day ahead.

Colonel Martin halted his caravan for a nooner when they came upon Lindsay Applegate and his family. The rugged country was taking its toll on wagons, and Lindsay's was the most recent victim. Late in the afternoon of the day before, Lindsay's wagon had broken an axletree when the left front wheel hit a large rock. The load in his wagon shifted, and the weight was too much for the weakened running gear. The front axletree cracked lengthwise, disabling the wagon. Lindsay did not carry a spare, so his only option was to convert the wagon into a two-wheeled cart by moving the remaining axletree forward to approximately the center of the wagon box. He was still re-stowing his baggage when the Light Column came up. The Cow

Column was now about a half day ahead, and Lindsay expected to catch up to them late in the evening.

"Abby, over here!" Betsy Applegate called and waved as Abby brought her wagon to a halt for the nooner. She set the brake and walked over to Betsy.

"A cart—Betsy, I'm sorry." Abby surveyed the broken axletree and array of baggage. Farm implements, stacked in a separate pile, did not look as though they would continue the journey. "Are you leaving these items behind?" She pointed to a plow, seed drill, and some hand tools.

"Can't be helped. We have to reduce our load, so we're hoping we can buy garden tools and farm equipment from the British at Fort Vancouver. If you can carry these things, you're welcome to 'em. I know you and Sam will need farm equipment, like this plow. If you can carry it, it's yours."

"Betsy, that's very generous, but my wagon is already full. I hope to make it across South Pass without having to discard anything. I'm afraid this iron would be too much. Your offer is very kind though, thank you."

"I understand—I wanted to offer it to you first. If you can't take it, then maybe somebody else in your column. I'd sure hate to leave such good equipment out here on the prairie."

"We should be here for an hour. I'll pass the word and see if anyone is willing to take these implements. Why don't you, Lindsay, and your children join Jacob and me for something to eat? You'll have a long day if you want to catch the Cow Column, and you can't do that on an empty stomach."

"Thank you, Abby, that's very kind." Betsy turned back toward her wagon, now a cart, and called out to Lindsay and her children. Soon Abby was serving bread, dried buffalo hump, and the beans remaining from a batch she had started back at Fort Laramie. With the beautiful blue-sky day and red-rock Western landscape as a backdrop, they all sat on the ground conversing about the new challenges and hazards of driving a cart over the Rocky Mountains.

"You're better off with a cart," Jacob said between mouthfuls. "They're easier to control no matter what the terrain—and with a lighter load, you're more likely to get through without any trouble. The first wheeled vehicles out this far were carts. Sublette brought them out for a Rendezvous one summer—I forget which one, Pierre's Hole, maybe Horse Creek. Anyway, he got through without any trouble, and so will you."

"Thank you, Mr. Chalmers, that's good to hear," responded Betsy.

"We could use some good news," said Lindsay. "When that axle-tree broke, I didn't know what to do. I thought I might have to abandon everything and use what few pack animals we have. A few men helped me convert it into a cart last night. I hate to leave all these implements and tools, but I've no choice—got to reduce the weight. I figure farm implements are something that the Hudson Bay Company will have."

"Maybe," replied Jacob. "They have several hundred mouths to feed, so they probably have a number of farms."

Silence fell over the group as they finished Abby's meal. Betsy's children were soon back to playing their game of tag while Abby and Betsy cleaned up.

"Jacob, do you see that rock structure up ahead, south of the trail?" asked Abby. "You know what that is?"

Jacob scanned the horizon, letting his eyes fall on a mound of rock to the southwest. "That's a rock bridge, first saw that back in '29. It goes over a creek—quite a curiosity. If we're still in the vicinity this evening, we can ride over and take a look."

"A rock bridge! Did you hear that Betsy? That's something I have to see."

"Oh, Abby, you're so adventuresome—like no other woman I've ever met." She smiled at Abby's enthusiasm. "If anyone gets through to Oregon safely, it'll be you, Abby. That's for certain."

"Betsy, let's get rolling." Lindsay called back as he started his cart in motion.

"He's right," Betsy responded, "we have a long day ahead to catch the Cow Column. Now, Abby, I owe you a meal sometime—and thank you for being so kind when we needed a little help."

"You're most welcome. Maybe we'll camp near each other tonight."

THE ENDLESS PRAIRIE BEYOND FORT LARAMIE.

"Maybe." Betsy started running to catch up to Lindsay. The rest of the Light Column and Chiles's California Column were just finishing their nooner, so it would be another ten minutes before their wagons began to roll.

Jacob checked the hooves of one of the oxen while Abby lazily stood by, surveying the landscape.

"Jacob, you think we might break an axletree? I have the weight distributed evenly. What more can I do?"

"Be on the lookout for rocks, the kind that broke Lindsay's. We could break one, but not if we're careful."

"I heard a few people arguing again this noon—tempers are getting a little thin on this rocky road. I hope there aren't any more fights like the ones we had at the start. I don't think I could take much more of that."

"Their complaining has bothered me since we left Independence. I don't see how a bunch of greenhorn farmers ever thought they could migrate over two thousand miles and not have any trouble. That broken axletree of Lindsay's probably just made things worse. Now people are thinking that it might happen to them—and it might. There's no sense in getting angry at people you may need to depend on."

"I've noticed that the wheels on a lot of these wagons seem like they're about to fall apart. They'll need patch jobs before this journey ends. Did you see all those wheels soaking in Sand Creek last night? I just don't see how some of those wheels will ever make it all the way to Oregon."

"You did well in buying this wagon. Hasn't given us much trouble at all—and it won't. We've only had a few loose spokes, and I was able to shim those. The wheelwright used well-cured wood for those spokes."

Abby was silently grateful for spending a little more to get a good wagon. The experience of seeing Lindsay's wagon and all the problems other people were having served to convince her that she had made a wise choice.

"I wish Zachary hadn't rejoined our column. You hear the way he was cussing his wife earlier? I don't know what she did, if anything.

He needs to be horse-whipped for treating anyone like that. If I was her …"

"The whole column heard him," interrupted Abby, "but it's none of our business."

"Well it disgusts me. If I hadn't given my word to you, Abby, I'd have left this migration weeks ago. Listening to this constant complaining is worse than driving these wagons across the Rocky Mountains." Jacob paused for a moment, first shifting his weight, then looking directly at Abby.

"You should know that I'm proud to be associated with one of the few hardy souls in this migration. It's an honor to go to Oregon with you, Miss Meacham."

Without saying another word he mounted his horse and rode back to his usual position, leaving Abby speechless. A minute later the order to move out came down from Martin and the advance guard. With a crack of her quirt, the Western Passage lurched forward, continuing up the rocky road toward the Rocky Mountains.

When wagon corrals formed that evening, they had made sixteen miles—a good day for a rough road. That evening Jacob received fresh bread and an extra helping of dried buffalo tongue. Abby would not let his earlier compliment pass without a thank-you. When Sam stopped by there was extra for him too.

After dinner Abby stacked the dishes in a bucket of water, while Jacob and Sam brought in their horses and one of Jacob's pack animals for Abby. The rock bridge was only a few miles away, and it would make a good diversion from the difficulties of the trail. A number of other people were also riding over to the bridge to see this curiosity. Several even took their dinners. When Abby, Sam, and Jacob arrived, they walked over to join a group of people sitting on a high mound with a good view of the bridge.

Abby absorbed the surrounding sandstone country—the hills and vegetation, and the most curious spectacle of all, the rock bridge, which formed an arch over a small body of water. The structure was solid rock, about thirty feet high in the center and seventy-five feet

ROCK BRIDGE ENCOUNTERED ON JULY 17, 1843

wide, and almost barren on top, permitting several young men to climb it and cross the bridge. Beneath it, the small pond received water from an intermittent stream. Some cottonwood trees grew around the pool, lending a quiet, glade-like atmosphere to the surroundings. Unlike the prairie grass that had thinned out since leaving Fort Laramie, thick, luxurious grass lined the pond—more like the rich plains they'd seen before reaching buffalo country. This oasis presented a quiet respite from the dusty work of driving wagons.

"Abby!" Dave Lenox called and gestured for Abby and Sam to sit down next to him and his family. When they got closer, he slid over next to his wife, Louisa, to make more room.

"I hear you two are planning on getting married out in Oregon," said Dave. "Congratulations!"

"Thank you," replied Abby. "Louisa, I've been so busy I don't think we've talked in three weeks."

"Say, I wanted to find out what church denomination you two are," Dave cut in. "All they got out in Oregon to do the marrying are Methodist ministers. I've always been a Baptist myself, and I plan to start a church as soon as I get there. It would be an honor to have you and Sam as my first parishioners. If you don't get a cabin built next winter, then you could marry in my church. You'd be the first vows in a new church—what do you think of that?"

"My family's never had a denomination, so your offer sounds wonderful," Abby replied. "Sam, how do you feel about that? We can get married in a brand new church!"

"How soon can you get that church built?"

"Sam!" Abby gave him a playful shove. "Thank you for the offer, Dave. We'd be proud to be the first couple married in your new church."

"Do you know where in Oregon you'll settle?" asked Louisa.

"Not yet," answered Sam. "We'll go to Oregon City first and find out where most of the farms are locating. We need to have roads or rivers to get our products to market, and the people there will know where we can find the best land. We plan on staking out 640 acres with a good stream and a woodlot. Abby's going to teach, so we'll be building a schoolhouse nearby. I'm sure all the neighbors will help us do that—same with your church."

"We'll be giving considerable business to the sawmill at Fort Vancouver," added Louisa.

"Just look at this bridge." Abby's thoughts shifted away from Oregon as she stared at the rock bridge. "How could this have ever formed? It's just a solid piece of rock! I never heard of anything like this back in Ohio. Even all those tall tales of Oregon never spoke of this. Good thing, too, cause I never would have believed it!"

"I'm with you, Abby," replied Louisa. "I never believed half of what I heard about Oregon. Now that I'm starting to see things like this, maybe all I heard is really true."

At several places near the base of the rock lay a number of Indian artifacts. At first Jacob suspected the items to be offerings for strength in battle, since they consisted of various warring articles such as lances, arrows, and shields. After a few moments he changed his original assumption.

"No, not offerings for strength. These are tributes to fallen warriors. Hard to tell how many. The local tribes consider this place sacred, so we shouldn't disturb anything."

"How will they ever know that we've been here?" asked Dave Lenox. "A storm could scatter these heathen objects—looks like a lot of rubbish to me."

"They'll know," Jacob responded. "Desecrating these memorials would be like desecrating one of your cemeteries or churches. Don't imagine you'd be too happy about that. We'll leave everything just as we see it—which means I don't want to see anyone taking any souvenirs."

"Jacob's usually right about these things, Dave," Sam said as he pointed to one of the memorials with a blade of grass. "If that was something like a gravestone, I wouldn't want anyone messing with it."

"Louisa, call those kids back and make sure they leave everything there." Dave motioned toward a group of about six children. Louisa hurried over to the children.

"Jacob, you think those Indians really believe in those heathen religions?" Dave posed the question while watching Louisa round up their children.

"As much as you believe in your religion. I've never been religious myself, so I've learned to respect all religions, Indian or white. They all have their special ceremonies and beliefs, whether it's Indian tribal differences or your denominational differences. They all deserve respect. Just because we don't understand a particular religion doesn't mean its wrong—it's just different. If it's helpful to those that believe, and it doesn't do physical injury to anyone else, then it's a good thing."

He stopped short, knowing that he had said enough. Sam, Abby, and Dave sat in silence, contemplating his words. Dave knew they were words of wisdom, the product of intelligence and experience. They did not sound like words from an old trapper—yet they were. Only Abby sat admiring Jacob's resolve. After two months his words could not surprise her. She always delighted in hearing his philosophies.

About an hour before sunset, folks slowly began to head back toward their respective wagons. Tomorrow would be another long day on a hard, rocky, dusty trail.

On Tuesday, July 18, Chiles's California Column broke camp at seven o'clock and started rolling west. They had eaten the dust of the Light Column for two days, which were two days too many for Chiles. He wanted to get at least one day ahead, so they planned to travel without a nooner and possibly late into the evening. Several other men in Chiles's column wanted to get ahead of Applegate's Cow Column, so their wagons lurched forward with an air of urgency, leaving the Light Column amid their morning chores.

By ten o'clock Martin's Light Column had traveled only three miles when they came upon a steep hill of solid sandstone. The advance guard, in charge of determining the best route, had surveyed the area and found this hill to be the best choice. The three columns ahead of them had all used the same road, so everyone knew it was passable—but not without difficulty. The hooves of oxen and mules slipped continuously as they strained under their loads going up the hill.

It took the efforts of both Abby and Jacob to keep their animals in line and moving. Jacob, walking on the left side of the team, urged them on with shouts of "Hee-yaa! Yaa! Get up there! Yaa!"—along with slapping his hat against their rumps. Abby used her quirt on the right side of each yoke, vocalizing in her own way. "Come on Lashes, get up there! Loafer, not today you don't." The quirt came down on Loafer's rump. "Dinnertime, you're plenty fat to pull up this hill, now get!"

It was a short hill, yet provided sufficient trouble as teamsters urged their oxen and mules forward over the hard sandstone. By noon the column had moved well past the hill and seven miles closer to Oregon. In the distance they could see Chiles's California Column and ahead of them the Cow Column. They, too, had halted for a nooner. At least that's what Colonel Martin and the rest of the Light Column thought. Soon a rider came in giving the news. "Joel Hembree's boy's dying, probably be dead by morning." Wes Howell, a seventeen-year-old young man traveling to Oregon with his parents, dismounted and walked forward to meet those moving in to hear the news. "Some of you know Joel and Sally, so I thought you might want to attend the services. We'll bury him tomorrow."

"Is he sick? How do you know he'll die?" asked Sarah Jane Hill. Like many of the women of the migration, Sarah Jane was a farmer's wife, just twenty years old, following her husband's dreams for a better life in Oregon.

"Got run over by a wagon." Wes replied. "We were moving along without much trouble, and it looked to be a good day—wagons were single file with most people walking. Well, you know how these kids can't walk all the time, so Joel Jr. was standing on the tongue of his father's wagon, balancing with his hands on an ox's rump—done it a hundred times before." Heads nodded among the small group of emigrants. They had all seen children do this.

"The wagon jolted over a rock and little Joel fell off. He screamed and the oxen took off running. The front wheel ran over his right leg, then he squirmed around and the rear wheel ran over him again. We got the wagon stopped, but it was too late for little Joel. The wheels crushed his hips and he was unconscious, losing a lot of blood. We've made him comfortable; still, it's just a matter of time before he dies. I hate to say it ... but I hope he dies without regaining consciousness."

"Can Reverend Whitman or Doc Long do anything?" asked Liz Hewitt.

"What can they do?" Wes said. "We're just making the boy comfortable. If he comes around, we've got laudanum ready. Otherwise, we've halted until the boy dies and we can get him buried proper. Those of you that know Joel and Sally might want to pay your respects today or tomorrow."

"Was anyone else injured?" asked Maggie Enoch.

"Almost," answered Wes. "Joel's eight-year-old brother Isham fell off the tongue too. He was able to get out of the way."

"Come noon with us, Mr. Howell." Mary Keizur, an older, quiet woman with the concern of a grandmother, offered a midday meal to Wes. "I want to hear more about what you're doing for services."

"Thank you, ma'am, that's right kind of you."

The crowd quietly dispersed into their respective noontime social groups. They had known back in Independence that not everyone would make it to Oregon, however, it was a topic not discussed. Now they could no longer ignore the subject. People asked the boy's age. "Six" came the response. Heads shook slowly back and forth: "So young, so young."

The Light Column moved on and made another eight miles, for a day's total of fifteen. They passed the Cow Column, and camped nearby on a dry creek bed between the North Platte and a grove of cottonwoods. On the north shore of the river stood more high, rocky bluffs. It was a somber evening as people rode over to the Cow Column to pay their respects and see the boy. Sam talked to Joel Sr., while Abby joined a group of women who were making a headboard. The board was part of a side slat from the Hembrees' wagon. The boy's coffin would be a bureau drawer. The ladies had carved the boy's name, birth date, and death date (except for the day) into the headboard. They wanted to add a short verse, but could not think of anything appropriate because of the tragedy of the circumstance.

"I know one," Abby said. "It's short enough for your headboard, and it's the one I wrote for my baby." She put her hand on the headboard, pointing out where the words would fit.

A flower, budded on earth,
Now blooming in Heaven.

"I like it," replied Mary Ann Holmes. Her husband, Bill Holmes, had been induced to travel to Oregon by Pete Burnett. The economic depression, and Pete's encouragement, had been enough for Bill and Mary Ann to change the direction of their lives and cast their lot with the Oregon migration. "What do you other ladies think?"

"It's perfect," said Jane Linebarger, an older woman with graying hair. "It's sweet and touching. Sally will like it too. Is that acceptable with everyone?"

There was an immediate agreement, and in another hour the headboard was complete, minus the death date.

Sam and Abby returned to their encampment to find Jacob quietly sitting next to the fire smoking his pipe. Cottonwood logs made a refreshing change from chips, with the sweet smell of burning wood filling the corral and surrounding area. They both sat down on the ground near the fire, cross-legged like Jacob. Rather than converse, they took comfort in the mesmerizing flicker of the flames—each sitting in quiet reflection, knowing that the Oregon Emigrating Company would soon have its numbers reduced by one young boy. Shortly after dusk, Sam said his good-nights and slowly walked back to his outfit at the Copenhavers' wagon. Abby wrote a few paragraphs in her diary, along with Joel's verse, then retired.

The next morning, Wednesday, Joel was still alive. He remained unconscious and now his breathing had become erratic—it would not be long. Colonel Martin wanted to get underway by ten o'clock, so people from the Light Column paid their final respects to Joel and Sally, then hitched up their teams in preparation for the day's march.

Poor Sally Hembree had been beside herself since the accident. Other women tried to comfort her, but only time could heal this wound. Abby went to see her early in the morning, but she was not able to speak. There was nothing that anyone could say to alleviate her pain. She looked at Abby through teary eyes as Abby mentioned her own loss of a daughter the year before. In parting, Abby recited the verse.

"We ladies wanted something so that Joel would not be forgotten and would be known to future emigrants traveling to Oregon." Sally nodded in appreciation. "My column will be leaving this morning, but I'm sure we'll talk again soon." She let go of Sally's hands, backed away, then turned to walk back to the Light Column.

Joel died at two o'clock in the afternoon. It was too late in the day to make any distance, so Jesse chose to stay in camp one more night. The funeral would take place in the morning. Gravediggers began their sad task on the left side of the trail next to Squaw Butte Creek. The spot had a sweeping view of the surrounding prairie and red rock buttes. After services, they planned to cover the grave with a large pile of stones to prevent wolves from digging up the corpse.

The Light Column continued their journey through the Black Hills, with red rock bluffs in every direction and a red, rocky road for the wagons to negotiate. It was a scorching hot day, so almost everyone walked on the north side of the column, in the shade of their wagons.

While stopped for the nooner, a man named Tom Naylor allowed his lead yoke of oxen to drink from a small puddle of alkali water. Tom thought they would stop drinking as soon as they tasted the water; unfortunately, they were too thirsty. By the time he pulled them away they had both drunk enough to cause a serious problem. He moved his wagon and team away from the water, then staked them down until the end of the nooner.

Abby and Jacob did not need the full hour for a noon stop, so they always made sure each of their animals had a drink of water, even if it was only a gallon. Each evening when they were near fresh water, Jacob refilled the twenty-gallon barrels to capacity. With his three horses, Abby's milch cow, and eight oxen, forty gallons of water would only last two days, three at the most. Since leaving Independence Jacob had always taken special precautions to make sure the stock had adequate water and feed. Now, in the Black Hills area west of Fort Laramie, that diligence was paying off. Although the oxen were showing wear, they were all still healthy.

At three in the afternoon the Light Column crossed a small creek that Captain Gantt referred to as Deer Creek. They continued a few more miles and camped on Big Rock Creek, twenty miles from last night's camp. The stream contained fresh water and flowed north into the North Platte.

Tom Naylor's lead oxen began showing signs of the scours that afternoon and were considerably weakened. He unhitched them before crossing Deer Creek and tied them to the back of his wagon. Later that evening they lay down and could not get up. Jacob and Captain Gantt came over to look at the animals, a sight they had seen all too often in the past.

"They'll be dead by morning—there's nothing we can do." Gantt was blunt as usual.

"I suggest you butcher them out and dry whatever meat you can salvage," added Jacob. "Wolves will finish off the rest. No sense in wasting all this meat." Jacob, too, was painfully blunt.

Tom knew they were right. Without speaking he nodded his recognition of the bloody task ahead, then walked back to his wagon to retrieve a gun and butcher knife. Henry Hunt offered to butcher one of the animals, and to help Sarah slice the meat and tie it over their white-top for drying. Lavinia Brown also offered Sarah help in cutting and drying the meat. It was good to have friends.

That evening shortly after dark, some young men, in a show of youthful foolishness, started firing their guns near one of the corrals. Nobody knew if they were simply trying to frighten people or were challenging each other to a shooting match in the dark. Their actions did not impress Captain Gantt and Colonel Martin. The gunshots caused an alarm and an unnecessary panic among the column's platoons. Colonel Martin immediately confiscated the guns and placed the boys under house arrest. They protested loudly, calling for their parents to intervene and retrieve their guns. Wiser heads prevailed, and soon the conflict was over. Parents took the guns and boys back to their respective wagons.

The Cow Column buried Joel Hembree Jr. on Thursday morning, July 20, after a simple graveside ceremony. In attendance were Joel Sr.'s two brothers, Absolom and Andy, and his sister, Sarah Pennington. The numerous Hembree clan, along with many of the adults from the Cow Column, made up the funeral assemblage. Reverend Whitman read a short verse, then said a few words of kindness to comfort Joel and Sally.

"Little Joel has gone to a better life," Whitman said as he looked out to the gathered crowd. "We all undertook this journey with courage and fortitude, but knew that not everyone would make it. We wanted Little Joel to stay with us and enjoy the bounty of Oregon, but the Lord had different plans. The young and innocent will always journey to that Eden we call Heaven." After a few more well-worn cliches, Orus Brown stepped forward to add his thoughts.

"Little Joel is already in Oregon," Orus addressed his remarks directly to Sally and Joel. "In a few months we'll all be enjoying that land of eternal beauty, and you'll be joined again with your little boy." Orus had left his family back in the United States, wanting to get established in Oregon before risking the lives of his wife and children. Little Joel's death demonstrated that he had done the right thing. He paused for a few seconds, then said, "Now let us all say a quiet prayer before getting back on the trail."

After a moment of silence they lowered the coffin and people walked slowly back to their wagons.

Before the gravediggers could finish filling the grave and erect the headboard, Jesse gave the order to march. Wranglers headed up the herds, and the long column of white-tops started moving west. Teamsters, women, and wranglers occasionally glanced back at the lonely grave of a little boy slowly disappearing in the distance. The men completing the grave would have to catch up. The Cow Column was now twenty miles behind the Light Column, and even farther behind Chiles's and Waldo's Columns. Everyone knew it would be a long day's march.

A morning for the Cow Column usually started at four o'clock with the discharge of rifles by the early morning guards. At this time of year the sun would not be up for another hour, yet there was sufficient work to do before the caravan could begin another day on the trail. The funeral of Joel Hembree slowed their usual morning chores by less than an hour. When people arose at four o'clock, men rekindled campfires and women prepared breakfast. The vast herds could stray up to two miles from camp, so rounding them up was no small chore. As wranglers approached the outer perimeter, they watched for any disturbance in the grass, indicating that some animals might have wandered even farther.

By five o'clock the herds began to take shape as wranglers tightened the perimeters, bringing the animals together and turning them in a westerly direction. Other men rode through the herd collecting working oxen and driving them back toward the wagons. This was a delicate task, since they did not want to spook the remaining animals, yet had to be firm enough to move those oxen not entirely satisfied with going back for yoking and another day of hard labor.

Plains Indians did not have much use for domestic cattle, so there was never any theft from the herds. Missing animals could always be found in some nearby ravine or around a hill. Indians knew that cattle meat was not as tasty as buffalo, and it was nearly impossible to enact a rapid retreat should they be discovered. When there was any stealing, Indians confined their acts exclusively to horses, pots, blankets, and other useful items. For many tribes, stealing constituted acceptable social mores for gaining wealth at the expense of an enemy. This could explain the disappearance of several items each week. The missing items could be the result of an occasional rogue Indian extracting a toll for crossing tribal lands. More than likely, though, the missing items were lost by careless emigrants. Small things such as cups or knives were inadvertently left behind during the rush to get ready each morning. Occasionally someone forgot an article of clothing that they previously draped over a bush to dry after washing. Such carelessness could account for almost all missing items; however, it was easier to blame the local Indians.

People in the Cow Column struck camp between the hours of six and seven. During this time everyone ate breakfast, boys packed tents and other equipment, women and girls cleaned and packed kitchen equipment, and the men yoked and chained working oxen to the wagon tongues. By seven o'clock all wagons were usually ready for the order to march. Those families lagging behind ate the dust of others, for the company could not delay simply for one or two families. To the casual observer the final few minutes before seven o'clock looked to be mass confusion, with each family appearing to be at a different point of readiness. As the hour approached there was a final mad rush to finish the morning chores and prepare for the march. Thursday morning presented a little more activity than usual, since the column had been in camp two nights. Some baggage needed to be repacked and, more importantly, people wanted to attend little Joel's funeral.

On most mornings, one of Jesse's lieutenants blew a trumpet to signal the order to march. Today would be different, for the end of funeral services marked the time to move out. Jesse, his pilot, Jim Cave, and several forward guards mounted their horses and took the lead. White-tops fell into place as the caravan slowly moved out, leaving little Joel's lonely grave and an area of trampled grass as the only reminder of their presence. Before long the column of wagons echoed with the sounds of wranglers and teamsters urging their beasts of burden westward. Women and children walked alongside the column, out far enough to escape the dust. It would be another day of exhausting travel, with thoughts of leaving a little boy's grave far behind and approaching the land of Oregon far ahead.

Shortly before noon on Thursday morning, the advance guard of the Light Column encountered five trappers returning from Black's Fork of the Green River. They had several pack animals loaded with furs belonging to a Mr. Vasques of the party. Two of the men were returning from Oregon and were carrying letters for three different families in the migration. These families had relatives who had journeyed to Oregon the year before.

Colonel Martin halted the column for an early nooner, so he could learn more about the road ahead and acquire the latest news from Oregon. Jacob, Pete Burnett, and Jim Nesmith joined Martin and the advance guard as they sat down with jerky, bread, pipes, and tobacco for an extended nooner.

The news from Oregon was not good. Both trappers talked about the deplorable condition of supplies and the incessant winter rains.

"If you like mud, you'll like Oregon," one trapper growled.

"The farmland's not all that productive," added the other. "It gets hot and dry in the summer, and you'll lose most of what you plant. In the spring the fields are just a sea of mud, not plowable until June."

Their talk of a lack of basic necessities such as clothing and tools might have served to discourage a number of people were it not for the letters they carried. The letters told a different story—a land of eternal green where cattle could graze all winter, and a land of immense agricultural potential. The letters encouraged their family members to come to Oregon if they had not already started. They boasted of a mild climate where only a light jacket could get a person through winter—and a country devoid of sickness. It was a repeat of the stories people had heard back in the United States, and it still sounded good. Confirmation of the Eden-like nature of Oregon from relatives already there was more than adequate to offset any bad news carried by the trappers. Their opinion was clearly in the minority, and as some people put it, "These men are trappers, not farmers. What could they know about our needs?"

Their poor description of Oregon Country was overshadowed by news that Oregon was about to become part of the United States.

"May second, that was the date," one trapper said. "I'll never forget it. We sent out word there would be a meeting on May first at Champooic on the Multnomah River, down there on the French Prairie. It was the next day before everyone finally showed up. Things had gotten pretty bad without any government and laws. When someone died there was no way to distribute the dead man's property. I never thought that could be a problem, but it is when the person owns a fair amount of livestock and land. So we got together there at Champooic to discuss what to do." The trapper filled his pipe with more tobacco before continuing.

"The first thing we had to figure out was what country we belonged to. Old Man McLoughlin controls most everything within eight hundred miles, and we knew that would be a problem. There were Hudson Bay people at that meeting and they wanted British rule, so the first vote ended up in a tie. Then old Joe Meek started in haranguing the boys about all the trouble the HBC trapping brigades gave us in the Rockies—always coming across the Divide to take our beaver and stir up the Blackfeet. It didn't take long before we had another vote, this time going toward the United States. I forget the final count—it was close. The American trappers won, so Oregon is now part of the United States." The men listening buzzed with surprise and satisfaction.

"That's how it happened," the other trapper nodded while packing down some pipe tobacco. "We're on our way East to let people know. Not sure if the United States will accept land that far away—surely not as a state, so maybe as a territory."

"Was Doc Newell there?" Jacob posed the question to the trappers.

"Sure was, old Doc was there."

"How 'bout Caleb Wilkins?"

"Caleb was there too," the first trapper replied. "Just about everyone was there."

Jacob addressed Captain Gantt. "John, you oughta come out to Oregon. There's nothing in California but a lot of greasers. Oregon's the new land."

"Maybe—there's land in California too. You remember what Jed Smith told us before he went and got himself killed. Maybe I'll go to Oregon next year—maybe you'll come to California."

"Maybe. For now it looks like I'm heading for the United States."

News about Oregon joining the United States left their noon circle and spread through the Light Column like a prairie fire. People broke out their brandy, previously packed for medicinal purposes only, and toasted the new land. It wasn't long before Sam came over to the Western Passage where Abby met him with a hug and a kiss.

"Sam, did you hear? Oregon is part of the United States. You were right! We're going to be living in the United States!"

"Now we can settle down just like we planned, and we'll have a local and territorial government along with the protection of the United States Government."

"I'll be teaching school in the United States." Abby was still hugging him with the grip of a brake shoe. "Isn't it wonderful? Come, join me for the nooner." She grabbed his arm with both hands, pulling him into her noon kitchen and setting him down on her overturned washtub.

Colonel Martin allowed the midday break to continue for over two hours to ascertain the condition of the road ahead and allow everyone a few moments of celebration. It was after two o'clock before the column began to move west, making a short day of only twelve miles.

For the animals, wagons, and emigrants, it was a tough twelve miles. The rocky road created more dust than usual, so wagons spread out wherever possible to avoid choking on dust from the wagon in front. Over most of the terrain, traveling in single file was the only choice. Jacob joined over thirty other men walking ahead of the lead wagons to roll the larger stones out of the way. There would be a visible road for later wagons. For now, no road existed. It was an exhausting day, so everyone was thankful for the long nooner and short afternoon.

Chiles's California Column, traveling with the Light Column today, did not care to stop so early. They continued toward the North Platte to look for a place to cross.

That evening's camp was dry, so Jacob watered the stock from Abby's barrels. The lack of water and firewood could not dampen many spirits after hearing the news from Oregon. Sam and Abby went for their usual walk away from the column for some private moments together, yet their conversation tonight was all about Oregon. If Oregon became a territory, then the next step would be statehood! It was too good to be true. They had dozens of questions, but few answers. Would they have all the comforts they knew back in the United States? Would foreign markets develop for a West Coast trading center of the United States? How many more people would now migrate to Oregon?

"I'm glad we're going to be the first," Sam said while walking with his arm around Abby's small waist. "That means we'll have first choice at the best farmland. Maybe in ten years there won't be any land left. Once people hear about Oregon becoming a territory, they'll come out here like a flood."

"Which means there'll be places to sell our crops, and children for my school."

Sam pointed to a few tufts of grass as a place to sit down. From there they could watch the sunset and continue to talk about Oregon.

"This great adventure of mine is turning out better than I ever imagined," Abby said as she snuggled her head into Sam's shoulder. "I have a good outfit, a good man in Jacob, a wonderful new future husband, and now I'm going to be living in the United States! As soon as I get the chance I'm going to write my family back in Ohio. I want them to know all the good things that are happening. Maybe my brother will come out to Oregon next year, or the year after. How about you, Sam, you think your brothers might come to Oregon?"

"I suspect William will. By the time he gets to Oregon, we'll have a farm and some children."

"All in good time, Sam, all in good time. Right now, I just want you." The conversation ended with Abby putting both arms around him and expressing her love and affection in a nonverbal manner. They lay back on the scant grass while another hot summer day came to a close.

People in the Light Column were up early on Friday, July 21, with a renewed vigor for going to Oregon. Complaints still surfaced about worn oxen, sore muscles, and fragile wheels, but the energy to move forward was decidedly greater. Today Abby unpacked a new bonnet. The bonnet she had worn since leaving Independence was getting a little threadbare, and the news of Oregon becoming part of the United States required some celebration. A new bonnet to continue the journey West was appropriate.

With this new energy, the Light Column was on the march by eight o'clock. They continued through a rough, rocky terrain that taxed the hooves of oxen and the shoes of emigrants. The wear on Abby's moccasins prompted thoughts of making a new pair, especially whenever she stepped on a small stone. Her sewing basket and possibles sack with the extra hides would be accessible during the nooner. She vowed to complete as much as she could before the afternoon march, since even one moccasin would be a vast improvement.

"I'll cut an additional sole for each moccasin," she thought. "This will help some. If I can get one or both made while nooning, then I'll have more time with Sam this evening." Walking alongside her oxen provided ample time for daydreaming of Oregon and thinking about the many chores to keep her outfit in good shape.

Sarah Rubey stopped by at midday to borrow a spoonful of oil for medicinal purposes. In this hot, dry climate, eyes became sore and lips chapped while facing a dry wind and the relentless hot summer sun. Rather than starting a new pair of moccasins, feeding Jacob and herself and socializing with Sarah took most of the hour. With only a few minutes left in the nooner, Abby found time only to cut two new soles and pack them inside her currently worn moccasins. This proved to be more than adequate for the afternoon.

The Light Column stopped for the evening along the south shore of the North Platte after a fifteen-mile day. Jacob drove the animals over to the river and allowed them to drink and wade in a shallow area for over an hour. He then hobbled them close to the river where they could get plenty of grass and water all night. While he was staking out the horses, Abby came down to the river with her milk can.

"I've noticed Spotty is giving less and less milk since we left Fort Laramie." She knelt down to milk what she could from Spotty's shrinking udder. "She's getting enough water, and the grass hasn't been too bad—but it could always be better."

"She's wearing out like all these other animals," Jacob said as he finished hobbling the stock. "I want to check her hooves for stones."

He lifted each leg, scraping the dirt and any small stones away. By the time he finished, the milk can was as full as it was going to get.

"Looks like less than a quart. She was giving over a gallon a day when we left Independence."

"She'll dry up by the time we reach Fort Hall and maybe even before Fort Bridger," Jacob stood back with his hands on his hips. "If we can get her to the Wallamet Valley and put her on good feed for the winter, well, by next spring you could breed her to get her producing again."

"Hear that, Spotty? You'll be eating good all winter. So for right now you need to do the best you can, and we'll get through to Oregon." She turned toward Jacob and with a smile added, "We'll all get through."

Jacob gave his usual nod. Then without speaking, he started walking back toward the wagon. By the time Abby returned, he was mounted and heading out for buffalo.

"Don't wait dinner for me, I grabbed some jerky. Should be back by dark." He dug his heels in and was off in a cloud of red alkali dust, downriver in search of buffalo.

Abby too grabbed some jerky, then went to work on her moccasins. By the time Sam arrived she was wearing a new pair.

"No dinner tonight?" Sam asked.

"Jacob went hunting, and I had better things to do than cook. What do you think?" She held up a foot, now wrapped in a new moccasin.

Sam shook his head, smiling as she wriggled her toes. "That's my wife—come on."

Abby grabbed his arm with both hands and they were soon out of sight of the wagon corrals.

Colonel Martin continued moving up the North Platte on Saturday, July 22, as Captain Gantt scouted for a safe place to cross. By noon they had made only six miles. During the morning, a constant stream of wagons had pulled out of line and stopped to repair wheels with loose spokes and tires, with Abby's wagon being one. Jacob shaved a few shims off the wagon bed and hammered them into the loose spoke holes. Only four spokes needed attention, so they were ready to continue in only twenty minutes.

Along with failing wagon wheels slowing the caravan, three men had come down with fevers since leaving Fort Laramie. They were Ed Stevenson, Clay Paine, and Dan Richardson. Clay and Dan rode in their respective wagons, now being driven by their wives and friends. Ed, who was traveling alone with a horse and two pack animals, rode with Clay in his wagon. The jostling along this section of rocky road took its toll on both men and equipment, forcing Colonel Martin to call a halt for the day after traveling a total of ten miles. Wagons that had pulled out of line in the morning could use the afternoon to catch up, while the sick men could spend some quiet time recovering. Additionally, Captain Gantt had not returned from his scouting foray, so Colonel Martin did not want to get ahead of a good crossing.

Jacob had come in the previous evening without securing any buffalo. Such was the luck with other hunting parties. Sir William Drummond Stewart's entourage was in the area and had run off all the buffalo. His hunting party was advancing ahead of the migration and had passed through the area about a week earlier, scaring off all the game.

That afternoon Abby made an entry in her diary concerning the scarcity of game: *"Our hunters have to travel many miles from the trail to secure meat. Stewart's hunting party may be making sport of the abundance of game, yet their disruption of the herds is costing us dearly. If there are emigrating parties in future years, and I'm sure there will be, they should take precautions to place all hunting parties far to the rear!"*

The afternoon saw tempers flare in the hot summer sun. The breakdown of wagon wheels and running gear, the death of several working stock, and the lack of buffalo all coalesced to create a volatile situation. To Abby and Jacob, there appeared to be another mutiny on the horizon. Some emigrants wanted to travel faster to get away from this rocky section of road and nearer to the buffalo herds. Other people wanted to slow down to reduce wear on wagon wheels and running gear. Still others wanted to cross the North Platte where they thought the road would be better and they could find buffalo.

Everyone seemed to find supporters for their ideas, so the discussions and arguments continued well into the evening. As Abby and Jacob finished their evening meal, Jim Nesmith stopped by in his general capacity as orderly sergeant to see how Abby's outfit was holding up.

"Jim, please come in." Abby motioned for him to sit on the wagon tongue. "How about some coffee? I just made a fresh pot."

"Thank you, Miss Meacham, that's very kind." He looked over at Jacob, who was sitting cross-legged on the ground. "Jacob."

Jacob nodded his acknowledgment. "So, Jim, what do you think of all these farmers cussing the trail?" Jacob spoke, holding his cup with both hands. "We gonna have another split?"

"I hope not, we're too fragmented already." Jim took the cup Abby handed him. "Thank you, Abby. If we were to get attacked, I think the Indians could do whatever they pleased. We have no more defense than a herd of sheep."

"It's not all that bad, Jim," Abby said as she sat back down on her overturned washtub. "This road is giving us some hard times now, but that will pass. Soon we'll be back near the buffalo herds and onto a smoother road. People need to be patient."

"Patience is something people forgot to pack back in the States," said Jim. "Everyone except you and Jacob—I've never heard you two complain about anything. Yes sir, these people have their own destruction within them, and it's called independence."

Jacob nodded, setting his cup down on the ground and pulling out his pipe.

"Indians aren't going to bother us. We could use some cooperation in getting across the North Platte and other areas between here and Oregon City. These farmers are not too fond of cooperating."

"That's probably why they're all going to Oregon," added Abby. "They're too independent to be cooped up in a civilized society. Even the name Oregon sounds like freedom. No wonder they were attracted to undertake this journey."

"We'll find a place to cross the North Platte in the next day or so. If we find good grass, buffalo, and a smooth road, then things should calm down. Did you hear that Applegate's Cow Column crossed only a few miles from here?"

"No, we hadn't heard," Jacob looked up with concern. "Any problems?"

"Plenty—the tongue on Bill Newby's wagon broke loose, and the oxen went one way and the wagon went the other. It rolled over several times and washed downriver three miles before it hung up on a sandbar. I heard they recovered most of his gear but not everything.

Lost his gun and shot pouch, an axe, tar bucket, and an ox yoke. Probably lost more than that, but the inside of his wagon was such a mess that it'll take Sarah several days to straighten things out."

"Did Jesse halt?" asked Abby.

"Kept going. They lost too much time with the Hembree boy getting killed. Bill will have to roll on with his baggage in a jumble and soaked clean through—probably have to discard some food. I suspect wherever they are right now he's got most everything laid out on the ground, drying before dark. Still got a few more hours of daylight—and this dry air should help. Poor Bill and Sarah, I do feel sorry for those folks, so I hope they have friends to help."

"I know Sarah Newby, and she'll have all kinds of help," said Abby. "She's made friends with just about every lady in the company. She'll have more help than she needs."

"If Bill hadn't switched columns that tongue would have still broke loose—probably loosened up from this road. It's a good warning. I'll check the bolts on our tongue before I turn in tonight." Jacob addressed his remarks to Abby, then looked over at Jim. "You hear if Colonel Martin wants to use the same crossing?"

"Not a chance. After that incident with Bill's wagon, we'll be looking for a better place than that. We'll be pulling out in the morning, so I'm checking to make sure everyone will be ready." He looked up from the fire with a smile and added, "Tomorrow's my birthday. I'll be twenty-three, and I want a good day of travel with as few problems as possible."

"We're in good shape, Jim, only a few loose spokes. And we'll check all the bolts on that tongue and our running gear. My ox teams are showing wear, but I think we'll get through in good health."

"Glad to see your wagon is holding up so well, Miss Meacham. You did well in buying such a fine wagon."

"Jim, you know you can call me Abby."

"You're engaged now, so I thought I better keep it formal."

"Well you can just unformalize it. I consider you a good friend, and I want you to call me Abby."

"In that case, Abby, thank you for the coffee. I'll try to stop by more often. I need to make my rounds to see if anyone needs help doing repairs." Jim handed his cup back, tipped his hat and walked over to the next kitchen, leading his horse.

As Jim made his exit, Sam made his entry. Whenever Sam showed up before Abby had the dishes put away, she recruited him as kitchen help. Jacob had done the heavier chores requiring strength for the first month after leaving Independence. Now those jobs fell to Sam too. Anything that kept him near Abby, even kitchen duties, was acceptable.

On Sunday morning Colonel Martin had the Light Column moving down the trail before nine o'clock. The alkali soil continued to stir up a cloud of red dust as the wagons and stock moved in single file through the red rock country. Teamsters and drovers covered their mouths and faces with handkerchiefs, a use Abby had not considered when buying hankys back in Independence. Now, along with her bonnet, she wore a handkerchief tied around her face so that only her eyes peered out from under the bonnet's visor. Jacob too covered his face against the wind and dust.

At about midmorning Jim Nesmith and Ed Otey left the caravan and headed south in search of game. They caught up again when the company stopped to noon along the North Platte where the Cow Column had crossed the day before. Jim had secured an antelope that he generously shared with the other people in his platoon.

In the meantime, Colonel Martin, Captain Gantt, Joe Walker, and Jacob were off reconnoitering the crossing to determine if they should chance it or continue upstream looking for a better ford. When they returned, they informed each platoon that the column would continue looking for shallower water. It was a good decision, for just then two men from Chiles's California Column rode in and informed everyone that there was a shallow crossing about ten miles ahead. The California Column had forded the river there without any trouble.

"Did you find that boat Stewart used?" Colonel Martin asked one of the men.

"If that royal buffalo stampeder left a boat, we couldn't find it anywhere," came the reply.

"It's some type of gum or elastic boat," said Captain Gantt. "We heard they were going to leave it in the fork of a tree."

"If that's where it is, we never found it. Maybe they crossed farther upriver. We never saw any boat in any tree. You can cross where we did, so you won't need a boat. Chiles thought we better come back and tell you."

"We thank you kindly," said Captain Gantt. "You can tell Joe we'll be coming up shortly."

The two men turned and headed back upriver to catch up with Chiles's California Column. Before they were out of sight, Colonel Martin roused his column from their nooner. They might not be able to get to the crossing today, but they would make a good effort.

During the afternoon, drovers had to make a special effort to keep the loose stock away from pools of alkali water. The hot summer sun took its toll on both the thirst of tired animals and the frayed nerves of exhausted teamsters. Abby always filled her canteen before leaving in the morning and again at noon, so she had water all day. Over the past month she had become adept at keeping her oxen moving while retrieving the canteen from its hook on the side of the wagon. The past few days had been so hot that she chose to sling the canteen over her shoulder. This afternoon as she took a drink, her eyes wandered over the backs of the oxen and settled on the beautiful Laramie Mountains to the south.

"Ahead lie the Rockies," she thought, "and they're even taller, with snow all year. That I have to see." She re-slung the canteen while bringing her quirt down on the rump of Lashes. The entire motion had the smooth movement of a well-rehearsed act.

Around three o'clock, a slight wind blew the trail dust away long enough for everyone to see the Cow Column marching along the north side of the North Platte. They were crossing a ridge and kicking up a cloud of dust that spoke of an alkali road as difficult as the one on this side of the river. Seeing the Cow Column in the lead further irritated those who had originally been convinced that the herds of cattle slowed the entire caravan. Now Jesse was not only in the lead, he was on the north side of the river!

Colonel Martin halted for the day on a small creek about a mile from the North Platte, and twelve miles from last night's camp. The creek provided fresh water for the stock, although there was a serious deficiency of good grass. Jacob scrounged what he could from the banks of the stream to supplement other meager shoots. It was not enough, but better than nothing. Although the crossing used by Chiles was still ahead, the availability of fresh water was reason enough to halt for the day. If they continued, they might not reach the crossing before dark and have to make a dry camp. Weakened stock needed water, especially on this alkali desert. Continuing on was not a viable option.

As soon as the wagon corrals formed and Jacob was down at the creek watering the stock, Abby began to make a small cake. She had been planning it ever since Jim Nesmith had mentioned that today was his birthday. Before mixing ingredients she gathered fuel, mostly chips, to start the fire. By the time her batter was ready, the fire was hot with glowing coals for her Dutch oven lid. In the background she could hear several men insulting their wives about the quality of cooked meals, insults she had become accustomed to hearing. She kept on with her chores, now setting up a fresh pot of beans for tomorrow, then roasting another pound of coffee beans for Jacob, and now preparing jerky and bread for tonight's meal. She checked the cake and could see it needed a few more minutes—just enough time to go down to the creek to wash the dirt off her face and rinse out a handkerchief. When she returned, she could see Jacob coming back from watering the stock.

"We're electing some new councilmen tonight," Jacob announced as he walked into the kitchen. "Maybe that'll quell some of the arguing. Seeing old Jesse up on that ridge today didn't help matters any."

"What will new councilmen do, make the dust disappear?" Abby showed annoyance over a frivolous election.

"I suspect the old councilmen are tired of all the complaining. Maybe if some of the complainers become councilmen, they'll start singing a different tune."

"I should be complaining for not being allowed to vote!"

"I'll vote for you. Who do you want?"

"It doesn't matter. Once we get past this dust, things will get better. We sure don't need a new council."

"The election's only for five members. I guess the rest are staying on, even with all the complaints. If this little formality will quiet people down, then I say, let's do it. We're all meeting over at Colonel Martin's wagon after dinner. You're certainly welcome to come."

"I'd rather spend the evening with Sam, but I suppose he's going to be there too."

"Probably."

"After the election I want you and Sam to bring Jim Nesmith back here. Today's his birthday and I've baked a small cake for him. He's had a tough job managing this platoon, and the least we can do is show some kindness, especially on his birthday."

Twenty minutes later dinner was ready, and twenty minutes after that Jacob was on his way to Martin's wagon. The election took less than a half-hour, after which Sam and Jacob showed up promptly with Jim in tow. The Otey men, Ed and Morris, also joined the group for cake.

"Please come in." Abby invited everyone into her kitchen as they approached. "Ed and Morris, I have cake for you too—I figured you'd be here. Happy birthday, Jim! I hope your day has been a pleasant one."

"Abby, you didn't have to go to all this trouble."

"No trouble at all—we have to have some civilization out here on the trail, and what better way to do that than by having cake and coffee to celebrate your birthday."

With six people the cake lasted for only one round. Everyone stayed and talked until dusk. The socializing helped to boost everyone's spirits and give Jim a memorable birthday. As the daylight faded, the guests excused themselves, thanking Abby for her cake, coffee, and hospitality. Tomorrow would be a busy day with the North Platte crossing, so even Sam said his good-nights.

Abby wrote a few paragraphs in her diary about seeing the Cow Column on the north side of the river, the alkali dust, her handkerchief mask, Jim's birthday celebration, and the kindness of Sam. There was no need to write about hardships and the irritable complaining of others. Memories like that do not need recording.

On Monday, July 24, the Light Column continued up the south side of the North Platte, arriving at the crossing in time for their nooner. The current at this place was fast, but the river was shallow. After reconnoitering the crossing Colonel Martin, Captain Gantt, and the platoon leaders determined that it would not be necessary to chain wagons together. They would cross single file with each wagon hitched to its maximum team.

As soon as they finished nooning, Jacob brought the fourth yoke of oxen around to the front while Abby stowed the food and utensils. As he finished hitching the additional yoke, he looked up to see two large clouds of dust moving west on the north side of the river. One cloud belonged to Jesse's Cow Column; the other was Colonel Fremont's government survey party. Hunters had run across Fremont two days earlier, so everyone knew they were in the area. Their group, along with Sir William Drummond Stewart's hunting party, was more than adequate to scare off every buffalo for miles around.

The North Platte now made a large horseshoe turn, referred to as Bessemer Bend by Captain Gantt. The first wagons entered the river before everyone finished nooning. Colonel Martin understood the independence of farmers and kept his frustration under control. Over the next three hours they completed the crossing in relative ease. By three o'clock the last wagon had pulled up on the north bank, with everyone ready to continue for a few more miles. Unfortunately, the road ahead was unknown, and the availability of water questionable. Because of this, Colonel Martin chose to spend the remainder of the day here on the north bank of the North Platte. There was ample feed along the banks for people to recruit their stock and prepare for another few difficult days until they could get through this red-rock alkali desert. The total of today's travel amounted to only six miles.

On Tuesday, July 25, the Light Column left the North Platte and headed for the Sweetwater. Martin had the column moving by eight o'clock with the intention of going as far as the terrain or their stock permitted. They nooned at an area Jacob called Rock Avenue, in tribute to the quality of the road. Late in the afternoon they arrived at Willow Springs, a distance of eighteen miles from last night's camp. With the availability of fresh water, Colonel Martin chose to halt for the night.

Willow Springs was a clear, cold source of fresh water with ample grass along its banks. It was named by trappers years ago and stood out as an oasis in this red rock country. After dinner Jim Nesmith came by to inform each wagon in the platoon that Colonel Martin and Captain Gantt had decided to stay here for one day. People could rest their stock, make repairs to their wagons, wash clothes, do other camp chores, and send out hunting parties to replenish their dwindling supply of meat. It was a wise precaution after the strain of travel since leaving Fort Laramie.

That evening while on their secluded walk, Sam and Abby came across a large area of soda. They had both heard about such phenomena while back in Independence—and here it was, no longer a tall tale. Abby noted the location and told Sam they could return the next evening to collect a quart or two.

"Both Hannah and Mrs. Skow told me I could use it in place of saleratus—won't hurt to try. I've still got plenty of flour and if it doesn't turn out, we'll eat it anyway. Like Jacob says, meat's meat."

They returned to the corral shortly after dark, with Sam grabbing a quick kiss before the flicker of campfires revealed their intimacy. It had been a long day's march for Abby, but not too long for a few more paragraphs in her diary. The natural soda needed recording, along with the smoother road as they approached the Sweetwater River, and of course, Sam. The original purpose of the diary was to record the adventure of going to Oregon, and Sam was never part of that plan. She needed to express her new love with someone, and the diary was as good as an older sister.

On Wednesday Captain Gantt organized a large contingent of men for a buffalo hunt. Buffalo had again become numerous within a few miles of the trail, and none too soon. The meat supplies of most people were running low. Within an hour after leaving the column and heading north, the hunting party came upon a small herd grazing along a dry creek bed. Without any concern for strategy, five men took off at a full gallop, scattering the herd for miles and not securing a single animal. Captain Gantt, Jacob, Joe Walker, and a few other experienced hunters became so disgusted at the display of greenhorn foolery that they chose to separate into smaller hunting parties for the remainder of the day. Greenhorns made up one party, while experienced hunters made up two others.

Jacob returned to camp by noon with both his packhorses laden with meat. It would be a busy afternoon of cutting, salting, and drying. By late afternoon sliced red meat completely covered the wagon's white-top. Other strips hung down on all sides of the wagon bed. By the time they finished cutting, there was still an hour or two before dinner, so Jacob headed down to the creek to catch some trout—a refreshing change from their daily fare. Abby used the time to roast and grind another pound of green coffee beans.

Shortly before dusk Sam and Abby returned to the spot marked earlier to gather a tin of soda. As they walked out away from the Light Column's wagon corrals, they scanned the western horizon for a monolith Jacob referred to as a "great rock like a giant snail". The horizon gave no token of its existence. After gathering the soda they slowly walked back, enjoying a few moments of solitude on a warm summer evening.

As they got back in sight of their corral, Jim Nesmith came riding in with his packhorse loaded with meat. He had killed a single buffalo after a long day's hunt. He dismounted and walked the remaining distance.

"Tomorrow we should get to that large rock that lies next to the Sweetwater River."

"We've heard," Abby replied. "Jacob said it's a good place to camp and usually has buffalo."

"Maybe we can stay a day or two," said Sam. "We need to recruit the stock some more and continue laying in a supply of meat before crossing South Pass."

"Maybe—I'll mention it to Colonel Martin."

"Jacob says we'll be crossing South Pass in a week," said Abby, "and that's the start of Oregon Country!" Her voice contained the excitement of a child about to see the circus. She tightened her grip on Sam's arm. "What are you going to do when you get to Oregon, Jim?"

"Don't rightly know, Abby. There should be work with starting a new territory and, hopefully, a state! Never was much of a farmer. I'll find something." He paused a moment to move the conversation away from himself.

"Gantt and the others say South Pass is easy to get across. I'll reserve judgment about that until I see it. I can't imagine a mountain range being easy to cross. I heard it gets cold up there in the pass—elevation, you know."

"We'll be ready," said Abby. "Did you know that after we cross this pass, all rain eventually flows into the Pacific Ocean? Back in Ohio I taught my classes that, but I never thought I'd actually live to see it."

"I want to see those mountains that everyone's been talking about," added Sam. "If they've got snow on them, maybe we're already too late to cross those Blue Mountains that Gantt's mentioned. You know, on the other side of those Snake River Plains."

"Oh, we'll get through. It won't be easy, but we'll get through. Now, if I can excuse myself, I've some butchering to do," Jim said as he started leading his horse toward the Oteys' wagon. "You two have a pleasant evening."

"We'll be ready at first light tomorrow," said Abby. "Ready for the Sweetwater!"

"Ma'am," Jim tipped his hat and moved off.

It was raining lightly the next morning, Thursday, July 27. With Colonel Martin's encouragement the column was on the move by eight o'clock, a good start for a rainy day. By noon they had traveled eleven miles and could now see a small hump on the horizon.

"Feels good, feels right," said Jacob as he scanned the horizon toward the giant monolith. "Feels like I've finally returned home."

"You really love the wildness of this country." Abby was sitting on her overturned washtub enjoying bread and buffalo hump meat.

"You can go out hunting this afternoon if you've a mind to. I can handle the wagon on this road."

"Thank you, Abby, but we have enough meat drying for now—any more would be wasteful. If we get close enough to that rock tonight, you, Sam, and me can ride over to it. It's easy to climb and you can get a good view of the surrounding land. A number of us trappers signed our names on it years ago, and I want to see if my name is still there."

"That sounds like fun, Jacob, a good diversion from this trail. If we stay in camp then maybe we can ride over the next day when we're fresh. I mean, this looks like it's going to be a long day of travel."

"Probably, probably." Jacob was looking at several riders coming up from Henry Lee's platoon: Jim Nesmith, Ed Otey, Morris Otey, Jacob Chimp, John Jackson, and Wes Howell.

"We're heading out for some buffalo, Jacob," said young Wes as they came riding up. "You want to join us? You seem to know how to find and kill buffalo better than any of us. Thought we could learn something from you, rather than repeat that foolishness of the other day."

"Thank you, Wes, that's right kind of you to ask. I was just telling Abby here that we got enough meat. You keep track of the wind and you'll get meat."

"Then maybe some other time," replied Jim.

"Maybe, maybe after the Sweetwater."

Each young man greeted Abby with a "Ma'am" and a tip of their hats as they turned their horses to ride north.

"Jacob, I think it's time you take me out hunting with you. I want to learn how to secure buffalo, too, and you said you would do that weeks ago."

"That I did, and I always keep my word. I'll have you putting those young bucks to shame. By the time we get over South Pass we should be able to take on more meat. One of your lady friends can look after your outfit while we go for meat." He paused for a few seconds, then added, "Better take Sam too."

"That sounds wonderful. Sam's told me how he wants to learn to hunt as good as you."

The nooner ended quickly as they both put the kitchen back in order and prepared for the afternoon march. By six o'clock they had come twenty miles from last night's camp and were now on the Sweetwater River. Normally, this river was small and placid, but a recent rain had caused it to swell and boil in muddy swirls. It appeared to still be rising, a condition that Jacob attributed to either distant rains or snowmelt.

Wagon circles formed within an easy ride to the giant monolith. This rock stood alone, or rather, lay alone as a lazy sentinel amid a vast desert prairie. It rose from the surrounding desert in a rounded oblong knob, smooth from eons of erosion. Nobody knew or could even imagine how such an uncommon object could form. It rose about a hundred feet without any transition zone from the flat desert. Its width varied, up to a few hundred feet, while it extended almost a quarter-mile in length. Jacob's description of a giant snail was appropriate. The rock was extremely hard, and people could easily climb and walk its entire length.

From on top one could see the surrounding prairie, or desert, extending to the horizon—a distance that defied estimation for the slow-moving wagon train. The Sweetwater River wound through the desert, disappearing to the southwest. Although it had overflowed its banks in many places, one could see that it was normally a placid, calm stream of fresh, drinkable water. Buffalo grazed lazily throughout the surrounding area as far as the eye could see. The grass was thin and could not support the massive herds seen before Fort Laramie; however, the Sweetwater River provided the drawing card to keep the herds nearby.

As soon as Abby's wagon corral formed, Jacob unhitched the oxen and drove all their stock down to the Sweetwater. Most of the women, Abby included, chose to skip their washing chores due to the muddy condition of the flooded river. Instead, they readied their kitchens and camp in hopes of having a layover day.

After dinner Abby took about four pounds of cooked buffalo hump over to Pierson Reading's wagon as a gesture of kindness. He had recently come down with a fever and was traveling with Chiles's California Column, now camped within a quarter mile of the Light

Column. They had halted there the day before to rest their stock and hunt buffalo. Joe Chiles referred to Pierson's condition, and that of the other ill men, as "mountain fever"—an illness that none of the Eastern emigrants had ever known. Joe Walker claimed that, with time, the illness would pass.

Shortly after Abby arrived, Dr. Long came by to bleed Pierson. Dr. Long was traveling with the Light Column, but moved between the other columns as needed. The Cow Column had arrived at the Sweetwater the day before and was spending a few days recruiting their herds before heading up South Pass. The roughness of the road from Fort Laramie had taken its toll on all columns, both people and stock. The Sweetwater River and surrounding country provided a needed respite of which everyone now took full advantage. Abby greeted Dr. Long, then excused herself to do other chores—the truth being that she did not care to see Pierson bled.

The buffalo within sight of camp were so numerous that hunters decided to wait until morning before securing meat. Instead, Captain Gantt and Bill Martin, and platoon leaders Hank Lee, Dave Lenox, Dan Matheny, and Jim Waters rode over to the giant monolith to record for history and posterity the passing of the migration. After riding completely around the rock, Bill picked out a place of prominence to engrave the company's name. He came equipped with a cold chisel and hammer, since the rock was solid granite and very hard. Shortly before dusk he completed the following inscription:

THE OREGON CO.
ARRIVED
JULY 26, 1843

They decided to carve yesterday's date since that was when the other columns had arrived. Although traveling in different groups, they still felt a general sense of belonging. They all belonged to the Oregon Emigrating Company.

Sam and Abby chose to stay in camp on this evening, resting their road-weary muscles. There would be time tomorrow to see the great rock and carve their names. Jim Nesmith had come by earlier informing everyone of Colonel Martin's decision to stay in camp for two nights. They would cross the Sweetwater on Saturday morning, then continue toward South Pass.

The evening passed quickly and soon Sam was ready to say his good-nights. Abby walked out with him, away from the flickering light of the many campfires. By the time she returned, Jacob lay under his buffalo robe next to the fire.

After a quick check of her kitchen's security, she crawled into the back of the wagon and lit a candle to write a few paragraphs.

"Today we arrived at a giant rock, laying on its side in the middle of this great desert. It is devoid of vegetation and shows signs of some powerful force, like a great flood, smoothing and rounding its sides. Nearby is the beautiful Sweetwater River. This river provides life-giving water to the vast numbers of buffalo, all within view of our camp and too numerous to count. We plan to stay here tomorrow, so I'll have a chance to catch up on baking and other chores, but mostly, I'll get to spend the day with Sam. We're planning on climbing the rock and exploring this desert guardian."

Before long the diary was back in its case, the candle extinguished, and all was quiet throughout the Light Column's camp.

Sam stopped by early on Friday, July 28 to help Abby finish her kitchen chores so they could ride over to the monolith. It was a cool, rainy morning that did not dampen their spirits for a day of exploration. Jacob readied Mud Flat, one of his packhorses, for Abby to ride. By nine o'clock the three were riding over toward the rock through a light drizzle. On the way several other people joined them for a morning of adventure, including Bill Fowler and Becky Kelsey. Ever since Bill had announced their engagement, Becky and Abby had become good friends.

As soon as they arrived at the rock, Jacob rode directly to a section of outcrop to see if his earlier inscription remained. It read:

J CHALMERS
FREE TRAPPER
1834

The inscription was still readable, but fading, since it consisted

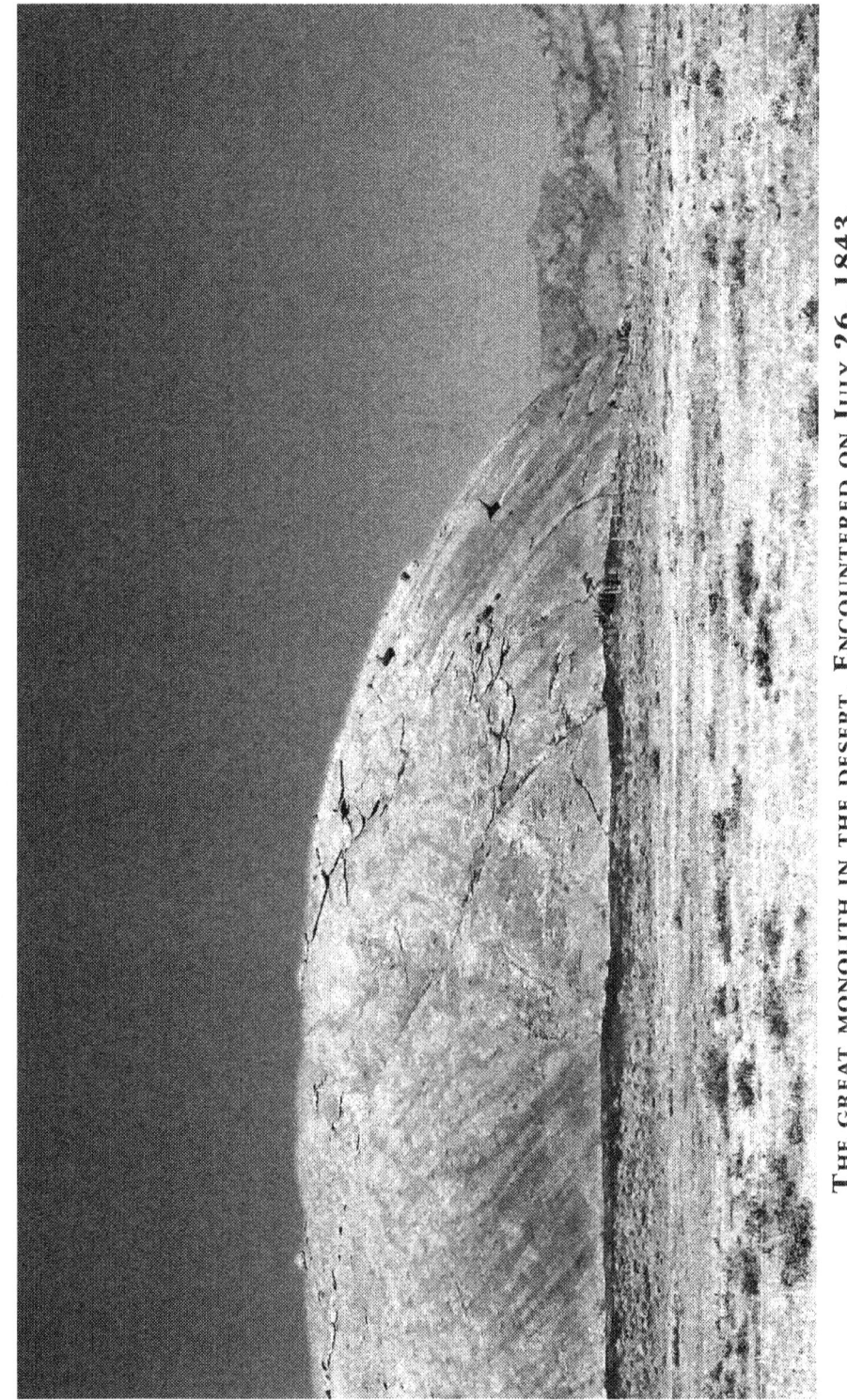

The great monolith in the desert. Encountered on July 26, 1843.

of a solution of buffalo grease, pine pitch, and ash. With Abby's cold chisel he immediately began converting the inscription to a permanent status. In the meantime, Abby and Sam climbed the large rounded end of the rock and walked along its entire length. They scanned the desert for any sign of buffalo which, to the dismay of many hunters, had again disappeared overnight. In particular, Abby was looking for snow-covered mountains. The rainy day reduced visibility, obscuring any outline of distant mountains. Earlier, Jacob had reaffirmed that they would soon be in sight—and snow in July was something to see.

"Not yet, Abby," responded Sam to her search. "We'll have to wait a few more days before seeing those mountains."

"They're the Wind River Mountains. Jacob's told me all about them. He said they had several summer Rendezvous near there when beaver filled the land. Those animals have been trapped out now. There's still buffalo—at least that's what Jacob says. He's going to take me out on his next buffalo hunt, and I'm sure he'll want you to join us."

"I wouldn't miss it. Did he say what Indian tribes inhabit those mountains?"

"Crow mostly. He says Crow land extends from here all the way north to the Big Horn Mountains and west to Yellowstone Country. I've never heard of any of those places. You should hear some of the stories he's told me about that Yellowstone region—stories about boiling mud ponds and steam vents coming straight out of the earth. One place they named Colter's Hell after one of the first trappers. Then there's Jackson's Hole, Pierre's Hole, Henry's Fork, the Musselshell, and so many others that I couldn't possibly remember them all. I don't suppose I'll ever see all of that—but I plan to see as much as possible, starting with this here rock."

"We should give it a name, Abby. A monument like this needs to have a name, so other people will know what to look for."

"If you come up with a name, I'll put it in my diary. When we get to Oregon, I'll write my family about all these wondrous things so they'll get printed in our local paper, and maybe even a Cincinnati paper. That way the names will stick."

By noon they returned to find Jacob completing the 4 in 1834. Abby retrieved enough bread, jerky, and water from her saddlebag for the three to have a nooner and enjoy a clearing in the day's weather. Afterwards, Sam took the chisel and headed back up the rock to an area he had picked out earlier for an inscription. After two long hours he completed his mark in history:

ABBY M—SAM O
OREGON 1843

"It looks wonderful, Sam." Abby stood back, admiring his work. "We'll be old and gray before that inscription weathers off."

"Oregon will be a state, and our children will be taking care of the farm, so we can take a train back here to see this place."

"Sam! A train! Don't be foolish. It will be a hundred years before railroad tracks extend all the way out to Oregon."

"If Oregon becomes a state, and I'm sure it will, the United States will have to build roads and railroads. You wait and see, or 'mark my words,' as Jacob would say."

"You're starting to sound like a teacher, Sam, not a farmer." She looked back at the inscription. "No matter what happens to Oregon, these words will be here for all future emigrants to see. We're two of the first, Sam. What do you think of that?"

"I want to chisel a circle around it so everyone will know that you're mine." He put his arm around her waist and pulled her in close.

"Sam! Not up here, the whole camp can see us!" She pushed him back while moving back a few feet herself. She continued smiling, looking directly at him.

"They can't see us."

"They can too." She pointed back toward the camp. "Some of those people have spyglasses."

"Abby, you worry too much, but I love ya anyway. Let me finish here, then we can go see what Bill and Becky wrote. Earlier, I saw them walking off in that direction." He motioned to the southeast side of the monolith.

On their way to find Bill and Becky, they came upon Jim Nesmith, who had returned with his hunting party around noon. With him were Mary Zachary, Laura Jane Mills, and Richard Arthur. Mary, Alex Zachary's daughter, showed the same frustration over her father's belligerence as did other people in the company. Spending a few hours with friends came as a welcome outing. Laura Jane, the nineteen-year-old daughter of Isaac Mills, was following her parents to Oregon. The abundance of young single men in the migration provided an easy inducement to brave the hardships of the journey. Richard, also following his parents to Oregon, was one of those single men.

Jim used a mixture of gunpowder, axle tar, and buffalo grease to make his inscription. After a half-hour of work, it read:

J W NESMITH
FROM MAINE

Next to the inscription he drew an anchor, signifying his origins from a coastal town in the state of Maine.

"We got two buffalo this morning," Jim announced as they came up. "You're welcome to some of the meat if you're running low."

"We have enough, Jim," replied Abby, "but thank you for offering. It's good to see you, Laura Jane, we haven't talked in days."

"People are quarreling down in the corral again, so we came up here with Jim to get away from all the fuss," said Mary. "It's so beautiful up here, even with this little rain."

"When are those men going to learn?" said Sam. "Quarreling won't get us any closer to Oregon. What are they arguing about this time?"

"Don't really know," said Laura Jane, "we just wanted to get away from it all."

"I wouldn't be surprised if there's another split before we get to Oregon," said Abby. "I don't know how many times this company can split and still stay together. We started out with over one hundred wagons. Now people switch between our four columns with no concern for cooperation or simply helping one another."

"It's not all that bad," said Jim as he stood up to admire his work. "Things will work out."

"I know, Jim, and I shouldn't say bad things about people—we're all trying our best. I guess I sometimes get tired of all the quarreling."

"Say, Wes Howell took ill last night when we were out on our hunt. We almost had to tie him on his horse before we got back today. He's over with his kinfolk now. This cool rain probably got to him after all those hot days since we left Fort Laramie. Have you seen the Sweetwater? It's come up a few feet since yesterday. Crossing tomorrow might be trickier than I first thought."

"We'll be ready," added Sam, "I think this group could cross just about anything."

"About four miles from here the Sweetwater cuts its way through some solid rock," said Jim, "and it don't make any sense. The river could have easily gone around those rocks. Captain Gantt calls it Devil's Gate. You and Sam should ride over and see that."

"We're heading over to find Bill Fowler and Becky," said Abby. "You folks are welcome to join us. We can't get any wetter in this rain, so we thought we'd stay out here a little longer."

Mary and Laura Jane looked at each other, then responded almost in unison, "Yes, we'd love to join you." They, too, were enjoying the time away from the caravan, even in the rain. Jim agreed to join them, for he could not pass up an opportunity to spend time with eligible ladies.

After Bill and Becky were located, the seven friends sat down on top of the rock to view the surrounding country. Soon Jacob joined them.

"Seen any buffalo?"

"Not a one," replied Abby.

"They surely got wind of all our camps and moved out last night. Can't hardly blame them—if this many people came into my home, I'd move out too!"

"I saw several hunting parties leaving early this morning," said Bill. "They should be back tonight loaded with meat. I mean, the buffalo couldn't have strayed too far."

Jacob did not reply. Rather, he continued scanning the horizon in all directions as if looking for something familiar.

"Look there!" Abby pointed to several wagons pulling out from one of the Light Column's corrals and heading over to an area farther down on the Sweetwater. "I hope this doesn't mean another split."

"Looks like one of those is the Oteys' wagon," Jim said. "They've got all my gear. I better get down there to see what's going on. If you ladies will excuse me."

"We better come down with you too," said Mary.

"Maybe we all better head down," said Sam. "How about you, Jacob?"

"I need to water the stock and move them to better grass—see you back at the wagon, Abby."

"We're right behind you," Abby called out as Jacob started back down. "You want to join us for dinner, Sam? We've more food than we can eat."

"Tell me when and I'll be there."

As they started back down, Becky quizzed Abby about how much help Jacob was in driving the wagon. She had never seen him working as a teamster and supposed he was of little value.

"I couldn't have found a better man," Abby disappointed her. "He's always giving me advice, good advice. He helps with the wagon whenever we get on a rough road or when we cross water, and he takes good care of the stock. I think my oxen are in the best condition of any oxen in our corral. They're easy to isolate in the morning 'cause they look so much better than the others."

"I've heard other people comment about that, Abby," added Bill. "You've been a bur under the saddle of quite a few of these men."

"That's not my problem. Jacob's advice has always been sound, and I plan to follow it all the way to Oregon."

"I don't think we're doing anything special to get across the Sweetwater tomorrow," said Sam. "I don't like that it's still rising, but we're experienced now. Crossing shouldn't be a problem."

"In a week or so we'll be across South Pass," added Bill.

When they returned to camp Jacob was already there, stoking up a fire with sagebrush. Buffalo chips were plentiful, but wood was scarce. Sagebrush was an acceptable substitute, yet it burned too quickly to give a hot steady cooking fire. Still, collecting sagebrush was easier than collecting chips.

"Too much saltwater around here. I had to rehobble two of your oxen that broke loose. I don't think they got into any alkali, but I took them back to the Sweetwater just in case."

"Thank you, Jacob. What were those wagons moving for?"

"Another split."

"No, not again. Who was it this time?"

"Different folks. They think Colonel Martin is moving too slow, since Jesse's Cow Column's been able to keep up with us. They split off with Lew Cooper as their leader. Coop's half Indian, so he should do well as a leader. Some of the wagons from the Cow Column joined him, so not everything is well over there. I think Coop's got about nineteen wagons now. Guess we'll have to call it Cooper's Splinter Column."

"We could see them forming a corral as we came down from the rock—they're just below Jesse's Cow Column. Poor Jim, he has no say in the split, yet all his gear is in the Oteys' wagon. What are we going to do for an orderly sergeant now?"

"Colonel Martin can figure that one out. We'll have to keep feeding this fire 'cause sage burns like kerosene." Jacob shoved another sage trunk onto the fire.

"Sam's coming over for dinner." She looked up from the fire and fixed her gaze on an animal about a half-mile distant that did not appear to be part of the emigrant's stock.

"Jacob, what's that?" She pointed toward the distant animal. "Looks too small to be an ox."

Jacob squinted as he viewed the animal. "Hold dinner for a few minutes, Abby. I think were going to have a change of fare."

Jacob grabbed Dog Town and rode off, angling downwind from the animal. Thirty minutes later he returned with it draped over his horse's rump. Abby met him on the outskirts of the corral, along with a number of other people. Here was an animal that nobody had ever seen, or even heard about. Its color was a cross between brown and gray, with a white rump, white snout, and hooves like a deer. The most unusual feature was its horns. They were thick and rough, curving back and out in a single, sweeping form without branching. Jacob called it a Rocky Mountain sheep.

"Some of the boys call them Big Horns," he said, "not as good as buffalo, but meat's meat. Abby and I want the shoulders and hide—you other folks can split the remainder."

He untied the animal and let it fall to the ground. With his Green River knife he quickly skinned it and cut enough shoulder meat for several meals. The other men soon butchered the remaining carcass for their own kitchens.

After dinner Sam helped Abby clean up, so they could have a few quiet moments together before the rain began again. Thunderheads were building up in the southwest, and it looked to be a wet night. They walked out arm in arm on the desert to be well away from prying eyes and the flickering light of campfires.

"It's wild, Sam, and young like us. I think we picked the most perfect place on earth to fall in love. I don't think any country could be as romantic as this."

"Wouldn't you rather have a cabin and schoolhouse?"

"Of course—but not right now. With all the hard work of getting to Oregon, finding you is making it all worthwhile. Even those angry clouds out there look beautiful—and Oregon will be even more wonderful."

"You get more and more romantic every day, Abby. For me, I want to get to Oregon. The Copenhavers keep me busy doing this and that, and it's getting old. I'm ready to start doing things for us—like starting our farm. It'll be hard work at first, we both know that."

Abby looked back toward the wagon corrals, then up at Sam. "Sam, nobody can see us now."

It was an hour after sunset before they returned to the wagon. Tomorrow would be a busy, tiring day and they wanted to be ready.

On Saturday, July 29, Colonel Martin called the remnants of his command together for an early-morning meeting. It had rained hard all night and was still raining lightly when everyone gathered on the outskirts of Bill Martin's corral. Bill started out by apologizing for the confusion, saying that there was nothing he could do about the split and that in the end it might be for the best. From now on there would only be three wagon corrals making up the Light Column, and they needed to get that organized this morning. After some discussion among the remaining leaders, Hank Lee came around informing each teamster which platoon (and subsequent corral) they would be in that evening. People took the change in stride and adjusted their marching positions accordingly.

The morning delay proved beneficial for Nancy Hembree, Sally Hembree's thirty-year-old sister-in-law. At ten o'clock she gave birth to a little girl—a plump healthy baby who was immediately named Nancy Ann after her mother. Abby and a few other ladies brought some food over to the Hembrees' wagon, helped to clean the new baby, and prepared a comfortable bed for the mother and baby to ride in that day. Even with the split, the appearance of a new life brightened everyone's morning as they prepared to cross the Sweetwater River by early afternoon.

Jesse's Cow Column broke camp early in the morning and was across the Sweetwater by the time of Nancy Ann's birth. Their crossing was not without incident as the Sweetwater had risen again overnight and was now a swollen, muddy, swift river. Several wagons stuck fast in the mud along the near bank and needed double-teaming to make it to the far shore. The herds swam the river with the loss of only one calf, which they retrieved, quickly butchered, and distributed.

Cooper's Splinter Column chose to stay in camp that day and spend their time drying meat, cleaning guns, and making repairs to clothing and wagons. Additionally, these people needed to organize and get to know their new leaders, wagon corrals, and marching orders. Jim Nesmith was in this new column, not by choice but by circumstance, and his status had changed. Tonight would be the first night since crossing the Kansas that he would only be a private, and no longer an orderly sergeant.

Shortly after nooning, the Light Column moved out and began to cross the swollen river. Abby and Jacob were the third wagon in line, and were as ready as they could ever be. Earlier, Jacob had hitched all four ox teams to provide the extra power needed to get through the mud. Now, mounted on his horse, he rode alongside the teams on the upstream side, trying to block some of the current. Abby rode in the front of the wagon using a long quirt she had made several weeks earlier when they had access to some willows. It was a rough crossing, with the water pushing violently on the wagon bed, especially in one deep hole. For a few moments the wagon appeared to be riding on only two wheels, with the two upstream wheels not touching the riverbed. Jacob kept the teams moving steadily forward, and they were soon out of danger and climbing the opposite bank.

They drove the wagon over to a spot of high ground, where Jacob could move the fourth yoke to the back of the wagon and Abby could begin straightening out the wagon contents that had shifted around during the crossing. As soon as everything was secure, Jacob rode back down to the river to help other teamsters. People were now tying ropes to the upstream side of their wagons to prevent them from tipping over in the deepest part of the river. Abby came down shortly after Jacob to watch the crossing and help in any way she could.

The Copenhavers' wagon had only two ox teams, but Sam and John Copenhaver decided that they would be adequate. Sam attached a rope to the upstream side of the wagon, intending to ride his horse across, parallel to the wagon and about twenty feet out. If the wagon started to tip in the current, he figured that he and his horse would have enough strength to keep it upright.

They misjudged the strength of the current, for when the overloaded wagon began to tip, the weight was too much for Sam and his horse. Sam had the rope tied around the saddle horn and was unable to release it before the river pulled both him and the horse over. The horse quickly regained his footing, but Sam floated downstream, striking his head on the underside of the partially tipped wagon. The current then pulled him under the wagon into a muddy swirling torrent. People looking on from the shore expected to see him come up on the downstream side of the wagon. John grabbed the rope and Sam's horse just in time to prevent the wagon from upsetting completely, then called out to the people on shore, asking if Sam was on the other side of the wagon.

"No," came the answer.

Abby watched in disbelief, looking for Sam to come up on the downstream side.

"Sam!" She screamed his name several times and began running downstream looking for any sign of him. As she ran she glanced wildly across the river to Jacob, screaming for his help.

Jacob was already moving. He dropped the yoke he was helping John Howell with, mounted his horse in one smooth motion, and galloped downstream, digging his heels into Dog Town's flanks. When he reached the area where Sam should be, he plunged into the river, urging his horse on to the deepest and swiftest current. He reached down into the water, feeling for any sign of Sam, wheeling his horse around as it lunged into several muddy swirling holes. All this time Abby was running along the bank, frantically screaming Sam's name and looking for any sign. She tripped several times on sagebrush, catching herself with her hands, then jumping up and continuing on in a desperate run to save Sam's life. As she reached the area Jacob was searching, she collapsed to her knees, continuing to scan the muddy current. There was no sign of him. Jacob continued his search, but he, too, knew there was little hope of finding Sam alive.

Other men came down to help with the search, but everyone knew it was hopeless. Five minutes went by, then ten. The current was not going to release him, and by now he was drowned and lost somewhere downstream. Jacob finally looked back at Abby with eyes of courage and despair, knowing that she knew Sam was gone. It had all happened so quickly—there was no time to prepare.

Abby, still on her knees, collapsed down onto the ground in disbelief. The man she loved, the man she was going to spend the rest of her life with had been taken away again. She stared at the muddy current not knowing what to do or what to think. She felt the swell of her heart as when a lover enters the room, a feeling of love that was now empty and alone. For the love was still very much alive, but the lover was gone.

Jacob, still on his horse, came out of the river and up to where Abby sat. He dismounted and stood next to her, holding the reins of Dog Town. No words were spoken. He continued to squint in the summer sun as he looked far downstream for any trace of Sam's body. Finally, he looked down at her.

"I am sorry, Abby, I truly am." He paused for a moment looking back downstream, then added, "He was a good man."

Abby said nothing. Not even the sound of despair she sometimes made could surface from her crumpled body. The tears had not yet come, for she was still filled with shock and disbelief. Becky Kelsey came running up and dropped down beside her with a supportive hug. That broke her hypnotic stare, and she began to cry uncontrollably. Becky looked up at Jacob while holding Abby in her arms. He simply nodded his understanding—an understanding that there was nothing more he could do and that Becky would stay with her. He walked back to the crossing, meeting Colonel Martin and informing him of the loss.

Bill Martin looked far downstream at the two small forms of Becky and Abby. "We'll set up camp here," he quietly said to Jacob, not removing his stare from the two women. "Probably take the rest of the day to cross anyway." He looked back at a group of about thirty people who had come running when they had heard Abby's screams. "We'll camp here," he shouted. "Form your corrals."

There would be time for friends to express their sympathies. For now, everyone gave Abby the room she needed, not disturbing her or Becky. Jacob returned to the wagon, moved it into place for the night, unhitched the teams, and tended to the stock. Three hours later Becky came walking into camp to inform Jacob that Abby wanted to be alone. The entire column was across the Sweetwater with their corrals formed, kitchens organized, and fires lit. Jacob thanked Becky for her help and asked that she look in on Abby over the next few days.

"Of course I will, and if there's anything I can do to help, please, let me know."

As Becky spoke, Bill Fowler came up and took Becky's arm.

"Jacob, if you need someone to drive this wagon, I'd be pleased to help, and there are women ready to do Abby's chores."

"Thank you kindly, Bill, we'll get along. It may take a week or two. Abby's got sand—she'll come back. If I need any help I'll surely call on you two. She cares about you two—she told me that. I'm sure she would be pleased to accept your offer."

"Come, Becky." Bill tugged on Becky's arm as he turned to walk back toward their kitchen.

Jacob could see Abby in the distance, still sitting on the ground next to the river where Sam had disappeared. He unloaded her kitchen, stoked a fire, and warmed up the beans remaining from last night. While they were warming he cooked the remaining mutton using a skewer. With a dish of beans, mutton, and bread, along with a canteen of water, he walked down to where Abby sat and placed the food on the ground next to her. Abby sat with her arms wrapped around her knees as she turned her head just far enough to see the food. Her dirty face was streaked with dried tears and still held the blank stare of disbelief. Without saying a word, Jacob stood up straight and again looked downstream as if searching for Sam. After a few moments he turned and walked back to the wagon. There was nothing he could say to make the hurt go away. Silence and solitude were the best medicine now.

The evening passed slowly. Abby thought about the time she had turned Sam away when she was tired, wishing for that evening again—and how she had never told him about the Kaw Indian that wanted to buy her. If she could only share that moment with him now. It was an hour after dark before she walked back into camp carrying the empty dish and canteen. Jacob was in his buffalo robe next to the dying fire, watching her every move. She placed the dish and canteen on her overturned washtub, then crawled into the back of the wagon.

There were no words spoken.

As the last embers of the fire flickered out, Jacob could hear muffled sobs coming from the wagon. He knew she was tough. Even so, she would need time to get through this.

Sunday, July 30, was a beautiful, sunny day. Captain Gantt requested that the column stay in camp one more night to continue recruiting the stock and to allow Clay Paine, Dan Richardson, and

Ed Stevenson more time to recover from their fevers. Colonel Martin quickly complied, especially with the tragic loss of Sam. Everyone could use the time for repairs, baking, and other preparations for the long climb up South Pass.

Abby arose later than usual, having only bread for breakfast. Jacob was already down at the Sweetwater making sure the stock had adequate grass and water. The grass here was thin and dry, not like the lush prairies before Fort Laramie. Recruiting stock on such poor forage took time. Although Abby's oxen were not as emaciated as others, they still needed rest before continuing the journey.

Colonel Martin sent a party of five men downriver to look for Sam's body. It was a gesture of sympathy and kindness, one which Jacob thanked him for.

"I'll let Abby know," Jacob said to Bill. "If you find him we can have the funeral tomorrow. If not, then I suggest we move out toward South Pass. It'll be best for Abby to get away from here."

Abby spent the day sick with grief. Her friends, Becky and Sarah Rubey, spent most of the day with her by helping with kitchen chores, repairing torn clothes, and baking bread. Abby began to soak a fresh pot of beans, but didn't have the energy to do much more. Several times during the day she wandered back downriver to the spot where Sam drowned, only to sit for a few minutes before returning. At midmorning Jacob went over to a small grove of aspen growing along the Sweetwater and cut a post that could be used as a headboard. With Abby's hewing axe, he shaved off an area for Sam's name and a small inscription. When she returned from her walk, he had Sam's name and death date inscribed.

"It's not much, but I thought it proper that we leave a marker."

Abby said nothing, staring only at Sam's name.

"I thought you might want to add a verse or some inscription."

She nodded, still not speaking. She walked over to her overturned washtub and sat down. Becky watched the proceedings while checking the progress of several loaves of bread cooking on the fire. Sarah, who was sitting on the wagon tongue mending a torn dress, came over and sat down on the washtub with her.

"Other people should know what a good man he was," she softly

THE SWEETWATER RIVER NEAR SOUTH PASS.

said. "Even if there's no grave it's good to have a marker to show our existence here on this earth."

Again Abby nodded, quietly reflecting on what to say. "He just wanted to go to Oregon, to have a family and a farm." She brushed her jet-black hair back. "It should be something simple."

"Maybe just 'OREGON,' or 'GOING TO OREGON.'"

"Now his Oregon dreams end here. He'll never see Oregon."

"When the Hembree boy died, we all thought that he was already in that promised land of Oregon," Sarah said. "You have to believe that Sam is there too."

"Thank you, Sarah." Abby glanced over at her with a slight smile. "You are a good friend. I think 'OREGON BOUND' will be adequate. Oregon Country doesn't start till we get past South Pass, so he's still on his way. Future emigrants will know he tried."

"'OREGON BOUND' sounds fine," said Sarah. "Becky and I can carve it out."

The men sent out by Colonel Martin returned that evening without finding Sam's body. After reporting to Martin, they came over to Jacob to give him the news.

"Martin wants to pull out in the morning," said Nat Sitton. "I realize that doesn't give Abby much time, but …"

"I understand, Nat." Jacob had walked out to meet him rather than disturb Abby's kitchen with more bad news. "Bill and I already talked it over. We'll be ready first thing tomorrow."

Abby fixed dinner that evening, and Jacob let her. There had been a constant stream of visitors during the afternoon and now into the evening, all expressing their sympathies for the loss of Sam. Jacob's calm manner and strength served Abby well as he greeted each visitor and accepted their kind words—a behavior that was no small feat for a hardened trapper. He had watched men die for the last twenty years, and none received a headboard and few received sympathy. It was part of a trapper's doctrine. About ten years before, a man had been killed while running buffalo, so they merely rolled him up in a blanket and cast him adrift on the Powder River. It was easier than digging a grave.

The evening passed quickly and soon the camp was quiet. Tonight

Abby lit a candle after crawling into bed. She wanted to write a few paragraphs in her diary—private thoughts of love, strength, and tragedy. Soon the light was out, and she was fast asleep.

The next morning, Monday, July 31, the Light Column hitched up their teams and started toward South Pass. Jacob tied his horse to the back of the wagon along with his two pack animals, the extra yoke of oxen, and the milch cow. Today he would drive the wagon, with Abby walking alongside.

Jesse's Cow Column and Chiles's California Column had left the day before and were well ahead by now. Cooper's Splinter Column, still in camp when the Light Column pulled out, was having difficulty getting organized. A number of men were already expressing dissatisfaction with Cooper. They had split from the Light Column to get ahead of the Cow Column. Now they were at least a day behind. When they saw the Light Column pull out ahead of them, tempers flared and arguments ensued. It was eleven o'clock before they finally got underway. Their wagons were the last vestiges of the Oregon Emigrating Company to leave the area of the great rock monolith.

Clay Paine, Dan Richardson, and Ed Stevenson appeared to be getting weaker each day. They rode in their wagons while some of the older boys took over responsibilities of driving their teams. Ed continued to ride in Clay's wagon. Though other people in the column were ill, most were able to walk or at least ride a horse. At the noon stop Colonel Martin visited both Clay and Ed, then decided to stop for the remainder of the day. It was a difficult decision, but if an afternoon of rest could help save their lives, it was worth it.

At two o'clock Cooper's Splinter Column caught up with the Light Column. The meeting was fortuitous, for now six of the nineteen wagons that had deserted chose to come back to the Light Column. Cooper was left with thirteen wagons, thirty-one men, and their families. He continued only another three miles before making camp for the night.

One of the six wagons to rejoin the Light Column belonged to the Oteys. Jim Nesmith was grateful to be back with his friends, but the joy would not last for long. The Oteys were still not happy with Colonel Martin's command and considered trying to catch up to Jesse's Cow Column.

Alex Zachary had shifted between columns several times and was now back traveling with the Light Column. While in camp the day before, he had managed to defraud Walt Matney of his remaining provisions and packhorse by means of a card game. Walt was single and traveling to Oregon to make his fortune. He was well-liked by everyone, and always willing to lend a hand during river crossings or road building. Sadly, his lack of education made him an easy target for unscrupulous people—a target that Zachary could not resist. Walt still had his horse and gun, so he would survive—but it was a cruel deed played by Zachary. Friends quickly came to Walt's aid with offers of dried meat, bread, and another packhorse to carry his gear.

Over the past two months Zachary had obtained the reputation of being the orneriest farmer in the entire migration. He never had a kind word for anyone and was usually in the fray of an argument. For the leaders of the Light Column, defrauding young Walt of his remaining provisions was the final insult. This time the Oregon Emigrating Company Council decided to take action. After dinner they gathered around Colonel Martin's wagon, where they convened a trial to determine what to do with "Old Prairie Chicken."

Pete Burnett read the charges, then anyone with a grievance spoke their piece. After a short deliberation the council found old Zachary guilty of defrauding Walt and stranding him to die in the desert. For punishment, they banished him from the company. As Pete Burnett read the decision, a cheer came up from the gathered crowd. Ridding their ranks of old Zachary was good news.

Zachary hitched up his oxen before dark and moved about a mile ahead for the night. To Jim Nesmith's dismay, the Oteys chose to join Zachary rather than travel with Martin's Light Column. Jim exchanged some peaceable words with both Ed and Morris, explaining that he did not share their opinions but had no other place to stow his gear. They understood his dilemma, but still refused to travel with the Light Column. Once again Jim said his farewells to friends in the Light Column, especially to Abby.

"Jacob will see to it that you'll get to Oregon safely," he told her in parting. "We won't be traveling so far apart that we can't get back together before long. We'll probably all meet at Fort Bridger." It was difficult to make conversation knowing she was still mourning the loss of Sam.

"Jim, if I were a man, Old Prairie Chicken would get a worse punishment than having to travel by himself. He was going to leave poor Walt to starve out here on the desert. I don't understand why anyone would do that. Don't we have enough difficulties as it is? I just don't understand a man like that."

"Nobody does, Abby. With just the Oteys it'll be a small camp for a big rascal. Wish I could stay here with you kind folks, but they've got all my gear."

"We understand, Jim, and we don't blame you for anything. There's nothing you can do." Smiling, she added, "When we get together down the road, you can come by for dinner."

"I will do that, Abby, I will do that." Jim mounted his horse, tipped his hat, glanced over at Jacob, and then rode off to catch up to the Oteys.

On the following morning, Tuesday, Abby began the day by driving her own wagon. She thanked Jacob for his help, but thought it was time she got back to her chores and her share of the work. Before beginning the day's march, she located Walt Matney to give him a loaf of bread. During the previous day he had acquired a fair amount of food from the many people coming to his aid. There were still many good and generous people in the company.

Before organizing camp the night before, they had to cross the Sweetwater again. The flow had dropped four feet in just thirty-six hours, so the crossing went without incident. Jacob had handled the team while Abby rode his horse. Today there would be several more crossings of the same river—crossings Abby could manage herself as the river continued falling and the flow slowing. The first crossing would be more emotional than physically difficult. The challenge of driving her wagon provided a needed diversion. Like the death of any loved one, she would never get over the loss. Rather, she would learn to live with it.

Women of the column took turns walking with Abby as the caravan wound through a rocky, sparsely vegetated desert. Sarah Rubey had been her constant companion since the death of Sam and remained a source of strength. The appearance of the Wind River Mountains in the distance brought their conversation back to the wonders of the journey. These snow-capped peaks extended to the north as far as one could see. For Abby and many other emigrants, their majesty evoked the feeling of entering a new world, unexplored and pure. Jacob too walked with her for part of the day. His stories of the Rendezvous held at the base of the Wind River Mountains captured her and Sarah's imagination like no other.

"Back in '29 we were up on the Popo Agie having a game of Old Sledge. After a few hours things started getting out of control, with all the grain alcohol Sublette brought in. Words were passed, and before long some poor child got killed. So we rolled him over and used his back as a table to finish the game."

"Jacob!" snapped Sarah. "I think you could find another subject to talk about."

"I don't mind, Sarah," Abby quickly responded. "I'm quite accustomed to Jacob's stories, no matter how wild they are. The more wild, the better I like them." She was smiling now, hoping Jacob would continue with his adventures.

"You don't actually believe any of his tales, do you?"

"I've never told an untruth, ma'am," Jacob responded. "If I said it happened, then it surely did."

"The stories are wild, Sarah, but you must admit they are plausible. A few months ago I had my doubts, but I know Jacob now, and if he said it happened, well, I believe him."

As Jacob continued his stories of the Popo Agie Rendezvous, Marcus Whitman came riding in from the Cow Column. He was spending the morning riding between the various columns encouraging each teamster to keep moving, much like he had done before Fort Laramie.

"Travel, travel, travel!" Marcus exclaimed as he rode up. "This is the only way you will get to the end of your journey, the only way you will get to Oregon. Avoid anything that slows you down, for anything that causes a moment's delay is not good."

When he came up alongside Abby, Jacob, and Sarah, he slowed his pace to that of Abby's team.

"I heard of your loss, Miss Abby, and I am sorry. We can have a service this evening if you wish."

"Thank you Reverend—I think not. Sam was never partial to religion, and we are moving forward now. I'd prefer not to return to the past."

Marcus showed a puzzled look as he considered her situation. "You are a strong woman, Abby, stronger than any I have ever known. There are many people here to help you along, and I'm sure Jacob has been a great comfort. I'm traveling with the Cow Column. You can come see me anytime."

"Thank you, Reverend, that's very kind."

"Ma'ams, Jacob." Marcus tipped his hat to the ladies and rode off to repeat his encouragement of "travel, travel, travel" to the next teamster in line.

"Look there." Sarah pointed to a small mountain topped with a rock that appeared to have split.

"Looks like the top broke in two," said Abby. "Does that rock have a name, Jacob?"

"Not that I know of. I've seen it before but never paid it any attention—just a rock to me."

"I will call it Split Rock," Abby said. "How does that sound to you, Sarah?"

"Split Rock? When we stop for a nooner I'll tell the other ladies. That way the name might stick, especially if we get it written down in our diaries."

The Wind River Mountains, and now Split Rock, were in view all day. By the time wagon corrals formed that evening, the column had traveled twenty miles from last night's camp. People continued to repair wagon wheels as the dry air shrunk spokes and felloes. Where possible, teamsters drove an extra piece of hoop iron or wooden wedges between the rim and felloes in a tightening process. After driving in the wedges, they punched holes through the rim iron and drove nails through to the felloes to hold the wedge in place, along with wedging loose spokes. Other emigrants removed wheels from their wagons and weighted them down in the Sweetwater River for an overnight soaking.

The columns were still paralleling the Sweetwater as they climbed toward South Pass. The livestock had fresh water each evening, but this would not always be the case.

Dinner that evening consisted of cornmeal, bread, and dried buffalo tongue. Abby stayed in camp straightening up her kitchen, getting ahead with baking bread, starting another pot of beans, and roasting another pound of green coffee beans for Jacob. These domestic chores had been ignored far too long, and it felt good to be needed. Bill and Becky stopped by, along with Richard Arthur and Laura Jane Mills. This couple, too, had met on the trail and were now seeing each other as more than friends.

Lancaster Clyman and Mary Manning dropped by before dusk as a gesture of kindness. They had been considering getting married in Oregon, but were now hesitant after the harsh reality of Abby's loss. Abby wasted no time in telling them not to hold back on their plans for starting a family.

"We'll be in the Wallamet Valley in a few more months, and all these troubles will be behind us," she said. "Now, I want you two to invite me to witness your vows."

"We will, we will," responded Mary.

After a pleasant conversation, the couple excused themselves and headed back to their respective wagons for the night. Abby pulled out her diary to record the events and sights of the day, including Split Rock and the Wind River Mountains. Tomorrow would be another long day of travel, so before long the camp was quiet, campfires had died, and the only sounds to be heard were the occasional grunt of an ox or bray of a mule.

On Wednesday morning, August 2, Abby could see all five columns camped within sight of each other: Applegate's Cow Column, Chiles's California Column, Waldo's Straggler Column, Cooper's

Split Rock. Encountered on August 1, 1843.

Splinter Column, and her own Light Column. The splits were maintaining peace between the independent emigrants, while allowing them to stay close enough for friends to visit. Also in the distance were Alex Zachary and the Oteys. Miles Eyre continued to camp by himself, although he always traveled with the Light Column.

The trail along the Sweetwater was level and easy to negotiate. During the day the Light Column crossed the river four more times, with three of the crossings close together as they cut off oxbows to shorten the journey. During the nooner about twenty oxen broke loose from their restraints and ran down to the Sweetwater, where there was both grass and fresh water. The owners quickly rounded them up and were ready to go before Colonel Martin gave the order to march.

At three o'clock the lead wagons encountered Jesse Applegate. Jesse's provisions wagon had broken an axletree, so he was now converting it into a cart, just as his brother Lindsay had done shortly after leaving Fort Laramie. George Beale, Jesse's teamster, had propped up the wagon with rocks, and was removing a wheel when Abby and Jacob came up alongside. Jesse wanted to keep one of the wheels as a hedge against future trouble. Unfortunately, that would not be possible. Cynthia, his wife, was already going through their possessions and eliminating weight wherever she could. With a cart, they would have to reduce their load by at least five hundred pounds. Several people in the Light Column offered to buy part of Jesse and Cynthia's stores—an offer that they refused. They would need those supplies for their own family. Instead, farm implements and other heavy items went to anyone willing to carry them.

Abby spent a few minutes talking with Cynthia, catching up on news, and offering encouragement. They had not talked in several weeks, and the current situation did not lend itself to a long discourse. Both women had suffered hardship and loss. A few friendly words provided comfort and strength; then Abby and Jacob were on their way.

The Light Column continued up the Sweetwater drainage, leaving Jesse and George to finish the work of moving the rear axle to the center of the box and then reloading the remaining provisions and possessions. They caught up with the Light Column that evening, but continued for several more miles, trying to catch up with the Cow

Column. Jesse and his brother Lindsay were not the only teamsters in the Oregon Emigrating Company who were now driving carts. The road to Oregon was taking a toll on many outfits.

On the following morning, August 3, Cooper's Splinter Column passed by before the Light Column was ready to begin their day's march. Everyone was busy with morning chores and preparing their outfits for the day, when Cooper veered his group around the Light Column's corrals.

Jacob brought the oxen around just as Abby finished packing her kitchen. With the kitchen gear stowed up front, it had to be loaded before yoking and chaining the ox teams. Nearby, Harriet and Pete Burnett were busy unloading half of their remaining cornmeal and giving it to their oxen as feed. It had gotten wet a few days earlier during the first crossing of the Sweetwater and was now too spoiled for human consumption. Their hungry oxen were more than willing to finish it off. As Abby watched the famished oxen gorge themselves on the cornmeal, she couldn't help but think about the good advice she had received from Hannah Greer and Mrs. Skow back in Independence. None of her supplies had suffered water damage, and the short-lived provisions, like bacon, had been consumed within the first month. Now, at the foothills of the Rocky Mountains, her outfit was still in good shape and ready for the rough road ahead.

During today's travel the Light Column crossed the Sweetwater, now just a shallow creek, another three times. Abby had no trouble handling her ox teams as she plunged the wagon into the shallow water, crossing without delay. Each crossing cut off an oxbow and shortened the journey up toward South Pass.

Abby thought back to each crossing over the last few days. "Eight, we've crossed this river eight times." The work of driving the oxen and managing her wagon over rough terrain provided ample challenge to keep her mind and body busy. It was good medicine.

The day of travel was long, and everyone was glad to see it end after twenty miles. They again camped on the Sweetwater. The grass here was so poor that the hungry stock did not receive much comfort. Cooper's Splinter Column camped only two hundred yards ahead. It was a quiet evening in camp as friends visited between the columns, resting and preparing for another long day tomorrow.

Clay Paine spent the day riding in his wagon, still too ill to walk. Tom Brown drove the wagon while Clay's wife walked alongside, managing her four small children, two of which were twin babies. Tom, a young man going West to make his fortune, was traveling with his friends Nat Sitton and John Cox. While in Independence, Nat had hired out as a teamster for an emigrant named Sam Vance. John and Tom could have hired out, too, but preferred to avoid the problems associated with a wagon. They packed their outfits on horses.

On the following morning, Friday, August 4, everyone woke to learn that during the night Clay Paine had died from an inflammation of the bowels. There was nothing anyone could do during his final hours except make him as comfortable as possible. Tom Brown pulled a plank off Clay's wagon to make a headboard, while Joe Garrison, a Methodist in the company, provided comfort to Mrs. Paine. Other ladies quickly took over the chores of caring for her children and cooking. Sam Gilmore, a 28-year-old farmer taking his family to Oregon, located a spot of high ground south of the trail. With the help of John Cox and Nat Sitton, he began to dig the grave.

The funeral was a sorrowful, impressive scene. Joe Garrison delivered the eulogy, with almost every adult from the Light Column in attendance. The lonely site lay out on the dry prairie, hundreds of miles from civilization. As the men lowered Clay's body into the shallow, rocky grave, Joe expressed his wish that whatever Clay had died of not be contagious. The gathered crowd responded with "Amen," and soon it was over. Nat, Sam, and John began filling in the grave while Tom Brown wrote Clay's name, birth, and death dates on the headboard with a mixture of ash, grease, and gunpowder. Abby supplied another verse, which Tom inscribed:

> *Precious darling, you have left us,*
> *Left us yes, forever more.*
> *But we hope to meet you once again,*
> *On that bright and happy shore.*

It was a verse she had learned back in Ohio as a little girl. Mrs.

Paine appreciated the gesture. She and her older children stood by until the men seated the headboard and packed down the dirt hard enough to prevent wolves from exhuming the corpse. Several ladies helped the widow back to the column while Tom and John told her that she did not need to worry about her outfit. They would take it through to Oregon.

The order to march did not come until ten o'clock, due to the funeral delay. The column pulled out, with people once again looking back at a lonely grave disappearing in the distance. Most ladies took turns paying their respects by walking with Mrs. Paine or taking care of her children. The need for advancement toward Oregon was a harsh reality in the face of death. The stoic teamsters and drovers continued to move their wagons and herds up the gradual ascent toward South Pass, making a road as they went.

Shortly after nooning, at around two o'clock in the afternoon, a loud, sharp boom sounded overhead. Following this sound was a rumbling like distant thunder. The column came to an instant halt as people looked around to see what might have caused the boom. In the sky they could see an object moving extremely fast, disappearing in a white flash toward the west. George Brooks described it as a ball of fire with a long tail of blue smoke. John Baker described the sound like that of artillery, while others said it was a Godly sign of Clay's death. The lack of clouds eliminated the possibility of a nearby thunderstorm. George Gray, a botanist originally from Germany, proclaimed it to be a meteor passing through the atmosphere. The sound, he thought, could have been made when it struck the earth. However, people had seen the object after the boom. The Light Column remained stopped for ten minutes as people tried to solve the mystery and collect their emotions. Finally, Colonel Martin gave the order to continue the afternoon's march.

George Gray, like others in the migration, had become mesmerized by the tales coming out of Oregon County. However, unlike other people, George was not journeying West to make his fortune. A new land with previously unknown flora provided the irresistible draw that convinced him to break the ties of family and friends and undertake the adventure. George planned to send detailed descriptions of the native plants found in Oregon Country to the scientific community back East.

After dinner Abby got her diary out and wrote about Clay's funeral and the passing of the meteor. It had been a short day of travel, only about ten miles for both the Light Column and Cooper's Splinter Column. The Splinter Column had expected to travel considerably faster, leaving the Light Column well in the rear. To the surprise of many, they were no faster than the Light Column and could not even catch the Cow Column.

With trail exhaustion taking its toll, another quiet evening passed in camp. Ladies wrote in their diaries while men discussed the road ahead and the need to stay together when death occurs. Ed Stevenson was still very ill and continued to ride in Clay Paine's wagon. Bob and Isaac Smith, two brothers traveling to Oregon, had been managing Ed's packhorses since leaving Fort Laramie. They would continue to do so until Ed could ride or walk on his own.

The next morning, Saturday, August 5, the Light Column veered away from the Sweetwater and began the final ascent up to South Pass. The morning was colder than usual, prompting most people to break out their heavy winter coats. Abby dug out the thick wool coat she had bought at the Skow's store back in Independence. This was the first time she had needed it. She relished the smell and feel of new wool, a feeling of warmth and security, as she stood next to her lead team waiting for the order to march.

The final climb to South Pass was steeper than previously experienced, yet not exceptionally difficult. Nobody had to double-team at any time. As Jacob had predicted weeks before, the Blevinses had to unload all the goods they planned to sell in Oregon before beginning the day's march. Their oxen were spent and could go no further with their current load. It was a difficult decision, one that Alex Blevins had put off since leaving Fort Laramie. If he had unloaded his goods at the fort, his oxen would not now be so exhausted. Sadly, it was too late to correct past mistakes. Plows, scythes, and other farm implements littered the side of the trail as the column began their day's march.

The snow-capped Wind River Mountains had been in view all week. The awe-inspiring peaks captured the attention of everyone. Jacob, Joe Walker, and Joe Chiles spent a good part of the day answering questions about the size of the mountain range and the oddity of snow in the summer. Some folks thought the snow should melt, since it was closer to the sun, while more educated people reveled in seeing something that they had only heard about back in the United States.

Abby could not stop staring at the mountains as she walked alongside her team. They were a sight to see—something she wished her family back in Ohio could see. Colonel Martin halted the column after advancing fifteen miles up the gradual incline to South Pass.

After dinner Abby put on her wool jacket, grabbed her diary, and headed out onto the dry desert to get a better view of the mountains—along with a few private moments of peace from the column. Soon she found a high spot of ground with a large rock to sit on. The snowy mountaintops and surrounding sage-covered desert provided a surreal scene of majestic beauty and mystery—a scene that needed recording. A slight breeze blew Abby's black hair back as she stared at the distant mountains, trying to make out distinct features such as trees and streams. The smell of sage hung heavy in the dry air, while cooking odors from the many campfires drifted up to where she sat. The difficulties of the journey stood in stark contrast to the breathtaking beauty of the land. With all her hard work, loss, and tears, Abby was still moving forward, glad to be going to Oregon. She felt no regrets, only a hunger to see and learn more—a hunger to leave the past behind and move forward to a new and better life in Oregon.

It was dusk when she returned, only to find that Jacob had cleaned up the dinner dishes and put everything away, in addition to caring for the stock.

"I guess I've been somewhat forgetful of my chores."

Jacob was sitting next to the fire, smoking his pipe.

"Weren't no trouble. I remember the first time I saw those mountains, I couldn't stop looking at them either. Say, Lashes is showing more wear than his partner, so I think we should give him another few days' rest."

Abby looked over at the hobbled oxen, wishing they had better grass. "Whatever you say Jacob; I trust your judgment. How soon before we get down from this pass and back into an area of good grass?"

"Another few days, not long."

"Have you been warm enough in that buffalo robe?"

"Plenty warm, plenty warm."

Abby looked around at the quiet scene of corralled wagons, grazing stock, drifting campfire smoke, and the last remnants of a beautiful orange and red sunset.

"Good night, Jacob."

He, too, had been gazing at the reddish western sky ever since the sun had dipped below the horizon. He slowly nodded, "Abby."

Abby crawled into the back of her wagon, put her diary away, and was soon asleep. The cool, thin air and hard day of travel had taken their toll.

On the following morning, Sunday, August 6, a thin sheet of ice lay on top of the water left in a cooking pot overnight. Again today, Abby wore her wool jacket and gloves against the chilly mountain air. Jacob had the wolf hide wrapped around his shoulders as he kindled a morning fire for her to cook on. Morning chores were routine and did not require conversation. While Abby heated biscuits, Jacob worked on the left front wheel by wedging another piece of scrap iron between the rim and the felloe, and then securing it with a nail. A few minutes later Joe Chiles rode by each kitchen informing people that they would be crossing South Pass sometime during the day. This came as welcome news to everyone. As soon as they crossed South Pass, the road would start to descend and, hopefully, they would encounter water. Most of the stock had gone without water the night before; that is, most except Abby's. She and Jacob had made sure each animal received at least one gallon of water, taken from the water barrels.

Colonel Martin started the column moving early, before eight o'clock.

THE WIND RIVER MOUNTAINS AS FIRST SEEN FROM THE TRAIL

Teamsters had already taken their designated positions, and were eager to get across the pass and into an area with water and grass.

At ten o'clock they passed Applegate's Cow Column, still in camp and trying to round up all the strays from the night before. With little grass and no water, their herds had strayed over five miles from camp. Rounding them up on that morning required every wrangler in the column.

By noon, the Light Column had traveled only five miles. They had not yet reached South Pass, so Colonel Martin halted for the Sunday nooner, a stop that was usually two hours in length to accommodate religious services. Dave Lenox and Bill Beagle formed a small Baptist contingent, while other groups were mostly Methodist. Abby, Jacob, and about half of the remaining, nonchurchgoing emigrants spent the time doing repairs or just resting in the warm summer sun. By midday the air temperature was warm and comfortable, a considerable change from the overnight frost. Heavy jackets had been put away several hours before as it became a beautiful, blue-sky summer day. A slight breeze now blew from the southwest, the smell of sage was everywhere, the snow-capped Wind River Mountains rose in the distance, and the air was so dry that not a single insect could be found. Abby used the time to walk out away from the wagons and sit down on a rock to again stare at the mountains. It was a sight that she could not get over. Reading about snow-covered mountains in the advanced school readers did not do them justice. This was a sight that one had to experience.

While the Light Column continued their Sunday services, Jesse's Cow Column passed by. A quick exchange of news revealed that the Pennington's wagon had pulled out of line when Sarah Pennington went into labor. Reverend Whitman was with her. They expected to spend the night, so Sarah's husband, John, was already stoking a fire. Sarah had been having a difficult time over the last few weeks, and several ladies in her column expressed anxious concern for her safety, even with the help of Reverend Whitman. Sadly, there was nothing anyone could do. The Cow Column needed to get over South Pass and back into an area with grass and water before losing any more cattle. The Penningtons would simply have to catch up.

When wagon corrals formed that evening the Light Column had made twelve miles—and somewhere during those miles they crossed the Continental Divide at South Pass. The trail undulated up and down small hills as they crossed the pass, so the exact point of crossing, the highest elevation, was unknown. Although they were still working their way through the rise and fall of the landscape, the general trend was now down. For these trail-weary emigrants, the exact moment of crossing did not matter. The important point was that everyone knew they were now traveling on the Pacific side of the continent!

The general health of the people in the Light Column had gradually improved since leaving the giant rock monolith. Most people attributed their improved health to the clear, cool, mountain air, while others thought the cause to be the dryness of the air. Nobody knew for sure, only that they were feeling stronger, healthier, and more energetic.

As on previous evenings, tonight's camp was cold and dry. People again wore their winter clothes, and most of the stock went another night without water and very little grass. Abby placed several pans out that evening to collect dew, even though it had seldom appeared on past mornings.

Shortly after dinner the Pennington wagon came up with Reverend Whitman, John and Sarah Pennington, and a new arrival named Mary Jane. The Penningtons chose to camp with the Light Column that evening, while Reverend Whitman quickened his pace to catch up with the Cow Column. The ladies in the Light Column made dinner for the Penningtons, along with donations of bread and dried meat to tide Sarah's family over for the next few days. Abby provided two loaves of bread and did not leave until she had a chance to hold the infant girl. This precious, domestic moment had been absent from her life for too long. The moment was short lived, for almost every lady there wanted to hold the baby.

After dinner Abby again walked out from the wagons to write in her diary and look at the mountains. She found a small rise with some rocks to sit on.

"*One out and one in,*" she wrote. "*Clay Paine dies and Mary Jane is born. Clay died in Atlantic waters and Mary Jane is born in Pacific waters. Pacific waters! Yes, I'm now in Pacific waters. From now on all the rivers will flow toward the Pacific Ocean. I will never again drink Atlantic water—for as long as I live!*"

She wrote a paragraph, then looked up at the mountains, then another paragraph. A gentle breeze blew her hair off her face, while the atmosphere was thick with the smell of sage. Again tonight a brilliant orange and red sunset lit the sky as the sun slowly dipped behind the snow-capped Wind River Mountains.

"*It's a beautiful, peaceful evening on the Pacific side of the continent,*" she wrote. "*Maybe tomorrow we will encounter water and grass for the stock. The nights up here are cold, as cold as early winter. In a week or so we should be back down to a warmer climate.*"

After writing a few more paragraphs, she returned to the wagon while there was still enough light to see each of the corrals, now dwarfed by the majestic mountains and unending Western landscape.

On the next morning, Monday, August 7, the column was again on the march before eight o'clock, looking for water and grass. They traveled six miles before encountering a fresh spring, the headwater of a small creek. Colonel Martin stopped the column for an early nooner, and teamsters allowed their stock to drink liberally. Captain Gantt notified everyone that, from this point, the trail headed out across a twenty-mile stretch of barren desert without water or grass.

Stock stirred up the spring so that the water was quite muddy, too muddy for human consumption. Jacob emptied one of the water barrels into the other, then filled the empty barrel with muddy water for the stock. Everyone expected to spend tonight in another dry camp.

Abby helped Jacob secure the barrel to its perch alongside the wagon, then stepped back displaying a broad smile. "We've Atlantic water in one barrel, and Pacific in the other. What do you think of that?"

"I expect that remaining Atlantic water will be the last I ever taste. I've no stomach for those Eastern settlements."

SOUTH PASS.

"Probably the last I'll ever have too. Oregon will be my home now."

"Did you know you're in Oregon now?"

"That's what you said some weeks ago. This isn't the Oregon I've heard so much about. The Wallamet Valley must be very different from this area. It just has to be!"

"Once you cross the Divide the land's considered Oregon Territory. You can now say you've made it to Oregon!"

"I'll put in my diary that I've arrived in Oregon, even though I'm far from stopping. Nobody could scratch out a living here on this desert. The Wallamet Valley and Oregon City are my destinations."

"What then? Still planning on becoming a schoolteacher?"

"Of course; I've never given that up. I just don't know where. I'll have to see where all these people set up their claims and where they need a schoolteacher."

"You've got sand, Abby, I'll give you that. I'm going over to see if Ed Stevenson or Dan Richardson need any water."

"Here." She reached into the back of the wagon and pulled out part of a loaf of bread. "Take this with you. Those poor men have been down since we left Fort Laramie. Maybe this cool mountain air is helping."

"Maybe. If the column starts before I get back, make sure your milch cow is secure. I'm letting her get her fill right now."

"Give my best to Dan and Ed."

The Light Column continued for ten more miles that afternoon, camping in a level area where they could form their corrals. The camp was dry, with scattered sage for fuel. Jacob doled out a single gallon of muddy water to each of the oxen, the milch cow, and his horse and pack animals. Most of the other emigrant stock went without water. The grass remained poor with only a few clumps here and there, clumps that the hungry animals quickly mowed down.

The lofty summits of the Wind River Mountains, with their eternal glaciers and fields of snow, ran parallel to the trail off to the northwest. The trail at this point headed in a southwesterly direction over sagebrush-covered hills dotted with dry clumps of nutritionally poor grass. Over each rise came another small rise, so nobody could see where the trail would come out as they descended from South Pass. The water from the spring at noon flowed west, and the general trend of the land was down, a marked decrease in elevation. They were on the other side of the continent, and it felt good.

Overnight many of the stock wandered off in search of grass and water. Teamsters spent the first few hours on Tuesday rounding up strays. Jacob had hobbled their stock overnight and was able to get them hitched for the day's march long before the other wagons and teamsters were ready. After yoking and chaining three teams, and tying the fourth yoke, the milch cow, and packhorses to the back of the wagon, both he and Abby chose to walk out onto the desert and sit down on some rocks to wait for the column to finish morning preparations.

"It's been over twenty years now since I went up the Missouri with Henry. The following year they sent a group of men down this way to scout out the fur resources and a way to cross the Rocky Mountains. Old Gabe and Bill Sublette were in that party—came right across South Pass here. Some people say Aster's expedition back in 1811 discovered the pass. If they did, then it was lost for the next ten years. I'll give Bridger and Sublette credit for finding it and making it known to others."

"Is this Bridger fellow the same man we'll meet at Fort Bridger?"

"The same—and I hope he's there 'cause it's been a long time. He probably thought this child's gone under by now—and I just about did back there in St. Louis."

"What about supplies? Since he started that fort to supply emigrants, do you think he has it stocked by now?"

"Not a chance, not unless he's been able to buy supplies from the Hudson Bay Company, and I doubt if he'll ever stoop that low. He probably just got the place built this year. Now that we've shown the way for other wagons to get from Independence to his fort, he can have supplies sent out next winter. He'll be ready for the emigrants of 1844, but not for us. That's the way I see it."

"You're probably right, at least that's logical—and the emigrants of next year won't have to clear sagebrush or build road like we've had to do."

"I imagine they'll make better time." He paused to light his pipe. "Probably get past Fort Laramie before Independence Day."

"None of us would have been able to find South Pass were it not for Joe Chiles or you, and I wouldn't have known when we crossed it if you hadn't told me. Looking back now, I can see that the general lay of the drainage is west."

"Joe Walker could have shown you where to go."

"This certainly doesn't look like the Oregon Country that people talked about back in Ohio. Nobody could ever live out here. There's no need for this desert to become part of the United States—just the Wallamet Valley and those coastal forests I've heard so much about. With all this desert between the good part of Oregon and the United States, I don't see how we could ever communicate or take an active part in our country."

Jacob slowly nodded, quietly listening to her concerns. "El Dorado is yet to come Abby. We've a lot of dry land to cross before we get there. We won't see a single forest until we get across the Snake, past Fort Boise. I'm not sure how we're going to get wagons up through those mountains."

"Is there a pass, like here?"

"There's a route alright, but not for wagons. We'll have to send a team of cutters out front to make a road. That will be another thing that people in coming years won't have to build."

"When we get to Oregon City, I'm going to write my family that this area beyond South Pass is a poor example of El Dorado. People shouldn't despair though, just keep going. Future wagon trains will have a much easier time than us, and the forts will be filled with supplies."

"Probably so, probably so. Looks like people are about ready to go." Jacob stood up and looked around at the horizon. "Isn't that Cooper's Splinter Column coming up behind?"

Abby squinted as she looked up toward South Pass. "It is—let's get back. Colonel Martin will probably want to stay ahead of them."

The Light Column moved out and did not stop for a nooner until three o'clock in the afternoon. After an hour rest, they resumed their march down from South Pass. As they moved slowly forward at about two miles an hour, Colonel Martin rode back along the line of wagons informing everyone that they would continue through the evening and into the night until they found water.

"We lost eight head of oxen last night and will probably lose more than that tonight if we don't find water soon."

Jacob rode up alongside Abby as Colonel Martin spoke.

"We'll stop for an hour rest just before dusk, then keep going. There'll be a full moon tonight and the road's not bad, so we should be able to do another ten miles or until we reach water, whichever comes first."

"We're ready," Abby replied. "Our stock needs grass. I don't think they've had full stomachs since we left that big rock on the Sweetwater."

"That's true for everyone, Miss Meacham." Bill Martin tipped his hat and rode off to inform the next teamster.

After a short stop before sunset, the Light Column continued across a sandy, sage-covered, rolling plain under a sky filled with stars and a full moon. The moon provided enough light so that sage plants were easily visible, along with rocks and other obstacles. At two o'clock in the morning the advance guard came across the Big Sandy River. They halted and waited for the wagons to come up, ordering corrals to form as best they could for a makeshift camp. Over the next hour Jacob and the other men moved their stock down to the Big Sandy for both water and grass. The floodplain area of the river contained the best grass anyone had seen since before Fort Laramie. Most of it was dry, yet it provided the nutrition needed by starving animals.

Cooper's Splinter Column was still behind and Applegate's Cow Column still ahead when people began to stir the following morning.

The Light Column members arose late, around eight o'clock, only to learn the sad news that Ed Stevenson was near death. Close friends paid their respects even though he was only semiconscious. Death came about midmorning. Colonel Martin had already decided to stay in camp the remainder of the day to allow stock to rest. Now there would be a funeral to attend.

Shortly after Ed died, Jim Nesmith, with the Oteys and Alex Zachary, passed by on their way to Fort Bridger. Like everyone else, their stock were gaunt, thirsty, and hungry. After speaking with Jacob and learning that Ham's Fork was ahead by ten or twelve miles, they decided to keep going and camp on that stream. The Light Column was not about to allow Zachary to camp with them. Poor Jim had to continue with the Oteys until late in the evening before stopping for a needed rest.

John Shively, one of Ed's good friends, located a gravesite near the banks of the Big Sandy River. He and Bob Smith dug the grave, while Sam Painter prepared a headboard from a board supplied by Clay Paine's wife. These men had met Ed Stevenson back in Independence, each planning to make his fortune in a new land. Now, they would continue their journey knowing that Ed's fate might await them all.

Nobody knew Ed's birth date, so Sam inscribed only his name and death date. Abby came forward with a few words to let other people know that Ed was a good man. The final headboard read:

EDWARD STEVENSON
DIED
AUG 9, 1843
GOOD, KIND, AND TRUE

Colonel Martin held funeral services late that afternoon. Most of the adults from the Light Column gathered along the banks of the Big Sandy River to hear Pierson Reading give a short eulogy.

"Nobody knew Ed before we left Independence, and he traveled without a wife, children, and wagon," Pierson began. "He was always willing to help during river crossings and any number of breakdowns. He was a good man. I believe he came from Kentucky, and if anyone knows of his family, let Colonel Martin know so we can send a letter after we get to Oregon City. He didn't leave much in the way of property, so we decided to wrap him in his best blanket. I'm sure he can use it on that journey beyond." He paused for a moment.

"We don't know what Ed died of, but I think I speak for everyone here when I say that I hope it wasn't contagious." Pierson continued with sincerity, "Everyone knew that not all of us would make it to Oregon—and there will probably be more deaths before we reach that green Eden of the Wallamet Valley. We need to stay together and stop our quarreling to better our chances of getting through. We're all split up now and we're only halfway. I don't like that one bit but don't know how to change things."

"We don't need to hear about that," Colonel Martin interrupted, pointing to Ed's body. "This is Ed's funeral."

"Well, that's all I've got to say. Ed was a good man who was willing to help. We'll miss him. Now let's have a few moments of silence."

Everyone bowed their heads as several men lowered Ed's body into the grave. As people began to disperse and return to their respective outfits, John Shively and Bob Smith stayed behind to fill in the grave and seat the headboard.

The disagreeable task of going through Ed's belongings to determine what to keep and what to throw out fell to Colonel Martin and Captain Gantt. They designated Ed's horse and two pack animals as property of the Oregon Emigrating Company, offering them to the highest bidder. The only other possessions of value included two blankets, Ed's rifle, his saddle, and some small items such as lead rifle balls, gunpowder, and a few cooking pots. Colonel Martin distributed these items to the most needy families, without cost.

The grass in this camp was not abundant, so by evening the stock had consumed virtually everything edible. They were able to satisfy their thirsts, but were still hungry and gaunt. Tomorrow morning the column would have to move.

Abby and Jacob spent a quiet evening around their kitchen and fire, with Jacob smoking his pipe and Abby writing in her diary. Earlier she had walked up the Big Sandy—above the stock, for the sole purpose of drinking Western water. It was cold and clear, tasting good after the long, hot day. Writing remembrances in her diary sufficed for an evening respite. She had not known Ed, other than for a few dances back at Fort Laramie. She made a note of his passing, along with his headboard verse. After a few more paragraphs about the scenery here on the west slope of the continent, she closed today's entry with, *"Western waters taste better than eastern waters."*

On Thursday morning, August 10, the Light Column was back on the trail by eight o'clock, still descending from South Pass. Shortly after nooning they came to a creek with clear, cold, fresh water and an abundant supply of grass growing on the banks. Colonel Martin ordered the wagon corrals to form, with the expectation of staying at this camp for at least two nights to make repairs and recruit the stock.

"Jacob, does that creek have a name?" Abby asked as she helped him unchain and unyoke the teams.

"Not that I know of, it's just a creek—too small for beaver."

"Then I will call it Pacific Creek. This water must flow into a bigger stream, then into a river like the Snake, and from there into the Columbia and the Pacific Ocean. That ocean is so far away, yet this water will eventually get there."

"Not this water—this creek's heading toward the Gulf of California. From here it'll work its way to the Green, then the Colorado. I've never been down that way, but I hear it's dry as bleached bones—like the desert we crossed going to California."

"If that's true, then we're very near to the top of the whole continent." She released the hoop from around Lashes neck. "Back across South Pass, those waters go to the Atlantic. If these waters go to the Gulf of California, then it can't be far from here that waters will go to the Snake and then to the Pacific. We have to be near the top of the continent, Jacob. What do you think of that?"

"The Snake gets its start up in Yellowstone Country, same as the Yellowstone River. Just below that is the headwaters of the Green, so I suspect that steaming caldron around Yellowstone Lake is really the top of the continent."

"You've never given me cause not to believe you, although I must say, some of those stories you've told about boiling mud and steam shooting out of the ground are a little wild. If you've seen it though, then I believe you."

"The Yellowstone flows northeast to the Missouri, and the Snake flows south through Jackson's Hole, then west to Fort Hall and Fort Boise. We won't see the Snake till we get to Fort Hall, since we'll be south of our Green River Rendezvous site when we make Fort Bridger."

"We've still half a day left, so what do you think about going out for some buffalo? I've been seeing sign all morning, and you did promise that you'd take me out."

"That I did, and I've been looking at that sign myself. If you could unload those packhorses, I'll water and hobble your stock. Bill Fowler won't mind looking after your outfit in case we're out late. I'll talk to him."

"Sometimes you hunters don't get back until late the next day. What if Colonel Martin changes his mind and decides to travel tomorrow?"

"That could be a problem," replied Jacob as he scanned the other kitchens. "John Cox has offered to help on a number of occasions. I'll talk to him. If we're not back and Colonel Martin wants to move, Cox can take your outfit forward. Better get it ready to travel, so all he has to do is yoke and chain the oxen."

Abby unloaded both pack animals, but kept the packsaddle on one of the horses for hauling meat. She would ride the other packhorse. After a few more minutes she was ready with her Hawken, a blanket, and coat, in case they were out overnight, plus a few additional possibles. She also stacked the yokes next to the wagon tongue, in case they did not return before the column moved out. Jacob finished watering the stock and was ready to go as she mounted one of the packhorses.

"John will take care of moving your outfit forward if Martin decides to leave in the morning. You and I will head northwest from here, toward the Wind River Mountains. That should put us downwind of any herds." Abby did not reply, only looked off in the direction he indicated.

They started riding northwest, with both of them carrying their rifles across their horse's necks. Around the corrals several people interrupted their chores to watch while other hunting groups prepared to leave.

"Sarah Hill invited me to pick gooseberries with the other ladies. They're going to make gooseberry dumplings tonight. When I told her I was going out buffalo hunting, I don't think she believed me. That's her over there." Abby motioned toward several women in another corral who were watching them ride out. "She certainly believes me now."

"They've families to take care of, and you don't—that will always make a difference. Don't you pay them any mind."

"They'd never admit it, but I'll bet a few of them would like to join us. Not the older ladies like Millie Arthur or Becky Cason, but the younger ones like Sarah Masters and Becky Stewart. I think Sarah got married just so she could go West. They're not like the other ladies." Abby paused while thinking about the adventure these newlyweds were having. "I guess they're more like me."

They rode on in silence, both watching the horizon for signs of buffalo. Jacob had not mentioned Sam for over a week, not wanting to bring back memories. Abby's strength had returned, and the added diversion of a buffalo hunt could only help. Before an hour passed they took up the trail of a small herd heading in a northerly direction. After two more hours they dismounted, tied their horses to some sage, and carefully walked up a small rise. On the other side were over thirty head of buffalo, lazily grazing in the summer sun.

They both lay down and crawled forward to get a better view. As soon as they were in place, Jacob pointed out the animals that would have the best meat. These were young bulls grazing on the outskirts of the herd. Jacob and Abby were now only fifty yards from the nearest animal. By staying downwind, none had detected their presence.

"Take that one on the right. He's far enough from the other animals that dropping him might not spook the rest."

Abby was already pointing her Hawken at the center of the herd. Now she seated the rifle against her shoulder and took aim at the bull Jacob indicated. She pulled the hammer back, then grabbed the pistol grip with her right hand. By balancing the barrel in her left hand and pushing her left elbow into the soft soil, the barrel remained steady.

"Now don't just shoot it in the side. You'll look like some of those other greenhorn farmers," Jacob said. "Take aim at that spot behind his shoulder and about a foot up from his underside. See where I mean?"

"Got it." Abby drew a breath, lined the sights on the spot Jacob described, and squeezed off a shot. The gun's recoil pushed her whole body back, while the bull fell over sideways and did not move.

Jacob nodded. "Can't do better than that." The herd looked up at the downed animal, smelling the wind for any sign of danger. Now Jacob took aim at another bull and dropped it. That was enough for the remaining animals; they took flight in a headlong race over the undulating sage desert. In a few moments they disappeared in a cloud of alkali dust. The hunters stood up and looked down into the draw at the two dead buffalo.

"That'll be enough meat for several weeks, won't need any more," said Abby. "Let's get the horses."

"Reload." Jacob started reloading his rifle while motioning for Abby to do the same. "You might need it before we get back to the horses."

Abby started reloading without hesitation. "After listening to your stories about grizzly bears and mad wolves, I don't doubt your sincerity. I'm loading."

Over the next hour Abby learned how to skin a buffalo and which parts are best for butchering. She had helped to butcher livestock back in Ohio, so she knew this was something she could do, and do well. With Jacob's help she took the hump, tongue, and flanks, along with both hides. By late afternoon they had everything loaded onto both packhorses. On setting out for the wagon, Abby had to ride behind Jacob on his horse.

They no sooner started back for the column when a small band of Crow appeared directly in their path. When they came to within two hundred yards of each other, Jacob halted, as did the Indians. He eased Abby down, then dismounted himself. After handing her his rifle, belt pistol, Green River knife, and leg sheath, he took off his shirt and approached the Indians. Their chief did likewise, leaving his weapons with his horse and approaching Jacob half-naked. As they came to within fifty yards of each other, Jacob recognized the chief from an incident years before. He immediately turned to Abby and signaled for her to bring the horses up. The chief did the same.

In English the chief's name was Three-Fingers. During a scrape with the Blackfeet a number of years before, the Crow and the white trappers of the Rocky Mountain Fur Company had fought side by side. At one point during the battle, Jacob had killed a Blackfoot just as he was about to run his spear through Three-Fingers, then a young Crow warrior. Three-Fingers had not forgotten the incident and now sat down with Jacob for a smoke. They communicated with sign, since Jacob knew very little Crow and Three-Fingers knew even less English. When the Crow learned that he was traveling with a large group of farmers, they both smiled with a half-laugh.

"How could a great warrior travel with farmers?" the Crow chief signed.

"With patience," Jacob signed back. "With patience."

Three-Fingers invited Jacob and his squaw (Abby) to the Crow village for a feast. It was not far away, and they would be honored guests. Jacob immediately accepted the invitation without bothering to consult Abby. To get away from the migration and spend a night as a mountain man was too tempting to turn down. Besides, Three-Fingers would have been insulted had he refused the offer. Theirs was a debt of friendship.

After Jacob explained that they would be spending the night at a Crow village, Abby grew both irritated and frightened, yet said nothing. These were real Western Indians, living a hunter-gatherer nomadic life—far different from the reservation Indians she had seen back in Ohio and Missouri. Jacob had previously related stories in which the Crow and white trappers were not always on the best of terms. Abby also knew that mountain men considered the Crow to be the finest horse thieves between the Black Hills and the Yellowstone. Her curiosity overcame her apprehensions. To spend a night in a Crow village would certainly be an adventure.

Three-Fingers assumed that Abby was Jacob's squaw, which was fine with Jacob. On the way back to the village, Jacob informed the chief that she had lost her brave and was now accompanying him on a buffalo hunt. The face of the Crow chief grew serious as he looked at Abby, recognizing her situation.

"She is welcome at my village," he signed. Turning to one of the young braves, he gave orders to ride back to the village and make preparations. It was only a few miles away, and the chief wanted to repay Jacob with a feast for the courage he had displayed years before. The brave would also inform the village squaws about Abby, so they would be ready to take care of her needs.

Upon her arrival at the village, the squaws surrounded Abby, looking at her dirty, drab brown cotton dress and filthy hair. Two older squaws took her by the arms and started to lead her off, away from Jacob. She turned to Jacob with a look of uncertainty and fear. His nod indicated that she should go with them. There was nothing to fear.

The Crow village sat on the banks of a fast-moving stream. It had been set up only a few days ago, since the village was traveling with the buffalo herds. Outside of a number of teepees stood the owners' primary horses. The majority of other horses grazed together in a nearby herd. Teenage boys rode on the outskirts of the herd for protection and to keep them from wandering too far. The entire village consisted of fifteen teepees, about fifty to sixty people, perhaps two hundred horses, and an odd number of dogs.

The teepees were constructed from long pine poles of about sixteen to eighteen feet in length and covered with buffalo hides with the hair removed. The skins hung heavy on the poles, sagging slightly between each pole. They were sturdy structures, with the thick skins and geometric forms providing ample support against strong winds. Over the top fourth of the teepee were several sewn buffalo robes with the hair still attached. Indians were well aware that heat rose, and knew that the top of the teepee needed to be insulated to keep the heat in.

However, on these long hot summer days, skin teepees could become insufferable. But the skin sides, rather than stopping at ground level, extended for another eight to ten feet. Short poles, five to six feet in length, supported these flaps, or vestibules. This allowed air to circulate through the teepee, keeping the contents as cool as possible. The skins were sewn together, and the seams sealed with a mixture of pine pitch and ash. The entire covering lay as a single garment over the pole framework, coming together in a vertical seam over the door. Squaws brought this seam together with pegs of about ten to twelve inches long. A round hole was cut as a doorway, while another skin flap acted as the door.

The Crow painted the outside of their teepees with various figures depicting buffalo hunts, battles, warriors, peace pipes, tomahawks, and other items peculiar to their culture. An additional long pole controlled the top flap, which covered the smoke hole. Around the entire teepee, about three feet off the ground, was a fringe for ornamentation. This fringe consisted of animal fur, hide, and pieces of scalps—a tribute to the warrior who resided within the teepee. To Abby, at least from a distance, the teepees appeared to be cozy homes for a nomadic people.

The Indians presented a menagerie of forms, a cross section of the difficult, hunter-gatherer existence of Plains Indians—from papooses to the very old. Abby noticed a blind woman with a deerskin strap wrapped around her head to shield her eyes. One boy had a deformed arm that appeared to have been broken and failed to heal properly. Two Indians, an adult and a small boy, were lying on buffalo robes outside their teepees, too ill to rise for the visitors. Another man was clearly blind in one eye. This small tribe, like others, acted as a single family unit, watching each other's children and caring for each other's welfare.

The Crow men had long hair, often extending down below their waists. They parted it on both sides, with an additional crop of hair extending halfway down their forehead and about three inches wide. Each man wore several rawhide necklaces decorated with beads, bones, and tufts of white fur. One warrior had the full hide of a small white weasel dangling on his chest. Their only clothing at this time of year was a piece of hide about a foot wide and five feet long. It was worn through the crotch and secured with a single strap of leather around the waist. As darkness came on, the squaws brought their men buffalo robes to wrap in. For decoration, most of the men wore two or three eagle or hawk feathers in their hair.

The squaws wore a similar dress, consisting of a single piece of hide about two feet wide and eight feet long. They wore it over their shoulders with a hole cut in the center for their head, and then laced up the sides to the waist, leaving the upper torso open. This gave nursing mothers easy access for their babes. The clothing of both squaws and warriors displayed colorful images depicting important events in the lives of the owner. Babies were secure in papooses, and small children played naked.

The ears of all the Indians, children included, held a number of piercings, decorated with pieces of metal, rawhide, and bone.

On the ground outside each teepee were numerous buffalo robes, staked to the ground and drying in the summer sun. The squaws had been busy scraping these hides when Jacob and Abby arrived. They now interrupted their work to see the strangers and satisfy their curiosity toward the white female.

Abby disappeared into one of the teepees while Jacob, Three-Fingers, and seven other warriors sat down for a smoke. It was early evening, with another hour of daylight. As the sun went down, the men moved into the chief's teepee and continued their smoke and discourse. Shortly afterward, squaws entered carrying food. Abby followed Three-Fingers' squaw, carrying a basket of food for Jacob. It consisted of cooked buffalo tongue and boiled roots.

Normally, Jacob would not pay any attention to the squaws in such a male-dominated society—but there was Abby. Rather than the drab brown dress she had arrived in, she now wore traditional Crow garb, along with a new pair of sturdy moccasins. Her clean, combed, jet-black hair made her look more Crow than a woman from Ohio. However, her clean white face with European features and her embarrassment at the openness of her new Crow dress revealed her true identity.

As she squatted to give Jacob his dinner, she kept her left hand strategically placed to prevent the dress from opening and exposing her breasts. Three-Fingers, watching Abby's movements and new look, smiled at her embarrassment. As she handed Jacob the basket she could feel the eyes of every man on her every move. She quickly looked around, grabbing her dress with her right arm to prevent the other braves from seeing her. This movement resulted in a hearty laugh from everyone, including the attending squaws. They had all been watching her. Abby said nothing, only looked back at Jacob's eyes to see his approval—a nod, ever so slightly, but definitely there. He knew that during the last hour she had been receiving the education of her life, an education that would continue into the night. The men continued their discourse as soon as the squaws and Abby left. By tomorrow, Abby, too, would be a Crow squaw.

After another two hours, Three-Fingers' squaw reentered to announce that a teepee was ready. The men finished their smoke and discourse, then disbanded for the night. Three-Fingers walked with Jacob to the specially prepared teepee. The regular occupants had removed to a relative's teepee.

Jacob entered to find Abby stoking the fire, considerably apprehensive about spending the night in the same teepee with him. Her nervousness evaporated as she began describing the last four hours since arriving at the village. Her ability at signing was still poor, so there had been a slight language gap between her and the squaws. Yet she knew enough to communicate adequately. Jacob had spent a number of hours over the last few months teaching Abby sign language. Her skill so far was barely enough to carry on a normal conversation. For the most part, she had simply done what the squaws had physically shown her to do.

Upon arriving at the village, getting cleaned up had been her first task. The squaws took her down to the nearby creek and gave her an ice cold bath with soap obtained from one of the fur trading posts up on the Missouri. This was not a usual trade item, more of a novelty. Yet it was an article native to whites, and the squaws thought she would appreciate its use. After Abby emerged from the stream, shivering and wet, they threw a Hudson Bay blanket around her and led her back to the village and into a teepee. There they gave her a traditional Crow dress. Rather than being decorated for ceremony, this was an everyday dress held on with a rawhide belt and side lacing up to the waist. The upper half remained open on both sides. Then they sat her down on a buffalo robe and began combing her hair with a trade comb. After four months on the trail, it was now nearly shoulder length. Other squaws began preparing food for the council of braves and Jacob. Squaws always ate after the braves and with whatever food was left over. Abby's initial anxiety had been replaced by a combination of interest and gratefulness. She could see that the squaws did not present a threat. Rather, they were doing their best to welcome her into their society.

Abby explained all of this in intimate detail as Jacob sat cross-legged on one side of the teepee.

"They'll expect you to be up with the sun tomorrow—probably show you how to dress a skin, make moccasins, and how to prepare some of their foods."

"I already know how to make moccasins," Abby replied with confidence.

"Not the Crow way—every tribe's a little different."

"Then dressing a skin is probably different too—especially out here where we don't have any of the needed tools."

"They just returned from a buffalo hunt—that's where all these hides came from. You'll probably spend some of your time scraping, but they'll have you doing a number of things. They'll probably want to show you what roots and shoots they use for food. I'll let Three-Fingers know we need to get back to our outfit tomorrow, that should give you most of the day. Well, at least till early afternoon before we leave."

"What will you be doing?"

"Nothing, maybe have a smoke. If they go out for more buffalo, I'll join 'em. Otherwise I'll stay around the village."

"You can't help with the work?" Abby wasn't annoyed, just inquisitive.

"Men don't do women's work, and all work around the village is women's work. Warriors provide meat and protection, squaws do everything else."

"No wonder you were so quick to accept Three-Fingers' invitation," Abby replied with a teasing smile. "This is just a pleasure excursion for you!"

Jacob lay back and pulled a buffalo robe over himself.

"Better get some sleep, you've got a big day tomorrow."

Abby knew he was right. After stirring the coals of the fire, she settled back onto another robe. In a few moments the teepee was dark and they were both asleep.

The next morning Jacob roused Abby just before two squaws came in to fetch her. She spent the morning learning various domestic duties relegated to squaws in their tightly knit society. The first two hours were spent scraping buffalo hides with a shoulder-blade bone. One of the squaws helping to scrape the hides carried a papoose in a canopied reed basket, suspended on her back by a band across her forehead. When the baby cried, the mother took the infant, basket and all, and slid it under her dress for the infant to suckle.

About the time Abby's fingers felt like they were about to fall off, two other squaws took her into a teepee to show her how to cut hide to make moccasins and other clothing. After that came the preparation of several types of foods. It was a busy, exhausting day, as Jacob had predicted.

The men did not go back out for buffalo, so Jacob spent the day lounging around with the other warriors—conversing, smoking, and eating. Early in the afternoon he brought his three horses around and started packing them in preparation for the trip back to the Light Column. Abby joined him with relish after a grueling morning of work and domestic education from the village squaws.

Before they finished packing the last horse, Three-Fingers came up with a spirited Indian pony to give as a gift, in payment for Jacob saving his life many years before. Jacob stood straight and proud as he surveyed the gift.

"He is a fine buffalo horse," he signed and spoke simultaneously. He walked around the animal, running his hand down a foreleg, then looking at its teeth.

"He is fleet and will serve me well. He is a handsome gift."

Three-Fingers also looked pleased to eliminate an old debt.

"My squaw is poor. She has no husband and no horse." Jacob continued to speak while signing. "She will need a horse to get to Oregon. I will let her ride on our journey." It was a generous offer and one that Three-Fingers understood. He too nodded his approval that the Crow Nation's newest squaw should ride the horse.

Abby too was admiring the pony—it was one of the finest horses she had ever seen. Nobody back in Ohio owned horses of this quality—it was truly a superb gift.

"This is an Indian pony, Abby," Jacob said quietly as she came around to the left side of the horse. "That means he's plenty skittish and only half broke."

"I'll be careful. Give me a leg up."

"You know you have to ride astride?"

"Yes, I know," she snapped back. "Help me up."

Jacob took hold of her left knee and gave her a boost. She swung her right leg over the bareback horse and took hold of the rawhide bridle. The horse nervously stepped around while Abby got comfortable. Jacob and Three-Fingers stepped back while she walked the horse around in a small circle, stopping next to Jacob.

"Jacob, this is the finest horse I've ever seen. It would bring five hundred dollars back in Ohio. Three-Fingers is simply going to give it to you?"

"Three-Fingers is a good man. You can have the horse, Abby. I don't need it, and you'll need a horse when you get to Oregon. Three-Fingers thinks you're my squaw, so seeing you ride is good. Family relationships are important to these people—and to them, you're my family.

Abby looked at Three-Fingers, smiled, and signed her appreciation. This pleased Three-Fingers. He backed up while nodding his approval of her riding the pony.

Abby then looked over at Jacob and announced, "We need to be getting back."

Jacob mounted his horse, taking the two pack animals in tow. He then turned to Abby to explain some final protocol.

"Follow behind the pack animals while we ride out. They will not accept you riding alongside me."

Abby did not respond, since his request made sense. This was a different culture, and one must adhere to and respect the cultural needs of others. Riding behind the pack animals was a small price to pay for the kindness shown by this small band of Crow over the last twenty-four hours.

As they slowly rode out, Jacob noticed one of the Indian squaws wearing Abby's old brown dress. She stood away from the other squaws and was clearly pleased with her new acquisition. Abby was wearing her Crow dress, and was also pleased with her new acquisition. It was a good trade.

As soon as they were out of sight of the village, Jacob stopped and waited for Abby to catch up. Earlier she had tied a piece of rawhide around her midsection to keep her dress closed.

"The women thought it was funny that I did not know how to do such simple chores like dressing a skin or preparing some of their foods. I wanted to learn how to weave those grass baskets, but there simply wasn't time."

"You did fine, Abby. I suspect you're the first white woman those squaws have ever seen. They probably don't understand how you can expect to ever find a husband when you don't have the skills that every woman should know."

"This dress is more comfortable than my old cotton dress. It's simple to make and more than adequate."

"The women back in the column might not be so understanding. You've already gained a reputation for being unconventional."

"I don't care what they think. Most of those women never wanted to go to Oregon to begin with. Jacob, are you really giving me this pony?"

"It's yours, Abby. I don't need another horse, and you'll need something out in Oregon. I suspect you'll be selling that wagon and whatever oxen you have left, so you'll need a horse, and that's a good one."

"I will name him Crow." She glanced a smile at Jacob, then looked back down at the horse, admiring her newest possession. He was right, she would need a horse out in Oregon.

When they arrived back at their previous camp, it was empty and the Light Column was en route. A massive cut of wagon wheels and trampled vegetation heading in a southwest direction provided an easy trail to follow. It was now five o'clock, allowing another three to four hours of daylight for travel. So they picked up their pace in order to catch up before dark.

They passed Jesse's Cow Column only a mile before encountering the Light Column. The toll taken in dead animals and broken-down wagons while crossing South Pass had brought the Cow Column to a halt. They needed an extra day to repair wheels, tongues, running gear, and to give their stock a chance to recover before moving on to Fort Bridger. With darkness rapidly approaching, Abby and Jacob hurried on to the Light Column.

"I never thought a wagon would look so comfortable," Abby said as they came in view of the column. "It's good to be home."

"I'll unload the meat and start cutting. We'll have to dry it while on the trail tomorrow."

"Here they come." Abby motioned to several women walking toward her outfit.

"We've work to do before turning in. I'll check with John Cox about your oxen. Don't let those women get in your way, we've got a lot to do."

With Abby dressed in Indian garb, the women had a myriad of questions to ask. Nobody had seen any Indians since before Fort Laramie, so this was news. While Jacob checked on the oxen he conversed with Colonel Martin, Captain Gantt, Al Hill, Ransom Clark, and several other men, relating the events of their buffalo hunt and their stay at the Crow village. After the women got a chance to see the Crow dress, Abby changed back into a cotton dress. This Crow dress was a treasure that she wanted to protect. The other ladies started unloading and cutting meat to make themselves useful while questioning her and hearing about her adventure.

Abby pulled out some jerky and bread for dinner while explaining to Sarah Hill, Sarah Rubey, Harriet Burnett, and the other ladies her experiences of the last day. They all listened intently as they sliced and stacked the meat, looking up occasionally in disbelief.

"You stayed in a teepee?"

"They had soap, real soap?"

"You scraped a buffalo hide? I don't believe it!"

The questions and conversation continued until well after dark when Abby excused herself. It had been a long and busy day. All the meat had been cut and strung up to dry, so the few remaining chores could wait until morning. Colonel Martin wanted to get back on the trail at an early hour, so tomorrow would be another long day of travel.

Jacob thanked the ladies for their help, which was a clear signal to leave. It had been an exhausting day for everyone. In a few minutes all was quiet throughout the Light Column's corrals.

On Saturday morning, August 12, the Light Column continued their journey down from South Pass toward Fort Bridger. Both Abby and Jacob arose early to finish yesterday's chores before beginning the day's march. Abby placed her Crow dress inside a trunk for safekeeping. It would provide a fine example of Plains Indian culture for her schoolchildren in Oregon. She then bundled and tied the two buffalo robes and threw them on top of her kitchen gear. Jacob agreed to fashion some small stakes so she could scrape the hides in the manner taught by the Crow squaws.

By eight o'clock they were on their way, winding down from South Pass over a parched desert of scattered sage and scant grass. The billowing clouds of dust prompted the teamsters and drovers to cover their faces with handkerchiefs. Other people, mostly women and children, walked one or two hundred feet out from the wagons to avoid the choking alkali dust.

After a morning of twelve miles, they stopped for a nooner on Ham's Fork of the Green River. The stop proved to be an emotional one, for one of Abby's ox lay down and was not able to get up. Jacob removed the yoke while Abby tried to get him to drink. It was too late. Within a half-hour, Loafer was dead. The extra stops for grass and water had not been enough for Loafer to recruit his emaciated frame. It was their first loss, but far from the first in the column. Oxen had started dying shortly after Fort Laramie, and by now most everyone had lost one or two. Even with this misfortune, Abby's oxen were in better shape than most. Since leaving the rock monolith, she and Jacob had expected to lose Loafer. He did not eat well when he had the chance, a sure sign that his days were numbered. Jacob tied Loafer's partner, Jumpy, to the back of the wagon and hitched up the fourth yoke. From now on, only the weakest ox would get to walk behind the wagon.

Shortly before the afternoon march began, Miles Eyre came by to look at the ox.

"You gonna butcher him?" he asked, looking at Jacob.

"No," answered Abby.

Miles spun around to face her.

"We've got buffalo, don't need any ox." she said. "This meat's probably no good anyway, considering how he died."

"Well, it's plenty good for me and my family," responded Miles. "I haven't got any buffalo, and we're running low on all our other food supplies."

"I'm sorry, Miles, I didn't realize that. You're always so quiet that I didn't realize you and Eliza needed meat. Yes, certainly—take all the meat you want."

"Thank you kindly, ma'am. Eliza and I appreciate your generosity."

"I don't want to see it—that ox was a good friend. Come on Jacob, let's move ahead."

Abby picked up her quirt and moved the wagon out of line and ahead a ways. Jacob grabbed the few items unloaded for their noon meal and followed her. Soon they were sitting down to finish their nooner.

"You know, that's the first time old man Eyre ever spoke to me," Abby said after sitting down. "Whenever I've gone over to visit with Eliza, he would go out with his oxen, not even coming in to learn of news or the trail ahead. Just about the most unfriendly man I've ever met—and now this. I don't understand people like that."

"He's hungry, and so is his family," Jacob replied. "Hunger will do strange things—make friends out of enemies, beggars out of gentlemen, and turn friend against friend."

"Next time we go out for buffalo, let's check if they need meat."

"He can go for buffalo the same as anyone else. It might be that he's afraid, might be that he never shot a gun—don't know. I've never seen him go out with any of the other hunting parties."

"He must have been buying meat from the other hunters. Everyone's probably running low by now. I haven't seen many hunters heading out since we left that monolith."

"That's probably why he ran out. If he doesn't want to hunt for himself, then he'd better hire someone to hunt for him. When we get up on the Snake River Plains, we'll be west of the herds. He'll be in a fix if he doesn't stock up before then."

"We should go out hunting whenever we get the chance from now on. When we get to Fort Hall, I want my wagon filled with as much dried meat as possible—I mean as much as we can carry. I don't plan on getting caught short."

Jacob nodded his understanding. They would be in good shape before venturing out onto the Snake River Plains.

After nooning, they crossed Ham's Fork and were soon on Black's Fork of the Green. The flow was low this time of year, providing only a minor obstacle for the wagons. They crossed the river and continued on without ever slowing below their usual two-mile-per-hour pace.

The desert beyond Black's Fork was even drier than previous areas, if that was possible. The summer heat bounced off the ground in waves of images appearing like small lakes or rivers, just out of reach. Now and then a team of oxen would bolt forward toward this imaginary water, only to be forced back in line by the quick action of a sharp quirt and yells from a teamster. Clouds of choking, billowing, alkali dust continued to rise all afternoon till they came to Black's Fork again. At this point they had made twenty-three miles and were at a stream with good water. The grass was marginal, but there was no other place to stop. Everyone was showing exhaustion, especially the thirsty oxen and remaining stock. Colonel Martin halted the caravan and ordered wagon corrals to form for the night.

A number of people spent the evening tightening iron rims that had worked loose due to a combination of the dry desert air and rough road. Also, almost every teamster took time to grease their running gear from their tar buckets. While Jacob took care of that, Abby spread the two buffalo hides on the ground and secured them with several small stakes that Jacob had made from sage. Rather than scraping with a shoulder blade bone, she used the metal scraper that had come in handy a few months earlier when she and Jacob first caulked the wagon.

When Jacob finished greasing the running gear, he moved the stock to another area of grass along the creek. Due to the poor condition of the grass, the stock needed to be moved several times before they had their fill. After returning to the wagon, Jacob pulled out his pipe and sat down on the ground, leaning up against one of the wagon wheels.

"You gonna make something from those robes?"

"Don't know," Abby panted between scrapes. "They'll come in handy if we get caught in snow crossing those Blue Mountains after Fort Boise."

"You hear that?" Jacob looked over at a nearby corral. Another argument had broken out, this one between Dan Delany and Jesse Looney.

"They've been arguing on and off all evening." Abby glanced over at the wagons, then back down at the hide as she continued to scrape. "Jesse's going to Oregon to get away from slavery, and people like Dan Delany, Miles Cary, and Pete Burnett are bringing their slaves with them. Since Oregon doesn't have any government, it could become a free state. I suspect that's what Jesse's arguing for."

"Those other people want to protect their investments. Should be some interesting discussions when Oregon draws up a constitution."

"If they want real progress ..." Abby stopped and looked up at Jacob. "If they want real progress they'll outlaw slavery and allow women to vote!"

Jacob took in her stern expression, knowing that she was serious. "Abby, I suspect when that happens you'll be right in the center of the ruckus."

"We pioneers have a chance to correct the mistakes made back in the United States, and I don't see why we can't do just that."

"No doubt." Jacob lit his pipe and looked off to the north at a distant hill. "Good to start out with a clean slate. The Green River Rendezvous site's not far from here, and there's good grass over there.

That's why we kept having our summer fairs on that river. Had more Rendezvous there than anyplace else."

"Will we be closer tomorrow night?"

"Not if we're going to Fort Bridger—that's south of here, maybe another twenty miles. I'm not entirely sure of its location, since Jim just built it. We'll run into it tomorrow or the day after. From there we'll be heading northwest, up past Bear River and Beer Springs."

"A number of people could use some blacksmithing on their wagons. I think we're in good shape—the patch jobs you've done on those wheels are holding up. The rims might work loose if we try to have them reset."

"They'll hold up."

"I never thought I'd say this, Jacob, but I miss not having chips to cook on. The dinner tonight was half-cold. I can't seem to get a hot fire started from this sage. It burns too fast to give off much heat, then it's gone."

"Fuel's gonna be a problem till we get past the Snake River Plains. After that we'll be into timber."

"We haven't seen a forest since we passed that island back on the Platte River," Abby said as she stopped her scraping and sat up to rest. "I'm glad the Wallamet Valley is not like this part of Oregon Country." She scanned the horizon of rolling hills as if looking for a tree or some other sign of fertility.

"Oregon has to be more productive than this, it just has to be."

"It is," Jacob replied as he stood up. "We wouldn't have heard all those stories if it looked like this. I'm going down to move the stock."

"Thank you." Abby watched him walk down toward the creek, then leaned over and continued scraping. By dusk she had completed both hides. She decided to let them continue drying overnight, then bundle and pack them in the morning.

Colonel Martin started the column early on Sunday in the hopes of reaching the fort before nightfall. By late that afternoon they had made twenty-three miles and were setting up their wagon corrals in the shadow of Fort Bridger. For Abby, she had placed enough mileage and time between her and the loss of Sam that she was essentially back to normal. Evening chores of washing, cooking, sewing, and miscellaneous repairs were now receiving her full attention.

Grass and water were plentiful around the fort, so much so that Colonel Martin decided to stay until Wednesday morning before resuming the journey. This interval stood in stark contrast to their short stay at Fort Laramie, when the stock were still in fairly good condition. The delays at crossing the Kansas and South Platte Rivers had still been fresh in everyone's minds, and there was an urgency to make up for lost time. Now, everyone needed a rest—especially the gaunt and starving stock. The Snake River Plains were ahead, and everyone knew of the lack of water and feed along that stretch between Fort Hall and Fort Boise. A two-day, three-night stopover at Fort Bridger would be a welcome respite for making blacksmithing repairs, washing clothes, mending harnesses, baking bread, and otherwise preparing for the push to Fort Hall.

Jacob watered the stock and hobbled them in a pasture of two-foot-high grass. Then, with rifle in hand and striding like a man on a mission, he went up to the fort to find Jim Bridger.

The area where Bridger had located his fort was mostly flat. The nearby creek, Black's Fork, wound its way through the valley providing the necessary water to support the grassy plains and the fort's garden. During the first year the garden contained only enough food to support the fort's occupants for the coming winter. At this time of year, nothing was ripe, so it would not present a temptation to the provision-poor travelers. In coming years Bridger and his partner planned to expand the garden and put up preserves—preserves they could sell during the following season. Off toward the south stood more snow-capped mountains, similar to the Wind River Mountains and appearing impassable.

Jacob walked up to the only structure, a small log cabin, and boomed out a loud demand. "I've come all the way from St. Louis, and I'm here to see old Gabe!"

With that announcement, a lanky gentleman in full buckskins stepped out of the cabin with rifle in hand, expecting trouble. "Jacob, you old horse thief! Joe said you was comin' in." It was Jim "Gabe" Bridger, the fort's proprietor and former bourgeois of the Rocky Mountain trapping brigades.

"Walker and Chiles arrived yesterday. Come on in, this old child could use some decent company."

Amid backslapping, minor wrestling, and some shots of pure-grain alcohol, Jim Bridger and Jacob got reacquainted after a year's absence. Another one of Jacob's cronies from the fur-trapping era, Louis Vasquez, was also at the fort. Louis was Jim's partner and played a necessary part in building the fort to service Oregon- and California-bound emigrants. Construction of the fort had begun that spring and was still underway. Supplies were almost nonexistent, and would remain so until a supply train could be brought out from St. Louis during the following winter. Next summer's emigrants would be able to resupply, but not the current migration. For each of the columns of the Oregon Emigrating Company, the only value of Fort Bridger was a blacksmith shop to make wheel repairs, and grass and water for the stock.

Louis excused himself from the camaraderie when shouts of an argument near the blacksmith lean-to caught his attention. The other members of the column had arrived. Joe Hess, the farmer from Germany who feared Indian attacks several months back, had been trying to explain to Pete Stewart that he needed to reset a wheel rim. Pete told him he'd have to wait. Joe got agitated, causing him to lose control of his English, and started in on Pete in scathing German. Now they were embroiled in a heated exchange that nobody could understand. Sam Cozine, who had been nearby helping another man with a wheel, tried to intervene, but could not speak German either. Louis, who could speak French, German, and English, quickly assessed the situation and set up a numbered priority of who would get to use the pit and tools. He also struck up an agreement and price at which Sam Cozine would do the blacksmithing work needed by Joe. It was a peaceful resolution that everyone could agree on.

Darkness was quickly approaching, so Joe left his wheel at the shop along with numerous other wheels dropped off by teamsters. There was no need to work through the night like they had back at Fort Laramie. With several days' rest ahead, tomorrow would be soon enough to begin repairs.

Jacob, too, wandered back to the wagon corral before he and Jim had drunk too many welcoming shots of grain alcohol. Other columns would be arriving tomorrow, so it would be a busy time at the fort, and especially at the blacksmith shop.

On Monday, August 14, both Cooper's and Applegate's Columns arrived. For the first time in weeks, Martin's Light Column, Chiles's California Column, Cooper's Splinter Column, Applegate's Cow Column, and Zachary's Outcast Mess were all camped together. Tomorrow they expected Waldo's Straggler Column to arrive. If so, this would be only the second time since leaving Elm Grove that every member of the full Oregon Emigrating Company had come together. The first time had been at Fort Laramie. Fortunately for all columns, the area Jim Bridger had chosen for his fort contained enough pasture for the working stock, milch cows, horses, and large beef herds.

Abby was busy making bread when Jacob rolled over in his buffalo robe to sit up and view the scene around him. Yesterday's pure-grain alcohol had taken its toll. Smoke drifted up from a hundred campfires, kindled for breakfast and a day of baking. Herds of beef cattle grazed into the distance, with drovers trying to keep some semblance of order and to prevent the herds from mixing. Clanging sounds drifted up from the blacksmith shop along with the sounds of several hundred children playing in the surrounding grass, the first they had seen since leaving the great rock monolith.

It was a scene of civilization with all the smells, noises, and sights of white-sheeted wagons and cattle—all new and never before seen out here in this remote oasis on the road to El Dorado. Ahead lay the Snake River Plains, then the Blue Mountains, then the swirling, boiling Columbia River. Never before had a wagon ventured into those outreaches of the North American continent. The emigrants felt a quiet pride that they had arrived at Fort Bridger with minimal loss of equipment and life—deaths that were offset by three births. Everyone knew that the worst was yet to come, and with provisions running low there could be no room for error. Wagon wheels, running gear, and the working stock were all tired and in need of rest or replacement—but such was not the luxury of these wayfarers. By Wednesday morning the columns would start pulling out, regardless of their preparedness.

"I've breakfast here as soon as you're ready," Abby said as she stirred a pot over a cottonwood fire. "Cornmeal. What did you learn at the fort last night?"

Jacob threw off his buffalo robe and pushed his hair back out of his eyes.

"Not much. The Sioux and Cheyenne paid a visit here a few weeks ago. Ran off all the buffalo, so we won't be going for meat. They killed three Snake Indians—good workers, according to Gabe. The worst of it was that they stole about sixty horses. Most of these farmers could use fresh mounts."

"The entire migration should be here today, so let's make sure we've hobbled the stock where they can get good grass and water."

Without saying a word, Jacob stood and, with rifle in hand, started walking out toward the stock.

"He can eat when he wants," Abby thought. "This pot will be here all day."

Abby planned to spend the day busy in her kitchen, stocking up on bread, repairing torn clothes, doing laundry in the nearby creek, making several new pair of moccasins, and taking care of any other chore that showed itself. Jacob's patch jobs and her wise choice of wagon wheels precluded any need for blacksmithing. The two-day respite would be wisely used in preparation for crossing the Snake River Plains.

The morning passed quickly with the completion of each chore as a signal of being one step closer to Oregon. While people paused for their nooner, word passed between the corrals that Catherine Cary, the three-year-old daughter of Miles and Cyrene Cary, had died of a fever. People greeted the news with quiet sadness that so young a life should be taken. Strangely, nobody knew that Catherine was near death. With over six hundred children, at least twenty-five were ill in bed at any one time. Catherine's death prompted more worries that there might be a contagious fever among the migration.

Abby stopped eating when the news came in. She sat holding a piece of bread, staring in the direction of the Cary wagon.

"I'm not sure Jacob, but I think that was the Cary's only child. I don't know Mrs. Cary very well, only talked to her once."

"I've seen her carrying an infant. What did we start out with," Jacob asked, "wasn't it 602 young 'uns?"

"About that, just over six hundred."

"We've had three births and now two deaths."

"I'm going over to see if Mrs. Cary needs anything."

Abby set her plate down on the washtub and walked over to the Cary wagon. In ten minutes she was back.

"Sarah Jane Matheny wants me to write a verse for Catherine. I guess I've earned a reputation for that."

"We should all leave something behind, you said it yourself. Little Catherine is only going to leave a few broken hearts. A verse will help give comfort to her parents."

"Jacob, sometimes I don't know if you're a mountain man, a father, or a preacher!"

Jacob was sitting on the ground cross-legged as Abby spoke. He straightened up and gave her a worried, furrowed-brow look, an acknowledgment of her confusion. He knew he presented an enigma of qualities to her and the other emigrants. He enjoyed the mystery about his past and preferred to keep it that way.

Abby retrieved her diary box and began drafting a verse. It did not come easy. After twenty minutes it was ready.

> *Beneath this stone in soft repose,*
> *Is laid a mother's dearest pride.*
> *A flower that scarce had waked to grow,*
> *To see light and beauty, ere it died.*

She handed it to Jacob for his opinion. "It's long, but we've time to fix up a nice headboard."

"It's a fine verse, Abby. It will give the Carys some comfort. They could probably use my help digging a grave." He stood up and handed the paper back. "Come on. Gabe probably set up a cemetery for those three Snake, assuming he buried 'em. If not, then we'll start a new one. Little Catherine will be the first occupant—not much of an honor."

Abby jumped up, briskly walking after him and carrying her verse. "If he didn't bury those Snake Indians, what did he do with them?" As soon as her words were out, she thought she might not want to know the answer.

"I suspect the other Snake took them out and buried them according to Snake custom. Type of burial depends on the tribe and the availability of materials. Sometimes bodies are put up on scaffolds, other times they're buried under large boulders—large enough so that wolves can't get at the corpse."

"Really."

"Yup, we'll probably have to start a cemetery. Poor Catherine."

They walked over to the Cary wagon in silence. Bridger was already there, along with about ten other emigrants. Miles sat apart from the other men, while three women tried to comfort Cyrene. Miles's slave, Button, sat on the wagon tongue—brave, stoic, and with tears running down both cheeks. She had taken care of Catherine since the day she was born. Now she had lost her very best friend.

Abby joined the ladies and presented the verse to Cyrene while Jacob went over to Jim to learn the funeral plans.

"Catherine's the first alright," said Bridger. "This fort's so new I never considered locating a cemetery."

"That high ground on the other side of the creek looks good as any," said Bill Day. Upon hearing the news of Catherine, a number of men had come over to the Cary's wagon to offer their help. "Good view of the surrounding valley and high enough to avoid flooding."

"What do you think, Jacob?" asked Jim. "If that were your child would that ground be acceptable?"

"As good as any around here," Jacob replied. "Let's go take a look."

It was a good site for a cemetery, so Jacob, Jim Huck, and George McCorkle each retrieved a shovel from their outfits and returned to the spot designated by Bridger. Jim Huck was traveling with pack animals and did not need the time to make equipment repairs. He was always willing to help with company needs, and offering his services to dig a grave seemed only fitting. George McCorkle was traveling with his extended kin, the Howells. There were already several men in his family taking care of repairs, freeing George to help with Catherine's funeral.

By late afternoon the grave was ready. Jim Athey, a carpenter, made a small coffin from some boards donated by Bridger, while Mary Ann Holmes and Ruby Looney inscribed the headboard. Later that evening, everything was ready for a Tuesday-morning funeral.

After dinner Jacob took up his rifle and walked back down to the fort to be with his trapping cronies, swapping stories between shots of pure-grain alcohol and challenging each other to feats of strength and skill. Catherine's death had weighed heavy on him, more so than the death of a trapper. He had seen men die in battle and sickness before, and it was of little concern. Eventually, everyone goes down under—yet the death of a child was different. He had been able to hide most of his empathy for little Joel Hembree, since they were on the move and the Hembrees were traveling with the Cow Column. The second death, Catherine, was more difficult. Jacob needed time with his old compadres.

By dusk Abby could hear the shouts of a drunken brawl drifting up from the fort, a good quarter-mile away. Jim Nesmith rode up as she stood looking at the fort, arms folded in a defiant stance.

"You're not going to be too happy when Jacob gets back," Jim said as he dismounted.

"So I hear. What's going on down there?"

"When I left they had finished off most of the alcohol and were planning on seeing who had the fastest horse. I thought it best to …"

Just then the crack of a rifle shot came up from the fort.

"Now what?" Jim turned around to look at the fort.

"I think they're target shooting," said Abby.

There was another shot.

"Target shooting! How can they see the target? It's almost dark and they're blind drunk!"

"Blind is a good word for it," Abby said. "I'm going to secure all my kitchen gear before he gets back, and I'd appreciate it if you'd camp nearby tonight. You know, in case I need your help."

"Yes, ma'am," said Jim. "I don't know how much help I'll be against a drunken mountain man."

"Being here is enough, Jim."

Two hours later, after several more horse races around the fort and another challenge of target shooting, Jacob came stumbling in, leading his horse by the reins.

Abby stood by her wagon, arms folded.

"Mr. Chalmers," she said with authority as he came into the light of the campfire. "This is a side of you I have never seen. I'll talk to you in the morning." She turned and climbed into the back of her wagon, pulling down the canvas flap in a manner replete with disgust.

Jacob said nothing. He dropped the reins of Dog Town, then fell face first on top of his buffalo robe—passed out until morning.

On Tuesday morning Abby walked down to the fort, leaving Jacob to "sleep it off." At the fort she learned that several farmers had sold their lame oxen the day before and received almost nothing in return. One man received only a coarse hat. The fort's supplies were clearly inadequate for this first year of emigrants, however, next year things would be different. Lame oxen this year would be strong and healthy for next year, fetching top dollar from teamsters with no other option than to pay the fort's price.

While Abby conversed with some of the ladies at the fort, Waldo's Straggler Column arrived. As they approached the fort from the northeast, Chiles's California Column pulled out in a northwesterly direction. With both Chiles and Joe Walker along, there was no need to wait for the company's guide. Gantt would continue to travel with the Light Column. Waldo had stayed in camp for several nights on Ham's Fork to make wheel and wagon repairs. It was a wise precaution, since he correctly deduced that the fort's facilities would be inundated with requests from other teamsters repairing wheels, hounds, tongues, and skidders. As the Straggler Column approached, they could see Catherine Cary's funeral procession walking up to the new cemetery. Four men served as pallbearers for the small rough-hewn coffin.

To the people in Waldo's Straggler Column, there appeared to be a scene of ordered confusion around the fort. Those not attending the funeral continued to finalize preparations for leaving on the following morning. Everyone knew that they would be traveling northwest upon leaving the fort, away from the snow-capped mountains to the south. Still, the trail ahead presented a new set of difficulties, such as the climb between the Green River drainage and the Bear River Valley. Everyone knew a tough road lay ahead, so preparations at the fort had taken on an urgency of life and death.

Abby chose to join the people at Catherine's funeral. It was a simple ceremony with very few words spoken on behalf of the little girl. Reverend Whitman made a few statements of comfort for Miles and Cyrene, then men lowered the coffin into the grave and everyone dispersed. Nat Sitton, John Cox, and Tom Brown, the three friends traveling together to make their fortune in Oregon, stayed behind to fill in the grave.

People spent the remainder of the day doing chores and completing equipment repairs for tomorrow's departure. With a desire to keep moving, Dan Waldo and his Straggler Column agreed to join Martin's Light Column. That gave them only one night at the fort. The small straggler group had kept their wagons in good shape by following the trail blazed by the columns in front of them, so one night at the fort was adequate.

In the early evening Fred Prigg walked up to Abby's kitchen, announcing himself as he approached.

"Good evening, Mr. Prigg," Abby replied. Please come in—here, you can sit on my washtub."

"Thank you, Abby, and you can call me Fred, you know that." Fred was a well-educated man, traveling to Oregon to begin a tool supply business to service all the new Wallamet Valley farms. With news of Oregon becoming part of the United States, Fred and a few other men had begun planning more politically oriented careers.

"I know, Fred. With all the work of traveling, I don't think we've talked in several weeks—and I've been even busier since we got here to Fort Bridger. I've finished all my chores now, and tomorrow looks like it will be a beautiful day to continue our journey."

"That's what I'm here to talk to you about. You being the schoolteacher, you're probably better educated than any woman in this company and most of the men. Some of us are talking about starting a literary club when we get to Oregon—you know, a library. Since Oregon is nothing but a vast wilderness, it's important that we establish a civilization we can be proud of—and that means good schools and a library. What do you think of that?"

When Fred mentioned the word *library,* Abby stopped kneading a large pile of dough and sat down on the wagon tongue to listen. She looked directly at Fred, holding both hands out in front of her since they were covered with dough. "A library! Yes, that's wonderful. I never dreamed you good people would want to start a library so soon. What can I do to help?"

"We want you to be a member of our club."

"Really." She hesitated with a look of surprise, first glancing over at Jacob and then back to Fred. "It's open to women?"

"Yes, ma'am. We want everyone to have access to the finer works of literature."

"Fred, I'm flattered that you would ask. Yes, definitely. I would be honored to be a member of your club—and you can call me Abby."

Fred let out a laugh. "I knew you'd want to be part of us. Jim Wair and I've been talking to all the educated men, and all these people have signed up." He produced a small piece of paper from under his shirt and held it out. Abby quickly wiped the dough from two fingers on the edge of the bowl and took the paper.

"Do you want me to sign?" She opened the paper and read:

The Pioneer Lyceum and Literary Club

Underneath this heading were the signatures of Asa Lovejoy, Jesse Applegate, Jim Nesmith, Ed Otey, Henry Lee, Bill Dement, Hiram Straight, Ransom Clark, Henry Hyde, John Campbell, Pete Stewart, Isaac Smith, Sam Holderness, John Brooks, and Dan Waldo.

"I don't have pen and ink with me," Fred apologized, "but if you've ..."

"I've got pen and ink," Abby said. She stood and stepped back toward the wagon to wipe her hands off and retrieve her diary box, continuing to read the list as she walked.

"We felt it important to have a library with a circulating collection." Fred continued as she sat back down with her diary box. "This is the foundation of any civilization—I mean, the promotion of literature in a new territory is important."

"Fred, this is wonderful. You want me to sign under Dan Waldo's name?"

"If you don't mind. We'll probably have our first official meeting in Oregon City sometime during this coming winter."

"I'll be there!" She looked up after signing, with a smile that could light the day. "I will definitely attend that meeting. Thank you so much for inviting me to join. I think it's wonderful what you're doing, and I will be a credit to your new club."

"I'm sure you will. This should open the door for other women, don't you think?" Fred took the paper back while getting up from the washtub.

"By all means, classic literature is for everyone."

"Well," said Fred, "I need to get back to the wife. I'll let everyone know you're a full member of our literary club. Good night now." He tipped his hat and turned to leave.

"Fred, did you ask Jacob if he would like to join?" Her question came as a surprise, rendering Mr. Prigg momentarily speechless. Everyone had simply assumed that an old mountain man could be nothing more than illiterate.

"No, I, well—it never occurred to me." He turned to Jacob who was quietly sitting at the fire, enjoying his pipe. "Would you like to join our literary club, Mr. Chalmers?" Fred held out the piece of paper with confidence that he would refuse. Even if a mountain man could read and write, he certainly would not support the creation of a library.

"Sure, I'll join." Jacob stood, took the sheet of paper, and walked over to Abby, who held out the pen for him to sign.

"I didn't realize you had an education, Mr. Chalmers," Fred said in a somewhat apologetic manner.

"He's gone all the way through secondary school," announced

Abby. "Probably one of the most educated men around here." She was smiling now at Fred's uneasiness.

Jacob signed and handed the paper back to Fred. "Have you thought about how you're going to fund such a library?"

"I guess we can count on you to come right to the point," Fred said smiling as he took the paper. "That's what we'll talk about at our first meeting."

"Should be interesting. I'll be there."

"We'll both be there," Abby said as she stood. "Thank you again for stopping by. I'm sure we'll formulate many plans for a library before we reach Oregon City."

"No doubt we will. Thank you, Abby; thank you, Mr. Chalmers." Fred again tipped his hat as he retreated into the dusk.

Jacob walked back over to the campfire to finish his smoke while Abby vented her delight.

"Did you see how nervous he got when I asked about you joining?"

"You're giving out my secrets, Abby. By tomorrow morning this entire camp will know I've been to school."

"As well they should. You've helped these ungrateful farmers since we left Independence. The least they could do is show you some respect."

"It don't matter."

"Does to me. My, they asked me to join their club. Me! A woman! Maybe things will be different in Oregon. Maybe I'll even get to vote!"

Abby's excitement was clearly evident. This new country of Oregon had an appeal for her that went beyond anything the men in the migration could ever appreciate. With the formation of a new government, old institutions based on prejudice and misconceptions could change. It was an exciting prospect.

"Anything's possible, Abby, anything's possible." Jacob tapped the burned ashes from his pipe. "Got a long day tomorrow—I'll see you in the morning." He got up to pull his buffalo robe out from underneath the wagon and move it over near the fire.

"Good night, Jacob."

Before turning in, Abby lit a candle inside the wagon and recorded the events of the day. The hours had been long and busy with Waldo's Straggler Column arriving, Catherine Cary's funeral, the completion of all needed repairs and chores, and now a membership in the new Pioneer Lyceum and Literary Club. Another half-hour passed before she put her diary away, extinguished the candle, and was fast asleep.

Colonel Martin had the Light Column back on the trail before eight o'clock on Wednesday morning. As the wagons slowly moved past Fort Bridger, Gabe came out to watch the procession. Jacob rode ahead to say a few parting words of friendship while Abby brought up the wagon. As she caught up with them, she called out a farewell while keeping a firm quirt on the rumps of her oxen.

"Thank you for your hospitality, Mr. Bridger. You will soon have the finest fort between Independence and Oregon City! It will be a lifesaver for many emigrants."

"I enjoyed meeting you, Abby Meacham. You will do well in Oregon."

Abby smiled, then brought her quirt down on Flowers's rump. She had to keep moving to avoid disrupting the column.

The trail blazed by Chiles's California Column was wide and smooth, allowing the Light Column to make almost fourteen miles before stopping for a nooner. The Uintah Mountains lay ahead, and beyond them the Bear River. The noon stop took place by a small stream that Jacob referred to as Muddy Creek. The name fit its turbidity, and only the stock could get a drink before the afternoon march.

The stay at Fort Bridger had satisfied Abby's need for a rest and a chance to catch up on repairs and baking. Now, being back on the trail felt good. She was still moving forward, still going to Oregon.

After nooning, the column continued to follow the trace of Chiles's California Column, heading up Muddy Creek in a west, northwesterly direction. The country was generally barren of forage except for a few small willows along the draws of Muddy Creek. The country was so dry that even the sage was sparse. Toward the north stood a flat-topped mesa where small conifers grew; from a distance, they appeared to be juniper. To the south lay sage-covered rolling hills, and beyond them, snow-capped mountains. Jacob estimated the mountains to be over a hundred miles away. Ahead, painted layers of red rock spoke of a difficult climb to the divide between the Green and Bear River drainages. Above, raptors glided over the windy, high-elevation landscape. At various points along the route the travelers could see for over a hundred miles in any direction. Although they were heading away from the snow-capped mountains in the south, the road ahead was just as unknown and dangerous. The beauty and wildness of the region belied the difficulties to come.

As they ascended the Muddy Creek drainage, there were numerous dry washes to cross, similar to their journey over South Pass. These depressions presented the most trouble during the climb. Weak oxen struggled to pull wagons through soft sand, while the teamsters and other men did their best to prevent wagons from tipping on the steeper slopes. Each mile seemed to be more demanding than the previous as they continued their slow climb up the drainage.

The Light Column continued for a day's total of twenty miles before forming their wagon corrals. The road since noon had begun a slow climb up the divide that separated them from the Bear River Valley—a valley that, according to Jacob and Captain Gantt, was lush with grass. It would be a good place to spend a few days before challenging the Snake River Plains.

After all the stock were let out to forage as best they could, several groups of men rode out on horses in hopes of obtaining an elk. The advance guard had spotted a large bull earlier in the day, and there was still daylight enough for the chance of a lucky shot. Provisions were running low for almost all families, and elk meat would provide a welcome change. At dusk the hunters returned, still hungry and wishing for elk.

On Thursday morning, August 17, Cooper's Splinter Column left Fort Bridger. By evening they were camping in the same area used by the Light Column.

The Light Column that day continued moving up Muddy Creek another ten miles. They crossed the Muddy shortly after breaking camp, then continued up the creek as far as possible before striking out in a westerly direction toward the Bear River Valley. The road was both rough and uphill, making the distance of ten miles an exhausting effort.

At the point of leaving the Muddy, the Light Column encountered and passed Chiles's California Column. Several of their wagons were experiencing problems with wheels and running gear since beginning the climb up this low arm of the Uintah Mountains. When the Light Column passed, men from the California-bound column had two wagons propped up on large rocks while they tended to both wheels and running gear. To Abby, it looked as though Chiles's Column might be here for a day or two.

Three miles later Colonel Martin halted near a small stream—the only one, it appeared, for miles around. Wagon corrals formed, teamsters watered their stock and put them out to pasture (what little there was), and families completed their dinners long before dusk. It had been another long and tiring day, so most everyone bedded down as soon as the sun disappeared behind the crest of the divide.

Friday, August 18, proved to be another exhausting day as the Light Column continued to climb the divide separating them from the Bear River Valley. By evening they had made only ten miles.

Behind the Light Column, Cooper's Splinter Column overtook Chiles's California Column while the latter were still at the head of Muddy Creek. The Splinter Column continued in the tracks of the Light Column and managed to catch up shortly before dusk.

Zachary's Outcast Mess, consisting of only the Zachary outfit and the Oteys' wagon, traveled a few hundred yards behind the Splinter Column. While crossing the Muddy earlier in the day, the Oteys' wagon tipped over, delaying their advance for over an hour. With the help of Alex Zachary and his son, John, the two Otey brothers and Jim Nesmith were able to recover all their gear and save the remaining flour. The men's gear and personal belongings were all wet—a minor inconvenience. Everything would dry quickly in the summer heat and dry air. The wagon had not been damaged, and they were able to continue, camping a few hundred yards behind the Splinter Column that evening.

On Saturday, August 19, the Light Column finally breached the crest of the divide. It had been a long hard climb. From this commanding position they were rewarded with the sight of a beautiful, lush green valley with a substantial stream meandering down the center. This was the Bear River Valley, an oasis in this sagebrush desert. The Bear River was about twenty yards wide and three to five feet deep, not a big river, but more than adequate considering the surrounding desert. The valley itself was about five miles wide and provided an opportunity to allow oxen and other stock to regain their strength before venturing out onto the Snake River Plains.

The trail leading down to the valley floor was steep and rough, with intersecting ravines and dangerous hillside angles—each threatening to topple the wagons and send them tumbling down. For Abby and Jacob, along with other members of the Light Column, it seemed a repeat of the dangerous hills they had first learned to negotiate back on the Platte. Jacob tied a rope to the center of the wagon's sideboard, then rode on the uphill side, keeping a tight line to prevent tipping. They both knew the routine well.

By midafternoon the column was forming their wagon corrals on the valley floor near a grove of black cottonwoods. It had been a seventeen-mile day, and everyone was ready to stop and enjoy the respite of green grass and a cool, clear river.

Good pasturage lay in every direction, so after watering the stock, Jacob hobbled the animals in an area of grass that came up to their bellies. Before nightfall he moved them to another area of tall grass. Their chances of survival on the Snake River Plains were directly dependent on the nourishment each animal could take in now.

"You just missed Hank Lee," Abby said as Jacob came riding in. "He says we're going to go up this valley for as far as possible before turning west to the Portneuf River. We can probably go quite a ways each day if this type of ground holds out. He wants all the stock to eat as much as they can before leaving this valley."

"Should take us about a week. We had the 1827 and '28 Rendezvous south of here on Bear Lake—good grass there too. There're not many places out here with enough pasturage to feed the several thousand horses we had at each Rendezvous. Pierre's Hole has enough, and the Green River near Ham's Fork, along with the Popo Agie in the Wind River range. That's about it."

"Tonight at dinner I want you to tell me about the Rendezvous you had at Bear Lake. Then I want to hear about the country ahead between here and Fort Hall." The seventeen-mile day had not tired Abby's enthusiasm for knowledge. Jacob would have a time explaining all the details she desired.

After dinner and the regaling of some Rendezvous adventures, Abby retreated to the banks of the Bear River to write in her diary. The coolness of the grass and availability of fresh water only helped to enhance the beautiful summer evening. After dark she planned to return for a bath. The long hot day closed with another magnificent red and orange sunset and the welcome relief of shade and a cool breeze.

The next morning, Sunday, August 20, the Light Column continued up the valley in a northerly direction. The flat ground provided easy going for teamsters, drovers, and stock. By noon they had made ten miles and expected to make another ten before evening.

One day behind the Light Column was Cooper's Splinter Column. Once again they camped in the same area used by the Light Column the night before. Grass was so plentiful that the depletion by the Light Column stock was hardly noticeable. There was still adequate feed for the Splinter Column and the others to follow.

During the morning Jacob, John Gantt, and several other men went out in search of elk and deer, for there were sign everywhere. Abby nooned alone. By midafternoon Jacob came riding back in with a small deer and, to the surprise of everyone, a Plains Grizzly. He kept enough meat to restock Abby's dwindling supply, then gave the rest away to needy families in their platoon.

The column continued for a twenty-mile day before forming their corrals. During dinner everyone in Abby's corral proclaimed grizzly meat to be as tasty as fresh buffalo. Jacob's usual low stature with the emigrants had improved immensely over the last few weeks when provisions had started running low. Now, they looked to him for guidance—asking any question that entailed survival in this Western landscape.

After dinner Abby staked out the bear hide to scrape and preserve it as the Crow had taught her. In the meantime, Jacob went down to the Bear River, returning shortly with two trout for breakfast the next morning. It was a quiet evening, and a day closer to Oregon.

Monday was uneventful, yet productive. The Light Column moved another twenty miles north along the Bear River Valley on a flat and easy trail. Behind came Cooper's Splinter Column, Chiles's California Column (finally on the move again), Zachary's Outcast Mess, and Applegate's Cow Column. The Light Column had absorbed Waldo's Straggler Column, with each wagon assigned to a specific corral, along with a position for each day's march.

John McHaley, who traveled with the Cow Column, had his wagon upset while crossing an oxbow of the Bear River during the morning's march. He did not lose any equipment or possessions, and suffered no damage because of the quick help of nearby men. John was back on the trail within the hour, wet but safe.

John McHaley was an older gentleman who was pushing the extent of his physical endurance by journeying to Oregon. Without the help of younger men, he might have lost everything. This was not the first mishap he had experienced while crossing a river. There had been several other near-tragic incidents, especially the one on the South Platte. McHaley's original request for the Oregon Emigrating Company to buy and carry two large boats for river crossings still loomed in his mind, yet it was too late now. He thanked the men who had saved his outfit, then continued, snapping his quirt on the rumps of his lead team. Sarah, his wife, could only walk along thinking about all the cleaning she would have to do with waterlogged trunks and possessions, now in a jumbled mess.

The company continued through the rich green pasturage of the Bear River Valley all day on Tuesday, a welcome sight for the desert-poor travelers. Unfortunately, the easy road could not help Cooper's Splinter Column, whose wagons were continually breaking down.

The breakdowns only served to frustrate those men who originally split off from the Light Column for the purpose of getting to Oregon quicker. Early in the morning, damaged wheels on two wagons threatened to keep everyone in the Splinter Column in camp for the entire day. That was enough for seven wagons and their resident families. They broke ranks, leaving the Splinter Column behind in an effort to catch the Light Column. Cooper's Column now had only six wagons and a considerably diminished stature.

As evening came on, the seven teamsters and their families caught up with the Light Column just as they were forming their corrals. Colonel Martin welcomed the deserters back into the fold, assigning them to their old corrals and marching positions. It had been another twenty-mile day for the Light Column. With such a good road and with water and forage to keep them moving, Captain Gantt and the other leaders thought it not likely that any of the other columns would catch up until Fort Hall—including the two wagons in Zachary's Outcast Mess.

On Wednesday, August 23, Colonel Fremont's government survey expedition caught up with and passed the Light Column. This came as quite a surprise, since nobody knew his expedition was in the area. Fremont had not been seen since the company crossed the North Platte, and most people thought that he and Sir William Drummond Stewart's hunting entourage were well off the road to Oregon. Nobody had expected to see either of these groups again.

Fremont's rapid march toward Fort Hall alarmed and discouraged those people hoping to buy badly needed supplies. Fort Hall was the furthest outpost of the British Hudson Bay Company, which had organized and managed a monopoly on the fur trade in the Pacific Northwest ever since the War of 1812. The company supported a series of trading posts that covered an area extending to the upper reaches of Blackfoot Territory, south to the Great Salt Lake and west to the Pacific Ocean. Among the ranks of the Oregon Emigrating Company, it was generally believed that the posts of Fort Hall and Fort Boise would be well stocked and able to sell provisions at a fair market value. Unless, of course, Fremont arrived first. He might consume most of the available goods, leaving nothing for the company. Also, the fort would now know of the migration's approach and possibly take action—such as caching some supplies. The prospects were not bright, yet there was nothing anyone could do.

Since Fremont traveled with pack animals and no wagons, the Light Column was no match for their speed. Fremont would arrive at the fort in two or three days, at least a day ahead of the first emigrants. The best they could hope for was a post fully stocked with provisions and supplies, too much to be exhausted by Fremont.

After Fremont's expedition passed, the Light Column resumed their journey down through the Bear River Valley. At noon they stopped at a place Jacob called Beer Springs, just north of Bear River. Here they caught up to Fremont, who had stopped to record this oddity of nature. Jacob, Captain Gantt, and Joe Walker did not hesitate to fill their cups and drink liberally from the spring. It had been several years since any of these men had enjoyed its rich beer flavor. Before long, and much to the chagrin of Fremont and the many wives, most of the men in Fremont's command and in the column were partaking of this natural ale.

Near Beer Springs were several steam vents and other geological curiosities that everyone wanted to see. A soda-covered soil extended over a flat area about ten acres in size and devoid of vegetation. Steam and boiling water shot up in a ten-foot geyser near one of the vents. Around this geyser were cones encrusted with soda and sulfur, many of which appeared to be dried up—geysers from a bygone era. They varied in diameter from three to thirty feet. The entire region looked like the product of violent and recent volcanic activity. As folks gathered around the largest geyser, Joe Walker began to pontificate for the curious onlookers.

"This here's Steamboat Springs," Joe announced. "We named it back when we were rendezvousing down on Bear Lake—must be fifteen years ago. From a distance Sublette thought it looked like a steamboat coming up Bear River."

Just as people began to get fully engrossed in Joe's tales of Steamboat Springs, the geyser erupted, sending everyone scurrying for cover. The quantity of water thrown into the air was not great, yet it was hot enough to cause serious burns. The water squirted from a small conical rock that appeared to have formed around the vent through many ages of eruptions.

Smaller, secondary eruptions came about every fifteen seconds, allowing people to gather some of the boiling water. While Joe continued, Abby walked over to another nearby cone where sulfuric gasses expelled through the vent, then drew back in, much like someone breathing. To Abby, it would be an interesting challenge to describe the spectacle in her diary and later for her students in Oregon.

Jacob, too, took an interest, following Abby around to the various conical structures. His prior visits had been with small trapping brigades more interested in Beer Springs than in the local formations.

"If you can imagine an area like this for miles around, that's what's up there in Yellowstone Country."

"Jacob," Abby exclaimed, "I will never again doubt any of your stories, no matter how wild they may seem. They must all be true!"

"If I said it, then it's true. That Yellowstone region doesn't have just one of these steamy spots, its got boiling mud and shooting steam over an area ..." he hesitated, "must be twenty miles across."

"Really!" Abby did not look up. She was too busy examining one of the smaller dried cones.

"There's this one vent, the water there shoots up over a hundred feet about every hour or so. It's up on a large outcrop of rock, so we could get up close and take a good look before it erupted."

"Can you tell when it's going to erupt? I mean you must have to get back!"

"The horses can tell alright. When they start getting jumpy, you better move back."

The noon stop at Beer and Steamboat Springs lasted for almost two hours before Colonel Martin got everyone collected and back on the trail. Abby produced some bread and jerky for her and Jacob to eat as they set out for the afternoon march. Their explorations of the steam vents had consumed the entire nooner without a thought of food.

At six o'clock the wagon corrals formed after another twenty-mile day. They were still in the Bear River Valley, with good forage and fresh water. Over the last two days the trail had veered slowly west, and the column was now moving due west. The journey from South Pass to Fort Bridger had taken them more than fifty miles south of a line drawn directly west from South Pass to this place. Some men thought that future emigrants might find a suitable route directly over to Beer Springs from South Pass, thereby eliminating Fort Bridger from the route. Others argued that even if a more direct route could be found, the availability of supplies at Fort Bridger would force people to take the longer route. This idle campfire conversation continued as men imagined larger migrations should Oregon ever become a state.

The various contingencies of the splintered Oregon Emigrating Company were now camping across a fifteen-mile section of the valley. Although the white-topped columns were not within sight of each other because of the distance and contours of the land, smoke could be seen rising from a hundred campfires. Cattle grazed serenely near each camp, and a slight breeze cooled the air and kept the black flies down by the river.

All seemed to be quiet until near dusk when the Light Column, still in the lead, received a visit from a small band of Snake Indians. They were en route from Fort Hall to see the new Fort Bridger. They had had a brief meeting with Colonel Fremont a few hours earlier, only to learn that he was unwilling to engage in trade. His supplies were running too low for even a small exchange. Instead, he was quick to describe the Oregon Emigrating Company and their desire to trade. With the company only a few hours away, the Indians chose to press on. They reached the Light Column at sunset.

Captain Gantt and Colonel Martin rode out to meet them, with Joe Walker and Jacob coming up behind. Among the Snakes was an old trapper named Peg-leg Smith and his squaw. He was a former employee of the Rocky Mountain Fur Company and an acquaintance of Gantt, Walker, and Jacob. After the usual greeting formalities, the Snake chief and his warriors sat down with the migration leaders to have a smoke and discuss news of the past winter and surrounding region. The chief wanted to trade some of their horses for blankets, knives, and tobacco—a trade that the horse-poor emigrants quickly obliged. All of the tradable items in possession of the company were of a higher quality than what was available at the Hudson Bay posts. The Indians realized this and eagerly engaged in a trading circle.

Other than the Crow Indians seen only by Jacob and Abby near South Pass, these Snake Indians were the first natives encountered by the company since leaving Fort Laramie. The trading continued until the Indians' stock of horses and trade items were exhausted and the day's light began to fade. The Snakes then chose to make their camp next to the Bear River, sufficiently distant from the other camps to avoid contact.

Shortly after dawn the next morning, Thursday, August 24, the Indians resumed their journey to Fort Bridger. As each of the columns was still preparing for the day's march, Peg-leg Smith rode up to talk with Captain Gantt. Jacob and Joe Walker watched the quick exchange from a distance. Before long, Peg-leg was riding back to join his Indian companions.

Within a mile after the Light Column started the day's march, the Bear River turned southwest away from the route to Fort Hall, then south to the Great Salt Lake. Jacob walked with Abby for most of the morning, describing the country beyond Fort Hall and south toward the lake.

"Bridger was the first to see the lake," Jacob said as he walked alongside of Abby. "It all happened back when we went up the Missouri with Andrew Henry. The next year General Ashley had Henry send out a party of men from the mouth of the Yellowstone to reconnoiter this region for fur production. After discovering South Pass, they split up to cover more country. Sublette went up toward Jackson's Hole while Bridger headed south. They made bullboats and floated down the Bear River all the way to the Great Salt Lake. When Bridger tasted the water, well, he figured he'd discovered the Pacific Ocean. Yup, old Gabe was the first white man ever to see this country. That he was."

"Where were you? Didn't you go with them?"

"Up on the Missouri. We set up a fixed trading post that year, but it didn't take—too much trouble with the Blackfeet. Old Ashley tried several schemes before he finally settled on the Rendezvous system."

"Where was your first Rendezvous?"

"Bear Lake."

So the morning passed with Jacob relating tales and Abby questioning him on regional geography, Indian tribes, their customs, and the land ahead.

At noon the Light Column stopped short of a lava field. The rough rock terrain appeared to extend for several miles, so before embarking, Colonel Martin thought it wise to rest the stock. During the nooner, Abby and Sarah Rubey walked over to the edge of the lava flow to examine this novelty of the West.

Sarah's comment described it best. "We're seeing the elephant, Abby. Yes we are, we're seeing the elephant."

"I don't know how long our wagons will hold together crossing rock like this. If this stretch goes on for a distance, then some of the wheels in our column will certainly fall apart!"

Abby's concern was shared by all of the teamsters. This lava field was worse than the red rock road west of Fort Laramie. If an easier way could not be found, then the hope of getting wagons through to the Wallamet Valley might end here, north of Bear Lake.

Fortunately for the entire column, they came to the end of the lava field shortly after Martin began the afternoon march. With a much improved road, the Light Column was able to make twenty miles before forming their wagon corrals along the Portneuf River. It had been a long, hot, and tiring day for everyone—and a dry one for the stock. Jacob hobbled all their stock such that they could reach the river while feeding.

The Portneuf flows directly into the Snake. News of this geographical fact spread through the column and helped lift the spirits of everyone. The thought of completing the journey to Fort Hall and moving out onto the Snake River Plains was a major step closer to Oregon City and the Wallamet Valley.

The evening passed quickly, with Abby spending her time baking and adding another page to her diary. Jacob's stories made good copy, along with his colorful descriptions of the surrounding country.

The next day a hunting party attached to Fremont's expedition nooned with the Light Column. With them was Kit Carson, a trapping friend of Jacob's whom Abby had met a few days earlier. With the demise of the fur trade, trappers had scattered to the four winds in search of employment or adventure. Similar to Captain Gantt, Carson signed on as a guide with a Western expedition. It was easy work for someone already familiar with the country. After a regaling nooner of Indian news, trapping information, and geographical descriptions, Carson and his hunting party went on toward the Bear River Valley while the Light Column moved north along the Portneuf toward Fort Hall.

The day continued uneventfully. Camp corrals were set up that evening along the Portneuf in an area of tolerable grass and plenty of water.

On Saturday, August 26, the Light Column crossed the Portneuf and continued in a northerly direction along the river. At this time of year the Portneuf was at its lowest flow, providing only a minor obstacle for the seasoned teamsters. In midafternoon Captain Gantt turned the column due west, away from the river and in a more direct route toward Fort Hall and the Snake River. Ahead of them, Colonel Fremont arrived at the fort and set up his camp for a stay of several days—recruiting stock and repairing gear.

After a long day's march, the Light Column camped on the open prairie without water and with only poor grass for the stock. As he had often done in the past, Jacob watered the stock from one of the twenty-gallon barrels, then hobbled them for the night. Before dusk he watered them again and moved each animal three times to ensure they got as much forage as possible. Other emigrants may have resented Jacob's knowledge and prowess of the West, but his care for Abby's outfit was evident. Here, over one thousand miles from Independence, that extra care was obvious to everyone. Abby's outfit was probably more capable of meeting the difficulties of the Snake River Plains than any other in the company.

"What have you heard about Fort Hall?" Jacob asked as he lit his pipe. Abby was cleaning up the dinner dishes while he took his pleasures at the campfire.

"Not much more than what you've told me—a British post that probably won't have enough supplies for our company."

"That worries all of us." The surprise interruption came from Miles Cary, walking past Abby's outfit while relocating his stock to an area of better grass.

"Oh, Miles, please come in," Abby said. "I've been meaning to stop by—how's Cyrene?"

"Better—not much energy after losing Catherine. She's a strong woman though. She'll come around."

"Please sit down—here, on my washtub. Jacob was going to tell me about Fort Hall."

"Thank you, Abby, I'd like to hear that. Let me relocate these animals and I'll be back directly."

Sarah Rubey, Bill Fowler, and Becky Kelsey came in for a visit just as Miles was returning. They all sat down to hear Jacob relate his tale about the origins of Fort Hall.

"It's a British fort alright, Hudson Bay Company." He stared into the fire, collecting his thoughts.

"Nat Wyeth built it back in '34. That child had sand—as much as any trapper. He was just a greenhorn businessman from New England, ice business, I think. He wanted to get into the trapping business, and so formed his own company and headed out to the Rendezvous in '32—Pierre's Hole, that's where we had it, at the western base of the Tetons. As I recall, in addition to trapping beaver Wyeth wanted to dry or smoke salmon on the Columbia and send barrels of it back to the United States. How he planned to get those barrels across the Rocky Mountains is a mystery. He couldn't change fate though, and the best of plans don't always weigh in. Old Nat met with one trouble after the next. He was persistent, I'll hand him that."

"Eleven years ago?" Miles looked up, running his fingers through his beard. "That was long before any talk about Oregon Country."

"Nat Wyeth was a thinker," Jacob continued. "When he started out, he planned to have fifty men on a five-year expedition. Recruiting wasn't easy, so he offered to share eighty percent of the profits. Still, only about twenty men signed up. He mustered up the start-up capital and called his outfit the Pacific Trading Company. When he got to St. Louis, he was so green that McKenzie and Sublette hired him to help them get supplies out to our Rendezvous. He must not have realized that he was in competition with Sublette for our annual catch. From St. Louis he went up to Independence to complete his outfit. He even went so far as to buy sheep to take along for food—even then, a couple of his men deserted. I guess they didn't have the stomach for adventure.

"Did he have any wagons?" asked Bill.

"None, only pack animals back then—it was 1832, May probably. Sublette and Bob Campbell were leading the pack train out to the Rendezvous that year, so Wyeth and his men got the guide they needed. It was a tough trip out, especially when Wyeth lost gunpowder and equipment while crossing the Laramie River. Sublette told him to use bullboats. Instead he decided to make a log raft. The towrope broke and he lost everything on board. After that they were attacked by Blackfeet and lost a number of horses. With all that trouble, they didn't get to Pierre's Hole until a few days after the Glorious Fourth. We had the usual Rendezvous with trading, drinking, racing, and other competitions—competitions that turned out to be quite a draw for his men. The next week a few more deserted, deciding to become free trappers. By the time Wyeth was ready to leave for the Columbia, he only had eleven men remaining. I believe Osborne Russell was one of those boys. Ozzie eventually turned out to be one of our better trappers."

"Mr. Wyeth must have given up his plans for barreling salmon," said Abby.

"Not yet. He hooked up to a trapping brigade led by Bill Sublette's brother Milt, and Henry Fraeb, heading west. On the south end of Pierre's Hole they ran into a party of Gros Ventres. That's the battle I told you about back in Independence."

"I remember," said Abby, "although I've been trying to forget. You don't think we'll run into any Gros Ventres out here, do you?"

"Maybe." Jacob continued without giving Abby's question much concern.

"Wyeth chose to cache his goods not far from here. They followed the Portneuf to the Snake River Plains, then west to the Owyhee River. The Hudson Bay Company had trapped out the Snake and its tributaries, so Sublette and Fraeb parted company from Wyeth. Nat wanted to go to the Columbia, and our men needed to find beaver. I don't much know what happened to Wyeth after that, except that he eventually made it to Fort Vancouver. The ship coming around the Horn with his supplies wrecked somewhere in the South Pacific, so that was the end of his plans for packing salmon. By then the remaining men in his party quit, and I don't blame them one bit."

"So is this Wyeth in Oregon now?" Becky asked.

"No, ma'am. He spent that winter in Oregon, but the following summer he showed up at the Rendezvous. We held it on the Green River in '33, near Horse Creek. Captain Bonneville was there that year, along with Sir William Drummond Stewart."

"Stewart?" exclaimed Miles. "The same Stewart that's been dogging us since Independence?"

"The same," replied Jacob. "After Rendezvous, Wyeth followed Milt Sublette and Tom Fitzpatrick back East. Somewhere around the Wind River Mountains they struck up an agreement for Wyeth to supply the next Rendezvous with goods from Boston and New York, since he claimed he could get them cheaper."

"Could he?"

"Don't know. He went all the way back to Boston that year and reorganized a new outfit, calling it the Columbia River Fishing and Trading Company. The next year he set out with supplies for the 1834 Rendezvous. That was the year Sublette left some men at the Laramie River to construct a fort. You remember those burned timbers down by the river?" Jacob looked up as he asked the question. "Well, that was Sublette's fort."

He paused to relight his pipe before continuing.

"As usual, Bill Sublette was also on his way to the Rendezvous that year. Whoever got there first would get all the trade and Bill knew it, so beating Wyeth wasn't a problem. By the time Wyeth arrived the trading was complete—and there was Wyeth with all those goods and nobody to trade with. We had the Rendezvous on Ham's Fork of the Green that year, and as I recall, that was the summer the Rocky Mountain Fur Company sold out to Fitzpatrick, Sublette, and Bridger. That left Wyeth out for good."

"Where are those supplies now?" asked Becky. "We could use them."

"That Wyeth was not a man to give up. I'll never forget what he said to old Gabe. Something like, 'I'll roll a stone into your garden that you will never be able to remove,' and he meant it. From the Rendezvous he headed west and built Fort Hall as a trading post for his supplies. About that time, the Hudson Bay Company built Fort Boise, and a few years later they bought Fort Hall. I guess old Wyeth's back in Boston by now—probably selling ice again."

"Then he was right," added Abby. "He did roll a stone into the trappers' garden, since Fort Hall now belongs to the British traders."

"That he did. It don't matter though—beaver trade is dead."

"Tell us some more about Fort Hall," asked Sarah. "It feels good to know we're not the first people out here. I mean, it feels like civilization."

"I know what you mean, Sarah," said Miles. "My woman could use some solace in seeing a building or a farm."

Jacob continued his stories until well after dark, when people excused themselves for the night. Tomorrow would be a busy day.

The next day, Sunday, August 27, the Light Column arrived at Fort Hall in time for their noon meal. From a distance the fort's adobe construction shimmered against the blue sky and dry sage plain, giving the appearance of a mesa of chalk, dwarfed against its Western backdrop. As the column approached, it became apparent that there was good forage around the fort and a plentiful supply of water from the confluence of the Portneuf and Snake Rivers. Fort employees kept their vegetable garden fenced against wandering stock and jackrabbits. Sadly, most items were not yet ripe and ready for harvest—but even if they were, the fort could not afford to feed so many emigrants. The fort's personnel needed food from the garden for the upcoming winter.

Fremont's party camped near the confluence along with the lodges of a few visiting Snake and Nez Perce Indians. The chief factor of the fort was a man by the name of Richard Grant. He was a long-time employee of the Hudson Bay Company, starting on the frontier in Quebec and working his way up the ranks from trapper to brigade leader and finally to chief factor of Fort Hall. Grant's tall, muscular frame gave him a commanding appearance, which served him well when dealing with visiting bands of Indians and the often-rowdy free trappers from America. There was seldom any trouble at the fort, and each year it produced a tidy profit for the company from the variety of furs exchanged for trade goods.

Mr. Grant, regaled in buckskins and a fur hat, came out to meet Colonel Martin and Captain Gantt as the Light Column approached. He was welcoming and kind, offering his fort's facilities to help the emigrants—but as expected, he did not have enough supplies for both himself and the emigrants.

"I'll sell what I can afford to do without," he said to Colonel Martin as they rode toward the fort. "It won't be much, and your people will have to pay the standard Hudson Bay price."

"We expected that," said Captain Gantt. "Your prices are probably similar to what we found at Fort Laramie. I don't think our people will be surprised."

"Fremont took most of the coffee. I've still got flour and rice, so I'll have my storekeeper put out a sign."

"We have a couple ill people with us," said Colonel Martin. "They need a physician familiar with mountain fever, and medication—anything you can spare."

"Nearest surgeon is at Fort Vancouver—I've some laudanum if you think that'll help. People usually don't get sick out here in the mountains."

"We've got laudanum," said Gantt. "One of our men has been down since Fort Laramie, and his condition has worsened since we left Fort Bridger."

"You mean Richardson?" asked Martin.

"That's the man," said Gantt. "A few days' rest here at the fort would do him good. He can't walk or ride, so we've carried him in his wagon since before South Pass."

"Like I said, I've only got enough supplies to get my people through next winter," Grant said with concern. "I can't be taking on any sick pilgrims."

"We understand that," said Martin. "Several of our young men have been helping to drive his wagon. He's got a wife and two children to care for, so if he doesn't improve, I'm sure those young men will be pleased to drive his wagon all the way to Oregon City."

"Oregon City! With all these wagons?" Grant's expression was filled with doubt.

"We know it's never been done," said Martin. "We plan to be the first. Once we open up a road, others will follow."

"Well now, that's not entirely true," Grant said. "Wagons rolled west from here three years ago when the American trapping brigades broke up. It was the summer of 1840. Silk hats had just come in, and those trappers knew their way of life was over. There were some wagons here at the fort, left over from one of the Rendezvous. Actually they were carts, but they had wheels. Doc Newell decided to go to the Wallamet Valley to try his hand at farming, so he enlisted the help of Joe Meek and a guy named Nicholas to drive those carts. I think Caleb Wilkins was also with them."

"So you're saying there's a road?" Colonel Martin was obviously excited at the prospect.

"I didn't say that. They got to Fort Boise, then to Waiilatpu. They were a small party, so building a road wasn't necessary—and those men were mountain men, not farmers. They're accustomed to privations and hardships. They abandoned the carts at Waiilatpu and used pack animals the rest of the way. Men on the supply train last year told me that in '41, old Newell went back to Waiilatpu for one of the carts and took it on to the Wallamet Valley. Those were the first wheels to ever roll south of the Columbia!"

"That news hasn't reached the United States," said Captain Gantt. "We thought we'd be the first."

"They was carts, mind you," Grant emphasized, "not wagons—and they were driven by mountain men, not farmers!"

"Still, it's good news to me," said Colonel Martin. "I'm on my way to California along with a number of other people, so it don't much matter to us—but these folks going to Oregon could use some good news. They might not have such a difficult time, knowing that carts made it through. They expected to build a road in the Blue Mountains, so this will come as welcome news."

"I'll make sure our platoon leaders pass the word," added Captain Gantt. "I'm almost sorry I won't be continuing on with those people. I'd like to see this road through the mountains."

"So, you're going to California too?" asked Grant.

"Yup, me and eighteen other men and their families. Joe Walker knows a better route, so he's taking over as guide. Marcus Whitman's guiding these farmers to Waiilatpu."

"Whitman!" Grant stated emphatically. "Is he here? Can't he do anything for your sick?"

"He's not been much help to some of our sicker people, same with our other surgeon, Doc Long. We thought you might have someone that knows more about this mountain fever."

The conversation continued as the men approached the fort and Colonel Martin gave the order for his platoon leaders to form their wagon corrals. As soon as teamsters unhitched their teams and women got their kitchens in order, people wandered over to the fort to get a taste of civilization.

Fort Hall existed purely for the fur trade business, much like Fort Laramie. Its facilities were considerably better than Fort Bridger's, since it had the full support of the Hudson Bay Company. Still, it could not support the enormous needs of an unexpected one thousand Americans.

The internal buildings contained crude and uncomfortable furnishings made at the fort's carpenter shop. Considering the remoteness of the outpost, the quarters were as accommodating as possible. There were warehouses for furs and trade goods, a trading house, a blacksmith shop, internal corrals for the fort's stock, small residences for the workers and their families, and a larger residence for Chief Factor Grant.

Outside the trading house hung a sign itemizing the few scant items available for sale, along with their inflated frontier prices:

Flour, unbolted	25 cents /pt
Sugar	50 cents /pt
Brown sugar	50 cents /pt
Coffee	50 cents /pound
White beans	$1.00 /pound
Rice	33 1/3 cents /pound
Salt	50 cents /pound
Powder	$1.50 /pound
Lead	75 cents /pound
Percussion caps	$1.50 /box
Calico	$1.00 /yard
Rawhide	10 cents /yard
Blankets	$5.00 each
Thread	10 cents /spool
Rough calico	75 cents /yard

After dealing with the prices at Fort Laramie, most people thought the Fort Hall prices were a bargain.

"These people aren't out to cheat us like back at Fort Laramie," stated Nat Sitton.

"We can use their blacksmith shop for free," added Levi Boyd. "I've already checked—and since we got our own blacksmiths, it won't cost us a thing."

Most emigrants, accustomed to the profiteering of frontier merchandisers, accepted the moderate prices and the friendliness of the Fort Hall residents as a welcome relief. Even though prices were considerably higher than what could be found back in Independence, they were certainly reasonable this far out from a manufacturing point or seaport. Each family bought what they could, knowing that the other columns were close behind and would surely finish off whatever supplies remained. The fort's ability and willingness to help appeared to be adequate. That impression would soon change.

Later that evening the Oregon Emigrating Company Council paid off John Gantt for services rendered between Independence and

Fort Hall. He had been a fair and dependable guide, one that many people would miss during their final five hundred-mile push to the Wallamet Valley. Marcus Whitman, the new Light Column guide and leader, decided to allow people a few days to make repairs and recruit their stock. Families parting for California would be afforded a few more evenings with lifelong friends whom they had met only a few months earlier.

On Monday, Cooper's Splinter Column arrived and rejoined the Light Column. Their original intent to travel faster had proved to be a failure, and there was no need to continue the split. With all the unknowns associated with the upcoming Snake River Plains, rejoining the Light Column was the better part of valor.

Applegate's Cow Column and Zachary's Outcast Mess also arrived that evening. With Waldo's Straggler Column and Cooper's Splinter Column rejoining the Light Column, and Chiles's California Column breaking off to head for California, the Oregon Emigrating Company was almost back to their original two columns, organized on June 9 after crossing the Big Blue. The only exception was Zachary's Outcast Mess. By Monday evening most of the remaining stragglers had arrived at the fort with their crippled and patched wagons. These teamsters, associated with one of the various columns, had suffered wagon breakdowns of one sort or another that had caused them to fall behind their respective columns. They would keep the blacksmith shop busy for the next few days.

As expected, these stragglers and a number of other people were not able to buy supplies from the Fort Hall warehouse. The Light Column had exhausted Grant's excess stores, and all that remained would be needed for the fort's personnel during the upcoming winter. Grant locked the door to his supply house, turning away the remaining emigrants.

The need for supplies and Grant's refusal to sell was more than the Williams brothers could take. Jim, Isaac, Squire, and John Williams and their companions were about to embark onto a vast unknown desert on their trek to California, and food supplies were essential for survival. Walker had told them that they would not find game until reaching the foothills of the Sierra Nevada Mountains, a good six to eight weeks away. Most of the men felt that their survival depended on Fort Hall providing for their needs.

Chief Factor Grant remained steadfast in his refusal to sell more supplies—even over the protests of the Williams brothers, who considered this a matter of life and death. Before too many words passed, Squire Williams pulled his rifle and threatened to shoot if Grant didn't reopen the trading house. Grant immediately sent for Colonel Fremont in hopes that a show of military force would discourage the determined emigrants. Fremont quickly arrived with ten men, all armed and ready for trouble. To Grant's dismay, Fremont stood on the side of the emigrants!

The War of 1812 had not been that long ago, and several men in the migration had served in the conflict. The Hudson Bay Company's incursion into United States territory for purposes of trapping did not set well with anyone, and now was as good a time as any to make up for past irritations. The thought of the British taking control of Oregon Country provided an additional frustration. The British had been persistent enemies of the United States for over fifty years, so Fremont was not about to afford them protection.

Grant surveyed the situation and realized it was hopeless. Fremont's men outnumbered and outgunned the entire fort's personnel. Even Colonel Martin and Captain Gantt failed to come to Grant's aid. Their initial friendliness quickly reverted to nationalist interests and country allegiance.

With the reopening of Fort Hall's supply house, people bought additional powder, lead, blankets, shirts, flour, axes, dried salmon, and elk meat—showing little concern for the fort's residents and their need to survive the upcoming winter. Abby considered their behavior self-serving and uncaring, but there was nothing she could do. She left the fort determined to subsist on what little she had, no matter what. Such selfishness was repulsive, and she did not want anything to do with the situation.

After dinner that evening, Grant paid a visit to the column leaders, who were meeting with the main council of the Oregon Emigrating Company. Colonel Martin, now just Bill Martin again, would be heading to California with Joe Walker, John Gantt, Joe Chiles, and the other California-bound families. Marcus Whitman sat with the council as he learned of his responsibilities as the new guide and leader of the Oregon Emigrating Company between here and Waiilatpu. Taking on the responsibilities of both Captain Gantt and Colonel Martin was well within the scope of Reverend Whitman's self-image.

There were no apologies given for the behavior of the needy emigrants, and Grant did not expect any. His purpose was now to try to convince the council that driving wagons west from Fort Hall would be an exercise in futility. He offered to provide a fair trade between wagons and pack animals for those teamsters wise enough to take the offer.

"How we gonna carry farm equipment and household goods on packhorses?" asked Jesse Applegate. "Me, my brother, and quite a few other people are driving carts now, and we expect to get through without any more trouble."

"What would you do with over one hundred wagons?" Dave Lenox posed a good question. "Why do you want to be so helpful after the way our people behaved?"

"You don't need that many wagons," added Hank Lee. "If we switch to pack animals, we won't be able to carry as much and you'll get most of your supplies back!"

"I don't consider reclaiming my property as a crime," asserted Grant. "I'll be hard pressed to replace those stores before the snow flies—and if you clean out the warehouse at Fort Boise, we might as well burn the forts and head back to Vancouver!"

The conversation continued, heated, yet civilized, with Grant trying to recover a part of his supplies and the leaders of the migration not willing to give ground. Marcus Whitman intervened with the most compelling argument to keep their wagons.

"I've been over these plains several times on horseback. I say a wagon can make it, all the way to Waiilatpu. We've the manpower to overcome any obstacle, else we'd have never gotten this far—and once we get a road through the Blue Mountains, that'll encourage thousands of people to follow in coming years."

"I'm with Marcus," said Dan Matheny. "We keep our wagons!"

The meeting broke up at dusk, with Grant showing obvious frustration at the loss of his supplies and the bleak prospects for the upcoming winter. Tensions had always run high between Great Britain and the United States, and this incident only served to exasperate Grant and reaffirm his dislike of Americans. Now, his only hope to survive the coming winter was to send a runner back to Fort Boise for emergency supplies, to send hunting parties out to restock food stores, and to depend on local Indian tribes to trade for smoked salmon.

The next morning, Tuesday, August 29, Bill Wilson took up Grant's offer and sold his wagon for five packhorses. With his current stock, including oxen, he was able to load almost all of his family's belongings. Larger, heavier items such as their heirloom rocker, a spinning wheel, and two trunks had to be abandoned. He was able to load most of the trunk contents onto makeshift packsaddles. Bill's wife, Polly, and their three children would have to sleep out under the stars and walk the final five hundred miles.

Wilson was the only man to switch to pack animals. Everyone else felt they could get through without too much difficulty. Besides, a wagon afforded the only protection against foul weather. After they entered the Blue Mountains, the weather could easily turn to snow or sleet.

The arguments for and against wagons did not diminish Abby's determination. She had made up her mind to take hers through to Oregon long before they ever reached Fort Laramie. Fort Hall was a mere way station where her stock could find forage, water, and a few days' rest. She was still moving forward, and with Jacob's help, would make it to Oregon City.

After dinner and chores, and after the various camps had quieted down, Abby recorded the tumultuous events of the day. Because of Jacob's advice on conserving food and his prowess as a hunter, she did not need to buy a single item at the fort—this she noted with an underline. The weather was a constant subject for her diary, as was the condition of the road and descriptions of the surrounding country. Tonight's entries included the uncivilized anger of emigrants wanting supplies versus the civilized appearance of adobe buildings. After so may weeks on the trail, this tiny outpost brought out a homesickness she had not felt since leaving Independence—a feeling of being lost, with no place to call home. Not since she had left her wedding dishes with Hannah Greer had such an emotion shown itself. The Western Passage now served as home and shelter. Seeing it, along with her kitchen and campfire, provided some measure of comfort.

Earlier that evening, Reverend Whitman had come around informing everyone that they would leave on Friday morning. That meant a few more days of rest and time to make needed repairs. After recording that, and a few more items, Abby put her diary away and extinguished the candle. Tomorrow would be a busy day of baking, sewing, repairing a tear in the white-top, and making some attempt to remove dirt and straighten the interior of the Western Passage.

The next morning brought the sad news that Dan Richardson had died during the night. His wife, Dorcas, stayed by his side all night trying to give comfort as his breathing became more shallow and sporadic. He died in her arms just as the morning sun began to rise. Friends carried the body into the fort while Dorcas stayed with her two children. Cyrene Cary offered her support, and Eliza Eyre and Sarah Goodman fixed breakfast for the ladies and all their children. Abby joined the group, contributing a fresh loaf of bread.

The hot dry days of summer seemed to be coming to a close with the cool, rainy weather of Wednesday morning. The rain felt good after so many dusty days on the trail, and the change in weather seemed appropriate as people prepared for another funeral. Reverend Whitman set the services for early the next morning. In the meantime, a coffin and headboard had to be made. Even after the way people had treated Chief Factor Grant, he generously offered to supply the needed planks. Once again the ladies requested Abby to write a verse. Dorcas's children, Gallatin and Alonzo Linn, needed something by which to remember their father and his courage to provide his family with a better life. Shortly before noon the verse was ready.

Dearest father, you have left us,
On our journey to El Dorado.
But we will see you once again,
When we reach that blessed land.

Jim Athey finished the coffin by midafternoon, along with the headboard. Lucinda Beagle and Catherine Baker made the inscription:

DANIEL RICHARDSON
DIED AUG 30, 1843
IN HIS 33ʳᴰ YEAR

They added Abby's verse while Nat Sitton, Tom Brown, and John Cox dug another grave, this time in the fort's cemetery. As the dinner hour approached, everything was ready for tomorrow's funeral.

Reverend Whitman held the funeral at nine o'clock on Thursday morning under another cold and rainy sky. As he delivered the eulogy, he spoke about Dan's dream of a good life for his family in Oregon. His words gave some solace to Dorcas and her children, though they were only empty, well-worn clichés. The funeral ended quickly, with everyone going back to their wagons to get out of the rain. Nat, Tom, and John stayed behind to fill in the grave and erect the headboard.

Everyone spent the remainder of the day trying to avoid the rain while preparing to get underway. This would be their last day at the fort.

The next morning, Friday, September 1, Reverend Marcus Whitman roused the Light Column at an early hour and had everyone moving west by eight o'clock. Not far behind was Jesse Applegate's Cow Column. The weather continued cold and rainy, with teamsters slogging through mud as they urged their teams forward. Their stay at Fort Hall had been uncomfortable at best, and it was good to be leaving. The weather, funeral, and conflict over securing supplies formed a flood of memories to leave behind. Before pulling out, people abandoned a number of oxen and milch cows because of lameness or simply weakness. Had these animals continued on, they would soon have been food for vultures and coyotes. By leaving them at the fort they could recruit their strength and be available to help some other poor, hapless emigrant next year.

Abby kept her milch cow tied to the back of the wagon, along with Jacob's two packhorses, the extra ox, and Crow. Jacob figured the cow would never give milk again. Whether it did or not, it would have value in the Wallamet Valley.

After an hour on the trail the rain had completely soaked Abby's clothes, bonnet, and moccasins. She struggled to stay warm and keep her oxen moving through the muddy, rough terrain. She and Jacob spent the nooner seeking shelter in the rear of the wagon.

The afternoon continued much like the morning with a steady, gentle rain and an occasional strong gust of wind. The rain fell in stark contrast to the surrounding sagebrush desert, but even the desert receives some rain. Whitman's desire to return to Waiilatpu made his first day as guide a long one, with the Light Column not forming their wagon corrals until after seven o'clock. It had been a grueling, miserable twenty-mile day.

That evening after the dinner hour, members of Chiles's California Column received a visit from many of the adults from both the Light Column and Jesse's Cow Column. Tonight would be their last night together, since tomorrow Joe Walker would turn the California-bound emigrants south toward the Humboldt River and California. Although the main Oregon migration had traveled and camped separately from the California-bound emigrants ever since leaving Independence, they were all part of the Oregon Emigrating Company. The journey had created friendships that would last a lifetime. After an hour of farewells, congratulations, and best wishes for a safe and speedy journey, folks wandered back to their wagons to escape another light drizzle and prepare for another long day on the trail.

The next morning was cloudy, but not raining. Although yesterday had been chilly and uncomfortable, it had come as a welcome change from the weeks of hot sun and alkali dust. The rain had washed dust from the wagons and stock, and now the desert had the smell of new growth. The white-tops were decidedly cleaner, making a picturesque image as they meandered their way West through swales and around sage. The refreshed column moved due west this morning as they began to cross the great Snake River Plains.

Abby hung her wet clothes over several of the interior wagon hoops before starting out on the day's march. The usual morning preparations, marching rotation, nooners, camp corrals, and other orders remained in effect. Whitman did not change any of Bill Martin's command structure. The organization worked, and considering the independence of the emigrants, it was not wise to change anything that worked.

About an hour down the road, Joe Walker turned the lead wagons in his column in a southwest direction, while Marcus Whitman kept the Light Column pointed due west. People from the Light Column who were now traveling to California included Captain Gantt (now simply John Gantt), Colonel Martin (now Bill Martin), Pierson Reading, and the Williams brothers (Isaac, Jim, John, and Squire). Most of the people of the Light Column were relieved to see the Williamses heading south. They had always traveled with the Light Column, and their independent ways had been a point of contention on more than one occasion.

Not all emigrants were unwavering in their destinations, however. Bill Baldridge, John Boardman, and Tom Hensley had left Independence with every intention of going to Oregon. Somewhere along the trail their plans had changed, and they now joined Joe Walker and the California-bound pilgrims. Apparently, the stories of mystery and wonder from California had outweighed the same stories filtering out of Oregon. The main concern was that California remained under Spanish control, while the future of Oregon was more certain. Since the vote at Champooic, everyone knew that Oregon would eventually become part of the United States. These men going to California were betting their futures that California would also someday join the union.

John Mills was just the opposite. He had left Independence intending to go to California. Something had changed his plans, possibly the news from the eastbound trappers that Oregon was to be American, not British. Mills now decided to join the Oregon-bound emigrants under the command of Marcus Whitman. The difficulties of trail life had not diminished his independence or that of any of the emigrants. Changing his future plans and destiny was only natural.

Abby watched as the small contingent of eight wagons and about fifty people veered away from the main trail. She waved as individuals looked back to see her and their Oregon-bound friends continue west, paralleling the Snake River. Her thoughts were of the friends she would never see again, and many unanswered questions. *Who will reach their destination first? What dangers will the others face in crossing that great desert before the California mountains? How will they ever get through those mountains?* The questions kept coming with no answers to soften their mystery.

Jacob rode up to ride alongside.

"What will become of those people?" Abby asked as they watched the column march off into the distance.

"I suppose most will remain as farmers and merchants. Some will become successful and some will fail." Jacob speculated.

"Will the Spanish government even allow them to settle?" Abby fervently wished that someday the entire Pacific Coast would belong to the United States.

The silhouette of the California-bound column kept getting smaller and smaller, until only an occasional flicker of movement on the horizon betrayed their location. The ground was still damp from the rain of the past few days, so trail dust gave no token of their position. Soon they were gone from sight. Abby faced forward, snapping her quirt on the rumps of her lead oxen and scanning the western horizon for signs of the land ahead.

"We are pointed directly at Oregon City," she thought. "Another five hundred miles and I'll be there!"

After dinner Abby sat down with her diary to note the names of the California-bound emigrants: *"Today we said goodbye to our California friends. Joe Walker is guiding them down the Humboldt River on a route he learned years ago while working as a trapper. He said it's a long and difficult route, through a desert with almost no game for food. The journey to the California mountains should take them about six weeks. Then they need to get their wagons up through those mountains, just like we will have to cross the Blue Mountains after we pass Fort Boise. I will probably never see my California friends again. In addition to those I mentioned last night, other men include Joe Chiles, John Atkinson, Vern Dawson, Milt Little, Julius Martin, Frank McClelland, John McGee, and John McIntire.*

"Tonight is the first night in many months that the Oregon-bound folks in our company are back together! Jesse's Cow Column is encamped only one mile upriver, and will probably be nearby all the way to Fort Boise. Waldo's Straggler Column and Cooper's Splinter Column have dissolved and joined our Light Column. The only exception is Zachary's Outcast Mess. There are no complaints that he is no longer traveling with us, although I do miss the company of Jim Nesmith."

Abby's words easily filled two pages as she took solace in the comfort of a campfire and a quiet evening. Tomorrow looked as though it would be a sunny day for travel.

On Sunday, September 3, the Light Column continued over a broken, rocky plain devoid of timber and game. There was a slight delay at midmorning when Lew Cooper got into a knock-down-drag-out argument with his teamster, John Jackson. The cause of the dispute was a mystery, but had something to do with an incident that took place when Cooper was in charge of the Splinter Column. Whitman immediately intervened, since their argument had brought the entire column to a halt. After a warning from Marcus that he would not tolerate such dissent, Jackson solved the problem by leaving Cooper's employ. He unhitched his horse from the back of Cooper's wagon, mounted, and rode over to Zachary's Mess. Zachary and the Oteys were traveling parallel to the Light Column, about a quarter mile to the south. With the Oteys' permission, Jackson would move his belongings from Cooper's wagon to the Oteys' that evening.

Cooper was now left without a teamster, a prospect that did not please him. With five head of cattle, two horses, and a milch cow, Cooper was in need of help. Dave Arthur, one of Bill Arthur's sons, stepped forward and offered his help for the same wage paid to Jackson. Cooper agreed, and the Light Column was again in motion.

The road here, if it could be called that, was simply a vague trace that led out through the sage toward Fort Boise, another Hudson Bay post about two hundred miles distant. The terrain was strewn with rocks and boulders as if scattered by some ancient volcano. Marcus referred to this area as the Devil's Garden—a name used by the trappers he accompanied back in 1835. That was the year he traveled West with Reverend Sam Parker, representing the American Board of Commissioners for Foreign Missions. Their purpose was to establish missions among the Columbia River Indians.

Wagons of the Light Column inched their way forward in a braided pattern as they went around the larger boulders and sage. A force of about thirty young men walked out in front of the lead wagons to push smaller stones to the side, creating the beginnings of an actual road.

The swales gave way to a level area, barren of grass and other nourishing vegetation. Sagebrush in this area was over three feet high and so sturdy that in some places the young trailblazers had to cut a trail. Whitman alternated the five lead wagons, to distribute the work of breaking down and crushing the sage where they actually had to plow through it. Abby took her turn at the lead three times over the course of the day. Each time, Jacob came in and helped handle the teams.

Marcus allowed almost two hours for the noon stop so that various religious factions could gather and worship. Nobody questioned the importance of traveling on the Sabbath, for winter snows were rapidly approaching—but extending the nooner for Sunday worship had come to be expected. As usual, Abby and Jacob sat alone as people gathered into their denominational groups.

"I can't stop smelling this sage," Abby said as she prepared some bread and dried buffalo meat. "It must be good for something, but I don't know what. It burns green and much too fast to be a good fuel—and the stock won't touch it."

"It'll tell you where to plant," said Jacob. "It needs soil to grow in, and the deeper the soil then the taller the sage. When we get near some hills, you take a look. On the hillsides where the soil is shallow there's almost no sage. Down in the valleys it can grow to five or six feet."

"Really."

"If you could get a water source, then some of this land might be good for farms."

"There lies the problem, Jacob—no water. Maybe the stringy bark fibers of this plant are useful for something."

"Already are—the Paiute make baskets, sandals, mats, and other articles from the bark." He stopped abruptly, self-conscious at expounding his knowledge so liberally.

"Have you noticed the leaves?" Abby asked, holding up a sprig, wanting to continue the conversation. "There're two different kinds, but I think one is just a juvenile leaf. The older ones have three rounded teeth, and if you crush them the smell of sage is so strong it's hard to breathe."

"You're starting to sound like a teacher again."

Abby laughed at his tease, tossing the piece of sage toward him.

"My students in Oregon are going to learn all about this land. I've been keeping a detailed account in my diary, so when I get settled I can write it up in the form of a grammar school learner."

"I'm sure you will, Abby, and your students will be the best-taught in Oregon!"

Abby smiled, taking the compliment with modesty. They continued their conversation about the surrounding country and the road ahead until Marcus rode by to rouse everyone from the nooner. It was time to get underway.

After a long afternoon of road building and blazing, wagon corrals formed on a rough basaltic plain high above the Snake River. The distance to the river was approximately one mile, downhill over a sage-covered incline. After a long day on the trail, this was a distance most of the tired emigrants chose not to negotiate. Jacob, with Abby's help, decided to descend to the river with all their stock. Oregon City was still a long ways off, and dead stock were of no use. After an hour of watering, they brought the animals back up and hobbled them near the kitchen just as the sun began to set. There was very little forage in the area, so hobbling in one place was as good as the next. Jacob staked them close to the wagon to shorten the morning preparations. Abby made a quick cold dinner, then retired to her wagon and diary. A half-hour later the entire camp was asleep for the night.

Early the next morning, Fred Prigg tried to ride one of his mules down to the river to fill a water jug and give the mule a drink. During the descent, the trail became so steep that his saddle slipped forward over the mule's head, sending him into a somersault while still hanging onto the saddle. He landed on his back and rolled another fifty feet before stopping his fall by grabbing onto a sage bush. He escaped without injury to either himself or the mule. After standing up and catching his breath, he picked up the saddle and led the mule back to camp. A drink of water could wait another day.

Today's road was much like yesterday's. The rocky plain continued, as did the ubiquitous sage. The five lead wagons continued to alternate to the back of the column, while young men walked out in front doing whatever they could to improve the road. The dry washes in this area were clear of both rocks and sage, no doubt washed out by annual floods, providing a smooth surface and a brief reprieve from the work of road building.

At noon the column stopped about a quarter-mile from the edge of a vertical drop-off that ran along the Snake River canyon. Here the river compressed into about two-thirds its usual width, spilling over the rugged volcanic rock that made up the region. Jacob called this spot the American Falls. It was a name trappers used to describe the rapid descent of the river. The water fell about twenty-five feet for every one hundred feet of river length, and was split into three chutes by two large boulders. The center chute presented a roaring whitewater rapids, while the two outside chutes contained waterfalls with a drop of about ten feet. In its entirety, it was magnificently beautiful.

The power and strength of a rushing rapid pitched against the blue sky and surrounding desert was a contrast that awed those emigrants accustomed to the slow-moving Ohio, Mississippi, and Missouri Rivers. The Snake was wild and untamed, rushing headlong into the unknown. They all knew the water would eventually reach the Pacific Ocean, and certainly before anyone in the migration could get there. If only they could build rafts and ride the wild water to their El Dorado! It was easy to dream of a quick end to the difficulties of the journey. Such dreams were short-lived, though, as reality set in. From conversations back at Fort Hall, everyone knew there were other dangerous rapids and falls downriver, and on the Columbia as well—too dangerous to survive on a mere raft.

During their one-hour nooner, the majority of emigrants took what food they could carry and walked over to the precipice. It was a sight too spectacular to miss. After drinking in the beauty and wildness of the scene for as long as they dared, they wandered back to the column shortly before Whitman gave the order to march.

The next morning, Tuesday, September 5, the Light Column stopped at several water holes after traveling for only an hour. The water holes had probably formed from the rain of the week before and were a fortuitous encounter. Many of the animals had been without water for two days, so stopping was not a matter of choice. Marcus halted the column for two hours while teamsters tended to their stock. The Snake River was still not accessible because of the depth of the canyon. Water in these holes was poor at best, but it was the only water available.

The water came too late for several oxen in the migration. After drinking, they could not continue and had to be killed. Their wasted frames precluded their use for edible meat, at least by humans. The owners butchered each animal and gave the meat to those people with dogs. At this point in the journey, even the dogs were near death. They had gone over fifteen hundred miles with only orts for food. When Marcus called for the caravan to move out, Joe Davis, a farmer from Illinois, had to leave his dog behind. Brownie was simply too exhausted to continue. Joe's wife, Lucy, tried to coax him along, but he refused to leave the water hole no matter what command or encouragement came from his masters. To Lucy, leaving Brownie behind was better than watching him die on the trail. Besides, he could feed off the remains of the ox carcasses. If a party of Indians should pass by, the dog might be strong enough to accompany them and gain a new home.

Later that day, Zachary's Mess came upon the water holes and Brownie. Alex Zachary had few morals and certainly no concern for another man's dog. In an instant he dispatched and butchered poor Brownie, providing himself and his family some poor meat for the next two days.

Rain returned during the afternoon, turning the road into a quagmire for the final wagons of the column. Everyone vied for a lead position to avoid the muddy ruts created by the forty-some wagons now comprising the Light Column. Jesse and the Cow Column, coming up behind, blazed their own trail to avoid the trace of the Light Column.

That evening's camp was again dominated by a lack of good forage for the several hundred head of working livestock, milch cows, and beef cattle. While Abby cooked a pot of rice, Jacob drove their livestock south for several miles before finding enough grass to provide a mild subsistence. It was still raining lightly when he returned shortly before nightfall, hobbling each animal near the kitchen. Abby had kept his dinner warm, for which he kindly thanked her as he took a heaping plateful and crawled under the wagon to escape the rain. She had already put his buffalo robe under the wagon, his usual place of residence during stormy weather.

The rain continued during most of the next day, Wednesday, September 6. Whitman began the march by making a rather large detour around a deep draw created from a creek running in from the south. A few miles beyond this, Abby noticed several large springs on the north side of the Snake River, coming forth from an embankment and rushing down to the river. As the column drew nearer, she could see additional springs emanating from several places along the ridge, which extended for about a half-mile. There appeared to be four major springs and numerous small ones. The hill they flowed down was about 150 feet high, 75 feet back from the river and perfectly flat on top. Small willows bordered the north shore of the river at this point, taking advantage of this additional source of water. From a distance, the springs and their rushing waters looked like banks of unmelted snow, hidden from the sun by the shade of a draw. It was a stark reminder that winter was on the way. This uncommon sight of fresh, clear water was visible for over an hour as the Light Column slowly moved down the south side of the river.

"Look at that, Jacob," Abby said as Jacob rode up and dismounted. "We need some springs like that on this side of the river. It's almost not fair that there can be so much good water, all within sight, and our animals can't have any."

"We'll have water by tonight," Jacob replied. "Salmon Falls is just ahead, and it'll be crowded with Indians. Those falls are an important fishing ground for tribes as far away as the Beaverhead. We'll probably use a good part of your trade goods stocking up on smoked salmon. We're beyond buffalo country now, so our meals will shift to fish. Hard to say when we'll have fresh meat again, maybe in the Blue Mountains. After the falls there probably won't be any more Indians to trade with until we reach the Columbia. The fish we get tomorrow will have to last us five to six weeks."

"I've never had salmon. I've had smoked fish back in Ohio, but never salmon. After hearing so much of this fish, it must be good food. Five to six weeks? We better figure," she hesitated while doing the math in her head, "better trade for at least 125 pounds. That should give me a pound and you two pounds a day. I've still got rice, flour, and beans. Probably not enough unless we're successful in getting plenty of salmon."

"Tribes along the Snake and Columbia use salmon as their main diet. After you've tried it you'll know why—it's right tasty, fresh or smoked."

Before long, signs of Indians became more numerous. There were heavily worn trails coming in from the south and leading downriver. In the distance, Whitman and the other pioneers in the advance guard could see wisps of smoke rising from thirty or forty fires around the perimeters of several Indian villages. The column was moving straight toward them. Marcus stopped to take his bearings, then realized they were approaching Salmon Falls. He ordered the column to continue for five more miles before forming their wagon corrals, close enough to the Indian villages for people to prepare for a day of trading.

Salmon Falls was another spectacle everyone wanted to see, and

Marcus knew they had to obtain needed food to cross the remaining Snake River Plains and the Blue Mountains. He had each platoon leader pass the word that they would stay two nights. Tomorrow folks could engage in trading, then on Friday morning they would be back on the trail.

Abby knew exactly what to expect, since Jacob had enlightened her in detail concerning the falls, Snake Indians, and trading opportunities. During that evening she went through the trunk containing trade goods—a trunk not opened since crossing the Big Blue. Jacob helped sort out which items to trade and which ones to hold back for trading on the Columbia.

The appearance of such a large contingency of white people with their strange-looking wagons and even stranger-looking animals had considerably alarmed the Indians the day before. As wagon corrals formed, several Indian chiefs came out to meet the column and determine their purpose. Whitman communicated that they were merely passing through on their way to the Columbia. To the Indians, the presence of women and children confirmed these peaceful intentions. War parties never traveled with women and children. Nonetheless, it was a frightening incursion into a land where the only exposure to whites were an occasional trapping brigade and the Hudson Bay Company outposts. Some of the Indians had seen Spanish cattle at the missions. Most had not. Even the trading posts did not have any of these strange-looking "buffalo." Chickens were another oddity, since none of the Indians had ever seen a domesticated bird.

The emigrants presented a heavily armed and superior society with their white-topped wagons, iron tools, cloth, and curiosities of a seemingly infinite nature. The Indians back at the falls spent an uneasy evening in fear and foreboding of what might happen in the morning. Warriors readied for battle while realizing they had no chance against such a large force. Their only hope for survival was flight. Soon their returning chiefs allayed their fears by ordering everyone to prepare for a day of trading.

A light drizzle fell that evening, so everyone corralled and stayed in their wagons. Tomorrow would be soon enough to trade for salmon and see the falls.

On Thursday morning, September 7, Jacob saddled his two packhorses with trade goods brought all the way from Independence. Shirts, beads, trade knives, and other paraphernalia bought at Skow's General Store would now prove their worth. Abby had sorted and tied the trade goods she wanted to use as Jacob had instructed. Now they would be exchanged for enough smoked salmon to get them to the Columbia, where they could procure more. Getting enough salmon now, 125 pounds, depended upon skill at trading. This was Jacob's area of expertise and Abby knew it. Her presence was merely as an observer.

The Snake squaws set up their trading circles in an area halfway between their village and the wagon corrals. Squaws piled their stores of salmon along a makeshift street that gave the appearance of a farm market from back in the United States. It was a welcoming sight to the emigrants, even if the traders and their wares were unfamiliar. A day of rest and shopping at a "farmers market" was a refreshing change from the difficulties of travel. Besides this marketplace, watching the Indians fish at the falls would provide hours of entertainment.

As they walked into the trading market leading their two packhorses, Abby tried hard to drink in all the sights, sounds, and smells around her. It was a blue-sky day in a sea of pale-green sage—and here within this wild country was a piece of civilization. Her gaze wandered across a wide area, taking in the river, Indian shanties, white-top wagons, herds of cattle from the Cow Column, the hundreds of Indians, and even the surrounding hills. There were several low-lying hills on either side of the river, although nothing of consequence. The country was rough, strewn with volcanic rock and deficient in both grass and trees. Near the south shore of the river stood several hundred Indian shanties made from sage, rocks, wood, skin, and any other material available for such a purpose. As far as the eye could see, both upriver and downriver, there were Indians—all engaged in the occupation of harvesting and curing salmon.

The Indians conducted their activities from the south shore. The steepness of the land on the north shore, a climb of about three hundred feet, precluded approaching the river from that direction. Out in the river on every available rock, young braves engaged in spearing fish as they swam upriver. After spearing a fish, children brought it to shore, where other children dispatched it by cutting off its head and clearing out its entrails. Another group of younger children carried the gutted fish up to waiting squaws. The women then cut the fish into boneless strips, placing part of the flesh out on grass mats to dry and the rest on scaffolding above smoldering sage fires. After drying or smoking, they wrapped the strips in woven grass mats for storage or trading.

The Snake Indians, like many of the tribes in the Northwest, subsisted almost entirely on salmon. During the fall when the salmon were running, times were good and stomachs were full. In other seasons, such as late winter, the tribes suffered greatly. It was a hard life. Their culture, whose origins had been lost to the dust of time, persisted through the centuries with annual migrations determined by the season and availability of food. Trappers moving through their country offered an opportunity to acquire goods not otherwise available. Consequently, these Indians were always ready to help travelers, both in kindness and with trading. Over the last twenty years, trading with the white trappers had become a major commercial activity. They acquired trade goods of clothing, knives, and guns that considerably improved their impoverish lives.

As the trading began, it was obvious that these Indians were trading for their very existence. They had little use for baubles such as hawks' bells, beads, or vermilion. Instead, clothing was their main focus of attention. The garb they wore was a strange combination of traditional skins and woven grass, interspersed with colored cloth, homespun shirts, and pieces of military uniforms.

The market soon became a bazaar of ethnic diversity coming together in a dozen different languages, cultures, and manners. The common thread was that they were all people, people with families and the basic needs of life. So the trading began in earnest as everyone communicated as best they could—mostly through hand signals—for only a few, such as Jacob, could speak in sign language. Although the traders at each bartering point could not understand each other's language, everyone continued to talk as if they could. A farmer would hold up a shirt while pointing to a stack of dried salmon. The squaw in turn would request to examine the shirt, then divide out an amount of salmon equivalent to its worth. The bartering went back and forth until both parties agreed to the exchange.

Abby and Jacob approached one of the squaws who, with hand signs, showed her approval of the shirts and disapproval of beads. It was clear that if they were to obtain 125 pounds of salmon they would have to trade with shirts, tools, ball, and powder. Baubles for these Indians were a worthless commodity. Abby placed these items back in their sack before their presence caused any additional irritation on the part of the Indian squaw.

"I believe you still have some sewing awls," Jacob said as he looked up at Abby. He sat cross-legged on the ground, signing with the squaw while Abby held the reins of the packhorses.

"Yes, I do—several." She quickly looked at the squaw, knowing that this would be an extremely valuable item for an Indian who had almost nothing compared to the Americans.

"Get two of them, they'll be worth a great deal to these people—and here," he handed her a sack of beads, "you can take all these back. Maybe we can use them on the Columbia. Bring an extra two shirts and five more loads of ball and powder. We can get about one dried fish for a single load of ammunition."

"How about tobacco?"

"Bring some. These people might be too savvy for that—but it's worth a try."

Abby handed him the reins, then quickly disappeared through the crowd on her way back to the wagon.

While Abby was fetching the additional goods, Jacob traded three shirts for almost 50 pounds of salmon. When she returned with two awls, four plugs of tobacco, and two more calico shirts, he easily secured another 75 pounds of fish. Most of this was smoked salmon, which carried a higher price than the dried salmon.

The sewing awls brought the most, even more than the calico shirts. With awls, the squaw could make or repair clothing all winter. Sewing awls were a grand prize for such a poor people.

John Shively traded all the goods he could afford to part with. His stores were almost gone, and he needed the salmon simply to survive until they reached Fort Boise. He, along with a number of other emigrants, deeply regretted his wastefulness early on in the journey. With an opportunity to restock their consumables, now was no time for recounting past faults. People traded whatever they could part with to secure the food needed for survival.

Several emigrants requested buffalo meat for trade but were told there was none. Buffalo skulls had been seen along the trail since leaving Fort Hall, so their absence was hard to believe. Nobody had seen any buffalo, and the poor condition of these Indians fell as proof to the animal's absence. Jacob informed the few demanding farmers that there had not been any buffalo west of Fort Hall since fur trappers first entered the region thirty years ago. The skulls along the Snake River Plains were old, yet well preserved because of the dry air.

"You'll see buffalo sign until we get to Fort Boise," Jacob informed the farmers. "The herds are long gone from this region, so trade what you can for as much fish as you can carry. We're out of buffalo country for good."

It was sage advice. Trading continued all morning with folks dropping off cured salmon and picking up more trade goods from their wagons before returning to the market.

As Abby and Jacob were leaving the market with both packhorses loaded down with both dried and smoked salmon, the shouting of two squaws brought them to a halt. One of the agitated squaws was berating two of the emigrant mothers. Nobody could understand what the squaws were saying, although they were obviously angry at the way the white women were treating the emigrant children. These children stood by in their torn and tattered clothes, looking gaunt and filthy from so many days of forced marching with only a minimum amount of food for the last month. Neither of the squaws could understand why anyone would treat children with such callousness.

As one squaw belittled the women's competence as mothers, the other squaw handed one of the emigrant women several pounds of smoked salmon. The woman thanked the squaw, then turned to walk away, not understanding that the fish was meant for the children. The squaw's shouts got louder as she pointed to the children. Still the woman did not understand. Jacob was about to step in when one of the squaws took the fish back and walked over to the children and handed it out—one piece to each child. Jacob knew the white mothers now understood, so he stepped back to watch the proceedings.

The reason for the squaw's anger was now all too obvious to the white mothers. Their children did look neglected, and this was intolerable to the Indians. Here, a culture of people so poor they barely had clothes to wear were more concerned about caring for these children than were the "rich" white travelers. It was a tough lesson. Before the end of the day, every child in the migration enjoyed a meal of smoked salmon. Only the adults needed to pay in trade goods for such food.

The Snake Indians viewed these trail-weary emigrants as being poorer than themselves—not poorer in material goods, but poorer in culture and spirit. It was the emigrants who needed help, not the Indians, and it was the emigrants who needed to learn that their children were the future.

Abby watched intently as the squaws berated the white mothers, then handed out salmon to their children. It was a lesson she would never forget.

Back at the Western Passage she stowed the parcels of salmon in the front of the wagon next to her other remaining food stores. The woven grass wrappings were more than adequate for storing the fish; however, the packages needed to be secured to prevent their bouncing free over the rough road. After tying the salmon down, she returned to the falls to watch the Indians fish.

Salmon Falls was not perpendicular, rather it dropped 25 feet over a distance of 300 yards. The river was about 150 yards wide and intersected by a long island. Indian men waded between the major rapids, staking out their positions on favorite rocks that jutted out into the rushing water.

As Abby sat watching the busy spectacle of hundreds of Indians engaged in obtaining salmon, one emigrant, Amon Hoyt, decided he could do the job himself. To the amazement of everyone, Amon produced a three-pronged harpoon from the bottom of his wagon. This type of harpoon was called a "gig," and he had brought it all the way from Portsmouth, New Hampshire, for the sole purpose of procuring salmon. He had heard about the vast salmon fisheries in the Pacific Northwest and had come prepared to indulge in the harvest. It would be considerably cheaper, he thought, than trading store-bought goods for salmon.

Amon found a good rock to stand on, then repeatedly thrust the gig into the water trying to spear a fish—but the salmon were too fast. The fish could see him throw the harpoon and so quickly darted out of the way. About the only thing Amon did was to provide great entertainment for his Indian audience. With each thrust of the gig, a loud resonance of laughter came forth with Indians cheering him on to try again. After an hour he returned to his wagon, both humbler and wiser.

After trading and before the dinner hour, Bill Wilson severely burned himself while lighting a fire. Like other people in the migration, he used a small amount of gunpowder to start the fire. His carelessness tonight caused a spark to ignite a nearby two-pound powder keg. The ensuing flash severely burned his face, closing both eyes. Dr. Long tended to his injury with cold compresses and animal grease. Bill was now an invalid with no way to travel. Leaving his wagon back at Fort Hall had seemed to be a good idea at the time, but now it was needed. Isaac Mills stepped in and offered Bill a bed in his own wagon—an offer Polly Wilson quickly accepted. Several other boys said they'd help drive the Wilsons' stock. Bill would live, although it would be a long, hard journey to the Wallamet Valley.

After treating Bill, Dr. Long graciously offered his medical skills to the Indians. There were a potpourri of maladies—the most common being sore eyes. The constant flashing glare of the sun off the moving river current was a menace for all Western tribes who subsisted through fishing. Dr. Long did what he could, which was very little, considering the meager condition of his medical supplies.

Abby spent part of the evening organizing the Western Passage in preparation for leaving the next morning. Opened trunks needed to be repacked and the salmon tightly secured for the bumpy road ahead. After nightfall she lit a candle and recorded the events of the day. It had been a busy, productive, and informative day—one that easily filled several pages. Of special interest were the local Indians:

"The fishing method these Indians use is very efficient, probably developed over centuries of use. The men have spears that consist of a strong, smooth pole about ten to twelve feet long, and a couple fingers in diameter. Jacob says they make it of hard, tough wood secured from the mountainous forests north of this region. On one end of the spear they fasten a piece of sharp-pointed buck horn which contains a barb. They hollowed the larger end of the horn so it can be fastened to the end of the pole. The pole, in turn, is tapered to fit snugly into the horn. Tied to the middle of this horn is a thong of securely fastened sinew. The other end of the sinew is attached to the pole just back from the tip, leaving a considerable slack in the line.

"The Indian takes this weapon out into the river and crouches down on a rock next to the water, holding the point of the spear near where he expects a fish to appear. When a fish swims in front of the spear, the Indian thrusts it rapidly into the fish before it has a chance to escape. The buck horn always comes off, embedded in the fish by the barb and held on by the sinew. Their skill at taking fish in this manner is a smooth and graceful operation that they performed flawlessly. I never saw a single fish escape."

On Friday morning, September 8, Reverend Marcus Whitman had the Light Column moving west by eight o'clock. The land continued much the same with basaltic boulders, sage, and swales hindering their forward progress. Young men continued to walk out in front, clearing a road as best they could.

"Jacob," Abby addressed him while they were stopped for the nooner, "have you thought about what you're going to do when we reach the Wallamet Valley?"

"Don't rightly know. I'm too old to start farming, and I don't much care for the idea of clearing new land."

"You won't need to. This land is supposed to be free of trees!"

"Maybe so, but it's never seen a plow. That first pass will wear down animals and equipment—and then there's always rocks to clear. I suspect I'll look up old Joe Meek, Doc Newell, Caleb Wilkins, and the other boys that are out there—see what they're doing."

"You think they've become farmers?"

"Don't know for sure, so I'll wait and see for myself. There should be work in Oregon City, especially with all these new people coming in. If there's a large migration next year, well, a savvy businessman could make a good living."

"I suppose. I need to find out where most everyone will locate. Wherever that is, they'll need a school. Those trappers we met, must be two months ago by now, they said there were new farms on an area called French Prairie—south of Oregon City, I believe. I almost hope they haven't got a school, so I can be the first."

"Build your own?"

"The families in the area will build the school—that's the way it worked back in Ohio. I doubt if Oregon will be any different. I mean, we're all Americans."

"They'll have to. A new provisional government probably won't get organized enough to collect taxes for a couple years."

"I've been thinking that, since Sam died, I'll be needing a place to stay. If we build a new schoolhouse, it shouldn't be too much trouble to build a room on the back for me. I could have a fireplace and a small stove. I won't need much."

"Some items might be hard to come by, like a stove. Manufactured goods like that will have to come around the Horn."

"I've cooked on a fire hearth before—that won't bother me."

"Manufactured goods." Jacob repeated the words, then paused as he considered the possibilities.

"If new emigrants come out every year," said Abby, "the demand for manufactured goods will keep increasing. Maybe you could start some type of trading company."

"It's something to think about—maybe contract with a shipping company."

"Five minutes, we roll in five minutes!" Dave Lenox came riding back along the column, rousing people from their nooner. Folks scrambled to put food away and gather loose children in preparation for the afternoon march.

"You think about that, Jacob. If I can be of help when we get to Oregon City, you let me know."

Jacob nodded. He was too reserved to show excitement. The thought of engaging in commerce while settling a new land was a tempting venture that needed more consideration.

The afternoon was exhausting, although it passed without incident. After a sixteen-mile day, wagon corrals formed in an area where the stock could be taken down to the river. Since leaving Independence, the availability of water often determined the location of wagon corrals—and here along the Snake River Plains, locating near water was more important than ever. Marcus could have made a few more miles, but there was no guarantee of water. Here they had water, so here they made camp.

Anna Hembree, the daughter of Andy and Martha Hembree, was celebrating her third birthday today. Martha purchased a single cup of flour from Abby's dwindling supply to make a small cake for Anna. The child had walked with her mother most of the way from Independence, only riding in the wagon when her small legs became too tired to continue. Today was her special day, so for dinner the entire Hembree clan gathered to celebrate her birthday. The meal, like most of the meals that evening, consisted almost entirely of salmon. It was a happy time for Anna and her family—very different from the tragedy their clan had experienced eight weeks earlier.

Martha Hembree was not the only woman running short of flour and other cooking supplies. In the past five months, people had learned about spoilage the hard way. Even though dried and smoked salmon could last for months, nobody wanted to tempt fate. Without barrels in which to carry the fish, consuming it before other food seemed to be only prudent. Everyone knew they could trade for more salmon on the Columbia, so the current stock could be consumed before then.

Campfires surrounded each wagon corral, while a cool breeze kept the smoke away. People sat around their kitchens resting weary muscles, talking of the home they had left behind, and the home yet to come. While everything seemed most peaceful, Ed Otey came riding in, looking for Dr. Long.

"It's Newt Wheeler," Ed announced as he rode up to Abby's kitchen. "Old Zachary just stabbed him! Where's Doc Long?"

"Over in Hank Lee's corral," Abby said, pointing toward the nearby wagon corral. "Is it bad?"

"Doesn't look serious, but he needs some doctoring." Ed tipped his hat, "Thank you, ma'am."

He turned and spurred his horse toward Lee's corral. As she watched him ride off, Dog Town came galloping by, with Jacob in the process of mounting. The horse had been hobbled a short distance away when Ed rode up with the news. Without saying a word, Jacob caught the horse, unhobbled it, pointed it toward Zachary's Mess, and whipped it forward. While coming up to full speed, Jacob hung onto the mane, then let both his feet touch the ground, providing just enough force to throw him up onto the horse's back. Zachary had run afoul of Jacob several times on the road from Independence, and now Jacob's patience had run out. This latest incident was not something that a trapper could ignore.

"Be careful!" Abby called out as he rode away. She watched him disappear behind a cloud of dust as he sped toward Zachary's Mess, about a half mile to the rear of the Light Column.

"I've never seen a young man mount and ride off that fast," Abby thought, "much less an old man. And he's carrying his rifle!"

Jacob found Jim Nesmith and John Jackson tending to Newt's wound, with Alex Zachary standing by his wagon along with Sarah, his wife, and Mary, his daughter. John, his eighteen-year-old son, stood by as if ready to offer his father help, if needed. Jacob's appearance was nothing short of intimidating for the boy. He backed off a little as Jacob came riding in and dismounted next to Newt.

"It's not bad, Jacob, looks like a glancing blow." Jim was holding a pressure bandage against Newt's side.

Jacob glanced over at Zachary with a look that made him wonder if the old trapper was going to use his rifle. It was a cold stare that established right from wrong. Alex knew that if he showed any defiance, it might be his last act on earth. He remained motionless for what seemed an eternity. Jacob looked back down at Jim, then knelt to talk to Newt.

"Doc Long is on his way. What are you doing over here, Newt? You want me to shoot Old Zack? It wouldn't be no trouble."

"No, Jacob, no. I should have known better than to befriend that murdering old thief. I just came over here to see if Jim and the Oteys' got enough salmon. When I looked in the back of the Oteys' wagon, Zack must have thought I was going to steal something. He came at me with a knife, and I couldn't get out of his way in time. When Ed yelled at him, he backed off. I don't know, Jacob. That man's crazy. You know that? He's just plain crazy."

"That he is. Where's Morris?"

"Out with the stock," said John Jackson. "Must be a distance, else he'd have come a-running."

Jacob looked up to see two horsemen riding in from the Light Column. "Here comes Ed and Doc Long. I'll let your wife know you're not injured too bad."

"We'll bring him back," said Jim. "Have Elizabeth prepare a bed—he'll probably be down for a week."

Jacob nodded to Jim's request, stood, and mounted just as Ed and Dr. Long rode up.

"You're near going under," Jacob called over to Alex as he wheeled his horse around. "You stab another one of these farmers, and I'll put you under myself!"

Alex knew that was no idle threat. Coming from a mountain man, they were words to heed. He remained motionless, for he did not want to give Jacob any reason to take action. Sarah and Mary stood frozen with embarrassment, humiliated by Alex's behavior.

An hour later Nesmith, Jackson, and the Otey brothers carried Newt back to his wagon, where Elizabeth Wheeler was waiting. Several groups of men, along with the Oregon Emigrating Company Council, were having an impromptu discussion of what to do with Zachary. Since he was already an outcast, they couldn't cast him out again—and since he was no longer a member of the migration, they had no jurisdiction, especially in a land without law. The discussions went back and forth, with some men, such as platoon leader

Dan Matheny, claiming that the council was the law, while others, including Bill Beagle were more in favor of vigilante justice. After looking in on Newt, Marcus Whitman joined the discussion.

"We'll have a formal meeting of the council tomorrow night, and maybe a trial. This is nothing short of attempted murder, and we can't let that go unpunished. Dan, you pass the word to meet over at Dave Lenox's wagon tomorrow evening."

"You'll have our support," said Bill McDaniel. Bill was a quiet man, traveling to Oregon by himself, with only the possessions he could fit on two packhorses. But he was an honest, good man, and Zachary's behavior was enough to bring him into the fray of the discussion.

"All of our support," added Aaron Layson. "Zack needs to be put in chains."

"We'll all be there, Marcus," said Sam Gilmore. "I'll make sure Nesmith, Jackson, and the Oteys are there—we've got witnesses." Back in Independence, Sam had hired a teamster, Solomon Emerick, to drive his wagon to Oregon. With this added help, Sam had always had spare time to serve on the council. He and his wife, Martha Ann, had fared well during the recent economic depression, but a land like Oregon was not something that he could ignore. He and Martha Ann planned to take advantage of all the business opportunities available in a new land of emigrants.

"I'll ride back and let Jesse and the other men in the Cow Column know about the trial," said Dan Waldo. "They should know to keep their distance from Old Prairie Chicken."

"Then it's settled," said Marcus. "Now let's break this up and get back to our families." As the men turned to leave, Morris and Ed Otey, John Jackson, and Jim Nesmith came riding in.

"That's it for me," said Morris as he dismounted and walked up to the council members. "If you don't mind, me and my brother would like to come back with the Light Column—Nesmith and Jackson too. I don't know what made me think we could get to Oregon quicker. That old thief can burn in hell, as far as I'm concerned."

"You bring your wagon over to my corral," said Dave Lenox.

"We appreciate that, Dave," said Ed. "We'll move while we still have some daylight." Both brothers started back toward Zachary's Mess, with Nesmith and Jackson close behind.

The event could have been more tragic. The injury was not serious, and Newt would be up in a week. The incident came as a relief to Jim Nesmith, for traveling with Zachary was something he hated. Now he was going to rejoin the Light Column, where he could again socialize with his friends and especially the young ladies.

On Saturday morning the Oteys, Nesmith, and Jackson were ready to go an hour before everyone else. There was still talk about what to do with Zachary—talk that was mostly venting. The council would have the final word.

As teamsters moved their oxen into position for yoking, one belonging to Jim White lost its footing near a rocky ledge along the Snake River canyon and fell about twenty feet. That was all it took, for the ox had a broken neck and had to be destroyed. White and several other men stayed behind to butcher the animal. They would catch up to the Light Column during the nooner.

Jim White took an amount of meat that he and his family could consume before spoilage, then gave the rest away. Unlike some emigrants, he took pride in helping his fellow travelers without asking for compensation.

That evening after dinner, Marcus, platoon leaders Hank Lee, Dave Lenox, Dan Matheny, and Jim Waters, along with the Cow Column leaders and council members gathered to determine what to do with Alex Zachary. The discussion centered on punishment, since there was no question as to his guilt. After having twenty-four hours to cool down and consider the situation logically, it was obvious that there was nothing anyone could do. They had no jail, no court, no law, and not even a pair of leg irons. Casting Zachary out of the company made no difference, since he merely followed behind. Leaving him unpunished was a bitter pill to swallow, but there was nothing else they could do. With the Oteys, Jackson, and Nesmith rejoining the Light Column, Alex Zachary and his family were now truly alone.

Councilman Aaron Layson summarized the meeting, then added his own comments.

"If he breaks an axle or needs help in any way, he's not going to receive it from anyone here. Are we agreed?"

"Agreed," came the response.

"We can take in his wife and children," added John McHaley. "They don't need to be left behind to die."

"That we should—it's not their fault," said Aaron.

"We can decide on that if the time comes. From now on old Zack's not getting any help from us." Marcus scanned the gathered men for any sign of dissent.

"Then it's unanimous; this meeting's adjourned."

The sun was just setting as the men returned to their respective kitchens. Jacob filled Abby in on what they decided, then retired. It all seemed fair to her, for Zachary, she thought, was not fit to associate with civilized people.

Soon the camp was quiet, the last candle extinguished, and the campfires reduced to a few glowing embers. Abby closed her eyes with the one thought that often helped give her strength: *We're another day closer to Oregon!*

On Sunday morning, September 10, Whitman and the Light Column were moving west down the Snake River Plains before eight o'clock. The road at this point ran along the south shore of the river, hemmed in by five hundred-foot-high, sage-covered hills to the south. The impassable hills kept getting closer and closer, indicating that the road would soon be forced to cross the Snake River. In addition to these hills, several rocky buttes stood on the north side of the river, lone sentinels to the passing river below. The general ruggedness of the terrain gave no token of comfort to the tired traveler, other than wild beauty in an endless Western landscape.

After an hour of travel they came to where the trace to Fort Boise crossed the Snake. The river here was wide and shallow, consisting of three islands dividing the current into four channels. The ford was about thirty miles downriver from Salmon Falls and presented one of the greatest challenges between Fort Hall and Fort Boise. The surrounding land still consisted of sage-covered high bluffs with occasional water holes found away from the river. In the distance, to the north and west, were larger hills approaching the description of mountains. There was little forage, little cover, and beyond the Snake River, very little water. The vastness of this unproductive land encouraged everyone to keep moving—keep moving until they reached the cool, timbered mountains west of Fort Boise—an area where deer and other game might be found. Such were the forces pushing them forward. For the present, they faced the difficult challenge of crossing the Snake River.

Whitman, the platoon leaders, and the council gathered on the south shore to discuss the logistics of crossing. The experience gained in crossing the Kansas, the Big Blue, and the South Fork of the Platte would now be put to use at this wide and dangerous section of river. The trace left by trappers moving between Fort Boise and Fort Hall entered the south shore of the river opposite the first of three islands that spanned the river. The crossing went out to the west end of this first island, then east across the island before entering the next channel. The second and third channels were not as wide as the first, and the next two islands were also not as large. They were actually sandbars that provided a chance to rest before entering the fourth and most dangerous channel. This last channel was the widest, the deepest, and contained the strongest current.

Whitman directed Dan Matheny and Aaron Layson to ride across and determine the best route. Besides river depth, they were to look for sections of riverbed that had the best footing. In the meantime, Dave Lenox and Hank Lee started organizing the wagons into groups of six and seven. Each group would be chained together for safety. Reverend Whitman could only stand by and watch, since he was not familiar with the particulars of such an operation. Although he was the migration's current leader and guide, for now, he was only in the way.

Bill Hobson, after conversing with Dave Lenox and Hank Lee, called over to Whitman. "Marcus, you ride your horse on the upstream side of the wagons. We're going to run two groups at once, side by side. That should give us more protection against the current. If any animal flounders, try to help as best you can."

Whitman agreed and took his post next to the first group.

Matheny and Layson returned just as teamsters completed chaining and readying the first two groups for crossing. Abby was in the first group, and had enough time for her and Jacob to recaulk both the foregate and tailgate with a mixture of mud, sage, and axle grease. Abby took her place behind the foregate while Jacob mounted his horse and stood ready next to the oxen. They had three yokes of oxen chained and ready to go. The two packhorses, Crow, the milch cow, and the weakest ox would have to swim on the upstream side of the wagon.

"That first island's about seventy-five yards from here," Dan Matheny shouted as he addressed the first group. Teamsters quickly moved in closer so they could hear better. "Point your wagons straight toward it and directly into the current. The current's not strong, so you shouldn't have any trouble. There's decent footing on the riverbed and on that first island. Then travel the length of the island before entering the second channel. We've tied a piece of cloth where you should enter the second channel. It's only about fifty yards wide, and shouldn't give you any trouble. Aim a little upstream," he advised, "so you'll come into the second island directly across from the first."

Dan looked over the crowd to make sure everyone was listening. "The second island's not very big," he continued, "so the lead wagons in your chained groups will be back in the water before the final wagons are out of the second channel. That means the lead wagon will have to keep moving—don't stop on the island. That shouldn't be a problem as long as nobody tips over." There were several murmurs of concern from the teamsters.

Dan raised his voice. "The third island is even smaller, so the lead wagons will have to keep moving there too. Don't bother to hesitate at the shore 'cause you'll be stranding the other wagons behind you out in the channel—just keep moving. Now, the fourth channel is the wide one. Aim upstream slightly, and don't slow down! This is where the current is strongest. You can land almost anywhere on the north shore, it's not steep." He paused. "Any questions?"

There was silence among the gathered teamsters. Everyone knew this would be a difficult crossing. With so many unknowns, and the potential for skittish animals, the chance of a mishap was high. Their silence was a shout of fear and foreboding, yet they had no choice. The river needed to be crossed. People turned and walked back to their wagons, ready for the order to move out.

Abby's wagon was third in line. The second group of seven entered the river parallel to her group, on the downstream side. Whitman chose to stay back and cross with the third and fourth groups.

The first channel had a slow current and did not present any problems, especially since at this initial point of crossing the wagons were pointed directly upstream, against the current. Each wagon came up onto the first island, dripping with water but safe. In the next three channels Abby's group would be on the upstream side. Jacob carried a six-foot willow switch to prod the teams, while Abby did the same to the rear team with her quirt. The packhorses, Crow, the spare ox, and the milch cow stayed next to the wagon as they crossed, not getting too far ahead or behind.

The second channel was easily crossed, much like the first. In this channel the wagons were perpendicular to the river with the current pushing on their starboard wagon planks. The lead wagons kept moving as ordered, and crossed the second and third islands without stopping.

The fourth channel presented a more difficult and dangerous challenge. Water rose ten inches up the sides of each wagon, causing them to intermittently flounder as wheels lifted off the riverbed. The first two groups made it to the north shore without any problems. They pulled up on land and moved away from the river far enough to make room for the next two groups. By the time they stopped, the third and fourth groups were entering the first channel on the south side.

As the emigrants on the north shore watched the next wagons enter the fourth channel, a horse near the last wagon bolted for deep water. The man on the horse, Alex Stoughton, was riding alongside his wagon on the upstream side. As his horse started to lose its footing and was about to roll over against the force of the current, Marcus

Whitman grabbed the reins and turned the animal downstream. It was lucky that Marcus was nearby, for the horse would have surely floundered and Alex couldn't swim. More than likely, Marcus saved Alex's life.

The wagons in the third and fourth groups made it to the north shore without further incident, coming up alongside the first two groups.

Next came Miles Eyre. Independent as ever, Miles was crossing on his own, just in front of the fifth and sixth groups of wagons. Following orders to keep moving, he did not stop on any of the islands. He easily crossed the first three channels, then plunged his mules into the fourth channel, pointing them slightly upstream. By the time he reached the center, the swiftness of the current caused the mules to panic and bolt for deeper water. As the wagon turned upstream, the two upstream wheels lifted off the bottom, causing the wagon to roll over, with Miles trying to jump out of the way. Cal Stringer, a young man traveling with his parents, was leading the chained wagons directly behind Miles and spurred his horse forward in an attempt to help. Soon his horse also floundered, sending him under as the horse rolled over on top of him.

The emigrants in the twenty-six wagons up on the north shore watched helplessly as two of their own drowned. Several men rode downstream to try to save Miles and Cal while everyone else looked for any sign of the two. It was no use. All they could see were the remnants of the Eyre wagon, still rolling over and over in the current, along with the carcasses of four mules and three horses.

Eliza, Miles's wife, had been too frightened to ride across with Miles. She and her three children had ridden in the Burnett's wagon among the third group. Now, she and her children watched their husband and father drown in a moment of disbelief and confusion. Several women rushed to Eliza's side. In the space of only a few seconds, she and her children were alone and destitute. They had no food, clothing, or shelter, and were still four hundred miles from the Wallamet Valley. Along with being made a widow, Eliza lost all of her worldly possessions, including the money belt Miles was wearing. She did not have so much as a change of clothes for her and her children.

Her condition and tragic loss prompted quick offers of clothing and food by a number of families. Although Miles had always camped by himself and had little use for friendship, Eliza had made numerous friends among the women of the migration. These women were now her salvation.

Cal Stringer's father, Cornelius, had wanted to take advantage of the free land in Oregon, so Cal had gone along in hopes of making his own fortune. Now he would never get the chance. When a distraught Cornelius Stringer got his wagon to the north shore, he handed the quirt to his wife, Mary Jane, then ran down the shoreline looking for Cal. It was too soon for reality to set in, and he thought he might be able to save his boy—but the river would not release him. Neither Miles nor Cal ever surfaced within view of the company.

After the last group of wagons crossed and unchained, the shaken column continued for eight miles in a northwesterly direction before making camp. The bodies of Miles and Cal could not be found, and Miles's outfit was a total loss. Stopping there for the night to console the surviving Eyres and Stringers, and continuing to look for Miles and Cal, would have been the decent thing to do. Sadly, Whitman's desire to travel went beyond decency. He could not see the value of another delay in looking for two drowned men. Their journey had ended here on the Snake River, and they could no longer help the remaining travelers. Whitman's attitude was callous and crude, although everyone followed his orders without question. The constant exposure to the elements of weather and difficulties of travel had calloused almost everyone. Folks were tired of the hard work, dangers, and tragedies of the journey and felt that the sooner they could get to the Wallamet Valley, then the sooner these troubles would end. When Whitman gave the order to march, everyone followed.

Jim Etchell invited Eliza and her children for dinner that evening. His wagon had run over a large salmon that day, providing a fortuitous meal of fresh fish. Margaret Garrison offered a bed in her wagon for Eliza's children, while Sarah Goodman made room for Eliza. Other women helped to console Mary Jane Stringer, Cal's mother, and help with her chores and feeding her family.

Young Cal had been carrying his outfit on two packhorses rather than in his parents' overloaded wagon. These two animals had also drowned in the incident, taking all of Cal's worldly possessions with them.

The campsite chosen by Whitman afforded good forage, of which Jacob was quick to take advantage. He hobbled the stock in an area of belly-high grass after allowing each animal to drink liberally from a nearby creek. With the formation of wagon corrals, the campsite looked the same as it had for many weeks—with one exception. Miles Eyre's wagon was not on the outskirts. Its absence was a sober reminder to everyone of the day's tragedy and the difficulty of realizing their original dream—a dream to take wagons all the way to Oregon.

Abby spent part of the evening with Eliza, Mary Jane, and the other ladies. After getting back to her wagon she sat by the campfire, diary in hand, wondering how to record the day. There were two less people in the migration than the night before.

"Today the Snake River erased these poor men from the face of the earth," she wrote. *"Everything they were, everything they had, and everything they would be is lost forever. They left no trace of their existence on this earth. Death is always with us. It is following us to Oregon and will probably be there when we arrive. Death is that one constant companion that we can never leave behind."*

Abby looked up from her diary and around at the wagon corrals, then to the outskirts where Miles's missing wagon should be. Quiet pervaded the camp as people adjusted to the deaths of Miles and Cal. Thoughts of Sam came flooding back.

"Nobody should leave this earth without leaving some sign of their existence," Abby wrote. *"Even if it's only a few words on a headboard, everyone should be remembered."*

Fifteen minutes later she finished composing two verses. She wrote each verse on a separate piece of paper so she could give them to Mary Jane and Eliza. For Miles she wrote,

> *Dear friend, in earth's thorny path,*
> *How long your feet have trod.*
> *To find at last this peaceful rest,*
> *Safe in the arms of God.*

Abby had never known Cal; few did—but he had helped a man in need and paid for it with his life. For Cal she wrote,

> *Asleep at last, blessed sleep,*
> *From which none ever wakes to weep.*

As she looked at the verses, she added another paragraph to her diary about the cause of the tragedy: *"Those people back in Independence were right. Never travel with mules. They're too stubborn and will give you nothing but grief!"*

Without the bodies of Miles and Cal, there would be no delay for funeral services in the morning. Everyone expected the column to continue its march west and so prepared for another long day on the trail.

The next morning, Monday, September 11, Jesse Applegate's Cow Column crossed at the same three-island ford without incident. Before entering the channels they chained fifteen wagons together—a precaution that proved wise against the strong current. They made the entire crossing without loss of equipment and minus only a few head of stock from their large herds of beef cattle.

As a surprise to most in the Light Column, Reverend Whitman chose to stay in camp an extra day to recruit the stock. There was good grass here, something they had not seen since Fort Hall. As a belated gesture of kindness he sent a small party of men back to the Snake River to look for the bodies of Miles and Cal, although nobody expected to find them. Whitman may have been regretting his callousness of the day before. As the company guide and leader, making an effort to look was the appropriate thing to do.

The extra day in camp came as an unexpected but welcome respite to most of the teamsters. Behind the Cow Column were several stragglers who needed to catch up. For one reason or another, their independence or poor equipment had caused them to lag behind. Because of their inability to keep up, they would have to cross the Snake River on their own. With an extra day some might catch up, at least to the Cow Column.

Abby spent the day drying out articles that had got wet in the crossing. She spread clothes and a blanket over the top of her wagon, then laid other items out on the ground. For the most part, the day was quiet, with livestock getting their fill of forage and water, and women doing domestic chores—chores long ignored from days of travel. The deaths of Miles and Cal did not affect folks as strongly as the first death of little Joel Hembree before South Pass. People went about their business as if it were a day no different than any other.

By early afternoon Abby was again sitting on her washtub, diary in hand, taking this rare opportunity to put down more thoughts of her journey and the surrounding land. Before long she had composed another verse for the country. It read:

The Snake River flows in its wild way,
Where it will end, no one can say.
Over rocks and shores, it's westerly bound,
So we follow its course to the land beyond.

This river is peaceful in its march to the sea,
But can rise up in anger when rocks impede.
Rushing headlong in a foaming wrath,
Not the tallest mountain can block its path.

It gives life to the thirsty, whether man or beast,
And greens the hills in a harvest and feast.
It gives food of abundance to this wild land,
And supplies life itself to the Indian bands.

One should not be fooled by beauty this way,
For the life it gives, it can take away.
Then, with no thought to its ruinous force,
Continues on, peaceful and calm, along its course.

We have come so far to pay our respects,
To a river so wild, so bold in its quest.
And like the river itself, we can never turn back,
Forward is destiny, the unknown our pact.

We are orphans in a land resplendent with charm,
Passing with care to avoid any harm.
Soon we will come to the land of our dreams,
And a rest, dear rest, for the weary and lean.

We walk like children in this boundless land,
Learning to live with the gifts at hand.
Civilization is gone, left far behind,
Now, forward we look, but what shall we find?

Unending hardships shall come to pass,
As we enter a land of trees and grass.
We will build our homes with love assured,
Yet never forget the troubles endured.

We are the first, but there will be more,
People with dreams of that distant shore.
They will look with awe at the road we dared,
And say we had courage, more than our share.

Abby gazed back at the verse, changing a word here and there. "It will do for now," she thought. She looked up from the paper to the nearby wagons, livestock, and emigrants—then back down at the verse. These moments with pen and paper provided a brief escape from the difficulties of trail life. Living from a wagon, and with a constant push to move forward, had taken its toll on everyone. Now, in mid-September, people looked to the end of the journey more than ever.

"But there are still so many weeks to go!" Abby went through the remainder of the journey in her mind. "Fort Boise is next. Then the Blue Mountains, then the mission at Waiilatpu, or is it called the Waiilatpu Mission?" She hesitated, trying to remember. "Then Fort Walla Walla, then the Columbia." Again she paused, thinking of that great river. "The Columbia, it must be magnificent. Whenever someone talks about Oregon, they surely talk about the Columbia. Then comes the mission at Wascopam, then Fort Vancouver, and finally Oregon City. The only things I really don't know about are how to get over the Blue Mountains and how to get down the Columbia." The magnitude of the undertaking struck her. "The Blue Mountains and the Columbia! Goodness, how will we ever get through?"

It was now late afternoon as she reread the verse. It seemed appropriate. She could go back to the verse in later years as a remembrance of this time and place. Soon she closed the diary and put it away. It was time for evening chores.

This evening the Cow Column came within sight of the Light Column. People from both columns visited friends and exchanged news, and spent a quiet evening reflecting on the loss of Miles and Cal.

Clouds moved in on the following morning, Tuesday, September 12, as the Light Column got underway before eight o'clock. At midmorning they arrived at an area Jacob and Marcus called Boiling Spring. This boiling hot spring issued forth from basaltic rock at three different places near the head of a small ravine. The water came out clear, but had a strong sulfur smell and was unfit to drink.

Against Whitman's orders, the entire column stopped to view this spectacle. This geological oddity did not vent steam like Steamboat Springs, yet it was still a curiosity that could not be missed. The boiling hot water flowed down a small creek, giving rise to ghostly images as it made its way toward the Snake River. Like others, Abby could not resist the attraction. She hobbled her lead team, set the brake, and walked over to the spring with Jacob in tow.

"You never told me about this," she said. "Look here, this water is nearly boiling. I could cook an egg with this water!"

"The Snake Indians use this area for ceremony, mostly religious. These springs are big medicine."

"With all the signs of volcanoes we've seen, that must be what's heating the water!"

"Probably, don't know what else could. It's not good for drinking and not even good for bathing—you'll just smell like sulfur."

"It's a wonderful marvel, Jacob. It seems as if almost every day we find something new and wondrous."

"Come on folks, let's go!" Marcus rode up on his horse shouting commands. "Take a quick look and get back to your wagons. Daylight's burning, and we've got a long way to go!"

"Jacob, I think there must be enough water here to run an overshot mill. Power for a mill and hot water too!" Abby had become so fascinated with exploring the spring that she and several other people failed to hear Whitman's calls. Soon they noticed others heading back to the trail, marking the end of their explorations.

"Every day I have something new to write about," Abby said to Jacob as they started walking back. "I want my students in Oregon to know about this place. Do you think they have any of these hot springs in Oregon?"

"Don't know 'bout that—maybe. Never heard of any, but Oregon's supposed to have absolutely everything. Haven't you heard people talk?"

"Jacob!" She jabbed him in the ribs for his tease.

Soon they were back at the wagon and moving west. The road began to change now, with a greater quantity of small rocks, causing difficult footing for oxen and other draft animals. To make things worse, shortly before noon it began to rain—not hard, but enough to provide a chilling cold. After the noon stop, the rain started coming down harder and continued for the remainder of the afternoon. Abby wrapped herself in her wool jacket, a jacket that provided warmth, but no protection against the rain. In a short time the wet jacket hung heavy on her shoulders. It was a miserable, cold, wet, and muddy afternoon. Exhaustion overcame the migration by the time wagon corrals formed at six o'clock. Rather than relaxing in the usual kitchens, people curled up inside their wagons trying to stay warm, eating whatever cold food they had. Those without wagons sought shelter underneath the wagons of friends. Smoked salmon was a tasty change from their usual fare, so there were few objections about a lack of cooked food. There were, however, numerous complaints about the lack of campfires and the cold, wet accommodations.

Shortly before dark, the rain eased and people ventured forth to take care of their stock. The Snake River had risen noticeably since the night before and now presented a formidable obstacle to cross. Unknown to most members of both the Light and Cow Columns, there were still a few wagons on the south side of the river, back at the three-island crossing. Overton Johnson, one of the farmers who had been so impatient back at the Blue, was one of those emigrants. Rather than chance a risky crossing in another flooded river, he chose to continue moving west down the south shore, hoping a better crossing would present itself before too long.

Abby speculated in her diary about the possibility of stragglers not being able to cross. *"Maybe those stragglers crossed earlier today,"* she wrote. *"If not, they will have to wait for the flow to drop, for no man, wagon, or beast could cross this churning torrent. Maybe they will catch up at Fort Boise!"*

By the next morning, Wednesday, September 13, the rain had stopped, but now the air was hazy due to a distant forest fire far to the north. A group of men gathered to discuss the conditions. Jacob considered the distant country to be Hudson Bay territory and, as such, it was unknown to most American trappers. But Jacob was familiar with fire. Upon being questioned, he informed the teamsters that forest fires out West were common this time of year.

"This smoke could stay with us till the Blue Mountains or beyond," he stated to the several men looking toward the north, trying to see the source of the haze. "Then again, it might be gone tomorrow. Looks like that rain moved east, so she's probably still burning."

"The country's changing," said Aaron Layson. "There's more grass around here than back at the falls."

"The road's no better," said Nat Sitton. He was one of the young men who had been helping to clear a trail. "It's different, with smaller rocks, but no easier to get through."

"Well, I think we're heading into better grass," added Dan Matheny. "That's probably why they built Fort Boise where they did—there's good grass. Maybe we'll get there sometime next week!"

"Closer than that," said Jacob, "but not if we stand around here jawing." He turned and walked back to the wagon to hitch the teams. With hardly a word, the other teamsters moved out to do the same.

The day was cool and dry, providing a pleasant change from yesterday's rain. Haze from the distant fire blocked the sun for most of the day, keeping the temperature down by five to ten degrees.

Since passing Fort Laramie almost seven hundred miles back, folks noticed that the lack of humidity had an affect on the air temperature, or what the air temperature seemed to be. When a cloud passed in front of the sun, it felt as if the air temperature dropped ten degrees. The emigrants soon learned that humidity holds heat. Without humidity, the sun's radiant energy made the air feel warmer than it actually was. Without direct sunlight, people felt the true temperature. This difference made the day seem hot, then cold, and then hot again as clouds passed in front of the sun. In September, as the days grew shorter, people looked more and more for sunlight to keep them warm.

The evening camp provided tolerable forage and adequate water for all the stock, including the herds in the Cow Column.

"Jacob," Abby said as they sat near the campfire, eating a meal of smoked salmon, "with a secondary school education, whatever made you go West to become a trapper?"

"I guess I never took to civilization." His slow manner gave him time to consider what to say before speaking. "Tried a few ventures in the freighting business but never made much of a go at it. That was back in Kentucky, 'bout the time Lewis and Clark got back. That was the first we ever heard about what was west of St. Louis."

"So you headed west then?"

"No, not then. I had a wife and a boy—couldn't leave them."

"Really, I never thought of you as being married. I mean you don't seem like a husband type."

"Husband type? What type is that?" He was smiling.

"Oh, you know what I mean." Abby too was smiling. "What happened then? I mean why did you leave?"

"I didn't—Susan left. That was my wife. She run off with a banker and took the boy."

"Just like that? You didn't go after her?"

"Not this child. I figured if she run off, then she wouldn't be much good as a wife. I missed the boy, though. Don't know what happened to him. If he's still alive, he'd be, let's see, thirty-eight now."

"How long has it been since you've seen him?"

"Thirty years. That's when I took stock of my situation and headed to St. Louis. I worked on and off with free trappers for a few years, then hooked up with Manuel Lisa. He was into the fur business in a big way. I guess ten or more years went by before I went up the Missouri with Andrew Henry as part of General Ashley's outfit."

"You've been out here ever since?"

"All but last winter. This child's been living under the stars too long to ever go back. I should have known that."

Their conversation drifted back and forth between Jacob's past, what they expected to find at Oregon City, and the difficulties of crossing the Snake River Plains. With the roughness of the road, they had only made seven miles from last night's camp and were now thirteen miles past the hot springs. It had been a long and exhausting day. These quiet moments in camp provided a comfort much like home.

Near the corrals tonight was a large rock that prompted a few people to carve their initials. For most, the day had been long and hard—and resting near a campfire was reward enough. By dusk most everyone was bedded down for the night.

The next day, Thursday, September 14, was cool and sunny. The road remained rocky and the pace slow. Even though the grass was improving, a number of oxen in the company were too gaunt to continue. Teamsters knew this, yet there was nothing they could do. Winter was quickly approaching, and the company needed to get across the Blue Mountains. That meant traveling as far as possible each day. For Abby, she knew that Patchy would not last much longer. For some reason, he had not been able to maintain his strength like the other oxen. For the last week, Jacob had allowed Patchy to walk behind the wagon to conserve his remaining strength. This morning it took both their efforts to get him on his feet and tied to the back of the wagon. It was almost as if he had given up on life. They knew his time would come soon—and just like many other oxen in the company, he would soon be meat.

This evening's camp provided adequate forage, for the land had begun to show noticeable changes. Sage was becoming scarcer and grass more plentiful. To the farmers, this was clearly better land due to the added rainfall, yet still not good enough to support farming. Trees remained scarce except along streambeds, and a land without trees could not support farming or any accompanying civilization.

Overton Johnson and the other stragglers caught up with their respective platoons late in the afternoon. As the sun turned daytime into a brilliant red and orange dusk, everyone in the Oregon Emigrating Company camped within sight of each other. The Cow Column was one mile behind the Light Column, close enough for friends to visit. In addition, the only outcast, Zachary, was also in sight, his lone wagon and campfire silhouetted against the southern horizon. He was close enough to not get lost, yet far enough that he no longer bothered anyone in the company.

Dan and Mary Matheny took in Mrs. Eyre and her children. The Mathenys were heading to Oregon with their extended family, including the Laysons and the Hewitts. With such a large group, there was enough room and caring for an additional mother and her three children.

At this point in the journey, Abby was counting one or two dead stock every day. She noted in her diary that evening, *"Whether man or beast, we are paying a terrible price on our journey to El Dorado!"*

The next morning, Friday, September 15, Jim Nesmith came by looking for his horse. Apparently the horse had escaped his hobbles and wandered off during the night. Without a horse, Jim would be walking the remainder of the journey to Oregon.

"Jim, if you can't find him, you're welcome to ride Crow. He's a bit spirited, but a good animal."

"Thank you, Abby, but I don't want to be a burden. He shouldn't have wandered off too far."

"He might have headed toward the Boise looking for better grass," added Jacob.

"Maybe so, maybe we'll come across him during the day. I'll let you know if I find him. Good day, Miss Abby." Jim tipped his hat as he turned to walk back to the Oteys' wagon.

Marcus Whitman moved the column out at eight o'clock, urging everyone forward, as the Cow Column was in close pursuit. The September days were getting shorter, reducing the amount of available travel time. Marcus passed the word to his platoon leaders, and from them to the teamsters and drovers, that everyone should be ready to leave at first light from this day forward.

"We'll probably spend a day at Fort Boise," Dan Matheny informed Abby as he rode alongside her. She was at her usual station, walking on the right side of her lead team and urging them on with her quirt. "This grass keeps getting better, so it's too bad we can't take more advantage of it."

"We've still got those Blue Mountains to cross," Abby said. "Only one day of rest probably won't help most of these animals—they're too far gone."

"Maybe so. That's what Marcus is talking about. People keep falling behind with busted wheels, stuck brake shoes, cracked tongues, and everything else. We could use several days to repair wagons and other gear."

"Can't argue with that—there's a few things Jacob and I need to do. One of my axles has worked loose from the bed, so we need to drill new holes for the bolts."

"I think we'll reach the Boise River by tonight," said Dan. "There's good water there for everyone."

"Do you think we'll have good water the rest of the way? My animals have suffered enough with this desert. Just the idea of entering mountains and a timbered region sounds inviting."

"Amen to that, Miss Meacham." He tipped his hat as he turned his horse to ride back to the next wagon. "Have to pass the word. Good day to you, ma'am."

"Thank you, Dan." She watched as he rode back to the Rubeys' wagon, the next wagon in line. Sarah had taken ill and was riding in her wagon—a bumpy ride, but better than walking. Abby continued walking backwards, watching Dan ride up to the Rubeys.

"Tonight I better make some dinner for Phil, Sarah, and her two children," she thought. "Poor Sarah, she never wanted to come along on this journey." Abby turned around and brought her quirt down on Lashes' rump.

"Come on, get on there," she ordered—a command the oxen knew well.

During today's nooner, Patchy lay down and could not get up. Abby knew there was nothing she or Jacob could do, so without saying a word, Jacob backed off a few steps, raised his rifle, and dispatched the ox. Abby stood by watching. She had gone through too many difficulties, seen too many deaths, and shed too many tears to shed any more for Patchy.

"He was a good ox, Jacob. He did his share as best he could."

"That he did." Jacob leaned his rifle against the wagon and pulled out his Green River knife.

"If you don't mind, this here's meat and it's been a long time. Salmon is good, but I would ..."

"I understand," Abby interrupted. "You cut whatever meat you can find that's still good, and I'll fix it tonight."

"Thank you kindly. We'll be here past the nooner unless you want to take the wagon on ahead."

"I don't much care to see Patchy butchered. You can use Crow to pack the meat. I'll see you when you catch up." Abby quickly began to put her kitchen items away in preparation for the afternoon march.

Jacob untied Crow from the wagon, then tied him to a sage bush alongside his own horse. As the column moved out, each wagon made a slight jog around Jacob and the dead ox, since Patchy had died in the middle of the road.

Abby continued to use six oxen to pull her wagon. It was considerably lighter now than when she left Independence, but the oxen were also considerably weaker.

"Thank goodness I started out with eight animals," she thought as she surveyed her outfit. "I could never make it with less! I'll give some of that meat to Phil Rubey. Maybe that will help Sarah regain her strength."

At three o'clock the column started down a slight incline into the Boise River floodplain. The grass here was dry from the summer drought, although thick enough to serve as some of the best forage since leaving Fort Hall. Whitman turned the column southwest to parallel the river, then halted after only a half mile. The immediate area provided flat ground for their wagon corrals, easy river access for watering the stock and refilling water barrels, adequate forage, and wood along the riverbanks. It had been a long time since anyone had enjoyed such lush surroundings.

As soon as the wagon corrals formed, Jacob rode up in time to unchain the oxen and take them down to the river for their first drink of the day.

"We haven't had a stop like this since the Bear River Valley," announced Abby as he dismounted. Her spirits were noticeably higher from the change in vegetation.

"Here's the meat," Jacob said as he tied both Crow and Dog Town off on one of the wagon wheels. "There's more here than we can eat, so you might consider giving some to the Rubeys."

"I'm already planning on doing that," she said with a smile. "If you don't mind, I'll stay with salmon. Patchy was more than just meat to me. I'll cook you up three or four pounds tonight."

"Thank you kindly."

As people organized their kitchens, tended to stock, and put up tents for the night, the vacant valley became a warm and inviting home. Jim Nesmith rode up on his truant horse and dismounted just as Abby was turning over her washtub for her evening chair.

"Lew Cooper had my horse," Jim explained, "had it all day! He found him in amongst his own stock this morning. Now I've walked all day, must be twenty miles, and Lew had my horse all the time. I told him what I thought, and they're not words I'd use around a lady like you, Miss Meacham."

"At least you got him back, Jim. You'll be riding tomorrow."

"That I will."

"Would you like to stay for dinner? We have fresh meat tonight—

one of my poor starved oxen didn't make it. It's poor meat, but meat's meat."

"I could never turn down an invitation from you, Abby." He was smiling proudly that she should want his company. "Let me water my horse and get him hobbled."

"Oh, it won't be ready for an hour or so, no hurry."

"If you don't mind, Abby, I prefer your company over that of the Oteys. I'll be back shortly."

As he walked down toward the river leading his horse, Abby could not help but laugh at his situation.

"So you had to walk all day," she murmured. "I've walked since we left Independence!" Her smile quickly faded as her gaze wandered over to Crow. He was loaded down with meat. Dinner and evening chores were beckoning.

During dinner a small band of Snake Indians on their way to Salmon Falls stopped for purposes of trading. They had smoked, dried, and fresh salmon to trade for clothing, tobacco, and ammunition.

"Jacob, you stay and enjoy your dinner," Abby said. "I've watched you trade, and it's time I try my hand at such bargaining."

"Remember what I've taught you 'bout signing. They'll respect a woman who can communicate."

"I will. Jim, you can stay or come along. Maybe you have something to trade."

"I do indeed, Abby. I got one whole salmon for a load of ammunition back at the falls. I'll get five loads and meet you there."

Abby retrieved one calico shirt and three plugs of tobacco from one of her trunks, then headed over to the trading circle, leaving Jacob to watch.

"That woman's come a long way," Jacob quietly said aloud. "She's not the same woman I met back in Independence. She was strong then," he paused, "but stronger now—she's got sand, alright. All she needed was knowledge."

The Indians presented a poor and squalid appearance. Their clothes were in rags and heavily infested with lice, yet they did not beg or complain of their condition. They were a proud people, ready to help travelers through their country. After an hour of trading, they had successfully converted their entire supply of salmon into trade goods—trade goods that made them "rich." Encountering such a large contingent of emigrants was something none of these Indians expected or had ever seen. Like previous tribes and the men at the forts, they were amazed at the sight of such a large group of white men, women, and children, traveling with wagons through a country without roads. It was a day they would never forget.

Abby returned with twenty-five pounds of salmon. She set the woven grass packages down on the ground, then took her place on the washtub to finish dinner. A few minutes later Jim walked in with over twenty pounds of salmon.

"You know Jacob, that Abby's a right smart trader," Jim said as he picked up his dinner plate. "Those Indians wanted to short her, but she wouldn't have nothin' to do with that. I think they admire you, Abby." He looked over at her. "They never seen a white woman trade that good. I'd say you were as good as the squaws."

"Really," she said with surprise, not knowing if his comment was a compliment.

"I mean it. Those squaws are good traders, and you're every bit their equal."

It was a compliment. "Thank you, Jim."

"We should have enough food to easily make the Columbia," said Jacob. "You got enough goods left to trade with those Columbia tribes?"

"I think so," Abby said. "I'm not worried though—we always seem to get by."

Dinner passed quickly, and soon Abby was off to the Rubeys' wagon to check on Sarah. Earlier she had taken a plate of cooked meat over to Phil. He now returned the empty plate and thanked her for her generosity. Sarah was sitting up, enjoying the cool evening air with Harriet Burnett and Cyrene Cary. Abby picked a seat on the wagon tongue and joined in. It was a conversation in which Phil knew he was not welcome—a ladies' conversation. He excused himself and went to check on his stock.

It was dusk when Abby returned to her kitchen, only to find all the dishes washed and put away.

"Jacob, you? You washed these dishes?"

"I certainly did—and don't go expecting that kind of help every night. I only signed on to take care of your stock and wagon."

"And you do the best job of stock tending in this entire migration. I thank you for the kitchen help, and I promise not to expect it. I surely do appreciate your help tonight, thank you."

Abby retrieved her diary and sat down to capture a few paragraphs before the end of the day's light.

"Thank you again for dinner, Abby." Jim Nesmith startled her as he walked into the kitchen. "Didn't know if you'd be coming back, so I did the dishes. Jacob even helped a little with the drying. Maybe when we get to Oregon and I've built a good home, I can pay you back with a home-cooked meal."

"That sounds wonderful, Jim." Abby was all smiles as she looked over at Jacob. "Maybe we could invite Jacob—we can always use some extra help in the kitchen."

Jacob had no response. He took a puff on his pipe, stared into the campfire with raised eyebrows, and shook his head in an affirmative manner, acknowledging his guilt.

Jim sat down to talk for awhile. After spending six weeks away from the Light Column with the Otey brothers and Zachary, he had a strong need for intelligent conversation with an educated woman. Traveling with the Oteys had its advantages, but intelligent conversation was not one of them. Abby closed her diary, and the three talked about the road ahead, problems with the stock and wagons, and their dreams of a home in Oregon. The flickering campfire provided a source of warmth, memories of the homes they had left behind, and the comfort of a warm, secure life—it felt good. The western sky was still hazy from the distant forest fire, so the sunset became a magnificent dance of orange and red images of flowers and dragons. The trio watched the display while keeping silent for a few minutes, mesmerized by the beauty.

When the last flicker of orange and red had disappeared, Jim excused himself for the evening. It had been a long day of walking, and tomorrow would be another day on the trail. In a short time the entire camp was quiet for the night—although not entirely silent. Within the hour, Abby and several other ladies emerged and went down to the river for a bath—a bath long overdue.

On Saturday morning, September 16, Abby and Jacob were ready to go before the first rays of sun flickered over the eastern horizon. Whitman wanted to be on the trail at sunup, and they had no intention of holding anyone back.

The trail today wound its way down the Boise River floodplain over soft ground. Soft, that is, in comparison to the road traveled from Fort Hall. Dry forage was still abundant, as was water. Loose animals continually stopped to munch as drovers prodded them along. Even the working stock would nip off blades of grass as they moved forward at their usual speed of two miles an hour.

For the nooner, teamsters drove each wagon out into an area of thick grass rather than holding their place in line as they usually did. By moving into grass, the working stock had a chance to graze during the one-hour stop. The children reveled in the new environment with games of tag, hide-and-seek, running through the grass, and just exploring along the riverbank.

After an eighteen-mile day, camp was again a comfortable change from the two long weeks spent on the Snake River Plains. Abby made sure Jacob had his fill of meat, while she stayed with the smoked salmon. She again took some cooked meat over to Sarah, who was gaining strength fast. After dinner the camp settled into a quiet routine, with smoke drifting up from a hundred fires. The scene reminded Abby of the South Platte, so many weeks and so many miles ago. After visiting with Sarah, she wrote a few paragraphs and retired as the sun once again set against a canvas of ghostly orange and red images.

On Sunday, September 17, the column continued down the Boise River at sunup. As on previous Sundays, Reverend Whitman stopped at eleven o'clock for a combined nooner and prayer meetings.

During the nooner, a runner from the advance guard returned with news that the Boise River crossing was five miles ahead. Whitman had crossed there both in 1836 and the previous year, and did not consider it dangerous. At this time of year the deepest water was less than four feet, and the put-in and take-out trails were well worn and did not require double-teaming. Word passed throughout the column that each wagon should yoke up all their oxen. There was no need to chain wagons together.

At three o'clock the lead wagon, driven by Solomon Emerick, entered the Boise River. The second wagon, belonging to Pete Burnett, waited until Solomon had made it across. It was a simple safety precaution to make sure the riverbed was solid and able to support a loaded wagon. Pete then snapped his team forward, with the other wagons of the Light Column following one by one. The entire crossing took place in no more time than if the river had not been there at all.

After another five miles, Whitman halted the caravan for the night—this time on the north side of the Boise River. Wagon corrals formed, stock were put out to graze, and children gathered firewood from the brush and small trees along the north bank. The camp provided another pleasant evening after a productive day on the trail.

Tonight people began to show noticeable excitement about the prospects of reaching Fort Boise. With a good day tomorrow, Marcus expected they would arrive sometime in the afternoon. This meant that by tomorrow evening the migration would be enjoying the comforts and offerings of another Hudson Bay Company outpost—including its stores, and especially its blacksmith shop. Tires, tongues, brakes, harnesses, axles, and a myriad of other equipment needed repair. Everyone knew they would not find a well-supplied general store, but that was not needed. Trading with the Snake Indians had replenished the food stores of almost everyone. With the Blue Mountains ahead, there was more concern for making wagons ready than in acquiring more food. As long as there were Indians to trade with, everyone knew that food would be plentiful.

Besides dinner and other kitchen chores, Abby used the evening to do her wash down at the river. She joined almost thirty other women engaged in the same task. Conversation and work made the evening pass quickly.

Later, after the red western sky faded into dark, Abby lay down on her wagon bed, gazing up at the canvas white-top.

"Another day closer," she whispered. "Another day closer."

On Monday, September 18, the Light Column arrived at Fort Boise shortly after two o'clock in the afternoon. With the experience gained at Fort Laramie, Fort Bridger, and Fort Hall, everyone knew the procedure. Smithies and people with blacksmithing needs descended on the blacksmith shop with wheels, axles, and other items in need of repair. Ladies organized their kitchens, then put on clean dresses before visiting the fort's trading house.

Emigrant provisions were low, although not as bad as back at Fort Hall. Most food stores, augmented with salmon, would last all the way to the Columbia. Trail clothes were threadbare, but people had become accustomed to such inconveniences—and they were only inconveniences, not hardships. After so many weeks of struggling to build a road to Oregon, everyone defined hardships as keeping broken-down wagons moving, crossing dangerous rivers, and standing up against stormy weather. Even the lack of a roof over one's head was simply an inconvenience. People concentrated their efforts on having enough to eat, enough to wear, and the need to keep moving forward until the end of their journey.

Similar to earlier forts, Fort Boise was in no position to help such a large group of emigrants. Their arrival came as a stunning surprise for the fort's employees. During 1842 only about 100 emigrants, all with horses and pack animals, had passed by in September. The fort's employees expected a similar migration this year. Instead, the arrival of over 900 Americans with almost 90 wagons, 2,000 head of beef cattle, and numerous working stock easily overwhelmed the fort's supplies. Similar to Fort Hall, this was a fur trading post of the Hudson Bay Company, and their supplies were reserved for trapping brigades made up of single men. Supplying the needs of families with over 600 children was simply not possible.

Monsieur Francois Payette, the chief factor of the fort, welcomed Whitman and Jesse Applegate into his quarters and agreed to help the emigrants as best he could. He immediately ordered his men to open the blacksmith shop for use by the teamsters. There was more work to do than the fort's blacksmith could handle, so allowing the men to do their own repairs was an easy solution. Payette's lack of food supplies was not a problem, since most everyone was fully stocked with salmon. More importantly, emigrants with enough food were not as volatile as they had been back at Fort Hall. Fortunately, the news of their behavior there had not yet reached Fort Boise. Had Chief Factor Payette known, he might have met the migration with an armed force.

Fort Boise was constructed of fifteen-foot-high adobe walls surrounding a parallelogram of about one hundred feet to a side. The white adobe stood in stark contrast to the brown country all around. Trees along the banks of the Boise River and the nearby Snake River were enough to provide fuel, but had not been numerous enough to build a fort. Adobe was the only available material. The fort stood on the north side of the Boise River, near its confluence with the Snake. The surrounding country contained low-lying hills, thick with dead grass—dried from the summer drought. When the caravan came within view of the fort, emigrants could see a number of Hudson Bay employees stacking piles of hay and grass in preparation for the coming winter. Other men were harvesting crops from the fort's nearby garden.

The sight of fresh vegetables and other foodstuffs was deliciously tempting to people in the migration. They traded what they could, but Monsieur Payette kept most of the garden crops for the fort's employees. People had learned back at Fort Hall that their United States currency would be of no value here at Fort Boise. Fort Hall had only accepted United States coin because they did a majority of their business with American trappers. Fort Boise was well within the domain of the British Hudson Bay Company and did not need to pander to American needs. British trapping brigades sent out from Fort Vancouver on the Columbia constituted the majority of business for Fort Boise. To secure available items from the fort's warehouse, emigrants engaged in barter by using the skills they had gained out on the Snake River Plains.

Reverend Whitman informed everyone that they would spend two nights at the fort. The column would leave on Wednesday morning, even if some teamsters were not yet ready. This would provide enough time for most men to complete their blacksmithing needs and for people to effect other repairs in preparation for crossing the Blue Mountains. During the remainder of the day, people not engaged in blacksmithing tended to their stock, making sure they had good forage and water. Other chores included making repairs to harnesses, clothes, canvas white-tops, tents, shoes, and other items worn and tattered from weeks on the trail.

Abby spent the evening in her kitchen baking cornbread and roasting another pound of coffee beans for Jacob. It was a quiet, pleasant evening and a good camp for another day closer to Oregon. Resting in an area with grass, wood, and water was a welcome relief from the many harsh camps along the Snake River Plains. Another day in camp would give everyone a well-deserved rest from the constant demands of travel.

The next morning Jacob drilled four new holes in the wagon bed to secure the rear axle. With wooden plugs and a combination of axle grease, ash, and tallow, he sealed the four old holes to be waterproof against future river crossings. The quality of his work would be tested shortly, since the migration would have to recross the Snake River in just twenty-four hours. He recaulked the tailgate and planned to do the foregate after loading the kitchen gear in the morning.

People spent the day making repairs while seeking shelter from a strong, cold wind from the east. Drovers continued to allow their stock to graze on the best available forage along the banks of the Boise and Snake Rivers. During this short stay at the fort, stock from Jesse's Cow Column mixed in with the stock from the Light Column, much as the migration had done before crossing the Blue River many weeks earlier. The Oregon Emigrating Company was truly reunited.

At noon, word passed through the columns that Monsieur Payette was having a dance in the fort's courtyard that evening and everyone was welcome. There had not been a dance since Fort Laramie, and only three in all since leaving Independence. This would be the fourth, and long overdue according to several single men. Jim Wair, Nat Sitton, Tom Brown, John Cox, Jim Nesmith, and many others had been paying special attention to Abby since the loss of Sam. A dance was a perfect way to show the schoolteacher their charms in a publicly acceptable manner. During the afternoon, fiddlers tuned their instruments, and men set up benches around the fort's courtyard. Women prepared dinners early so that everyone could begin the dance at six, two hours before sunset.

It was cool and windy when the emigrants returned to the fort. The high adobe walls kept the wind out and provided a warm and festive atmosphere for the dance. Abby was again the belle of the ball, with her dance card filling up first. Ladies of the migration, well aware of Abby's charm, knew that she was no threat to their marital bliss. Over the summer months the ladies of the migration had become good friends with Abby, sharing in both tragedies and triumphs. If their husbands wanted to dance with the schoolteacher, it was quite alright. Everyone had earned an evening of entertainment after the long weeks of travel and the many difficulties of trail life.

The fiddlers began promptly at six o'clock, with everyone joining in. Three fires were kept burning on the outskirts of the courtyard to warm those not in the dance circle. The entertainment continued until well after dark when folks out on the dance area, especially Abby, became too exhausted to continue. Tomorrow would be a tough day on the trail, so Marcus and Jesse went around the courtyard urging people to have one last dance, then call it a night. For Abby, their request came as a lifesaver. Her legs were about to give out, for the men had not allowed her to sit out a single dance all evening.

Jacob sat on the outskirts enjoying the music, but not joining in with the dancing. He had spent too many years alone in the mountains to feel comfortable around such gatherings. When the music ended he showed a sophisticated courtesy in collecting Abby from the arms of her several admirers. Jim Wair, Nat Sitton, and Andy Baker were about to take to blows over who would get to walk Abby back to the corral. Jacob quietly stepped between them and Abby, then held out his arm much like a gentleman from the social elite. Smiling,

Abby took the arm of her rescuer, said her good-nights to the disappointed men, then walked back to the wagon with Jacob. The three men knew better than to cross paths with a mountain man.

"Courting Abby may have to wait until we get to Oregon," said Nat.

Jim Wair looked at Nat, then at Andy Baker, a young man traveling West with his parents. "You two might as well turn back to Independence. When we get to Oregon, that woman's mine!"

Andy was considerably younger than Abby, a situation that did not dampen his enthusiasm. He headed back to the corral, knowing that courting Abby would be a considerable challenge, both in winning her charm and in fighting off all the competition.

Back at the wagon, Abby thanked Jacob for his rescue and gentlemanly ways, then retrieved a bar of soap, a warm jacket, a clean dress, and headed down to the river.

The next morning, Wednesday, September 20, Whitman had the Light Column moving toward the Snake River shortly after sunup. A few wagons remained behind with unfinished repairs, however, that could not be helped. The owners of these outfits expected to be ready later in the day, so they would simply have to catch up.

The Snake River at the point of crossing was about six hundred yards wide and four to five feet deep. Wagons again chained together in groups of six or seven, with all working stock yoked or harnessed for added power. The crossing went without incident, with the last group of wagons pulling up on the far shore shortly after ten o'clock. While people unchained their wagons, Marcus passed word that they would stay for one hour. This would allow people to organize their stock, drain water from leaky wagon beds, and get something to eat before the afternoon march.

Back at the fort, Jesse Applegate decided to have the Cow Column spend an additional three days recruiting the health of their herds. The Snake River Plains had taken a devastating toll on all animals, leaving the remaining stock as walking skeletons. Oregon was still a long way off, and there was no telling what type of forage they would find in the Blue Mountains. The stronger each animal could become now, then the better their chances of survival to the Wallamet Valley.

During the afternoon, the Light Column moved northwest for twelve miles and camped on the banks of the Malheur River. They spent the first seven miles (the majority of the afternoon) in a long uphill climb as they left the Snake River floodplain. Upon arriving at the top of the drainage, they could see the surrounding country and get a good sense of the land they were entering. To the south they could see where the Owyhee River entered the Snake, several miles upriver from where they had just crossed. To the north they could see where the Malheur entered the Snake, and beyond that the route they would take to reach the Blue Mountains. At this overlook, the Blue Mountains were merely distant waves on the western horizon—and indeed, they were blue. The conifer-covered slopes cast a blue hue in the afternoon sun, beckoning the desert pilgrims to a new and welcoming world. Directly before them were more rolling hills speckled with a tree not unlike eastern juniper. Grass remained plentiful enough to feed all the stock, although water could only be found at the bottom of major drainages, such as the Snake and its tributaries.

The road was only a trail used by trappers and pack trains moving from Fort Walla Walla on the Columbia to Forts Boise and Hall along the Snake. While the Light Column crossed the pass, each teamster and drover reconnoitered the surrounding country without bothering to stop. The next drainage and tonight's camp lay in the Malheur floodplain, directly ahead.

Similar to camps along the Boise, there was adequate forage and fuel along the Malheur River. The grass away from the river was dry, yet still nutritious. During the evening three more straggler wagons caught up with the column. One wagon belonged to Overton Johnson, who informed Whitman that the Keizur clan he'd left behind planned to travel with Jesse's Cow Column for safety until they could all reunite. Besides, this gave them three more days to make repairs and recruit their stock at Fort Boise.

Another hot spring along the south bank of the Malheur River attracted the curiosity of everyone. This spring was larger than the previous one encountered, spewing forth boiling hot water, steam, and a sulfurous smell. Indians had constructed three different pools between the spring and the river, providing baths of three different temperatures. The upper bath, nearest the spring, was almost too hot to enter. Jacob quickly informed the onlookers that these pools represented big medicine.

"I've seen pools like this up on the Bitterroot in Blackfoot Country," he said to the men and women dipping their hands in the water to test the temperature. "They get into the hottest pool and stay there as long as possible. Then they run down to the river and jump in without hesitation. It's supposed to be both a sign of strength and to have some religious significance."

"I don't much care what the Indians do," said Susan Cochran. "This is hot water and I plan on doing my wash." Susan was a homely woman, and had married a younger man who showed very few prospects. When he decided to start a new life in Oregon, she did little to discourage his first step toward employment and a future.

"I'll be joining you," added Eliza Eyre.

Other women agreed—this would be an ideal place to wash clothes, kitchen items, and even children.

The vegetation near the hot spring was green and lush, reminding people of the farms and land they had left behind. Several kinds of daisies grew there, along with a white flower that looked like a bunch of pearls. Abby decided to join the ladies and give her kitchen gear a good washing. Later, back at the wagon she ground the coffee beans she had roasted while at the fort. The dance had interfered with normal chores, although it was well worth it. Most women spent this evening catching up on the domestic activities that they had put aside the previous day.

In the morning, Thursday, September 21, the Light Column crossed the Malheur River without incident. The flow at this time of year was low, allowing wagons to cross without having the water line rise much above the hubs.

The road this morning was over rough terrain, up and down desert swales. The afternoon was equally slow, and by the time wagon corrals formed, the Light Column was only ten miles beyond the Malheur River. Tonight was a dry camp, so teamsters moved their stock around to scattered water holes as best they could. For the most part, only the working stock received adequate water.

Jacob watered all their stock from one of the water barrels. The column expected to encounter the Snake again on the following night, so he was liberal with the water, allowing each animal one bucket or about three gallons. The milch cow was gaining strength since reaching the Boise and would probably make it to the Wallamet Valley.

On the next day, Friday, September 22, the Light Column continued through rough, broken country consisting of dried grass, scattered juniper, and loose volcanic rocks of all sizes. No wagon had ever trod on this ground, and a road of any sort did not exist. Wheels and stock trampled the grass, while a lead team of young men rolled large stones out of the way in an attempt to make a passable route. Small water holes could be found along the way, although not enough to give relief to the stock. At the end of another long hard day, the column had made only twelve miles. It did not matter, though, for they were once again on the banks of the Snake River!

Marcus Whitman passed word down through his platoon leaders that this would be their last view of the Snake River. From here the migration would start up a long, steady incline through an area called Burnt Canyon. It was a well-chosen name due to a catastrophic fire that had swept through the area about twenty years earlier. Viewed from a distance, the route had few trees and appeared to be a long slow climb through dried grass, up into the Blue Mountains.

The grass near the river's edge was excellent, some of the best the migration had seen since before Fort Laramie. Several people requested a layover day, and Whitman quickly concurred. With Burnt Canyon and the Blue Mountains dead ahead, an extra day of rest for the stock couldn't hurt.

After forming wagon corrals and hobbling the stock in an area of lush forage, Jacob rubbed oil on the sore hooves of each exhausted animal. He had done this many times before since passing Fort Laramie, and the improved condition of his and Abby's animals was evident. They were gaunt, tired, and lean, yet in the best condition possible considering the hardships. Oxen, mules, horses, and other stock in the migration were in worse condition, with one or two animals dying every day.

"Jacob, this is a wonderful place to lay over," Abby said as she stood up from hobbling Lashes. "Look at those hills over there," she pointed to the mountains on the far side of the river. "Not a tree on them, yet they're magnificent. I never knew a mountain could be so barren and still so beautiful!"

"It is a sight. One could start a farm down here in the floodplain, but those mountains are only good for looking at."

"If only my family back in Ohio could see this area. It looks as if someone took a brown carpet and laid it down over that mountain. Each little draw and swale is perfectly covered, not a wrinkle to be found."

They paused in silence for a moment, looking at the mountains. Then Jacob said, "I'll water the stock again before dark."

"I don't know why I should be in such good spirits," Abby pondered. "It was a long, hard day, and I should be more tired. I just feel we're getting closer to our goal. The Snake River Plains are behind us now, when for weeks they were in front of us—and now we get this beautiful camp before crossing the Blue Mountains. I should be more cautious in my optimism—but I just know we'll get across those mountains. We couldn't have come this far and gone through so many troubles only to be stopped by some mountains. We'll make it!"

"We've got the Columbia River after that. Have you decided if you want to float down on rafts or blaze a trail?"

"I'll wait until I see the country and find out what other people are doing. Blazing a new trail might not be too bad if the ground is open. I just don't know right now."

"I've heard talk of people wanting to float the remaining distance. Their animals are spent and so is their muster. Some of these folks will take any kind of a risk to ease their workload and shorten the journey."

"How are they going to get rafts around the rapids and falls?"

"Don't know," replied Jacob. "I've never seen the Columbia."

"Our outfit is in good shape, better than most of these wagons. We can go either way. I'd prefer to talk to people at the Waiilatpu Mission and Fort Walla Walla on what they think about floating the Columbia. Then I'll decide."

Jacob nodded his approval, resealed the tin of oil, and headed back to the wagon. Abby continued to look at the mountains, mesmerized by their beauty. They extended from the north shore of the Snake River in an undulating climb to a horizon of blue sky, making for a most unusual and magnificent sight indeed.

After dinner Abby visited Sarah Rubey, who was still down with a fever and unable to eat. Their conversation wandered between the beauty of the region and all the troubles endured.

"You were one of the first people I met," said Abby, "back there in Independence. You were so kind to me, right when I needed a friend."

"We thought you were crazy, and here you've done better on this journey than most. I mean with your wagon and stock. That was a terrible thing with Sam."

"Jacob told me the Indians revere their dead but don't dwell on it. They think it's bad luck to talk of the dead. I never heard of such a thing."

Sarah sighed. "It's a hard life we've chosen. If you could have the last year over again, would you still go?"

"Yes!" Abby answered without hesitation, startling Sarah with her abruptness. "Look at all we've seen since leaving Independence. We've seen sights so wondrous I never would have believed it had I not seen them with my own eyes."

"Well, I could do without them, dear. I never did want to come out here—and for what? We had a good farm back in Illinois!"

"If I were in your situation, I wouldn't want to have come out here either. My life was different. I had nothing back in Ohio. Oh, my parents and brothers were there—but I should have my own family by now. Without a family, there was nothing holding me back."

"You're a brave one, Abby."

"Brave? I think more curious. I've always enjoyed learning, and I knew this trip would be a school like no other."

"It's been worth it?"

"Yes, yes, many times over—and in just a month or so we'll reach the Wallamet Valley, where they say people are seldom sick. You'll regain all your strength and be better than when you left Illinois."

She smiled at Abby's enthusiasm, hoping her friend was right and wishing for some of her strength. After an hour, Abby said her good-nights to allow Sarah a restful evening. She went back to the wagon to retrieve her wool jacket, then walked down to the shore to look at the river and mountains. She had not been there long when Jacob came up.

"Too bad we can't float down this river," he said. "It enters the Columbia downstream somewhere."

"Didn't Monsieur Payette say it's impassable? Didn't he say something about a falls, or rocks and rapids?"

"He did. Personally I wouldn't trust any of those company people. He might be doing right by us, but I've had too many encounters with their trapping brigades to do much trusting."

"Marcus has been this way, and if it was passable, well, he'd know—and he says to cross the Blue Mountains."

"That we will. This child could use the clear health of mountain air. I've had my fill of desert dust."

"That climb into Burnt Canyon looks plenty dry. I'll be glad when we're past it."

"We should be able to get enough water from mountain streams. When we pull out, you can say farewell to the Snake. This here bend will be the last we'll ever see of this river."

"The next major river will be the Columbia! Imagine, the Columbia!" Abby let the words drift out over the water, as if by some magical force she could visualize the river she had heard so much about.

"That water feel good?"

Abby had removed her moccasins and was dangling both feet in the river. "It feels wonderful. My poor tired feet have come a long way."

"We'll probably have to cut a road through timber when we get some elevation. It'll be rough going, but not so rough on your feet.

Mountain trails are always soft, ask any trapper. We trappers will take mountain life over deserts and farming anytime."

"I'm sure you would." Abby smiled back at him, then looked out across the Snake. The sunset was throwing shadows over the carpeted mountain in a spectacular display of colors and shapes. Paragraphs for the diary would have to wait. This evening's display of Western beauty was too good to miss.

People rose late the next morning, kindling fires and moving stock to areas of new grass. It was a quiet day, with teamsters preparing their outfits as best they could for the coming climb into the Blue Mountains. Those with flour or cornmeal, such as Abby, used the opportunity to bake as much bread as possible. In the afternoon she took two loaves over to Sarah Rubey, since it was the only food she could keep down. Her husband, Phil, was of no use in the kitchen. He offered to give his remaining flour to any woman willing to convert it into bread, as long as he could receive half of the loaves for his family. Several women took him up on the offer, while Abby chose to spend another hour with Sarah. With bread and smoked salmon, Sarah, Phil, and their two children would be ready to cross the Blue Mountains.

The sunny day passed quickly for people of the Light Column, with both stock and emigrants getting their fill of food and rest before the final push. Back at Fort Boise, Jesse's Cow Column got underway at an early hour. They crossed the Snake without incident and made it over to the Malheur drainage before sunset. By camping at the same spot used by the Light Column, women of the Cow Column made good use of the hot springs. They, too, washed clothes and kitchen equipment that had not seen hot water and cleanliness since leaving Independence.

After dinner that evening, Abby again watched the sunset from down at the river's south shore. This time she waded out to her knees, holding up her dress and feeling the sand squeeze between her toes. The surrounding mountains stood as giant sentinels, watching over the river and those that depended on it for subsistence. It was a sight she tried hard to commit to memory. In the distance, she could see Jacob moving and hobbling the stock.

"He's a good man," she thought. "I could not have done better!"

While there was still some daylight left, Abby sat down on the shoreline grass to record her thoughts and the beauty of the camp. The Snake River had been their constant companion since Fort Hall. From here they would push northwest up Burnt Canyon while the river turned due north.

The Snake had provided both the water and subsistence needed to make it this far, yet it had taken the lives of two men. It was a contradiction of good and evil. Even so, the beauty of the country could not be denied. This river was the lifeblood that allowed survival for both man and beast. Without it, crossing the last two hundred miles of desert would not have been possible, and the great experiment of taking wagons to Oregon would have ended in failure. The same could be said for the help received from Indians along the Snake and elsewhere. Without their assistance, the journey to Oregon would have ended in disaster many weeks ago.

Abby recorded these notes of fact, since future travelers would face the same obstacles. After a few more paragraphs describing the magnificent beauty of this bend in the river, the light faded to dusk and it was time to return to the wagon.

The next morning, Sunday, September 24, Reverend Whitman had the Light Column moving up the trail at first light. Traveling on the Sabbath would have angered other preachers; however, other preachers did not have Marcus's knowledge or experience. This was a country where there were no days of the week—only days and seasons of the year. Weeks and months were conventions of civilization, used to measure time in a faraway land. They had no place in a country that followed only daily and seasonal weather changes. One could easily lose track of the day of the week or month, for these time divisions were of no consequence. Summer was now giving way to winter, which provided the driving force for the emigrants to cross the Blue Mountains—cross before they became locked in winter's grip. Survival depended on knowing the land and the gifts it offered.

At this time of year, with snow approaching, a one-day layover along the Snake was risky at best. It was time to move on.

The people of the Light Column bid farewell to the Snake River and the green, inviting campsite at the bend in its course. The long, slow climb into Burnt Canyon began almost immediately. Dried grass covered the land in every direction—dried from the summer drought, yet still nutritious enough to feed hungry stock.

The climb began with difficulty due to intersecting ravines that forced the column to create their own roadless switchbacks. Men attached stabilizing ropes to each wagon with the other end tied to a mounted rider on the uphill side. Those without horses tied the rope around their waists and held on as best they could. This technique had worked well back on the Platte and would probably be needed many times before reaching the Columbia River.

The only trees in the region grew in watered ravines. Abby noted the western hackberry, some type of willow, an unusual hawthorn, a western-style cottonwood, and a small bushy tree that nobody had ever seen before. It had narrow leaves about three inches long and with the edges curled under. For lack of a good name, Abby decided to call it curl-leaf. The name would help to provide a description for this evening's diary entry.

After five miles the column encountered Burnt River, and stopped for a nooner and Sabbath services. The road so far had been steep and rocky, described by some as the worst yet.

"I'm beginning to see why nobody has brought wagons up this canyon," Abby said as she prepared the noon meal. "We've only come five miles, but we must have traveled ten. All this winding around steep slopes is exhausting."

"Old Joe and Doc Newell had carts when they came through here," said Jacob. "I can't see them spending time struggling with a wagon."

"Here," she handed him a plate of smoked salmon and cornbread, "we're out of meat again, and so is everyone else. Seems like whenever someone's ox or mule dies, it's gone in a day."

"I suspect they'll start killing stock for food from here on. Haven't heard much remorse for all their wastefulness."

"Everyone's probably too tired—can't change the past. People seem to be moving forward by habit and not motivation. They aren't quarreling as much. That might be because they're too tired."

"The quarreling never settled a thing."

"Amen to that!" Abby smiled at her response, adding, "And that will be our sermon for the day!"

Jacob nodded with a half-smile, too busy eating to respond.

The nooner lasted two hours, after which the column continued up Burnt River Canyon. This river, more like a small creek, had carved a ravine rather than a wide canyon—and the steep hillsides threatened to topple each wagon. It was not uncommon for the two uphill wheels of a wagon to lift off the ground with only a taut guy line preventing a disaster.

As the caravan ascended into the Blue Mountains, people could see signs of an old fire from burned-out stumps, now surrounded in a sea of dried grass. In the recent past this region had supported more trees; however, the dry climate prevented a quick recovery from a disastrous fire. It would be decades before trees could encroach back into the open areas, and only then with an extended period of above-average moisture and the absence of fire.

The sandy soil gave way under the hooves of hundreds of stock and heavy wagon wheels. By the time the last wagon passed, the beginnings of a trail, or road, showed where before there had been nothing. The pioneer guard did their best to pick the easiest route, but did not have time to survey all possibilities. They picked a route that looked passable, then moved on before the first wagons arrived.

For everyone, it was a long and exhausting day, ending with only an advance of ten miles from last night's camp. The steepness of the country prevented their usual wagon corrals. Since steep canyon walls on either side hemmed them in, teamsters simply stopped where they were and unchained and hobbled their stock for the night. Abby took note of it in her diary: *This is the longest and narrowest camp yet!*

Lew Linebarger killed his milch cow that evening. She had stopped giving milk two months ago and was now so gaunt that Jane, Lew's wife, decided it was better to use her for meat now rather than wait until she died. Animals dead from exhaustion produced very little good meat.

A number of people did not take to salmon and were now looking at their loose stock as potential food. A few had not bothered to secure salmon, thinking it was inferior food because it was the main diet of Snake Indians. Cultural prejudices and ignorance still pervaded the migration. With only one mountain range left to cross, many people saw no need to change their social proprieties.

After one of the hardest days yet, several men discussed abandoning their wagons and using their oxen as pack animals until reaching the Columbia. At that point they could build rafts for their baggage and sell their surviving stock to Fort Walla Walla, another Hudson Bay Company post on the Columbia. The discussion died quickly as wives voiced their protests concerning household goods that would have to be left behind. Marcus also intervened by reminding the men of Bill Wilson's misfortune after selling his wagon at Fort Hall. Calmer voices soon prevailed, and the long, narrow camp became quiet. Everyone retired at sunset, for they expected tomorrow to be just as grueling.

The next morning, Monday, September 25, the column moved forward at first light. Most people never bothered with campfires due to the scarcity of wood and the steepness of their camp. The single-file camp lacked any of the comforts or social amenities of their usual camps, so Whitman had no trouble in starting the column early.

High-side guy lines continued to help balance wagons as the emigrants resumed their precarious slow climb into the Blue Mountains. In several places the column halted as men double-teamed wagons to get over an especially steep incline. The steepest required eight and nine yoke of oxen to pull a single wagon over a ridge. Gaunt and weak oxen did the best they could against their heavy loads. The gaps over some ridges were so narrow that they allowed room for only a single wagon, and no room for a teamster. The day was slow and exhausting, fraying the nerves of people longing for an end to their journey.

As the column moved up Burnt Canyon, they crossed Burnt River a number of times in an attempt to avoid the steepest ground.

Shortly before noon they came to a patch of black haws on the river. Here was an appropriate place to stop for a nooner, for the berries provided a food luxury that most people had not tasted for a year.

During the afternoon they came upon a small village of Nez Perce Indians situated on a fork of Burnt River. Jacob quickly joined the advance guard, who wanted to learn about the condition of the road ahead and if it was passable by wagons. The Indians did not give a hopeful description for an ascent up the river they called the Brule. Mostly, they were in disbelief that anyone would try to take wagons through to the Columbia. Few of the Indians had ever seen a wheeled vehicle, having spent their entire lives in the mountains. They crowded around the lead wagon, reaching out to touch the wood and metal, and alarming some of the teamsters.

The chiefs quickly ordered their people back, possibly fearing for their lives. They knew through instinct that anyone who could build such a curiosity must have great powers. One of the chiefs offered three good horses for one of the wagons. The owner, Rich Goodman, nearly accepted before his wife stepped in. Sarah would have nothing to do with abandoning her household goods and using pack animals—even if they were the finest horses anyone had seen since leaving Independence.

The column continued climbing up Burnt River Canyon and set up camp near a spring that flowed into the river. Here was enough flat ground for the wagons to break rank, but not enough to form their corrals. The water from the spring was clear, cold, and refreshing after the long, hard day. Jacob only half-filled the barrels with fresh water. This would help keep their load light while distributing the weight to both sides of the wagon. Water appeared to be plentiful in the mountains, so there was no need to keep both barrels full.

Whitman informed his platoon leaders that they would leave Burnt River in the morning and make a seven-mile detour around an impassable section of the canyon. By tomorrow evening they should again be on Burnt River, which would also be their last night on that stream. From there, Burnt River turns due west, while the trail into the mountains continues in a northwesterly direction.

The hard day resulted in moving twelve miles closer to their goal—a fact not missed in Abby's diary.

On Tuesday morning, September 26, members of the Oregon Emigrating Company awoke to see a thin veil of white on the mountains ahead. It was the first snow of the season and a sobering reminder of the potential for tragedy. People hastened their breakfasts and started forward as quickly as possible. The weather this morning was cold and rainy, which made travel over the slippery, steep slopes especially dangerous. It was a danger they chose to face rather than chance getting caught in an early snow.

At midmorning, Jesse Looney's wagon hit a rock and tipped over. The contents spilled out from both ends, and the inside was a jumble of opened trunks with clothes, equipment, and household goods scattered everywhere. The column halted, and with the help of almost thirty men, they were able to right the wagon and return its contents. Ruby Looney figured it would be several days to a week before she could get her house on wheels back in order. At least nothing was lost. The column continued after a half-hour delay.

Overton Johnson, the Newbys, and several other teamsters were also having trouble managing their broken-down wagons over this rough terrain. While crossing the North Platte, Bill Newby's wagon had rolled over several times before getting stuck in the shallows—and Overton Johnson had been having a hard time keeping up with the column ever since leaving Fort Bridger. The difficulty of crossing the Blue Mountains would be the death knell for these wagons and several others. If they could get through to Waiilatpu, these teamsters would have to make other arrangements for getting to the Wallamet Valley. Their only two options would be to continue with pack animals or to risk the dangers of the Columbia in a boat or on a raft.

Rain continued intermittently all day, and snow-covered mountains were visible to the west. By evening they had made another twelve miles and camped on a ridge overlooking an immense valley extending to the northwest. In the northwest corner of this valley, they could see a river entering from a gap in the mountains, then meandering throughout the valley, gathering water from numerous side streams. It was a magnificently beautiful valley, nestled between lofty mountains and rich with water and forage.

Due to a lack of flat ground, people set up their kitchens wherever they could. Rainy weather and no water for the stock made for another uncomfortable camp—except for views of the surrounding mountains. These mountains, now covered in a light snow, contained thick stands of conifer timber. The view came as a welcome relief, for these dense forests were the first timber of any consequence they had seen since passing Grand Island on the Platte, over a thousand miles ago. With the valley stretched out before them, several farmers started entertaining ideas of stopping and building their homes right here. The discussions were short-lived, for calmer minds and logic prevailed. Markets were too far away, and roads were nonexistent. For the present, the valley would remain as a beautiful oasis for travelers passing through the country.

After dinner, Abby took her diary and walked up to a rise of ground where she could get a good view of the valley ahead. Jacob was already there enjoying a smoke.

"Look there!" Abby pointed to a large, single pine growing in the center of the valley. It was the only tree for about a five-mile radius.

"How do you suppose that tree got started? There's not another tree anywhere near!"

"That's Lone Pine. I've heard talk of it from Nat Wyeth and Captain Bonneville. The Indians say this valley belongs to that pine."

"Lone Pine. Then this must be Lone Pine Valley."

"Powder River Valley. That's the Powder River over there." Jacob pointed to the river flowing through the valley.

"We should make good time tomorrow as soon as we can get off this ridge. Probably make it past Lone Pine."

"Probably."

"You think we'll go past it or stop for the night?"

"Don't much matter—those mountains on the other side of this valley got me concerned. I don't see any opening through that timber." Jacob pointed to a heavily timbered draw heading out of the northwest end of the valley, almost twenty miles distant.

"You said we might have to cut our way through."

"That I did." He paused, taking a puff on his pipe and looking up at the sky. "Looks like the rain's comin' back." Without saying another word, he stood and took a long look at the distant pass, then started back toward the wagon.

Abby stayed to write a few paragraphs in her diary, then headed back to the wagon. She arrived and climbed in just as a light drizzle began. Jacob was already in his buffalo robe underneath the wagon bed.

On the following morning, the Light Column began their descent into Powder River Valley. The downhill trail was slippery and treacherous, but everyone made it to flat ground without incident. As each wagon came down onto the valley floor and into a horizontal position, the teamster and family breathed a sigh of relief, and then continued on at a quickened pace through the lush grass of the valley. The route had been long and exhausting since leaving the Snake River, and this mountain oasis, or "hole" as the mountain men call them, was a welcome sight.

During the descent, movement along the column was extremely slow, with constant switchbacks allowing teamsters to maintain control. When a wagon made it to the valley floor and sped up, it wasn't long before the distance between wagons was over two hundred yards. By the time the last wagon was down, the Light Column stretched out in a single file for over five miles. Jacob untied and stowed the guy line, then mounted and took his usual position of twenty to thirty yards out from the column. Abby kept her oxen moving through tall grass that scraped along their bellies. The ground felt soft under her moccasins, a welcome relief from the hard, slippery slopes of Burnt River Canyon.

Abby's attention wandered between the beauty of the surrounding mountains, the long line of white-tops ahead, and keeping her oxen moving. Each animal nipped at the tall grass as they continued in a northwesterly direction. The light rain had ceased, and the afternoon looked to be much more pleasant.

Dan Matheny came riding back, telling people to stop where they were for a nooner. The column was too spread out and would probably not come together until evening. Without hesitation, Abby stopped her outfit and started fixing a meal for herself and Jacob. She was hungry and in need of a rest after the difficult descent into the valley.

The lateness of the season provided a stark contrast between conditions on the valley floor and in the surrounding mountains. A thin veil of snow blanketed the thickly timbered slopes, while the valley floor was warm and comfortable—so warm that waves of heat could be seen in the distance as the sky cleared and the September sun shone brightly. After eating, Abby stowed her kitchen gear and wool jacket, then sat waiting for Dan Matheny to come riding back ordering the column to continue. While enjoying the warmth of the sun, her gaze wandered up to the majestic, towering mountains.

"This would be a wonderful place for a town," she thought. "A town surrounded by farms—what a beautiful place to raise a family." She strained to see the details of each mountain, the subvalleys, draws, ridges, rocky crags, and timbered slopes—all for a later description in her diary.

Before long, word came down the long line of wagons to move out. Abby snapped her quirt and the wagon lurched forward. The soft ground and distance between wagons was a refreshing change from the choking, alkali dust of the Snake River Plains. Now and then Abby's gaze would come down from the mountains and look forward to the next wagon, then to the lead wagons way off in the distance—along with Lone Pine.

"Get on!" Her quirt came down on Dinnertime's rump. Grass in this valley was too tempting for him and his teammates to pay much attention to the work at hand. An hour passed with Abby trying to drink in every aspect of the scenery. Since passing Fort Boise, the land had changed rapidly. This valley presented a picture of the Eden described in the wild stories of Oregon heard back in the United States.

Clouds moved in and around the mountain ridges, yielding new sights and beauty. Abby continued to watch the mountains with only an occasional glance at the road and an urging quirt to keep her wagon moving. It was an easy, pleasant advance through a lush valley.

"If only this were the Wallamet Valley," she thought. "This is the kind of country I've dreamed of."

Again her gaze swept forward to the lead wagons, but this time the pine tree was gone! She quickly looked to either side, thinking it was merely hidden from view by another wagon. She glanced back to the wagon behind her, then forward. She was still traveling in the right direction, so the pine tree should be ahead!—but it was gone!

As she came up to the spot where the pine had stood, she quickly saw what had happened. Over the nooner some inconsiderate young men had cut the tree down. Their intention was to gather branches for their evening fire. Sadly, the branches were too green. The destruction of the tree was a terrible waste. By the time Abby's wagon passed, the fellers had moved on, leaving their destruction as a huge scar on the valley floor. For later entry into her diary, Abby noted that the tree was over three feet in diameter and had bark consisting of large, yellow plates. The needles were long and dark green, indicating a tree that had been exceptionally healthy.

Abby kept her frustration silent, but her anger was evident. When wagon corrals formed that evening, she learned that other people were equally angry. Jacob too showed irritation at the destruction of such an old landmark—and for nothing. The young men who had done the deed made themselves scarce that evening, a wise precaution to keep the peace.

After dinner and chores, Abby made the following diary entry: *"The beauty of this magnificent valley has been scarred by the wanton destruction of Lone Pine. This tree stood as an ancient resident of the valley, choosing one of the most beautiful places on earth to call its home. The valley belonged to that tree, and the tree belonged to the valley—but no more. Future emigrants will never know the beauty of Lone Pine."*

This evening's camp was sixteen miles from the previous night's ridge top. Wagon corrals formed along the banks of the Powder River, allowing the women to wash clothes and children after the challenging road up from the Snake. Stock received their fill of water and forage, while farmers continued to talk about the fertility of the valley. This valley was the Oregon most had come to expect. Finally, they had reached an area with fertile, flat ground already cleared of trees and ready for the plow. The surrounding mountains could provide an endless supply of lumber and fuel to feed a new settlement. Tonight was an evening for reminiscing about farms left back in the United States and dreams of new farms to come in the Wallamet Valley.

Clouds swirled around the surrounding mountaintops, dropping more snow here and there before moving out across the valley. The light snow turned to rain on the valley floor—rain that everyone knew would not last. In a few weeks the valley floor would be covered with snow. This prospect gave the emigrants the final emotional drive needed to push through to the Columbia.

After a quiet evening with people staying close to their kitchens, the camp settled down early and was asleep by dusk. Darkness came faster than usual as the sun set behind one of the tall, snow-covered mountains. Even with the abundance of forage and water in this valley, everyone knew they could not spend any layover days. The lateness of the season demanded they keep pushing forward to the next valley beyond and then to the Columbia.

On Thursday morning, September 28, the column continued their trek through the Powder River Valley, now with wagons traveling closer together. The flat ground provided an easy road for the first eight miles, before the column crossed one of the meanders of the Powder River. At this time of year the river ran shallow with numerous gravel bars. Chaining wagons or double-teaming was not necessary, as each wagon plunged into the river and crossed without slowing down. The banks on either side of the river were so gradual that they could hardly be called banks at all. The river wound back and forth throughout the entire valley, watering these natural pastures without the formation of steep banks.

Shortly after crossing the Powder, the column crossed two smaller streams and continued in a northwesterly direction toward the far mountain pass. As they approached the pass, the emigrants could see a break in the timbered slopes where the column could climb out of this valley and into the valley beyond. After crossing the third stream the column began a slow, although not exceptionally steep, climb into the next valley. After another seven miles Reverend Whitman came to an area of good forage where wagon corrals could form and there was a supply of firewood. Tonight was another dry camp—an inconvenience people had come to expect. Within the hour the Light Column's mobile settlement looked as it had for many weeks before, with only a change in the surrounding scenery to indicate progress.

After dinner Harriet Burnett stopped by Abby's kitchen in hopes of buying some cornmeal.

"Hattie cooked up the last of our parched corn tonight," Harriet said. "If you got any extra, I'll gladly pay you twice what it was worth back in Independence."

"I've some left Harriet, but Jacob and I will need it. We'll probably run out, too, by the time we get to the Columbia, or shortly after—and I'm sure we'll run out of flour."

"Well, I just don't know what we'll do. Hattie doesn't need to have any, but Pete likes his cornbread."

"Don't you have any salmon left?"

"Sure, but that's not good food. We need meat and bread. Pete and I don't much care for salmon. We'd eat it if we were starving, otherwise we give that to Hattie."

Abby's distaste for slavery was about to surface in a harangue when Jacob joined the conversation.

"I believe I saw a sack of white beans when Hattie set up your kitchen tonight. You've more than enough food to make it to the Columbia."

Harriet stood looking at Jacob, knowing that he was not a man to argue with. Besides, he was right.

"Then I'll tell Pete he'll have to do without cornbread."

"Everything will work out," Abby said. "Before long we'll be on the Columbia where there's all kinds of food."

"More than salmon?"

"Maybe. I heard Marcus talking about his garden at the mission. Everything should be ripe when we get there, so you might be able to buy fresh corn and squash."

Harriet was clearly not happy, yet she had no choice but to accept the situation. The Burnetts were unaccustomed to difficult times, and this journey had taxed their patience. Hattie had borne the brunt of the work, doing all kitchen, washing, mending, and cooking chores since leaving Independence. Now, Pete and Harriet would have to eat their slave's food, salmon, before reaching the Wallamet Valley.

On the next morning, Friday, September 29, the Light Column continued their ascent up the low-lying mountain pass in a north-by-northwest direction. Within six miles they reached the top of the pass and could see in the distance a wide, bold river winding its way through another magnificent mountain valley. The valley stretched out before them toward the northwest, looking to be another scenic place to establish a settlement.

The river was the Grande Ronde, and this was the Grande Ronde Valley. Seeing the valley and getting to it were two different things. The route down from the mountain pass was treacherous at best and impassable at worst. The advance guard split up to check several routes before agreeing on a course. Wagons slowly inched their way down from the pass, creating their own switchbacks wherever possible.

The valley was about twenty miles long and ten miles wide. Grass covered the valley floor, presenting a beautiful prospect for future farms and communities. The descent from the mountain pass required all of Abby's and Jacob's attention, so admiring the valley would have to wait. Jacob attached two guy lines to the wagon so he would always have a line on the uphill side. When Abby turned a switchback, he tossed the end of one line into the back of the wagon then pulled the other line out and took his position on the uphill side. This procedure repeated itself eighteen times before they finally reached the valley floor. As they had in the previous valley, wagons quickly sped up, leaving the column to stretch out for over five miles across the valley floor.

Upon reaching the Grande Ronde River the advance guard encountered a single Indian of the Cayuse tribe, traveling east from the Waiilatpu Mission. The Indian, named Stickus, had been sent to find Reverend Whitman. At an establishment called Tshimakain, a Mrs. Eells was having a difficult time in labor and was in need of a physician to help deliver her baby.

Stickus was one of the many Christian converts from the Waiilatpu Mission. He was employed by Whitman, as were other converts, as general laborers to tend crops and do all the other hard work associated with a frontier mission. The caravan met Stickus late in the day, so Marcus ordered the column to form camp. The site provided excellent forage, an easily accessible source of water, and flat ground for the wagon corrals. As the camp formed, poor Stickus stood agape at the spectacle before his eyes. He had seen two-wheeled carts at Fort Walla Walla, but never wagons—and certainly nothing with a white-sheeted top. He had also never seen cattle like the ones accompanying the caravan. The only stock at Fort Walla Walla and the Waiilatpu Mission were Spanish cattle, a breed inferior to these new breeds brought out from the United States.

Stickus walked around the campsite watching people organize their kitchens, pitch tents, and prepare for the night's camp. Members of the column set up their camp with the precision of a drilled military unit. Everyone did their assigned chores efficiently and quickly. Even the older children had specific duties each night in camp.

Along with the wagons and stock, Stickus had never seen so many white people, especially children. As he surveyed the amazing scene before him, his eyes fell upon Rachael, Dan Delany's slave. Not only had he never seen a black person, he had never heard that such people existed. He cautiously walked up to her to see if the color was her true skin or if she was wearing paint. He rubbed her face, then jumped back—it did not come off. From across the wagon corral he then saw Hattie, Pete Burnett's slave. That was quite enough. He started back to where Whitman stood, to question where these people came from. On his way he saw the slave belonging to Miles and Cyrene Cary carrying a bucket of water up from the river. It was a day Stickus would never forget.

Marcus calmed Stickus with assurances that these people were not dangerous and that they were only passing through the country on their way to Fort Vancouver. Stickus welcomed the assurances; however, for safety he located his one-man camp on the other side of the Grande Ronde River.

As women prepared the evening meal, several men dug holes to look at the fertility and rockiness of the soil, much like they had done in the previous valley. They determined this valley to also be an ideal location for a new settlement. The surrounding mountains could provide all the needed timber, while the valley floor contained excellent farmland with a year-round water source. With canals, they could irrigate the entire valley with this single river!

As it did during their stay in the Powder River Valley, the want of provisions would keep the column moving forward. The extreme distance to markets also precluded any wild dreams of starting a settlement. Some thought that in fifty years this valley might be a lucrative place to start a farm or business. Others thought that one hundred years might be more accurate. The distance from any established markets was simply too far.

Sarah Rubey's health had been steadily improving, but took a turn for the worse in crossing the last mountain pass. She rode lying down in her wagon, enduring the painful jostling from every bump. At one point when the wagon went over a particularly sharp rock, she felt a pain shoot through her lower abdomen that completely incapacitated her. She was not able to sit up that evening, much less walk or eat. It was evident to Phil and the other women that Sarah's time was near. Dr. Long looked in on her, as he had done on numerous occasions before. However, he said he was at a loss as to the cause of her condition and what to do. He and Reverend Whitman tried to give Phil some reassuring words and a glimmer of hope.

"Keep her warm," Dr. Long told Phil, "and try to get her to drink some water."

"I'll stay with her." Abby was standing behind Phil and overheard Dr. Long's discouraging diagnosis.

"Thank you, Abby," said Phil. "She always enjoys your visits."

"I need to get Jacob his dinner first, so I'll be back as soon as I can."

Abby returned after dinner carrying her canteen and a blanket. Throughout the evening, Sarah was not able to drink and kept dropping in and out of consciousness. When conscious, she made little sense and had difficulty completing sentences. Abby continued to hold her hand, talking about the good life yet to come.

"I'll be out here if you need anything," Phil said as he poked his head into the wagon. "My tent's set up over there, so you let me know when you leave, and I'll come sit with her."

"Thank you, Phil, but I'll probably spend the night—that's why I brought my blanket."

"That's kind and decent of you, Abby—you call if you need anything."

"I will."

The night was cold, so Abby curled up in her blanket, pulling it over her head to cover any exposed skin. By early morning she finally drifted off to sleep, only to wake three hours later when guards fired the morning volley. Sarah was still sleeping, and Abby could not discern any change in her condition. It was time to get back to the Western Passage and morning chores.

"I'll be around if Sarah needs anything," she told Phil as he crawled out of his tent. "Don't hesitate to call on me or any of the other ladies."

"Thank you kindly, Abby. You're a good friend."

It was now the last day of September, and the hours of daylight were getting short. The column struck camp and was back on the trail as the first rays of sun filtered over the mountaintops. It would be another two or three hours before the rays could reach the valley floor, so the air remained cool as the column moved off to the northwest.

Whitman continued to travel with the caravan, expecting to move ahead when they reached the end of the valley. As the caravan inched along, he informed Stickus that *he* would have to lead the emigrants to the Waiilatpu Mission and Fort Walla Walla. Marcus's instructions were as specific as possible, yet wagons had never traversed these mountains. The success or failure of the migration to get through the Blue Mountains was now in the hands of Stickus. It was a great responsibility—one the Indian accepted proudly. He would have to find a route by which wagons could travel through an area of heavy timber, with a lead team of fellers blazing a trail. Stickus had a more intimate knowledge of these mountains than Marcus did. So leaving the fate of the migration in the hands of Stickus was a fortuitous exchange.

The column traveled six miles before reaching the end of the valley. While stopped for a nooner, Whitman and the platoon leaders decided the company should make camp here and enter the mountains in the morning. The journey from this juncture would require a team of fellers to work in advance of the wagons. By stopping here for the night, platoon leaders would have time to organize volunteers, who could then get busy sharpening axes and crosscut saws.

Another reason for stopping was that nearby some Cayuse squaws were gathering kamash roots. Kamash roots were an important source of fresh plant food, something everyone had longed for since before Fort Laramie.

Abby used three plugs of tobacco to secure almost ten pounds of roots. Before leaving to trade for the roots, she asked Jacob to start a fire and get some water boiling. Upon returning she placed about a third of the roots in the water. When they were soft she mashed them down on a plate and took them over to Sarah.

"This is good food that Sarah won't have to chew," Abby said as she held out the plate for Phil. "If she's awake I can give it to her."

"She wakes up now and then. If she's sleeping, then just wake her. She hasn't eaten anything in two days."

Abby crawled into the back of Phil's wagon and woke Sarah. Sadly, she was still unable to eat. Her mind drifted in and out of conscious thought as she tried to speak. Most of what she said was unintelligible, except for one phrase: "Here my journey ends."

This she said several times against Abby's protests. Sarah could not hear as she drifted back into sleep without eating. Abby stayed with her for another hour, then gave the dish of roots to Phil.

"If she wakes up, she might want this."

"I'll be sure to give it to her," said Phil. "Thank you again for your kindness, Miss Meacham. You are one of Sarah's very best friends."

Abby forced a smile, then walked back to her kitchen. There were chores to do.

Later that evening as she sat writing in her diary, and Jacob smoking his pipe, Hattie came by to inform everyone that Sarah had died.

"My master asked me to pass the word to Miss Meacham."

"Thank you, Hattie," said Jacob.

Abby could not speak. Her eyes swelled up, and tears began to draw lines through the dirt on her face. She set her diary down, pulled her knees up, and buried her face in her dress for a good cry. Sarah had been a close friend since those first days at Independence. She was always supportive and quick to come to Abby's defense. She would be missed.

Marcus set the funeral for the next morning, while Nat Sitton, Tom Brown, and John Cox set about digging another grave—a task they were all too familiar with. They located the grave at the foot of the trail that the column would use to leave the valley. It was a beautiful spot and would stand as a marker for other travelers through the valley. With a good headboard, Sarah Rubey would not be forgotten.

Jim Athey made the headboard from a plank Phil tore off the side of his wagon. There was no time to make a coffin, so several men wrapped Sarah in a blanket. Before completing the headboard, Jim stopped by to see if Abby had a verse.

"Yes, Jim, I do," Abby said, "but give me a few minutes to finish it. I'll bring it over to your wagon."

"No hurry, take your time. We've got all night."

"Verse," Abby thought, "I need to write a verse." Her grief over the loss of Sarah had consumed all her attention. She had not given any thought to a verse.

"Here my journey ends," she whispered. "Those were Sarah's last words to me. Something with that would be appropriate." Another hour passed before the verse was ready.

Gone she has left us, her spirit has fled,
Her body now slumbers along with the dead.
She was sweet and kind, always willing to lend,
Now here in these mountains, her journey ends.

Abby delivered the verse to Jim, then returned to the Western

Passage without stopping to see Phil. There were already enough people with him and his two children. He certainly didn't need to see another sobbing woman.

Early the next morning, Sunday, October 1, the Oregon Emigrating Company buried Sarah Rubey. Reverend Whitman said a few words of kindness to Phil and the attendees, keeping the sermon short. He needed to hurry along to Tshimakain, and the rest of the column needed to start their long climb through timbered mountains to the Waiilatpu Mission. Nat Sitton and Tom Brown lowered Sarah's blanket-wrapped body into the grave as people dispersed back to their wagons to complete preparations for the day's march. By the time the column moved out, Nat, Tom, and John had the grave filled in and the headboard seated. Abby glanced back several times as she started to climb out of the valley. Soon Sarah's grave was out of sight.

Whitman left before the column started. The advance guard now had a new member and guide, the Cayuse Indian named Stickus. Without hesitation, Stickus boldly pointed out the direction to travel. His certainty helped assure the platoon leaders, although with or without confidence, they had no choice but to follow. Stickus was the only man who knew the way through the mountains. Unfounded prejudices had to be cast aside, since the migration would now succeed or perish depending on the knowledge of this Indian. Over four months of travel and numerous encounters with Western Indians had taught these pilgrims the value of knowledge of the land and its resources. Now, Stickus possessed the wisdom needed for their survival.

Stickus directed the column up into some sparse timber, where a group of young men began clearing brush and downed logs from in front of the lead wagons. Stickus's knowledge of the mountains was unerring. Whenever possible, he had the wagons traverse natural openings in the forest where there were few obstacles. He seldom looked for an alternate route. The advance guard quickly learned to trust Stickus implicitly, never questioning his directions. Wherever he told them to go, they would go. He was familiar with the land and knew exactly the best route for the heavy wagons.

At several points the timber grew too thick for wagons to penetrate. Platoon leaders quickly assembled the prearranged felling teams of forty men and placed Jim Nesmith in charge. It was slow going, with the column coming to a halt for an hour, then moving forward a quarter-mile before halting again as fellers continued their task. The men felled and bucked just enough timber to squeeze a wagon through.

Felling timber was difficult, dangerous work. Felled trees needed to be bucked into lengths short enough to drag out of the way. Most of the horses were too weak to pull a heavy load, so bucked lengths had to be less than eight feet.

The division between workers and shirkers was again clearly evident. Those individuals unwilling to contribute to the effort had ready-made excuses to avoid the work. These ranged from complaints of a sore back, or a bum knee, to a skittish wagon team that only they could handle. Other individuals, like Nat Sitton and Adam Matheny, willingly volunteered their services. Even Jacob, who could be excused due to his age, volunteered for the day. Phil Rubey, who could also easily be excused, came forward with an axe, offering his services. Jim Nesmith gladly accepted the offer, for hard work was a good healer.

It was an exhausting, slow day, with the column advancing twelve miles into the timbered regions of the Blue Mountains. Late in the day they came to a deep ravine that afforded enough open space to accommodate their night's camp. The advance guard ordered a halt for the day, and none too soon for the exhausted fellers. A nearby creek provided water for the stock, while forage was marginal and grew only where sunlight could penetrate the forest canopy.

After dinner that evening, Abby sat on her washtub with diary in hand, looking at the wagons and stock scattered throughout the timber. The unusual scene was unlike any previous camp.

"Tonight our company is scattered about this beautiful forest," she wrote. *"This is the first time that trees have prevented the formation of wagon corrals. I think we are over 1,500 miles from Independence, but still a long ways from the Wallamet Valley. Jacob has tied our stock to nearby trees, but the grass is too thin for them to get full stomachs. Some of the brush is edible,*

but not much. There will be even less food for animals when the Cow Column gets up here, but they won't have to build a road so they'll be able to travel faster.

"From here I can see pine, spruce, hemlock, fir, and tamarack as major trees of this forest, along with several species of berry bushes. The warmth of the campfire feels good under this cool forest canopy. We need the light it provides, since darkness comes on earlier than usual due to overhead trees. Tomorrow will be another slow day, but in a few days (maybe a week) we should be out of these mountains and into an area where our animals can get fed."

With the approach of night, Abby put her diary away and crawled into her wagon bed, covering up with two blankets against the cool mountain air. Jacob was already in his buffalo robe, next to the fire. The tiring day ended quietly with people knowing that tomorrow would be just as difficult.

The next morning, Monday, October 2, the column moved an additional five miles, penetrating deeper and deeper into the heavily timbered Blue Mountains before stopping for a nooner. During the stop, Stickus's Christian conversion was clearly evident through his verbal prayers before eating. He could not speak a word of English, so the Cayuse versions of traditional Christian prayers presented a curious addition to the column's nooner. The scattered wagons stretched for over a half-mile, with timber and distance preventing some family clans from getting together. After an hour of rest, the fellers were back at work under the authority of Jim Nesmith and the guidance of Stickus.

Nesmith communicated with Stickus through pantomime, except when Jacob was nearby and sign language could be used. After another seven miles the column set up their camp near a small mountain stream with clear, cold water. Stickus continued to camp by himself, away from the main body. It wasn't that he was unfriendly, rather he was uncomfortable. Cayuse society was very different from the ways of the Americans, and camping separately was a wise precaution to avoid potential confrontation.

While families and single men prepared their dinners that evening, Jim Nesmith paid Stickus a visit to express his appreciation. As was the custom with Cayuse, Stickus offered Jim a large piece of meat from his spit. It was tough, yet tasty. When Jim pointed to the meat in an attempt to discern where it came from, Stickus made a sign over his head that Jim interpreted as elk antlers. Jim nodded his appreciation and continued to eat. Without an ability to communicate, there was no need to stay after finishing the meal. Jim thanked Stickus as best he could, then started back toward the Oteys' wagon. He hadn't gone twenty feet when he noticed part of a mule carcass behind some brush. It was suddenly evident that Stickus had been signing mule ears, not elk antlers. The mule had been sacrificed for food by one of the emigrants, and Stickus had been given the head and neck for his services as guide.

Tonight teamsters were either careless or too tired to hobble or secure many of the stock. With thick timber surrounding their camp, men thought that the animals could not wander far. Camping within this forested region provided a feeling of security, since there was less exposure to weather and other potential dangers.

Abby took a loaf of bread over to Phil Rubey, then sat with him awhile along with Cyrene Cary and Fred Prigg. When she returned, Jacob had already bedded down for the night using several fir boughs as a mattress. After settling into her wagon she lit a candle, wrote a few paragraphs, then retired.

On Tuesday morning, October 3, people had difficulty locating about a hundred head of working stock. They had not wandered far, but had bedded down in dense thickets of brush. They were too weak to want to rise when teamsters began calling, so each animal had to be physically found and brought back for yoking. It was after ten o'clock by the time men had yoked and chained the last team. Although the two-hour delay grated on the nerves of those people tired of the journey and yearning only for a warm hearth on a Wallamet Valley farm, it did not present a serious problem. Fellers had cleared a stretch of road, so the wagons were able to quickly catch up.

Today proved to be more difficult than any before. The timber remained thick, so platoon leaders called for additional volunteers. Jim Nesmith took whomever he could get, for volunteers were not plentiful. Excuses continued as the shirkers did what they could to avoid being placed on work detail. When unable to find an adequate excuse, their contributions to the felling teams were minimal. They took frequent breaks and often went back to move their wagon forward, even though other members of their family could do that job. It was a frustrating day for Jim as he continued to direct the building of a road where Stickus indicated.

The discontent created by a lack of ready volunteers was disquieting to many women, especially Abby. Jacob was in the lead felling team, so she handled the wagon by herself. It was rough going through the broken terrain and brushed-out road. Stumps were cut low enough to pass over, but were too high to run a wheel over. Managing an ox team and heavy wagon was difficult work for every teamster. Abby's quirt usually sufficed, but at times she had to put her shoulder into the side of an ox to push and urge the yoked team sideways. The cut road was narrow, sometimes yielding only enough room for the wagon. Several times the oxen needed to be lined up and then urged through these narrow passages with a sharp quirt and hardy yells.

The weather since leaving the Grande Ronde Valley had been warm and clear during the day, with cool, even cold nights. Without such good weather, cutting a road through the forest would be considerably more difficult. The wagons were not getting stuck in mud, and work animals were not slipping. With all things considered, cutting and building a road through the mountains could have been more tedious, frustrating, and dangerous.

The column spent the majority of the day crossing a heavily timbered, steep ravine. Timber fellers had to cut a road down the side of the ravine in a zigzag pattern, constructing a number of switchbacks. Then they had to climb up the other side in a similar zigzag fashion. Bucked logs had to be dragged clear of the road rather than simply rolled downhill. Rolling them downhill would again put them in the way. By four o'clock in the afternoon the column had advanced only three miles from last night's camp. All wagons and stock had made it to the other side of the ravine so, out of pure exhaustion, the platoon leaders called a halt to the day's march. The three-mile advance had been the slowest day since leaving Independence!

Rough terrain took its toll on a number of wagons during the day. Several hounds broke, each one requiring two hours to repair. After stopping for the day, fellers and other men began to effect repairs to their damaged or crippled wagons. People set up their kitchens wherever their wagon happened to be when the leaders called for a halt. Family clans and friends simply joined up at a common kitchen for the evening meal.

"Stickus says we'll have one more day up here," Jacob said as he sat down with smoked salmon and the last of Abby's cornbread. "Looks like the timber might thin out. We'll still have some cutting to do."

"How much farther to Waiilatpu? Did he tell you that?"

"Day after tomorrow. Stickus's village is up ahead, and from there one can go to either the Waiilatpu Mission or Fort Walla Walla. The mission will probably add twenty miles."

"So we'll split up again? I mean the Light Column."

"No doubt. People low on supplies may choose to go directly to the fort. These pilgrims will do anything to shorten the trip."

"Risking running out of food is foolish, especially for people with families. What are they going to do for their children, let them go hungry?"

"Maybe, we'll see. How about you, Abby, Fort Walla Walla or the mission?"

"The mission. We can use fresh garden food. My wagon is still in good shape, and I want to meet Mrs. Whitman."

"Narcissa should be there, alright. I don't mind seeing her myself. She was a pretty one, yes ma'am, that she was."

Abby looked over at Jacob. "You knew her?"

"Back in '36, she and Marcus came out with the Rendezvous pack train. Some of us trappers hadn't seen a white woman in ten years, so she caused quite a commotion. After that summer fair, they went on to the Columbia to start a mission. I don't think they were too impressed with all of us Godless trappers, so they were probably glad to get out of there."

Abby smiled at Jacob's reminisce, then handed him another pound of salmon.

"If we can get some pumpkin, I've still got enough flour and sugar left to make a pie."

"You've pretty near spoiled me with your cooking, Abby. I must admit, I'll miss your good meals after we get to Oregon City."

"You still haven't decided what you're going to do when we arrive, and I still don't know where I'll be teaching."

"It'll work out. By being the first group of settlers and knowing what folks will need, we can get set up to do business with future settlers. I'm still thinking about the merchandising business. There should be a high demand for farm and household goods for a number of years."

"If you put your mind to it, then I'm sure you'll be successful. Hard work always pays off."

"How much coffee you got left?"

"I was going to roast the last of those beans tomorrow night. I should have bought a few more pounds—we'll never make it to the Wallamet Valley with what we've got left."

"You've still got flour and beans. With buffalo and salmon, you did alright. You'll have food left when you get to Oregon City."

"That might come in handy for the coming winter. I won't sell the wagon till I'm settled. Maybe I'll hang onto the stock till then too. They'll be fatter and stronger next summer and should bring a better price."

"You might get paid in barter if money's scarce, which I suspect it will be."

"You mean trade for food?"

"Could be. Maybe trade for land, too, don't know."

"Can't be land, land's free!"

"Before they form a provisional government, you might consider staking a claim. A new government might ban women from owning land. It would be wise to stake out 640 acres right away. That's what I say. If you're already the owner, then they'll have no choice but to accept you."

"I hadn't thought of that," Abby said as she took a sip of tea. "I'll do that. I'll claim 640 acres this winter!"

A few moments passed in silence, as often happened at the evening meal. It was a time to rest, a time to reflect, and a time to plan.

"You seen Becky Stewart's baby lately?" Jacob began to light his pipe.

"Not since the Powder River Valley."

"I'm afraid that little girl's not going to make it—she's lost all her baby fat. Poor Becky, she's tried hard to keep that baby alive—been carrying it every day since it was born. I suspect we'll be digging another grave in a day or so." Jacob's words were all too true. The little infant who had given new life and happiness to the trail-weary emigrants would soon become another sad footnote in the many diaries.

A cool wind blew through the forest this evening, cool enough for people to break out their warm winter clothes. Wagons, campfires, and stock lay scattered throughout the timber, presenting a peaceful scene that belied the labor of the day. To the relief of many, darkness, then sleep came early.

On the next morning, Wednesday, October 4, people of the Light Column woke to a barrage of cold rain, some hail, and some snow. With miserable, freezing weather, continuing the arduous task of cutting a road through the mountains was not a pleasant prospect.

The felling teams moved out as soon as there was enough light to see the tops of the trees. As bad as the weather was, it could only get worse at this time of the year. The emigrants' survival depended on getting out of these mountains as quickly as possible. Even with this need to move forward, most felling teams were missing one or two members, as shirkers stayed back as long as possible. In all, there remained no more than forty men engaged in felling and bucking at any one time.

The change in weather came as both an unpleasant surprise and a new incentive to finish the road and get out of the mountains. Deep snow would not be far behind, and with that came certain death.

The entire migration now teetered on the edge of winter, crossing the Blue Mountains just in time.

Jesse's Cow Column was catching up fast. Choosing not to spend an extra day at the final Snake River site, and with a road already blazed, their journey through the Blue Mountains was considerably easier. Yesterday's three-mile day had slowed the Light Column to where Jesse was now only one day behind. Some of the platoon leaders of the Light Column entertained the idea that Jesse had intentionally fallen behind at Fort Boise. By doing so, the hard work of road building through the mountains would be done by the time his column arrived. It was an idle thought that no one could prove.

The timber today thinned out, and the column started losing elevation in a twelve-mile advance before striking the Umatilla River. During the last three miles, the wagons descended from the mountains along a grass-covered ridge, precariously snaking their way down to flat ground. On either side of this ridge, the land dropped off in slopes too steep to negotiate. Should this singular ridge end in a similar vertical drop, they would have to backtrack and find another route down from the mountains.

Stickus's knowledge of the terrain remained unerring. The ridge brought the column down to the Umatilla River in a gradual and safe descent. Stickus turned the company downriver for another mile before the platoon leaders ordered a halt for the day. They were now at the base of the last mountain and out of the timber. Before them stretched a vast grassland of undulating hills, unbroken by a single tree. The only wood to be found grew along the banks of the Umatilla River. There was good forage for the stock, clear, cold water from the river, and just as important, warm weather. They had made it through the mountains before the first winter snows!

Two miles farther downriver lay Stickus's village. After the caravan halted, Stickus continued on to his village, returning in two hours with half the population in tow. Although many of the squaws brought fresh vegetables to trade for clothing, they were all there to verify the incredible story told by Stickus. His story of hundreds of white people with strange wagons, strange livestock, and people who had black skin could not possibly be true! Such exaggerations could not be believed, they had to be seen. The people of this Cayuse village were just as stunned as Stickus had been back in the Grande Ronde Valley. Those who had not believed Stickus stared, astonished at the spectacle before them. It was just as Stickus had described. He was also correct in his description that these alien people were rich with clothes and trade goods. After twenty minutes of greetings and gawkings, trading circles formed and the bartering began.

The Indians rode and carried their trade goods on horses that many of the emigrants described as some of the finest-looking animals they had ever seen. These horses were tall, strong, well fed, and healthy. None among the hundreds of emigrant horses could compare. Men immediately inquired about trading for horses, to which the Cayuse consented—but not these horses. Out on the prairie were several thousand additional horses of equal stature, all belonging to this single Cayuse village. One of the lesser chiefs ordered a young brave to bring in a number of horses for trading.

In an hour the brave returned with three herders and about fifty horses. It took two emigrant horses to secure one of the Cayuse horses, which was a fair trade, considering the condition of emigrant horses. After a year of recuperating with the Cayuse herds, the emigrant horses would be as healthy as their Indian counterparts. Today's trading would increase the tribe's wealth of good horses. Such was the nature of the situation. A dead horse was of no use to anyone, and many of these animals would soon be dead if forced to continue. The Oregon Emigrating Company still had 250 miles to go. Trading for strong healthy horses was simply common sense. Other working stock, namely oxen, would have to continue as best they could.

Trading continued until the Indians ran out of goods. The primary items accepted in trade were clothes. People without trade shirts simply traded their old, worn-out clothes. In return they received corn, peas, squash, and a type of potato. For tonight's dinner, the people of the Light Column would feast on food they had not tasted for months.

Abby used two trade shirts to secure twenty ears of corn, about a half-gallon of unshucked peas, and a gallon of potatoes. The squaws valued shirts and other clothing, since tobacco and gewgaw had little practical use. However, a few plugs of tobacco and a handful of beads helped to complete the deal.

"I'll boil half these peas tonight and the rest tomorrow," Abby said as she prepared her kitchen. "We should be at Waiilatpu after that, where we can get more vegetables."

"We'll be encountering Indians from here on," said Jacob. "You might not need much more of that food you're hauling, so I'd say it would be wise to conserve as much as you can for this coming winter."

"I will. Vegetables and fish from here on!"

"The road splits just across the river from Stickus's village. While you were trading, I rode down both trails for a piece. They look fairly firm and can manage a wagon. Both are well worn and wide enough that we shouldn't have any trouble getting wagons down either of them."

"I feel like we're getting back to civilization. First we'll get to the mission, where we can trade for more food, then Fort Walla Walla, where people can make repairs—but they can do that at the mission too! Then we'll get to the mission at Wascopam, then Fort Vancouver, and finally Oregon City. Since we'll be among Indians all the way, we can always trade for more salmon. It's not the same civilization as back in the United States—but this is a Western civilization, so I never expected it to be the same."

Jacob was leaning over the campfire, looking at the boiling peas as Abby continued to talk. She was visibly pleased with their good fortune. They had made it through the Blue Mountains, and now, on the very first night, they were enjoying fresh vegetables!

"This will probably be our last night as an organized migration," said Jacob. "We'll split up in the morning with some going direct to Fort Walla Walla and others to the mission. Everyone will be on their own from here on."

"So this is the end of the Oregon Emigrating Company?"

"That it is. We don't need a guide anymore, or anyone else giving orders. That should come as a great relief to these ornery farmers."

"Do you think we'll have any trouble? I mean what about road building? There's a number of us who want to get our wagons through to the Wallamet Valley."

"Well, I don't know for sure, but I suspect there's already some type of road between Fort Walla Walla and Wascopam. Seems like that would have happened by now, and I know there's a good road between the Waiilatpu Mission and Fort Walla Walla. Whitman himself told me."

Abby continued stirring the peas and rotating the corn that was heating alongside the fire.

"We're going to make it Jacob!" She looked over at him as he sat down near the fire to light his pipe. "We're going to make it just like I said we would back in Independence." Abby was smiling broadly now, like someone who had just won a great contest.

"That we are, and I don't mind telling you that I had my doubts. Back when people were racing their teams and throwing out good food before we ever reached the Platte, well, I figured those pilgrims would never make it."

"I thought some would turn back."

"Some did. At least they turned south to Taos."

"They could have made it just like the rest of us. They had more than enough food."

"That they did, but it takes more than that. They didn't have the will power—not enough sand. I don't know why anyone would start for Oregon with a wagon and family without being prepared for the worst."

"Hardships?"

"All of that. Emigrants next year will have it a lot easier, and each year after that until the road we blazed is no hardship at all. Before long, there'll probably be ferries across the major rivers and a whole string of supply stations stocked with goods. Going to Oregon shouldn't be any trouble at all."

Abby agreed while continuing to stir the peas. Having vegetables to cook was really quite exciting!

Across the compound several young Cayuse Indians were taunting the ox teams belonging to Lew Cooper. These animals were entirely new to the Cayuse people, as were the strange white-topped wagons.

Taunting the teams and having them pull a wagon provided great entertainment for the Indian boys. Abby, Jacob, and most everyone else had been ignoring the activity, attributing it to the noise of children at play. Folks started to take notice when the ruckus grew louder as the teenagers began to make the teams race around in a circle.

Bill McDaniel grabbed his pistol and came running to help, since Lew was off checking which road to take in the morning. As Bill came up, the fore axletree of Cooper's wagon broke, causing it to nearly upset. Bill raised his pistol and shot wildly, wounding one of the young boys in the mouth. With the sound of the shot, Jacob was up and running toward Lew's crippled wagon, rifle in had. Abby watched in disbelief as her peaceful world of fresh vegetables and a successful journey quickly shattered.

Other people came running too. When Jacob arrived, the Indian boy was on the ground holding his bloody mouth while two other men tended to his wound. The second Indian boy had disappeared, no doubt running back to his village. The wound was superficial, causing no permanent damage. The men bandaged it, then asked the chief to make his people behave before there was more trouble. The chief showed open embarrassment at the boys' behavior, claiming they would be punished severely. The whole incident was over within a half-hour, with people returning to their camps and the Indians packing up their new riches (clothes) and heading back to their village. The chief asked if they could come back in the morning for more trading, but was rebuffed due to the wagon incident. Dave Lenox explained that they would be leaving early and heading to Fort Walla Walla or the mission. He thanked the chiefs for their kindness and good trading, then bid them farewell.

The emigrants returned from the incident and settled down for a quiet evening in camp. When Jacob got back, dinner was ready. He and Abby sat down to eat and recapture the peaceful solitude of only an hour ago.

Due to the split in the road, people of the Light Column knew it would be their last night together. Tonight's camp was busier than usual as people moved between kitchens, visiting friends and talking about their good fortune of getting through to Oregon. It was an evening not unlike those first evenings near Independence, when everyone talked of their hopes and dreams of going to Oregon. Somehow, the deaths and difficulties of the last few months were now overshadowed by the triumph of success. Others were more cautious about euphoric feelings of victory. They were still 250 miles from the Wallamet Valley, and an unforgiving Columbia River was yet to come.

Several men helped Lew Cooper convert his wagon to a cart for the final push. Some thought he might be able to get a new axle at Fort Walla Walla. Most likely though, it would have to be made from scratch. Lew had been planning on going to Waiilatpu, but this incident changed his mind. The mission was twenty miles out of the way. With only a cart, he would have to take his chances in obtaining food at the fort or along the river from local Indians.

Unknown to these Indians was the presence of another emigrant, Alex Zachary. Zachary had been following the Light Column at a comfortable distance ever since leaving Fort Boise. His banishment from the Light Column allowed him to follow their road through the mountains while not contributing any labor to its construction. To avoid contact with the column tonight, Alex set up his camp where the trail down from the Blue Mountains first intersected the Umatilla River. The one-mile distance provided a comfortable margin to avoid further conflicts. His punishment of being banned from the Oregon Emigrating Company had little affect on his advancement to Oregon, and was now working to his advantage. Zachary had made it through the mountains in safety, and without having to do any of the work of road building!

Fires were kept burning a little longer that evening as people munched on vegetables and visited with friends. They knew they would still come together at various points before reaching Oregon City, yet theirs was a bittersweet farewell as the company began to break up for good. Those who suffer difficult times together share an undefined force that binds them in a lifelong friendship. These emigrants had started out as strangers, and had become friends, foes, and then friends again along the trail. They would build their farms in the Wallamet Valley and form the first provisional government for the new territory of Oregon. There was a great deal of empire building to do, and their binding friendships would serve them well for the rest of their lives.

On Thursday morning, October 5, people did not waste time waiting for one another. As soon as a wagon was ready, its teamster gave the command and it was off, either northwest to Fort Walla Walla, or northeast to Waiilatpu. The one major delay related to the stock. Overnight a number of emigrant horses had wandered in amongst the Cayuse herds. Teamsters now had to locate and separate their animals from the herd. It was easy to spot an emigrant horse for they were scrawny and weak with their entire rib cages visible; however, getting them away from their new-found friends proved to be quite a challenge. With help from the Cayuse herders they were able to round up all stray animals by ten o'clock. Shortly before noon the last wagon of the Light Column was on its way.

Abby and Jacob were moving by eight o'clock, heading toward the Cayuse village, where the road split. The village, consisting of numerous small lodges, controlled the only location on the Umatilla River that afforded easy access for crossing. Both roads intersected at this spot. Getting across the river at this point was not difficult, but did consume valuable time. By noon they were on the other side and up on high ground, moving toward the Waiilatpu Mission.

Jacob was right. This well-worn road was as easy to travel as any road back in Missouri. After nooning on cold corn, they were on their way in less than a half-hour. Without a leader there was no need to wait for the order to march. As soon as they finished eating, Abby quickly cleaned up her noon kitchen, stowed each item, and grabbed her quirt. The weather was good, and with luck, they could reduce the distance to Waiilatpu by half before stopping for the night.

Wagons going to Waiilatpu stretched for over five miles as each family moved at their own pace. Stickus chose to follow the group to Waiilatpu. Over the course of the afternoon he came up and rode alongside each wagon on the road. After their journey through the Blue Mountains, he considered everyone in the migration as a new friend and ally. His mission, given to him by Reverend Whitman back in the Grande Ronde Valley, was to lead the emigrants to Waiilatpu. Therefore, even though he was no longer needed, he was not about to abandon his post. He would see these people through to Waiilatpu no matter what.

By evening they had traveled a total of eight miles from the Umatilla crossing. Abby directed her lead team to an area of flat ground near a large cottonwood growing alongside a creek, about one hundred yards from the road. Like a seasoned teamster, she positioned the wagon with ease in an area that would allow her to set up her kitchen and have easy access to water. Jacob unhitched the team and, after watering them downstream, hobbled them out on the prairie. Conditions were now reminiscent of the early weeks back along the Platte. Grass and water were plentiful, and the road was fairly reasonable. The one big difference was food. Abby again prepared a meal of peas, corn, and potatoes. There was enough to feed four people, yet she and Jacob ate it all.

The evening passed quickly, with Abby catching up on diary entries of the last three days. She noted the importance of encountering the Cayuse village just when they needed food and help, along with the enormous life-saving help provided by Stickus in guiding the migration through the Blue Mountains.

"With future emigrants, the west side of the Blue Mountains would be a good place to organize a supply station," she wrote. *"By this point in the journey people need virtually everything from clothes and food to strong working stock. One could make a good living selling supplies to future emigrants along the trail!"*

Campfires could be seen glowing in the distance as members of the Light Column stretched across several miles of prairie. They would come together at the mission and other points between here and Oregon City—but for the most part, folks were now on their own.

The Cayuse village along the Umatilla was not without visitors for long. That afternoon Jesse's Cow Column had arrived with their wagons and over a thousand head of cattle. Once again the Cayuse engaged in trading food for clothes. Though this first migration would have a lasting effect on their culture that they could never have imagined, trading with these rich Americans now was an event of great importance. In only two days the village vastly increased its wealth of material goods and horses.

At noon on Friday, October 6, Abby and Jacob arrived at the Whitmans' Waiilatpu Mission. It was a rainy, misty day, so the sight of adobe buildings lifted everyone's spirits. The mission overlooked the Walla Walla River and a wide-open prairie of rolling hills covered with thick grass. Several buildings housed supplies, workers, and equipment, and one small building served as a gristmill. The Whitmans lived in a T-shaped adobe structure in the center of the compound. All quarters were comfortably furnished and well equipped with tools and supplies provided by the Hudson Bay Company. On a nearby hill stood a small cemetery with a large cross, erected so travelers could see it from a great distance. The mission garden was immense, full of corn, squash, potatoes, pumpkins, peas, beans, and a variety of other vegetables. Nearby were several farms belonging to former employees of the Hudson Bay Company.

Three miles from Waiilatpu the main road curved west to Fort Walla Walla. As directed by Stickus, Abby and the other mission-bound teamsters took the spur that led to the Waiilatpu Mission. Retired trappers and traders located their primitive farms along this road. These were the first farms anyone had seen since passing the Shawnee farms west of Independence. They reminded everyone of homes left back in the United States. Surely, this was civilization. After a journey of over two thousand miles, they were finally coming out of the wilderness!

When people of the Light Column began arriving, workers in the mission garden came over to greet the new visitors. Reverend Whitman had informed his chief overseer, a William Geiger, that a migration of almost one thousand souls would soon be arriving. In preparation, mission workers harvested ripened vegetables and readied them for sale to the needy travelers. Marcus had promised the availability of food, and he was right. What he failed to mention were the high prices. A sign hung on the main storehouse:

Beef	*10 cents /pound*
Pork	*15 cents /pound*
Potatoes	*40 cents /bushel*
Unbolted flour	*7 cents /pound*
Wheat	*$1.00 /bushel*
Squash	*40 cents /bushel*
Corn	*25 cents /bushel*
Pumpkin	*5 cents /pound*
Peas	*10 cents /pound*
String beans	*10 cents /pound*
Beets	*20 cents /pound*

These prices were about four times the going prices back in Missouri—a point that many of the farmers did not hesitate to tell Mr. Geiger. Raw wheat was of little value unless someone was packing a gristmill, and that was unlikely.

The farmers soon learned that Mrs. Eells's baby was doing fine and that Reverend Whitman was away on business at the Lapwai Mission, about 150 miles east of here at the confluence of the Lapwai and Clearwater Rivers. The heads of that mission, Henry Spalding and his wife Eliza, had accompanied Marcus and Narcissa when they had first ventured into Oregon Country back in 1836. Eliza and Narcissa had the distinction of being the first white women to travel into the American West. Currently, and much to the disappointment of Jacob and Abby, Narcissa was visiting the mission at Wascopam.

William Geiger was in charge of all operations while the Whitmans were away, and he had no intention of lowering the prices set by Marcus. Several men vocalized their dissatisfaction, saying that had they been aware of Whitman's "cut-throat prices" they would not have come twenty miles out of their way. Instead, they would have gone directly to Fort Walla Walla. Anger and complaints had no affect on Geiger. If the hungry travelers wanted food, they would have to pay.

Along with food, the mission had livestock. Geiger encouraged the teamsters to swap their worn-out animals for fresh ones—an offer that many could not refuse. Sarah Jane Hill traded two worn and tired cows for one Spanish steer. The cows no longer gave milk, and the healthy steer had more usable meat than both cows combined. Dave Lenox traded five of his emaciated oxen for two Spanish steers. Like those traded at the Cayuse village, the weakened stock would be given free range to recruit their strength. With the arrival of more emigrants next fall, these animals would be strong and healthy enough to be traded again. With a steady stream of fall emigrants, the mission could double or triple its herd every year.

Abby was able to get all the food she and Jacob needed by using United States currency rather than trade goods. Although Geiger and other British patriots were long-time enemies of the Americans, residents of the Waiilatpu Mission and surrounding farms could not pass up an opportunity to obtain actual currency.

Rather than giving the mission her business, Abby made her purchases from a local farmer by the name of Mr. Brewer. He offered the same prices as the mission, but his assortment and quality of vegetables were considerably better. He even offered to help carry the peas, beans, squash, beets, and turnips back to the wagon. After thanking him, Abby returned to the mission to buy a bushel of potatoes and a peck of corn, items that Mr. Brewer did not have. By four o'clock she was restocked and ready to move down the road toward Fort Walla Walla.

The purpose of stopping at Waiilatpu was to obtain garden food and to meet Narcissa. With Narcissa at Wascopam, there was no need to delay. Other emigrants were already at Fort Walla Walla, deciding how to continue their journey—by land or by river. The sooner Abby and Jacob could get to the fort, then the better their chances of hooking up with one of the small caravans going overland. Jim Nesmith and the Oteys, along with several other families, were also ready to move a few miles down the road before stopping for the night.

The road to Fort Walla Walla followed the Walla Walla River, which afforded clear, cold water and wood along its banks. After four miles, Abby picked out a spot near another large cottonwood for the night's camp. No sooner had she set up her kitchen than the sky cleared, with the sun coming out just in time to provide a beautiful sunset. Tonight she cooked up another meal of corn, this time with squash and beets. After dinner she roasted the last of the coffee beans. Crossing the Blue Mountains had been too exhausting to bother with roasting them earlier.

Later that evening, while Abby was stowing some of her kitchen gear along with the coffee grinder, Nat Sitton rode in with news that Becky Stewart's baby girl had died. Becky was still back at the mission, so the funeral would be tomorrow morning.

"Are they going to bury her at the mission cemetery?" asked Jacob.

"Probably, don't see why not," said Nat.

"Methodists can be mighty particular about who gets buried in their cemeteries. What religion was Becky?"

"I think she might be Methodist," said Abby. "Dave Lenox would know. He's camped about a quarter mile ahead."

"They have to bury the poor infant somewhere," said Nat. "I'm passing down the line letting everyone know. If you want to attend the services, they'll be tomorrow morning back at the mission."

"Thank you, Nat," said Abby, "but I think we'll continue to the fort. There's nothing we can do or say, and I suspect I'll be seeing Becky along the way—maybe at Wascopam. I can talk to her then."

"As you wish, ma'am. I'll be going now." Nat tipped his hat and continued down the Walla Walla River toward the next camp.

"Poor Becky," Abby said as she watched him ride away. "I know just how she feels."

"You going to write another verse?" asked Jacob.

"No. No, I don't think so. That little girl only lived a couple months and was sick every day. Becky won't have any happy memories from that baby. It's best forgotten."

That evening she made a note in her diary of the passing of Becky's baby, along with a description of the Waiilatpu Mission and the food they had acquired. The happiness of the day had been overshadowed by the death of a baby, so a description of the country could wait for another evening. For now, it was time to sleep.

On Saturday morning they continued down the road and Walla Walla River toward the fort. Back at Waiilatpu, mission workers buried Becky's baby in the cemetery on top of the hill. Only immediate family and friends attended the short service. By eight o'clock it was over and wagons were rolling away from the mission, down the Walla Walla River toward the Columbia.

With everyone on their own, folks traveled at their leisure. There was no longer any concern for getting caught in snow, and the prospects of being able to float the remaining distance helped to slow some people's conviction for speed. With a lack of leadership, it became evident to the more discerning that many never would have survived had it not been for the military discipline of the Oregon Emigrating Company. They all owed their success and lives to this makeshift trail government, yet, many would probably live out their days never realizing the true basis of their success. They would dwell on memories of the hardships, quarrels, and splintered columns of the last five months.

Abby and Jacob continued down the Walla Walla River road until three o'clock, when they arrived at a good place to stop for the night. Communication with a local Indian indicated that the fort was only a few hours ahead. Tomorrow would be soon enough. Abby pulled her wagon under some trees and set up her kitchen.

As soon as Jacob had the stock watered and hobbled for the night, a group of Indians rode in from the fort for purposes of trading. They carried smoked salmon, kamash roots, cured skins of salmon, plus rabbit, mink, and weasel skins.

Abby traded a single plug of tobacco for some kamash roots, then thanked the Indian in sign. This root was the same food she had acquired from the Cayuse squaws back in the Grande Ronde Valley. It was small and oval with a dark color and sweet taste—almost like a sweet potato or yam. Back at the mission she had heard that Indians made bread from it, although she had no idea how.

Not everyone chose to engage in trading. Jim Nesmith traded for a mink skin that he planned to make into mittens. He and Abby were the exceptions. Most of the emigrants were well stocked with food and had no need for additional salmon or other items. After the trading activities ended, the Cayuse set up their camp several hundred yards downstream. Then shortly after the dinner hour, three Cayuse returned, leading a milch cow belonging to Tom Keizur. Tom had not known she was missing. Trading had not gone well, and now the Indians wanted a shirt in exchange for returning the cow.

Tom reluctantly paid the requested fee and led the cow back to his wagon, rather than hobbling her out on the prairie. That's where he had left her earlier. He and several other men suspected that the Indians must have stolen her in retaliation for the poor trading session, however, nothing could be proven. Paying the Indians for returning the animal eliminated a potentially disagreeable situation.

The next morning, Sunday, October 8, Nesmith was missing a tin cup, and Lew Linebarger and Morton McCarver could not find their horses. After very little attempt to look for the items, emigrants immediately blamed the nearby Cayuse. With Fort Walla Walla just ahead, the explosive situation was defused when wagons got underway early. Abby and Jacob were on the road before eight o'clock and would arrive at Fort Walla Walla well before noon.

Fort Walla Walla was of adobe construction, and similar in appearance and makeup to Fort Boise and Fort Hall, the other Hudson Bay posts. Of the other two forts encountered, Fort Bridger and Fort Laramie, only Fort Bridger had a wooden palisade. With a dearth of timber, the usual Western construction material was adobe.

Fort Walla Walla overlooked the confluence of the Walla Walla River with the Columbia River. The surrounding country consisted of rolling hills devoid of trees, and prairie grass that was not as thick as the grass found back at Waiilatpu. The hills had a slight tinge of green from recent rains, but mostly the country presented a bleak and dreary backdrop. To the south were several high hills with rock outcroppings alongside the Columbia. Grazing at the foot of the hills were over a thousand head of livestock belonging to the Cow Column. While the others were at Waiilatpu, Jesse's Cow Column had made it to Fort Walla Walla.

As Abby and Jacob approached the fort, they spotted an additional group of men camped on the north side of the fort. Abby squinted to discern who it might be.

"Fremont!" she said aloud. "Where did he come from? He must have been behind the Cow Column!" She shuddered to think of the potential for trouble, since Fremont's brigade would be looking to buy food.

"That's Fremont!" Jacob called out from the other side of the wagon. "He must have been behind the Cow Column."

"I hope we don't have trouble like we did back at Fort Hall. We'll camp far enough away to avoid any conflict."

As Abby surveyed the scene before her, she noticed four empty, white-sheeted wagons lined up in single file next to the fort. Several had been converted to carts somewhere along the trail from Independence. She assumed that emigrants planning to continue downriver had sold their wagons to the fort in exchange for boats. The sight of the Cow Column boosted her spirits, for she'd be able to visit with ladies she had not seen since the dance at Fort Boise. The adobe fort, its immense garden, a few scattered farms, and the promise of familiar faces from the caravan beckoned her forward. But it was another sight that captured Abby's attention. There before her, wide and wild and dominating the entire scene, ran the Columbia River!

Here was the river Abby had heard so much about. The first stories of Oregon Country filtering back to Ohio had talked about this mighty and bountiful river. Now, it was no longer a word-of-mouth description. Here it was in all its glory. Abby brought her wagon to a halt and stood mesmerized by the river and the immense scene around her.

The Columbia River flowed from right to left in a southerly direction, cradling the fort and spelling home, security, and success. This was a river in a country so new that not even a drawing existed to help the imaginations of dreamers back in the United States. The channel and its valley stretched from horizon to horizon, the river's deep blue hue contrasting starkly with the surrounding barren, brown hills. The free-flowing water and majestic landscape were everything Abby had ever expected. *To see the beauty of this river,* she thought, *one must endure hardships a hundred times over, through a journey of many months and many miles.*

Only when Jacob rode up alongside her did she snap out of her trance and quirt the oxen forward. She smiled. Tonight she would set up her kitchen along the shores of the Columbia!

The twenty-four miles from Waiilatpu had shown poor soil and little opportunity for establishing a settlement. Some emigrants expressed their discouragement at this poor sample of Oregon. The country around the Columbia River did not look any better for farming. It was dry and barren, certainly not living up to the stories heard back in the United States. "Patience; be patient" came the word. The Wallamet Valley was still over two hundred miles away—surely, the land would improve!

Archibald McKinley, a long-time Hudson Bay employee, was the chief factor of Fort Walla Walla. Similar to his counterparts at Fort Boise and Fort Hall, he made all accommodations for the emigrants within his means. Unfortunately, he, too, was totally unprepared to address the needs of such a large migration. He informed the leaders that he had no food to sell, but could part with some tobacco. Back at Fort Hall such news would have been unacceptable. Things were different now, for almost everyone was well stocked with smoked salmon and fresh vegetables. Unlike at previous forts, several nearby farms of former company employees had food to sell, and the farmers hoped the emigrants would be willing to pay exorbitant prices.

Men accepted McKinley's situation and his need to preserve the food he had for the fort's employees. However, when they offered to pay for some tobacco, he balked. He did not want to sell tobacco on the Sabbath. After an exchange of a few heated words, McKinley conceded. Apparently it was better to sin than to anger the guests.

That afternoon Jim Nesmith, John Jackson, and the Oteys struck a deal with McKinley to trade their wagon for packhorses. They planned to go overland, but did not want to bother any longer with the difficulties of moving a wagon. McKinley informed everyone that there was a primitive road leading to the Wascopam Mission, and no road beyond that. Once at Wascopam, people with wagons would have to abandon them and continue down a pack trail, or build rafts and float their wagons down to Fort Vancouver. Between

Wascopam and Fort Vancouver were the impassable Cascade Falls. These, McKinley described, were a treacherous set of rapids interspersed with house-size boulders. To get around the rapids they would have to portage their possessions and line the rafts.

By trading their wagon at Fort Walla Walla, the Oteys could receive a fair price—something they might not be able to get at Wascopam. Additionally, the fort had strong, healthy horses to sell. Considering their situation, their desire to complete the journey successfully, and the opportunity to convert to pack animals, the Otey party chose the conservative approach. They would complete the journey without a wagon. With a gentleman's handshake, they left McKinley, promising to return the day after next with their empty wagon. In turn, McKinley would have five healthy packhorses ready for exchange.

Nesmith, Jackson, and the Oteys were not alone. A number of other people chose to sell their wagons and continue the journey using either pack animals or boats. The river at this point was wide, calm, and inviting—a temptation hard to ignore. After two thousand miles of struggling with a wagon through a roadless country, the idea of quietly floating the remaining two hundred miles was too much to resist. The fort only had a few boats, and they were sold to the first arrivals. Other families would have to build their own boats. Even with this inconvenience, for many, it still seemed like the best choice.

Abby had already made up her mind to take her wagon to the Wallamet Valley, so she was not swayed by activities at the fort or discouraging remarks from others. As she drove her wagon past the fort and down toward the wharf, she encountered Malinda Applegate.

"Malinda!" Abby called out, bringing her wagon to a halt and setting the brake. "It's wonderful to see you again. I hope you didn't have too much trouble crossing those mountains."

"None to speak of," said Malinda. "That road you people carved saved us a lot of time. Even so, I was glad we had these two carts rather than wagons." She motioned to the wagons that had been converted to carts.

"I assume you'll be going by land the rest of the way."

"No ma'am!" she replied sternly. "The drovers plan to take the herds overland, along with a few other people who have wagons.

We're floating the rest of the way. Jesse and Lindsay are up at the fort right now seeing what kind of price they can get for these carts and wagons. Looks like we'll have to build our own boats."

"How long will that take?"

"A week or so, I suspect. We'll make up for it on the river. I'm so tired of walking and all the trouble of driving wagons. Abby, you just don't know how ... well, I guess you do know."

"It's been rough, but I'm taking my wagon through to the Wallamet Valley. It will be useful this coming winter, especially if I can't find shelter—and I can use the food I have left."

"You get any more food at the fort?"

"They don't have any. At least that's what someone told me. The man in charge, an Archibald McKinley, offered to sell tobacco. I can't imagine a more useless item."

"Amen to that."

"I bought vegetables at Waiilatpu, so Jacob and I are pretty well-off. We should be able to make Oregon City without having to buy or trade for too much more."

"You eating that salmon?"

"Almost every day. The smoked fish is better than the dried. I'll probably trade for more as we move down the Columbia."

"Some of us Applegates like it, others don't. It's hard to feed such a large group, with everyone having their favorites. All these children are not easy to please. You kill any of your stock for food?"

"No. Thanks to Jacob my oxen are in fairly good shape—and with all the available salmon we shouldn't have to kill any. If I can get them to the Wallamet Valley and fatten them up, then next summer they'll be worth many times what I paid for them in Independence. I figure I can't go wrong."

"But there's no road from here to Oregon City!"

"Supposed to be some type of road to Wascopam, then Jacob and I will have to build a raft and float the rest of the way. We talked it over last night and that's our plan, at least for now."

"Well, good luck to you, dearie. This is the end of the road for me. If I can't float the rest of the way, then I'm going no farther. Charles can build his farm right here!"

"Malinda, you don't mean that."

"Don't be so sure. Our wagons and carts are in such poor shape that they'll never make it to Wascopam. That last pull over the Blue Mountains was their death knell, so here they'll stay."

"Did you hear about Sarah Rubey?"

"We saw her grave back in that valley. I'm so sorry, Abby, I know you two were good friends."

"She never wanted to come out here to Oregon. We buried her in one of the most beautiful valleys I've ever seen."

"She's in a far better place by now than we'll ever see in Oregon."

"Becky Stewart's baby died the other day, too, back at Waiilatpu."

"I hadn't heard that—that poor child. Is Becky on her way here now?"

"Probably."

"I'll bake some cornbread for her. It was expected though. That baby never was healthy."

"Looks like people are heading downriver to form a camp. I better get moving and claim a spot. Give my best to Cynthia and the rest of your clan."

"I will. Come visit again before you leave."

"I will." Abby released the brake and brought her quirt down on the lead oxens' rumps. The wagon lurched forward with the creaks and groans gained from so many miles of roadless travel. As she steered the wagon back toward the trail that passed in front of the fort, she turned and called back to Malinda. "We should be in camp for a couple nights, so I'll be back tomorrow!"

Jesse received a poor price for the Applegate wagons and carts, for they were no longer worth much. After the grueling journey from Missouri, they were all in need of serious repair—and in a region with no roads, their best use was for firewood. Jesse and Lindsay got what they could, while Charles procured the services of two Indians familiar with building the Mackinaw boats used to ply the Columbia. Before the end of the day, the three Applegate brothers had organized a boat-building brigade of young men and Indians. Work would begin in the morning.

Abby and Jacob moved two miles downriver before stopping for the night. They organized their camp on a flat spot of ground near the east shore of the Columbia next to five large cottonwoods. There was good forage for the stock and easy access to the river. Nearby were the Oteys, John Jackson, and Jim Nesmith, along with five other white-tops belonging to the Mathenys, the Hewitts, and the Laysons. Abby was not alone in her desire to get her wagon to the Wallamet Valley.

While Abby set up her kitchen, Jim Nesmith came by to welcome her to their camp. "We're going up to the fort tomorrow to see about trading for packsaddles. You want to join us?"

"I'd love to, Jim. I heard some of the outlying farms might have food to sell. It certainly wouldn't hurt to look."

"Yes, ma'am. We plan to buy food too." Jim adjusted his jacket and hat. "Sure is good to be here on the Columbia. I feel like we're almost there."

"It's just so wonderful to see this river." Abby stopped unloading her washtub full of kitchen supplies and turned toward the river. "I never knew exactly what to expect, except that it should take my breath away."

"Did it?"

"It did. Look at this country, Jim. I never knew anything could be so immense. I thought I was accustomed to the vastness of the West when we were back on the Platte, but nothing prepared me for this. The country around here seems to go on forever!"

"I don't mind telling you that I'm a little disappointed. Can't make a productive farm out of any of this land."

"The Wallamet Valley will be different. Remember people talking about all the trees and the mild climate and the land that doesn't need to be cleared for farms?"

"I do—but that's a far cry from this country."

"Everything is going to work out, Jim. All those wild stories I heard back in Ohio are all coming true. I never would have believed half the things I've seen."

"Did you ever hear people talking about the big trees in Oregon? Some stories say they're ten feet through!"

"That, I want to see," said Abby. "How can a tree that big ever get cut down? It would take ten men working a week!"

"Well, I don't see how trees can get that big. They weren't that big in the Blue Mountains. The trees back in Maine are just as big as Blue Mountain trees!"

"I've learned to be patient. You just wait, Jim—wait till we get to the Wallamet Valley."

"Here come the Oteys, I better see to our camp. Ma'am." Jim tipped his hat as he turned to leave.

Dinner that evening was another sumptuous meal of smoked salmon, kamash roots, string beans, and squash. Afterwards Abby did a quick job of evening chores, then grabbed her diary and headed down to the river. In a few minutes she had her moccasins off and was wading out to her knees, holding her dress up. The water was cool and refreshing, and the sand felt good squeezing between her toes.

"You gonna swim to Oregon City?" It was Jacob.

Abby turned back toward the shore with a broad smile. "The Columbia! We're really here on the Columbia!"

Jacob slowly nodded, looking downriver and drinking in the surrounding country.

"That we are, Abby, that we are. If what I hear is true, this peaceful river gets angry several times before reaching the ocean. You find out how those boat builders plan to get through?"

"They're hiring Indian guides. Malinda told me that if the Indians can make it, then so can the Applegates!"

Jacob nodded again. "With Indian guides they should make it alright. I've heard the road to Wascopam is passable with wagons. We shouldn't have too much trouble."

"What a relief that is. You must be exhausted from the work you did in the Blue Mountains."

"A little sore, but that'll pass." Jacob sat down along the bank and lit his pipe.

"You're enjoying this journey, Jacob, I can tell. You're always looking off at some distant mountain as if you're seeing your one true love."

"I'll never go back East—I learned my lesson last winter. Oregon is the only place for me. I'll find a home in Oregon."

"I'm sure you will." Still smiling, Abby turned and continued to wade along the shallow shoreline. After another few minutes she went up on shore to record the day's events. Encountering Fort Walla Walla and the Columbia would fill several pages.

On the next morning, Monday, October 9, Abby, Sarah Jane Layson, and Mary Matheny joined the Oteys, John Jackson, and Jim Nesmith in walking back to the fort to buy whatever food and equipment they could find for sale. Abby led Crow to pack her purchases, while the other ladies had three horses between them. Jim and Ed Otey also took their horses.

It was a beautiful, clear fall day with a deep blue sky and a slight upriver breeze. The freshness of the air and the scene at the fort combined to make their visit an exciting adventure. The fort was abuzz inside and out with nearly nine hundred people from the Oregon Emigrating Company, the fort's personnel, Fremont's expedition, hundreds of Indians, and a combined total of almost two thousand head of stock. Wagons and stock seemed to be moving in every direction at once.

The Applegate men were down near the wharf supervising the building of several large Mackinaw boats, using wood from cottonwood trees that grew along the Walla Walla River. The finished boats would be about forty-five feet in length, five feet wide at the center and three feet deep. They were light, thereby allowing the handlers to portage around rapids. The Indians described four treacherous areas of concern; the Umatilla Rapids, the Falls of the Columbia, The Dalles, and Cascade Falls. Both falls required portages, but Umatilla Rapids and The Dalles were runable in an empty or light canoe.

Abby found Malinda and caught up on recent news. She learned that late yesterday afternoon Jesse had made arrangements with McKinley to trade their herds for cattle vouchers. These vouchers were exchangeable for cattle in kind, both in sex and number, at Fort Vancouver. The gaunt cattle of the Cow Column would probably suffer greatly on their journey to the Wallamet Valley, with a probable loss that Jesse estimated to be as high as 25 percent. By accepting vouchers, Jesse and the other cattle owners were guaranteed live animals when they arrived at Fort Vancouver—and the animals at the fort would surely be in better condition. This was a deal Jesse and the others could not turn down. The only thing they now had left to do was to float their families and possessions down the Columbia.

Pete Burnett had bought an old boat from McKinley the night before. It was a boat several other emigrants had refused earlier, claiming it was not safe. Safe or not, Harriet Burnett would not have anything to do with more walking, so Pete purchased the only boat available. Harriet wanted to ride the remaining distance to Oregon City, and that, according to Malinda, had been final. The boat was smaller than those being built by the Applegates, but large enough to carry the Burnetts and Hattie. Abby estimated the boat to be thirty-five feet long by five feet wide in the center, and three feet deep. Bill Beagle signed on to work the tiller, while Pete hired several Indians as paddlers and one as a guide. Pete also decided to wait and travel with the Applegates for safety. That would delay their arrival in Oregon City, since the Applegates' boats would not be ready for a couple weeks. That didn't matter to Harriet—as long as she didn't have to walk.

Ed Lenox hired two Indians and their forty-foot canoe to transport the Lenox clan downriver. This Mackinaw was large enough to seat their ten family members and all their possessions. Hiring the Indians consumed all of Ed's remaining trade items and several blankets his family did not want to part with. Such were the emotional forces at play with exhausted emigrants and an opportunity to float the remaining two hundred miles.

Abby and Sarah Jane Layson were each able to buy a bushel of corn from a nearby farmer, while Mary Matheny secured a bushel of squash. For Abby, it was a friendly, relaxing outing with her friends. By noon they were back at camp, two miles downriver from the fort. There they met Jim Nesmith, who had been unsuccessful in buying packsaddles. He, the Oteys, and John Jackson were now making their own by tying carved willow and cottonwood branches with strips of rawhide.

Abby had no sooner got her corn stowed when Archibald McKinley rode up.

"Where's the man of this outfit?"

Abby looked up to see McKinley atop a tall Indian mount.

"This is my wagon."

"You tell your man that I'm having a feast tomorrow night and he's invited. Fremont's going to be there, along with all the emigrant leaders. I think congratulations are in order for making it all the way out here with these wagons."

"Am I invited?" Abby stood tall and firm with her arms folded.

"You!" He laughed. "Of course not. This celebration is for the men. Now you tell your man we'll be expecting him."

Abby had all she could do to restrain herself from picking up a rock and throwing it. Instead, she stood there watching him ride off, thankful that she would not be attending the dinner.

"I got my wagon through just like these other people. Nobody's congratulating me!" Abby quietly muttered aloud.

"I won't be attending." Jacob had been sitting under one of the cottonwood trees and had heard every word. His approach startled Abby who was concentrating on the disappearing form of McKinley.

"This is your outfit, Abby, and if he don't see fit to invite you, then I don't want anything to do with his feast."

"Thank you, Jacob. I appreciate your directness."

"I've had my fill of these farmers, so it's no trouble to stay away. He's got no cause to treat you like that. We'll be pulling out the day after tomorrow, and McKinley will be left far behind."

"Maybe he doesn't know any better—but he's familiar with squaws, so he knows what women are capable of!"

"Indian culture is highly defined." Jacob paused, not wanting to fuel a volatile scene. "I don't know, Abby. We'll be out of here soon, so forget it."

Abby continued staring in the direction of the fort, still standing with her arms folded. It was that unconscious stance of defiance that had served her well on many previous occasions.

"What if there are people like this in the Wallamet Valley?" she thought. "I'll have to establish myself early—certainly with property.

I can also get involved with the provisional government. I'm already a member of the Pioneer Lyceum and Literary Club!"

Two Indians walking toward the Oteys wagon broke her concentration. One of the Indians, named Yenemah, politely asked if they could follow along to Wascopam. Jacob came over to interpret, allowing them to join the caravan as long as they followed behind and didn't cause any trouble. Soon the Indians were making their camp a few hundred yards downriver.

On the next morning, Tuesday, October 10, Jim Nesmith and John Jackson helped Ed Otey drive his wagon up to the fort to exchange it for five packhorses. The animals were strong and healthy, just as McKinley had promised. By ten o'clock they were back in camp, fitting their new packsaddles to each horse.

The day passed quickly with people preparing for the push to Wascopam. Abby organized her new store of vegetables using old flour sacks and storage holes in her wagon that had formerly been filled with flour, cornmeal, and sugar.

As she finished preparations, several more wagons arrived from Waiilatpu. One of the wagons belonged to Pete and Becky Stewart. Abby wasted no time in welcoming them to her camp and consoling Becky. Pete thanked her for her kindness, then asked Jacob if they could join the small caravan to Wascopam. They had done their preparations before leaving Waiilatpu and would be ready to travel in the morning.

"Certainly," said Jacob. "We can always use additional help if this road turns sour. You can pull up over there." He motioned to a flat area underneath a tall cottonwood. Pete and Becky were traveling with Becky's parents, Fendall and Rebecca Cason, as an extended family. Both Pete and Fendall quirted their oxen forward toward their new campsite.

The small caravan going to Wascopam enjoyed one of the more picturesque spots along this stretch of the Columbia. The entire camp was on flat ground next to the river—ground that probably flooded each spring. At this time of year the grass and cottonwoods made an inviting temporary home. To the east was a high hill that ran north and south, paralleling the river. There were numerous rock outcroppings along the top, giving it a ragged and wild appearance. Nearby were two cylindrical rocks jutting up from the front edge of a hill. Each rock was about thirty feet in diameter and rose fifty feet above its base, appearing like two towers from a distance. When questioned, Yenemah explained that the rocks had magical powers and were greatly venerated in his tribe's religious rites. He said the rocks were really two Indian damsels, petrified so they could always watch for his tribe's safe passage on the river.

Shortly after dusk Harriet Burnett came by looking for her slave, Hattie.

"Pete sent her down to the river for some water just before going to that dinner McKinley's having. She never came back, so I'm checking each of the camps to see if she's run off."

"We haven't seen her," replied Jacob. He stood stoically, staring at Harriet. He didn't care for slavery any more than Abby did, and had he said anything else, it would probably have been in support of Hattie's freedom.

"She might have fallen in," said Harriet. "The current's strong along the shore up by our camp. You didn't happen to see her float by, did you?"

Abby, Jacob, and the Mathenys stood speechless. How could one answer such a callous question?

"Well, if you see her, you let me know. If she doesn't show up by tomorrow, then I'll assume she drowned. She was worth over five hundred dollars back in Missouri. I don't know how we'll ever replace her way out here. Well, you folks have a safe journey." She turned to walk down to the next camp.

The silence of the gathered group finally gave way to motion. People walked back to their kitchens without saying a word. What could anyone say? Poor Hattie—she was probably another casualty of the Oregon Emigrating Company.

With darkness came cold, one of the coldest nights yet. Abby curled up in a blanket inside her wagon as she wrote a few paragraphs, including some kind words for Hattie: *"She was a frightened young girl back in Missouri, but worked hard for her masters through uncounted difficulties and hunger. She deserves more than a watery grave!"*

On Wednesday morning, October 11, the small caravan broke camp at eight o'clock and started toward Wascopam. Their group consisted of eight wagons and about seventy-five people. The Oteys, John Jackson, Jim Nesmith, and the Wilsons were all using pack animals. Bill Wilson's facial burns from the gunpowder mishap were still healing, but no longer interfered with his activity. The lead wagon belonged to the Mathenys, followed by the Stewarts, Casons, Keizurs, Hewitts, Laysons, and finally Abby. Women and children walked behind the last wagon, while mounted riders brought up the end of the train. For the people on foot, this road provided easier passage than out away from the column, and the dust was minimal due to recent rains.

Ever since arriving at Fort Walla Walla, people had become aware of the change in behavior of local Indian tribes. Here on the Columbia, Indians held white people in contempt, trying to rob them whenever an opportunity presented itself. This was just the opposite of the Indians along the Snake River Plains. Jacob suspected it was probably due to less than friendly interactions from the Hudson Bay Company.

Unknown to the group, the day before, Indians had robbed the families of Bill Arthur and Ed Constable. Their party consisted of two wagons and about ten people. It happened shortly after they left Fort Walla Walla for Wascopam. The group was poorly armed and could not defend themselves against the Indian demands. The encounter resulted in the Indians confiscating everything of value—horses, tools, and food—leaving the cattle and flour, items useless in Indian culture.

Today Abby's caravan came upon their robbed and destitute compadres. Jim Nesmith quickly offered the protection of their group, allowing the Arthurs and Constables to bring their cattle and the few articles left by the Indians. After a short discussion with Jacob, the men in the caravan checked their weapons and vowed to carry them in full view all the way to Wascopam. They knew from discussions back at the fort that Indians never molested well-armed groups.

The road today was flat and easily passable with wagons. It followed the river's floodplain in a southerly direction through a country that varied little from the dry hills surrounding Fort Walla Walla. In the afternoon they passed the southern boundary of the high hills flanking the east side of the river. From here, the country widened out into more rolling hills of enormous size.

Around three o'clock the people in Abby's caravan could see Overton Johnson and Bill Newby plying their large Mackinaws down the Columbia. Overton and Bill had been two of the first arrivals at Fort Walla Walla and had bought the first two canoes. With an Indian guide in the bow and several more Indians as paddlers, they were the first to cast off and head downriver. They left among the cheers of well-wishers standing on the wharf. Soon the other people continuing by boat would join them, with everyone eventually meeting up in Oregon City.

Having set sail at noon, Johnson and Newby were already passing the land-bound travelers in their advance toward Wascopam. In the bow of the lead boat sat their Indian guide. His jet-black hair hung loosely over his shoulders as he hung onto a long-handled paddle used as a front-end tiller. Other paddlers and a rear tiller, all Indians, worked to maintain a speed slightly faster than the current. Only in this way could their front and rear tillers effect steerage.

The river at this point consisted of swift whitewater, careening around boulders varying in size from that of a small farm shed to as large as a house. As a boat approached one of the boulders, the Indian in the bow would thrust his paddle into the river at the last possible moment, causing the boat to veer out of the way. These intrepid guides knew exactly where to go. Without hesitation they directed the course of the boats through whitewater channels and boulder gardens considered impassable by most of the men watching from the shore.

Everyone watched keenly as the Mackinaws darted past in what looked like a race to the Wallamet Valley. Their Indian guides had floated this section of river a hundred times, yet all their skill and cunning could not prevent an occasional mishap. As people on the shore watched, the boat with Bill and Sarah Newby hit a subsurface rock and rolled over. The Indian paddlers hung onto the gunwales and angled the boat to the western shore as they had learned to do during previous incidents, for saving the Mackinaw boat was critically important. The Newby's gear, which had been tied in, was safe but wet. Bill and Sarah swam for the nearest boulder and crawled up on top, shaken and exhausted. Had they stayed with the boat they would now be safely on shore. Instead, they sat stranded on a boulder in the middle of a massive section of whitewater, which Yenemah referred to as Umatilla, the same name of the river whose confluence was a few miles ahead.

Abby's group was helpless to offer assistance to their friends. Some feared that Bill and Sarah's situation could only end in their deaths.

As soon as the Indians got their boat to the far shore, they unloaded it and began to carry it back upstream. The boat with Overton Johnson and his family landed downstream on the far shore to await the outcome of the Indian's rescue. They, too, felt as helpless as their wagon-bound friends.

Carrying the Mackinaw back upstream took over an hour, since they needed to get far enough above the whitewater to give them plenty of time to align with the boulder holding Bill and Sarah. Once there, the paddlers would have to hold the boat steady long enough for Bill and Sarah to jump on board. There could not be any hesitation on the part of the Newbys, for the boat would only be accessible for a second or two. The entire operation had to be carried out with flawless precision. No Indian could miss a paddle stroke, and their guide had to position the craft with pinpoint accuracy. To maneuver, their speed had to be faster than the current—but as soon as they reached the boulder, the paddlers would have to reverse their strokes and bring the Mackinaw to a halt, long enough for Bill and Sarah to jump on. Then once they were on board, the paddlers had to regain their speed to prevent the boat from being dashed to pieces as they floundered in the current.

The courageous Indians moved out into the current without hesitation. Their empty boat responded quickly to the force of their paddles, and they were soon approaching the boulder that held Bill and Sarah. The guide made a hand signal motioning for them to jump in as soon as the boat came alongside. In the next second they were there, scooping Bill and Sarah off the boulder and safely paddling back to the far shore. It was an impressive rescue, and the Newbys owed their lives to these fearless Indians. Without their help, the two would have surely perished.

At this area of whitewater, the river was a quarter-mile wide. Boulders and swift water separated the two camps of the trail-bound caravan and the Johnson and Newby boats. They could see each other and wave a greeting, but nothing more.

"Maybe," Abby thought, "we'll come together at Wascopam. Poor Sarah, she must be terribly frightened!"

A two-hour nooner and leisurely pace had resulted in Abby's group advancing only twelve miles closer to Wascopam. This short distance was in part due to the Arthurs and Constables needing time to gather their nerve after being robbed. They all understood that there was nothing left to do but continue downriver to Wascopam. Their camp that night was near a large rock outcrop they named Windmill Rock due to its similarity to a Dutch windmill. There was poor grass in the area and no trees for firewood. With clear skies and the lateness of the season, it would be another cold night.

After retiring, Abby crouched next to her candle trying to gather some warmth while writing a few paragraphs about the events of the day, especially the ordeal with Bill and Sarah. Despite the excitement, it was good to be moving again, moving closer and closer to the Wallamet Valley.

The little caravan started early the next morning, Thursday, October 12, on a clear, blue-sky day. After a few miles the Columbia widened to a half-mile and again presented the appearance of a calm and peaceful highway. By ten o'clock the wagons were again on the shore of the Umatilla River, only now at its confluence with the Columbia. Exactly one week had passed since the first crossing of this river—one week and a great deal of activity. They had pursued a circuitous route, causing at least five days' delay. Coming straight down the Umatilla River would have been a considerably shorter route, however, that could not be helped. Waiilatpu and Fort Walla Walla had provided needed food and services.

The caravan easily accomplished the crossing since the water flow was still running low after the summer drought. Without a great deal of scouting, Dan Matheny determined that the river bottom was firm enough to handle heavy wagons and the bank angle was low enough that double-teaming was not necessary. The small column boldly plunged in and was soon climbing the opposite bank, continuing down the trail toward Wascopam. During the crossing Abby took her usual position in the front of the wagon while Jacob rode alongside the lead team, keeping them moving with a willow switch for a prod.

During their nooner, a small group of trappers arrived from the direction of Wascopam. Their leader, a Mr. McDonald, stated that they were employees of the Hudson Bay Company and on their way from Fort Vancouver to Fort Hall with supplies and instructions. En route they would stop at Fort Walla Walla and Fort Boise. For the gathered emigrants, Mr. McDonald provided a stern warning to be on their guard against rogue Indians. Three days ago a small group had robbed five of their men of all they had. McDonald stated that the Indians had drawn their bows and arrows in a very disagreeable situation. Everyone took the warning as further support to keep their weapons loaded and at the ready.

During the afternoon, the caravan passed several stretches of boiling whitewater where the river narrowed due to basalt flows and other house-sized boulders. By the time they stopped for the day, the river was again a half-mile wide, calm and placid. The road still paralleled the shoreline and was easy going—easy enough to make twenty-five miles for the day. People could remember only one other day when they had traversed such a great distance—and that was back on the American Prairie, where few obstacles had blocked their advance. Dan Matheny, the self-appointed leader of the small group, called a halt to the day's march an hour before sunset at an area with flat ground for kitchens and wagons. They formed a corral by using wagon tongues to enlarge and close the circle. The surrounding area had poor forage except directly along the shore. With few animals, each was able to get its fill of grass and water.

Dinner again consisted of smoked salmon and corn. For Abby and Jacob, it was high living with such excellent food. Only buffalo could compete with salmon for taste.

While the small group enjoyed their evening meal and discussed the road for tomorrow, Yenemah and his companion went down to the river, surveyed the water, then entered and began swimming for the far shore. Nobody knew why they had changed their minds about continuing to Wascopam, or why they chose to cross. For some, it was a relief to see them leave. Those less trusting supposed their primary objective had been to steal whatever they could. The armed condition of the caravan provided a major drawback, reason enough for them to decide it was time to leave.

After dinner Abby went down to the shore to go wading. The water felt good on her callused feet, and the country had not lost any of its charm. The surrounding treeless mountains had a beauty all their own.

"Long day?" Jacob spoke as he came walking down to the shore, carrying his pipe and looking to spend a few moments by himself.

"Cold water just feels good. You were right about my feet getting tough in moccasins. It's going to be difficult to go back to shoes."

"Won't be long now—three, maybe four weeks."

"I've been thinking about that too. Looks like I'll get my wagon to Oregon City around the first of November."

Jacob did not respond. He sat down and lit his pipe.

"Back in Ohio I always thought I lived in the West, I mean the Western United States. Now I think of Ohio as being back East!"

"You think your brother will ever come out here?"

"He will after I write. As soon as I get to Oregon City, and there's some means of getting mail back to the United States, I'm going to write him all about this country. He'll come alright—he's not the kind to stay at home when there's an adventure to see."

"I suspect there'll be more people coming out here to Oregon every year. Once a government gets established, folks who are less than pioneering in nature will start arriving."

"If the land around here had trees and good soil, I think it might be the most beautiful place on earth. I don't think I will ever get accustomed to how big and open this country is. If someone had told me how beautiful barren mountains can be, I never would have believed them!" Abby stood holding her dress out of the water, looking around at the rolling hills on the far side of the river.

While Abby and Jacob were down at the shore, an Indian came into camp at about the same time Tom Keizur noticed one of his horses was missing. Tom sent a messenger to fetch Jacob to communicate the loss and ascertain if the Indian had seen the horse. Jacob went with him, leaving Abby to continue her wading.

"He says he'll find the horse in exchange for some clothing," Jacob stated after signing with the Indian.

"He probably stole it," said Dan Matheny.

"I paid with a shirt back at Fort Walla Walla to get an animal back," said Tom. "If he stole it, then it should be nearby. I say we shoot him and go find the horse."

"Tom!" scolded Dan. "You know better than that. Jacob, you tell him to bring in the horse and we'll give him a shirt. When we get the horse back, we'll put the fear of God in him. That should be enough."

Soon the Indian was back, leading the horse. Tom gave the Indian an old, worn-out shirt and took the reins.

"Jacob, you tell this scoundrel that if he steals another horse or if I catch him around our camp again, I'll shoot him dead. You tell him that!" Tom stood in defiance, scowling at the Indian so he could see that his threats were real.

The Indian nodded to Jacob's signing, then turned and left their camp as quickly as possible.

"He won't be back," said Jacob. "We might run into more Indians of similar character, but that one won't be back."

The gathered crowd broke up and Tom led the horse back to his wagon, tying it to one of the wheels. Dusk came early, and soon a quiet repose pervaded their small encampment. Dan assigned guard duties to several volunteers. With so many Indians in the vicinity, Indians not hesitant to steal, each man was more than willing to serve his share of guard duty.

While there was still some light, Abby came up from the shore, secured her kitchen for the night, then retired. It had been a long day, and the diary could wait till tomorrow. With the cool, crisp, clear air, she was soon asleep, as was the rest of the camp. Only guards remained to view the beauty of a full moon glittering off the Columbia.

The next morning, Friday, October 13, the caravan was back on the road by eight o'clock. The road continued down the Columbia floodplain over a sandy, dry soil, sturdy enough to support the heavy wagons without sinking in. The weather was clear, and it looked to be another good day of travel. By noon, the cool morning had given way to a sunny, warm afternoon. People shed their jackets before the afternoon march.

Following the river for the last two days had slowly changed their course from a southerly direction toward the west. As the caravan turned due west, they got their first view of Mount Hood. This mountain stood tall and majestic against a blue-sky backdrop. On the other side of Mount Hood was the Wallamet Valley. They were so close, yet so far. Eternal snows covered the mountain's summit, presenting a contradiction of beauty and hardship. The snows confirmed everyone's suspicions that they would have to build rafts at Wascopam and float the remaining distance to Oregon City. But the mountain added to that alluring Oregon landscape that they had heard so much about back in the United States. The timbered foothills contrasted sharply with the land they had been traveling through since leaving the Blue Mountains—but this splendor did not mask the dangers ahead. Floating down an unforgiving Columbia River presented a new catalog of troubles and dangers. Still, the sight of Mount Hood helped inspire the tired emigrants to push on to their final goal.

The mountain was visible until midafternoon when the caravan reached a place where canyon walls began to close in on the river. The road, flat and easy to this point, now began to wind up a gradual incline away from the river. True to the description given at Fort Walla Walla, they would now be on an undulating plain high above the river until reaching their objective, the Wascopam Mission. At various points the trail veered near the edge of the canyon, giving everyone a breathtaking view of the Columbia River and surrounding country below. From this commanding position, Mount Hood was again visible along with other snow-covered peaks to the north.

It was near dusk by the time they reached the plateau high above the river, twenty miles from last night's camp. As the sun began to set, they came to a small ravine where there was good grass and a small trickle of water. It was a good place to stop for the night. The day had been warm, and the climb from the Columbia floodplain exhausting. Shortly after stopping, people put on jackets against another cold night. Clear skies yielded little warmth after the sun went down. A full moon helped to extend the light long enough for folks to finish their dinners and secure stock for the night.

Indians, missionaries, and Hudson Bay Company personnel routinely traveled through this secluded ravine on the road from Wascopam to Fort Walla Walla. With such a potential for traffic, volunteers posted themselves around the camp to guard against the "pesky" Indians and anyone else who might venture into the area. Other men agreed to relieve the guards at midnight. Everyone, Abby included, had become tired of local Indians constantly begging, stealing, or insisting on trading. Guards checked their weapons and took their posts. With a full moon, it would be difficult to approach camp without being detected.

On Saturday morning, October 14, they were back on the road at first light, well before eight o'clock. The small caravan prepared for the day's march with the efficiency and precision of a military drill. Everyone was eager to see an end to their labors, and the sooner they could get to Wascopam, then the sooner they could begin building rafts for the final leg of their journey. Those back at Fort Walla Walla might get their boats built and arrive at Wascopam first. It was a clear incentive to keep moving.

The absence of Indians today was a pleasant change from last week. In addition to this good fortune, the road ahead, although both rocky and sandy, was easily passable with wagons. This, and their nearness to Wascopam, helped to boost the morale and determination of everyone. By evening they had advanced another twenty-five miles from last night's camp. The weather remained clear and sunny, good for travel but indicative of another cold night.

During dinner a Cayuse Indian traveling east from Wascopam came into camp for the purpose of trading smoked salmon. None of the kitchens he approached showed any interest in trading, since everyone was fully stocked with fish and vegetables. When he approached Abby, she produced a few trade baubles in exchange for five pounds of fish. The baubles had no value to her, and this was an opportunity to get rid of them before reaching the Wallamet Valley. It was a good and amicable trade.

Jacob instructed the Indian to make his camp down the road and not within sight of their caravan. With the extent of armed men throughout this small group, the Indian gladly heeded his request. He quickly moved down the road, leading his packhorse still laden with smoked salmon. There would be other people to trade with tomorrow.

The next morning, Sunday, October 15, the same Indian returned—this time begging for breakfast. Nobody was willing to part with food, especially since the Indian had plenty of salmon to eat. Abby had a small piece of dried bread left and offered it to him when he stopped at her kitchen. It was more a gesture to get rid of him rather than an act of humanity. He walked over to the side of the road and sat down to eat. He presented a curious sight, as he had been Christianized by the mission. He crossed himself, mumbled a few words in his native language, and then began to eat. Abby quickly looked around to see if other people had seen him pray—they had. The missionary influence was changing Columbia River tribes forever.

The road today became rugged in spots, yet still passable for wagons. Shortly before noon they began heading down a gradual slope toward the John Day River, named by the Astoria Expedition almost thirty years earlier. Due to the lateness of the season, the river was flowing at only a trickle, easily crossed by wagons. The deepest water only came up to the hubs, presenting no danger to wagons or stock. Abby again rode in the front of the wagon while Jacob prodded the lead team with a stick. The climb up from the river was another gradual incline, presenting little difficulty. Within a mile they were back on level ground, making good time toward Wascopam.

At this point on the road, the caravan was several miles south of the Columbia River. As the afternoon wore on, the road came near enough to the edge of the canyon for everyone to view the river below. The lead horsemen warned the others how dangerous it was for anyone to get near the edge. If a horse got frightened and bolted, it could slip or throw its rider over the edge. Others shared their concern and dismounted before walking over to the edge to view the scene.

After a sixteen-mile day, Dan Matheny halted the caravan in an area that afforded adequate grass, but no water. Though it was still fairly early, everyone was ready to stop. The previous day had been long and hard, and sixteen miles plus a river crossing was more than adequate for today. Stopping early gave both people and stock a needed rest.

Small sage covered the country, indicative of a prairie that had recently burned. There had not been enough time for larger sage to develop. The only trees, unknown types of juniper, hackberry, and alder, scrubby in form, grew near the John Day River and nowhere else.

After dinner Abby made a quick job of cleaning up and headed over to the canyon rim to view the river below. Jacob was already there having his evening smoke. Here, they could see the Columbia River extending east to the confluence of the Umatilla River, and west into a canyon that appeared to get increasingly narrow. Directly below, high rocks in the center of the river produced horrific, boiling whitewater. The sight of the difficult passage, and the earlier incident with the Newbys, confirmed to Abby that she had made the right decision. Continuing on with her wagon was infinitely better than braving such a wild and treacherous river.

The weather remained clear with no clouds in sight for tomorrow. After returning from the river and completing evening chores, Abby caught up on diary entries, then retired by dusk. Tomorrow would be here all too soon.

On Monday, October 16, Matheny's caravan made good progress during the morning march. By the time they stopped for a nooner, they had descended back down to river level and were now on the east bank of the Chute River, next to its confluence with the Columbia. This river flows in a northerly direction, emptying into the south side of the Columbia in one final torrent of angry, foamy whitewater. Although the flow was down at this time of year, the current was strong and dangerous where the Chute met the Columbia. The scene upstream from the confluence showed a wild, untamed river careening around tall, treeless mountains. This river, like many before, presented a highway into unknown and untamed lands. It beckoned the adventurer into regions known only to Indians and trappers. Such exploration would have to wait for future pioneers. Presently, the small caravan of wagons needed to cross, and the prospects looked dangerous.

A small Indian village, consisting of eight huts and about forty individuals, sat on the east bank of the Chute River. Dan Matheny quickly employed the services of three Indians to help move his wagons to the opposite shore, while other teamsters looked on to assess the dangers before crossing. Once safely on the western shore, the Indians returned to help with the rest of the wagons. Jacob employed two of them, one to ride on either side of the lead team. The Hewitts also hired two Indians. The Wilsons, who had sold their wagon back at Fort Hall, rode alongside Abby's wagon on the downstream side. Bill Wilson hoped that the wagon would minimize the strength of the current and provide a small margin of safety. Still, Polly Wilson became nearly paralyzed with fear. After months of hardships, and the incident with the Newbys, she was certain this river would finally claim her life or a family member's. The men ignored her pleas to find another route, for there was no other route. She would have to take her chances along with everyone else.

Midway across the rushing river Polly lost all control and began screaming wildly, pleading to go back. After two ear-splitting screeches, the Indian riding on the right side of Abby's team turned toward the woman with a scowl of irritation.

Before Polly could scream again, the Indian called out, "Wicked woman, put your trust in God!"

Stunned into silence, Polly gaped at the Indian, as did everyone else. This Indian was not only Christianized, but spoke excellent English!

Abby poked her head around the corner of the wagon canopy to look back at Polly. She was now riding in silence, no doubt just as frightened, but in control of her fears. Abby faced forward again, this time with a concerted effort to hide a smile. The incident would make good copy for tonight's diary.

After completing the crossing, the men and Abby paid their Indian guides in clothing and a few trade baubles. Colored beads and ribbons were of little value to these Indians—but the emigrants wanted to rid themselves of unused trade items and this was a good opportunity.

The Indians returned to the east shore while the small caravan set up their camp on the west shore. It was still only midafternoon, but ahead was a long, steep climb back up to the Columbia's canyon rim. After negotiating the Chute River, everyone was in favor of resting the stock for the remainder of the day. Tomorrow would be soon enough to begin the ascent.

Tuesday morning, October 17, was again bright and sunny. The coolness of the air helped give the stock extra strength as they began the long, slow climb back up to the top of the Columbia River canyon. By ten o'clock the last wagon breached the crest and stopped for a well-deserved rest. Before eleven, they were back on the trail, vowing to take a late nooner. The trail, or road at this point, wound its way over undulating ground, never veering too far from the edge of the canyon. In places it came close enough for drovers and teamsters to see the river below.

The late stop for a nooner occurred almost directly above the Falls of the Columbia. These falls were one of the most magnificent features of the entire Columbia River. They consisted of a series of cascades dropping about thirty feet into a boiling caldron of whitewater. The main falls formed a horseshoe and faced south, an oddity since the river flowed west. Some water escaped the torrent by flowing through a narrow channel on the north side of the river, the section where the river-bound emigrants would have to line or portage their boats. Directly below the Falls of the Columbia was The Dalles.

The Dalles, according to the men back at Fort Walla Walla, was a five-mile stretch of canyon where the river compressed into a narrow channel that forced water through in a mad torrent, much like water through a funnel. The speed of the current precluded any attempt of a safe passage. Seeing The Dalles from the canyon rim convinced almost everyone that their river-bound friends would have to portage the five miles, carrying their boats and all their baggage. Other men felt that with experienced Indian guides some boats might be light enough to risk running this section. The Dalles terminated at the Wascopam Mission, a wide spot in the river canyon that afforded enough space for the construction of mission buildings and a support garden. There the river made a large horseshoe bend, turning to the south before heading west, north, and then west again.

As Abby drank in the incredulous scene before her, she tried to memorize every detail for subsequent creation of a written record. Below were over a thousand Indians engaged in a myriad of tasks, all related to harvesting salmon. Their presence only helped to add intrigue to this wild, adventuresome scene. On the south shore at the foot of the falls stood a large village of various-sized huts. In every direction, Abby could see Indian children playing; women cooking, scraping hides, and curing salmon; older men relaxing; and young men and boys fishing. Smoke from what must have been a hundred salmon-filled huts rose above the village while extensive racks of salmon dried out in the sun. The intoxicating sight of this great river and the people who depended on it mesmerized Abby and the other emigrants, making the nooner go by all too fast.

During the afternoon, the small caravan advanced another four miles before making camp in a small ravine with water. The camp itself was not noteworthy, however, the surrounding country was. After dinner Abby returned to the edge of the canyon where she could get a good view of The Dalles below. The impressive, awe-inspiring scene demanded recording.

"From this distance," she wrote, *"it appears that the Columbia River Indians fish in the same manner as the Indians back on the Snake River. They use the same type of harpoon with a releasable antler horn as a spearhead. Each Indian stakes out a favorite rock where he can get close to the current and be able to see the salmon coming upstream. Those fish swimming near the shore are the unlucky ones. I suspect that hundreds of thousands of other fish, farther out in the river, escape this gauntlet. They'll get speared at some other point upriver. Salmon probably swim up most of the rivers on this side of the continent.*

"Because of the way these people depend on salmon, their lives and the life of each river seem to come together. Their dependence on the fish from this river has probably existed for thousands of years and will continue to exist for thousands more."

Overnight some clouds drifted in from the west, and in the morning a light drizzle fell—not enough to get soaked, but enough to become chilled and uncomfortable. But the mission was not far, so morale was high when the emigrants broke camp at eight o'clock. Within the hour they came to a large draw where the road led north, down toward the river and the Wascopam Mission. As they descended, it occurred to Abby that this final stretch of road would be the last few miles where she would have to walk alongside her lead team, urging them on with her quirt. From Wascopam, they would continue with rafts until reaching their final destination of Oregon City.

Abby looked back at her outfit, surveying the gaunt oxen, Jacob's two packhorses, Crow, and the milch cow. Back at Fort Walla Walla, Jacob had been assured that local Indians could move their livestock downriver on a narrow trail to Oregon City, a distance of about one hundred miles—but the wagons would require rafting. They could always abandon their wagons and use pack animals if rafting proved impossible. But many, including Abby, wanted to get their wagons to the Wallamet Valley. Upon arrival in Oregon City, the owners could reclaim their livestock and compensate the Indians.

"Jacob," Abby called out, and he quickly rode up and dismounted. He had often walked alongside her when giving his horse a rest.

"How much trouble will it be to build a raft large enough to hold this wagon?"

"Have to see the timber. Pine about a foot in diameter works best. Big enough for a sturdy raft, but small enough to cut and haul."

"How do you plan to secure the logs together?"

"We'll split some into rails and nail them down as crossties. Those nails you bought back in Missouri will come in handy."

Abby thought about the situation for a few minutes, quirting the teams and trying to imagine how they would secure the wagon. "I should have enough rope to lash all our belongings to the raft."

"We'll take the axletrees off and load the box first. You can put everything back in just like it's packed now. Then we'll set the axletrees and wheels over the top and tie them down with rope. That should prevent items from getting knocked around or thrown into the river."

"How long do you think we'll be delayed at Wascopam?"

"Few days, maybe a week. If we pitch in and help each other, the raft building shouldn't take too long. Make sure you got trade items ready for when we get to Cascade Falls. We'll need to hire Indians to portage your baggage."

"Then this is it, our last mile on the trail!" Abby affirmed the statement with a smile. "We did alright—and my wagon didn't cause us much trouble at all."

"No trouble at all. You did a right fine job of picking out a good wagon—stock too. We lost a few, but that can't be helped. I'd say you did better than most of these farmers."

"Thank you, Jacob. Now if we can just get by Cascade Falls without any trouble …"

"We will. Are you buying any more garden food at Wascopam?"

"I have a few holes I can stow some things in. People at Waiilatpu said they have dried rhubarb here. If I can get a half bushel, we'll be in fine shape."

The caravan continued down the draw, winding back and forth in a braided fashion, until the road entered a narrow pass between vertical rock walls. From here they could see the Wascopam Mission, perched back from the river on a wide, flat plain over five miles long and extending a mile back from the river. Several farms dotted the landscape along with the massive mission garden. There were also several orchards, too immature to produce any fruit. Orchards were something nobody had seen since leaving the United States.

Dan Matheny did not bother to stop the caravan for a nooner—there would be time for that later. Instead the group continued down the road directly toward the mission. Jacob surveyed the surrounding hills and saw there would be little trouble in securing enough logs for a raft. The long-needled pine had reappeared, absent since the Blue Mountains. It was still drizzling when Abby pulled her wagon up to the front of the mission and set the brake.

Wascopam was an outpost of the mission started several years earlier by Jason Lee in the Wallamet Valley. Lee hoped to convert the thousands of Columbia River Indians to Christianity, and so had instructed a Reverend Waller to construct and maintain this mission. The name, Wascopam, came from the local Indians and referred to the wide spot in the river's floodplain where the settlement was located.

Reverend Waller, a tall, lanky man, came out to greet everyone and welcome them to his mission. He wore an ankle-length robe and a smile that proclaimed an end to his lonely days as a missionary. Overton Johnson and the Newbys had already arrived, so the reverend was well aware of the surge of emigrants he could expect in the next few weeks. He walked between the wagons shaking every man's hand and tipping his hat to all the ladies, genuinely excited at the prospect of Americans coming out to colonize Oregon. He missed the comforts of civilization and knew his days in an isolated mission would soon be over.

Under directions from Reverend Perkins, Reverend Waller's assistant, Jacob unhitched the oxen and moved all the stock to an area west of the mission that had good forage and access to water. From there, arrangements would have to be made with local Indians to have the animals moved to Oregon City.

Abby checked the brake, shook some of the trail mud from her dress, and walked over to the mission. As she approached, she noticed a lady coming from one of the storehouses. She was a small woman, with shoulder-length blonde hair and a smooth, light complexion.

"That must be Narcissa." Without hesitation, Abby walked over to introduce herself. "Mrs. Whitman?"

"Yes?"

"My name is Abby Meacham. I've just arrived from the United States, and I've been so looking forward to meeting you."

"Really! Miss Meacham. It's good to meet you. You must have traveled with my husband."

"Yes, he was one of our guides, and you can call me Abby."

"Abby."

"My, you're just as pretty as I've heard."

"Heard, you don't mean Marcus was …"

"Oh, no, my hired man told me all about you. His name is Jacob Chalmers."

Narcissa gave a look of inquisitiveness, then surprise as she remembered the name. She rolled her eyes, shaking her head.

"Jacob Chalmers! Is he here?"

"You know him?"

"A bit too well. He and some of his trapping friends frightened me half to death back in '36. They came swooping down on our column, and I thought for sure they were Indians and we'd all be killed."

"He never told me that."

"Then there were those Rendezvous—nothing more than opulent debauchery from the Devil's own. You say Chalmers worked for you all the way from Missouri?"

"Yes, and he's been a good man! I'm glad I didn't know the details of his past, else I might not have hired him!"

"Well, everyone's entitled to change, and Lord willing, old Jacob could use a great deal of changing! Come, you look chilled and in need of soap. We have a fire in the main house where you can warm up and dry off."

Abby followed Narcissa into the mission, spending the next hour relating her triumphs and tragedies of the trip out from Independence. Afterwards, Narcissa arranged for one of the mission laborers to place a half-bushel of dried rhubarb under her wagon, compliments of Jason Lee. She felt it was the least she could do for the pain and trouble Abby had gone through in bringing her wagon out from the United States.

In the meantime, Jacob made arrangements for securing logs to build a raft. The Mathenys, Hewitts, Keizurs, Casons, Stewarts, and Laysons also needed rafts, so each family agreed to help the other. By late afternoon they had surveyed the surrounding timber and determined the best place to secure logs. The pines were tall and straight, about a foot in diameter and only a modest distance from the river. Felling would begin in the morning.

The river at this place was about sixty yards wide as it wound its way around a large horseshoe bend in front of the mission. The narrowness of the channel created a substantial current, although not as bad as at The Dalles. Mission laborers informed the men that the river widened out as soon as it turned west, after which the only problem they could expect was the difficult portage around Cascade Falls.

After meeting with Narcissa and getting warm, dry, and fed, Abby excused herself and went in search of Sarah Newby. It wasn't long before she found her, staying warm and dry in one of the mission's three storehouses.

"Abby, you should have seen it," said Sarah. "I thought for sure we would all be drowned!"

"I did see it, everything. I was over on the south shore. Those Indians deserve some extra payment for the way they risked their lives to get you and Bill off that rock."

"Bill's already planning to give them a little extra when we get to Oregon City." She paused to take a breath. "Abby, I was absolutely terrified. No matter how violent the water got, those Indians never flinched. They were calm and determined in their pursuit. They knew exactly where to steer those boats—and if something happened, they knew just what to do, like you saw."

"It was an amazing rescue, Sarah. None of us thought they could get their boat out there again."

"Me included. After that we never questioned any Indian. If the guide said paddle, we paddled. If he said stop, we stopped. You should have seen some of the other water we came through, like The Dalles."

"I saw that from the ridge. You didn't portage?"

"No ma'am, went straight through. I don't mind telling you I was terrified every inch of the way. We'd come at a rock, and as we were just about to hit it, the Indian in front would suddenly steer around it. I don't know why they couldn't turn sooner, it's just their way."

"You lose many of your possessions?"

"None. Those Indians rescued everything."

"Well, the worst is over, Sarah. That's what I've heard. From here the only bad water is Cascade Falls, and everyone portages that."

They continued their conversation until the dinner hour, when Abby excused herself to get some food prepared for herself and Jacob. Since Sarah, Bill, and Overton Johnson had no wagon to shelter them from the rain, Reverend Waller was allowing them to stay in the storehouse until they were ready to continue downriver. Joining them were the Arthurs and Constables, the destitute emigrants picked up by Abby's small caravan just after leaving Fort Walla Walla.

After dinner Abby spent the evening inside the Western Passage to escape the rain. A candle provided some warmth and enough light to write a few paragraphs:

"We arrived at Wascopam today! It won't be long now and my journey to Oregon will be over. From here we will float the Columbia on rafts. Indians will take our animals down a trail that leads all the way to Oregon City. It's hard to imagine this journey being over, but today was the last mile for my poor wagon. The next time it rolls, I'll be in Oregon City! The next few nights will be my final nights using the Western Passage as a trail home. After embarking on rafts, the stars will be my only roof. Not until after we arrive at Oregon City will the Western Passage again serve as home and bed."

After a few more paragraphs about the Wascopam Mission, it was time for sleep.

The next morning, Thursday, October 19, Jim Nesmith stopped by while Abby was preparing breakfast. He and Sarah Jane Matheny were going to grind some wheat at the mission's mill, and Jim knew that Abby could use a little extra flour. Jacob and the Matheny and Keizur men, along with Henry Hewitt, Aaron Layson, Pete Stewart, and Fendall Cason, were already felling trees when the trio set off for the gristmill.

Tree felling continued until early in the afternoon. By then the men had enough logs for four rafts. Adam Matheny used three horses belonging to the Matheny clan for skidding the logs down to a beach just west of the mission's dock. The horses were healthy Indian mounts acquired from the Cayuse after emerging from the Blue Mountains.

Young Adam Matheny had volunteered for numerous jobs since leaving Independence, from river crossings to building a road through the Blue Mountains. His sixteen-year-old bride, Sarah Jane, shared his desire for adventure. They had gotten married in Independence and planned to begin their new lives together in Oregon. The difficulties of the last two thousand miles had not dampened their spirits for settling a new land—and with only a short distance left, their enthusiasm for completing the journey was greater than ever. Winter was quickly approaching, and everyone wanted to get to the Wallamet Valley in time to build a cabin or some other shelter for the coming season.

During the morning Abby ground ten pounds of flour and stowed it in one of her empty flour sacks. This gain was an unexpected surprise, so that afternoon she converted some of the mission rhubarb, a few cups of flour, and her remaining sugar into a rhubarb pie. It would be a well-deserved treat for Jacob when he got back that evening.

Also during that afternoon Abby hired three Indians to move her six oxen, milch cow, Jacob's horses, and Crow down the south side of the Columbia all the way to Oregon City. This trail wound precariously along the south shore past numerous waterfalls and rocky ledges, too narrow to support a wagon road. Emigrants who were already using pack animals, such as the Bill Wilson family, chose to travel with the Indian drovers. Their conversion to pack animals weeks before was finally paying off. They did not have to build boats at Fort Walla Walla or rafts at Wascopam. They could leave for Oregon City as soon as they were ready.

Not everyone using pack animals looked forward to continuing their journey with the Indian drovers. Jim Nesmith, John Jackson, and the Oteys, who were having trouble with their hastily-made packsaddles, chose to trade their horses for a forty-foot-long Chinook canoe. They could fit all their possessions into the canoe, so the temptation to have a smooth ride all the way to Oregon City was too much to ignore. Joining them would be Bill McDaniel, who had wounded the Cayuse boy from Stickus's village, and another young, single man named Bernie Haggard. Without the responsibility of a family or wagon, Bernie did not hesitate to join his friends for an easy ride to Oregon City. The men traded their horses for a single, small canoe.

During the afternoon, forty or so more emigrants arrived by land from Fort Walla Walla. Those whom they'd left back at the fort building boats, including the Applegates, would not be ready to embark for another week or ten days. By then Jacob expected that he and Abby would be at Fort Vancouver, if not Oregon City.

Shortly before dinner Jacob, Layson, Hewitt, Stewart, Cason, and the Matheny and Keizur men completed moving all the felled and bucked logs down to the river. Construction of the rafts could begin in the morning. They planned to use ten to twelve logs of about twelve to eighteen inches in diameter and twenty feet long for each raft. Along with securing the logs with nailed-down crossties, Jacob instructed the men to use rope as lashing to provide additional strength. Dan Matheny had sized the logs so that three rafts could hold two wagons each, side by side. The fourth and largest raft would have to hold three wagons. There would be a tiller at either end, and men with long poles would be stationed on either side to provide additional power when needed, such as in landing. The duel tillers allowed the steersmen to move the raft from one side of the river to the other, much like a set of large oars. There was no need for forward power, since the river's current took care of that.

Moving downriver to Fort Vancouver would not be much of a problem, except for the portage at Cascade Falls. After that they would have to turn south at the confluence of the Multnomah River with the Columbia, then pole their way upstream to Oregon City. Should the current be strong, poling the raft might present a considerable challenge.

After dinner Jacob easily finished off half of the rhubarb pie. Progress on the rafts was moving faster than expected, an indication that tomorrow might be their last day at Wascopam. Abby cleaned up her kitchen and then retired to the Western Passage to escape a cold upriver wind.

The next day, Friday, October 20, construction on the rafts began at sunup. With everyone inspired to complete their journey to the Wallamet Valley, the rafts were ready for loading by early afternoon. Wagon boxes went first, then possessions such as trunks, tools, and food. Women directed the placement of these items back into the wagon boxes in their usual order. After that, men loaded the running gear and wheels over the beds, lashing them down with rope. Wheels remained attached to the axletrees.

Abby helped to tie down her outfit before placing her canvas white-top over the entire load to keep everything as dry as possible. She then secured the bonnet-top wagon hoops flat on the raft, extending around the wagon box. Sarah Jane Matheny did likewise, as they were sharing the same raft.

Jacob fashioned a small mast from a pole tree, and Adam Matheny offered his white-top as a sail. The other three rafts housing the remaining Mathenys, Keizurs, Hewitts, Stewarts, Laysons, and Casons were outfitted in a similar manner. By six in the evening, all wagons and baggage had been loaded and secured. They would set sail the following morning as soon as they could hire a guide.

At first light on Saturday morning, Jacob wasted no time in going up to a nearby Indian village to secure the services of a guide. By nine o'clock he was back with three young braves in tow. The additional help would be needed during the portage around Cascade Falls. At ten o'clock the small, four-raft flotilla cast off and headed downriver on the final leg of their journey.

The current grabbed the rafts, and soon they were heading downriver at a pace far quicker than any wagon road would allow. To Abby, it was good to be moving again. Moving like never before, for this time she wasn't walking. She sat on the edge of her wagon box in the bow of the raft, adjusting to the movement of the raft and acquiring her "sea legs". The smooth, swift ride was a marvelous change from the difficulties of the road. She looked back at Wascopam with its mission buildings, gardens and orchards, now quickly disappearing in the distance. Soon she faced forward again as her attention focused on the concerns at hand.

Before them was the massive, humbling presence of canyon walls rising eight hundred to a thousand feet on either side of the river. Grass covered the sloping ground within the confines of the canyon just past the Wascopam river bend. Most of it remained brown from the summer drought, although a slight tinge of green spoke of fall rains. Trees quickly became more numerous until after only five miles, thick conifer forests covered the canyon slopes on both sides of the river. For everyone in the flotilla, it was a mesmerizing scene of beauty as their tiny rafts sped headlong down the Columbia toward Oregon City and a new land.

Speed, comfort, and the state of riding, not walking, were not the only things Abby noticed. Drifting was quiet. There were no squeaking wheels, clanging pots, creaking wagons, or braying animals. The smooth, gentle ride down the Columbia was a feast of peaceful repose—and there was not the slightest breeze to disrupt the solitude and calmness of the river. After journeying hundreds of miles on a rough, broken, dusty, and sometimes nonexistent trail, today was a day to remember.

A ways below the mission they passed hundreds of dead trees standing in about ten feet of water on both sides of the river. The tops of the trees had eroded into points anywhere from a few feet to thirty feet above the water line. The trees, or rather stumps, lined both shores and extended as much as one hundred feet out into the river. The area appeared to be a forest that had recently flooded due to some type of dam or obstruction downstream. Such is the result of landslides and the subsequent creation of new rapids.

Upon Jacob's inquiry, one of the Indian guides told him that the river had once run in a continuous torrent of whitewater from the Falls of the Columbia, past Wascopam, to this place of ghostly stumps. Many years before, a tremendous landslide had dammed up the river, creating Cascade Falls and calm, slack water all the way back to Wascopam. According to this Indian, some of the elders in his tribe still remembered when the river flowed angrily past Wascopam.

Jacob related this information to Abby, who was still in the bow of the raft. She listened intently, then nodded her understanding.

"Cascade Falls must be huge," she said. "I mean, to dam a river this big, and for so many miles."

"As I understand it, we'll have about a three-mile portage. With luck we might secure the help of some of those livestock moving down to Oregon City. Drovers were leaving Wascopam every day, so some of them might be there when we arrive."

"How about the rafts?"

"Have to line them. We'll need three, maybe four lines on each raft. If the current's not too swift and we have good footing, it shouldn't be too bad. There might be some boulders and other obstacles along the shore that could give us trouble—we'll see."

"What's that?" Abby pointed to an island, ahead and to the starboard. On it were white objects glistening in the sun, not discernible at this distance.

In another half-hour they were close enough to see that it was a burial island. One of the Indians came forward to the bow.

"Memaloose," he said while pointing to the island. "Memaloose."

The island was large and oblong, extending in the direction of the current and located in the center of the channel. A small land bridge connected it to the north shore. During the spring runoff this bridge was submerged.

Abby watched intently as the small fleet of rafts slowly drifted by. The bones of hundreds of individuals, bleached white in the sun, were piled together inside cedar slab pens about eight feet square. The cedar slabs were set on end, much like the palisade of a fort. The builders had not removed the bark from the slabs, rather they ornamented them with carved images of birds, local animals, human skeletons, and various other grotesque images. Some of the pens had fallen down, no doubt from age or rot. Where a wall had collapsed, hundreds of bones and skulls spilled out over the ground.

Since leaving Independence, each day had brought new and wondrous marvels to see and write about, yet this was different. This was the sacred burial ground of a culture unknown to people back in the

United States. Abby stood in silence, staring at the enormous piles of bones; then one item caught her eye.

"Look!" she pointed to a fresh body. Family members had wrapped their recently departed in a Hudson Bay blanket and placed him on top of a pile of bones in one of the pens.

Jacob stood by, silently nodding his acknowledgment. He had seen many strange things in the mountains, but nothing like this. In the mountains, Indian tribes placed their dead on scaffolds to prevent wolves from eating the corpse. Wolves did not inhabit the Columbia Gorge, so this was not a precaution here. The island stood as a curiosity to the emigrants, yet a sacred tribal ground for the Indians of the river.

Soon the island was behind them and their attentions were again focused on the river. The tillers, bow and stern, positioned the raft into the center channel to capture the strongest current. Another mile passed, then a bend in the river and another mile. Movement was so swift that Abby and the others barely had time to reconnoiter the surrounding landscape before it changed. At times there were towering forests reaching up to the sky, then rocky crags hanging over the river, then small rivulets entering the Columbia through vertical-walled canyons. It was a scene of infinite variety and infinite beauty—a scene wild and untouched by the civilized hand of man, and that in itself was beauty.

The cool morning had given way to a mild and pleasant afternoon. The lack of wind prevented the use of sails, but that was of no importance. The river's current was moving them west at a pace faster than they had ever traveled. Additional speed was not warranted or even wanted. There was a general air of good feeling aboard the small flotilla, a feeling spurred by the magnificent beauty of the canyon and the sure-paced movement toward their final goal.

Several miles after Memaloose, Jacob again came up to the bow. Without saying a word, his stare wandered around the canyon drinking in its endless variety—yet his gaze was that of a mountain man. He searched the landscape as if memorizing each side canyon, making a mental map of the region and no doubt wondering what kind of furs the forests and side streams would yield. As he approached the bow and Abby's position, he could see that she was crying.

"Abby?"

Abby straightened her posture as she glanced over at him, then turned to look ahead at the canyon. "It's so beautiful." She wiped the tears from under her eyes and motioned toward the canyon downriver. "It's just so beautiful." Her arm dropped back down onto her worn brown dress. "If only my friends and family back in Greene County could see this." She paused for a moment, collecting herself. "If only Caleb and Sam could have lived to see this. It's just so beautiful."

Jacob looked ahead at the deep gorge through which the river flowed. He slowly nodded and in his quiet way added, "It truly is, Abby, it truly is."

As evening approached, the Indian guides continued moving them downriver, knowing they would reach an acceptable landing before losing all of the day's light. Just before six o'clock the tillers moved the rafts over to the north side of the river, then ordered the men to pole up onto a beach.

Six other Indians, en route to Fort Vancouver and Astoria to trade for blankets and other useful articles, were already camped on the beach. Smoked salmon filled their two forty-foot-long canoes. The beach was wide and broad, leaving room for both parties to camp without interfering with each other. Tomorrow the flotilla would gain the accompaniment of these two canoes and their occupants, company not unwanted considering the difficulty of tomorrow's portage.

The day had seen twenty-two miles pass with hardly any effort. With the clear weather still holding, Jacob had a fire going within minutes as Abby unloaded her kitchen gear and started to make dinner. Boiled vegetables were still a luxury that she and Jacob did not want to do without. Tonight there was the added delicacy of rhubarb pie.

After dinner Abby made her bed on the beach along with the other travelers. It would be a cold night, requiring several blankets. Jacob stoked the fire while Fendall, Pete, and Adam piled enough firewood nearby to last the night. The effort was not necessary, for it wasn't long before the entire camp was fast asleep.

On Sunday morning, October 22, the four rafts and two Indian canoes started downriver as soon as the first rays of sun began to light the canyon. The morning turned out to be a repeat of yesterday. Clear weather held and the air remained calm, leaving a peaceful, swift-flowing river to carry the flotilla downstream. There was no need to stop for a nooner, for the noontime meal could be prepared on the rafts. Furthermore, landing simply consumed time. Drifting an additional two or three miles downstream was a better alternative.

At two o'clock the Indian guides moved each raft over to the south shore and landed on a broad, wide beach. From the abandoned Indian huts and well-worn paths, it was obvious to everyone that this beach had special significance. This was the upper portage around Cascade Falls.

The small flotilla had now traveled forty miles from Wascopam in an almost effortless advance, and it had only taken a little more than a day!

Jacob and the other men secured the rafts to large conifers growing on the back side of the beach, then began the job of unloading. The running gear, wheels, and wagon boxes would be resecured on the rafts before lining. Trunks, food stores, farm implements, and other household items needed to be carried downriver over three miles of rough trail to the lower landing. It was an impossible task without the help of Indians and preferably, livestock. Unfortunately, the stock on their way to Oregon City were nowhere to be found. They may not have reached Cascade Falls yet, or they may have been beyond this point. There was no way to tell. The three Indians hired by Jacob began the task by creating a neat cache of Abby's possessions on the back side of the beach on a grassy knoll. Within the hour they had unloaded everything and Jacob was resecuring the running gear and wagon box to the raft.

The Indians completed their work with precision and expediency. It was clear to Abby, Jacob, and the others that these Indians possessed years of experience in portaging this section of river. They knew what had to be done and the amount of weight they could handle over the three miles of trail. It would take many trips before the neatly stacked piles reappeared on the lower beach.

Three hours of daylight remained, enough to make two round-trip portages. Jacob agreed to stay on the upper beach watching their outfit while Abby walked to the lower beach with the first portage. She carried blankets and food with the expectation of spending the night at the lower end. Jacob would stay at the upper beach until the Indians could portage all articles. At that time (probably tomorrow afternoon) he, the other male emigrants, and the Indians would line the rafts past the falls and down to the lower beach.

Other Indians at the falls came up to offer their services in portaging the emigrants' baggage, so Abby hired one additional man. She was quick to recognize how helpful these Indians were, very different from the Indians above Wascopam. These men were honest and, like the Indians encountered on the Snake River Plains, were desirous of getting paid in clothes. These people had a sense of value, in both their lives and material goods. They were careful and considerate of everyone's possessions, taking special precautions not to damage anything. No Indian ever deserted his post, and several assisted emigrant mothers by carrying small children down the portage trail.

Once again, without the help of local Indians, the emigrants' journey to the Wallamet Valley might have ended here. As soon as Abby reached the lower beach, along with her trade goods trunk, she separated the trade clothes for payment to the Indians. In addition to the three guides Jacob had hired at Wascopam and the young man just hired at the falls, the Indians moving their stock to Oregon City needed to be paid. She still had four trade shirts left, which would suffice as payment for the portage. The other articles of trade, including two worn-out dresses, could be disbursed at Oregon City. The Indians moving stock down to Oregon City and the three Indians helping to pilot their raft would be paid at that time. Abby assessed the extent of her trade goods, wishing she had more, but grateful for what she did have. There would be enough to pay for all the Indian labor.

While Abby sorted and separated her trade goods, a familiar voice called out from the lower end of the beach.

"I was wondering when you'd get here."

Abby turned to see Jim Nesmith walking up from an Indian village just below Cascade Falls.

"Jim! What are you doing here? I thought you and the others would be at Fort Vancouver by now."

"Oh, Ed, Morris, and the others might be. They wanted to chance running the boat through the shallows, but I wouldn't have anything to do with it—too much chance of wrecking. When I finally got down here to the lower beach they'd already gone by. Maybe they didn't know where to stop."

"So they just abandoned you! How long have you been here?"

"Since yesterday afternoon. I'm sure it was just an oversight, missing this beach and all."

"Jim, that's terrible."

"By the time they discovered their error I imagine they were too far downriver to come back. Sure glad to see you Abby—hope you don't mind if I ride with you down to Oregon City."

"Not at all, Jim, you're always welcome. Abby enjoyed the prospect of taking on Jim, but had to laugh at his predicament. "So they just left you," she said with a smile. "You done anything to make them angry?"

"Yeah, I'm a terrible cook."

"Jacob and I have food," she said laughing. "You're more than welcome to join us."

"Thank you, Abby. I can't think of a nicer person to rescue me."

Jim had spent the previous night with an Indian family in one of the huts near the lower beach. They provided food and a Hudson Bay blanket for the night, asking nothing in return. Thanks to their kindness, being stranded at this point in the journey was certainly no hardship.

Similar to tribes throughout the entire Columbia and Snake River drainages, the Indians on the lower beach were in pursuit of their main occupation of securing salmon both for food and trade. The squaws wore brass strings of beads of all colors, no doubt secured through trading with Hudson Bay personnel or any of the many tall ships that sailed up the Columbia to Fort Vancouver. This bodily decor was highly fashionable, with all squaws wearing some variation of beads or metal decorations. Their clothes also reflected European influence. Some Indians wore the leggings of a sailor, while others looked like bankers and others like farmers. This menagerie of discarded clothes was worn with no knowledge of how each item fit into European or American culture. This was not the first time Abby had seen such a display of cultural ignorance. The first Western Indians she had ever seen, back in St. Louis, had worn a similar display of trade clothes. The scene here on the Columbia would make for interesting copy in her next diary entry.

Although the portage was only three miles, Cascade Falls extended for four miles, with the river descending about fifty feet. The falls began where the water first picked up speed, a few hundred yards below the upper portage beach. Calm water did not resume until a half-mile below the lower portage beach. This last half-mile of churning water was swift, but not that dangerous. Rafts could be floated safely down to calm water.

Cascade Falls contained most of the drop, about thirty-five feet, but extended for a quarter-mile. The water in this narrow section of river churned in a boiling, foaming, angry mass strewn with shed-sized boulders, snags, strainers, and sawyers. It was in this area that the Indians secured salmon. They crowded onto favorite points of land and boulders jutting out into the river, spearing fish with an efficiency that would make any fisherman jealous. Abby was able to see some of the activity on her way down the trail where trees did not block the view. From the lower portage beach she had a clear view upriver to where the water cascaded over boulders in a headlong dash to the ocean. She had been told at Wascopam that no boat could ever negotiate the falls, and now she could see why. There was no visible route, and anyone attempting such a foolish undertaking would surely wreck. Portaging was the only option.

Around the falls on either side of the river stood high mountains, extending almost vertically for eight hundred to a thousand feet. Beyond this they continued on a more gentle rise, until reaching the alpine and treeless regions of Mount Hood to the south and Mount Adams to the north. At this point in the river a recent fire had burned the surrounding forests, leaving only the skeletal remains of a once-green landscape. Trees killed by surface fires retained their needles, but were now reddish brown. The scene, although wild, did not present the picture of beauty that everyone had enjoyed on their drift down from Wascopam; however, their stay here would be short. Jacob estimated two nights, and now Abby agreed. With the efficient manner in which the Indians were transporting her outfit to the lower beach, they would be ready to go the day after tomorrow.

Tonight was one of the few nights that Abby and Jacob had spent apart since leaving Independence. The other times had been during Jacob's solo hunting expeditions out on the prairie. Abby prepared her bed on a knoll of grass, wishing she had her diary to record the events of the day. The book was still in a trunk that would be portaged in the morning. Along with detailing the portage, she wanted to describe the immense salmon fisheries encountered here and elsewhere on the Columbia. At each obstacle such as the Falls of the Columbia or The Dalles, or here at Cascade Falls, Indians extracted huge quantities of fish. Salmon was truly the currency of the Columbia.

Jim Nesmith chose to spend the night out on the beach with Abby rather than with his newly adopted Indian family. She had enough blankets for him and welcomed the added protection of a trusted friend.

On Monday morning, October 23, Abby's remaining baggage arrived before noon. All that was left was the job of lining the rafts down the south shore.

Men secured each raft with four lines, long enough for two people to man each line. By working together as a team, eight men could line one raft down to the lower beach. There was a primitive trail alongside the river, since the Indians often lined their Mackinaws. Lining rafts was a novelty for the Indian labor, but one they mastered quickly. Their strength, knowledge of the lining route, and expertise in reading river currents allowed them to safely line each raft to the lower beach with minimal delay. Only on a few occasions did a raft come up against a boulder or get caught in an eddy. In each case they quickly extricated it with little damage. Abby's raft went first. Upon reaching the lower beach, Jacob secured the raft to a large conifer, then followed the Indians and other men back up to the upper beach to line the next raft. By evening all four rafts were on the lower beach.

Late afternoon saw the arrival of Nineveh Ford at the upper Cascade Falls portage. Nineveh was a husky 28-year-old business entrepreneur who was taking his wife and family to Oregon to start a tannery. With an annual influx of new emigrants, there would be an enormous demand for the hundreds of products made from leather. Everything from saddles and plow harnesses to shoes and other clothing would enjoy a ready market. Nineveh could not pass up this business opportunity. Traveling with Nineveh was his younger brother, Nimrod, his wife and children, along with their cousins, John and Ephriam and their families. The group had five wagons, carried on three hastily built rafts. With a desire to see an end to their journey, and to avoid the added expense of an Indian guide, they had cast off from Wascopam before the first morning light in an attempt to overtake and join Abby's flotilla.

The rafts the Ford men had built were poorly constructed and not holding together against the river's current. Lining past Cascade Falls early in the evening almost proved disastrous when two of the fragile crafts careened off of several large boulders, tearing out logs and almost destroying one raft. With the help of Indians, the men were able to get their rafts, along with their wagon boxes, possessions, and running gear, down to the lower beach before dark. They had not bothered to portage their belongings. Instead, they lined the rafts fully loaded. This added weight was simply too much for the men to handle during the long lining process.

By the time they arrived it was obvious that each raft needed major repairs before continuing downriver. As a result of this disagreeable situation, the Ford men chose to buy two canoes belonging to the Indians at the lower village. They took the beds of their five wagons and lashed them upside-down across the two forty-foot-long canoes, thereby making an extended platform on a multi-hulled craft. On top of this they placed their running gear, then tied their baggage on top of that. Their last job was to rig a mast, using one of the white-tops as a sail.

As people were reloading their rafts and the Ford men were constructing their new river boat, two bateaux arrived from Fort Vancouver. To everyone's surprise, Chief Factor Dr. John McLoughlin had heard of the emigrants' approach and plight. As a courtesy to the Americans, he sent two boats with provisions to help in the descent of the Columbia.

The Mathenys and several other men helped to land the bateaux, then spent the next hour talking to Mr. Douglass, the gentleman in charge. Douglass had come over from Britain on a supply ship over fifteen years before. After spending the first ten years as a trapper, he had finally worked his way up the Hudson Bay Company hierarchy to where he now acted as Dr. McLoughlin's attaché. Douglass handled much of the day-to-day business operations conducted with the outlying forts and numerous Indian chiefs. His stature of over six feet in height and two hundred pounds generated the respect he needed to carry out Dr. McLoughlin's orders.

"You won't have any trouble from here on," said Douglass. "The river widens out and is calm from here to the Pacific. Although it can get windy down here in the gorge, so that might cause you some delay. If it's blowing in the right direction, then you might consider rigging a sail."

"How about the Multnomah?" asked Jacob. "Can we pole these rafts up that river?"

"Can if you stick close to the shore. Multnomah's a big river and the current this time of year is slow. It'll be work, you can depend on that—but with enough polers you should make it without too much trouble. Oregon City is about thirty miles from Fort Vancouver, with twenty-five of those miles on the Multnomah. With these rafts you better expect to spend two days poling up that river."

Each emigrant listened intently, for they all had wagons they wanted to get to Oregon City and the Wallamet Valley. Wagons were a necessity for farming, and they had come too far to give up now. The conversation continued with questions about the land in the Wallamet Valley, farm markets, new settlements, and areas where retired trappers had begun their own farms. Mr. Douglass had firsthand knowledge and all the recent news of this new land, so it proved to be a valuable and informative evening around the campfire.

Mr. Douglass distributed dried salmon and apples to each of the travelers, compliments of Dr. McLoughlin and the Hudson Bay Company. Abby had enough smoked salmon, but accepted a half-bushel of apples, wisely maintaining a full cache of food.

Mr. Douglass made arrangements to have Indians carry his bateaux up the portage trail first thing in the morning so he could continue his journey to Wascopam and The Dalles. The emigrants on the lower beach would finish their preparations, then proceed downriver. It was now well after dark, so everyone gladly retired to the warmth of their blankets.

Abby and Jacob spent the following morning repairing some crosstie damage sustained by their raft during yesterday's lining, reloading the raft, and securing everything for the remainder of the journey. Their last chore was to have a meal of smoked salmon before casting off in the early afternoon. Jim Nesmith helped in preparing and loading the raft, for he would join Abby and Jacob for the float to Oregon City.

The warning of strong winds given by Mr. Douglass proved all too real that afternoon. A stiff, cold wind blew up the Columbia, producing whitecap waves across the entire river and slowing the flotilla's speed by at least half. It was a slow, tiring afternoon as the emigrants tried to keep their rafts in the main current as best as they could.

The drift today took them past a large vertical rock structure on the north side of the river, first described in the Lewis and Clark journals. As a consummate student, Abby had read many of the published excerpts from the explorers' journals and remembered this landmark. The rock was cylindrical, standing about five hundred feet tall and two or three hundred feet thick at the base.

"Jacob!" She called back to get his attention. He broke off his conversation with Adam and came forward.

"Look at that," Abby said as she pointed to the large monolith. "That has to be the rock I read about in the Cincinnati paper when they published parts of William Clark's journal. They described it as being along the north shore, but standing out in the river by itself. What do you think? It fits their description, so that must be it!"

Jacob scanned the large, ragged landmark. "Could be, there's nothing else along this river that matches that description."

"I read that when they first saw that rock they named it Beaten Rock. Then on their way back the next spring, they referred to it as Beacon Rock. Which name do you think will stick?"

"Name? Don't matter. What do local Indians call it? No need for us to keep changing things."

"Well, I think it's just magnificent. The description Clark gave couldn't begin to do it justice. I never thought I'd see it, and now there it is—right in front of us!"

The fire-scarred slopes had now given way to thick stands of timber, almost exclusively conifer. Even the top of Beaten Rock displayed several scraggly-looking fir. Abby's gaze continued to wander about the canyon as she tried hard not to miss any details.

"Jacob, look!" Abby pointed to a sea lion that had just surfaced about fifty feet in front of the raft. It had a salmon in its mouth, and with a few gulps the fish disappeared.

"There's more." Jacob pointed to several more sea lions on the north shore of the river.

"Now I know we're getting close. These are ocean-dwelling animals, Jacob! I read about them too!"

The windy day took its toll on everyone, and by evening they were only eight miles from the lower portage. The sky had remained clear, but began to cloud up as darkness approached. Tonight's camp was on the north side of the river on another well-worn beach. One of the Indian guides killed two grouse that he readily shared with everyone in the party. This, along with salmon and apples, made an excellent meal.

On Wednesday morning, October 25, the high winds continued, except they were now from the southeast. The night cold had sunk into Abby's bones, with two blankets proving woefully inadequate. Before morning she had retrieved two more blankets from her baggage, adding some comfort, but for the most part it was a sleepless night.

The shift in wind direction afforded the first opportunity to use the sail. When the single spar bowed under the weight of the sail, Jacob and Adam Matheny constructed an additional support using the tongue from Abby's wagon. Once in place, the sail added another two miles each hour to their drift speed.

Abby's excitement from the day before grew as the flotilla drifted past several more waterfalls coming in on the south side. She shaded her eyes from the noon sun to get a better view. Each display was slightly different as the water issued forth from the deep forest in a cascade of twenty or more feet. Some were partially hidden by trees, presenting intermittent flashes of white as they shone through.

"There it is, a double waterfall!"

Abby pointed to a falls described by William Clark as falling over six hundred feet in the first drop and an additional thirty feet in the second. The initial drop was a spectacular plunge over a sheer cliff almost seven hundred feet above the river. From there it formed a small pool before continuing down another thirty-foot drop to the Columbia. The wind today was strong enough to disrupt the upper falls and turn the water into a mist that seemed to disappear along the cliff's walls.

"It's just like I imagined it, Jacob. Have you ever seen such a beautiful waterfall?"

"Up in Yellowstone Country." Jacob paused as he remembered. "We called it the Falls of the Yellowstone. Only trappers and Indians ever seen it, and it's a match for this one. Doesn't fall as far, but it puts out considerably more water."

"I think this is just the most beautiful falls I've ever seen. No wonder there are so many tall tales about Oregon. People see things like this, and it's only natural to exaggerate."

"Looks like there might be more falls during the spring runoff." Jacob pointed to sheer cliffs west of the double falls. Eons of erosion and discoloration of the rock face indicated an intermittent cascade.

"I think we can finally say we're in the Oregon we've heard so much about. Can't be any more deserts, we're too close to the Wallamet Valley. I'll bet all of that valley is as beautiful as this canyon!"

"Don't know," replied Jacob in his slow and calculating manner, "but we'll be there soon if this wind holds. I'll pass the word to keep drifting for as long as possible. This wind might turn on us tomorrow."

They continued downriver until after dark, taking full advantage of the strong wind. The Indians piloting the raft knew each beach, river obstacle, and eddy, so drifting after dark did not present a serious hazard. Soon they saw a large campfire on the north shore—a campfire that the Indians referred to as a "Boston" fire. Jacob quickly discerned that Boston meant non-Indian, or rather, a white man's fire.

By using the forward and aft tillers as paddles, the Indian pilots started moving the flotilla of rafts toward the bright light. Included in their flotilla were three Indian canoes and Nineveh Ford's double-hulled craft. As they approached, Jim Nesmith drew his pistol and fired one shot into the air. The shore party answered back with another pistol shot.

Soon the rafts and canoes were scraping up on the beach. Indians jumped out with lines to secure each craft to trees while the people on shore came down to assist in the landing. As Jim threw a line out to an approaching man, he saw that the shore party consisted of his lost companions, Ed and Morris Otey, John Jackson, Bill McDaniel, and Bernie Haggard. They carried all of his baggage, so finding them was a great relief. Bernie caught the line and started pulling the raft up onto the sand.

"Bernie! What are you doing here?"

"Waiting for you. We figured you'd hook up with someone." Bernie looked around at the flotilla. "Miss Meacham, it's always good to see you."

"Bernie." Abby acknowledged his greeting while looking after the landing and security of her outfit.

"Jacob, I want to tie off with at least two lines," Abby said, pulling out another rope. "Three are better—this wind might get worse overnight."

Without speaking, Jacob grabbed a third line to triple-tie the raft.

Securing the rafts and unloading blankets for the night and food for dinner took less than twenty minutes. Ed Otey stoked the campfire for the added company as everyone gathered around for dinner.

The Indian guides set their camp downstream from the Boston fire—a wise precaution considering the many cultural differences.

"It won't be long now," said Jim, breaking off a piece of smoked salmon that his companions were sharing. Abby slid over to make room for him to sit down.

"If you hadn't gotten yourself lost," said Morris, "we could probably be at Fort Vancouver by now. Where'd you spend last night?"

Jim looked up. "Lost! You floated right by that lower beach."

"Saw it too late," added Ed. "This boat is just too heavy to pull over quickly, so we had no choice but to continue. Since you were able to hook up with Abby, we sure don't feel sorry for you."

"Spent the first night in that Indian village below the falls. And I might add that their hospitality and cooking is certainly better than yours! Abby showed up the next day—and her hospitality and cooking are better than yours too!" Abby gave Jim a playful elbow in the ribs as their eyes met.

"Today was a good day for travel," Abby said, looking over at Ed and Morris. "Too bad you men had to wait here."

"We'll make up for that, Abby," said John Jackson. "I'd just as soon push right on through to Oregon City rather than spending any time at Fort Vancouver. Seems like we've been traveling for a year."

"Jacob and I figure another week, maybe less," added Abby. "What plans have you men got for the coming winter?"

"First thing to do is build some kind of shelter," said Jim. "There should be plenty of game around to keep us fed until spring. By then we'll know the country and what the best opportunities are. There should be more emigrants arriving next fall, so I imagine a good businessman could make a respectable living."

The conversation continued amid the warmth of the campfire and the gentle sound of waves on the river shoreline. After an hour of eating and socializing, it came time to turn in. The day had been long, although that alone was not enough to move people to their blankets. The strong wind had not dissipated, and it was now cold and uncomfortable away from the fire. Rolling up in several blankets and hugging the ground would be the best way to stay warm until morning.

On Thursday morning, October 26, the cold wind continued from the east—a good power source for pushing the flotilla down to Fort Vancouver. At noon they arrived at the Hudson Bay gristmill on the north shore. The mill was approximately seven miles above the fort and had a good beach for landing. This was the first building encountered since leaving Wascopam, so Dan Matheny ordered the flotilla to land. Their primary purpose was to gain information about the river ahead, the distance to Fort Vancouver, and the difficulty of poling up the Multnomah to Oregon City.

Upon landing they encountered more emigrants from the Oregon Emigrating Company. Jim Waters (one of Bill Martin's platoon leaders), Lindsey Thorp, Jim Martin, and Nate Smith had their camp set up on the west end of the beach, waiting for the downriver wind to subside. After arriving at Fort Walla Walla, these men chose to hurry down to Fort Vancouver to secure a large boat from the Hudson Bay Company. They were now on their way back up the Columbia to Fort Walla Walla to retrieve their families and baggage. Abby broke out enough food for her and Jacob, then sat down with her dusty trail mates to discuss the details of the final miles to Oregon City.

Choosing not to stop for a noon meal, Jim Nesmith and his companions continued downriver with the intention of reaching Oregon City, or as near as possible, by evening. With a Columbia River canoe, they could make better time than the rafts, even with a downriver wind. Their desire to reach their final destination was far greater than their wish to remain with their traveling companions and stop at another Hudson Bay fort, namely, Fort Vancouver.

Jacob's earlier prediction was correct. After crossing the Blue Mountains, the Oregon Emigrating Company had disintegrated. As soon as people no longer needed a guide or mutual protection and help against the unknowns of the trail, their individual independence took control. Emigrant parties now stretched between Fort Vancouver and Fort Walla Walla, with each man or family making their own decisions on how to complete the journey. These men heading back upriver would meet others coming downriver, and still others were planning on going back to Fort Walla Walla in the spring to recover livestock.

The confusion of the final push was unsettling, yet Abby knew she was in better shape than most. She and Jacob were only a few days from their final goal, and they had their entire outfit with them. They would not have to travel back upriver, since their livestock would be in Oregon City waiting for them. After nooning, Abby bid her friends farewell as they continued their journey upriver, and she and Jacob their journey downriver. It was an easy farewell, for she would see these people again in the Wallamet Valley, and going back upriver was something she had no desire to do.

The flotilla arrived at Fort Vancouver in the late afternoon, about an hour before dark. Docked at the fort's wharf were three tall ships belonging to the Hudson Bay Company. They were the *H.M.S. Vancouver*, the *H.M.S. Columbia*, and a smaller schooner used to ply trade along the north coast. These were the first tall ships Abby and most of the other emigrants had ever seen. Their sense of wonder had not been dampened by the abundance of new sights along the journey; the adventure of seeing the elephant was still very real.

The rafts pulled up on a beach just east of the fort's main pier, where the men could secure them to several small pilings. Darkness was quickly approaching, leaving just enough time to walk up to the fort and announce their arrival.

Unlike at other forts encountered earlier by the migration, a high wooden palisade consisting of one-foot-thick logs surrounded Fort Vancouver. The interior contained numerous buildings serving as stores, warehouses, repair shops, and residences for agents, their families, and the chief factor, Dr. John McLoughlin. Extending back from the fort for about a mile lay numerous pastures, orchards, and fields of row crops belonging to former employees of the Hudson Bay Company. These farms supplied fresh milk, meat, and a variety of vegetables and fruit for the fort and surrounding population. The main dairy for the fort was several miles downriver on Sophia's Island. Every year this dairy manufactured several hundred pounds of cheese and butter, which the company sold to the Russian settlements up in Sitka along the north coast. In return, the company received the Russian fur trade. Tall ships maintained this trade route, along with a substantial trade in the Sandwich Islands.

Dr. McLoughlin greeted the emigrants, welcoming them to Oregon Country and congratulating everyone on their success in bringing wagons out from the United States. McLoughlin's husky voice, piercing eyes, and dominating stature easily commanded everyone's attention. He shook hands with each man, then invited everyone to a feast in their honor the next evening. It was an invitation the tired travelers could not turn down, no matter how much they wanted to complete their journey to Oregon City. Dr. McLoughlin controlled Oregon Country with dictatorial power, and his order to send two bateaux upriver to help the Americans was proof enough of their welcome. A layover day at the fort would not be an inconvenience. Besides, the fort's warehouses and store might be able to provide valuable items needed to build a winter cabin in the Wallamet Valley.

Everyone returned to their rafts for the night. Tomorrow would be a relaxing day among the comforts of civilization.

The next morning Abby and several of the ladies went up to the fort to see what they might have to sell. This was the Hudson Bay's main fort, which supplied all other establishments, including Fort Hall, now five hundred miles to the east. Abby and her friends entered the store, and as everyone had suspected, found blankets, food, lumber, various implements for farming, and tools for building a cabin. All available for sale and, of course, at a price considerably higher than what could be found back in the United States. With the experiences gained since leaving Independence, high prices hardly received a mention from the ladies.

The Western Passage was in good shape after the journey from Fort Walla Walla to Wascopam and did not need any attention from the fort's blacksmith, however, the trip down from Wascopam had demonstrated a need for more rope. Additionally, axes and knives needed sharpening. The sharpening wheel used by the Oregon Emigrating Company belonged to Sam Cozine who, at this moment, could be anywhere between Waiilatpu and Oregon City.

Abby bought one hundred feet of rope from the store, then located the blacksmith shop and made arrangements to use their wheel.

Upon returning to the raft, she shoved the rope into her wagon box and then pulled out one of the axes before Jacob came to her aid. Sharpening tools was strictly a man's job.

"Here, you give me that," he said as he took the axe. "They got a wheel up at the fort?"

"It's at the blacksmith shop. He's expecting me."

"Then let's go." He picked up a second axe, the shovel, and four knives. "You got anything else that needs sharpening?"

"That's it." Abby resecured the white-top over her wagon box and jumped off the raft to follow Jacob. The fort stood back from the river about a quarter-mile, high enough to avoid the spring runoff. A wide, well-worn road led from the fort's front gate down to the wharf.

"You learn where the confluence of the Multnomah is?" asked Abby.

"Five miles downriver from here near a Sophia's Island. Supposed to be hard to find."

"Our guide should be able to find it."

"That he should. We're probably seeing the north end of the Wallamet Valley over there on the south shore."

Abby spun around to look across the Columbia. Several miles upstream from the fort, the canyon walls along the river had given way to a flat country, bounded by scattered hills of distant timber.

"Probably," she said. "The Wallamet Valley! Aren't you getting excited, Jacob? We're almost there and you've hardly said a word."

"Nothing to say. I don't much care for the Hudson Bay Company, so I'll be pleased to shove off tomorrow morning."

"We're getting our tools sharpened, and I was able to buy more rope, and we're invited to dinner tonight. These Hudson Bay people aren't that bad, at least not that I've seen."

"Well, I'd like to get away before anyone recognizes me. We had some scrapes with their trapping brigades back in the Rockies, and I don't much care to run into anyone that I've previously shot."

"Jacob! Sometimes I don't know about you. You can stay down by the rafts if you wish, we have plenty of smoked salmon. I'll be joining the Mathenys, Laysons, and the others at Dr. McLoughlin's table."

That evening Jacob chose to stay down by the rafts as Abby suggested. She and the other flotilla emigrants joined Dr. McLoughlin and a brigade leader named Peter Ogden at a banquet fit for guests of great importance. A long table was set in Dr. McLoughlin's dining room, warmed by two fires and lit with eight lanterns.

Servants ushered the guests into Dr. McLoughlin's residence and back to the large dining room. Abby sat down, adjusting her worn dress and trying to look as ladylike as possible, considering her trail-hardened condition. She had washed her face, hair, and hands earlier, yet her worn dress told a tale of many weeks of rugged trail life. She sat speechless, looking up and down the long table, admiring the place settings, dishes, silverware, and baskets of bread. Then she put her feet together, sat up straight, and placed her hands down on the table, feeling the wood. This was the first table she had sat at since leaving Hannah Greer's boarding house in Independence five months ago. *It seems more like five years!* Abby thought. At first a smile came to her face, then tears as she remembered the comforts of her home back in Ohio. The emotion took her by surprise, so she quickly wiped away the tears before anyone could see. In the next moment she entered into a conversation between Mary Matheny and Becky Stewart. The distraction helped to hide the surprise of homesickness.

"Isn't this wonderful," said Becky with a smile that proclaimed her return to civilization. "I hope Dr. McLoughlin has enough food to feed all of us."

"I never expected such a formal dining room, did you? Abby stated emphatically. "And with servants! If only my family back in Ohio could see this."

"We'll all have homes like this in a few years," added Mary with resolve. "Maybe not with servants, but with enough food for any occasion."

Dr. McLoughlin sat at the head of the table; then came the men, and then the women. The men wanted to converse with McLoughlin about prospects in the Wallamet Valley, while McLoughlin wanted to learn about their plans for settling the valley. Women sat together at the other end, conversing among themselves. There were three main courses, one of beef, the other elk, and the third salmon. They were accompanied by cooked carrots, peas, string beans, potatoes, gravy, bread, butter, cheese, and squash, followed by pie and cake for dessert. Abby was so busy eating and conversing with the other ladies that she failed to hear her name when Dr. McLoughlin addressed her.

"Which one of you ladies came out here by yourself?" inquired McLoughlin.

"Abby," whispered Becky. "Dr. McLoughlin's talking to you!"

"I'd like to meet that woman!"

Someone pointed her out.

Abby spun around, looking to the head of the table, her eyes wide open and her mouth bulging with a spoonful of mashed potatoes.

"They tell me you came out here by yourself," the chief factor boomed. "Is that true?"

Abby covered her mouth as she tried to bolt down the food. "Yes." She swallowed again. "I've come from Ohio to teach school in the Wallamet Valley."

"A schoolteacher! Well now, that's excellent!" McLoughlin took a drink to wash down some food. "The children of all these farmers are going to need schooling," he said in a somewhat blustery voice. "A number of my trappers have settled down on French Prairie near Champooic. Their children need schooling too. What family did you come out with?"

"Nobody, sir. I have my own outfit, a good wagon and stock to pull it. I hired a man to help with the chores, but it's my wagon and I'll have it in Oregon City before long."

He sat staring at her for a few seconds. "Now that's the kind of woman we need out here." Other conversations had ended as everyone listened. McLoughlin then stood and held up his stein.

"I drink to your health, Miss Meacham—and wish you the best of success here in Oregon Country."

The other men immediately stood up with their steins, and everyone had a toast in Abby's honor. It was an embarrassing moment to say the least.

"Thank you, Mr. McLoughlin," Abby said with a smile, while choking back tears. "I'm looking forward to starting a school and,

and, it's wonderful to be here. This is a grand dinner. Thank you so much for inviting us!"

McLoughlin nodded and sat down, as did everyone else. Abby hoped that what she had said was acceptable. Her head was spinning with confusion and embarrassment, but she would look back on this as a dinner and evening to remember.

The men's conversation returned to the fate of the remaining emigrants at Fort Walla Walla. When McLoughlin learned that Chief Factor McKinley was holding American cattle in exchange for cattle here at Fort Vancouver, he voiced disapproval.

"All I have here are Spanish cattle brought up from California," he said, "and they're not worth the feed to keep 'em alive. An even exchange is not possible. Spanish stock are only worth about $9 a head, while your American breeds will bring $45 to $50 a head. When your Applegates and those other stockowners get down here with their vouchers, I'll sign a letter to McKinley telling him to return your cattle in the spring—and without any charge for pasturage. McKinley has no business defrauding you people."

When Abby heard this she thought of Malinda and her other friends. Were they still at Fort Walla Walla building boats, or had they left on their perilous journey down the beautiful but dangerous Columbia? There was no way to tell.

"Did you hear that?" Abby asked as she turned back to the other ladies. "Malinda, Jesse, McHaley, and the others will get their stock back next spring after they've regained their strength. They'll be happy to hear that. Those American cattle will be the first in the Wallamet Valley! They're really going to make it!"

Emigrant guests did not return to their flotilla until after ten o'clock. The dinner and conversation lasted for three hours, far longer than anyone expected. The people who had stayed with the rafts, mostly children, were already asleep when everyone got back. Abby pulled out four blankets and lay down inside her wagon box. It was too dark to find a good place on shore, and the wagon box was a familiar and friendly bed.

On Saturday morning, October 28, Abby sat up in her wagon box and peered out from under the canvas at the scene about. Sometime during the previous evening several Indians had landed two cedar Mackinaws next to her raft. In the early morning light she could see the details of these finely made crafts. Other folks were already up and preparing for the day, so Abby quickly produced her diary to record a description:

"These Indian boats are sleek and fast, made from a single hollowed-out cedar log. Each is about thirty feet long, three feet wide in the center, and two feet deep. The decorations on the outer hull display various carvings of grotesque heads and images of salmon, birds, and bears. The Indians have painted each image with a different color, using shades of red, blue, and black along with white trim. Besides having utility for navigating the river, these Indian boats are true works of art."

They had to get underway soon, so she jotted down a few more items from the previous day to jog her memory when she had more time to write. Time was short, and there was breakfast to prepare and a river to float. By tonight they would be on the waters of the Multnomah!

This morning, like each morning of the past week, held none of the usual chores of cleaning utensils, stowing kitchen gear, hitching stock, and the many other routine details of preparing for a day's march. Abby simply got out some apples and salmon for herself and Jacob. Ten minutes later they were ready to cast off. After last night's dinner she had no appetite for a large breakfast.

"Jacob, I don't think I've ever eaten so much in my life as I did last night. Everything was so good. We sat at a table with dishes and silverware, and there were servants that served the food, and all kinds of things to talk about with new farms and settlements."

"Anyone there from the trapping brigades?"

"One man—I believe his name was Peter Ogden. Dr. McLoughlin introduced him as one of his brigade leaders. Do you know him?"

"Not well. He could probably recognize me though. It was his brigade that we ran into down near the Bear River."

"Did you shoot him?" Abby said this with a half-sarcastic smile.

Jacob quickly changed the subject. "We should cast off while it's calm. That wind might shift when the sun gets high." He stood and walked over to Dan Matheny's raft to see if they were ready to leave.

Maybe he did shoot him, Abby thought. *I shouldn't have teased him!*

Her mind quickly diverted to the chores at hand. She stowed the remaining breakfast food and made fast the white-top over her wagon box. She attached one end of her new rope to one of the raft's crossties for later use as a shoreline. Five minutes later they were casting off, with their Indian guides using the tillers to move the rafts out into swifter water.

As the small flotilla drifted down toward the fort's wharf, Abby's raft came nearest to the tall ships. Several sailors soon noticed the group, and especially Abby. As they drifted past, one of the sailors tossed her an apple. She caught it and waved back.

"Thank you, that's very kind!"

Soon other sailors were tossing apples, and Abby was smiling and catching them as fast as she could. Jacob stood by watching the spectacle, as did the Indians and other emigrants. Had the other ladies been close enough to the ships, they too would have received apples. By the time they finally drifted out of range, Abby had almost a half-bushel of apples stacked on top of her white-top.

"Well, that was interesting," she said to Jacob with a smile. "We can always use a few more apples."

"Those sailors had more on their minds than just apples."

"Jacob! There's no need for unkind thoughts. I thought it was very sweet of them to give us these apples."

"You'll never go hungry, Abby, that's for certain."

"Someone once told me, meat's meat!"

When she said this, Jacob had to grin. She had caught him with his own philosophy. Nodding his approval, he walked to the back of the raft to get a pole and help with navigating.

As they drifted the final mile along the Columbia, another tall ship passed by on its way up to Fort Vancouver. The ship was a schooner named *H.M.S. Pallas.* Like the others, this ship belonged to the Hudson Bay Company's fur-trading fleet and was apparently returning from one of the remote outposts, loaded down with last winter's catch.

Everyone waved and shouted their greetings. The sight of wagons secured to rafts was as unusual a spectacle to the sailors as the ships were to the emigrants. The small flotilla's cargo of Eastern settlers, wagons, and farm implements foretold certain change, a portent of things to come. As the trapping era came to an end, these newest residents would begin to usher in a new era of settlement and civilization. It was a pivotal moment in the history of Oregon Country and the expansion of the United States domain, a moment that possibly only Dr. McLoughlin truly understood.

After another few miles the Indian guides moved the rafts over to the south shore, drifting near the shallows until they came to the head of Sophia's Island. Clearing a sandbar, they drifted around a bend and into the current of the Multnomah River. They were now approximately five miles from Fort Vancouver. Each man grabbed a pole and began to push the raft up the east shore of the Multnomah. After another mile, the Indian guides steered the rafts over to the west shore where the river was shallower and the current not as strong.

Along the west bank lay an immense conifer forest extending back to some low hills about a half-mile distant. On the east bank was a rolling prairie that appeared to have burned recently. By four o'clock that afternoon the small flotilla had painstakingly poled almost twelve miles upriver. The Indian guides pulled into a well-worn beach on the west side while there was still daylight to build a fire, get something to eat, and rest sore muscles.

The beach was not large, only about twenty feet deep and thirty feet long, with barely enough room for four rafts and the Ford's double-hulled craft. The men pulled each raft up on the sand as far as possible, then prepared to secure them with two lines to trees on the back side of the beach. Earlier in the day the other Indian canoes associated with the flotilla had left them at the mouth of the Multnomah, continuing down the Columbia to Astoria, located at the river's confluence with the Pacific Ocean.

With the concern over landing and securing the rafts, nobody had paid much attention to the surrounding area. Jacob handed Abby one end of her new rope to tie off on a tree. When she got halfway to the back side of the beach, she dropped the rope and looked up in amazement at the trees in front of her. There were several small shrubs and conifers, much like the forests along the Columbia River, but towering above these were trees of a magnitude she had never imagined. Abby stood agape in front of a conifer that was wider than a wagon and taller than anything she had ever seen. She leaned back trying to see the top, which disappeared into the forest canopy.

Jacob and the other emigrants now took notice of the trees. Everyone stopped what they were doing and stared in amazement at the forest in front of them.

Abby slowly moved forward, as if drawn into the timber by some unseen force. Reaching the nearest tree, she extended her arms as if to give it a hug. She threw her head back, again trying to see the top. The tree had a straight, cylindrical bole that extended vertically for at least a hundred feet before the first branches—then continued skyward, towering out of sight up into the canopy. Abby started moving around the trunk with her arms out, measuring the number of times the full width of her arms could fit around the tree before coming back to the start point.

"One, two, three, four, five." She counted out each span. "Almost six." She went back down on the beach and scratched out the math in the sand.

"I have a five-foot reach, so that tree's got a circumference of about 29 or 30 feet. That's …" She quickly scribbled a division of 30 by 3.1. In a moment she was again standing up straight, looking back at the tree.

"That tree is over nine feet across!" she called back at Jacob and the others. They were all standing in silence, staring in disbelief at these giants of the forest. The silence finally broke as everyone, except the Indians, started walking back into the forest to get a closer look at the massive trees.

"Jacob, it's like a park in here. What a beautiful place for a home."

"You could never cut one of these down," Jacob said. "They're too big—and if you could get one down, there's no sawmill large enough to cut it into boards."

"They can't all be this big," said Abby, "but they're incredible. Just incredible!"

"You ever hear stories of trees this big?"

"Yes," she replied, "but I never believed them. In fact I was quite upset that people should tell such outlandish tales."

"You'll be telling those tales now."

"I will. As soon as we get to Oregon City I'm writing my brother. He knows I would never exaggerate—and if I tell him about this, he'll be out here the first chance he gets."

After another twenty minutes of exploring, folks walked back out onto the beach to start preparations for the night. Jacob and Adam stoked up a single campfire for the whole group, mostly for warmth. For simplicity, the ladies prepared a cold dinner of smoked salmon and apples. It was almost dark when everyone finished and began to turn in for the night. Abby made her bed under the forest canopy on a thick mat of moss. It was, by far, the softest bed she had experienced since leaving her farm in Ohio.

On Sunday morning, October 29, the small flotilla continued their laborious task of poling up the west shore of the Multnomah River. Timbered slopes continued on the west side, with steep hills approaching the river, precluding the natural development of beaches. On the east bank, the dry-grass prairie landscape gave way to heavy timber. During the day several large islands broke up the river's current and lessened the labor of poling each raft.

By midafternoon they reached the confluence of a fast-flowing river coming in from the east. This river, called Clakamas by the Indian guides, created a shallow rapids where it met the Multnomah. Poling up the west bank of the Multnomah was the only passable route. Even with all hands working the poles, it took over an hour to get past the rapids. Once past, the Indian guides started moving each raft over to the east bank while the polers prevented the rafts from sliding downriver. As they passed the midpoint in the Multnomah, the emigrants were now able to see around a bend in the river ahead. There, on the east bank just above the Clakamas—a small settlement!

"Jacob," Abby called out in excitement while pointing at the small town. "Oregon City!"

Oregon City nestled precariously between the Multnomah River and a timbered hill running a quarter mile back from the river. Dr. McLoughlin had said it consisted of approximately one hundred residents, almost all associated with the fur trading business. A precarious trail led up the timbered hill on the south end of town, while the Clakamas River flowed into the Multnomah about a quarter-mile north of town. The town itself held no more than two dozen buildings of one and two stories built along a wide, muddy street. A small sawmill at one end of town no doubt produced the only source of lumber. The sawmill received power from a waterwheel extending out into the Multnomah. Various horses and pack animals patiently waited at hitching posts in front of several buildings while their owners secured supplies from the few businesses. This fledgling settlement beckoned to the weary travelers, and would soon become the furthest outpost of the United States. As Abby surveyed her final goal, she noticed one conspicuous absence. There was not a single wheeled vehicle in the entire town!

Everyone stared intently at their final goal. Could this really be Oregon City? This muddy, drab, frontier town without churches, schools, or other civilized amenities? Yes! This was it! Finally, this was El Dorado. From this wild and meager beginning, all dreams would come true.

The flotilla landed next to a small dock, where men could secure each raft to pilings, rocks, or trees. Dusk was rapidly approaching, and the day had been long and hard. Tomorrow would be soon enough to unload the rafts and reassemble the wagons. For now, the time had come to revel in the pleasure of attaining their final goal.

Townspeople crowded down along the beach and dock to see and meet their newest residents. The appearance of wagons had no small effect, for it meant progress—progress for a fledgling settlement on the edge of a vast empire waiting to yield its treasures to those brave enough to venture out here. Several of the locals had come West the year before using pack animals, convinced of the impossibility of moving loaded wagons over the Rocky Mountains, the Snake River

Plains, the Blue Mountains, and finally through the Columbia River Gorge. Now these residents stood in amazement, gawking at the small flotilla. Here were emigrants who had accomplished what few had thought possible. They had braved the uncrossable rivers, the bone-dry deserts, the rocky plains, and the impassable mountains. They had accomplished the impossible and proved all the doomsayers wrong. Yes, here they were—wagons from the United States!

CHAPTER 4

Oregon City

The fledgling town of Oregon City overlooked a beautiful waterfall on the Multnomah River. Flowing north from the unknown reaches of the Wallamet Valley, this untamed river plunged over a precipice extending from shore to shore with a drop of over thirty feet. The white, turbulent waters helped to accent the green backdrop of heavily timbered hills and the deep blue of an endless sky. Here was surely one of the most beautiful locations in all of Oregon Country. Everything about it was wild, new, and inviting. Nestled into the natural floodplain of the confluence of the Clakamas with the Multnomah, this infant settlement beckoned for its place in history.

From Oregon City, a wide trail led south to Champooic and French Prairie. Behind the settlement and extending up the Clakamas River were several farms belonging to former trappers and Hudson Bay employees. Beyond these few humble beginnings lay vast areas of timbered mountains and watered valleys, the extent of which nobody really knew.

On Monday, October 30, Abby awoke at dawn, ready to begin her new life in Oregon Country. Within minutes everyone in the flotilla was up and moving about with purpose in mind. Women prepared a quick, cold breakfast while the men began the job of unloading baggage and wagons.

Town residents returned to watch the unloading and to see the first wagons roll into their city. Comments quickly circulated that they were proof of Oregon's intention to join the United States. The presence of wagons meant a road now extended from Oregon Country all the way back to the United States—a road that future emigrants would be able to use. Some even predicted a flood of new emigrants every autumn for the next twenty years. The arrival of women and children surely signaled that civilization was here to stay.

Jim Nesmith, the Oteys, Bernie Haggard, John Jackson, and Bill McDaniel had arrived on Friday afternoon, October 27, two days earlier. Jim, as usual, offered his services to Abby and Jacob. While he and Jacob reassembled the wagon, Abby went off in search of her stock. She found them in a corral near the north end of town, along with their Indian drovers. Before Jim and Jacob were done, the Indians had moved all the stock down to the shore and were well paid with the remainder of Abby's trade goods, including the last of the tobacco. Jacob's insistence on buying a quantity of tobacco way back in Independence had been worthy advice, right to the end.

As soon as the wagons were reassembled and ready, family members began loading their cache of baggage as the men yoked and chained their ox teams. By early afternoon a total of fourteen wagons were rolling down the main street of Oregon City—Abby's and the Laysons', Hewitts', Keizurs', Stewarts', and Casons'; three belonging to the Mathenys; and five more driven by the Ford clan.

For the past six months Abby and her fellow adventurers had held a specific goal in mind. Each morning that goal provided the incentive to keep moving forward, no matter what troubles befell their effort. Now, they had finally reached their destination. Oregon City was not necessarily the end of the journey, for farms needed to be located and claims established; yet it was the goal of which they had always spoken. Reaching this city with their wagons and all their worldly possessions filled them with pride. It was a moment to be cherished.

Strange as it may seem, their arrival marked the end of that great incentive. As teamsters rolled their wagons down Main Street—the first street encountered since leaving Independence—they looked with both interest and disappointment at the scant offerings of Oregon City. The few businesses providing goods and services would have a difficult time meeting the needs of so many new residents. In the space of only a few weeks, the population of the entire Oregon Country was about to double.

Without that one constant incentive pulling the emigrants forward, there was confusion toward what to do next. Should they go into a store? Should they set up camp on the outskirts of town? Should they seek out advice on where to locate a farm? That singular drive to move forward was gone, and now came the realities of settling a new land.

The trail government of the Oregon Emigrating Company had dissolved over two hundred miles ago—and Oregon was still an unorganized, ungoverned country. Now, freedom was their only guide. There was the individual freedom to do what one wished, and the economic freedom allowing a market economy to find its own equilibrium. Where a demand arose, someone would come forward with a supply—and these pioneers had an unending list of demands as they began their new lives. Merchants and marketeers would soon enter the scene to supply this insatiable demand. Free enterprise did not require a government, only a medium of exchange. For the present, that need could be satisfied with the age-old system of barter.

Abby drove straight through town, noting businesses she would return to later. Finding a place for her wagon and stock was top priority. She planned to stay several nights, so the best choice was to camp on the outskirts of town near fresh water and forage. North of town, near the Clakamas and Multnomah Rivers, they had passed an area where the stock could graze and a campfire could be kindled. After all, the Western Passage was still home.

As soon as she and Jacob found an adequate place to set up camp, Jacob unhitched and hobbled the stock in an area of tall grass next to the Clakamas. Abby unloaded her kitchen equipment and then spent some time organizing the interior of the wagon. The trip down from Wascopam had played havoc with her usual orderly house. Living off a raft, sleeping on beaches, and portaging around Cascade Falls had taken its toll on her baggage. And eliminating all Indian trade goods had left considerably more room in one of the trunks. The absence of bulk quantities of flour, sugar, cornmeal, and other foodstuffs made for additional room. The hurried job of loading down at the Oregon City dock would never do, for this wagon might be home for the next few months.

Before long things were in order and Abby was on her way back to town. She placed twenty dollars in the small drawstring purse that she had not used since Independence. If Oregon City had anything to sell, it would probably be something she needed. She hadn't found a chance to do the wash or take a bath in several weeks, so with a tattered brown dress and an attempt to look presentable, Abby headed back to town. Although the dress was the best one left, it was threadbare and completely filthy. Purchasing a new dress was top priority.

Her first stop was a store bearing a sign that read, "General Merchandise." Four burly men in full buckskin regalia stood at the entrance to the store, leaning on their rifles and conversing about the expected flood of Americans. Animal grease, dirt, and a hefty stench covered the buckskins of each man. Like other locals, they, too, were curious about the new arrivals—no doubt wondering how things would change in coming years. These men had seen many years of lonely campfires, icy beaver streams, hair-raising battles, and a lifestyle that could challenge the hardships of an inmate from Botany Bay. With their long rifles, Green River knives, and scraggly beards, their occupation was unmistakable—they were trappers—trappers not yet given in to the life of a Wallamet Valley farmer. Abby had grown accustomed to such frontier appearances and paid little attention to them as she entered the store.

The men, however, noticed her. White women were scarce in Oregon Country, and any new addition was welcome. Abby's tattered dress, worn moccasins, greasy hair (now tied back with a bandanna), and dirty face successfully hid all of her charms. As she passed she could hear one of the men comment, "Well, at least it's female!"

The interior of the store gave off a familiar smell of new cloth, bulk foods, and iron tools, an odor Abby had not smelled since leaving the Skow's store back in Independence. She stood in the doorway surveying the merchandise and reveling in the smell, the scent of civilization. To her surprise and joy, the store held a number of needed items. A young woman, probably the half-breed wife of the store's owner, approached.

"Ma'am, please come in. We are well stocked with many of the items you can find back in the United States. The supply ships from Portsmouth this year had …" She stopped abruptly, surveying Abby's condition. "Ma'am, you'll be pleased to know we can offer you a bath for twenty-five cents, American."

"Hot water?"

"Yes, ma'am," replied the woman, "as hot as you want. Come."

Abby followed her into a back room where a large washtub served as the bath. Anything was better than nothing.

"I'm going to need a new dress," Abby said as she began to remove her moccasins. "A small size, do you have a small size?"

"Yes, ma'am." The woman placed a large kettle of water on the stove, then stoked the fire. "You can get the first layer off with cold water. By then this pot should be ready. You want to wear that dress now?"

"Yes, please, if you don't mind. The new cloth smells so good."

"Soap's over there." The woman motioned to a nearby shelf, then poured three buckets of cold water into the tub before going outside to fetch more. As soon as she left the room, Abby lifted her dress and took off the knife she had worn since crossing the Blue. *No need to frighten the poor woman,* she thought.

Almost an hour later Abby was clean and wearing her new dress. She turned down the woman's offer of a new pair of shoes, for her moccasins were considerably more comfortable, however, a new comb was irresistible. She started combing out her wet, jet-black hair, now squeaky clean. After a six-month journey from Greene County, it fell down to the tops of her shoulders.

The woman stood in the doorway, watching Abby comb her hair and prepare to meet the town. The unkempt lady who had come in was nowhere to be found. In her place was this stunning, charming beauty from the United States.

"You going out there?" asked the woman, pointing toward the front of the store.

"Yes. I'd like to buy a small cone of sugar, if you have one."

"We do," she replied. "I mean are you going outside—outside looking like that?" She motioned at Abby's person.

Abby quickly turned back to the small mirror, moving her head from side to side several times to see her entire face. Everything looked fine. She straightened up and turned back toward the woman. "Is there something wrong?" she asked, glancing down at her new dress.

"No," the woman said hesitatingly, then nodded her approval. "No, nothing. Sugar's out here."

After buying a cone of sugar, one more blanket (winter was approaching) and paying for the dress, Abby stepped from the store into the bright morning sunshine. The four trappers now came to attention as they took notice of her. The one nearest Abby removed his skin hat and crushed it against his chest. They said nothing, merely stood gawking at the woman they had failed to appraise an hour earlier. Abby had not seen such behavior since her walk down the streets of St. Louis, and it amused her. It felt good to be clean, to wear a new dress, and to be turning heads as she once did back in the United States. She walked briskly by, so the trappers could not see her feeble attempt to hide a smile.

Abby peered into the other stores as she walked down the board sidewalk, enjoying her time in Oregon City. Before returning to the Western Passage she learned that she could get a room at a boarding house for 25 cents a day or $4.50 for the month, not including meals. She also learned more about the area called French Prairie and the beginnings of a town at Champooic. Apparently Champooic was not a settlement, as she had originally thought. Rather, it was a spot along the Multnomah River where river travelers could easily reach the surrounding valley. Elsewhere, timber along the river's shoreline was too thick to penetrate. Farmers needed a ready highway to move their produce to market, and here in Oregon that highway was the Multnomah River, accessible at a point called Champooic.

During the afternoon, Abby reveled in seeing homes, farms, storehouses, mills, various shops, and hearing the sounds of civilization. Over two thousand miles separated this American outpost from its nearest American neighbor. Yet to Abby it could have passed for any rural town in America. It was almost like being back in the United States!

Back at camp she invited Jacob to stay for dinner.

"I have plenty of food, Jacob, and I'll probably be here for another day. The people in town told me I should locate down near Champooic. There are a number of trappers that built farms in an area called French Prairie, so they'll need a schoolteacher."

"You speak any French?"

"No, not a word. Most of the adults speak English, so the children must too. Probably not as their first language, but enough to get along."

"I talked to some men this afternoon who are building a road up the east bank of the Multnomah all the way to a dock across from Fort Vancouver. They can use my help."

"There you go," Abby smiled. "We haven't been in town for a single day and you've already found work!"

"Work for now—I've decided to go into merchandising. I have until next fall to get organized—I suspect there'll be another group of emigrants arriving by then. Might not be well supplied, since the orders I place this winter won't arrive till the summer after next, but it's a start."

"You'll do fine, and whenever I get back to Oregon City I'll be sure to visit your store." Abby smiled at Jacob's prospects as she continued to organize dinner. It would be a quiet evening around the campfire, talking over their accomplishments and planning for the winter.

Unknown to the new arrivals in Oregon City, their friends back out in the Columbia Gorge had not been so lucky. The Applegates and Burnetts had finished their boats and left Fort Walla Walla early that same morning. Bill Beagle worked the tiller for the Burnetts, while George Beale handled the tiller for the lead Applegate boat. Tragedy struck when they got to the rapids near the confluence of the Umatilla River, the same rapids that had almost claimed the lives of Bill and Sarah Newby. Jesse's Indian guide had directed the flotilla over to the right side of the river through a passable channel, however, the boat containing Alex McClelland and two of the Applegate boys was too far to the left and could not get over in time. Their boat struck a boulder and rolled over, sending the occupants swimming for their lives. Soon Alex, Edward Applegate, and Warren Applegate had all drowned. The full complement of emigrants from the Oregon Emigrating Company would not learn of the tragedy until later during the coming winter.

On Tuesday morning, October 31, Abby went back into town to gain more information on where to locate. The woman at the general store directed her to a man loading a pack animal with two fifty-pound sacks of flour. He was Doc Newell, a former trapper for the Rocky Mountain Fur Company and now a pioneering farmer on French Prairie.

"Dr. Newell?"

The man looked up at Abby standing on the board sidewalk, tall and straight, holding her drawstring purse with both hands.

"You are Dr. Newell, aren't you?"

"I'm Doc Newell, and who might you be, missy?"

"My name is Abby Meacham, and I've just arrived from the United States. I was told you could provide me with information about the area called French Prairie."

"I can. You and your husband thinking of starting a farm up there?"

"No, sir. I'm a schoolteacher and I would like to know the prospects of starting a school for the children of the area."

Newell proceeded to give Abby a positive description of the locale, acknowledging the need for a schoolteacher, especially one from the United States. He was a bit taken aback upon learning that she had made the journey out here by herself. Before he could question her honesty, she resolved his doubt.

"I believe my hired man is a friend of yours. His name is Jacob Chalmers."

"Chalmers!" Newell stopped securing the packsaddle and stared back at her. "Chalmers brought you out here from Independence?"

"Yes, sir."

"No wonder you're still alive."

"I did a fair amount of work myself, Mr. Newell. It's my outfit and ..."

"Where's Chalmers now?"

"He plans to hire on to help build a road up toward Fort Vancouver. You can probably find him at my camp this evening, north of town."

"I'll be there. In the meantime, you can plan on locating up near my place. I've got a farm just above Champooic with plenty of land for a schoolhouse. Maybe next spring we farmers can build you one. The road from here to French Prairie has never seen a wagon, but you shouldn't have much trouble. Once you get through that timber," he pointed toward the road leading south out of town, "it's a wide-open prairie with only a few scattered oaks. Shouldn't be any trouble for someone that's brought a wagon all the way from Independence."

Newell gave a slight smile to Abby, tipped his hat, then unhitched his packhorse and was gone—no doubt to reappear at dinnertime.

During the remainder of the afternoon, Abby walked up to a point where she could sit and watch the Falls of the Multnomah. This was the falls that Caleb and Sam had wanted so much to see. It was a peaceful scene, providing endless beauty to gaze upon while resting her tired frame. There was no need to hurry, for a lazy afternoon at the falls was well-deserved. Tomorrow would be soon enough to move out toward French Prairie.

Across from the falls stood another conifer forest of massive trees. Upstream, the river turned to the southwest, quickly disappearing through heavy timber on both shores. According to Doc Newell and other townspeople, the timber was not deep, opening up into an oak savanna within several hundred yards. Thousands of acres of open prairie were said to be available for new homesteads, plus regional timber to supply the needs of farms and settlements. All the wild stories of Oregon Country were proving to be true.

As Abby watched the falls, she couldn't help but reflect on how different this country was from her home back in Greene County. "This is such a new world," she whispered. "And I'm one of the first to be here. If only my family could see this place. There's so much to write them! If I tell them everything, they'll think I'm making it up." Abby looked down at the waterfall and the mist rising from the foam. "I'm one of the first," she again whispered. "And I'll be a part of settling and organizing this new land!"

Doc Newell showed up at Abby's kitchen in time for dinner. While enjoying one of Abby's meals of fresh vegetables and salmon, he and Jacob regaled each other with stories of danger and debauchery in the Rocky Mountains. Jacob learned that his friends Joe Meek and Caleb Wilkins had both settled farms in a valley northwest of here called the Twalatain Plains. Apparently, numerous subvalleys, all suitable for farming, intersected the Wallamet Valley. Their conversation continued into the night amid the warmth of a campfire. As darkness approached, Abby excused herself and retired to the wagon. The diary needed attention, and tomorrow she would set out for her new home.

On Wednesday morning, November 1, Doc Newell took his leave, with expectations of seeing Jacob in business during his next visit to Oregon City. Abby loaded her kitchen gear and secured everything for the journey south while Jacob brought in the oxen, and yoked and chained them to the tongue. It was a routine they both knew well.

When Abby had finished loading her kitchen and other gear, she climbed into the back of the wagon and withdrew $220 from one of the trunks. After a final check of her outfit for the day's journey, she met Jacob alongside the lead team as he finished chaining them to the tongue.

"I believe our agreement was for a payment of $200 upon my safe arrival here in Oregon City," she said. "I have learned a great deal traveling with you, Jacob, and I agreed to pay you extra for that education. Here is $220." She held out a handful of twenty-dollar gold pieces.

Jacob looked at them for a few moments, then at Abby, then back at the coins. Rather than taking all of them, he picked out seven of the gold pieces. "Traveling with you has been an honor, Miss Meacham. You can keep the rest of that money. This is all I need to get my outfit started."

Abby closed her hand on the coins, not quite knowing how to respond. She looked at him for a moment, then walked around to the back of the wagon, untied Crow and brought him up to the front.

"Here." She handed Jacob the halter lead. "I will not need a horse of this quality, and besides, he always liked you best."

Jacob was somewhat taken aback by her generosity. A horse of this stature was worth far more than $200 back in the United States. He took the halter lead, slowly nodding in his usual calculating manner.

"I thank you kindly, Abby. He is a fine horse—we will take good care of each other."

"I'm sure you will. You are good with animals, Jacob. I never could have made it to Oregon without your help." She hesitated while looking at Crow, then back at Jacob. "It has been a pleasure knowing you, Mr. Chalmers. You will always be my good friend."

The time had come to leave—certainly before any tears could be shed. Abby smiled slightly, then pulled her quirt from its hold. Without any long farewells she gave a snap on the rumps of her lead oxen, and the wagon lurched forward—moving south now, toward Oregon City and beyond, to French Prairie and the area of Champooic.

Jacob watched Abby's wagon move slowly up the road toward town. The groans and creaks from the running gear and bed told of a perilous journey from the United States, across vast expanses of prairies, deserts, and mountains where no road existed. With the end of the journey, there were now empires to build. A provisional government would soon form, with new towns, new farms, and hundreds more emigrants in the years to come. It was an exciting time to be in Oregon.

Jacob glanced at Crow, then back toward the wagon. Running his hand over Crow's mane, he gave his slow nod of approval and respect as he watched Abby and her wagon slowly disappear in the distance.

"She will do well in Oregon," he said softly. "She will do well."

Appendices

APPENDIX A

The Oregon Migration of 1843

After crossing the Kansas River on 1 Jun 1843, the Oregon Emigrating Company instructed Jim Nesmith to compile a list of all males sixteen years of age and older[3]. He lists 294 individuals, the same count given in an emigrant letter sent back to Independence on 10 Jun 1843. The letter was sent with a group of wagons heading east from Fort Laramie. Along with males sixteen years of age and older, the emigrant letter lists 130 women (age sixteen and older), 290 boys, and 312 girls for a total of 1,026 people.

Seven men, two women, and four children died before reaching the Wallamet (Willamette) Valley in Oregon. Three babies were born on the trail. One of the babies died at the Waiilatpu Mission. One man lost his way while on the South Platte River and was never found. Five men and their families turned south at Fort Laramie and went to Taos. Eighteen men and their families turned south after Fort Hall and went to California.

Mr. Kerritook, Ben Wood, Ed Constable, and Dave Lenox were not on Nesmith's list, but were mentioned in several diaries and other historical sources. Reverend Marcus Whitman was not on the list, but played a prominent role in guiding the emigrants from Fort Hall to the Grande Ronde Valley. Joe Walker joined the migration at Fort Laramie and acted as a guide beyond Fort Hall for the

---

[3] Nesmith, J. W. 1876. *The occasional address.* Transactions of the Third Annual Reunion of the Oregon Pioneer Association, Salem, Oregon. E. M. Waite, Printer and Bookbinder. pp. 49-51.

California-bound emigrants. This brings the final count (including births and deaths) to 1,021 people.

Names in parentheses below indicate unresolved spellings. The age given refers to the age of the emigrant (if known) when the wagon train left Independence on May 22, 1843. The convention "Wife was ..." indicates the woman was with the migration.

Compilation of the following information came from numerous sources including cemetery headstones, trail diaries, probate records, the Oregon State Archives, and several Oregon historical libraries. With patience, perseverance, and plenty of time, the accuracy and completeness of this list will improve.

—TJH

1. Charles Applegate: age 37[4]. b. 5 Dec 1805, d. 9 Aug 1879. Wife was Malinda Miller, age 31. She was b. 31 Mar 1812, d. 29 Jan 1888. Charles and Malinda are buried in Yoncalla, Oregon.

2. Jesse A. Applegate: age 31. b. 5 Jul 1811, d. 22 Apr 1888. Wife was Cynthia Ann Parker, age 29. She was b. 15 Aug 1813, d. 1 Jun 1882. Jesse was the leader of the Cow Column. He was also one of the original leaders of the Oregon Provisional Government between 1844 and 1849, and the first surveyor general in 1844. He served in the Oregon Territorial Legislature in 1845 and was a member of the Constitutional Convention for statehood in 1857. He served in the Oregon State Legislature between 1865 and 1866. Jesse and Cynthia are buried in the Applegate family cemetery in Yoncalla, Oregon.

3. Lindsay Applegate: age 34. b. 18 Sep 1808, d. 28 Nov 1892. Wife was Elizabeth Basham Miller, age 26. She was b. 27 Sep 1816, d. 6 Jul 1882. She was called Betsy. Lindsay served in the Oregon State Legislature in 1862.

4. David Arthur: age 23. b. 15 Mar 1820. Dave married Mary Jane Malone in 1846. She might have been the daughter of Madison

---

[4] Emigrant's age when the wagon train left Independence, May 22, 1843.

Malone, another 1843 emigrant. The Arthurs and Constables traveled together as an extended family.

5. Richard Arthur: age 19. b. 7 Jun 1824, d. 22 Jul 1869. Richard married Laura Jane Mills, age 19, on 23 May 1844. She was b. 26 Mar 1824, d. 15 Jul 1868. Laura was Isaac Mills's daughter. Richard and Laura may have met on the trail in 1843. Jim Nesmith erroneously recorded Richard Arthur as Robert Arthur. Robert was Richard's younger brother and son of William Arthur as recorded in William Arthur's probate file. Richard and Laura Jane are buried in the Union Point Cemetery in Banks, Oregon.

6. William Arthur: age 47. b. 9 Apr 1796, d. 14 Aug 1866. Wife was Millie, age 51. She was b. 1792, d. 30 Sep 1861. Bill married Catharine A. after the death of Millie. The spelling of Catharine is how she signed her name. William and Millie are buried in the Pleasant View Pioneer Cemetery in Oregon.

7. James Athey: age 26. b. 1817, d. 31 May 1897. Wife was Nancy P. Allen, age 16. She was b. 17 Apr 1827, d. 11 Feb 1897. James was a carpenter.

8. William Athey: age 25. b. 1818.

9. John Atkinson: John turned south after Fort Hall and went to California.

10. Andrew J. Baker: age 17. b. 2 Dec 1825. Andrew married Mary Ann Lake on 12 Oct 1858. He fought in the Yakima War, 1855-56.

11. John Gordon Baker: age 24. b. 17 Oct 1818, d. 4 Mar 1887. Wife was Catherine Blevins, age 19. She was b. 1 Jun 1823, d. 16 Jan 1912. John served as Sheriff of Yamhill County under the Oregon Provisional Government and later under the Oregon Territorial Government. The Bakers and Blevins may have traveled together as an extended family. John and Catherine are buried in the Masonic Cemetery in McMinnville, Oregon.

12. John W. Baker: d. 1870. John fought in the War of 1812.

13. William Baldridge: William turned south after Fort Hall and went to California.

14. Layton Bane

15. William S. Barker: age 27. b. 31 Aug 1815, d. 2 Jul 1869. Spouse was Aurelia A., age 17. She was b. 21 Sep 1825, d. 19 Feb 1907. William and Aurelia are buried in the Pioneer Cemetery in Salem, Oregon.

16. William M. Beagle: age 34. b. 16 Jun 1808, d. 18 Jul 1887. Wife was Lucinda Thompson. William is buried in the Baptist Cemetery in West Union, Oregon. The Lenox's, Mauzey's, and William Beagle traveled together as an extended family.

17. George P. Beale: d. 17 May 1865. George married Mariah S. Taylor on 18 Nov 1857. George was the son of a Missouri slave owner. During the 1843 migration, Jesse Applegate employed him as a teamster. Twenty years after arriving in Oregon, he was hung in a public square in Salem, Oregon on 17 May 1865 for murdering Dan Delany Sr. during a robbery. Dan was also a member of the 1843 migration. George was buried in the Waldo family cemetery east of Salem after both local Salem cemeteries refused his body. This family cemetery was recently destroyed by the current landowner.

18. Nicholas Biddle: Nicholas turned south at Fort Laramie and went to Taos.
19. David Bird
20. J. P. Black
21. Alexander Blevins: age 35. b. 1808. Wife was Levina. The Blevins and Bakers may have traveled together as an extended family.
22. John Boardman: John turned south after Fort Hall and went to California.
23. Levi Boyd: age 30. b. Sep 1812, d. 1913. Levi returned East during the Civil War and fought for the Confederacy. He relocated to eastern Washington after the war and lived to over one hundred years of age. He was a bachelor.
24. James Brady (Braidy)
25. George Brooks
26. John P. Brooks: age 19. b. 1824, d. 1905. John married Mary Ann Thomas on 24 Nov 1846. John is buried in the Pioneer Cemetery in Salem, Oregon.
27. Martin J. Brown
28. Orus Brown: age 42. b. 4 Sep 1800, d. 5 May 1874. Spouse was Lavinia Waddels. She was b. 12 Sep 1816, d. 4 Feb 1860. Orus

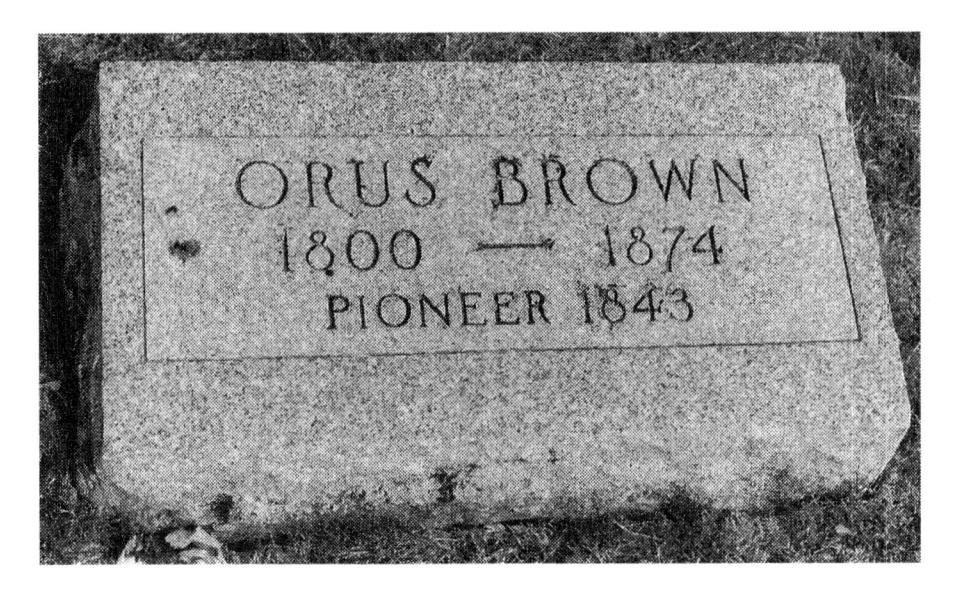

traveled to Oregon in 1843 by himself and settled a Donation Land Claim. In 1845 he returned to Missouri, and brought his family to Oregon in 1846. He married Sarah Meek Hayden on 7 Nov 1860. Orus and Lavinia are buried in the Mt. View Cemetery in Forest Grove, Oregon.

29. Thomas A. Brown: Tom traveled with his friends Nat Sitton and John Cox.

30. Peter Hardeman Burnett: age 35. b. 15 Nov 1807, d. 17 May 1895. Wife was Harriet Rogers. After crossing the Kansas River, Pete was elected captain of the Oregon Emigrating Company. In the following week he resigned the position. He founded the town of Linnton, near the confluence of the Multnomah and Columbia Rivers, with Morton McCarver shortly after arriving at Fort Vancouver in 1843. He and Morton named the town after Senator Linn of Missouri. He served as Supreme Court justice under the Oregon Provisional Government from 6 Sep 1845 to 29 Dec 1846. He moved his family to the California gold fields in 1848, and later became the first governor for the new state of California. During the 1843 migration he traveled with a slave servant by the name of Hattie. It is assumed that she drowned in the Columbia River near Fort Walla Walla.

31. Amon Butler

32. John Gill Campbell: age 25. b. 26 Mar 1818, d. 21 Nov 1872. John married Rothilda E. Buck on 25 Jul 1846. She was b. Oct 1828, d. 21 Jul 1894. Rothilda came to Oregon on an 1845 wagon train. John was called Jack, and his wife was called Ruth. "Jack" Campbell was an accountant. John and Rothilda are buried in the Mt. View Cemetery in Oregon City, Oregon.

33. Miles Cary: age 32. b. 15 Jun 1811, d. 26 Sep 1858. Wife was Cyrene Bundren Taylor, age 27. She was b. 24 Jul 1815, d. 1 Sep 1911. Miles traveled with a female slave servant. One of the Cary children, age three, died at Fort Bridger. The Carys also traveled with an infant son, born 2 Jan 1843. Miles and Cyrene are buried in the Pioneer Cemetery in Lafayette, Oregon.

34. Fendall Carr Cason: age 43. b. 12 Oct 1799, d. 29 Nov 1860. Wife was Rebecca Rawlings Holliday, age 40. She was b. 23 Jan 1803. The Casons and Stewarts traveled together as an extended family.

35. James Cason

36. Jesse H. Caton: age 23. b. 10 Dec 1819, d. 15 Jun 1863. Jesse married Precious Starr on 31 Dec 1848. She was b. 28 Feb 1832, d. 2 Oct 1908. Precious came to Oregon on an 1848 wagon train.

37. James Cave: d. 20 Oct 1861. Wife was Malinda Crump. James married Lucy Ann Matheny on 6 Dec 1844. Lucy was probably part of the Oregon Emigrating Company Matheny clan. James and Lucy may have met on the trail in 1843.

38. Manuel Chapman

39. William Chapman

40. Alfred Chappell

41. Samuel U. Chase: age 26. b. 1 Aug 1816, d. 2 Feb 1906. Samuel fought in the Cayuse War, 1847-48. He was a bachelor.

42. Moses Childers

43. Joseph B. Chiles: Joe turned south after Fort Hall and went to California. He led the California Column.

44. Jacob Chuny (Chimp) (Champ)

45. Ransom Clark: age 34. b. 1809, d. 24 May 1859. Ransom married

Lettice Jane Millican on 16 Feb 1845. Lettice was Elijah Millican's daughter. Ransom and Lettice may have met on the trail in 1843.

46. Lancaster Clyman: Lancaster married Mary Manning on 15 Sep 1844. Mary was also with the 1843 migration. She and Lancaster may have met on the trail in 1843.

47. Thomas Cochran: age 23. b. 1820, d. 10 Aug 1898. Wife was Susan, age 27. She was b. 1816, d. after 31 Aug 1898. Thomas became a minister.

48. Benedict Constable: The Constables and Arthurs traveled together as an extended family.

49. Edward Constable: age 26. b. 15 Jun 1816, d. 5 Aug 1895. Wife was Brazilla Arthur, age 21. She was b. 7 Apr 1822, d. 4 Oct 1893. Brazilla was William Arthur's daughter. Edward and Brazilla are buried in the Baptist Cemetery in West Union, Oregon.

50. Lewis C. Cooper: Lewis was half Mohican Indian. He assumed captain duties of the Splinter Column near the Sweetwater River. He was a blacksmith. Lew employed John Jackson as a teamster until 3 Sep.

51. John Copenhaver

52. John Cox: John traveled with his friends Tom Brown and Nat Sitton.

53. Samuel Cozine: age 22. b. 8 Jul 1820, d. 20 Mar 1897. Sam married Mahala Arthur, age 22, on 29 Mar 1845. She was b. 29 Jul 1820. Mahala was William Arthur's daughter. Sam and Mahala may have met on the trail in 1843. He was a blacksmith. Sam is buried in the Masonic Cemetery in McMinnville, Oregon.

54. Daniel Cronin (Cragan) (Cragin)

55. George Dailey

56. Burrel Davis: d. 10 Jun 1848.

57. Joseph H. Davis: age 30. b. 30 Aug 1812, d. 1 Feb 1877. Wife was Lucy Carpenter, age 26. She was b. 4 Dec 1816, d. 31 May 1884. Joseph and Lucy are buried in the Hill Cemetery near Laurelwood, Oregon.

58. Thomas Davis: d. 1875. Spouse was Sarah.

59. V. W. Dawson: Mr. Dawson turned south after Fort Hall and went to California.

60. William Day: d. 1843. William died at Fort Vancouver. The cause of death is unknown.

61. Daniel Delany, Jr.: age 17. b. 1826. Daniel married Eliza A. Walters on 28 Jun 1857. He fought in the Cayuse War, 1847-48.

62. Daniel Delany, Sr.: age 49. b. 1794, d. 9 Jan 1865. Wife was Elizabeth Magee, d. 1867. Dan was also married to Rebecca Parrish. He traveled with a slave servant by the name of Rachael, age 14, b. 1828, d. 12 Oct 1910. She was purchased for $450 on 3 Sep 1842. Dan carried the slave's purchase receipt with him to Oregon to prove his ownership. He was murdered by George Beale (teamster for Jesse Applegate) during a robbery. His probate file lists his worth at $31,049.56, of which $20,370.76 was in coin and dust. The reputation of his wealth prompted the robbery and subsequent murder by George Beale. His name is spelled as Delaney in historical records, however, his signature uses the spelling Delany. Daniel and Elizabeth are buried in the Cloverdale Cemetery south of Turner, Oregon.

63. William Delany: age 19. b. 24 Apr 1824, d. 1 Sep 1899. Wife was Cassandria E. G. McKoin, age 18. She was b. 3 Feb 1825. William's name is spelled as Delaney in historical records, however, his signature uses the spelling Delany.

64. William Clement Dement: age 23. b. 10 Mar 1823, d. 2 Jan 1865. Bill married Olivia Johnson on 4 Jul 1846. He died leaving

an estate worth over $63,000.00. William and Olivia are buried in the Mt. View Cemetery in Oregon City, Oregon.

65. Solomon Dodd

66. John Doherty

67. William Doke: William was involved in the accident at the Umatilla Rapids where Alexander McClelland (age 68), Warren Applegate (age 9), and Edward Applegate (age 9) all drowned. William survived.

68. Jacob Doran: age 31. b. 1812. Jacob married Amanda in 1851. She d. 15 Feb 1855.

69. William Paydon Dougherty: d. 16 Apr 1898. William married Mary Jane Chambers on 19 Nov 1846. She was b. 5 Nov 1828. Mary came to Oregon on an 1845 wagon train.

70. James Duncan: d. 30 Jan 1899.

71. John W. East: age 34. b. 1809, d. 19 Jan 1878.

72. Charles Eaton: age 24 b. 22 Dec 1818, d. 10 Dec 1876. Charles went to the California gold fields in 1849.

73. Nathaniel Eaton: age 19. b. 1824, d. 9 Mar 1883. Nathaniel fought in the Cayuse War, 1847-48, then went to the California gold fields in 1849. He fought in the Yakima War, 1855-56. He married Lestina Zilpha Hines on 15 Dec 1872. She was b. 26 Nov 1852, d. 1901. Lestina came to Oregon on an 1853 wagon train.

74. Ninian Alkanah Eberman: age 21. b. 9 Dec 1821, d. 19 Apr 1896. Ninian married Emma H. on 25 Jul 1850. He died from severe burns.

75. Elbridge G. Edson: Elbridge married Mary Garrison on 17 Feb 1848.

76. Solomon Emerick: age 21. b. 30 Nov 1821, d. 6 Feb 1899. Solomon married Lucetta Ann Zachary, age 18, on 17 Jun 1845. She was b. 28 Jan 1825, d. 22 Aug 1899. Lucetta was Alex Zachary's daughter. Solomon and Lucetta may have met on the trail in 1843. Solomon worked as a teamster for Sam Gilmore.

At Cascade Falls the Gilmore family portaged all their baggage, while Solomon and James Hayes shot the rapids in an empty thirty-foot canoe. Solomon fought in the Cayuse War, 1847-48. He was illiterate.

77. James Etchell

78. Miles Eyre: age 44. b. 1799, d. 10 Sep 1843. Wife was Eliza Turner, age 38. She was b. Nov 1805, d. Nov 1893. Miles drowned while crossing the Snake River.

79. Stephen Fairly

80. Charles Edward Fendall: age 22. b. 4 Jan 1821, d. 20 Apr 1894. Charles married Amanda F. Rogers on 8 Jan 1848 when she was fifteen. She was b. 27 Jun 1832. Amanda came to Oregon on a wagon train in 1846. Charles was a stockman.

81. Ephriam Ford: d. 25 Sep 1863. Ephriam married Martha Jane Garrison on 27 Feb 1851. She was b. 6 Nov 1836.

82. John Ford

83. Nimrod Ford: age 25. b. 11 Feb 1818, d. 15 Mar 1865. Nimrod married Mary Jane Kendall on 24 Oct 1860. Nimrod is buried in the Pioneer Cemetery in Salem, Oregon.

84. Nineveh Ford: age 28. b. 15 Feb 1815, d. 8 Mar 1897. Nineveh served one term in the Oregon Territorial Legislature in 1855. He served two terms in the Oregon State Legislature between 1866 and 1868. He also constructed the first tannery, shoe shop, and butcher shop west of the Rocky Mountains.

85. Henry Fowler

86. William Fowler: age 29. b. 13 Dec 1813, d. 1 Apr 1884. Bill married Rebecca Kelsey, age 24, on 20 Dec

1843. Becky was David Kelsey's daughter. Bill met Becky on the trail and married shortly after arriving in Oregon. She was b. 18 Feb 1819, d. 18 Feb 1890. William and Rebecca are buried in the Old Scotch Church Cemetery north of Hillsboro, Oregon.

87. William J. Fowler, Jr.

88. Alexander Francis: Alex turned south at Fort Laramie and went to Taos.

89. Abner Frazier

90. William B. Frazier

91. John Gantt: John turned south after Fort Hall and went to California. He acted as a guide for the Oregon Emigrating Company between Independence, Missouri and Fort Hall. Captain Gantt charged $1.00 per emigrant for his services as guide.

92. Samuel J. Gardner: d. 7 Nov 1891. Samuel married Eliza A. Smith on 3 Mar 1853.

93. William Gardner

94. Enoch Garrison: age 37. b. 20 Jan 1806, d. 11 Jul 1883. Wife was Margaret Herron, age 42. She was b. 24 Jan 1801, d. 26 Mar 1874. Enoch and Margaret are buried in the Masonic Cemetery in McMinnville, Oregon.

95. Joseph M. Garrison: age 30. b. 1813, d. 17 Jan 1884. Joe married Mary Matheny on 16 Apr 1846 when she was fourteen years old. She was b. 1832. Mary was Daniel Matheny's daughter, age 11 in 1843. Joe was presiding judge of Champooic County, 1847.

96. William J. Garrison: age 16. b. 13 Mar 1827. William married Cornelia Smith in 1849. She d. 1884.

97. Samuel Mattison Gilmore: age 28. b. 17 Mar 1815, d. 5 Nov 1893. Wife was Martha Ann Stevenson, age 24. She was b. 11 Sep 1818, d. 6 Mar 1909. Sam left his oxen at Fort Walla Walla and went down the Columbia River in a thirty-foot open canoe without a guide. At Cascade Falls the Gilmore family portaged all their baggage while their teamster, Solomon Emerick, along with James Hayes, shot the rapids in an empty canoe. During

the following spring Sam returned to Fort Walla Walla to claim his oxen and take them to the Wallamet Valley.

98. William Gilpin: age 40. b. 22 Feb 1803, d. 3 Feb 1897. Wife was Francis McGuire, age 40. She was b. 29 Nov 1802, d. 29 May 1895. William might be buried in the Hill Cemetery near Laurelwood, Oregon.

99. Richard Goodman: age 36. b. 18 Oct 1806, d. 1849. Wife was Sarah Conner. Richard was accidentally shot by John Umnicker in the arm on 2 Jul along the South Platte River. He went to the California gold fields in 1849, where he took ill and died.

100. Chesley B. Gray

101. George W. Gray: age 22. b. 5 Aug 1820, d. 23 Jul 1900. George married Prudence M. Berry. She was b. 11 Mar 1831, d. 17 Dec 1903. George was a German botanist. George and Prudence are buried in the Pioneer Cemetery in Salem, Oregon.

102. Bernard Haggard

103. Samuel B. Hall: Samuel settled on the Clatsop Plains, where he fell in love with a schoolteacher. She rejected him, after which he moved to California where he died. In his will, he left all his property to the school district on the Clatsop Plains.

104. Bartholomew Halley: age 41. b. 1802, d. 14 Jul 1883. Wife was Agatha.

105. William W. Hargrove: d. 12 Dec 1875. Spouse was Polina E.

106. Bernard Harrigas

107. Jacob Hawn: age 39. b. 13 Jan 1804, d. 27 Jan 1860. Wife was Harriet Elizabeth Pierson, age 24. She was b. 31 Aug 1818, d. 17 Apr 1883.

108. James Hayes: At Cascade Falls, James and Solomon Emerick shot the rapids in an empty thirty-foot canoe.

109. Absolom Jefferson Hembree: age 29. b. 14 Dec 1813, d. 10 Apr 1856. Wife was Nancy J. Dodson, age 29. She was b. 22 Jun 1813, d. 12 Jan 1886. Yakima Indians killed Absolom during the 1855-56 war. The Hembrees and Penningtons traveled together as an extended family.

110. Andrew T. Hembree: age 38. b. 1805. Wife was Martha Lorinda McCoy, age 28. She was b. 24 Jun 1814.

111. James Thomas Hembree: age 17. b. 13 Sep 1825, d. 12 Jan 1919. James married Malvina A. Millican, on 24 Sep 1845. She was b. 22 Sep 1832, d. 17 Mar 1916. Malvina was the daughter of Elijah Millican. James and Malvina, age 10, may have met on the trail in 1843. James and Malvina are buried in the Masonic Cemetery in Lafayette, Oregon.

112. Joel Jordan Hembree: age 38. b. 7 Dec 1804, d. 8 Sep 1868. Wife was Sally Payne, age 34. She was b. 2 Mar 1809, d. 15 Mar 1854. Their son, Joel Hembree Jr., age six, was killed when a wagon ran over his body on 18 Jul. Joel Sr. married Letitia Woolery on 2 Dec 1864. She was b. 1810. Joel and Sally are buried in the Masonic Cemetery in McMinnville, Oregon.

113. Abijah S. Hendrix: age 28. b. 1815, d. 1873. Abijah married Mary Jane Dickerson on 1 Mar 1846. She was b. 14 Feb 1830, d. 26 Jun 1915. Mary came to Oregon on an 1845 wagon train. The name is spelled as Hendricks in several historical references.

114. Thomas J. Hensley: Tom turned south after Fort Hall and went to California.

115. Joseph Hess: age 31. b. 1812. Wife was Mary Louisa Kaiser, age 26. She was b. 22 Feb 1817, d. 20 Feb 1903. Indians in California killed Joe, possibly during the gold rush. Mary Louisa is buried in the Pioneer Cemetery in Newberg, Oregon.

116. Henry Hewitt: age 20. b. 19 Nov 1822, d. 15 Jan 1899. Wife was Elizabeth Matheny, age 20. She was b. 26 Mar 1823, d. 13 Oct 1899. Henry was elected commissioner of Yamhill County in 1864. The Hewitts, Laysons, and Mathenys traveled together as an extended family. Henry and Elizabeth are buried in the Pioneer Cemetery in Hopewell, Oregon.

117. Almoran Hill: age 20. b. 26 Dec 1822, d. 3 Feb 1910. Wife was Sarah Jane Reed, age 20. She was b. 26 Jan 1823, d. 23 Jul 1913. Almoran volunteered for the Cayuse War, 1847-48. Almoran and Sarah Jane are buried in the Hill Cemetery near Laurelwood, Oregon.

118. Henry C. Hill: Henry married Mary A. Millican on 30 Nov 1845. Mary was the daughter of Elijah Millican. James and Mary may have met on the trail in 1843.

119. William Hill

120. John Hobson: age 18. b. 4 Dec 1824, d. 6 Dec 1896. John married Diana M. Owens in 1851. She d. 1873. He married again in 1875.

121. William Hobson: age 45. b. 28 Jun 1797, d. 10 Aug 1879. Bill married Eliza Turner Eyre, age 38, on 10 Nov 1853. She was b. Nov 1805, d. Nov 1893. Eliza was Miles Eyre's widow.

122. Samuel M. Holderness: Samuel served as secretary of state under the Oregon Provisional Government from 19 Sep 1848 to 10 Mar 1849. He was appointed to this post after Secretary Frederick Prigg drowned in the Clackamas River. Frederick Prigg was also a member of the 1843 migration. The Oregon Provisional Government outlawed dueling within the territory for the express purpose of stopping Sam Holderness from dueling with a man named Taylor.

123. Daniel S. Holman: age 20. b. 15 Nov 1822, d. 15 Mar 1910. Daniel married Martha Elizabeth Burnett on 31 Aug 1847. She was b. 11 Dec 1830, d. 27 Jun 1913. Martha came to Oregon on an 1846 wagon train. Daniel and Martha are buried in the Masonic Cemetery in McMinnville, Oregon.

124. John Holman: age 55. b. 11 Sep 1787, d. 14 May 1864. Spouse was Elizabeth Duvall. She d. 1841. John fought in the War of 1812. He went to Oregon alone, leaving his younger children under the care of his married children. In 1844 he sent word back to Missouri that he was settled and the children should join him. He married Martha Thomasson McGary, age 43, on 15 May 1844 or 1845. She was b. 21 Jan 1800, d. 4 May 1861. She was the mother of Garrett McGary, another member of the 1843 migration. John and Martha may have met on the trail in 1843. John and Martha are buried in the Masonic Cemetery in McMinnville, Oregon.

125. Riley A. Holmes

126. William Livingston Holmes: age 35. b. 30 May 1807, d. 12 Sep 1879. Wife was Mary Ann Louisa Campbell Williams, age 29. She was b. 9 Dec 1813, d. 25 Jul 1884. Peter Burnett induced William to travel to Oregon. William served as the sheriff of Clackamas County between 1844 and 1855. William and Mary are buried in the Mt. View Cemetery in Oregon City, Oregon.

127. G. W. Howell: The Howells and McCorkles traveled together as an extended family.

128. John B. Howell: age 55. b. 6 Dec 1787, d. 4 Oct 1869. Wife was Temperance Midkiff, age 47. She was b. 29 Apr 1796, d. 22 Mar 1848. On 14 Jun, John shot an ox belonging to Elbridge Edson. The Oregon Emigrating Company fined John twenty dollars and the forfeiture of an ox. John and Temperance are buried in the Howell Prairie Pioneer Cemetery, northeast of Salem, Oregon.

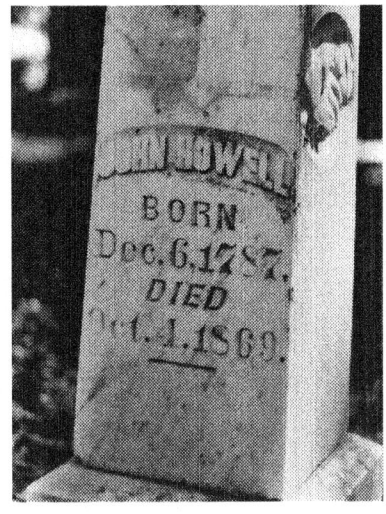

129. Thomas E. Howell: age 19. b. 1824. Thomas married Rachael M. She was b. 1828.

130. Wesley Howell: age 17. b. 1826, d. 4 Dec 1883. Wesley married Margarett McDaniel on 13 Jul 1848. He fought in the Cayuse War, 1847-48. The spelling of Margarett is how she signed her name. Wesley is buried in the Howell Prairie Pioneer Cemetery, northeast of Salem, Oregon.

131. William B. Howell: age 25. b. 1818, d. 1888. Wife was Sallie A., age 18. She was b. 1825, d. 1889. William and Sallie are buried in the cemetery just south of Scio, Oregon.

132. Amon Hoyt

133. James Huck: age 24. b. 1819. James left Oregon in 1845 for California, where he fought in the Mexican War of 1846. He returned to Ohio and married Mary Jones in 1857. She d. 1858. He later married Frances E. Albert. He returned to Oregon in 1875.

134. William P. Hughes

135. Henry H. Hunt: Henry and Ben Wood built the first sawmill on the Clatsop Plains of the lower Columbia River. Known as "Hunt's Mill," it was powered by a thirty-foot diameter overshot water wheel. Henry traveled with the Straight family.

136. Alanson Husted: Alanson married Mary Montgomery Saunders on 26 Apr 1848. She was b. 13 Mar 1813. Cayuse Indians killed Mary's first husband, Luke W. Saunders, during a raid on the Whitman mission at Waiilatpu on 29 Nov 1847. Mary survived the attack. This raid resulted in the Cayuse War of 1847-48.

137. Isaac Hutchins

138. Henry H. Hyde: age 31. b. 1812, d. 1881. Henry was married to Henrietta Holman on 1 Sep 1846 by Judge Peter H. Burnett. Henrietta was John Holman's daughter and came to Oregon on an 1845 wagon train. Henry went to the California gold fields in 1849, then returned to Oregon and ran a store in Prairie City. He married Susan Brock Kinzey on 23 Dec 1850.

139. John H. B. Jackson: age 23. b. 14 Mar 1820, d. 22 Dec 1869. John married Sarah S. Parker on 4 Jul 1846. She was b. 1828, d. 1917. Lewis Cooper employed John as a teamster. On 3 Sep while crossing the Snake River Plains, John left the employ of Cooper and joined Zachary's Outcast Mess. On 8 Sep he returned to the Light Column after Zachary stabbed Newt Wheeler. Sarah came to Oregon on an 1845 wagon train by way of Meek's Cut-off. John and Sarah are buried in the Baptist Cemetery in West Union, Oregon.

140. Calvin James

141. Overton Johnson: Overton served as secretary of state under the Oregon Provisional Government from 4 Mar 1844 to 25 May 1844.

142. John Jones

143. John B. Keizur: age 18. b. Nov 1824, d. 11 Apr 1870. John married Mary Jane.

144. Pleasante C. Keizur: Pleasante married Sarah Woodside on 5 May 1850.

145. Thomas Dove Keizur: age 50. b. 1793, d. 19 Jun 1871. Wife was Mary Girley, age 50. She was b. 1793, d. 1853.

146. Kelley

147. David Kelsey: David's daughter, Rebecca, age 24, met Bill Fowler while on the trail in 1843. They married on 20 Dec 1843 after arriving in Oregon. She was b. 18 Feb 1819, d. 18 Feb 1890. Bill and Rebecca are buried in the Old Scotch Church Cemetery north of Hillsboro, Oregon.

148. Kerritook: Mr. Kerritook was injured when his rifle breech exploded while shooting at an antelope on 3 Jul on the South Platte. He was half Cherokee Indian.

149. Isaac Laswell: age 23. b. 1820. Isaac married Rachael E. She was b. 1831.

150. John Lauderdale

151. Aaron M. Layson: age 23. b. 1820, d. 1886. Wife was Sarah Jane, age 17. She was b. 1826, d. 1849. Aaron initiated the first meeting to organize a provisional trail government outside of Independence, Missouri. The Laysons, Mathenys, and Hewitts traveled together as an extended family. Aaron and Sara Jane are buried in the Pioneer Cemetery in Hopewell, Oregon.

152. Henry A. G. Lee: d. 4 Oct 1850. Henry captained one of the platoons in the Light Column.

153. F. Legear (Legeer) (Lugur): Mr. Legear turned south at Fort Laramie and went to Taos.

154. David Thomas Lenox: age 40. b. 1 Dec 1802, d. 18 Oct 1874. Wife was Louisa Swan, age 36. She was b. 5 Apr 1807, d. 9 Nov 1879. Dave captained one of the platoons in the Light Column. He started the first Baptist church west of the Rocky Mountains and was deacon in this church for thirty years. The church is West Union Baptist Church near West Union, Oregon, and is still in use. David's probate file lists the year of his death

as 1874, however, his headstone lists the year as 1873. Since his body was moved to its current location years after his death, the headstone year of 1873 is probably incorrect. David and Louisa are buried in the Baptist Cemetery in West Union, Oregon. The Lenox's, Mauzey's, and William Beagle traveled together as an extended family.

155. Edward Henry Lenox: age 16. b. 19 Feb 1827, d. 8 Jan 1905. Ed married Eleanor Porter on 12 May 1850. He was the son of David Lenox. The Lenox's, Mauzey's, and William Beagle traveled together as an extended family.

156. Edward Lenox: d. approx. 1876. Wife was Louise, age 35. She was b. 1808, d. 16 Nov 1879. Ed served as judge in Washington County, Oregon. He may have been David Lenox's brother. The Lenox's, Mauzey's, and William Beagle traveled together as an extended family.

157. John Linebarger

158. Lewis Linebarger: age 42. b. 1801, d. 29 May 1883. Wife was Jane Henderson.

159. Milton Little: Milton turned south after Fort Hall and went to California.

160. John E. Long: d. 21 Jun 1846. Mary A. was his first wife. Elizabeth B. was his second wife. She d. Feb 1851. Elizabeth remained in Kentucky when John went to Oregon in 1843. Frances C. Campbell rendered services as his supposed and respected wife between Dec 1843 and Jun 1846. She received $500 from the settlement of his estate for these services. Dr. Long served as secretary of state under the Oregon Provisional Government from 25 May 1844 to 21 Jun 1846. He was a founding member of the Oregon Printing Association, which issued the first news-

paper west of the Rocky Mountains, the *Oregon Spectator*. Dr. Long drowned while crossing the Clackamas River en route to Oregon City to visit patients. He was thrown into the river after his spur got caught in the harness of a skittish horse.

161. Jesse Looney: age 40. b. 15 Dec 1802, d. 25 Mar 1869. Wife was Ruby Crawford Bond, age 35. She was b. 18 Mar 1808, d. 7 May 1900. Jesse was born in Knox County, Tennessee, and was a first cousin of President Andrew Jackson. He went to Oregon with his wife and children to escape the institution of slavery. He traveled with three wagons, twenty milk cows, and four brood mares. He spent the winter of 1843-44 at the Waiilatpu Mission, then traveled to the Wallamet Valley the following spring. On his tombstone is written, "His motto through life and last words to his children was do right, be honorable, and truthful". Jesse and Ruby are buried in the Looney Family Cemetery south of Turner, Oregon.

162. John Loughborough: John turned south at Fort Laramie and went to Taos.

163. Asa Lawrence Lovejoy: age 35. b. 14 Mar 1808, d. 11 Sep 1882. Asa married Elizabeth McGary on 17 Mar 1845. She was b. 10 Jan 1829, d. 4 Jan 1904. Asa served as attorney general for the Oregon Provisional Government in 1844 and as speaker of the House for the Oregon Provisional Government between 1844 and 1846. He lost to George Abernethy for the first governorship in 1845. He also served as mayor of Oregon City in 1845. During the Cayuse War of 1847-48, he served with the rank of adjutant general. After the war he served as Supreme Court justice under the Oregon Provisional Government, elected 16

Feb 1849. He also went to the California gold fields in 1849. After returning to Oregon, Asa became a member of the Oregon Constitutional Convention in 1857. He was a joint proprietor of the City of Portland. Asa is buried in the Lone Fir Cemetery in Portland, Oregon.

164. John F. Luther: age 26. b. 21 Apr 1817, d. 14 Mar 1880. Wife was Elizabeth A., age 18. She was b. 20 Nov 1825, d. 17 Nov 1903. John is buried in the Union Point Cemetery in Banks, Oregon.

165. Madison M. Malone: Madison's first wife died in 1850. He married Margaret Eaton in 1852 or 1853. Madison is buried in the Malone Family Cemetery in McMinnville, Oregon.

166. James Manning: James married Norma Richardson on 22 Jan 1847.

167. John Manning

168. James Martin: d. 25 Jun 1867.

169. Julius Martin: Julius turned south after Fort Hall and went to California.

170. William Jennings Martin: age 29. b. 2 Feb 1814, d. 26 Apr 1901. Wife was Catherine Crobarger. She d. 8 Mar 1884. Bill fought in the Seminole War in Florida, 1835. He married Margaret Trible in 1895 at the age of 81. She d. 16 Jun 1899. William commanded the Light Column from the Blue River to Fort Hall, then turned south after Fort Hall and went to California. He returned to Missouri from California in 1844 with John C. Fremont's expedition. During 1846 he took his family to Oregon.

171. Andrew Jackson Masters: age 27. b. 20 Mar 1816, d. 11 Oct 1856. Wife was Sarah Jane Jenkins, age 16. She was b. 4 Oct 1826, d. 26 Sep 1896. Sarah Jane and Andrew married on 1 Oct 1842, six months before leaving for Oregon. Andrew was killed by James Harvey McMillen with a gunshot wound to the head.

Andrew and Sarah Jane are buried in the Pioneer Cemetery in Hillsboro, Oregon.

172. Adam Matheny: age 22. b. 20 Dec 1820, d. 7 Nov 1895. Wife was Sarah Jane Layson, age 16. She was b. 27 Mar 1827, d. 30 Jan 1847. They married in April 1843 just before leaving for Oregon. Sarah Jane died, leaving a son and infant daughter. Adam fought in the Cayuse War, 1847-48. After the war he married Harriet Hamilton on 30 Apr 1850. Adam was the son of Daniel and Mary Cooper Matheny. The Mathenys, Laysons, and Hewitts traveled together as an extended family. Sarah Jane is buried in the Pioneer Cemetery in Hopewell, Oregon.

173. Daniel Matheny: age 49. b. 11 Dec 1793. d. 1 Feb 1872. Wife was Mary Cooper, age 43. She was b. 23 Feb 1800, d. 29 Sep 1856. Dan fought in the War of 1812. He helped with the original organization of the Oregon Emigrating Company at Independence, Missouri, then captained one of the platoons in the Light Column. He was the brother of Henry Matheny. Dan and Mary are buried in the Pioneer Cemetery in Hopewell, Oregon.

174. Henry Younger Matheny: age 39 or 43. b. 1800 or 1804, d. Sep 1849. Wife was Rachael Cooper, age 40. She was b. 26 Mar 1803, d. 25 Jun 1877. Henry went to the California gold fields in 1849, where he died. He was the brother of Daniel Matheny. Rachael is buried in the Pioneer Cemetery in Hopewell, Oregon.

175. Isaiah C. Matheny: age 17. b. 1826, d. 4 Sep 1906. Isaiah married

Emaline Allen on 14 Mar 1850. She was b. 1833, d. 1903. He was the son of Daniel and Mary Cooper Matheny. Isaiah fought in the Cayuse War, 1847-48. After his discharge he went to the California gold fields in 1848. In 1866 he moved his family to California. He again moved in 1871, to southern Idaho. In later years his last move was to southwest Oregon.

176. Jasper Matheny: Jasper married Mary Ring on 26 Dec 1852. He was the son of Daniel and Mary Cooper Matheny.

177. Walter Jefferson Matney: age 26. b. 1817, d. 1874. Walter married Martha Jane on 5 Apr 1847. She d. 28 Jun 1852, leaving two children. He married Julia Ann Cooper on 28 Mar 1853. Alexander Zachary defrauded Walt of all his provisions on the Sweetwater River on 30 Jul 1843.

178. William Mauzey: age 24. b. 10 Mar 1819, d. 4 Jan 1897. William married Eleanor Evans in 1847. She was b. 15 Apr 1828, d. 14 Feb 1861. William and Eleanor are buried in the Baptist Cemetery in West Union, Oregon. The Lenox's, Mauzey's, and William Beagle traveled together as an extended family.

179. William Mayes (Mays)

180. Morton Matthew McCarver: age 36. b. 14 Jan 1807, d. 17 Apr 1875. Wife was Mary Ann Jennings. Morton married Julia Ann Buckalen on 30 Jan 1848. She was b. 19 Nov 1825, d. 14 May 1897. Morton fought in the Black Hawk War in Wisconsin, 1832. There is a record of him leaving the Light Column and joining the Cow Column while traveling along the South Platte River. He founded the town of Linnton, near the confluence of the Multnomah and Columbia Rivers, with Peter Burnett shortly after arriving at Fort Vancouver in 1843. He and Peter named the town after Senator Linn of Missouri. Morton served as the first speaker of the House for the Oregon Provisional Government. He went to the California gold fields in 1848. Later he was a delegate to the California Monterey Convention that drafted the first California State Constitution. Morton also founded the city of Sacramento, California, in 1849. He was commissioned a general in the Rogue River War in 1853. He later founded the

city of Tacoma, Washington, in 1868. His second wife, Julia Ann, came to Oregon on an 1847 wagon train with her first husband, Garrette Buckalen, who died shortly after arriving in Oregon. Her youngest of two children died en route on the plains.

181. John Burch McClane: age 23. b. 21 Jan 1820, d. 19 Jan 1892. John married Helen C. Judson on 9 May 1849. She was b. 14 Apr 1834, d. 1 Oct 1903. John fought in the Cayuse War, 1847-48. After his discharge he went to the California gold fields, returning in 1849. He served as the first postmaster of Salem, Oregon. He also served as the county treasurer for Marion County between 1850 and 1851. His wife, Helen, came to Oregon in 1839 on the ship *Lausanne* as part of a Methodist missionary party.

182. Alexander McClelland: age 68. b. approx. 1775, d. Oct 1843. Alex drowned at the Umatilla Rapids on the Columbia River while trying to save Edward Applegate, age 9. The Applegate children called him Uncle Mack.

183. F. McClelland: Mr. McClelland turned south after Fort Hall and went to California.

184. George F. McCorkle: age 23. b. 10 Sep 1819, d. 26 Jul 1891. Wife was Elizabeth Brooks Howell, age 21. She was b. 24 Apr 1822, d. 26 Sep 1900. The McCorkles and Howells traveled together as an extended family. George and Elizabeth are buried in the Howell Prairie Pioneer Cemetery, northeast of Salem, Oregon.

185. William McDaniel: age 23. b. 1820.

186. Garrett W. McGary: age 21. b. 1822. Garrett's mother, Martha Thomasson McGary, age 43 or 44, accompanied her son to Oregon. She was b. 1 Jan 1799 or 1800, d. 4 May 1861.

187. McGee: Mr. McGee turned south after Fort Hall and went to California.

188. John McHaley: age 59. b. 1784. Wife was Sarah Frazier, age 40. She was b. 1803, d. 13 Aug 1857. John proposed the Oregon Emigrating Company buy two large boats, carried in each of two wagons, for crossing large streams and rivers. He owned a large herd of cattle and traveled with the Cow Column. Although Sarah was forty, she had an eighteen-month-old son. Sarah and her son are buried in the Twin Oaks Cemetery in Turner, Oregon.

189. John McIntire: John turned south after Fort Hall and went to California.

190. D. McKissic

191. Elijah Millican: age 40. b. Jul 1802. Wife was Lucinda Wilson Crisp, age 31. She was b. 29 Jul 1811.

192. Isaac Mills: Wife was Rachael Bales. Their daughter, Laura Jane Mills, age 19, accompanied them to Oregon. She was b. 26 Mar 1824, d. 15 Jul 1868.

193. John B. Mills: Wife was Mary.

194. Owen M. Mills: Owen married Priscilla Blair on 29 Oct 1847. She was b. 1812, d. Jun 1900.

195. William A. Mills: age 16. b. 1 Sep 1826, d. 10 Dec 1906. Bill married Rachael Joy Fisher in March, 1848. She was b. 20 Apr 1821, d. 11 Dec 1868. Rachael came to Oregon on an 1847 wagon train. Bill later married Mary E. Craghead Capps on 15 Oct 1874. She was b. 1841. Mary came to Oregon on an 1852 wagon train. Mary was postmistress at Clackamas from Jun 1876 to 1879. William was elected to the Oregon State Legislature in 1870. William and Rachael are buried in the Union Point Cemetery in Banks, Oregon.

196. Gilbert Mondon

197. Jackson Moore: Jackson turned south at Fort Laramie and went to Taos.

198. Jacob L. Myers: age 21. b. 22 Feb 1822.

199. Thomas George Naylor: age 28. b. 12 Oct 1814, d. 5 Dec 1872. Wife was Sarah Storey, age 22. She was b. 16 Jun 1820, d. 2 Feb 1853. They had seven children. After Sarah's death Tom married her sister, Catherine Storey, on 5 Apr 1853 and had nine more children.

200. James Willis Nesmith: age 22. b. 23 Jul 1820, d. 17 Jun 1885. Jim married Caroline Lucinda Pauline Goff on 14 Jun 1846. She was b. 7 Apr 1831, d. 30 Dec 1890. Caroline came to Oregon on an 1844 wagon train. Jim served as Supreme Court justice under the Oregon Provisional Government from 25 Dec 1844 to 9 Aug 1845. He fought in the Cayuse War, 1847-48 and in the Rogue River War in 1853. During these campaigns he attained the rank of colonel. He served as a United States marshal from 1853 to 1855. Between 1857 and 1859 he served as superintendent of Indian Affairs. He also served as a United States senator from Oregon between 1861 and 1867. President Johnson appointed him as minister to Austria, but the Senate refused to confirm the appointment. He served as a United States congressman from Oregon between 1873 and 1875. Jim and Caroline are buried in the Nesmith Family Cemetery in Rickreall, Oregon.

201. William Thompson Newby: age 23. b. 25 Mar 1820, d. 22

Oct 1884. Wife was Sarah Jane McGary, age 20. She was b. 1823, d. 1887. Bill and his wife almost drowned at the Umatilla Rapids on the Columbia River. He served as assessor under the Oregon Provisional Government in 1848. He founded the city of McMinnville, Oregon, in 1853. He also served as an Oregon state senator during 1870. William was able to leave the column and go on buffalo hunts with the other men. This fact suggests that he probably employed one of the other young men as a teamster to drive his wagon. William and Sarah Jane are buried in the Masonic Cemetery in McMinnville, Oregon.

202. Noah Newman

203. Hugh D. O'Brien

204. Humphrey O'Brien

205. Bennett O'Neil: Bennett lost his way while hunting on the South Platte River and was never found. His final whereabouts were never known, so people assumed he had been killed; however, he is listed in the 1845 census taken by the Oregon Provisional Government. If this is the same Ben O'Neil, how he got to Oregon is a mystery.

206. Abraham Olinger: age 31. b. 1812, d. 3 Jan 1874. Wife was Rachael Stout, age 22. She was b. 1821, d. 22 Oct 1861.

207. Neil Osborn

208. Edwin W. Otey: age 27. b. 1816. Ed married Martha J. Bunton on 4 Jul 1846. He worked as a millwright in Henry Hunt's sawmill. Edwin, his brother Morris, and Jim Nesmith traveled together.

209. Morris B. Otey: Traveled with his brother Edwin and Jim Nesmith.

210. Thomas Owens: age 29. b. 4 Jul 1813, d. 4 Dec 1892. Thomas married Emeline L. Young on 25 Dec 1850. She was b. 22 Sep 1827, d. 17 Sep 1903. Thomas and Emeline are buried in the Masonic Cemetery in McMinnville, Oregon.

211. Thomas Owens: age 35. b. 12 Jan 1808, d. 23 Jul 1873. Wife

was Sarah, age 23. She was b. 1820. Sarah sowed the first crop of flax in Oregon in 1844. It was used to produce shoe thread; elk hides were used for shoe leather. In subsequent years she traded the flax to local Indians for salmon. They used it to make superior fishing nets. Thomas went to the California gold fields in 1849.

212. Clayborn Paine: d. 4 Aug 1843. Clay died near South Pass of a fever contracted at Fort Laramie. He left a wife and four children.

213. Samuel Painter: Sam married Matilda Caroline Keizur.

214. Jesse Parker

215. William Glenn Parker: age 21. b. 1822, d. 4 Mar 1859. Bill married Lucinda Tetherow on 27 Jan 1847. She was b. 1 Aug 1830. He later married Cynthia Ann. Bill was involved in the accident at the Umatilla Rapids where Alexander McClelland (age 68), Warren Applegate (age 9), and Edward Applegate

(age 9) all drowned. William died leaving an estate worth over $30,000.00.

216. Joseph R. Patterson: age 22. b. 1821. Joseph married Sarah Lucintha Keizur on 13 Feb 1845. She d. 28 May 1850, leaving two children.

217. John Barton Pennington: age 24. b. 25 Apr 1819, d. 4 Oct 1910. Wife was Sarah Elizabeth Hembree, age 27 or 31. She was b. 10 May 1812 or 16, d. 23 Sep 1851. Sarah gave birth to a daughter on 6 Aug. The daughter was named Mary Jane. She d. 5 Oct 1899. John married Elizabeth Jane Sportsman on 25 Feb 1853 after his first wife died. He later married Margaret Fisher. The Penningtons and Hembrees traveled together as an extended family.

218. Charles E. Pickett

219. Robert H. Powe: d. 1846. In a letter from his parents dated shortly after his arrival in Oregon, they spell their family name as Powe. However all references, including his probate file, spell the name as Poe.

220. Frederick Prigg: d. 16 Sep 1848. Frederick served as secretary of state under the Oregon Provisional Government from 26 Jun 1846 to 16 Sep 1848. Governor Abernethy appointed him to this post after Secretary John Long drowned in the Clackamas River. Frederick also served as circuit judge of Clackamas County and as president of the court and probate judge of Clackamas County. Frederick drowned in the Clackamas River, the same as his predecessor, Secretary of State John Long.

221. Pierson B. Reading: Pierson turned south after Fort Hall and went to California.

222. Jacob T. Reed: age 28. b. 11 Mar 1815. Jacob married Patsy Williams on 5 Sep 1844. They may have met on the trail in 1843. He was a blacksmith.

223. Thomas Reeves: age 29. b. 6 Mar 1814, d. 1886. Thomas married Nancy Jane Lloyd in Jun 1846. She d. 1870. Nancy came to Oregon on an 1845 wagon train. He was a tanner.

224. George W. Rice: d. 30 Apr 1849. Wife was Anne.

225. Daniel Richardson: age 33. b. 1810, d. 30 Aug 1843. Wife was Dorcas Caldwell, age 27. She was b. 10 Feb 1816, d. 23 Jan 1887. Dan died at Fort Hall leaving a wife and two children. The cause of death was unknown. Dorcas later remarried a man by the name of S. W. Moss. She is buried in the Mt. View Cemetery in Oregon City, Oregon.

226. John Richardson

227. John Ricord

228. Emsley Roberts

229. James Roberts

230. Solomon Roberts

231. George W. Rodgers

232. S. P. Rodgers

233. J. F. Roe: Mr. Roe had a 9-year-old son named John Fitzgerald, who became a physician. Researchers might confuse him with his father, since they have the same initials. The son was b. 12 Apr 1834 and d. 23 Jun 1869.

234. Joseph Rossin

235. Philip Rubey: Mrs. Rubey died in the Grande Ronde Valley. The cause of death is unknown.

236. William Russell

237. Henry Sewell: age 24. b. 22 Mar 1819, d. 11 Dec 1869. Henry married Mary Ann Jones Gerrish on 29 Mar 1846. She was b. 1829, d. 21 Mar 1866. He was a Baptist minister who committed suicide.. Henry and Mary Ann are buried in the Mt. View Cemetery in Forest Grove, Oregon.

238. Cornelius Sharp: Cornelius ran a "house of ill fame" in Oregon City. On 7 Dec 1853 he shot and

killed a man named Robert McCarther at the house. The cause of the dispute is unknown.

239. William Sheldon

240. Samuel Shirley

241. John M. Shively: age 39. b. 2 Apr 1804. John married Susan S. on 30 Mar 1847. He was appointed as first postmaster of the Oregon Country in 1847.

242. Nathaniel Koontz Sitton: age 17. b. 2 Sep 1825, d. 10 Jul 1902. Nat married Priscilla A. Rogers on 22 Apr 1847. She was b. 28 Oct 1829, d. 22 Jun 1869. He later married Mary M. Shelley Laughlin on 31 Jan 1871. She was b. 8 Dec 1839, d. 1 Jul 1904. Mary came to Oregon on an 1848 wagon train. Nathaniel obtained the title of Doc while on the trail to Oregon. He worked as a teamster for Sam Vance during the 1843 migration, but was traveling with his friends Tom Brown and John Cox. He went to the California gold fields in 1848, returning the next year with $1,200.00. Nathaniel, Priscilla, and Mary are buried in the McBride Cemetery west of Carlton, Oregon.

243. Ahi Smith

244. Anderson Smith: d. 29 Jul 1875. Spouse was Ann, age 26. She was b. 1817.

245. Eli Smith

246. Isaac W. Smith: age 34. b. 1809. Isaac married Mary Northrup on 12 Feb 1846.

247. Robert Smith: d. 5 May 1888. Bob married Susan Applegate on 11 Mar 1851. She was b. 25 May 1831, d. 30 Dec 1907. She

was a daughter of Charles Applegate. Robert went to the California gold fields in 1848.

248. Thomas Smith

249. Thomas Hardman Smith: age 19. b. 1824. Thomas married Maria McKay on 25 Dec 1845. She was b. 10 Mar 1832. Maria came to Oregon in 1841 from Winnipeg. Thomas was a lawyer and a judge.

250. Chauncey Spencer

251. George Sterling

252. Edward Stevenson: d. 9 Aug 1843. Ed died near South Pass from a fever contracted at Fort Laramie. He was buried on the banks of the Big Sandy River.

253. Peter Grant Stewart: age 33. b. 6 Sep 1809, d. 27 Aug 1900. Wife was Rebecca Rawlins Cason, age 17. She was b. 13 Sep 1826, d. Oct 1863. Fendall Cason was her father. Rebecca gave birth to a daughter while on the South Platte. The infant was not well and died at the Waiilatpu Mission. Pete was elected to the Executive Committee of the Oregon Provisional Government on 14 May 1844. This office served the function of a part-time governor, with a salary of $100 per annum. Pete was elected Clackamas District Judge on 19 Aug 1845, and resigned on 5 Dec 1845. He went to the California gold fields in 1848 with Peter Burnett and the Casons. He returned in 1849. He married Eliza Rosencrans on 3 Sep 1876. He was a watchmaker and jeweler. The Stewarts and Casons traveled together as an extended family.

254. Christopher Stommerman (Stimmerman)

255. James Story

256. Alexander R. Stoughton: age 36. b. 1807.

257. Ephriam Stout: age 68. b. 1775, d. 1852. Wife was Jane Smith. He was a Quaker.

258. Henry (Hugh) Stout

259. Hiram Aldrich Straight: age 29. b. 4 Mar 1814, d. 8 Jan 1897. Wife was Susan Laswell, age 32. She was b. 1811, d. 2 Jun 1883. The Straights traveled with Henry Hunt. Hiram and Susan are buried in the Straight Family Cemetery in Oregon.

260. C. M. Stringer: d. 10 Sep 1843. Mr. Stringer drowned in the Snake River while trying to help Miles Eyre.

261. Cornelius Stringer: age 55. b. 1788.

262. George Summers

263. Milford (W. C.) Summers

264. Dean Swift

265. Stephen Tarbox: age 31. b. 1812.

266. Jeremiah Teller

267. Lindsey Thorp

268. John Thompson

269. Daniel Trainer (Trainor)

270. John Umnicker (Umicker) (Unicker)

271. Samuel N. Vance: age 36. b. 1807, d. 1888. Samuel married Mary Ellen Hamilton Willis on 4 Sep 1851. She was b. 1819, d. 26 Mar 1880. Mary Ellen came to Oregon on an 1846 wagon train with her first husband, Jacob Willis. Sam was a widower with children when he married Mary Ellen. He employed Nat Sitton as a teamster during the 1843 migration. Sam and Mary Ellen are buried in the Mt. View Cemetery in Oregon City, Oregon.

272. William Hatchett Vaughan: age 21. b. 17 Jan 1822, d. 11 Feb 1906. William married Susan Mary Officer on 27 Aug 1847. She was b. 3 Mar 1833. Susan came to Oregon on an 1845 wagon train. William fought in the Cayuse War, 1847-48. William, called Billy by his friends, almost drowned while crossing the Kansas River on 28 May 1843.

273. George W. Vernon: age 31. b. 1812. Wife was Rebecca. She d. 4 Aug 1870.

274. John Waggoner

275. Daniel Waldo: age 43. b. 1800, d. 6 Sep 1880. Wife was Malinda Lunsford, age 38. She was b. 1805, d. 15 Sep 1885. Dan served as captain of the Straggler Column that left Independence after 22 May. He served as justice of the peace under the Oregon Provisional Government. Daniel and Malinda are buried in the Pioneer Cemetery in Salem, Oregon.

276. David Logan Waldo: age 15. b. 15 Sep 1827, d. 1853. David was probably included in the list of men age sixteen and over because he would turn sixteen before reaching Oregon. He fought in the Cayuse War, 1847-48. David married Mary Porter on 6 Feb 1862.

277. William Waldo: Dan Waldo had an 11-year-old son named William in 1843. This individual might be a cousin or brother whom the son was named after.

278. Joseph Reddeford Walker: age 44. b. 3 Dec 1798, d. 13 Nov 1872. Joe Walker was not associated with the original Oregon Emigrating Company. Instead, he joined Chiles's California Column at Fort Laramie to act as a guide between Fort Hall and California. The trapping brigade he led to California discovered Yosemite Valley on 13 Nov 1833.

279. T. B. Ward: age 16. b. 1827, d. approx. 1896. Mr. Ward married Minerva P. She was b. 25 May 1831, d. 28 Jun 1866. He later married Mary Jane. Mr. Ward was committed to the Oregon State Insane Asylum on 23 Feb 1886. He was released on 5 Jun 1886, then recommitted on 31 Oct 1888. Minerva is buried in the Pioneer Cemetery in Salem, Oregon.

280. James M. Wair: d. Apr 1856. He was a bachelor.

281. James Waters: James captained one of the platoons in the Light Column.

282. John Watson

283. Newton Wheeler: d. 15 Aug 1849. Wife was Elizabeth. Alexander Zachary stabbed Newt on 8 Sep while traveling along the Snake River Plains. The cause of the dispute is unknown. Newton went to the California gold fields in 1849, where he died.

284. James S. White: d. 12 Jun 1886. Wife may have been Rhoda Kinze. Spouse was Isabel M.

285. Marcus Whitman: age 40. b. 4 Sep 1802, d. 29 Nov 1847. His wife, Narcissa Prentiss, was at Waiilatpu during the 1843 migration. She was b. 14 Mar 1808, d. 29 Nov 1847. Marcus, a missionary working for the American Board of Commissioners for Foreign Missions, joined the migration en route. He acted as a guide between Fort Hall and the Grande Ronde Valley. Cayuse Indians killed Marcus and Narcissa, an event that initiated the Cayuse War of 1847-48. Marcus and Narcissa are buried in the Waiilatpu Mission Cemetery, west of Walla Walla, Washington.

286. Benjamin Williams: age 26. b. 1817, d. 18 Jun 1852. Wife was Harriet Wingfield. Benjamin died at the age of 35, leaving a wife and four small children.

287. David Williams

288. Edward Williams

289. Isaac Williams: Isaac was found sleeping on guard duty on 9 Jul and had to forfeit his gun. The Oregon Emigrating Company

Council sold the gun at auction on 12 Jul. Isaac turned south after Fort Hall and went to California.

290. James Williams: Jim turned south after Fort Hall and went to California.

291. John Williams: John turned south after Fort Hall and went to California.

292. Squire Williams: Squire turned south after Fort Hall and went to California.

293. Joseph (James) Wilmot (Wilmont)

294. William Charles Wilson: age 23. b. 1 May 1820, d. 3 Oct 1899. Wife was Mary Jane Mills, age 23. She was b. 1820, d. 9 Jan 1849. William went to the California gold fields in 1849 after Mary Jane died. The next year, he returned, remarried, and became a farmer. His second wife was Sarah Phillips Tedwell. She was b. 28 Oct 1819, d. 18 May 1891. Sarah came to Oregon on an 1847 wagon train with her father after her first husband died in 1844. After William's second wife died, he married Sarah Hoard on 3 Mar 1893 at the age of 73. She died three months later on 18 Jun 1893. William and Sarah Hoard are buried in the Union Point Cemetery in Banks, Oregon.

295. William H. Wilson: age 20. b. 28 Dec 1822, d. 11 Feb 1902. Wife was Polly. She d. 9 Jan 1849, leaving five children. Bill sold his wagon at Fort Hall on 29 Aug and continued with pack animals. He fought in the Cayuse War, 1847-48. After his discharge he went to the California gold fields in 1848. When he returned, he married Hannah R. Dickinson Gilliam on 22 Oct 1850. Dickinson was her maiden name, and Gilliam the name of her first husband. She was b. 5 Nov 1832, d. 28 May 1919. William was elected territorial auditor on 16 Dec 1850. He also fought in the Rogue River War, 1853. William was an early member of the Oregon State Legislature. He also served as County Commissioner and Justice of the Peace in Yoncalla, Oregon. He was affectionately called Uncle Billy. William is buried in the Pioneer Cemetery in Yoncalla, Oregon.

296. Archibald Winkler (Winkle)

297. William H. Winter

298. Tallmadge Benjamin Wood: age 25. b. 5 Jul 1817, d. 1848. He was called Ben. Ben served as an orderly sergeant under the command of Colonel Bill Martin. Ben and Henry Hunt built the first sawmill on the Clatsop Plains of the lower Columbia River. Known as "Hunt's Mill," it was powered by a thirty-foot diameter overshot water wheel. California Indians killed Ben during the 1848 gold rush.

299. Alexander Zachary: age 41. b. 1802, d. 12 Apr 1859. Wife was Sarah. Alex was banished from the Oregon Emigrating Company after he defrauded Walter Matney of provisions near the Sweetwater River on 30 Jul. Alex stabbed Newt Wheeler on 8 Sep while traveling along the Snake River Plains. Alexander is buried in an unmarked grave in the Baptist Cemetery in West Union, Oregon.

300. John Q. Zachary: age 18. b. 23 Mar 1825, d. 10 Jan 1896. John married Teresa E. Brown on 2 Mar 1851. He was the son of Alexander Zachary.

APPENDIX B

Slave receipt

This is a copy of the slave receipt carried by Dan Delany for the purchase of his slave, Rachael. He needed the receipt to prove his ownership upon arriving in Oregon Country. The receipt reads:

Received of Daniel Delany four Hundred and fifty dollars in full payment for a negro girl named Rachael aged fourteen years the Right and Tittle of said negro I Bind myself my heirs Executors and assigns to warrant and forever defend also warrant the soundness of Boddy and mind of said negro this the 3 day of Sept 1842

   attest John Delany ___ C Campbell

APPENDIX C
Calendar for 1843

January

Sun	Mon	Tue	Wed	Thu	Fri	Sat
1	2	3	4	5	6	7
8	9	10	11	12	13	14
15	16	17	18	19	20	21
22	23	24	25	26	27	28
29	30	31				

February

Sun	Mon	Tue	Wed	Thu	Fri	Sat
			1	2	3	4
5	6	7	8	9	10	11
12	13	14	15	16	17	18
19	20	21	22	23	24	25
26	27	28				

March

Sun	Mon	Tue	Wed	Thu	Fri	Sat
			1	2	3	4
5	6	7	8	9	10	11
12	13	14	15	16	17	18
19	20	21	22	23	24	25
26	27	28	29	30	31	

April

Sun	Mon	Tue	Wed	Thu	Fri	Sat
						1
2	3	4	5	6	7	8
9	10	11	12	13	14	15
16	17	18	19	20	21	22
23	24	25	26	27	28	29
30						

May

Sun	Mon	Tue	Wed	Thu	Fri	Sat
	1	2	3	4	5	6
7	8	9	10	11	12	13
14	15	16	17	18	19	20
21	22	23	24	25	26	27
28	29	30	31			

June

Sun	Mon	Tue	Wed	Thu	Fri	Sat
				1	2	3
4	5	6	7	8	9	10
11	12	13	14	15	16	17
18	19	20	21	22	23	24
25	26	27	28	29	30	

July

Sun	Mon	Tue	Wed	Thu	Fri	Sat
						1
2	3	4	5	6	7	8
9	10	11	12	13	14	15
16	17	18	19	20	21	22
23	24	25	26	27	28	29
30	31					

August

Sun	Mon	Tue	Wed	Thu	Fri	Sat
		1	2	3	4	5
6	7	8	9	10	11	12
13	14	15	16	17	18	19
20	21	22	23	24	25	26
27	28	29	30	31		

September

Sun	Mon	Tue	Wed	Thu	Fri	Sat
					1	2
3	4	5	6	7	8	9
10	11	12	13	14	15	16
17	18	19	20	21	22	23
24	25	26	27	28	29	30

October

Sun	Mon	Tue	Wed	Thu	Fri	Sat
1	2	3	4	5	6	7
8	9	10	11	12	13	14
15	16	17	18	19	20	21
22	23	24	25	26	27	28
29	30	31				

November

Sun	Mon	Tue	Wed	Thu	Fri	Sat
			1	2	3	4
5	6	7	8	9	10	11
12	13	14	15	16	17	18
19	20	21	22	23	24	25
26	27	28	29	30		

December

Sun	Mon	Tue	Wed	Thu	Fri	Sat
					1	2
3	4	5	6	7	8	9
10	11	12	13	14	15	16
17	18	19	20	21	22	23
24	25	26	27	28	29	30
31						

Index

advance guard; 180
alkali; 125
American Board of Commissioners for
    Foreign Missions; 98, 424
American Falls; 426
American Fur Company; 270
American West; 143
Applegate, Jesse; 181
    wagon breaks an axletree; 344
Applegate, Lindsay:
    wagon breaks an axletree; 282
Arikaras; 112
Ash Creek; 200
Ash Hollow; 249, 250
Ashley, General; 140, 403, 458
Astoria Expedition; 541
August 1, 1843; 339
August 2, 1843; 342
August 3, 1843; 345
August 4, 1843; 346
August 5, 1843; 348
August 6, 1843; 350
August 7, 1843; 354
August 8, 1843; 357
August 9, 1843; 359
August 10, 1843; 362
August 11, 1843; 372
August 12, 1843; 376
August 13, 1843; 380
August 14, 1843; 383
August 15, 1843; 388
August 16, 1843; 393
August 17, 1843; 394
August 18, 1843; 395
August 19, 1843; 396
August 20, 1843; 397
August 21, 1843; 398
August 22, 1843; 398
August 23, 1843; 399
August 24, 1843; 403
August 25, 1843; 405
August 26, 1843; 405
August 27, 1843; 409
August 28, 1843; 414
August 29, 1843; 417
August 30, 1843; 418
August 31, 1843; 419

Bannock bread; 197
Bannock Indians; 139
bateaux; 565
Beacon Rock; 567
Beale, George; 137
Bear Lake; 396, 397
Bear River; 380, 393, 396, 403
Bear River Valley; 394, 395, 396, 400
Beaten Rock; 567
Beer Springs; 380, 400
Bent's Fort; 153
Bessemer Bend; 313
Betzar's Bluff; 263
Biddle, Nicholas; 277
Big Horn Mountains; 322
Big Rock Creek; 296
Big Sandy Creek; 166
Big Sandy River; 359
Big Spring,; 100
birth of:
    Becky Stewart's daughter; 240
    Nancy Hembree's daughter; 329
    Sarah Pennington's daughter; 352
black haws; 484
Black Hills; 264, 295
Black Vermillion River; 169

Black Warrior Creek; 141
Black's Fork of the Green River; 153, 299, 378
Blackfeet Indians; 404, 407
Blue Mountains; 161, 383, 483
Blue River; 180, 181, 197, 199
Blue River Valley; 208, 209
Boiling Spring; 454
Boise River; 460
Bonneville, Captain; 408
Boston fire; 569
Brewer, Mr.; 516
Bridger, Jim; 357, 382, 409
    Blanket Chief; 140
    Gabe; 138
British trapping brigades; 229
Brule River; 484
buffalo:
    first seen by migration; 195
bullboats; 238, 403
Burnett, Peter:
    election as captain; 159
    resigns as captain; 190
Burnt Canyon; 475, 483
Burnt River; 481, 483, 484

Camp Delay; 143, 145, 161, 164
Camp Disagreeable; 217
Camp Satisfaction; 218
Carson, Kit; 405
Cascade Falls; 522, 547
Catholic missionaries; 147
Cayuse Indians; 98, 492, 496
Champooic; 300, 576
Cheyenne Indians; 271
Chiles's California Column; 160
Chimney Rock; 257, 259
Chute River; 543
Clakamas River; 582
Clearwater River; 515
clothes for the journey; 50
Colter's Hell; 322
Columbia River; 383, 520
Columbia River Fishing and Trading Company; 408
Conestoga wagons; 39
confluence of the South and North Platte Rivers; 230
Continental Divide; 353
Cooper, Lewis; 327, 423

Courthouse Rock; 253
Courthouse Square; 40
Cow Column:
    organization of; 194
crossing the:
    Bear River; 398
    Big Rock Creek; 296
    Big Sandy Creek; 166
    Black Vermillion River; 169
    Blue River; 183
    Boise River; 467
    Chute River; 543
    Deer Creek; 296
    East Fork of the Blue River; 169
    John Day River; 541
    Kansas River; 140
    Laramie River; 269
    Malheur River; 474
    Powder River; 490
    Rockariski River; 121
    Snake River at Fort Boise; 472
    Snake River between Fort Hall and Fort Boise; 445
    South Platte River; 238
    Sweetwater River; 329
    Umatilla River; 512, 536
    West Fork of the Blue River; 180
Crow Indians; 138, 322
curl-leaf; 481

Davis, Burrell; 175
De Smet, Father Pierre-Jean; 147
De Vos, Father; 147
death of:
    Alex McClelland; 591
    Becky Stewart's baby; 517
    C. M. Stringer; 448
    Catherine Cary; 384
    Clay Paine; 346
    Dan Richardson; 418
    Ed Stevenson; 359
    Edward Applegate; 591
    Hattie; 531
    Joel Hembree, Jr.; 293
    Miles Eyre; 448
    Mrs. Rubey; 497
    Warren Applegate; 591
Deer Creek; 296
Devil's Garden; 424
Devil's Gate; 325

dog chases antelope; 215
Douglass, Mr.; 565

East Fork of the Blue River; 169
Edson, Elbridge; 206
Elm Grove; 73, 104, 107, 108, 111
equipment for the journey; 51
Etchell, James; 449

Falls of the Columbia; 544
Fitzhugh's Grove; 100
Fitzhugh's Mill; 94, 100, 104
Fitzpatrick, Sublette, and Bridger; 409
Fitzpatrick, Tom; 408, 409
Flathead Indians; 147
food for the journey; 54
Fort Boise; 139, 147, 161, 409, 468, 469
Fort Bridger; 381
Fort Hall; 139, 186, 409
　origins; 407
Fort Laramie; 153, 264, 267, 270
Fort Platte; 269
Fort Vancouver; 521
Fort Walla Walla; 473, 519
Fort William; 267
Fowler, Bill; 251
Fraeb, Henry; 407, 408
Francis, Alex; 277
Fremont, John Charles:
　at Fort Walla Walla; 520
　frightens buffalo; 313
　introduced; 72
　passes migration near Fort Hall; 399
　show of force at Fort Hall; 415
French Prairie; 300, 576

Gantt, John:
　introduced; 98
Geiger, William; 514, 515
Glorious Fourth; 245, 247
Goodman, Rich:
　wounded while hunting; 241
Grand Island; 212
Grande Ronde River; 492
Grande Ronde Valley; 492
Grant, Richard; 410
Great American Desert; 212
Great Salt Lake; 403
Green River; 139, 153, 408

Green River Rendezvous; 363
Gros Ventres Indians; 87, 407

H.M.S. Columbia; 572
H.M.S. Pallas; 579
H.M.S. Vancouver; 572
hackberry; 481
Ham's Fork of the Green River; 360, 376, 408
Hattie; 531
hawthorn; 481
Henry, Andrew; 112, 140, 403, 458
Henry's Fork; 322
honey trees; 127
Horse Creek; 153, 197, 198, 284, 408
Howell, John; 205
Howell, Wes; 325
Hoyt, Amon:
　tries to spear salmon; 436
Hudson Bay grist mill; 571
Humboldt River; 104, 271, 420

Jackson, John; 423
Jackson's Hole; 322, 403
Jailhouse Rock; 253
John Day River; 541
Johnson, Overton; 147, 182, 456, 533, 534
July 1, 1843; 239
July 2, 1843; 241
July 3, 1843; 242
July 4, 1843; 245
July 5, 1843; 245
July 6, 1843; 247
July 7, 1843; 249
July 8, 1843; 251
July 9, 1843; 256
July 10, 1843; 259
July 11, 1843; 260
July 12, 1843; 265
July 13, 1843; 266
July 14, 1843; 269
July 15, 1843; 271
July 16, 1843; 279
July 17, 1843; 282
July 18, 1843; 291
July 19, 1843; 294
July 20, 1843; 297
July 21, 1843; 303
July 22, 1843; 305

July 23, 1843; 309
July 24, 1843; 313
July 25, 1843; 313
July 26, 1843; 314
July 27, 1843; 316
July 28, 1843; 320
July 29, 1843; 328
July 30, 1843; 333
July 31, 1843; 337
June 1, 1843; 158
June 2, 1843; 160
June 3, 1843; 165
June 4, 1843; 165
June 5, 1843; 169
June 6, 1843; 175
June 7, 1843; 179
June 8, 1843; 183
June 9, 1843; 190
June 10, 1843; 195
June 11, 1843; 197
June 12, 1843; 198
June 13, 1843; 199
June 14, 1843; 200
June 15, 1843; 204
June 16, 1843; 206
June 17, 1843; 209
June 18, 1843; 211
June 19, 1843; 212
June 20, 1843; 216
June 21, 1843; 217
June 22, 1843; 217
June 23, 1843; 217
June 24, 1843; 220
June 25, 1843; 225
June 26, 1843; 230
June 27, 1843; 232
June 28, 1843; 236
June 29, 1843; 237
June 30, 1843; 238

kamash roots; 496, 518
Kansas River; 126, 140, 145, 169
Kaw Indians; 145, 147, 183
Kaw warriors; 180
Kelsey, Becky; 251
Kerritook:
    injured when breech bursts; 244

Lapwai Mission; 515
Lapwai River; 515

Laramie Mountains; 265
Laramie River; 269, 270, 407, 408
Lee, Hank; 194
Legear, Frank; 277
Lenox, Dave; 194
Lewis and Clark; 32, 149, 457, 566
Light Column:
    organization of; 194
Linebarger, Lewis; 482
Lisa, Manuel; 458
Little Red Wagon; 89, 136
Lone Pine; 486, 488
Looney, Jesse; 485
Loughborough, John; 277

Mackinaw boats; 524
Malheur River; 473, 474
Matheny, Dan; 194
May 22, 1843; 106
May 23, 1843; 111
May 24, 1843; 118
May 25, 1843; 124
May 26, 1843; 138
May 27, 1843; 142
May 28, 1843; 143
May 29, 1843; 145
May 30, 1843; 147
May 31, 1843; 157
McClane, John Burch; 240
McDonald, Mr.; 536
McHaley, John; 181
McKinley, Archibald; 521
McLoughlin, Dr. John; 410, 565, 572, 578, 583
Meat wagon; 136
Meek, Joe; 138, 139, 176, 301, 411, 481
meteor; 347
Moore, Jackson; 277
Mount Adams; 562
Mount Hood; 539, 562
mountain fever; 319
Mountain Lamb; 139
Muddy Creek; 393
Multnomah River; 300, 580
Musselshell; 322
Myers, Jacob; 207

Nesmith, Jim:
    appointed as orderly sergeant; 159

census on the Kansas River; 160
  introduced; 116
Newby, Bill; 533, 534
Newby's rescue on the Columbia; 534
Newell, Doc; 139, 411, 481
Nez Perce Indians; 484
North Fork of the Platte River; 249
North Platte River; 259
November 1, 1843; 594

O'Neil, Bennett:
  lost on the South Platte River; 251
October 1, 1843; 498
October 2, 1843; 500
October 3, 1843; 501
October 4, 1843; 505
October 5, 1843; 512
October 6, 1843; 514
October 7, 1843; 518
October 8, 1843; 519
October 9, 1843; 527
October 10, 1843; 530
October 11, 1843; 532
October 12, 1843; 535
October 13, 1843; 539
October 14, 1843; 540
October 15, 1843; 541
October 16, 1843; 543
October 17, 1843; 544
October 18, 1843; 546
October 19, 1843; 551
October 20, 1843; 554
October 21, 1843; 554
October 22, 1843; 559
October 23, 1843; 563
October 24, 1843; 566
October 25, 1843; 567
October 26, 1843; 571
October 27, 1843; 573
October 28, 1843; 578
October 29, 1843; 582
October 30, 1843; 585
October 31, 1843; 592
Ogden, Peter Skene; 410, 578
Old Prairie Chicken; 248
Old Sledge; 340
Oregon Emigrating Company:
  at Fort Bridger; 383
  auction of Isaac Williams's gun; 266

Bill Martin appointed as captain; 194
Chiles's California Column joins the migration; 186
elections on the Kansas River; 158
emigrants turn south to Taos; 277
encounters a dead Pawnee; 196
encounters five trappers heading east; 299
encounters the Platte River; 212
expulsion of Alex Zachary; 338
first Indians encountered after Fort Laramie; 403
formation of the Cow Column; 194
formation of the Light Column; 194
in the Bear River Valley; 402
John Gantt hired; 98
learns that Oregon will become part of the United States; 300
Marcus Whitman catches up; 210
organization of; 94
Pete Burnett resigns as captain; 190
reunification; 383
rules; 100
split at the Blue River; 194
Waldo's Straggler Column catches up; 209
Oregon Migration of 1843; 73
Osage Indians; 127, 141
Osage warriors; 141, 142, 180
Outcast Mess; 383
Owyhee River; 408, 473

Pacific Creek; 362
Pacific Trading Company; 407
Paine, Clay; 305
Paiute Indians; 150, 247, 425
pap; 135
Pappin's flatboat; 140, 141
Parker, Reverend Sam; 424
Pawnee Indians; 180, 207
Pawnee Territory; 200
Payette, Francois; 469
Pennington, John; 175
Pierre's Hole; 284, 322, 397, 407
  Battle of; 87
Pioneer Lyceum and Literary Club; 390
pioneers; 197
Plains Indians; 142, 146
Platte River; 209

Popo Agie; 340, 397
Portneuf River; 396, 404
Potawotomie Indians; 122
Powder River; 336, 486, 489
Powder River Valley; 486, 487
prickly pear; 150
Prigg, Fred; 426

Red Buttes; 280
Rendezvous; 153
Republican Fork of the Kansas River; 199
Richardson, Dan; 305
Rock Avenue; 313
Rock Bridge; 287
Rockariski River; 121
Rocky Mountain Fur Company; 8, 73, 74, 132, 366, 402, 409, 592
Rocky Mountain sheep; 327
Rossin, Joe; 175
Russell, Osborne; 407
Russian fur trade; 573
Russian settlements; 572

salmon:
    spearing by Snake Indians; 437
Salmon Falls; 429
Sand Creek; 280
Sandwich Islands; 573
Santa Fe traders; 39
Santa Fe trail; 111
Scott, Hiram; 262
Scott's Bluff; 260, 262, 263, 265
September 1, 1843; 419
September 2, 1843; 420
September 3, 1843; 423
September 4, 1843; 426
September 5, 1843; 427
September 6, 1843; 428
September 7, 1843; 431
September 8, 1843; 437
September 9, 1843; 443
September 10, 1843; 444
September 11, 1843; 451
September 12, 1843; 454
September 13, 1843; 456
September 14, 1843; 458
September 15, 1843; 459
September 16, 1843; 466
September 17, 1843; 466

September 18, 1843; 468
September 19, 1843; 470
September 20, 1843; 472
September 21, 1843; 474
September 22, 1843; 475
September 23, 1843; 479
September 24, 1843; 480
September 25, 1843; 483
September 26, 1843; 485
September 27, 1843; 487
September 28, 1843; 490
September 29, 1843; 492
September 30, 1843; 495
Shawnee:
    farmland; 143
    Indian Territory; 105, 108
sign language; 148
Sioux warriors; 130
Sitka; 572
Sleepy Grove; 238, 247
Smith, Jed; 229
Smith, Peg-leg; 402, 403
Snake Indians; 139, 403, 430
Snake River; 422, 475
Snake River Plains; 383, 394, 396, 408
soda:
    collected in place of saleratus; 314
Soldier Creek; 141
Sophia's Island; 572, 574, 580
South Pass; 139, 347, 348, 403
South Platte River; 230
Spalding, Eliza; 515
Spalding, Henry; 515
Spanish cattle; 493, 577
Splinter Column:
    formation of; 327
Split Rock; 341
Squaw Butte Creek; 295
St. Louis; 31, 32
Steamboat Springs; 400
Stevenson, Ed; 305
Stewart, Peter; 144
Stewart, Sir William Drummond; 145, 147, 182, 306, 408
    description of hunting party; 145
    frightens buffalo; 313
    introduced; 72
    near Fort Hall; 399
Stickus; 492, 498
stock to pull a wagon; 45

Stoughton, Alexander; 447
Sublette, Bill; 257, 270, 284, 340, 357, 400, 403, 407, 408, 409
Sublette, Milton; 407, 408
sulfate of soda; 237
Sweetwater River; 314, 318

Taos; 153
The Dalles; 545
The Gateway to the West; 32
trade goods; 431
Tshimakain; 492
turtle shells; 265

Uintah Mountains; 393, 395
Umatilla River; 506
Umnicker, John; 241

Vasques, Mr.; 299
Vasquez, Louis; 382
Vaughan, Billy; 144

wagon loading; 91
wagon requirements; 43
Waiilatpu Mission; 98, 509
Wair, Jim; 164
Waldo's Straggler Column; 160
Walker, Joe; 271
Walla Walla River; 514, 518
Waller, Reverend; 548
War of 1812; 415
Wascopam Mission; 521, 547
Waters, Jim; 194
West Fork of the Blue River; 180
Western Emigration Company; 246
Whitman Mission; 514
Whitman, Marcus; 515
　introduced; 98
　joins migration; 99
　leaves migration; 498
　leaves Independence; 160
　takes over as guide; 419
Whitman, Narcissa; 515
Wilkins, Caleb; 139, 411
Williams, Isaac:
　falls asleep on guard duty; 256
Willow Springs; 314
Wind River Mountains; 153, 322, 340, 341, 349, 408
Windmill Rock; 535

Winter, Bill; 147, 182
Wyeth, Nathaniel; 406, 407, 408

Yellowstone Country; 322
Yellowstone River; 138, 362
Yenemah; 530

Zachary, Alex:
　banished from Oregon Emigrating Company; 338
　defrauds Walt Matney; 338
　leaves Light Column; 248
　stabs Newt Wheeler; 440

CPSIA information can be obtained at www.ICGtesting.com
Printed in the USA
BVOW06s2121010715

407150BV00003B/8/P